"THE QUEEN OF ROMANTIC SUSPENSE."
—Crime and Publishing

Praise for *No One Left to Tell*

"An action-packed thriller from the opening homicide until the final confrontation . . . [a] twisting tale."
—The Mystery Gazette

"Nonstop action and drama . . . another engaging and exciting story by Karen Rose." —Joyfully Reviewed

"There is something about the way that Rose writes . . . that makes me *need* to read her books. . . . [It] has made me an addict."
—Crime and Publishing

Praise for *You Belong to Me*

"A fast-paced murder mystery that will keep you turning pages. If you are not already a fan of Karen Rose, then you will be after reading this book." —Fresh Fiction

"Grabs your attention from the first page until the very last."
—The Romance Readers Connection

"Fast-paced, with superb twists." —*Midwest Book Review*

"Karen Rose brings suspense to a whole new level!"
—Long and Short Reviews

"You will want to make sure the lights are on while reading this one!" —*Romantic Times* (top pick, 4½ stars)

continued . . .

Also by Karen Rose

No One Left to Tell
You Belong to Me

KAREN ROSE

DID YOU MISS ME?

A SIGNET BOOK

SIGNET
Published by the Penguin Group
Penguin Group (USA), 375 Hudson Street,
New York, New York 10014, USA

USA | Canada | UK | Ireland | Australia | New Zealand | India | South Africa | China

Penguin Books Ltd., Registered Offices: 80 Strand, London WC2R 0RL, England
For more information about the Penguin Group visit penguin.com.

Published by Signet, an imprint of New American Library,
a division of Penguin Group (USA)

First Signet Printing, February 2013
First Signet Printing (Read Pink Edition), October 2013

ⓇREGISTERED TRADEMARK—MARCA REGISTRADA

ISBN 978-0-451-46748-5

Printed in the United States of America
10 9 8 7 6 5 4 3 2 1

PUBLISHER'S NOTE
This is a work of fiction. Names, characters, places, and incidents either are the
product of the author's imagination or are used fictitiously, and any resemblance
to actual persons, living or dead, business establishments, events, or locales is
entirely coincidental.
  The publisher does not have any control over and does not assume any
responsibility for author or third-party Web sites or their content.

ALWAYS LEARNING   PEARSON

To my beautiful friends who have battled breast cancer—thank you for opening your hearts and sharing your stories with me. By your strength and determination, I am inspired. By your trust, I am humbled. And by your friendship, I am truly blessed.

To Claire Zion, Vicki Mellor, and Robin Rue—for seeing me through.

And, as always, to Martin. I love you.

ACKNOWLEDGMENTS

All the women who shared their individual cancer experiences, I thank you from the bottom of my heart, and wish you all the best.

Marc Conterato, for all things medical.

Kay Conterato, for asking me to create a heroine who was a bit different.

My friends who know me and love me anyway—Terri, Mandy, Sonie, and Kay—for your love, hugs, and the chocolate you sneaked to me when nobody was looking.

My amazing editors, Claire Zion and Vicki Mellor, for your patience and support. I am fortunate indeed to have the privilege of working with you both.

As always, all mistakes are my own.

DID YOU MISS ME?

Prologue

Cold. So cold. Ford curled into himself, instinctively trying to find some warmth. But there was none.

Cold. The floor was cold. And hard. And dirty. *Hard to breathe.*

The wind was blowing outside, rattling windows, sending jets of frigid air around his body. Over his skin. *So cold.* A shudder racked him and he struggled to open his eyes. It was dark. *Can't see. Head hurts. God.* He tried to get up, to push at whatever covered his eyes, but he couldn't. *Where am ... . What hap—*

Clarity returned in a rush and with it came blinding panic. He was blindfolded. Gagged. Tied, hands and feet. *No.* He fought wildly for a few seconds, hissing when the rope seared his skin. He slumped, his heart racing.

Kim. The image of her face broke through the pounding in his head. He'd been with Kim. Walking her to her car, so happy that she finally let him do so after three months of dating. Relieved that she finally admitted she needed him, because he'd quickly come to need her, to *crave* the way she could make him feel. He'd never known anyone to so perfectly match his interests. Wants. Needs.

Like she was made for me alone.

Fiercely independent, she always insisted that she didn't need a sitter, didn't need any guy to protect her. But not this time. *She asked me to walk her.* Because it was a bad part of town. *Because she needed me. She needed me and I fucked up.*

Where was she? *Don't let her be here.* Tied up. Gagged. *Please let her be all right.*

What the hell had happened? *There was an alley.* They'd gone through an alley because Kim parked behind the movie theater. *That damn foreign film.* She'd had to see some French film for class. Weird theater, sketchy part of town. He'd been angry with the prof for assigning the film to start with and was going to tell him so.

Kim didn't want him to confront the prof. They'd been arguing about it when he'd heard a noise. Felt . . . pain. *Oh God.* The fear in Kim's dark eyes. Her scream. Every nerve in his body fired all at once and then there was the shattering pain in his head, right before everything went dark.

Kim. He threw his body forward and grunted, the exploding pain in his shoulder sending him back to the floor, where he huddled, grimacing. *Where is she?*

He drew another breath, taking care not to inhale the dirt this time. Quieting himself, he listened for any sound—a whisper, a wheeze, a whimper. But there was none.

She's not here. He closed his eyes, fighting to control his pounding heart. *Please don't let her be here.* Because if she was here, she wasn't breathing. If she was here, she was hurt. Maybe dead. *No. No.* He shook his head hard, wincing when the pain spiked deep. *She got away. Please let her have gotten away.*

Away . . . from what? From whom? Where is here? The panic rose in his throat, choking him. *Calm down. Think. You know how to think.*

Thinking was what Ford Elkhart did best.

He closed his eyes, forced himself to calm. To think. To remember. *It's cold.* Which told him nothing. It was December, for God's sake. He could be anywhere north of Florida.

Why? Why me? He gave the ropes binding his wrists another hard yank, then swore when his frozen skin burned. *Why?*

He knew why.

Money. Ransom. It had to be. Kids of rich parents were prey. He wondered whether they were contacting his mother or his father. He hoped his mother. *Dad won't pay a dime to get me back,* he thought bitterly, then pictured his mother, and his heart clenched.

Mom. She'd be terrified. Out of her mind with worry. Because his mother had prosecuted enough of these cases to know what was happening to him right now.

Enough of these cases . . . *Oh no. Hell, no.* His stomach turned over as he considered the alternative. It was The Case. *Oh God.* The case he couldn't wait to see over. The murder case that had consumed his mother for months. Those trashy Millhouses. Reggie was the killer, but the rest of the Millhouses were probably just as bad—they just hadn't been caught yet. *They hate Mom.* They'd harassed her. Threatened her. *Threatened me.* If the Millhouses were behind this . . . *I'm fucked.*

I'm sorry, Mom. She'd urged him to let her hire a bodyguard, just until the case died down. He hadn't wanted anyone following him around, snooping on him and Kim. He hadn't needed a bodyguard. He could take care of himself.

Hell. He'd taken care of himself so well that he was trussed up like a Christmas turkey. Probably waiting for the same fate. He blinked hard, shook the tears off his face. *Stop it,* he barked at himself. *Crying won't help you get away.*

And he had to get away. *Kim needs me. So think. Breathe.* He forced himself to calm, willed his mind to hear the voice of his mother's friend Paige, who taught self-defense. He'd taken Kim to Paige for instruction because he'd wanted to keep her safe even when he wasn't there to protect her.

You were there, his mind mocked. *Standing right beside her. And it didn't make a bit of difference.*

He fought the terror that closed his throat. *Please let her be all right. I'll do anything. If something happened to her . . . because somebody was trying to get to me . . .* He'd never be able to forgive himself.

You might not get the chance to forgive yourself—or to save her—if you die here, so stop whining and think. He tried to remember what Paige had said, but he'd been watching Kim from the sidelines, admiring her body as she practiced the escape moves Paige had demonstrated. He'd been thinking about what they'd do when he got Kim back to his room.

He prayed that Kim had been paying attention, because he hadn't been.

So pay attention now. Eventually whoever brought him here would come back, if only to kill him. *You need to be ready to strike. To get away.*

Ford took an inventory of his injuries. His head—the back of his skull hurt like hell. *That's where the bastard hit me.* His right arm hurt, too, but probably wasn't broken.

His legs . . . He tried to move them within the confines of the ropes. They seemed okay. Stiff from being tied, but not injured. *So you can run. When you get the chance, hit with your left and run like a bat out of hell.*

To where? He could hear nothing, no sounds of the city. Seemed like he was far enough out that getting back might be a challenge. It was cold and he had no coat. At least he had shoes. He might have to walk a long way. But he'd do it. He'd get back. He'd find Kim and they'd get back to their lives. He'd take her home, introduce her to his mother and Gran. He wished he'd done so already.

But first he had to get away from here. *Wherever the hell here is.*

Ford froze. Someone was coming. *Stay calm. Pay attention to details.*

A door creaked as it opened, an icy blast rushing into the room. His teeth would have chattered had it not been for the gag in his mouth.

He heard footsteps. Coming closer. Heavy footsteps. A man. Boots. He was wearing boots.

The footsteps stopped close to Ford's head and he could feel warmth from the man's body.

"You're awake."

Gravelly. The voice was deep and harsh. Filled with . . . laughter? Yeah, laughter. *Asshole's laughing at me.* Ford bit back the fury that roared through him. *Pay attention.*

He heard the crack of knees and the warmth came closer. There was a scent. Aftershave. *Familiar.* He'd smelled it before, he was sure of it. *Where?* He tensed when fingers ran over his head, then hissed a curse when a fist grabbed his hair and yanked him up. *Fight. Dammit, fight.* Ford thrashed, flinging his body to one side. A heavy knee planted itself on his chest, holding him down. His head was yanked to one side, exposing his neck.

"I'm back," the man crooned. "Did you miss me?"

Mitch Roberts pulled the needle from his captive's neck and, breathing hard, counted down from ten. *Three, two, one, and . . . out like a light.* He let Ford fall, enjoying the sound of the bastard's skull cracking on the hard floor.

Slowly he stood, staring down at Elkhart's body. Kid had to be two hundred pounds of solid muscle. He capped the needle and slid the syringe into his pocket. Fully abled, Ford Elkhart would have put him in traction, but a little ketamine went a very long way.

"Time to get busy," he murmured. Kneeling, he cut the ropes from Ford's wrists, pulled another length of rope from his pocket, and retied him. Just looser. He loosened the blindfold as well, but just a little. Just enough.

He took a rusted box cutter from his pocket, quickly slit the tape from the box he'd brought in from the van, and dumped its contents on the floor, the foul odor making his eyes water. When the kid woke up, the first thing he'd smell would be death.

A nice touch, if I say so myself. He casually dropped the box cutter, watching it bounce and roll, coming to rest under a low shelf.

Locking the door behind him, he crossed the yard to the cabin and let himself in.

Wilson Beckett stood at the stove, frying bacon. It smelled good and Mitch realized it had been too many hours since his last meal. But he'd seen the old man's hygiene. There was no way he was eating anything touched by the guy's hands.

Stomping his feet, Mitch rubbed his hands briskly. "He's still not awake," he stated.

Beckett looked up from the skillet, his weathered face bent in a frown. "Hell, boy, how hard did you hit him?"

Not nearly as hard as I wanted to. "Maybe a little too hard. I have to get back to the city. Check on him in the morning. If he's still out, call me. If he wakes up, don't hit him anymore, understand? I want him lucid so he can talk to his mama."

"You phone in the ransom yet?"

"Yep." *Nope.* Nor would he. *Not part of the plan.* Although making the old man think there would be a ransom was definitely part of the plan.

Wilson's eyes gleamed at the prospect of sharing five million dollars. *As if.* "You think they'll pay?"

Mitch smiled. "I know they will."

One

The kid's hood was ice-cold. FBI Special Agent Joseph Carter lifted his hand from Ford Elkhart's Chevy Suburban, flexing his fingers to shake off the chill. The thin latex gloves he wore were no protection against the frigid wind, but he'd left his leather gloves at home. At least the latex kept him from contaminating what might be a crime scene.

Might be, but probably was not. Ford's boss was already convinced that something dire had happened to the boy, but Joseph considered it far more likely that the twenty-year-old college kid had gone home with his girlfriend last night for wild monkey sex.

However, Ford's boss was Joseph's father, so Joseph figured he could spare an hour to check on the kid, just to put his dad's mind at ease.

And, Joseph would admit to himself alone, his own mind. Because even though he mostly believed that Ford and his girlfriend were doing the horizontal tango in a nice warm bed, the uncertainty would nag at him until he knew for sure. Because Ford struck him as a little too soberly reliable to simply not show up to work without a phone call.

And if something dire had happened, the boy's mother would be devastated.

A woman like Ford's mother did not deserve to be devastated. A single mom, she'd raised her son while earning her law degree and now successfully juggled her job as a prosecutor with an impressive list of charitable activities. She was colorfully bold, warmly brash. Smart as hell.

And, of course, there were those legs of hers. Joseph let out a harsh breath that hung in the cold air, remembering his first look at Assistant State's Attorney Daphne Montgomery, more than nine months before.

No, he couldn't forget about those legs. He hadn't been able to forget about her at all. He'd tried. Many, many times. But she was taken. *Because I waited too long*.

Making sure that her son was unharmed was the least he could do for her. Hell, it was the only thing he could do for her. Because he'd waited too long and now another man got to see her legs up close . . . and the rest of her, too.

His phone buzzed in his pocket and he grabbed at it, happy for anything that would distract him from the direction his mind had taken. The caller ID was no surprise. That his father had waited this long before calling for an update was unusual.

The CEO of an electronics firm that had its fingers in everything from guidance systems to prosthetic implants, Jack Carter gave definition to the term "multitasking." The term "waiting," however, wasn't high on his vocabulary list.

"Well?" his father demanded. "Did you find him?"

"Found his Suburban," Joseph said. "About a block from Penn Station."

"Why was he at the train station? His buddy said he posted on Facebook that he took his girlfriend to a movie for her French class."

"Only two theaters in town are showing French films, one near the station. I searched until I found his SUV. Appears to have been here all night."

"That's a dangerous part of town."

"It's not bad during the day." Joseph watched a homeless man shuffle into an alley, a bag slung over his back. Probably all he owned in the world. "At night it can get dicey."

"That's why Ford went. So that Kim wouldn't be out alone after dark."

"I take it that you haven't heard from him."

"No, but I did just get a call from Andrew, the other student intern who Ford was supposed to drive to work this morning. Andrew called Kim's dorm and she's not there, either. Her roommate said she never came back last night."

Some people might think it odd that a CEO would take such an interest in the business of a college intern. Those people hadn't met his dad. Carter Industries was a giant in the manufacturing world, but Jack Carter was a scientist at heart and research was his life's blood. Interns generated a lot of new ideas and his father made it a point to listen to each one. That he'd know Ford Elkhart by name was to be expected.

That he'd care so much about the kid's safety . . . well, that was his dad. That there was a family connection hadn't hurt. Joseph's adopted brother, Grayson, was Daphne's boss and her friend. That made Daphne and her son like family.

That Ford shared Jack's interest in research had sealed the deal. Jack loved his four children unconditionally, but none of them had any interest in the family business.

Joseph's oldest sister, Lisa, ran a catering company with her husband. His middle sister, Zoe, was a police psychologist, and his youngest sister, Holly . . . well, Holly worked for Lisa. An adult with Down syndrome, Holly grew more independent with every year that passed, but she would never take the reins of Carter Industries.

Joseph was probably his father's biggest disappointment. He'd actually earned a degree in electrical engineering, only to join the FBI. His passion had never been wires and widgets. But Ford's was, and his dad had become fond of the kid.

"They probably checked into a hotel," Joseph said. "They're twenty-year-olds and he's rich. Maybe the movie gave them ideas they wanted privacy to try."

"No, Ford's been signed up to use one of the new robotic devices and this morning was his turn in the lab. It's all he could talk about. Something's not right here. I feel it."

Joseph felt it, too, that buzzing on the back of his neck that signaled trouble. "Has anyone contacted the parents of either kid? Maybe they went home."

"I've tried to call Daphne, but it goes to her voice mail. I don't have numbers for Kim's parents, but Andrew said they lived near Philly."

"I'll contact the university for the girl's parents' info.

Ford's mother is with the state's attorney's office, right?" Joseph asked, as if he didn't know exactly where she worked.

His father took a moment before answering. "Yes, Joseph," he said in a way that let Joseph know his coy move hadn't fooled the old man. *I never could.*

"I'll call Grayson." It was through one of his brother's court cases that Joseph had met Daphne in the first place. "He'll track her down."

"I already called Grayson, and got his voice mail, too. Seems they're both in court. It's that big trial that's been in the news."

"The Millhouse boy," Joseph said flatly. He'd been following the case, Daphne's first big solo trial since she'd been promoted to Grayson's old job. Reggie Millhouse, a high school senior, was accused of murdering a middle-aged married couple whose Mercedes had broken down on the side of a lonely road.

The case was top of the news because the married couple was African-American—and Reggie had ties to a local white supremacist group.

"The news said that the jury's reached a verdict," his father said. "City's gonna pop."

Because the evidence was mostly circumstantial and tempers raged on both sides. Whichever way the jury decided, there would be an outcry. Outside the courthouse was not the safest place to be today. Inevitably, that's where the protesters would gather.

If Daphne's son had disappeared on the eve of an important verdict . . .

"You're quiet," his father murmured. "Are you thinking what I'm thinking?"

"It could be coincidence." Joseph prayed it was. "I'll head over there, wait for his mother and Grayson to come out of court." He started walking to his Escalade. "Let's not borrow trouble until we know for sure that the kids are really missing."

"That's wise. I have Kim's car's make and license plate. She visited Ford here at the office for lunch a few times, so it was on file at the guard shack. Her full name is Kimberly MacGregor and she drives a ten-year-old Toyota Corolla. Blue."

"Fine. I'll call you if . . . Wait." Joseph turned, looking back to the five cars parked between Ford's SUV and the alley into which the homeless man had gone a few minutes before. Joseph started to run, abruptly stopping at the last vehicle in line.

"What is it?" his father demanded. "Joseph?"

Joseph stared at the blue Corolla. There was a dark brown smear on the passenger-door handle. Dried blood. Heart sinking, he crouched by the door, where he saw two more smears, hand-shaped, woman-sized.

"Read me the license plate number." His father did and it was a match. "I found the girl's car." The blood he'd keep from his father, for now. "I'll call you when I know—" A shrill scream from within the alley cut him off.

"What was that? Joseph, answer—"

Joseph ran to the alley entrance. The homeless man was running in the opposite direction, hands empty. Something had scared him so badly that he'd dropped his sack.

"Call you back," Joseph said curtly, dropping his phone into his pocket as he started after the man. But halfway into the alley Joseph stopped short.

A pair of feet wearing bright red socks stuck out from one end of a pile of flattened boxes, reminding Joseph ridiculously of the witch's red shoes sticking out from under Dorothy's house. Except the feet were big. A man's feet.

Grimly, he stepped around the pile of boxes, then let out a relieved breath. It wasn't Daphne's son. It wasn't anyone Joseph knew. But the man was unquestionably dead, the cause of death most likely the slit across his throat that went ear to ear.

Joseph swallowed hard. The victim's head clung to his body by about two inches of flesh on the back of his neck. He'd seen his share of slit throats in the course of his career, but this one . . . it was damn near decapitation.

No wonder the homeless guy took off. The sack he'd left behind sat a few feet from the victim's head. A pair of running shoes had rolled to the pavement. The shoe size looked to be a match for the dead man's feet.

That's cold. Stealing the shoes off a dead man. It appeared that the homeless guy had started to pull boxes off the victim when he'd seen the head and bolted.

About half of the victim's torso was uncovered. He was a black male, mid-thirties. About six feet and broad-shouldered. He wore a leather jacket, unzipped, and under it a gray sweatshirt with three big black letters.

The middle letter was a "P," visible where the jacket parted. To the left of it was what looked like an "M." To the right . . . it was a "D." Joseph sighed quietly. *Aw, hell.*

MPD. Metro Police Department. *This guy's a DC cop.*

Joseph crouched next to the victim. Carefully he probed the man's chest through the sweatshirt. And felt something hard. On a chain. In the shape of a shield. *A DC cop killed in the line of duty.*

"Goddammit," Joseph muttered, dialing his cell phone as he came to his feet. The murder of a cop was enough of a loss. That the victim had been on duty made it that much worse. That the victim was Joseph's own age . . . It hit damn close to home.

"Special Agent Lamar, VCET."

Supervisory Special Agent Boaz Lamar headed the Violent Crimes Enforcement Team, a joint task force staffed by Baltimore city and county cops and the FBI. Bo and Joseph went way back in the Bureau—Bo had been one of his trainers when Joseph had been a newly sworn agent.

Three years ago, Bo began preparing for his retirement and had asked Joseph to transfer from the domestic terrorism unit into VCET, with the plan being for Joseph to eventually be promoted to Bo's job. For reasons of his own, Joseph had declined, then and every other time Bo brought it up.

Until nine months ago, when everything changed and, again for reasons of his own, Joseph accepted Bo's offer, surprising everyone. When grilled by his family, he'd said he needed a change. When grilled by his bosses, he'd said he wanted to stick closer to home. Neither was a lie. But the real reason he kept to himself.

It had been a damn good reason nine months ago. Six months of paperwork and red tape later, Joseph had his transfer, but his real reason wasn't actionable anymore.

Because he'd waited too long and Daphne had chosen someone else.

Sometimes life's a bitch that way. He looked down at the body. He was pretty sure that Mr. Red Socks would agree, whoever he was.

"Bo, it's Joseph. I need CSU and the ME at this location. I've got a definite murder and a possible abduction with two missing persons. One is Ford Elkhart, the son of the state's attorney on the Millhouse case. The other is Kimberly MacGregor, his girlfriend." Joseph dreaded the fear he'd see in Daphne's eyes when he told her. "This dead guy was a DC Metro cop. Somebody all but separated his head from his body."

Bo exhaled. "Text me his face and we'll contact MPD to get an ID started. I'll get a team together and out to you within fifteen."

Tuesday, December 3, 9:57 a.m.

Most excellent. Mitch Roberts's customer was waiting, just where he was supposed to be. *It's nice when people follow instructions.*

George Millhouse wasn't waiting very patiently, though. He paced back and forth, checking his watch every five seconds. Which, had they been in a less secluded place, would have been a dead giveaway. *Fortunately, I planned for this.* George's frantic pacing would be seen by no one.

Mitch slipped into the alley, much like he'd slipped into the one down by the movie theater the night before. *Except there'd better not be any surprises like there were last night.* He didn't like surprises in general, and that cop had been a nasty shock.

Mitch grinned to himself. And then the cop had gotten a nasty shock. It all worked out very well, actually. Better than the original plan. "Hello, George."

George spun around, relief filling his eyes, followed by fury. "*Doug.* Where have you been? I've been waiting here for an hour. I'm going to be *late.*"

Using one's real name when selling illegal weapons would have been downright foolish, so Mitch had introduced himself to the Millhouses as "Doug" months ago. It had become something of a nickname during the years he spent in prison, so every time he heard one of the Millhouses call his name it rekindled his anger, reminding him that there was someone he hated even more than Daphne Montgomery.

Not that Mitch needed any reminders. He wore his anger like a second skin, his revenge a painful thirst that he could never satisfy. Until now. Everything was finally coming together and furious George here was an important piece of the plan.

Mitch kept his voice mild. "What you're going to be is

arrested if you don't calm down. You look like *you* did the murder, George."

George's eyes narrowed. "If you didn't bring my package, I just might."

Were I not armed, I'd be nervous. George was a big sonofabitch, yet still smaller than his brother Reggie, who was a fucking King Kong. The jury had seen Reggie that way, too. Which was why George was so anxious to get this delivery.

"Tsk, tsk, tsk. George, how many times do I have to tell you to hold your temper?"

George ground his teeth. "Did you bring the knife?"

"Of course I did." With a few modifications. "Did you bring the brace?"

George held out a plastic grocery bag. "Yeah. I did."

Mitch frowned. "Have you been wearing it?"

"*Yes.* Every goddamn day of this trial. Now *hurry*. I need to get to the courtroom."

Mitch took the wrist brace from the bag and winced. Yep, George had been wearing it all right. Every day. During which he'd never washed his arm. The brace was ripe.

"Do me a favor, will you, and slip the plastic plate out of the brace. The one that supports your wrist." George obeyed, carelessly leaving his prints all over the plastic. *Like taking candy from a baby,* Mitch thought as he produced an identical-looking plate from his pocket. Unlike George, he wore gloves, ensuring that the only prints the cops would find would be George's. "This is your knife."

George's face darkened. "*That?* That piece of shit plastic? *That's* what you've been promising us?"

"Watch. This plate slides apart—it's two layers." He took the pieces apart, but George was not impressed. *Idiot.* This was top-of-the-line polymer construction.

"It's plastic," George said flatly.

"But it's no piece of shit. The edges of the bottom layer have been sharpened to a fine edge. It will easily slice skin and muscle." Which it had done the night before. *Stupid cop. Sneaking up on me.* "If you use enough pressure, it'll cut through bone. Connect the pieces like this." Mitch snapped them together. "This other piece isn't sharp. Therefore it is the handle." He said it like he might to a kindergartner.

Giving him a dirty look, George crossed his arms over his chest. "Prove it."

I should prove it on you. But that wouldn't suit his goal. Mitch looked around the alley, spied a bicycle tire. He picked it up and tossed it to George, who dropped the original dull, fingerprint-riddled plastic brace so that he could catch it.

"What the fuck?" George exploded. "I gotta go to court. I might be on TV and you almost messed up my suit."

"If you hold the tire, you'll know how much pressure I'm using to cut it." The knife easily sliced through the tire and George's irate disbelief became greedy delight.

"Give it to me." George opened his backpack. "Small bills, just like you asked for."

"Very good." Just to mess with him, Mitch began to count the cash.

George growled. "If I miss the verdict, I promise you will be a very unhappy man."

"I don't want to be unhappy." Mitch unsnapped the handle from the blade, fitted the plates together, and slid them into the brace. "There you go."

"If I get caught with this thing, you'll be even unhappier." With that, George shoved the backpack at him and took off, fastening the brace to his wrist as he ran.

Actually, if you get caught I'll be exceptionally happy, you inbred dick.

Once alone, Mitch emptied the backpack, dumping the cash into the plastic grocery sack. He scooped up the legitimate plastic brace plate that George had dropped, put it in the backpack, and tossed the backpack behind a Dumpster, his plan on track.

The cops would inevitably find the weapon he'd just sold to George, either because George got caught in security or because the Millhouses' crazy Plan B actually worked and they ended up using it in the courtroom.

Regardless, Baltimore PD's CSU expert would be so excited—because in the crevice where the handle met George's blade, they'd find blood that matched a certain dead DC Metro cop. George and the whole Millhouse clan would be on the hook.

Sweet. One more thing to do and he could go home. Mitch took Ford Elkhart's iPhone from his pocket and slid the SIM card he'd removed the night before back into place. Turning it on, he checked Ford's texts. There were several, including two from somebody who appeared to be Ford's boss, asking why he hadn't shown up at his job.

Mitch had been surprised to find Ford had a job at all considering he was mega-rich. Granted, it was a nerd desk job, but the kid put in twenty hours a week. On top of his studies and sports and his girlfriend, he kept busy. Hard to find time for his mama.

Who would be in court, waiting for that jury verdict. *I'm so damn tired of hearing about that verdict.* But the Millhouses couldn't have come along at a better time. All the trash talk aimed at the prosecution gave him one enormous decoy to hide behind.

I want Montgomery to suffer. I want her to die. But I won't get caught. Prison was not for the fainthearted, which he knew firsthand. Much better for the cops to think the Millhouses were behind his evil deeds. *Much better if no one suspects me at all.*

Except for Daphne, of course. *She needs to know that I'm the one holding the gun to her head. Just like she held the gun to my mother's.*

Ford's phone held no new texts from his mother. Old texts asked how he was, how was school. Ford's responses were brief, so the text Mitch had in mind would fit right in.

Good luck, Mom! he typed, then removed the SIM card and turned off the phone. The cops would soon start hunting for Ford. When they checked his phone records, they'd think he'd sent a text from this very spot.

Unfortunately, all they'd find when they got here would be George Millhouse's backpack—and one plastic wrist brace plate with George's fingerprints all over it. *The same shape as the blade George is smuggling into the courthouse at this very moment.*

I love it when everything comes together. Now he could go home. He'd first check on the girls, make sure they hadn't died from exposure or blood loss during the night.

Then I have to sleep. He should have felt tired after driving so many hours, but he didn't. He felt juiced. On the verge. The plans he'd spent months constructing in painful detail were about to come to fruition. It was as if he'd spent months setting up dominoes in intricate designs and now stood poised to nudge the first one down. It was going to be one hell of a show.

And so even though he wasn't tired, he'd make himself sleep. He needed to be well-rested so that he didn't miss a single moment.

Tuesday, December 3, 10:10 a.m.

Assistant State's Attorney Daphne Montgomery glanced at the clock on the wall for the tenth time in as many minutes. The door to the jury deliberation room remained firmly closed and the tension in the courtroom seemed to double with every sweep of that slow-moving minute hand. *What the hell is* taking *them so long?*

"What the hell is *taking* them so long?" a male voice muttered over her shoulder. Daphne looked up to see her boss pulling out the chair next to hers. "Just a little moral support before the party starts," Grayson added in a murmur. "This is always the hardest for me. Waiting those last few minutes for the jury to file in."

"Assuming they're even still back there and haven't all fled to Tahiti or something," Daphne murmured back. Which would be par for the course for this case, a three-ring circus even before jury selection had begun, thirty very long days ago.

Grayson frowned. "What do you know?"

"Only that the jurors saw the protesters this morning, just like we did." The crowd had more than doubled that morning, their collective energy increasing by far more. "And the Millhouse contingent is smiling like canary-eating cats."

The Millhouse contingent included Bill and Cindy—parents of the accused—and a half dozen of their saner family members. "Saner" being relative, of course.

"More like vultures," Grayson said with contempt. "Circling."

Reggie sat at the defendant's table with an arrogant smile. *He expects to be acquitted.* The eighteen-year-old had beaten an African-American couple to death after finding them stranded on the road. His lawyer had the nerve to present a self-defense plea, claiming the couple lured an unsuspecting Reggie to their aid and had struck him first.

The media had stirred a frenzy in the city. Reggie's father, Bill, had worked the talk-show circuit, presenting his family as ordinary, hardworking, and middle class, struggling to make ends meet and pay the rent—just like everyone else. Bill Millhouse had made numerous pleas for support—and dollars—for Reggie's defense.

Has this country become so politically correct that a white man can't defend himself? had become Bill's sound bite. His followers had responded enthusiastically, donating a staggering sum through a Web site set up for that purpose.

African-American community leaders responded with rhetoric of their own and the battle spread from television to churches and civic halls, bars and beauty parlors, spilling over into the largely anonymous Internet blogosphere like . . . a cancer. Insidious and terrifying.

But defeatable, Daphne thought resolutely. *This I know for a fact.*

Because she'd beaten cancer herself. It was an empowering thing, beating cancer. It had left her with the feeling of *I stared death in the eye, so hit me with your best shot, asshole.* Earned arrogance, so to speak. Reggie's arrogance was nothing but a cheap imitation. *Like a ten-dollar Prada knockoff.*

She met Reggie's eyes across the aisle. Watched his smile fade to a grim snarl. *Too bad his online fan club isn't here to see it.* Reggie pretended to be a poster child for milk-drinking, clean-living, misunderstood American youth. A frightening number of people in TV- and Internet-land had bought his innocent act, lock, stock, and wallet.

And then you met me, you little sonofabitch.

"Well, sugar," she said softly to Grayson, "those vultures can circle all they want. I'm nobody's roadkill today."

"Atta girl, *sugar,*" he said, mimicking her twang. A glance up at him revealed the approval in his eyes. Because she knew the kind of man he was, his approval meant a lot. But his approval was tempered with caution. "Are you wearing your vest?"

"Every damn day, because either way this jury comes back, there'll be trouble."

"Either way this jury comes back," Grayson countered, "you've done a good job."

"I had good evidence." The detectives had been meticulous, the ME unshakable. Daphne had presented a solid case while the Millhouse clan stared with blatant malice, trying to intimidate her. That they'd succeeded was a secret she'd never reveal.

"You stuck," Grayson said simply. "A lot of prosecutors would have quit. A few did."

I almost did, too. Daphne had no doubts that the Millhouses were responsible for the threatening phone calls she'd received, but the police hadn't been able to prove it. The calls had started months ago, long before the first juror was chosen. At first they'd been annoying but quickly swelled into threats that left her shaken.

She'd started driving home a different way every night and her two newest—and now closest—friends had become concerned. A pair of PIs, they'd taken charge of the escalating situation, providing the kind of personal security that the police simply couldn't give her.

Clay Maynard had ensured that her house was wired with the best security system money could buy. Paige Holden drilled her in self-defense moves and had given her a very big dog. Things had settled for a while, and Daphne redoubled her efforts to build a case that would wipe that arrogant smile off the little bastard's face.

But when the callers had threatened her son . . . Daphne had come damn close to calling it quits. She'd begged Ford to accept a bodyguard, but her twenty-year-old, testing-his-wings son had point-blank refused and no amount of reason had swayed him. So, being a mom, she'd hired one anyway. *He'd shit a ring if he knew the truth.* But she wouldn't apologize if he found out. *Because I sleep better. A little.*

More important than her sleep, it had given her the strength to stay the course.

She'd been through a hell of a lot in her life and was proud that she'd never given up. There'd been a few times she'd had to hunker down and wait out a storm, but mostly she'd risen to whatever challenge had been tossed in her path. Giving up had rarely even entered her mind. But the thought of the Millhouses touching a single hair on Ford's head had given her serious pause.

"I don't give up so easily," she said, grateful she'd had the financial means to make that statement true. If she hadn't been able to afford protection for Ford, she might have run for the hills. Instead, she'd pushed forward, prosecuting an eighteen-year-old murderer who'd regarded her with chilling contempt from the first day of the trial.

Now the final decision lay with the jury.

"Miss Montgomery."

Daphne turned to the quiet voice on the bench behind her. It was Sondra Turner, the daughter of the victims. Barely twenty-one, she'd conducted herself with a dignity far beyond her years. Beside her was her younger brother, DeShawn, who sat slightly bent forward, his eyes closed. His clenched fists rested on his knees.

"Almost over, guys," Daphne murmured. "Soon."

Sondra folded her hands in her lap. "I wanted . . . we wanted you to know that whatever happens next, we know you did your best for our parents. Thank you."

"You're welcome." But even if they got a conviction, it wouldn't be enough. Sondra and DeShawn had lost their parents, brutally. Nothing would bring them back.

But a conviction was better than nothing. Better than no justice. *This I also know.*

Daphne sympathized with the victims who relived their trauma in the courtroom, but she also envied the closure they got from the process. She'd never confronted the man who stole so much from her. From her family. She'd been too young. Then too scared. And then he'd been too dead. The passage of time had taken the choice out of her hands.

"Did you make provisions for them?" Grayson whispered, facing forward so that the Turners' children could not see his face. *In the event of a riot*, was what he left unsaid.

"I did." Daphne lifted her eyes to the back of the standing-room-only gallery to the detectives who'd made the arrest, J. D. Fitzpatrick and Stevie Mazzetti. They'd promised to protect Sondra and DeShawn if courtroom tensions boiled over. The promise had not been easily won from J.D., who hadn't wanted to abandon Daphne should a melee erupt.

J.D. shouldn't even be here, she thought. *He should be home with Lucy.* J.D.'s very pregnant wife was due any day, and even though she was already on maternity leave, she'd come in to testify the week before. As the medical examiner who'd autopsied the Turners, Dr. Lucy Trask Fitzpatrick's testimony had been invaluable, painting the picture of a brutal attack on a middle-aged couple who'd tried to defend themselves, but had been overpowered by someone much bigger and stronger. Someone just like Reggie Millhouse.

J.D. gave Daphne a hard stare now and mouthed, "Vest?"

Daphne nodded, then her eyes flicked to the door at his right as it opened. The older Millhouse brother had arrived, uncharacteristically out of breath. George had been running, his face red and sweaty. He shot her a cold look before taking his place between his parents.

"Looks like George made it after all," Grayson murmured.

"Lucky us," Daphne muttered sarcastically. George had been escorted from the courtroom many times for his outbursts. She wasn't eager to see what he had up his sleeve today. She turned in her seat, facing forward. "At least Marina isn't here."

"Maybe she finally had that baby," Grayson said.

"Lucky us," Daphne muttered again. That child didn't have a snowball's chance in hell with a sixteen-year-old KKK groupie for a mother and Reggie Millhouse for a father.

Normally Daphne felt empathy for teen mothers, having been one herself, but she felt very little for Marina. Daphne clearly remembered what it had been like to find out she was pregnant at fifteen—the fear, the despair, the disappointment that her dreams would never be. But those feelings had quickly taken a backseat to the need to protect her unborn child, to give him the best life she could. It had been one of the greatest challenges in her life.

Marina—and the Millhouses—seemed to view pregnancy in a far more calculating way, using her baby to manipulate public opinion in their favor. There were some who pitied Marina, believing that the Millhouses controlled her actions, but Daphne had seen the sly gleam in the girl's eye. Marina not only knew what she was doing, she reveled in it. Daphne worried about the baby, worried about the life the child would lead. If Reggie was acquitted, the baby would be raised to become another Millhouse, racist and violent, but with that shiny veneer of charm that had fooled so many. If Reggie was convicted, his baby, who *in utero* had already become the symbol of the Millhouses' "hope for a purer America," would become . . . Daphne shuddered to think about it.

Marina had been absent for the past few days, a welcome relief from her soulful sobs. A pretty girl, she was a media favorite who used those baby blues of hers to influence anyone on the fence.

Unbelievably, there were people on the fence. Hopefully none were on this jury.

Daphne sucked in a breath when the door to the jury room opened. *Finally.* Clearing her mind, she studied the jurors, noting that some were pale. All were grim.

"I'm going back to my seat now," Grayson whispered. "If things go south, you will not act the hero. You tuck and roll. Got it?"

"Sugar, if things go south, I'll be dusting the floor. Guaranteed."

The bailiff entered solemnly. "All rise."

They did, then sat when the judge had been seated. Daphne held her breath as the judge asked the jury foreman for their verdict. The foreman stood, the paper he held fluttering as his hands shook. But he wasted no time in reading the verdict.

"We the jury, on the charge of murder in the first degree, find the defendant, Reggie Millhouse, guilty."

Yes. Daphne closed her eyes as cheers and cries of outrage rose around them.

"No!"

Twisting in the direction of the shriek, Daphne could only stare. One second Cindy Millhouse was hugging her son over the bar, sobbing, then suddenly she was barreling through the gate.

"Bitch!" Fingers like claws, face contorted with rage, Cindy lunged, coming for . . .

Me. Oh my God. She's coming for me.

Tuesday, December 3, 10:10 a.m.

Joseph texted photos of the dead cop's face to Bo, but didn't think they'd do much good toward an ID. The pics were too grainy because the alley was too damn dark, the rooftops of the buildings blocking what little natural light there was. The sky was gray and darkening by the hour, the forecasters calling for more snow. *Which is all we need.*

He was about to put his phone away when a string of very terse texts came through. *Hell.* He'd forgotten about his father. Joseph sent a quick answer: *Working a case. Victim is not Ford. Will call when I can.*

He aimed his flashlight at the victim's face and upper

torso—all he could see until CSU processed the scene and removed the pile of boxes covering him to his ankles.

There didn't seem to be any injuries to the face and head. Nothing but that mawing slice across his throat. The blood that had pooled behind the victim's neck and head had frozen. The cop had been lying here for hours. Probably since last night.

Why were you here, man? Why are you dead?

Joseph frowned. And why was the blood frozen in a pool close to the man's head? He stood, shining his light on the walls and pavement, looking for spatter, but saw none.

The blood had seeped, not spurted. Which meant Red Socks was already dead when his throat was slit. This guy was big, his neck thick and muscular. So how had his killer taken him down? And why slit his throat if he was already dead?

Joseph searched the area beyond the victim and found part of the answer. AFID tags, about an inch in diameter, littered the ground five feet from where the victim lay. Like confetti, twenty to thirty of the brightly colored anti-felon identification tags were ejected from a Taser when a cartridge was deployed. Serial numbers on each tag matched the cartridge, intended to deter anyone from firing a Taser unlawfully and to track them if they did.

It obviously hadn't deterred Red Socks's assailant. Still, a Taser blast wouldn't have killed the victim. So what happened in between the Taser and the knife?

Joseph lifted his head when he heard a car door being closed. CSU was still five minutes away. But it could be somebody returning to the scene.

Drawing his gun, Joseph stepped into the shadows behind the Dumpster closest to the alley entrance. And waited. He didn't have to wait long.

A man crept into the alley. He was as big as Joseph, and the collar of his leather jacket was pulled up, hiding his face. Still, there was something familiar about him. The way he moved. Like a soldier. The way he held his gun at his side. Like a cop. A recent memory flickered and Joseph narrowed his eyes. *No way. Couldn't be.*

"Tuzak," the man hissed. "Are you here?" He paused, tilting his head to listen.

The movement exposed his face and Joseph's suspicion was confirmed. Clay Maynard.

Joseph knew this guy. Resented the fucking hell out of him. Came perilously close to hating him. *So of course he shows up.* He'd worked with the PI once before. The day he'd met Daphne. Clay Maynard had met her that same day. Except it was Maynard she'd come to rely on in the months that followed. Months when Joseph had flown all over the country, tracking domestic terrorists, waiting for his transfer into VCET so that he could stay close to home. Close to her.

What the hell is he doing here? That he was carrying a semi-auto didn't bode well.

However, as much as Joseph would have liked to believe the guy was dirty, he knew better. He could hate Clay Maynard for sharing Daphne's bed, but the man had earned the respect of the Carter clan. Of Joseph's brother, Grayson, specifically.

Clay's partner in his PI firm was Grayson's fiancée, Paige Holden. Paige trusted Maynard with her life. Importantly, Grayson trusted Maynard with Paige's life.

Maynard continued toward him. In another few steps, he'd discover Red Socks.

Remaining concealed, Joseph kept his voice even, not wanting to surprise a man with a gun in his hand. "FBI. Drop your weapon."

"Fuck," Maynard muttered. "Let me see the badge."

Joseph held it out and Maynard's chin came up, his eyes wide. "Carter?"

"That would be me. The gun, please."

Maynard handed it over, handle first. "Why are you here?"

"I was going to ask you the same thing." Joseph pocketed Maynard's gun.

"I have a permit to carry," Maynard said, eyes narrowing.

"You'll get it back when we're done. Why are you here?"

"I'm looking for someone."

He'd called the man *Tuzak*. "A friend?" Joseph asked.

"An employee." Maynard hesitated. "And yes, he's a friend, too."

Joseph thought of the slice across the victim's throat. As much as he resented Maynard, he hated for the guy to see his friend that way. "Is he a cop?"

Maynard's narrowed eyes turned wary. "How'd you know?"

There was no good way to say the words. "He's dead, Clay. I'm sorry."

Maynard's eyes closed, shoulders sagging as if he'd been expecting it. "How?"

"Throat slit."

Maynard's eyes flew open, denial warring with grief. "What are you doing here?"

"I'm also looking for an employee." Ford Elkhart was his father's employee, but it was close enough for now. "Why was this man here? What was he doing for you?"

"Where is he?" Maynard pushed past Joseph.

Joseph grabbed his arm. "No. Clay, wait."

Maynard snarled, pain in his eyes. "Let me go or I'll break your fucking arm."

"He . . . looks bad. If he was your friend, you don't want to see him this way."

Clay's lips thinned. "I'm sure I've seen worse. Let me go."

Joseph released him, following to make sure he didn't disturb the scene. Maynard probably had seen a lot worse, but it was different when you knew the victim.

Maynard abruptly stopped when he saw the victim's red socks and sucked in a strangled breath as he walked around to see the head, the color draining from his face.

"Oh God," he whispered. "Not again." Slowly he fell to his knees. "Not again."

Not again? What the— Oh, shit. Maynard's story came back to Joseph in a rush. He'd lost the partner before Paige, discovering her body gutted by a vicious killer and left to rot. Now this partner was nearly decapitated. *If I'd remembered, I would have held him back harder, kept him from seeing this.* But Joseph knew it would have been fruitless to try to control Maynard. *I would've pushed him away under the same circumstances.*

"They cut him." Maynard uttered the words in a choked whisper. "They cut his head off. Oh my God. Fucking hell." He lurched to his feet and stumbled backward, his expression a mixture of shock, nausea, and pain.

Joseph turned him so that he no longer stared at his dead friend. "Who is he?"

"Isaac Zacharias. Sergeant, DCPD. Oh God. What am I gonna tell Phyllis?"

"What was he doing for you?" Joseph shook his shoulder. "*Clay*. What was Zacharias doing for you that got him killed?"

Maynard drew a breath and pulled himself together. "Bodyguard duty."

Bodyguard duty. The sick feeling in Joseph's gut spiked. That Daphne would trust Maynard to protect her son made sense.

New horror mixed with the grief on Maynard's face. "Oh God. Ford. Daphne's son."

"Zacharias was protecting Ford?"

"Ford is the employee, isn't he? Your father's employee." It was calmly stated, but the vein in Maynard's neck visibly throbbed. "Where is he?"

"He appears to be missing," Joseph said grimly.

"Does Daphne know?"

"Not yet. We've tried to contact her. She hasn't answered her phone this morning."

"She's in court. Jury verdict today on the Millhouse case."

"How did you know to come here?"

"Tracker on Tuzak's car. All my people carry one, just in case they need backup. His relief called to say he hadn't phoned in Ford's location. I called Phyllis to see if he'd come home from his night shift. He hadn't, so I tracked him here."

"Tuzak is Zacharias?"

"Isaac Zacharias. Two Zacs. We called him Tuzak at the academy. It stuck."

"You were in DCPD together?"

"Yeah. I left, he stayed. He was a good cop. Smart. He never would have let some punk get the drop on him. How the hell did this happen?" He turned to Joseph, his eyes suddenly suspicious. "And how did *you* know to come here?"

"Ford didn't show up for work this morning. Dad asked me to check it out. I found Ford's SUV on the street at the other end of the alley. It's probably been there all night."

The suspicion faded from Maynard's eyes, replaced with a weary dread. "This is going to kill her," he murmured.

"She was terrified something like this would happen." He turned, his gaze returning to his slain friend. "How do I tell her? She's pregnant."

Joseph's teeth clacked together, hard. "Daphne's *pregnant*?"

Maynard shook his head. "No. Phyllis Zacharias. The baby's due in a few weeks. Tuzak was just looking to make a little extra . . . for expenses."

Joseph pointed his flashlight to the AFID tags, noticing there were even more a few feet away. Zacharias's killer had fired multiple cartridges. "Taser."

"Sonofabitch," Maynard swore viciously, then swallowed hard. "Sonofabitch," he repeated, this time in a whisper. "Phyllis can't see him this way. She can't."

"We won't ask her to do the ID," Joseph murmured. "But we have two missing persons and I'm going to have to ask questions."

"Then ask me," Clay said harshly. "Phyllis only knew that he was working for me."

"Okay, we'll start with you. Did Zacharias see anything weird? Anyone suspicious?"

"No. He said it was a cream puff job, following around a squeaky-clean kid who didn't even know he was there."

"Ford didn't know he had a bodyguard?"

"No. Daphne tried to get him to agree to have one, but the kid is stubborn. She started getting threats and—"

"What kind of threats?" Joseph demanded. "From whom?"

"Violent threats. You-have-to-sleep-sometime threats. Isn't-that-son-of-yours-a-handsome-young-man threats. I'm certain they came from the family of the murderer she's prosecuting. Millhouse. I have to tell her."

"No, you don't. Let us handle this."

Maynard glared. "This is my business, Carter. My employee. My friend. My goddamn responsibility."

"I know," Joseph said quietly, knowing he was dealing with a man on the edge of control. *I'd react the same way.* And he had. "And you have my word that I'll respect that. But this is my case and you're going to have to trust me. I know my job."

"Wait. You're Homeland. You're out of your jurisdiction. Why is this your case?"

Joseph wasn't surprised Maynard had known he'd been
Homeland Security. He did have to admit to being a bit
surprised—and impressed—with his brother's fiancée's discretion. Paige hadn't mentioned his transfer to her own
partner. *Good to know.*

"I'm VCET now. FBI/Local task force."

"I know what VCET is," Maynard said, jaw clenched.
"And for the record, I trust Feds about as much as I trust
most cops. Which is about nil."

"Look, you're standing here talking to me and not cuffed
because my brother trusts you. And because he does, I'll
explain how this is. Before Homeland, *this* is what I did—
finding missing people and killers. If you don't trust me,
you'll have to trust Grayson."

Maynard said nothing, so Joseph tried a different tack.
"Clay, Isaac was your friend. You're not objective. You
know it's true."

"And you'd step aside if you were me?"

*No. If somebody killed someone I cared about, I'd find
the sonofabitch and kill him with my bare hands.* And he
had. And he wasn't sorry. It was remembering . . . no, savor-
ing the sound of the neck he'd snapped all those years ago
that got him through the nightmares, then and now. And
the loneliness. Then and now.

A flutter at the corner of his eye caught Joseph's attention and he barely stifled his groan. A man stood in the alley entry, his snow-white hair and goatee sharply contrasting
with his bronzed face. His black leather trench coat whipped
in the wind and wraparound sunglasses covered his eyes.
His hand rested on his holstered gun as he assessed the situation, looking like a freaky cross between a sun-bleached
Blade and Wyatt Earp.

Maynard followed his gaze, stiffening. "What the hell is
that?"

A pain in my ass. "Special Agent Deacon Novak." Joseph looked back at Maynard. "Are you going to let me
handle this? Ford's life could depend on it."

"For now," Maynard said evenly.

"Fair enough." Maynard's concession would do. For
now. "Let's get to work."

Two

Frozen, Daphne watched Cindy Millhouse clear the bar like it was a track-and-field hurdle. Then her reflexes kicked in and Daphne was on her feet, her left arm swinging up, deflecting Cindy's fingers. *Not the hair. You're not touching my hair.*

She grabbed Cindy's wrist, struggling to keep the woman's sharp fingernails away from her face. From the direction of the defense table came a loud crash and Cindy's eyes flickered with satisfaction, her nails inching closer.

Then Cindy was yanked away and forced to the floor. Grayson glanced up, his face hard with fury. "Are you all right?" he asked as he restrained Cindy—an effort even for him, a guy who could bench-press a small truck. Reggie's mother was in wildcat mode.

Daphne nodded unsteadily. The defense's table had been overturned—the crash she'd heard. Edward Ellis, Reggie's attorney, lay on the floor, his foot pinned by the table. Stunned, Ellis stared up at his client, who grappled with the courtroom deputy. Reggie's arm was locked around Deputy Welch's throat as he grabbed for Welch's gun. For a horrified moment Daphne thought Reggie might succeed in getting it, but Welch threw his head back, cracking his skull into Reggie's face. The deputy broke free as five more uniforms charged through the gate. Four ran to subdue Reggie while the fifth veered off to assist Grayson.

Daphne had started to back away when she saw Deputy

Welch crawling back toward the overturned defense table, where Reggie continued to wrestle with the four new deputies. Welch was leaving a trail of bloody handprints behind him.

Dropping to her knees, she crawled over to Welch. "What are you doing, Deputy? Get back."

Welch's arm was bleeding profusely, dripping on the floor. "Shiv," he said, pointing.

Daphne could see it lying against the leg of the overturned table, hidden from the deputies' view. It didn't shine, wasn't metal. It looked like plastic. It looked harmless. But it couldn't be, because every time Reggie lunged, that was what he reached for.

"Get back. I'll get it." Going flat on her stomach, she reached out and closed her fingertips over the strange-looking knife, then crawled backward, away from the fray. She held the knife over her head. "He had a knife," she yelled, then placed it on the floor, far away from the action.

The deputies holding Reggie stared, eyes flaring wide. Two of the deputies drew their weapons, one aiming at Reggie's chest, the other at his head. A third smacked Reggie in the back of the head with his club, stunning him long enough to cuff one wrist.

Daphne turned back to Welch, who was lying in the shadow of the judge's bench. His arm still bled, but wasn't gushing, so that was good. She was more worried about the blood pooling at his hip. "He got you twice," she said.

"No shit." Welch tried for a smile but grimaced instead. "Hurts like a bitch."

"I guess so." The court reporter had left her sweater on the back of her chair when she'd fled the courtroom and Daphne grabbed it, pressing it to Welch's hip, surveying the courtroom as she applied pressure.

By the prosecution table, Cindy kicked and screamed even as she was being cuffed. On the other side of the aisle the deputies finally cuffed Reggie's other wrist, having had to use a stun gun first. They shackled his ankles with plastic restraints and Cindy abruptly ceased her thrashing, breathing hard. Her shoulders sagged as she stared at her son, her face grim with impotent rage.

Realization dawned. *That conniving bitch. She attacked me to create a diversion so that Reggie could escape.*

Cindy glared at Daphne, venom in her eyes. "You'll pay

for this," she spat as the deputy jerked her to her feet. "You took our son from us. I swear to the living God, you will know how this feels."

Daphne's composure remained intact as Cindy was removed from the courtroom, even though her heart hammered like a wild thing. She maintained her outward calm only because she knew that Ford was protected. A well-trained bodyguard had her son's back, whether he'd wanted one or not.

Plus, she'd learned the hard way that losing it at times like this didn't help anything. Welch still needed her to keep pressure on his wound. As long as she had a task to focus on, she'd be able to keep herself together. After that, she'd find a private place to fall apart.

The four deputies who'd subdued Reggie dragged him back to the holding cell while the second wave of uniforms finished clearing the gallery and moved the table off Reggie's defense attorney.

When the courtroom was finally emptied, a team of EMTs rushed in and Daphne stepped back to give them room to work. She didn't realize how rigidly she was holding herself until Grayson gently took her hands, making her flinch violently.

"I'm sorry," Grayson murmured. "I didn't mean to scare you. Your hands are covered with Welch's blood." He began to clean her hands with disinfectant wipes.

"He's going to be okay, right?" she asked, more for reassurance than anything else.

"Looks like it. When you're less tense, I'm going to yell like hell at you for grabbing that knife. You could have been killed." He released her hands, clean now.

"You would have done the same thing," she said shakily.

Grayson shrugged. "I'm still going to yell like hell at you. Once I'm able to breathe, that is."

"Join the club." Daphne fought the trembles she felt coming on. She cautiously ran a hand over her hair and exhaled, relieved. Her smooth twist was still in place. *Good thing Cindy didn't get her claws in my hair. That would have been embarrassing as hell.*

One of the EMTs came over to them. "Either of you need medical attention?"

"No," they answered together.

"Is Deputy Welch going to be okay?" she added.

"He should be fine. We've got a rig waiting outside for him. Mr. Defense over there will need to wait for the next one, but it's not far behind."

Grayson crouched beside Reggie's attorney. "How badly are you hurt?"

"Arm's busted," Ellis muttered, gritting his teeth. "Bastard snapped it. Ankle's probably busted, too."

Daphne could feel no sympathy for Edward Ellis. He'd had no legitimate defense, so he'd smeared the victims' good names ruthlessly. Because she couldn't think of a single nice thing to say at the moment, she kept her mouth shut.

Grayson must have found himself in the same position, because he fell silent, too.

Ellis shot them both a hostile look. "You think I deserved this."

"No," she denied quickly. "You didn't deserve to be hurt, but I guess I don't think you deserve to be terribly shocked. You're not a public defender. You chose to represent this killer."

Ellis's eyes narrowed. "I wasn't born with a silver spoon in my mouth and I wasn't lucky enough to grab one out of the mouth of a rich judge in a divorce settlement. You can afford to take the high road. I have to pay the rent, so I take the cases that come and I don't apologize."

Silver spoons, she thought, her temper boiling up. *If he only knew.* Clamping her mouth shut, she was grateful for the arrival of the second EMT team, who took Ellis away, leaving Daphne and Grayson staring at the doors that closed behind him.

"If he only knew what I paid for that silver spoon I got in my divorce settlement," she muttered, then shrugged uncomfortably.

If it had just been her, she would have walked away from her ex-husband's millions. But it hadn't been just her. It had been about Ford, about securing his future. So she'd fought hard and was mostly glad she had. Her divorce settlement had made it possible for her to achieve her own dreams. To get her law degree and to stand for victims like the Turners.

Grayson lifted his brows. "From what little I know about your ex, I'd say the silver spoon you got in your divorce settlement was well earned."

"Living with Travis Elkhart for twelve years was hard

work," she agreed, keeping her tone light. "Living with his mother was even harder. And speaking of mothers . . ." Daphne sat on the edge of the prosecutors' table, ready to change the subject. "Cindy Millhouse scares me shitless. *I swear to the living God, you will know how this feels,*" she quoted, then shivered. "I guess I'm lucky she didn't swear to any dead gods."

"Cindy smuggled a knife into the courtroom, threatened a state's attorney, and resisted arrest. I doubt she'll get bail."

"Yeah, but she and Bill have minions. And speaking of Bill, where was he when all hell broke loose? I saw George fighting with a cop and getting cuffed. Where was Bill?"

"He left the courtroom as soon as the verdict was read, probably to give his version to the press before you could."

"So he's out there somewhere. That makes me nervous." But being nervous wouldn't fix anything and she'd be damned before she'd hide. "Do you want to give a statement? The press will be mobbing the courthouse steps."

"Do I *want* to give a statement? Hell, no. But we will. Actually, you will. It was your case. Which you hit out of the park, by the way. Congratulations."

"Thank you," she said. "At least I'll be able to sleep tonight."

"I imagine you will at that," he said with a small secretive smile.

"What is that supposed to mean?"

"There's a bottle of champagne in our fridge that has your name on it. Paige bought it the day they started jury selection. She's very proud of you."

Grayson's face softened every time he mentioned his fiancée. It made Daphne all warm inside to see how close he and Paige had become.

Nine months ago Paige had exploded into their lives, seeking justice for Ramon Muñoz, a man wrongly convicted of a brutal murder. Now she was not only Grayson's fiancée, but she was also Daphne's best friend. Together she and Paige had started Women Serving Women—first as a cover for Paige's investigation to clear Muñoz, but once that job was done, their foundation grew legs. At the moment WSW housed only Paige's karate school, but the two of them had big plans.

The day Daphne had been assigned to the Millhouse case she'd told Paige she was afraid the case was too big, that she couldn't handle it. That her friend had bought champagne before the trial had even started . . . Daphne swallowed the lump in her throat. "That was so sweet of her."

"Although I think she'll be more proud when I tell her about that fancy blocking. I didn't realize you'd gotten so good."

"She kept drilling me with that one move. 'Keep your hands up,'" Daphne mimicked. "'You want to protect that beehive of yours? Then keep your damn hands up.'"

Grayson chuckled. "You mean the beehive you *used* to have. I'm glad she taught you so well, but I have to say that I do *not* miss the beehive."

Daphne had retired her trademark hairdo when she'd accepted the promotion into Grayson's old job as lead prosecutor the spring before. Back then, she'd sat second chair, taking notes, preparing briefs. Preparing witnesses to sit on the stand, to address the jury. Now, she addressed the jury, and their focus needed to be on her arguments and not her big hair. "I guess Cindy coming at my hair triggered my protective instincts."

"Then I'll never diss your hair again," he promised. "Ready for the cameras?"

"Hell, no. I am not facing the press looking like I was just in a barroom brawl. Give me a few minutes to put myself back together." *And to call my son.*

Hearing Ford's voice would dispel some of the fear that churned in her gut. It was time to tell him that he had a bodyguard. It didn't matter if he didn't want one, because as long as Cindy and her clan were a threat, he'd have one. It was non-negotiable.

Marston, West Virginia
Tuesday, December 3, 10:20 a.m.

Ford's nose burned, his eyes watered. *So cold. Shithead chem majors left the window open again. Gonna kick their—*

Awareness abruptly returned. The floor was hard and he was freezing. This wasn't his dorm and the chem majors were not doing another lab in the communal kitchen.

I'm still tied. Still blindfolded. Still gagged. But the smell was new. He drew a breath through his nose and tried to keep from throwing up. Something had died. *Kim.*

No. His mind immediately rejected it. Whatever had died was decomposing. Long dead. *Not Kim. So calm down before your head explodes.*

The throbbing pain in his skull had been joined by another new sensation—his scalp burned. *He grabbed my hair last night.* It felt like he'd yanked out a handful.

Who was that guy? He blocked the pain and concentrated on what he'd said. *I'm back. Did you miss me?* The memory of that mocking, singsongy tone made Ford's skin crawl. *Do I know him?* There was something familiar, but he couldn't think what.

Keep going. Come back to him later. Think back before the creepy guy. What happened before that? The alley. He'd heard Kim's scream. His stomach twisted.

Don't think about what they're doing to her now. But he was. Every sick thing he'd ever read in the news flew through his mind. *Please be all right. Please.*

Concentrate. They'd been walking to her car and there was a noise. *A sharp crack. Like a gun, but not as loud.* And then every nerve in Ford's body had fired.

Shit. Sonofabitch tased me. Then hit my head. Then drugged me. Suddenly he remembered the needle after *"Did you miss me?"* The sonofabitch had drugged him twice! He needed to have a plan before the SOB came back to make it three times.

Sitting up, Ford scooted on his ass in a circle until he saw light through the blindfold. *A window.*

He twisted his body, finally rising to his knees and crawling until he felt a slight warming of the floor that was in the direct path of the sun streaming through the window. Lifting his chin, he felt the sun on his face and held still for a few seconds, absorbing a little warmth before continuing. He'd barely moved a foot more when the floor grew cold once again. *Dammit. The window's high and small.*

He crawled until he hit the wall. It was cold against his cheek. Textured. *Concrete block. Not good.* Concrete would be hard to break through.

Ignoring the pain at the back of his head, he rubbed his temple against the wall, vigorously working the blindfold until finally he was free of it. He could see! *Yes.*

He was in a garage, about twenty feet square. Behind a stack of firewood was a garage door. But it hadn't been used for years if the rusty chains securing it were any indication. Heavy padlocks hung from the chains. *Not a way out.*

Ford looked up. *Dammit.* The window was five feet

above the ground and not even big enough for a toddler to escape through. He turned to look over his shoulder, his eyes squeezing closed of their own volition. *Don't want to see what's causing that smell.* He forced himself to look and the breath he held shuddered out.

Not Kim. Not human. Maybe a dog or a cat. Maybe. But not human.

To the left of the carcass was a door. He started crawling, then stopped. Behind the carcass were bones. Whoever left that animal had done so before. Many times.

I'm back. Did you miss me? Ford swallowed hard. What kind of sick freak was he dealing with? *The kind that tases people,* he thought grimly, *then kidnaps them.*

And he's got Kim. Unless she got away. Please let her have gotten away.

He crawled to the door, leaned hard against it. It didn't budge. Worn, Ford pressed his back to the door and slid down to sit. *This is hopeless.*

Stop it. He closed his eyes. *Get your bearings. You need to cut these ropes. You'll never get out of here unless you can move. So find something sharp. Anything will do.*

He opened his eyes. *Hello.* Under a set of plastic shelves was a box cutter. Hopefully it was still sharp.

He crawled back across the room, slowing as he passed the carcass again. Why was it here? Because it hadn't been last night. *I would have remembered a stench like that.* He made himself look. It was a cat. Or had been. But there didn't seem to be any blood. It was covered in dirt. The cat had been buried, then dug up. *That's just sick.*

The animal wore a collar with a tag attached. The collar was old, but the tag was new. Shiny. Engraved with FLUFFY, in a flowery script. *What the hell?*

Consider it later. He needed that box cutter.

Baltimore, Maryland
Tuesday, December 3, 10:20 a.m.

Giving Clay Maynard a cursory glance, Special Agent Deacon Novak removed his wraparound sunglasses and walked the alley like he owned it, as was his way.

Joseph found the man's way annoying, but Bo Lamar

swore that Deacon had "skills." Joseph wondered if Bo counted dramatic flair as a core skill.

Once he'd explored the scene, Deacon doubled back, crouched down, and studied the body. "So who exactly is this guy?" he asked over his shoulder.

"His name is Isaac Zacharias," Joseph said. "He was a DC cop, moonlighting as private security for Mr. Maynard here, guarding SA Montgomery's son, who's missing."

Deacon noted the AFID tags. "Taser." Rising, he lifted his uncovered eyes to Maynard, who flinched, a common reaction when seeing Deacon's eyes for the first time.

Deacon knew it and, Joseph suspected, used it to his full advantage. The man was only about thirty, but his hair was snow white and apparently had been for years.

However, it was his eyes that really threw people off. His irises were bicolored—both of them. Half brilliant blue and half chocolate brown, each iris looked like two different eyes had been sliced, mixed, and spliced.

Of course they're contacts, Joseph thought. *Nobody has real eyes like that.*

Deacon lifted his brows to Clay. "Not much of a body-guard, was he?"

Maynard drew a sharp breath, let it out. His whole body vibrated with anger, but he kept his clenched fists at his sides and his voice to a low growl. "This was a good man. A family man. A good cop. He doesn't deserve this. He doesn't deserve you." He cast an angry glance at Joseph. "'For now' is officially over."

"Maynard was a cop," Joseph muttered. "This was his friend. Have some respect."

Deacon's odd eyes flickered. "I'm sorry for your loss," he said quietly.

Maynard just shook his head. "Go to hell."

"Planning on it," Deacon replied evenly. "So how did SA Montgomery hire you? She find your ad on craigslist or something?"

Maynard gritted his teeth. "She and I are friends."

And lovers, Joseph thought, bitter envy welling up. Then swiftly came the shame. They had one man dead and two college kids missing. Who Daphne Montgomery bedded was not his focus. Bringing her son and his girlfriend home—alive—was.

"How did Zacharias come to work for you?" Joseph asked Maynard.

"I recruited him years ago. We served together." Maynard's gaze dropped back down to the body, pain in his eyes. "Rode together on patrol."

Damn. Partners, too. Joseph's resentment ebbed. Maynard may have won who Joseph wanted, but he wasn't such a bastard as to strike out at a man in pain.

"So this wasn't his first job for you," Deacon said.

"No." Maynard swallowed hard. "He worked for me each time his wife was pregnant. They needed the money for expenses. Diapers, formula. College funds. Phyllis has got to be out of her mind by now. She needs to be informed. So does Daphne."

"Before it breaks in the media," Joseph agreed. "Deacon, stay here and coordinate with CSU—and get some uniforms canvassing this area. I want to know who was home last night at eleven and what they saw or heard."

"Eleven?" Deacon asked. "Significance?"

"That's when the film Ford and Kim went to see was over." Joseph checked his phone for messages, finding the be-on-the-lookout bulletin. "Bo's put out the BOLO. He attached photos of both of them, if you need to show them around." He opened the photo of Kimberly, surprised to see that the girl was Asian. "Not what I expected with a name like MacGregor."

"She was adopted," Maynard said quietly. "She friended an organization for Chinese adoptees in Philadelphia on Facebook. Her parents are Caucasian, based on the photos she's posted. She's got one sister, Pamela, about fourteen, also Chinese."

"This is why I don't have a Facebook page," Deacon said.

Joseph shrugged. "Makes our lives easier. Who needs a warrant when you've got the social network? Questions before I go do notifications?"

"Several. I—" Whatever Deacon had been about to ask next was interrupted by slamming doors and the appearance of CSU. "Stay here, Mr. Maynard," Deacon said. "I'm certain that I'll have more questions for you."

"He's with me," Joseph said. "Officer Zacharias's wife will need someone to stay with her. She's pregnant. We don't want to make this situation even worse."

Deacon had been ready to argue, but closed his mouth when Joseph gave him a pointed look. "Okay." Deacon shrugged. "I'll keep in touch."

"Can you wait next to my SUV?" Joseph asked Maynard, pointing to the alley entrance. "It's a black Escalade, parked on the street. I need to coordinate a few things with Agent Novak before we go."

"Whatever. Let's just get this over with." Maynard walked away, shoulders bowed.

Joseph frowned at Deacon, who studied him, bemused. "What?"

"I'm trying to figure you out," Deacon murmured. "When I walked up, you looked like you wanted to rip Maynard apart, and yet you yell at me for not being Mr. Sensitive."

Joseph blinked, taken aback. "I did not look any such way."

Deacon's odd eyes widened. "You thought you'd hidden it. Oh, that's rich. News flash, Carter. You didn't. So what did your boy do to you?"

"Nothing." Joseph swallowed his annoyance when Deacon made a show of biting back a smile. "Maynard works with my brother's fiancée. My brother trusts him, which means I do, too. Maynard didn't kill Zacharias."

"Maybe, maybe not. I'm inclined to agree, though. So what did he do to *you*?"

Joseph counted backward from ten, grateful for the appearance of a fiftysomething woman in white coveralls who carried a tackle box in each hand, her back bowing under the weight. Barely five feet tall, Dr. Fiona Brodie looked too fragile to be carrying her own equipment, but Joseph had learned long ago never to presume to carry it for her.

Brodie had thirty years with the Bureau, all in forensics. Joseph had known her since his academy days when he'd sat in her classroom studying blood spatter patterns. She reminded him of his mother, possessing that ageless quality that made her appear unchanged. Dr. Brodie had joined VCET because she wanted to do something different before retiring. *This case should grant that wish,* Joseph thought grimly.

He met her halfway. "Dr. Brodie. I'm glad you're here."

She stopped at the body and took it all in, her face creasing in a mighty frown. "Who touched him? Who removed these boxes?" She looked over her shoulder, disappointed. "*Some*body has compromised evidence."

Joseph felt compelled to defend himself. "It was the homeless guy who found him." He pointed to the sack. "He stole the victim's shoes and was scavenging his clothes."

"Oh. Sorry. Wouldn't have been the first time an agent mucked up a crime scene." She angled a look up at him. "But it would have been the first time *you* mucked one up. Glad to see you haven't slipped." Her brows lifted, her ire dissipated. "Bo tells me that you're leading this investigation."

Well, what do you know? Bo hadn't actually told Joseph that he was lead on this case, but he'd hoped it was true. "Yes, ma'am."

Brodie dropped her eyes back to the body, dismissing him. "Then don't you have something better to do than get under my feet?"

"Yeah, I do," he said. "Notifications, both to his victim's widow and the parents of the abducted college kids. It should take me at least an hour."

She sighed. "I should have him uncovered by the time you get back."

"Thanks." He turned to find Deacon crouching in the middle of the alley, staring at the pavement. "What is it?"

"Blood," Deacon said. He shined his flashlight at the area. "And what looks like hair. What color is Ford's hair?"

"Blond." Like Daphne's.

"Could be his. Looks like somebody bashed his head into the asphalt." He stood up. "So what's the plan, boss?"

"We start with the Millhouse case. It's the most obvious connection for now and they were suspected of threatening Montgomery. I'll get a warrant started for the Millhouse home and business, but I'm not sure we have enough for a judge to sign off."

"Unless we can prove the threats. Did Montgomery document them?"

"No idea, but Maynard should know. We also need to check out Ford Elkhart's life, every nook and cranny, just in case this isn't connected to the trial."

"Any indication that the kid's dirty?"

"None whatsoever. But we can't ignore the possibility that whoever did this had a score to settle with him. Or the girl. Or Maynard, even."

Deacon frowned. "You said he didn't do this."

"I don't believe he did. Doesn't mean somebody else

didn't have it in for him. Wouldn't be the first time a killer struck at his target's inner circle first."

"I'll request cell records and financials while Brodie's doing her thing," Deacon said. "Has anyone checked SA Montgomery's house? Could the kid have gone back home? Maybe the killer knocked him out and he came to later, flagged a cab home."

"Possible, I guess. Unlikely, though, as he would have seen Zacharias's body. I can't see Ford ignoring something like that, but I'll check it out. I'll call you when I've done the notifications. We'll regroup here."

"And the girlfriend?" Deacon asked. "Kimberly Mac-Gregor?"

"Family is near Philly. Call the field office up there. Have them send someone out to the parents, then proceed according to SOP."

"Phone tap, trace all incoming. Just in case this is about the girl." Deacon looked up from his notepad. "But you know it's not, don't you?"

"Yeah. I know. Later, Novak." Joseph hurried to his Escalade, where he found Clay leaning against the front passenger door, looking ill. "You gonna be okay?"

"Yeah. Let's get this over with."

Joseph started his SUV. "Where's Zacharias's house?"

Maynard's hands shook as he buckled in. "Silver Spring."

A forty-five-minute drive. "Okay. I'm going to stop by Miss Montgomery's house first." It was about twenty minutes away, in Roland Park, an exclusive neighborhood north of the city. "I want to be sure Ford and his girlfriend aren't there."

Maynard's gaze was fixed out the window, in the direction of the alley. And his dead friend. "How do you plan to get into her house?" he asked tonelessly.

"My brother mentioned that her mother and an aunt live with her."

"Not anymore. They stay there sometimes, on weekends, but Simone bought a condo in Roland Park, not far from her dress shop. She's there now. Maggie should be there with her. Maggie's not Daphne's aunt, though. She's an old family friend. She lives at the farm."

Joseph knew about Mrs. Montgomery's dress shop. He'd actually shopped there, for his mother. But Maynard knew all the details. *Leave it, Carter.* "We can stop at the dress shop for a key to Daphne's house."

Maynard hadn't looked away from the window. "No need to stop. I have a key."

Joseph swallowed hard. *Of course you do.* "That's convenient, then."

"Ford's not at the house or Simone's condo in the burbs. I saw Daphne this morning and she was feeling guilty for ignoring him. She hasn't seen him in two weeks. I thought he might be at the condo here in the city, but he's not."

Joseph blinked. "How many houses does Daphne have?"

"Too many to keep safe," Maynard murmured. "The condo here in the city is pretty basic. She bought it as an investment, but her old tenant moved out. Now she keeps it for when she works too late to drive home. Ford uses it when he needs to study and the dorm is too loud. It's next to the Inner Harbor."

Whoa. Those places weren't cheap. Joseph owned a few investment condos there himself. His own apartment truly was basic—just a place to lay his head, located close to his family's home. "Those condos on the harbor aren't what I'd call 'basic.' They rent for a couple thousand a month."

Maynard turned to look at him. "From a security standpoint, I meant. The building provides a lot of the security, so I don't worry so much about her there."

"Oh. They'd have a record of Ford coming and going, then. Even if he's not there now, I can call to see if he and Kimberly have been there."

"They haven't. I called the desk to ask while you were talking to Novak. Last time the condo was used was last week. Daphne crashed there after working most of the night."

Did security tell you that or were you there with her? The question danced on the tip of Joseph's tongue, but he swallowed it back. "What other properties does she have besides her house, her mother's condo, and the condo on the harbor?"

"She owns a farm in Hunt Valley, twenty acres. That's where Maggie lives, along with the horses. Maggie takes care of the animals. The farm is the worst, security-wise. Too many entrances and outbuildings."

"Four properties. But she lives in the Roland Park house?"

"Yeah. It's a Victorian, built in the 1880s. It had no security system until the Millhouses started their threats. I installed one. Anyone comes or goes, I know."

"How?"

"The system sends a text message to my phone."

Joseph was reluctantly impressed. Maynard was taking care of Daphne. That was good, right? *Yeah,* he thought glumly. *Right.* Then he shoved his mind back on track. Hunt Valley was a half hour northwest of her house. "Would Ford go to the farm?"

"Probably not. Especially without a car. Did you check his dorm?"

"Roommate says he never came back last night," Joseph said. "I need you to text all of Daphne's addresses to my boss." He dialed Bo on his cell. "It's Joseph. We need uniforms at the kids' dorms and all of Miss Montgomery's properties. Her security manager is texting you with the addresses. I want to preserve any evidence while we sort through all this."

"So it's what you thought?" Bo asked. "Abduction?"

"Looks that way."

Three

Daphne gripped the sides of the sink in the ladies' room, grateful that it was deserted—at least she'd have a little privacy to clean up after losing what little she'd eaten for breakfast. And possibly last night's dinner.

She rinsed her mouth with a grimace. *I'd kill for a toothbrush right about now.* She shook some Tic Tacs into her mouth, the minty burn making her feel human again.

The adrenaline crash had hit five feet from the washroom door with violent trembling and nausea. She was still trembling, but the heaving had passed.

She'd gotten accustomed to controlling her nausea during chemo using both medication and meditation, but this episode had caught her by surprise. There'd been no time to prepare. No time to get her Zen going. Just . . . *bleh.*

I look a fright. Her wig had stayed in place during her tussle with Cindy, but the post-fight worship of the porcelain goddess had knocked it askew. The sleek blond French twist was sliding halfway down her forehead, her real hair a tangled mess that defied every attempt to crimp, curl, or straighten it into submission.

Seven years since chemo and her hair was still not smooth and silky like it had been before. It had been so lush and gorgeous—and stylable—once. It probably never would be again.

Don't worry! everyone had told her when it all fell out.

It'll grow back! And it had, which was the problem. At the beginning, the new growth made her a walking ad for salon perms—*Just say no to home perms or this could be you!* Over time the curls had become less coarse, but her hair wasn't the same.

Looking at herself in the mirror no longer brought tears to her eyes, but her hair was still an ongoing source of annoyance. She never knew which way the waves would choose to go. Taming it into anything remotely court appropriate would sap precious minutes from her morning routine. The wigs that had been a necessity during chemo had now become a time-saving, sanity-saving convenience.

And a shield of sorts. She liked being able to choose which Daphne the world got to see. She liked being in control, having had so little of it in years past. She depended on appearing put together and confident on the outside, even if on the inside she still fought panic attacks.

They were a lot less frequent than they'd once been, but she never knew when one would hit. Sometimes they were triggered by one of those ubiquitous pink ribbons, a stark reminder that her cancer could sneak back. Every now and then an underground parking garage sent her into a mental spin, flinging her back into her fear of confined spaces and childhood terrors.

When panic attacks took root, she relied on the facade, hiding behind it while she wrestled with her fears. The facade normally held firm.

Unless she heard The Phrase. The four little words uttered in a mocking singsong still had the capability of reducing her to rubble inside, so absolutely that the outside facade crumbled, too. She'd trained her mind to block it if she heard someone start to say it. *Did you—*

Stop. She frowned at herself in the mirror, yanking her mind back to safe ground. *Fix your hair, Daphne. Repair the facade.* It was a crutch, she knew. But fixing the facade kept her grounded and didn't hurt anyone, so it was a crutch she embraced.

She repositioned the wig, setting it firmly into place. Then she pulled her real hair into the wig's hairline, combing it until real blended with fake, the colors a perfect match. Nobody could tell she wore a wig except for hairdressers with a very good eye.

Or bitches who tried to grab the wig off her head. She scowled. If Cindy Millhouse had touched her hair, she'd have been a dead woman. *Guaranteed.*

With some measure of control restored, Daphne reapplied her makeup, cursing the TV cameras that caught every blemish. Briefly she considered escape through the back door of the justice building, but that would be letting Cindy win.

She twisted the top off her mascara. *Not today, baby.* Except her hands still trembled, jerking when her cell phone suddenly vibrated in her pocket. She gave up on the mascara, checking her phone with a frown. She had a million voice mails.

Reporters. She'd given up changing her phone number. It never seemed to even slow them down. Ignoring the voice mails, she checked her texts and smiled. One from Ford, sent while she'd waited for the jury. *Good luck, Mom!* He was such a good kid.

She steadied her hands enough to type. *Thx. Call me later. Love u.*

There were many texts from Paige. The first three were notes from yesterday's meeting with the contractor they'd hired for their foundation's newest project—the rehab of an abandoned school into a facility that would serve twenty single mothers undergoing chemotherapy. It had been one of Daphne's dreams for years, ever since she herself had faced the big C as a newly divorced woman with a twelve-year-old son.

Daphne's mother had taken care of her and Ford, but the single moms who had no support system weren't as lucky. Back then she'd vowed that someday she'd change that. With the help of Paige and a lot of other people, that someday had become today.

Paige's other messages were increasingly more urgent. She'd seen the news and heard about the courtroom drama. No one was releasing information and she hadn't been able to reach Grayson. *Poor kid,* Daphne thought. *She must be frantic.*

Grayson and I are fine, she typed. *I'll have him phone you asap.*

Unsurprisingly, there were a whole slew of messages from her mother, most of them in the last ten minutes.

Daphne knew her mother—she'd have had the TV on in the shop and all of her customers would be watching.

Working in a dress shop had been her mother's dream when Daphne had been small and her mother had also been a single mom, cleaning hotel rooms for a living. Now her mother owned her own shop and it was her pride and joy.

Both she and her mother had come a long way from the hills of West Virginia. Being a prosecutor had been Daphne's goal since she was old enough to understand what "justice" really meant. And what happened to victims when justice was denied.

Think about that, Daphne. About the good you were able to do. Smell those roses. Today she'd felt the thrill of delivering justice. And it felt powerful. *I feel powerful.*

Daphne dialed her mother's number, knowing her mother would need to hear her voice, just like she needed to hear Ford's. *I'll call him next.*

"Mama, it's me," she said when her mother answered. "I'm fine."

"Daphne! I was so worried."

Daphne frowned. "Are you crying, Mama?"

"Course I'm not," her mother declared with an indignant huff.

Of course she had been. But Simone Montgomery would never admit to tears, even on the rare occasions that she shed them in front of people. Especially on those occasions. "Of course you weren't," Daphne said apologetically. "How silly of me."

"The news said someone got stabbed." This came from Maggie, her mama's best friend. *And my mentor, teacher, confidante. Savior.* "Are you hurt, too?"

"I'm all right, Maggie. I'm just a little rattled, but I'll be fine."

"Of course you will," Maggie said matter-of-factly. Then her voice softened. "Should I leave the barn light on for you?"

Daphne let her mind drift until she could hear soft whinnies and smell sweet hay. When she was a little girl in West Virginia, when she was most upset, she went to the barn to brush Maggie's horses, whispering her darkest secrets and deepest fears in their ears. They always listened and never told a soul. They never criticized or terrorized. She'd worked through many a panic attack by brushing a horse.

When she'd gotten sick, her mother had moved to Baltimore to take care of her. Maggie had soon followed, bringing her horses. Now Maggie had a new barn not far from Daphne's house and Daphne got out there as often as she could. She didn't always ride, but she always brushed the horses.

It hadn't always been easy to get away to the quiet of the barn over the years, so she'd learned to go there in her mind. It was her own version of meditation and it had worked in hospital rooms, law school classrooms, and most recently at her desk in the SA's office as her schedule became fuller and tighter.

It was working now, her rocketing pulse having slowed to almost normal. Today she'd go to the barn in person. *I've earned the respite.*

"It may be late, Maggie," Daphne said, "but I'll be by."

"Good. Reese tolerates me riding her, but she's been watching for you."

Reese was Daphne's horse, a mare she and Maggie had rescued several years before. Healthy now, Reese loved a quiet trail ride. "Now that this case is finally over, I'll have more time for her." *And for myself.* Daphne needed to store up some quality time before the next big case fell in her lap and her schedule became hectic once again.

"We saw the verdict on the news," her mother said. "We're all very proud of you." Her mother's voice cracked slightly, her emotion making Daphne's eyes sting in turn.

"Thank you, Mama. Look, I have to finish putting my face on for the cameras and y'all are going to make me smear my mascara, so I have to go. Love you. Bye."

She dropped the phone into her purse and reached for the mascara, tranquillity restored. She'd brushed on the first coat when the washroom door creaked loudly.

"Daphne?" a male voice whispered loudly.

Her cheeks flamed. "Grayson? Tell me you are not in this ladies' room."

"Okay, I'm not. Not all the way, anyway. One foot's still in the hall. I wanted to be sure that you're all right."

"Why wouldn't I be?" she asked.

"Um, all the heaving?" he asked and she closed her eyes.

"You heard that?"

"Kind of hard not to."

"God," she groaned. "This day just keeps sucking worse and worse."

"If it makes you feel better, no one else heard. This floor's been evacuated."

It did help, a little. "I was wondering why I was all alone in here. I'm almost done." She slapped on lipstick and exited in the most dignified manner possible, under the circumstances. Grayson was holding her coat.

"I figured you'd want to cover up Welch's blood on your blouse," he said.

"Thanks." Daphne shrugged into her coat. "Paige texted me. You need to call her."

He showed her his phone, the screen splintered. "Cindy's boot. Phone's dead. I called Paige from one of the offices. And I called my mother, too, so don't nag me."

Daphne often nagged him about calling his mama, because she empathized with the woman. She checked her phone, frowning. "Ford hasn't tried to call me."

"I'll return the favor and nag him for you."

"Nah, you don't have to do that. He's a pretty good kid." Even though he got all absent-minded-professorish when he got involved in a project. "He's probably gotten sucked into one of his experiments in the lab and lost track of time." She dialed Ford's number, got his voice mail, and left him a message to call her when he got the chance.

Grayson pushed the button for the elevator. "It better be one hell of an experiment not to call you after something like this hits the news."

"He'll call. He always does. Eventually," she added with a wistful smile.

"My mother wouldn't be so magnanimous," Grayson said.

Actually, Daphne was thrilled that Ford got so preoccupied with his studies and experiments these days because there had been a lot of years when he hadn't allowed himself to. Days when she'd needed him to run errands, or make dinner, or pay the bills when she'd been too sick to write a check.

He'd had to grow up far too quickly, which was exactly what she hadn't wanted for him. She'd wanted him to be a child, to be secure and to feel safe. She'd wanted him to have a mother *and* a father. She vaguely remembered what that was like. Her father had left them when she was eight, but the years before that had been happy ones.

After she was eight . . . not so happy. Her father had left them without saying good-bye. Not that she could blame him. *He'd been ruined. Maligned. I'm sorry, Daddy. I'm so sorry. Wherever you are.* She lifted her chin, rewinding her story to the part she could stand to remember. But before she'd been eight . . . *We were happy.*

Daphne wanted that remembered stability for her son, but it hadn't worked out that way. Her ex-husband had wealth and privilege, breeding and education. But Travis Elkhart was a selfish, cold man who'd given nothing of himself to his only son.

Or to me. Pregnant at fifteen after a bewildering one-night stand, Daphne had found herself in possession of something very valuable—the next Elkhart heir.

And then she'd found herself the possession of the Elkharts. From the moment Travis's mother had learned of her pregnancy, Daphne had been absorbed into their world, whether she'd wanted to be or not.

From that day forward, Daphne had been keenly aware that she had very little control over her own life. Travis's mother called the shots, forcing her son to marry a "provincial" he didn't love, then molding that provincial into someone who would bring no shame to the Elkhart name.

Daphne had also been keenly aware that she wasn't part of their world. She was an outsider looking in, merely tethered to the Elkhart family through Ford. She had not complained. How could she? She got an education, had her own room. Food, clothes.

She had everything, but no one to call her own, except her son. She'd made a few friends on the estate and she still had her mama and Maggie, but they'd been back in West Virginia. They might as well have been on the moon.

Daphne hadn't been a prisoner per se. She had been free to leave the Elkhart estate—with her mother-in-law's permission and if accompanied by a bodyguard. Which was Elkhart-ese for a chaperone. She could leave on her own terms anytime she chose—but only if she left Ford behind. That was something she would not do.

So she'd stuck it out for twelve years. Flanked by a cheating husband and a despotic mother-in-law, Daphne had been lonely every day of her marriage. If it hadn't been for Ford, she wasn't sure what she'd have done. Taking care of him, watching him grow, had made each day worth waking up to.

Now he was a man nearly grown. *He doesn't need his mama anymore. And as thrilled as I am that he's becoming independent, I'm as alone as I've ever been, with no prospects in sight.*

Prospects. Her mind seemed to go there often these days and it didn't take a rocket scientist to figure out why. Her nest was empty and the years ahead were looming even emptier. The nights were starkly silent, the murmur of the television and the bark of her dog the only things separating her home from a tomb.

But days were worse. Working with Grayson meant overhearing the phone calls with the woman he loved, the *I-love-you*s and the *Bring-home-a-carton-of-milk*s. The phrases that, quilted together, made a life.

A beautiful life. The kind of life she'd always wanted.

I envy Paige. Daphne didn't begrudge her friend an ounce of happiness, but seeing the joy in Paige's dark eyes every time she spoke Grayson's name . . . *It shines a spotlight on my table for one.*

It wasn't like she had no options at all. She'd had a number of offers—most for no-strings flings. *Not interested.* She wanted a man who could go the distance. A keeper. She wanted for richer and poorer. In sickness and in health. *Dream on.*

Since her divorce, there had been a few men along the way who'd wanted the same. Nice guys. But there was no . . . spark. *I want spark. I deserve some spark.*

She'd thought she found some spark, months ago. He'd made her eyes widen and her heart race. Still did, every time she'd seen him since. Which, as fate would have it, had become frequently. The brother of her boss and the future brother-in-law of her best friend, he'd become damn near unavoidable.

At first she'd considered this a boon. She'd see him at fund-raising events, the sight of him in a tux—all tall, dark, and dangerous—taking her breath away. In the past three months he'd become a regular at Paige's karate school, watching his youngest sister, Holly, with a pride that had her eyes misting. Daphne would notice him. Always.

But he never seemed to notice her. *I guess he doesn't find me as compelling as I find him.* Because every time she ran into him at the karate school, he kept his distance. *Like I've got the damn plague.*

Although it was far more likely that he found her too brash. *Provincial.* That was the word her ex-husband had used—often and with a sneer. She'd learned early in her marriage that "provincial" was just an upper-crust way of saying "white trash."

She'd found as the years passed that no amount of polish could make her a true Elkhart, with their *Mayflower* pedigree and their refined manners. She'd go to her grave a "provincial." So when the marriage was over, she'd embraced her provinciality.

I'm me again. Love me or leave me. Beehive hair, bold colors, and a sassy twang had become her trademarks. She softened her image a bit when it came to court, but inside . . . *I'm me and I'm not changing.* Not even for a man who set her heart pumping like a bat out of hell. Especially not for him. *Love me or leave me. Just the way I am.*

She'd expected more of Joseph Carter. His family was lovely—giving, open, and friendly. Down-to-earth, despite their wealth. And he was, too—with them. *With me . . . well, there isn't anything to comment on there.* He ignored her. *Like I don't exist.*

Which stung. *Okay, it hurts. A lot.* But not what she should be thinking about now.

She was at the front door, seconds from a wall of flashing lights and reporters screaming their questions. She ran a nervous hand over her hair, fidgeted with the top button on her coat. All buttoned and tucked, none of Deputy Welch's blood showing.

"You look fine," Grayson murmured, "but sad. You won today. Don't let the Millhouses take that away from you or from the Turners. May they finally rest in peace."

He was wrong about the direction her mind had taken but right in what he'd said. Daphne's selfishness shamed her. *This is not about you.*

"Thank you," she murmured. "I needed a little perspective adjustment."

The door opened and immediately the yelling began. The mikes and the cameras.

"Showtime," Grayson whispered in her ear. "You earned this success, so knock 'em dead." He stepped to the side, leaving her to face the media cameras alone.

Tuesday, December 3, 11:00 a.m.

Clay stared out the passenger-side window of Joseph Carter's Escalade, trying not to think of his friend. Lying in an alley, his throat sliced open. All night. Alone.

But the picture was there in his mind, joining the others that haunted him when he couldn't sleep. Which was most nights of his life. *Tuzak. I'm sorry, man.*

A wave of grief squeezed his chest. *Don't think. Listen to Carter.* Who was on the phone with his CO. *Listen, learn. So that you can find who did this.*

"He might have a decent eye," Carter was saying to his CO, grudgingly. *He's talking about that asshole Novak. Not much of a bodyguard, my ass.* "He found what looks like Ford Elkhart's hair and blood on the asphalt in the alley. But he's about as tactful as a bull in a china shop."

Clay tensed. That they'd found Ford's hair and blood was bad news, but news.

News was the reason Clay sat in Carter's fancy SUV and not his own car. He didn't have to be here. Carter wanted him here so that he didn't "go cowboy," but the Fed had no authority over him, here or anywhere else. *I'm here because I want to be here.* He'd hear Carter talk about details that he'd never know about working solo.

They'd been in the car less than five minutes when Joseph had told his CO that Tuzak's killer had slit his throat after he was dead. Clay hadn't noticed the lack of spatter. Carter had a good eye, too. And he'd been right. *I'm not objective right now.*

Tuzak's killer had all but cut off his head *after* he was already dead. There'd been no need. No benefit. Just a viciousness that deserved to be returned in kind.

And I will, he vowed. But first he had to find Ford and Kimberly. *I'll find them. I have to.*

He couldn't allow himself to think about the alternative. He'd seen with his own eyes what their abductor was capable of doing. As hard as he tried, Clay couldn't get the picture out of his mind for even a moment—Tuzak lying in the street, covered in garbage, his head barely . . . *The monster who did that has those kids. I'll get them back.*

And then? He didn't know. He only knew the man who did this had to pay.

Clay jerked when something landed in his lap. A box of tissues. He lifted his hand to his wet cheek. He'd been crying and hadn't even realized it.

He put the tissue box on the console between them and scrubbed his palms over his face. Carter had finished his call with his CO. How long ago? They'd driven several blocks, headed away from downtown. To where Phyllis was waiting for word.

"Oh God," Clay whispered. He'd have to tell her that her husband was never coming home. He'd have to tell Daphne her son was missing. He'd promised to keep Ford safe. *I failed.*

There was a long space of silence, and then Carter sighed. "Be careful, Clay."

Clay whipped around to stare at the Fed's profile. "Be careful of what?"

Carter kept his eyes forward, tapping one finger on the wheel as he drove. He looked like he was choosing his words carefully. "Of revenge," he finally said. "If you find him before we do."

"I don't know what you're talking about," Clay lied.

"Uh-huh. Right. I told my CO that I'd removed you from the scene so you didn't slug Novak, which was true, but he knows cops. And ex-cops. Knows that seeing a partner brutalized like that will stir a man up. He told me to keep an eye on you. And that if he finds you going cowboy, he'll slap cuffs on you faster than you can blink."

He'd have to catch me first. "I understand."

"Good." They drove another few blocks before Carter spoke again. "Of course, should the suspect attack you first, you're entitled to defend yourself." And then Carter turned and met his eyes for a brief moment. There was understanding there. And truth.

He realized what the Fed was telling him. Carter had killed before. To avenge. Not in cold blood, but his self-defense had been dual-edged. And he wasn't the least bit sorry. The Fed rose dramatically in his estimation. Clay nodded. "I understand."

"Good." Carter reached into the console between them and pulled out a Baggie filled with brownies. "My brother-in-law made them," he said, as if they hadn't just discussed killing a man. He bit into one with gusto. "Help yourself. They're damn good."

Clay couldn't eat. Still, he appreciated the gesture. "This is the brother-in-law that owns the catering business? Brian?"

"One and the same. You know him?"

"Ate at his place once, when Paige and Grayson were involved in the Muñoz case. I've met him a few times since then. He caters all the charity functions Daphne's been throwing for her women's center. His food makes it almost worth wearing a tux."

Carter's jaw froze midchew. His throat worked as he swallowed hard, then resumed chewing, although it now appeared to be a chore. "Brian's good about that, donating food to good causes," he said.

Clay frowned. It didn't take a PI to see he'd said something that annoyed the Fed. "You got a problem with charity functions, Carter?"

"Nope. Get dragged to them from time to time. Miss Montgomery usually throws a good one." But Carter's jaw was clenched so tightly that the muscle in his cheek bulged.

If Carter didn't have a problem with charity functions, then he had a problem with Daphne. And nobody had a problem with Daphne. Except the lowlifes she sent to jail. And her ex-husband, the asshole. Everybody else loved . . .

Oh. Comprehension dawned and Clay found the weight on his shoulders easing a fraction. At least something good might come of this day.

Carter had stopped at a traffic light and was dialing his cell, his expression intense in its attempt to be bland. "Grayson's still not picking up." His tone changed when he left a message. "Gray, call me. It's urgent." The light changed and he proceeded, outwardly calm except for the forefinger that tapped the wheel in a rapid staccato. "How long can it take for a jury to read a damn verdict?"

"She's not mine, Carter," Clay said quietly and watched the Fed's finger abruptly still. "Not that you asked. Just thought you should know. We're friends. That's all."

Carter drew a deep breath and held it for several seconds before slowly releasing it. "I see." He kept his eyes fixed forward. "Not that I asked."

"She's got no one right now. Not that you asked that, either."

"No. I didn't."

"But I have to warn you . . ." Clay waited for Carter to look at him. Finally the Fed did, just a glance, but long enough for Clay to know that he'd guessed right.

"Warn me about what?" Carter asked levelly.

"She's been hurt. Badly. But she has one of the kindest hearts I've ever known. If anyone were to hurt her again . . . I wouldn't wait for him to attack me first."

Carter nodded solemnly. "I understand."

"Good." Good deed done for the day, Clay fixed his gaze on the passing houses. The weight that had momentarily lifted returned with a vengeance. Clay closed his eyes, pictured Phyllis's face. Pictured himself sitting her down, the terror in her eyes, because she'd know. "They always know, cops' wives."

"I know. I hate this part. People say 'You're just the messenger. You're not the one ripping their lives apart.' But it sure feels that way."

Clay looked over at him. "Then why are you here?"

Carter's brows lifted. "Like I should send Novak to do the notification?"

"Good point. The man's an ass. No offense."

"None taken. But he's got a sharp mind. And Brodie, the woman leading the CSU team? She's simply the best. Been with the Bureau's lab for years."

"Longevity doesn't mean skill."

"No, it doesn't. But I know of twenty murderers that we couldn't have caught or convicted without her evidence, and that's just my history with her. If the man who killed your friend left an eyelash in that alley, she'll find it."

It was the best thing the Fed could have said. "Thanks."

"Now I need to ask a few questions. I'm assuming that the Millhouses kidnapped Ford. My CO is working on the warrant to search their home and business to see if they've hidden him there. I'd have a better chance of getting a judge's John Hancock if I had proof that Daphne and her assistant were being threatened by the Millhouses."

"The cops have all that. Daphne kept every note, every taped cell phone call."

"Daphne's taping her cell phone calls?"

"She got a judge to sign a wiretap order."

"Then getting the search warrant won't be a problem."

"I wouldn't think so. What other questions?"

"Tell me about your agency. I knew you did PI work, but I didn't know about the personal security side. I'll need the number of your employees, your areas of expertise, anyone who'd want to take you down."

Clay laughed bitterly. "Who'd want to take me down? That's a ripe question. How much time do we have?"

"Not enough for me to be asking idle questions."

Again the Fed was right. "I do personal and corporate security, which includes investigating custody fights, cheating spouses, employers checking up on clients after money goes missing. We're sometimes hired by the defense and we're often hired by businessmen to secure their homes and businesses. Occasionally we travel internationally with a client who is going into a known danger zone. Why?"

"Number one, *I* need to know. Daphne trusts you and my brother trusts you and that takes me about ninety percent of the way. But *I* don't know you and we've all been fooled by liars over the course of our careers."

"True." That the Fed hadn't claimed it was routine satisfied him. "Number two?"

"You probably have complete confidence in your people, but they can betray us. I need to know who knows about your business."

Clay thought of his last partner, the one before Paige. Nicki had fucked up, big-time, paying the ultimate price. Unfortunately she dragged good people into the crossfire.

"I have a few full-time employees. Paige, of course. My office assistant, Alyssa, who I've known since she was a kid. On the security side I have Alec Vaughn, a network geek I hired about six months ago. I've known Alec since he was twelve years old, and his godfather is my best friend. Alec's solid."

"Who else?"

"That's it. I bring in contract help as needed. Old pals, usually. Some I served with on the force in DC." *Like Tuzak.* "Some I served with in the Corps."

"Marines?"

"Sure as hell wasn't the Peace Corps. I'll have Alyssa print you out a list."

"That would be great. I need to take this," Carter said when his cell rang. "What do you have, Bo?" A minute later his expression changed. "Oh my God. Fatalities?"

Clay straightened in his seat. "What?" he demanded.

Carter ignored him, abruptly swinging across traffic to the left lane. He flipped a switch and the blue lights on his dash began to strobe and flash. "Tell them we'll be there in less than five." He hung up and, barely slowing down, did a hard U-turn at the next light. "Hold on," he told Clay grimly.

"Where are we going? What's happened?"

"My CO's sending another agent to notify Mrs. Zacharias. We're going to the courthouse. The jury returned a guilty verdict and all hell broke loose. Defendant's mother slipped him a knife and he stabbed a deputy. Not fatally, thank goodness."

"Daphne?" Clay asked, his heart in his throat.

"Defendant's mother attacked her. She's not injured. The mother's attack was a diversion. Millhouse was trying to break free."

"Does Daphne know about Ford?"

"Not yet. The priority was subduing Millhouse and his mother, then transporting the injured. My CO says he's contacted BPD about Ford. They're sending word to the cops on duty at the justice center. Daphne and Grayson are about to talk to the press."

"Standing in front of a crowd that hasn't gone through security." Clay was imagining all the ways this could go wrong and from the look on Carter's face, so was he. "But why would the Millhouses take Ford now? The jury's reached their decision. Daphne couldn't meet their demands if she wanted to."

"I don't know. But they'll have to go through me to get to her. Hang on."

Tuesday, December 3, 11:00 a.m.

Mitch turned into the drive that led to his home. *My home.* It had always been *home.* But it hadn't been *his* until last year. It was the first time anything had been *his.*

It was a great old house, built by his mother's grandfather in 1915 on what had at the time been a fifty-acre dairy farm. Douglases had always lived here. Although his last name was Roberts on paper, Mitch was a Douglas. *And now this belongs to me.*

Betty Douglas, Mitch's mother's aunt, had been the last to bear the Douglas name. Great-aunt Betty had been born here. His mother, orphaned as an infant, had grown up here, too. Aunt Betty had given her a home until she was old enough to live on her own. When his mother found herself widowed with an infant son, Betty welcomed them back.

It had been a hell of a place for Mitch to grow up. They'd still had a few cows then. They were geriatric cows, true, but he'd liked them. But by the time his mother had remarried, moved them to Virginia, and birthed two more sons, the herd was all gone.

When her second husband cheated on her, his mother brought Mitch's youngest brother, Cole, back to this place. She'd come home to lick her wounds, find herself again.

Mitch, at eighteen, had just joined the U.S. Army when his mother came home. The middle brother, Mutt, stayed with his father, too wrapped up in his high school friends and the learning of his father's trade to take care of their mother.

Cole had been only three, too young to give their mother any solace.

Aunt Betty had been her support once again and Mitch knew his old aunt had done the best that she could. But in the end, there had been no solace for his mother. Two years after she'd come home here, to this place, she had left again.

But permanently. She'd taken her own life. That had been eight years ago and it still made Mitch's chest so damn tight . . .

Mitch drew a breath, then another, until he could breathe normally once again.

Time had passed. His grief had dimmed and he'd gone on, taking care of Cole.

But Mitch had made some mistakes. Some worse than others. For those he'd paid. Dearly. And when things had become more than he could bear, he'd followed in his mother's footsteps. He'd brought Cole back here. *I came home.*

There'd been changes, of course. The property had been whittled away over the years, Aunt Betty having sold it to pay her bills, but they were still surrounded by five acres. Lots of privacy.

After sharing a mega-tent in Iraq with forty guys for most of his Army deployment, Mitch had developed a real appreciation for privacy. Later, after sharing a six-by-eight for three years with another convicted drug dealer, he had come to crave it.

Betty had understood that, which was why she'd left the old house solely to Mitch in her will. Not to share with his brothers Mutt and Cole. *Just to me. Mine.*

Pulling the van into his garage alongside his old Jeep, he shut off the engine. He got out of the van and stretched his neck, grimacing. *He wasn't even thirty yet— too young to feel this damn old.*

But revenge had a revitalizing side effect. His back might be killing him and his neck might be stiff, but his heart was beating fast and strong, his mind still crystal clear. A painkiller chased by a quick nap would take care of the aches.

But first, he had a job to do. He pulled at the shelves on the far wall of his garage, smiling when the entire unit swung out effortlessly. Perfectly balanced, the false wall could still be moved with the strength in his pinkie, almost sixty years after it was built.

Mitch's great-grandfather Myron Douglas had been one hell of an artisan.

This garage was a later addition to the property, built by his great-grandfather in the 1950s. Back when Aunt Betty and her friends were taught to hide under their desks in the event of a nuclear bomb. And back when a man built a bomb shelter for his family, but didn't want the neighbors to know. Only so much room down there. So much air.

So his great-grandfather had built the shelter, then slapped a garage on top of it, hid the doorway behind the swinging bookshelf, and swore his daughters to silence.

Betty had told Mitch about the shelter and given him the entry combinations on his sixteenth birthday. It had been her gift to him, indicating he was now the man of the house.

His middle brother Mutt knew nothing about the shelter and that always made Mitch feel good. Cole knew about the place, but Mitch didn't worry about him coming down here. Cole's first and last visit to the shelter had been a horrific one. Even if his little brother did remember the combination, he wouldn't be coming down anytime soon.

Mitch twisted the dial on the lock that secured the latch and climbed into the access tube, hopped off the bottom of the ladder and went in. About eight by eight, it contained a desk and chair and three vintage Army cots circa 1957. Shelves covered three of the walls, laden with canned goods. Two of the shelves were hinged, replicas of the one in the garage. Both hid doors that led to tunnels.

One escaped to the outside, ending fifty yards from the house. The other tunnel led to the existing basement, specifically to a room that had been originally used for storage when the house was built. His great-grandfather had hidden the basement access by yet another swinging bookshelf.

If an idea worked, his great-granddad had run with it. Not a bad approach, all in all.

The shelter was how Betty had left it, which was how Mitch's mother had left it.

Minus the blood and brains, of course. Mitch had done the cleanup and it had not been pleasant. He remembered it every time he came down here. Given the room wasn't much bigger than his prison cell had been, that wasn't all that often. But each time his hate was renewed.

His mother had killed herself in this room. He still had the gun she'd used, eventually returned by the police. He'd hidden it where his younger brother couldn't find it. Cole had enough bad memories of that time, because, at only five years old, he was the one who had found her.

Mitch had been twenty-one, stationed in Iraq. It had taken him a week to get home for her funeral. A week that the mess his mother left behind had remained, putrefying. The cops took the gun and the ME took the body, but nobody had cleaned.

Aunt Betty didn't. To hire a company to clean the mess hadn't occurred to her because she was in shock. Even if she hadn't been, there'd been no money to pay anyone else. And she couldn't have cleaned it herself—she was too old by then to climb down the ladder. Which was why she'd given Cole the lock combinations in the first place—their mother had been missing for four days and her fits of alcoholic depression down in the shelter had never lasted so long before.

So the cleanup had fallen to Mitch and the memory of that day was never far from his mind. For a long, long time Mitch hated his mother for being a drunk, for taking the easy way out, for leaving her body for her little boy to find. *For me to clean.*

He'd hated his stepfather for breaking her heart and driving her to suicide, for refusing to acknowledge Cole as his son. After having cheated on her for *years*, his mother's husband had accused *her* of cheating.

It wasn't true. Mitch knew his mother would never have done such a thing. But even if it were true, Cole was a child, undeserving of the cruelties heaped on him by the man Mitch's mother had loved to distraction long after he'd cast her aside.

But Mitch had picked up, moved on. He'd had to—there was a small boy who'd needed him. He'd finished the last few months of his Army tour and had come home to care for Cole, getting him counseling, trying to be both mother and father to the boy.

And through those horrible years, Mitch had learned a lot of things the hard way.

Like what he'd thought was hate for his mother was really grief, and that time did heal. Eventually the grief of losing his mother had dulled, the hate softening to anger, then to sad disgust for a woman who'd loved a man who never wanted her.

He'd learned that sometimes people aren't as bad as they seem—they could be worse. This was definitely true of his stepfather.

Mitch had returned home from Iraq to a horrible economy. In desperation, he'd accepted what was to have been a temp job from his stepfather. Mistake number one.

Mistake number two was learning the true nature of the family business and not running like hell the other way. *Drugs are bad, Mitch,* Aunt Betty would say with a wag of her finger. *Just say no.* Man, did he ever wish he had.

Because mistake number three had been the biggest one. Lured by the promise of a fast buck, Mitch had actually believed his stepfather would allow him to make a place for himself in the family drug empire. Mitch had considered the temp job a foot in the door. Then, once he had a toehold, he'd find a way to take it all, leaving the bastard crying and alone.

He'd had time to reflect on the colossal stupidity of that third mistake. Three years, to be exact, as he'd served his sentence for distribution.

A delivery had gone bad and Mitch had been caught. He hadn't been worried at the beginning. Employees—even ones without family connections—got the company's legal support. But no attorney showed up for Mitch. Just the public defender. *And me.*

Mitch's revenge had taken root the day he cleaned his mother's blood and brains from this very room. It had taken form and substance as he'd listened to the jury declare him guilty of possession with intent to sell. It had become a fully fleshed-out plan during the years he'd been incarcerated. His endgame—to see his stepfather suffer, excruciatingly. And to see him dead.

To jump-start his plan he'd needed a little spending money. Fortunately prison was chock-full of guys with connections. Mitch had landed a highly illegal but highly lucrative job on the outside before he'd walked through the prison gates, a free man once again. But first he'd come home, to this house. He loved this house.

What had greeted his eye only served to harden him further. Betty had grown too old to properly care for a growing boy and Cole was thin, hungry, and dirty. Mitch had arranged for a neighbor to check on her and then taken the boy with him, settling in Florida to implement the first phase of his revenge. Building his nest egg.

But things had gone wrong once again and he'd had to run from the law to avoid another prison sentence. He'd come home once again. This time to his house. *Mine.* Because a week after he came home, Aunt Betty had died peacefully in her sleep.

In her nightstand drawer he'd found the will in which she'd left the house to him, God bless her. But bundled with Betty's papers he'd also found his mother's diary and when he'd read *that*, everything changed. Well, almost everything changed.

He still loved Cole and still hated his stepfather. That hadn't changed.

But now he understood the pain his mother had endured. Mitch had always thought his stepfather was a player, screwing a different woman every night. What he learned by reading his mother's diary was the opposite. His stepfather had one woman, all those years, one who was also married. He'd left Mitch's mother every night for a woman who'd rubbed the affair in his mother's face. Who'd laughed at her, considered her a joke.

Mitch now knew that woman's name.

He sat down at the old desk and pulled the drawer out, revealing the leather-bound volume. Carefully set it on the desk and opened it to the page he knew by heart. Read the words penned in his mother's hand on an autumn night eight years before.

> *Tonight I followed him. I did. I put the baby in his car seat and I followed him. To the Motel 6 in Winchester, VA.*
>
> *Motel 6? Really? I was so relieved. Just a prostitute, I thought. He's not in love with someone else. And then her car pulled up. A Bentley. A Bentley in the lot of Motel 6. I would have laughed if I hadn't been crying.*
>
> *Because Daphne Elkhart got out of the car. He took her in his arms. Right there in the parking lot.*
>
> *How do I compete with a woman like her? She's beautiful. She's rich. I can't compete. But I can't just give up without a fight. I'll give her one more chance. I'll go see her. I'll ask her to leave my man alone. I'll take Cole with me. She'll see he has a child. That she's wrecking a home. And if she doesn't back away, I'll tell her husband. He'll fix her. He'll make her behave. And if Travis won't, his mother will. I'll make someone listen if it kills me.*

Mitch closed the diary, put it back in the drawer. The entry was dated two nights before she killed herself. There was one more entry, the following night. His mother had confronted Daphne, begged her to leave her husband alone. And Daphne had laughed at her.

The ME had placed time of death as sometime on the day after that last entry.

Knowing who had destroyed his mother's life had rocked him soundly, making him hate his stepfather all the more. He and Daphne deserved each other. So he'd started to plan how he could get them both. All at once. If he could use them against each other? Even better.

Mitch had been setting things up for months. His stepfather's endgame. Daphne's endgame. The Millhouses taking the fall so that nobody suspected him. Things had finally started to cook last night. The next days would bring the payoff.

He walked to the only area of the shelter he'd changed, walling off two small rooms, lining them with extra insulation. They were three feet underground with concrete walls twelve inches thick, but cops had sophisticated equipment these days. He didn't want to risk that anyone searching above might pick up a heat signature. They were to hold his stepfather and Daphne, once he had them both. But at the moment someone else inhabited one of the rooms.

Kimberly MacGregor looked up when he unlocked her door, hate in her dark eyes. He'd tied and gagged her, so she couldn't speak, not with her mouth anyway. Her eyes expressed everything she couldn't say. She hated his guts. Which he could live with.

She was sitting on the cot, back against the wall, shivering even though she was wrapped in a blanket.

"Hi, Kimberly. Just wanted to see if you're still alive." He removed the gag, then stepped back. He'd had to stab her thigh to keep her from running to her car the night before, but she'd got in a couple of good kicks with the other leg. "Let it all out," he said.

"Where is my sister?"

"Safe. For now. But close enough that I could get to her before my temper dies down. So don't make me angry, Kim."

She glared, but toned it down. "You said you were going to *talk* to Ford, only *talk*!"

"You wanted to believe it, because it made it easier for you to justify betraying him."

She swallowed hard. "Is he alive?"

"Last I checked." He studied her carefully. "Who was the cop?"

"I don't know." But she looked away briefly as she said it. *She's lying.* "You saw what I did to that cop last night. If you want to save your little sister from a similar fate, you'll tell me what I want to know. Who was he?"

"I don't know his name, but I don't think he was a cop. I think he was a bodyguard."

"Ford hired a bodyguard?"

"His mother did. She was afraid for him. He didn't know about the bodyguard."

"But you did?" he asked silkily. "And you didn't tell me?"

"I didn't know about him," she insisted, "until all of a sudden he was there and you tased him. His mother must have hired him without telling Ford."

"You gave me away," he said quietly. If he'd been a second slower, if he hadn't been so well prepared, things would have ended very differently.

"I didn't mean to. I was surprised. Look, I got Ford to the alley when you told me to."

"Only because I took your sister. You got cold feet and nearly ruined my plans. I'm surprised and disappointed. I didn't take you for a coward." He studied Kim's face. "Or maybe it wasn't fear. Maybe you've developed feelings for Ford Elkhart?"

Kim's cheeks flushed a dull red. "No. Not like that. He's . . . just a nice kid. I didn't want him hurt."

"Better Ford than Pamela. You're lucky I wasn't caught. Then nobody would know where I stashed your sister and before long she would run out of air. That would be bad."

She glanced up at him, fear in her eyes. *Now, that's what I'm talking about.*

"I did what you said. Let Pamela go. She's just a kid. She didn't do anything wrong."

He retied the gag. "When did age or innocence ever matter? Technically, Ford didn't do anything wrong, except trust you. If you're nice and behave, I'll let you see your sister later. If you cross me again, I'll gut her and make you watch."

He locked her door and checked the empty room that would soon belong to Daphne Montgomery. He hadn't realized she was Daphne Elkhart until her son won some stupid horse jumping contest and they got written up in the paper.

Daphne wouldn't like her new home. She didn't like being underground. *Can't say that I blame her.* He'd mounted a CD player on the wall. The CD was mostly a mix of white noise, but every so often a voice would say, "I'm back! Did you miss me?"

Thanks to his stepfather's painstakingly kept records, Mitch knew exactly what those words meant to her. When he'd read her story, Mitch's first inclination was to feel pity for the poor little mountain girl, kidnapped and terrorized. But then he remembered cleaning his mother's blood and brains from this room. He remembered his brother's nightmares, and all Mitch's pity vaporized as if it had never been.

Daphne had a hard time as a kid. *So damn what? So did I. So did Cole.* The judge hadn't cared about Mitch's sad story when he'd gone on trial. As Daphne's judge and jury, Mitch didn't care, either.

Four

Ford's hands sprang free, his lungs heaving. *Thank God.*
The box cutter had been damn dull. Rubbing his wrists
over the blade had taken forever, but it was done. He pulled
the box cutter from the logs where he'd wedged it. He
sawed at the ropes around his ankles, rubbing his legs to get
his blood circulating again, then ran a hand over his hair,
unsurprised to find a bald spot where his scalp burned.
What the hell? Gingerly he touched the sore spot on his
head. At least it had stopped bleeding.

Call for help. But of course his cell phone was gone.

Thump. Thump.

Ford stilled. The sound came from close enough to rattle
the window above his head. He rose, standing to one side of
the glass so he couldn't be seen.

It was an old man, splitting logs. From the way he swung
his axe, he looked to be in damn good shape. He was about
sixty-five, maybe seventy.

He gathered up the wood he'd split and carried it into
his house, a cabin with a front porch, complete with a rocking chair. Just when Ford had started to wonder if he had
anything to do with his kidnapping, the old guy reappeared,
a rifle over his shoulder.

Coming this way. *He'll have to come through that door.*

You'll have one chance to overpower him. If you fail, you're dead. So don't fuck it up, Ford.

Ford searched the shed, looking for a weapon. The box cutter might work, but he'd have to get too close and the man had a gun. He needed something with more reach. *The logs in the corner.* He tested one, then another, until he found one that was longer than the rest. It was nowhere near baseball bat length, but it would have to do.

Standing at one side of the door, he heard the creak of the rusty hinges. *Wait . . . wait for it . . .* Ford swung the log, smacking the man upside the head. The guy teetered, then went down on his knees. *Don't wuss out now. Finish it.*

Ford hauled back and smacked him again. The man fell forward, his rifle sliding out of his grip. The old man pushed himself up on his hands and knees, reaching for his weapon. Ford hit him in the head a third time. This time the man didn't get up.

Ford stood there, panting, staring down at the old man. *Oh my God, I killed him.*

So? He's a sick fuck who would have killed you.

No, wait—he's breathing. I didn't kill him. Now what? Run. Ford grabbed the rifle and burst through the doorway, gasping at the cold air outside. *Need a coat. You could die out here without a coat.* He ran around the shed, toward the cabin. There was an old truck parked out front. *Keys. Dammit. I should have taken his keys.*

He ran into the cabin. There was a phone on the wall, but it was an old rotary-style set. "No way," he murmured. Would it even work anymore? He lifted the receiver—but heard nothing. The line was dead.

Turning slowly, he looked for the keys to the truck. His heart was pounding so hard it was all he could hear. *No keys. Not okay.* For a ridiculous moment he wished he'd run with a rougher crowd in high school. *Then I might know how to hot-wire an engine.*

Gran would know. His mother's mother knew how to do lots of things that would be useful in this situation. *Wish I'd paid more attention during all those hiking trips.* She'd tried to teach him survival skills, but he'd been too addicted to his Game Boy to listen.

He opened drawers, looking for keys, a knife, anything.

Hello. Boxes of ammo. *This could come in handy.* He pulled one out and frowned. Empty. They were all empty.

His back was to the open front door when he felt the floor tremble under his feet. He wheeled around to see the old man stagger through the doorway, an axe clutched in both hands. For a second they stared at each other, and then Ford remembered he still held the guy's rifle. Not breaking eye contact, Ford lifted it to his shoulder.

Luckily I did pay attention to all Gran's target-shooting lessons. They'd given him the edge over all his friends, making him a living legend at Xbox *Medal of Honor*.

"Where's the girl?" Ford asked quietly.

The old man hesitated, then shook his head. "Don't know what you're talking about." But there was a flicker of unease in his eyes.

Liar. "The girl who was with me last night. What have you done with her?"

Unease flashed to relief before settling into feigned confusion. "There wasn't any girl. Just you."

"There was a girl. Where is she?"

"You're crazy," the old man said. He took a tentative step forward, then another.

Ford took one step back, then stopped himself. "No more. I will kill you if I have to."

"No you won't." He took a third step, his confidence growing. "Give me the—"

The man was a yard away from grabbing the barrel of the rifle. *Do it. Shoot him now.* Ford prepared for the recoil and the earsplitting blast, and squeezed the trigger.

Nothing happened. No recoil. No blast. Ford cocked the lever, fired again. Nothing.

The gun wasn't loaded. Ford wasn't sure who was more surprised, him or the old man. But the old man recovered quickly and charged, swinging the axe up as he'd done with the logs outside.

Ford stepped to the side and when the old guy rushed past, he jabbed his back with the rifle stock, knocking him off balance, then swung the weapon by the barrel to smack the back of his head again. The old man went down and Ford followed, shoving his knee into the guy's kidney. *Hope it hurts, you bastard.*

He wrenched the axe from the old man's grip and

pressed the blade up under his grizzled jaw. "Where's. The. Girl?"

"I. Don't. Know."

"You have to know. You shot me in the back with a fucking Taser. She was there. What did you do with her?"

"I didn't shoot you with nothin'. I signed on to babysit only you and that's all."

Ford frowned. *I'm back. Did you miss me?* This wasn't the same man that talked to him before. The voice was way different. "Who's the other guy?"

"Don't know."

He pressed the axe blade harder against the man's flesh until a line of blood appeared. "You don't want to push me, buddy. Who's the other guy?"

The man hesitated, then his shoulders sagged as if he'd given up, which Ford didn't buy for a second. "Archie Leach."

That named sounded really familiar. "Why did he kidnap me?"

"Money. Both your parents are richer than God."

"What's your name?"

"Marion Morrison," he drawled.

That name Ford knew. Fury bubbled up. *Asshole.* Morrison was John Wayne's real name. Who knew who "Archie Leach" really was? "Where is Archie now?"

"Went to the city to collect the ransom."

"Which he'll *share* with you?" Ford let the sarcasm ooze in.

"Marion" had gone still. Sincerely still this time. He said nothing.

Ford laughed bitterly. "You already know that somebody unloaded your gun. Did your Smithsonian phone over there actually work before?"

The surprised jerk of the old man's shoulders said that it had.

"Well, it doesn't now," Ford said flatly. "So your partner left you alone, with no way to defend yourself and no way to call for help. He collects the ransom and leaves you high and dry. And even if you take this gun from me, it doesn't matter, because he's taken your ammo. Yeah," he added when the old man exhaled sharply. "All the boxes in the drawer? Empty. You think you're a fucking John Wayne? You're just the fall guy."

"If you're gonna use that axe, boy, do it now. I'm gettin'
tired of listenin' to you."

Ford frowned, not sure what to do next. He probably
couldn't kill the old bastard, not on purpose anyway. *And I
don't have any ammo, either. Which the old guy now knows.
Way to go, Elkhart.*

The subtle tightening of the old man's back was the only
warning Ford had before he twisted out of his grip, rolling
away from the axe blade and grabbing the handle with both
hands. But although his captor was strong for sixty-five,
Ford was twenty years old and pissed off. With a hard yank,
Ford took the axe back and, holding it like a bat, walloped
John Wayne's head like he was going for a home run.

The old man was out cold—but still breathing. It was
probably a good idea to keep him that way. He might know
who had Kim. He definitely knew the other kidnapper.

I need to get help before the other guy comes back.

Hold on, Kim. Just a little longer.

Baltimore, Maryland
Tuesday, December 3, 11:10 a.m.

Mitch climbed back up the ladder, secured the door, and
pushed the shelves back into place. Wearily he let himself
into the kitchen, then stopped short, stifling a curse.

His middle brother, Mutt, was sitting at the table eating
cereal. The TV was on and his brother frowned as he
watched. *What the hell is he doing here?* Mitch closed the
door hard enough to startle him. Mutt wheeled, sending a
splash of milk onto the floor.

"Where have you been?" Mutt demanded. Mutt's given
name was Matthew, but Mitch always thought of him as
Mutt, since his middle brother was the only legitimate son.
Mitch and Cole were bastards, or so his stepfather said.
Takes one to know one.

"I had a delivery. It was on the schedule," Mitch replied.
Appropriating his stepfather's goods was an important
part of his plan. Being a delivery driver gave him access
and opportunity.

As the logistics manager and accountant, Mutt was only
too happy to have Mitch's help, especially when the deliv-

ery was a dangerous one—it meant Mutt didn't have to call in any favors from the drivers he kept on the actual books.

It also meant Mutt could pay his brother half of what he paid everyone else and pocket the difference. Mutt didn't know Mitch knew about that. It pissed Mitch off to high heaven, but he'd bitten his tongue. It had also eliminated any lingering affection he felt for his brother. Things were about to get real bad for Mutt's daddy. If Mutt got caught in the crossfire . . . *Well, I won't cry too hard about that.*

"Your delivery was to *Richmond*. You should have been back hours ago."

"Got a legit job," Mitch lied smoothly. "Last-minute emergency. Woman's heat pump went out and she has a baby. I fixed it on my way back. Why are you here, anyway?"

Mutt lived in one of his daddy's fancy houses in the city. He'd never lived out here. His daddy didn't even like him driving out here, "slumming it" with his half brothers.

Mutt frowned. "Because the school called. They tried to get in touch with you, but you were AWOL, so they called me since you put me as an emergency contact."

Mitch's heart stuttered. "Why? What's wrong?"

"Cole didn't show up to school today. He's skipped nine of the last ten days. They've called the house and sent home letters. Cole's about to get expelled. I drove out to see if something was wrong, like you guys had food poisoning or something."

Expelled? Hell. "And? Did you find him?"

"Yep. He was in the basement. I sent him to his room."

Mitch's shoulders slumped in relief as anger boiled in his gut. His youngest brother had become a real problem recently, finding every way possible to keep from going to school. *I'm glad he's okay, because I'm gonna kill him.*

Of course he'd never do that. But he would take away every privilege his little brother still had. Which wasn't many.

"The school never called me." Mitch patted his pockets for his cell phones. He kept four—two throwaways he used to communicate with the Millhouses and Beckett, respectively, and one he used to communicate with Mutt about deliveries. The fourth was the number he gave to Cole and to the middle school. He found the right phone, then glared at the display. "Battery's dead." Then he realized what Mutt had said. "Cole was in the basement? Why?"

Mitch kept stuff in the basement. Important stuff. Like cash. Guns. And as of last night, Pamela MacGregor, Kim's little sister, who was now his leverage.

Mutt pointed to the TV in the corner. "Damn, would you look at that?"

Mitch looked up and saw that Mutt was watching the very thing he wanted to see. "What's happening?" Mitch asked, very aware Mutt had dodged his question about Cole and the basement. He'd come back to it later.

"It's that damn jury verdict on the Millhouse case," Mutt said. "I've got an appointment downtown and I wanted to be sure there was no riot in the streets."

"Is there?"

"Not yet. Jury found the little bastard guilty. But the real excitement was what happened after. The killer knifed a cop and his mom attacked the prosecutor. There was a brawl in the courtroom while the Millhouse kid tried to escape."

So the Millhouses' Plan B actually worked? *Oh. My. God.* "Did he get away?"

"Nah," Mutt said, "but I gather it was touch and go for a minute. Kid's a fucking psycho. At least two people have been taken to area hospitals."

His heart did another stutter, dip, and roll. "What about the prosecutor?"

"Not clear yet. There's supposed to a press conference in a few minutes."

If Daphne was badly injured, I'll kill every last Millhouse I can find.

Pouring himself some cereal, Mitch sat down next to Mutt and pointed to his brother's laptop. "What's that?" he asked, even though he knew.

"I'm doing the books," Mutt said. "Figured I'd keep busy while I waited for you to get your ass home."

"Well, I'm home now," Mitch said blandly. "Need any help with that?"

Mutt rolled his eyes. "As if. You can't even balance your own checkbook."

That Mitch couldn't balance his own checkbook was not true. He did his own personal accounting, he just didn't advertise it. It was better to let your adversaries believe you were stupid and technically challenged. It made them less careful around you—after all, what harm could you do with a P&L statement or a page of passwords?

Mitch shrugged. "Guilty as charged."

"You need an accountant, Mitch," Mutt said, serious now. "I found your stash of cash in the root cellar when I was looking for Cole. You can't just leave that kind of money lying around. Anybody could come in and steal it."

Mitch narrowed his eyes. "Wait. How did you get in? I never gave you a key."

"The back door was unlocked. I just walked in."

Mitch ground his teeth. *Cole.* "Damn that boy. Where's your car?"

"I parked around back. Didn't want Cole to know I was here in case he was up to no good. I'm serious about that money, Mitch. I knew you'd pulled some from that last job in Florida, but I had no idea you just had it lying around. You've got to have a couple hundred thousand down there, just piled up in plastic storage tubs."

There was three times that, actually. Most of it was in the basement room where he'd hidden Pamela, but he'd hidden a few tubs full of cash in the root cellar, located in the basement's back corner. The money was what he'd been able to load onto a U-Haul trailer right before the Feds crashed the "pain clinic" business he'd worked for in Miami. Florida was the go-to state for pill poppers. Dealers and addicts alike swarmed in from the Midwest to buy cheap prescription pills doled out by doctors on the take. There was huge money to be made and Mitch had needed huge money.

His original plan when he'd been paroled was to set up his stepfather to be arrested for the same crime that had robbed Mitch of three years of his life—possession with intent to distribute. He basically planned to gather as much money as he could, buy as much heroin as he could with it, plant it on his stepfather, and call in an anonymous tip. They'd raid his stepfather's compound, seize his books— both sets—and bring his empire crashing down. Simple yet elegant.

He'd stuck it out in Miami as long as he dared, working for the uncle of his cellmate until the Feds began raiding the pain centers and hauling away the dirty doctors. Mitch had been skimming cash off the top—there was so much money floating around that nobody missed it. Over the course of two years, he'd skimmed a hell of a lot of money, which he vacuum-sealed into tidy little bricks and stored in plastic tubs in his Miami garage. When the raids started, he rented a U-Haul, loaded it up, packed a protesting Cole into the truck's cab, and hightailed it for Aunt Betty's house. For home.

Only to find things had changed within his stepfather's business. No longer were drugs his principal source of revenue. To Mitch's delight, his stepfather had gotten himself involved in something even better—gun running. Highly lucrative and extremely dangerous. And perfect for what Mitch had in mind. Plus, he didn't have to spend any of the money he'd hidden in the root cellar. Money that Mutt now knew about.

Part of it anyway. Mutt hadn't found all of it, not by a long shot.

"It's not like I can walk into a bank with tubs of cash," Mitch said grumpily. "I've been depositing it slowly, staying under the bank's radar."

Mutt blinked at him. "You've been depositing it ten grand at a time?"

"That's the magic number, isn't it? Over that and they have to report it to the IRS?"

Mutt sputtered, nearly speechless. "Well, yeah, that's the number if you care about being legal, but . . . My God. Ten grand at a time, *in the same bank*? With no business charter, no P&L? Mitch, that's . . ." *Stupid,* his brother clearly wanted to say. "Incredibly inefficient," he said instead. "I can set you up so the money doesn't raise any flags and works for you instead of sitting in plastic tubs in your root cellar."

Out of the goodness of his little heart, Mitch thought. "For how much?"

Mutt shrugged. "A third of whatever I process."

You rotten little sonofabitch. A third? A tenth would be highway robbery. But Mitch just smiled. "That sounds more than fair." He'd let Mutt set up the business paperwork and then he'd take over the deposits himself. And then when Mutt wasn't looking, Mitch would log in to Mutt's accounting software and wire the money back to himself. No harm, no foul.

Knowing that his brother kept all of his passwords in a file on his iPhone was useful. Knowing Mutt's phone pass code was more useful still. This password Mitch had gotten the old-fashioned, totally low-tech way—he'd gotten Mutt drunk and looked over his shoulder as his brother had entered it into his phone.

So getting his money back would be no problem and the opportunity would come sooner rather than later. In just a few more days Mutt and his daddy would be in hot water with people far more dangerous than the cops and the Feds put together.

While Mitch was in prison, his stepfather had entered into a business association with a Russian named Fyodor Antonov. Antonov ran one of the Eastern European crime families that were quickly taking root up and down the East Coast.

Mutt's old man had been expanding his drug business, but an independent could grow only so much on the East Coast before encroaching on one of the big guys. He'd skated too close to the edge and got smacked back by Antonov's goons.

His stepfather had been given a choice: work for the Russian or surrender his entire business. He'd gone for the first option and now claimed stockpiled rifles shipped from Ukraine into the Port of Baltimore, transporting them south, presumably to the Mexican cartel.

Mutt had been put in charge of the drivers and he'd offered "poor big brother" Mitch a route. Driving for Mutt offered a much better way to destroy his stepfather than his original plan of simply framing him for drug distribution. Mitch had been skimming rifles from shipments for months. He'd also hacked into Mutt's computer to make the invoices match what he'd actually delivered, forging his stepfather's signature on all the reports.

Because Mutt believed him to be stupid, he'd never been suspected, not even once. Because Mutt's daddy had no clue that he was a driver, he'd never been concerned about him. It was perfect.

The rifles would soon be discovered by the cops—again, part of Mitch's plan. The cops would see AK-47s and think "Russian." Because they weren't stupid, either. When the Russians got wind of an investigation, they'd hunker down and check inventories. His stepfather's books would be audited and the discrepancies discovered. Antonov would believe Mitch's stepfather was a thief.

From what Mitch had gleaned in prison, the Russians didn't take kindly to thieves. If they didn't kill his stepfather, the old man would wish they had.

Mutt packed up his laptop, a gleam in his eye. "I think I'll go down to the root cellar to see how much cash we're talking about."

Mitch just smiled at him. Mutt would be so focused on all that pretty money that he wouldn't think to look for anything else, like Pamela MacGregor. "I appreciate the help."

Mutt grinned at him. "What are brothers for?"

Ask me in a week. I'll have a really good answer then.

Tuesday, December 3, 11:10 a.m.

The cold wind felt good. Daphne drew a deep breath of fresh air and scanned the crowd. All the reporters were here. About twenty feet to her left stood Detectives Stevie Mazzetti and J. D. Fitzpatrick along with half a dozen deputies, their eyes watchful. After what had happened in the courtroom, it looked like the cops were taking no chances, for which Daphne was grateful.

Still, there was a tension, a foreboding that crawled up her spine. Ignoring it for the moment, she cloaked herself in her composure.

"Ladies and gentlemen, I'm sure you've all heard that a jury of Mr. Millhouse's peers returned with a guilty verdict this morning. We are exceptionally pleased and hope this sends a clear message. We will not allow the murder of innocents to go unpunished and we will fight to bring justice to those who believe themselves above the law." She forced a small smile. "Now, it's been a very long morning. If you'll excuse—"

"Miss Montgomery!" It was Phin Radcliffe, the alpha dog of all the reporters. "Is it true that Reggie Millhouse's mother slipped him a knife?"

Somehow Radcliffe managed to be in the front row, every time. *Pact with Satan*, Daphne thought darkly. But he was good about giving their women's center on-air coverage, promoting their fund-raisers, so Daphne bit back her dislike.

"There was a knife, but who gave it to whom, I don't know for certain. The police acted swiftly to contain the threat, but there were injuries." She knew the media had gotten the EMTs on camera as they'd entered and exited the justice center. "I appreciate your discretion until the families of the injured have been notified."

Another reporter piped up. "Is it true Reggie's mother attacked you?"

"No comment," Daphne said, her smile faint.

"Miss Montgomery!" A young woman pushed her way to the front, at the far edge of the crowd.

Daphne caught a flurry of motion from the corner of her eye. Stevie Mazzetti had answered her phone, her expression going very still. Her eyes flashed to Daphne's. Something was wrong.

"Miss Montgomery!" The young woman raised her voice, her tone abrasive and accusatory. "I have a question for you."

Daphne ripped her gaze away from Stevie and back to the young woman, who stood far enough away that she had to squint.

The woman smiled and Daphne had a flash of recognition, but it was too late. Her gaze dropped to the gun in Marina Craig's hands. Reggie's sixteen-year-old girlfriend, pregnant with his child, held the weapon at her hip with an ease that suggested she'd done so many times before.

"Don't do—" Gunfire cracked the air and Daphne gasped, thrown backward against the concrete step as pain radiated from the center of her chest, then the back of her head. She tried to breathe, but her lungs weren't working.

Get up. Get away. Daphne struggled to open her eyes, flinching at the loud noise. More gunfire. Screams. *She's shooting people. Fucking hell.*

She pushed herself to her elbows and looked around, blinking. People, running away. People on the ground, not moving. *She's shooting people. Somebody stop her.*

Daphne watched Stevie run toward her, the movement almost slow motion, then another shot cracked the air and Stevie was down, her hands gripping her thigh. There was blood. Lots of blood. Where was J.D.? Grayson? *Don't be dead.*

Daphne rolled to one side, her lungs starting to function again. *Kevlar,* she remembered. The vest she'd complained about wearing. She blinked hard. *Oh God.* Next to her lay Radcliffe's cameraman, his white shirt now crimson.

Fear rose up to choke her. *Not now.* Glancing around frantically, she saw the cameraman's bag. It was heavy. It would have to do. She rolled farther, edging her fingers forward until they closed against the bag's strap.

"Stop," Marina barked. "Put it down, now."

Daphne froze, then realized the girl wasn't talking to her. She lifted her eyes, and her heart stopped. *Grayson.* He stood five feet away, the gun in his hand pointed at Marina. The laser sight of Marina's gun was centered on his forehead.

Daphne looked past him. And had to swallow back the bile. He'd taken the gun from a dead cop. How many had Marina killed? Where was J.D.?

"I said, put it down," Marina said furiously. "I will shoot you right here and now."

"No," Grayson said. He was pale, but his hand didn't waver.

"I can drop you before you even pull the trigger," Marina boasted.

This stops. Now. Daphne tightened her fist around the camera bag's strap, gathered her energy, and flung it as hard as she could.

It went only about three feet, skittering along the ground. But it was enough. Startled, Marina spun, pulling the trigger, spraying bullets as she turned in an arc.

Back to me. Nowhere to run. Nowhere to hide.

And everything happened at once. Gunfire erupted from everywhere as a dark blur flew through the air from her left. A man. It was a man.

The air was crushed from her lungs again as he landed on top of her, shielding her. Daphne felt the jerk of his body against hers—once, twice. Marina was shooting him.

No. Daphne tried to shout, but there was no air. She could only stare horrified as he twisted, his arm extended toward Marina in a straight, unwavering line, a gun in his hand and grim resolve on his face. A final shot rang out and Marina dropped to the ground.

And then it was quiet. No gunfire, just the sound of heavy breathing. Some moans. Sobs. A voice shouting for someone to call 911.

Dazed, Daphne looked up. He hung over her, supporting his weight on his elbows. He was tall, dark, dangerous. And familiar. She blinked, wondering if she was dreaming.

"Joseph?" she gasped.

Tuesday, December 3, 11:13 a.m.

Stunned, Joseph pushed himself to his knees, looking over his shoulder. The woman with the gun was dead. But he'd never pulled the trigger. He looked to his right. Stevie was propped up on one elbow, her arm still extended, the gun slipping from her bloody hand. She'd fired. She fell back and Maynard was suddenly at her side.

Holstering his gun, Joseph looked down at Daphne and his heart stopped beating. She'd been hit. *Bullet holes.* There were bullet holes in her coat. He ripped at the buttons and his heart stopped. *Her blouse was covered in blood.*

The sight of it flung him back to a different day, a different place. A different woman. *Same blood. So much blood. Can't make it stop.*

"Joseph?" The whisper yanked him back. Daphne stared up at him, her blue eyes wide with confusion and disbelief. His breath shallow and too fast, he stared back.

Different day, he told himself. *Different woman. Different end.* Daphne was not going to die. He simply would not allow it.

"You're going to be okay," he told her, his voice somehow steady. But she was bleeding and he needed to make it stop. Grimly he set to working on the tiny buttons of her blouse. Her eyes popping wide in shock, she smacked his hands away.

"I'm not hurt," she insisted, huffing out every word on a rasping exhale.

She'd been hit by at least three bullets, maybe more. He could hear several people on their cell phones with 911. He looked over his shoulder and swore. Where were the goddamn EMTs?

"You're hit. You're covered in blood." He was always

calm. Unshakable. But not now. Not with her. Not like this. He flexed his fingers, then tried to work the buttons again, glaring when she grabbed his wrists to stop him.

"Not my blood," she said, her voice a rasp. "Came from earlier."

Grayson dropped to his knees beside them. "She did first aid on the deputy who was stabbed by Millhouse," he said. "It's the deputy's blood, not hers. She's wearing a vest. Do you hear me, Joseph? I made her wear Kevlar."

Joseph blinked at his brother for a moment, his shoulders sagging with relief as the words sank in. *Kevlar. Oh God.* He willed his heart to slow down, then realized the blood on her blouse wasn't spreading. It wasn't even wet. "The blood is dried."

"Because it's not mine," Daphne muttered, still rasping. "And you didn't make me do anything, Grayson. I'm not an idiot. I wore the damn Kevlar . . . on my own."

Ignoring her, Grayson checked Joseph's eyes, then inspected his back, blanching at what he saw. "Bullet holes. But no blood. You look okay. Are you okay?"

"I'm all right. I'm wearing a vest, too. Never leave home without it." Joseph didn't even feel the pain. Yet. But it would come once the adrenaline ebbed. Getting shot while wearing Kevlar still hurt like hell. But it was better than the alternative.

He twisted around, taking in the scene. It looked like a lot of battlefields he'd been on. He saw one dead, a cop. Half a dozen more were injured. The crowd had scattered, only law enforcement and a few reporters remaining. Cops were checking the wounded, administering first aid. Two uniforms were crouched over the cameraman, working to stop the bleeding. Everyone who needed help seemed to have it.

Joseph looked back at Grayson to find his brother staring at him. "What are you doing here, Joseph? Not that I'm unhappy to see you, but . . . What's going on?"

Joseph glanced down at Daphne, who stared at him as well, but her gaze was clouded with pain. She was tentatively reaching for the back of her head where she'd hit the concrete when the impact of the bullets had knocked her down.

"I need to check her head," he said, but Grayson grabbed his arm.

"Dammit, Joseph," he said through clenched teeth. "Don't you dare ignore me."

Joseph looked around, then leaned close to Grayson's ear. "I have to get her out of here. Her son's been abducted. I was on my way to tell her when all hell broke loose."

Grayson pulled back slowly, his face shocked. "What?"

"You heard me. Keep the reporters away. They may not have picked up on the BOLO yet, but only because this story is bigger. Soon somebody's going to connect the dots. I need to get her out of here before that happens. I can't let her find out that way."

Grayson visibly pulled himself together. "You stay here. I'll get an EMT to you as soon as we can."

"I won't leave her," Joseph promised, then pulled latex gloves from his coat pocket and gave them to his brother. "You never know what you'll find in this kind of situation."

Grayson took off at a jog and Joseph dropped back down to his knees, angling his body to shield her from cameras as best he could.

"You don't need to stay with me," Daphne mumbled. "Other people are hurt worse."

"Other people aren't a killer's target. I'm staying." Now that he knew she wasn't bleeding out, his fury rose anew. "What the hell were you doing, throwing that bag at her? She would have shot you."

When he and Maynard had arrived, Daphne had just started taking questions. And then bullets started to fly. By the time he'd fought his way through the fleeing crowd of reporters and protesters, she was on the ground beside a man with a hole in his chest, grappling for a camera bag. Joseph had taken a running leap across the courthouse steps—and none too soon.

"I was trying to stop her," Daphne said thickly. "Somebody needed to. Thank you. I think you saved my life."

"If I'd been a second later . . ." His blood ran cold. "You'd be dead."

"How many did she kill?" Her voice was a little less raspy, but still slurred.

"One. Maybe a half dozen injured."

"Sweet Lord." Daphne whispered it, disbelieving. Then her memory reconnected. "Stevie!" She tried to sit up, but Joseph gently pressed her back down. "She was hit."

"In the thigh," Joseph said. "Your PI's with her now."

Maynard knelt next to Stevie Mazzetti, putting pressure on her thigh. His coat was rolled up, pillowing her head. He'd taken off his shirt and ripped it into strips. He had to be freezing, but showed no sign that he even noticed the cold.

The PI had told him that Daphne wasn't his, that they were just friends. Looking at Maynard's agonized expression as he treated Stevie's wound, Joseph believed him. *If I look like he does . . . Might as well wear a neon sign over my head. Down for the count.*

"Is she all right?" Daphne started to sit up again, then fell back, hitting her head on the step before Joseph could reach her. She groaned softly, touching the base of her skull. When she pulled her hand away, it was covered in blood. Fresh blood this time. She stared at her hand, not quite seeing. "I think I hit my head." She closed her eyes, grimacing. "I don't feel so good. You might want to step back. Really."

"You need to throw up, go ahead. Nothing I haven't seen before." He'd started to probe the back of her head to determine the damage when her eyes flew open.

Alarmed, she grabbed his wrist again. "No," she pleaded desperately. "Don't."

"I need to know you're okay," he said firmly, then gentled his voice. "I won't hurt you, Daphne, but I need to check. You might have a concussion. Don't fight me."

She angled her face away and closed her eyes again. Her cheeks grew flushed, the bright red in vivid contrast to her pale face. "Just . . . hurry. Please."

Frowning at her tone, he touched the back of her head. Then his frown sharpened when his fingers slid up under . . . her wig. *She's wearing a wig. Why?* For a moment he wondered what he should say, then realized there wasn't anything he could say that wouldn't embarrass her further. So for the moment he said nothing. Later, he'd ask. "Open your eyes. Let me see your pupils."

She opened her eyes, looking everywhere but at him. "I guess you're wondering—"

He laid his finger across her lips. "Your pupils are looking more normal and you're sounding less drunk. You've got a bad gash," he said matter-of-factly and watched her swallow hard. "You probably hit your head on the edge of the step, and even small head wounds bleed like a bitch. I doubt you'll need stitches, but you need to get checked."

He needed to wipe the shame from her expression. Whatever her reason for the wig, it didn't change the fact that she was the most beautiful, the most . . . compelling woman he'd ever met. He'd tell her someday. Because this was definitely not the time.

"Stevie's snarling at Maynard," he said, redirecting her attention, "so I think she's okay." Daphne shot him a look of gratitude that grated. *What did she think I'd do? Yank the damn thing off her head and hold it up for everyone to see?* But she was hurt, so he stowed his irritation. "Maynard's applying a tourniquet. Boy knows his first aid. He's doing everything he can without a med kit."

"Clay's seen gunshot wounds," she said. "He did two tours in Somalia."

"He told me he was in the Corps." The PI moved up further in his estimation. Now that Maynard wasn't a contender, Joseph could feel all kinds of friendly toward the guy.

Now that he knew Daphne wasn't going to die, he could breathe again. *And in a minute, I'll destroy her. I'll have to tell her that her son is missing, his bodyguard slain.*

His ears pricked at the sound of sirens, starting soft but growing louder. "EMTs are coming," he said, looking over his shoulder to the street. "J.D.'s meeting them." He'd get her in one of the ambulances, away from prying eyes. And he'd tell her there.

She frowned. "He wasn't with Stevie when she was shot. Where did he go?"

Joseph pointed to a man lying facedown on the pavement, his wrists cuffed behind him. "J.D. was subduing him when we got here."

"Help me up."

Joseph guided her to vertical, placing his hand against her back in case she got dizzy again.

She sucked in a surprised breath. "That's Reggie's father."

"He had a Glock just like the one the girl used, plus an

assault rifle. Good thing J.D. saw him when he did, because even after we'd stopped the girl, he might have kept on firing. We'd all be dead."

"Now I know why he left the courtroom after the verdict. They planned this."

Joseph thought of the dead cop in the alley and Ford and Kimberly. *This and more.* "I need to get you out of here," he said. "They might have other surprises in store."

He tugged her arm, but she didn't move. Eyes wide, she was viewing the scene, not realizing that, for her, the worst part was still to come.

"Oh my God," she whispered, flinching when she saw the dead shooter.

A lot of shots had been fired in those final few seconds. There was a lot of blood. He expected her to look away, but she shifted to her hands and knees, crawling down one of the steps by the time he'd recovered from his surprise.

He grasped her shoulders. "Stop. She's dead. There's nothing you can do."

"But what about the baby?" Daphne grabbed his arm. "Her baby might be saved."

Baby? Joseph whipped around to stare at the dead shooter. "She was pregnant?"

"You didn't notice?" she asked, dumbfounded. "She was due any day."

"I was busy noticing the modified Glock she was using to shoot people." It had been more than five minutes. If by some miracle the baby had survived all the bullets shot at its mother at the end, it would almost certainly be dead or suffering brain damage by now. He almost told Daphne this, but her eyes were pleading with him.

"We don't have much more time," he told her instead. "Another minute or two at the most." Pulling on a pair of latex gloves, he turned the shooter on her back. And sighed. "Aw hell. She's just a kid."

"She's sixteen. Reggie Millhouse is the baby's father."

Joseph rapidly unbuttoned the girl's coat. "What was her name?"

"Marina Craig," Daphne said. She crawled closer, grimacing. "Good God. How many times did you shoot her?"

"Me? None. The others shot six times. After you threw the camera bag, she lost focus and wasn't aiming at anyone.

That's when everyone got a clear shot." With his pocket-knife, he sliced the girl's shirt open and did a double take. "What the hell?"

"Is the baby dead?" Daphne asked, peering over his shoulder. "Please say no."

"No." He lifted the pad she wore, designed to look like a nine-month-pregnant belly.

Daphne's mouth fell open. "She faked being pregnant?"

Underneath the pad the girl's belly was soft and fleshy. "I think she was pregnant, and recently. But not today."

"But why?" she asked, bewildered. "Why would she do that?"

"So people wouldn't consider her a threat or they wouldn't shoot to kill. Which most of the cops didn't. There are no bullet holes in her torso, only in her legs and arms."

"And her head. Who shot her there?"

"Stevie did," Joseph said, waiting for her to look appalled.

Instead her lips firmed, her eyes hardening. "Good. She saved a lot of lives."

EMTs were everywhere, but he could now see there weren't enough ambulances for the wounded. He'd take her to the ER himself. "Do you think you can walk?"

"Yes." She said it defiantly, as if trying to convince herself.

He gently pulled her to her feet. "Come on. Let's get your head taken care of." She leaned into him, resting her forehead against his chest.

"Give me a second. The world is spinning and . . . God. I'd really like to not throw up in front of all these people."

He indulged himself, wrapping one arm around her protectively, keeping his free hand on his weapon. Just in case.

"Hey, Carter, wait one second."

Joseph checked over his shoulder, relieved to see J. D. Fitzpatrick approaching. Joseph had known Stevie Mazzetti for years, as she'd been among his brother's circle of friends. J.D. had quickly joined that circle the year before. J.D. was a damn good cop.

"I'm taking her to the ER," Joseph said.

"Good." J.D. met his eyes and Joseph knew that he'd had been apprised of their situation, that Ford was missing. "I'll find you at the ER to take your statement."

Joseph glanced down at Daphne. Her eyes were tightly closed and she clutched his coat like a lifeline. He mouthed

his next words to J.D., not wanting her to hear. "Send someone to get her mother. Take her to Daphne's house. Set up
a guard. I'll call you."

"Got it," J.D. mouthed back, then said aloud, "You okay,
there, Daph? You're looking a little green around the gills."

"Mostly," she muttered. "What are you two are talking
about over my head?"

"Joseph just asked me to make sure your mother knows
you're okay."

"Oh. That's sweet. Ford, too? He'll be worried sick. Ask
him to walk Tasha for me."

"You bet," J.D. said lightly, but his mouth was grim.

"Who's Tasha?" Joseph asked.

"My dog," she said against his coat.

"Protection dog," J.D. mouthed. "Fucking huge."

Which meant that any agents who went to search the
house should be prepared.

"You took down Bill Millhouse," she said, still not looking up. "What happened?"

"He left the courtroom before everyone else and I knew
he was up to no good. We got the Turner kids out and I saw
Bill skulking around. Followed him, found his stash. In the
trunk of his car he had ten more assault rifles. He'd planned
something big."

"Dear God," Daphne mumbled. "This is craziness."

"I need to get her to the ER," Joseph said, pointing at
the reporters who were venturing toward them now that
the bullets had stopped flying. "I'll keep you updated."

Tuesday, December 3, 11:40 a.m.

That stupid little bitch. Mitch stared at the television screen
in stunned disbelief. He'd known Marina Craig was a wild
card. But . . . the girl was fucking nuts.

Luckily enough, she was now fucking dead. She'd come
seconds from ruining everything. *Be glad you're dead. If
you'd killed Montgomery, I would have killed you myself.
And I would have made it hurt a hell of a lot more.*

The video wasn't the greatest quality. Whoever operated
the camera was far away, across the street from the courthouse steps. At least the picture was now stable, the camera

mounted on a tripod. Before, it had shaken, the cameraman obviously rattled.

The crowd had scattered, media and protesters ducking for cover. After her initial hit on Montgomery—and thank God for Kevlar—Marina had started taking out cops.

The door behind him creaked, giving him only a second's warning before Cole flopped on the sofa beside him, sending the frame shuddering. "Whatcha watching?"

He frowned at Cole, but didn't look away from the screen. Daphne Montgomery had yet to get up. There was a guy kneeling next to her, looking like he was doing first aid. *I need to see her get up.* "You're going to break this sofa one of these days."

"And my eyes'll get stuck if I roll them," Cole said. "What movie is this?"

"It's not a movie," Mitch said dryly. "It's the news."

"No shit? This is real life? I thought it was . . ." Cole pitched forward, squinting.

Montgomery was on her feet, so he turned the TV off. "Nothing you need to see."

Cole gave him the look. "I'm thirteen and a half. Get a grip."

"Oh, I'm about to. Why aren't you in school?"

Cole shrugged. Scowled. Said nothing.

Mitch's temper boiled up. "You've skipped nine of the last ten days. You're going to have that social worker on my ass, boy. And I don't like that. They're always poking in other people's business." *And when they poke, they find shit I really don't want them to see.* "Isn't it bad enough that you spend half your time suspended because you can't stop looking for fights? You're gonna skip the other half? I don't think so."

Cole set his jaw, his expression mutinous. "I don't go lookin' for fights."

"They just find you," Mitch said sarcastically and stood up. "I don't need this right now. Go to school, or so help me God, I'll drag you."

Cole stood up. And looked down at him. *Whoa. When did he get bigger than me?*

"I do not go looking for fights," Cole said through his teeth. "But I ain't gonna run from one if it comes looking for me."

"Go to school. If you leave now, you can still make your last two classes."

Cole's eyes flashed with fury, but he turned for the door. Visions of nosy social workers had Mitch flinging a few parting words. "And if you try real hard, maybe you can stay out of trouble till the Christmas break."

"If you'd wanted me to stay out of trouble, maybe you never shoulda dragged me back to this godforsaken hellhole. Everything was fine in Florida. *Just fine.*" He swept out of the room, slamming the front door so hard that the house shook.

Mitch stood looking at the door. Behind him he heard the door to the basement open, then close softly.

"Boy's got a point," Mutt said mildly. "You packed him up in the middle of the night, dragged him into a U-Haul truck, and never let him say good-bye to his friends. You wouldn't have reacted nearly so well at the same age."

I would have killed me in my sleep. "Your point?"

"The kid's not stupid. He knew something was wrong then. He does now." Mutt's brows lifted. "He nearly stumbled on your stash this morning."

Mitch's jaw tightened. "Dammit."

"This surprises you? You hid storage tubs filled with cash in the root cellar. It's not exactly the most diabolically secure hiding place."

Mitch did have a more secure hiding place in the basement—the small room that connected to the tunnel—but until recently it had been filled with the guns he'd skimmed from his stepfather's shipments. Now the guns were gone, making room for Pamela MacGregor.

"Why was Cole in the basement to start with?" he asked, remembering that he'd tried to ask once before.

"Hiding from you. He didn't want you to catch him skipping school. Or smoking."

Mitch's jaw dropped. "When the *hell* did he start smoking?"

Mutt started laughing. "You're hiding a quarter million in your root cellar and you're worried about Cole *smoking*? Oh, come on, Mitch. You gotta see the irony in that."

No, I really don't. But he made himself chuckle. "I guess I do." He made a point of looking at the suitcase in Mutt's hands. "I see you're starting on my deposits."

"After my meeting. I'll e-mail you a receipt."

I wonder what number Mutt will write on that "receipt." Mitch knew to the dollar what he had downstairs, so he'd know exactly what his brother had just stolen from him. Only the knowledge that he knew exactly how to break into Mutt's precious accounting program to take his money back kept the easy smile on his face. "You do that."

When Mitch had closed and locked the door, he let himself snarl. *Does Mutt think I'm that stupid? Does he really think I don't know what he's doing? Or does he just think I'm too weak to tell him no? Probably all of the above.*

I'm not stupid. I'm a helluva lot smarter than he is. And I did it on my own, without a fancy college degree or my daddy's money. Mitch marched up to his bedroom. *If I was stupid, I wouldn't know how to do this.*

Sitting on his bed, he pulled up Beckett's garage Webcam on his phone. The shed was empty and Mitch was reluctantly impressed. It hadn't taken Ford nearly as long to escape as he'd expected.

Now, let's see if I was right. He'd predicted Ford would escape, leaving Wilson Beckett alive. Because Ford was oh-so-kind. Which was really too bad for the kid. Ford Elkhart had the brains and brawn to be somebody someday, but that tender heart he wore on his sleeve would relegate him to the pussy ranks forever. *Just ask Kimberly.*

The girl had enchanted Ford with her brains and enticed him with her bod, but it was her whispered tale of the abuse she'd suffered at the hands of her mother's boyfriend that had cemented her hold.

Kim's stories were, of course, pure fabrication. Her parents lived together in a rich suburb of Philadelphia. There was no boyfriend, abusive or otherwise.

It had been a risk, having Kim lie about her family. Ford might have had her checked out. If he had, her true connection to Ford's mother would have been revealed and because she'd already lied, he wouldn't have believed anything else she'd said.

But Mitch knew people and was damn good at predicting what they'd do. Ford hadn't checked her out, because he wanted to believe the girl. Kim's stories had roused the kid's inner white knight, ensuring that he would follow her anywhere. Even into an alley.

Mitch switched to the camera feed in the cabin and

grinned. *Am I good or what?* Beckett was on the floor—alive, tied, and gagged. And naked as the day he was born.

Mitch chuckled. *You go, Ford.* Stealing the old man's thermals took chutzpah—and a strong stomach because the guy stank like he hadn't bathed in a long time.

Now I can sleep. But not for too long. If Ford wasn't found by nightfall, Mitch would need to drive back and help the kid out. He couldn't have Ford dying before he took his message back to his mama.

I'm back. Did you miss me?

Tuesday, December 3, 11:47 a.m.

Cole flattened himself against the side of the old house, holding his breath. He shouldn't have worried. Matt didn't look his way as he walked to his Mercedes.

He drives a damn Mercedes. It wasn't fair. Matt got the money, and he and Mitch had to scratch for everything. Cole wasn't stupid. He knew that Mitch was a drug dealer. He knew that Matt was too—he just did it in a suit and tie.

Cole knew that Mitch was on the run right now because of that botched job at the pill-popper palace in Miami. Mitch had forced him to leave his friends behind without saying good-bye and part of him hated Mitch for that.

I wish he weren't involved in any of this illegal shit. But Mitch was, and Cole found himself wishing that if Mitch was going to be bad, he would at least be better at it. Then they wouldn't have to be running from the law all the time.

They could stay in one place. Have a decent house. A decent life. *Like Matt has.* But Mitch sucked at being bad and they were on the run, hiding in this piece of shit house that Mitch called "home." Cole called it "hell."

Mitch loved this hellhole and Cole had no idea why.

I hate it here. I hated it when I had to live here before. His mother's aunt had been so old. Betty had tried to take care of him, but she couldn't even take care of herself. *I had to do it all.* And he'd only been a little kid. Only eight when Mitch went to jail. Because of Matt's father.

Who says I'm not his son. It shouldn't matter. But it did. It mattered because Matt got everything. *And I have to live here and keep up the act.* Mitch wanted everything to look normal, wanted people to believe he really did HVAC work with that black van he drove. *He wants me to go to school and have friends.*

Sure, like I'm gonna invite the guys to hang here at Hotel Hell where my brother's hiding a quarter million in cash in the root cellar and a pile of pistols in that room in the basement that's supposed to be secret.

Mitch thought he didn't know. Mitch thought he was stupid. Sometimes Cole let people think that because then they didn't expect as much.

It worked sometimes. Sometimes it didn't. Recently it hadn't mattered. A few of the guys at school had bothered him last year, stealing his lunch, pushing him around. He'd grown over the summer and he'd thought things would be better and for a while they were. Until the head asshole at school found out that Mitch had gone to prison.

The bullying had started all over again. And now it was more personal. Calling Mitch a fag was bad. Saying Mitch was doing me was a hell of a lot worse.

Shoving me against a wall . . . Cole shuddered. They'd ganged up on him in the stairwell. *If that janitor hadn't come along when he did . . . God. I was so lucky.* But he wouldn't be next time. The guys had told him so. They'd wait until nobody was looking.

And Mitch wonders why the hell I don't go to school? Cole didn't know what to do. It wasn't like he could go to the cops. Not with a quarter million in cash in the root cellar and all those guns in the secret room.

Well, there was one fewer gun in that room now. Cole patted his pocket, comforted by the hard steel he'd kept hidden there for the past three days. *Let them try to touch me again,* he thought fiercely. *They'll be sorry.*

Five

Ford had found the keys to the old man's truck in his pants pocket. It had been easier to strip the pants off his body and dump the contents than to go rooting around and risk the old guy coming to. Once he'd ripped off the pants, it occurred to him that the old guy would have trouble following him in the snow if he had no clothes at all. So he'd stripped him to the skin. And hadn't that been fun? *That would be a big no.*

Tying the old man up had been considerably more satisfying. Ford had found some strong twine and tied it *tight*. No way was anybody getting free from those knots.

Then Ford had searched the place, looking for any hint to where this cabin was or where they'd taken Kim. He'd found nothing and began to worry that the creepy guy would come back. *I'm back. Did you miss me?*

Ford shivered, grasping the steering wheel of the old guy's truck, his hands covered with a pair of ratty gloves that were too small. He wore the old man's coat and had dumped every article of clothing he'd found in the cabin into the bed of the truck so the man couldn't put clothes on and follow him should he manage to escape.

Then he'd rounded up the old man's weapons and any food he could easily carry. The unloaded rifle was on the seat next to him. Still unloaded, because he hadn't found any ammunition. He'd taken every knife in every drawer, his final action being to roll the old man's fingers across one of the blades.

So the cops would know who the hell they were dealing with. Or at least one of the two. Hopefully the old man would roll on the creepy guy once the cops got involved.

Marion Morrison my ass.

Now he held his breath as he turned the key in the ignition, then let it out when the engine turned over. *Thank you, God.* At the end of a mile-long unpaved driveway he came to an actual road. Right or left? *East.* Eventually he'd end up at the ocean.

He didn't think he'd been taken too far west. The rock formations were shale and sandstone . . . *Which you're only gonna find in Appalachia, son.* With a start he realized that it was Gran's voice he heard. *I guess I was listening better on all those hiking trips than I thought. I'm in Appalachia.*

Ford's lips curved in a smile for the first time since he'd left the theater the night before. Assuming it had been only one night. From the way his head had started to heal, that made sense. Plus, he'd be a lot hungrier had it been more than one night. And he was damn hungry as it was. All he'd found was some beef jerky and canned beans and he'd save that for when he was positively starving.

Don't think about being hungry. Just drive until you see a house or another car. A call box on the side of the road. Something. Just drive.

Baltimore, Maryland
Tuesday, December 3, 12:00 p.m.

Daphne shivered despite the fact that the heater in Joseph's Escalade was set on high and she wore his coat.

She'd need a new coat, because hers had Mike the cameraman's blood on the sleeve and one of the detectives had taken it as evidence. *My coat is evidence.* And her blouse would be, too, once she got to the ER. It was soaked with Deputy Welch's blood.

"I'd almost forgotten," she murmured.

"What?" Joseph asked. He stared straight ahead, his expression grim. He might have been a statue were it not for his forefinger that tapped the steering wheel.

"About the courtroom fiasco. Reggie and his mother. Deputy Welch. I feel . . . disconnected. Like I'm dreaming. But I'm not."

"No. You're not."

She bit her lip. "I left my phone in the pocket of my coat."

"J.D. will get it back to you."

"If it survived my fall. Grayson's didn't survive the court-room brawl. Reggie's mother kicked the screen in."

"So that's why he didn't call me back," he muttered to himself.

"Can I use *your* phone?" she asked when he didn't offer.

He handed his phone to her. "Just don't look at texts or any of my call logs."

"I won't. I just need to call my mother. She was worried before. She'll be worried sick now." Daphne dialed, then frowned when the name of her mother's dress shop appeared on the screen. "Joseph, why do you have my mother's shop in your contact list?" she asked him while her mother's phone rang.

The shop's answering machine picked up before he answered and she heard her mother's voice, stating the store's hours. "Mama," she said when the tone had beeped. "Mama, it's me. Pick up the phone. Mama? Okay, now you've got me worried. Call me so I know you're all right." She hung up, her frown deeper. "She should be there."

He glanced at her, his expression unreadable and intense all at once. "She's okay. The squad car J.D. sent to check on her reported back. She's fine."

"How do you know they reported back?" He'd taken no calls.

"J.D. texted me a few minutes ago."

Something didn't feel right. Okay, lots of things didn't feel right. Joseph was acting strange, even for Joseph. "But she should be there. She never closes the shop early."

"She's probably been bombarded by calls from the press, so she's screening her calls. I know for a fact that she's okay. So don't worry about her."

"All right." Still, something wasn't right and she didn't know what it was. "Why do you have my mother's shop in your contact list?"

"Because Paige bought Grayson's mother a hat to wear

to one of those fund-raisers you two are always having for the women's center."

Daphne had to think. Hats? "Oh. The one at the race-track last summer." All of the ladies had worn hats, à la Derby Day. "What a nightmare. Never seen so many big hats in my life. They kept whackin' each other over the punch bowl. One stabbed the other with her hatpin. It was awful." *And you weren't there,* she thought, watching him. She knew every fund-raiser he'd attended by heart. *Because I'm just that pathetic.*

She still hadn't gotten over the shock of looking up to see his face. She'd thought herself a goner for sure. But he'd saved her. *Which is a good thing.* So what was bothering her so much? "I still don't get why *you* have Mama's shop in your phone."

She was missing a detail. It wasn't *this* detail, but she had to start somewhere.

"My mother liked Grayson's mother's hat, so when it was her birthday Paige took me to your mother's shop." He said it like he was reading from a police report. Stiff and formal. Flat. Too polite. "Your mother was helpful and my mother was pleased."

"I see. Well, that's nice. Let me call Ford. I'm sure he's worried, too."

The finger that tapped the steering wheel froze and the breath backed up in her lungs. *Ford.* Something was wrong with Ford.

Wait. Joseph said he'd tried to call Grayson when they were in court. *Why?* And then she knew what had been bothering her. Suddenly terrified, she forced herself to ask, "Joseph, why were you at the courthouse today? And with Clay? Why?"

"We're here." He pulled into the ER, but didn't drive up to the door. Instead, he pulled into a parking place reserved for law enforcement, underscoring the fact that he wasn't just Grayson's brother. He was FBI.

Oh my God. The fear rose in her throat, choking her. *He's FBI.* "Tell me," she demanded, fighting the wave of hysteria. "Dammit, Joseph, why were you there?"

He turned to meet her eyes. And she knew. Her breath was coming too fast. *Can't be. Won't let it be.* She shrank away from him, her hands over her ears. "No."

Joseph leaned across the seat and pulled her hands away, his dark eyes intense. "Daphne, listen to me. Ford's bodyguard was found dead this morning. Murdered."

"No. It's a mistake. Whoever found him made a mistake."

"I found him. It's no mistake."

"Isaac is a cop. He wouldn't let that happen. It wasn't him. It wasn't Isaac."

"Clay was there. He identified him."

Clay was there. They'd come together. *To tell me.* It made sense. *No, it didn't.*

"I can't hear this." Ford was gone. Gone. Taken. *Just like me. I can't do this again.*

The years rushed back and she was *there.* That cabin with its shed . . . and the steps going down into the earth. It was dark. *I was so cold. This can't be happening again.*

"I can't hear this," she repeated in a harsh whisper.

"You have to. Daphne, Isaac Zacharias was murdered near the theater that Ford and Kimberly went to last night. Ford's and Kim's cars were still at the scene. They didn't show up where they were supposed to be today."

"So?" *Can't breathe. Gone. Taken. He's wrong.* "Doesn't mean they're missing."

He closed his eyes for three hard beats of her heart. When he opened them . . . she saw regret. "We found blood on the ground near Isaac's body. And blond hair. Ford's color. And . . . blood on the handle of Kimberly's car. We're treating it as an abduction. I'd come to tell you, when . . . when all hell broke loose."

A sob built up inside her and broke free. "Joseph."

"I know," he said quietly. "I'm so sorry."

Then Daphne saw Cindy Millhouse in her mind, face twisted with hate. "*You'll know how this feels.* That's what Cindy said. She's got Ford. She's got my son."

"We'll find him," he promised fiercely.

"I've got a folder. All my trial notes, profiles, research. Everything I gathered for Reggie's trial. It's in my desk. Take me there. I'll get it."

"Grayson went to get it. I need you to go to the ER and let them look at your head."

"No, I can't. I have to find him." She grabbed the door handle and wrenched it open, but he was out of the car and around to her side before she could slide to the ground.

He grasped her shoulders and held her fast. "Daphne, you can't help your son if you're in pain. I need you to be alert. I need you to be able to think."

"Let me go. You don't understand. I need to go. I have to find him." Furiously she jerked away, stumbling backward. "Let me go. You can't make me stay. You don't understand." *I was there in that dark little room. I was there.* "You don't understand."

Joseph pulled her to him and held her there, one hand cradling her head, the other stroking her back. "I'm sorry," he kept saying. "I'm so sorry."

"Joseph." The agonized cry was ripped from her chest. "They've got my son." The sobs broke free and she sagged against him, her knees folding. He caught her before she hit the pavement, lifting her into his arms like she was a child.

"I know, honey," he whispered. "And I do understand. Better than you think."

Tuesday, December 3, 12:40 p.m.

Joseph paced in front of the ER bay in which they'd placed her. He'd carried her himself, snarling at the med tech who approached with a wheelchair. He'd had to force himself to calm, to allow the man to wheel her through the double doors.

His cell rang and it was Bo. Joseph had called his CO asking for a bigger team—for security and investigation. They had to find Ford and Kim. They had to protect Daphne. And her family. *Family. Oh no.*

Daphne was the original target, but Grayson had worked right beside her. *Now Grayson's family—my family—is at risk.* His parents, sisters, nieces, nephews.

His sister Lisa had four kids under the age of twelve. And then there was his sister Holly, who was vulnerable in a different way. A high-functioning adult with Down syndrome, Holly had a lot of independence, which made her accessible. Joseph's protective instincts flared. *There's no way the Millhouses are touching my family.* If VCET personnel were stretched too thin to cover his family, he'd hire his own security. *Just like Daphne did.*

"This is Carter. Status?" Joseph asked.

"I've assigned Hector and Kate to provide security for

Miss Montgomery. They'll be there in twenty. I've got two
agents en route to her house. They'll secure the perimeter
and set up the phone systems in case the abductors call.
Her mother and aunt are being taken to the house as well.
We can cover them more efficiently that way."

Joseph's tension lessened considerably. Both Detective
Hector Rivera and Special Agent Kate Coppola were
VCET, handpicked by Bo Lamar to serve on his joint task
force. Hector had come from Baltimore PD, most recently
working Vice. Kate had served on an FBI SWAT team.
They'd been Joseph's first choices.

"Good. We'll also need to cover Grayson's family. By
keeping Cindy Millhouse from attacking Daphne, he dam-
aged their plan to divert deputies away from Reggie."

"I hadn't thought of that. Especially your sister. She had
a rough time last spring."

Last spring, when Holly had become a killer's pawn,
used to hurt Grayson. *Maybe law enforcement shouldn't
have family at all. We're lousy prospects.*

"Holly's better now, but I'll be damned before I put her
in the crosshairs again." At least Holly had a protection
dog. Peppermint Patty never strayed more than a few feet
from Holly's side and a ninety-pound Rottweiler was a hell
of a deterrent. It made the family feel safer and—*Oh, hell,
I forgot about the dog.* "Daphne's got a protection dog. If it
came from where I think, it's going to be well trained, but
deadly."

"Very good to know. I'll have the agents at her house
wait for her mother before they go in. Hopefully the mother
can control the dog."

"Again, if it came from where I think, it'll be family
friendly. Where are we on the warrant to check the Millhouse properties?"

"Signed. BPD's got two of their Homicide guys at the
Millhouse residence. I've got two of ours on their way to
the business."

"That's good. You'll call me as soon as you know anything?"

"Of course. Now, I have a question for you, Joseph, and
I need you to be honest. Are you capable of leading this
investigation? You went looking for the boy because of his
connection to your father. Anyone who saw the video of

the attack saw you protect Miss Montgomery. Do the two of you have a personal connection you'd like to disclose?"

"It's true that I went looking for the boy because my father asked me to." Although he would have done the same had the request come from his worst enemy. Ford was Daphne's heart. "But I would have protected anyone in Miss Montgomery's situation."

"I know, Joseph, because I know you. But you have to admit it was a little extreme."

"I saw the shooter pointing a gun in Miss Montgomery's face and I reacted. And no, there's nothing I have to disclose." *Not now anyway.*

"All right. What's your next step?"

"I'm going back to the scene at the alley. The priority is finding Ford and Kimberly. I doubt the Millhouses have stashed them in their basement. And I doubt they're going to simply tell us. We need all the data we can get to encourage their compliance."

"I agree. Keep in contact. And tell Miss Montgomery that we have every available resource working to bring her son home."

"Thanks. I will." Joseph hung up and listened. Daphne had grown very quiet behind the curtain. He wanted to give her space, but he was going out of his mind worrying, imagining the worst. And that she wore a wig was now back in the front of his mind, tying knots in his brain. Why? What was wrong with her? Was she sick? Dying? Did she have cancer? Something worse? What would this stress do to her?

He'd pulled the curtain back an inch to peek in when a young blonde wearing a white coat approached. She looked familiar. Her name tag read "Dr. Charlotte Burke."

"Just a minute, please," he said softly, stepping in front of the curtain's edge.

Burke looked up, studying his face. "I'm the doctor Daphne requested."

"You know her, then?"

"Yes, from the women's center. I'm on the board."

Now he remembered where he'd seen her. It had been at a fund-raiser and the doctor had been standing next to Daphne, who'd worn a gown of the deepest blue he'd ever seen. The same color as the suit she wore today, actually. *Maybe it's her favorite color. It's certainly mine.* Daphne had looked like a goddess that night. Burke he barely recalled. "You look different here," he said.

Burke smiled up at him. "I get that a lot. Are *you* okay, Agent Carter?"

"I'm fine." He drew a breath. "She hit her head. Didn't feel like too deep a wound, but she might have some broken ribs from the impact of the bullets. She was wearing Kevlar . . ." He could see that she already knew all of this. "I'm rambling. I'm sorry."

"I'll take good care of Daphne. Don't you worry."

He swallowed hard. "You need to know . . . She might be sick. She's wearing . . ." He leaned down to whisper. "A wig. I don't want her embarrassed, but I'm not sure why she's wearing it. If she's on meds, chemo . . . I thought you should know to check."

Burke nodded, her gray eyes remaining calm. "Thank you. If you'll excuse me . . ."

"Wait. Her son has been abducted. I'd love to tell you to give her something to sleep, but I need her sharp."

"Got it. Now, let me pass, Agent Carter. I need to tend to her." She pushed past him and standing there, feeling helpless, he listened shamelessly.

"Hey, girl," Burke said quietly. "What can I do for you?"

"Get me out of here. Please. I have to get out of here. I have to find my son."

"That agent lurking outside said you hit your head. Let me see if you need stitches. And then I'll get you out of here."

"Agent Carter." The male voice had come from behind him and Joseph turned to see a nurse standing next to the elevator with Stevie Mazzetti, who lay on a stretcher. One leg of her pants had been cut away, her thigh heavily bandaged.

"Stevie." Joseph rushed to her side, grabbing her hand. "Are you okay?"

"Just pissed off." Her eyes fought to stay open. She was so pale. "Need surgery."

"Shit. What did the bullet hit?" She'd been gushing like a damn geyser at the scene.

"Artery. Dammit. Am not happy 'bout this."

"Neither was Maynard," Joseph said, remembering the PI's face.

Her jaw tightened. "Damn that man."

"You mean you don't . . . You and Maynard aren't . . ."

She forced her eyes open and stared at his face. "Don't go there, Carter. Don't."

"Okay." He wanted to take a step back. Her eyes were wild, whether from the pain or something she'd been given for it, he couldn't say. "You just sleep now."

"Wait. Don't go yet. I have a message. From Clay. He said to tell you that he was going to . . . somebody's house. Two-something. Notification."

"I understand." The elevator opened, the nurse giving him a move-your-ass look.

"Joseph." She grabbed onto his sleeve. "If I die—"

He was surprised to hear her fear. "You're not going to die, Stevie."

"Everybody does sometime. And surgery and me . . . we don't mix so good. So if I do . . . you tell Cordy that I love her. *Promise me.*"

Joseph's throat closed at the thought of having to say those words to Stevie's little girl. "Stop this, right now. You are not going to die."

"And J.D. . . . You tell him if he names that baby of his Stevie, I'll haunt him."

"She needs to go to surgery," the nurse said. "You have to go."

"Wait," Stevie growled. "Not done. Tell Clay . . . I wish I'd been ready. That I . . . wanted . . . you know." Her eyes fluttered shut. "If I don't die, you tell nobody nothin'."

"I promise." He stepped back, watched the elevator take her away. Stevie was a good cop. A single mother, having lost her husband and five-year-old son to a random shooting while still pregnant with Cordelia. She wasn't ready to risk her heart again.

Joseph knew the feeling. He hoped for both Stevie and Maynard's sake that she'd work through her grief faster than he had. His heart had broken ten years ago and it had only started beating again nine months ago. When he'd seen Daphne for the first time.

"Agent Carter?" Dr. Burke leaned around the curtain. "Can you come here, please?"

He was at the curtain before she finished the question. "Is she all right?"

"No stitches were needed. She can go home or wherever you can keep her safest."

"And she's not . . . sick? Nothing I need to do?"

Burke checked her clipboard. "I have to see to other injuries. She can go home."

Guess that means it's not my business. Joseph pulled the curtain, finding Daphne standing by the bed, coiffed but fragile. Her head was bowed, her shoulders heavy.

"Daphne?" When she met his eyes, his heart clenched. He'd seen too many parents of abducted children with that look in their eyes. The agony, the envisioning of what could be happening to their child at that very moment. The fear that they'd never get them back. The fear of what their lives would be like if they did get them back. He saw the parents' eyes in his nightmares.

The adults whose spouses or lovers had been abducted wore a different look, just as agonized. It was the look that said they knew that a vital part of themselves had been ripped away, never to be regained. That look he'd seen in the mirror.

"Go," she whispered fiercely. "Don't you stay here another second."

"I'm not leaving you unprotected."

"There are a dozen cops in the waiting room, here for the cops who are hurt. All of them have guns. I am protected. My son . . ." Her voice broke. "My son is out there somewhere, Joseph. So don't you dare waste another second babysitting me."

"All right. My boss is Special Agent Bo Lamar. He's got federal agents on their way to your house. They'll trace any call that comes in. A security team will escort you home. We have Bill Millhouse in custody. I'll personally question him and his wife."

"There's another son in custody. George. He came in late to court today. He'd been rushing. He was out of breath. Seemed more wired than usual. And then Cindy somehow had a knife in the courtroom. There has to be a connection."

"I'll check it out."

"You said Kimberly was missing. She's the girlfriend that Ford hadn't brought home."

He frowned, surprised. "You didn't know about her?"

"No, I knew about her. Ford told me. He said she was

nervous about meeting me. Something about bad prior experiences with the mother of an old boyfriend. Ford's been giving her space. But he's told me bits and pieces about her."

"Is that why he didn't want a bodyguard? Because he wanted to give her space?"

"I think so. Have you notified her family?"

"An agent from the Philly office should be there now. I'll be by your house to update you as soon as I can." He hated to leave her, but knew he had to go. "Be careful."

She nodded numbly. "You, too."

Marston, West Virginia
Tuesday, December 3, 1:00 p.m.

Frustrated, Ford smacked the steering wheel of the piece-of-shit truck he'd stolen from the old man. "Out of gas." *Of course it is.*

He'd driven miles, not passing a single house or another vehicle. He had passed a rusty West Virginia highway marker, so at least he knew where he was. At the same time, he had no idea where he *was*. The nearest city could be fifty miles away.

He could stay or he could start walking. He had a few hours of daylight left. Once the sun went down it would become dangerously cold. *Like frostbite and losing-my-fingers cold.* Not good. *So start walking.*

He shouldered the pack he'd taken from the cabin, then stopped and looked back at the truck. If he could find a scrap of paper and a pen, he could leave a note in case somebody came by. At least someone would know where to look for him.

He opened the glove box, found it empty. There was no registration. Nothing to ID the SOB. *I should memorize the license plate. At least the cops will have a place to start.* He felt under the passenger seat and pulled out a small gold purse, the kind with a loop that a girl wore around her wrist. Kim had a couple, but this didn't look like hers.

Ford unzipped it and dumped the contents on the seat. And the hairs on the back of his neck stood up. He picked up the ID first. The girl was young and pretty, with long, dark hair. Heather Lipton. It was an ID card from a high school in Wheeling, in northern West Virginia. Heather was a senior, due to graduate in six months.

Oh. Something finally made sense. He'd demanded that the old man tell him where the girl was. The guy's eyes had flickered, like he was trying to figure out the best way to lie. *I was talking about Kim.* But his gut told him that the old man hadn't been.

Was Heather back there somewhere? Part of him screamed that he should go back to save her. But he needed help, and he'd passed none back in that direction. *I can help her better if I move forward. If she's still alive.*

It was possible that he was overreacting, that the old man had stolen this purse and that Heather was home right now, safe and sound. But Ford didn't really think so.

Her purse held a tube of red lipstick that looked brand-new, five dollars, a folded piece of paper, and an unused concert ticket dated August 27 of that year.

Ford blinked at the ticket. The band was hot, tickets incredibly hard to come by. Every show had been sold out weeks in advance. If Heather had missed this concert, something was seriously wrong. He unfolded the piece of paper and it all became clear.

The paper was a receipt from Mountain Jack's Towing and was dated the day of the concert ticket. On it was scrawled: *Picked up, one 2004 Honda Civic, brown.*

Her car had broken down, Ford thought. With a ticket to the concert of the summer, Heather had probably decided to hitchhike. She'd never made it to the show.

What should he do? *Keep to the plan. Get help.* He returned the items to the purse, except for the lipstick. For a moment he hesitated. What he had in mind would destroy it. What if there was DNA on the lipstick?

If he died out here, the lipstick wouldn't matter, so he twisted the lipstick tube and wrote on the windshield in big letters—HELP. Below it he wrote his name and the date. And his mother's phone number. Finally he drew a big arrow down the middle of the truck's hood, showing the direction he'd gone.

With my luck the old man will find me first. Or the did-you-miss-me guy.

At least he was somewhat armed. He had several knives in his pack. And a few strips of beef jerky and a couple cans of beans—the best of what he found in the old man's cupboards. He took one of the jerky strips and started down the road, munching as he walked. He'd have to ration what was left. Who knew when he'd be found.

I hope to God it's soon. It's getting really cold.

Baltimore, Maryland
Tuesday, December 3, 1:05 p.m.

Joseph arrived back at the movie theater to find the alley crisscrossed with twine, creating a precise grid that CSU would use to record the crime scene, layer by layer.

In an alley filled with garbage, cataloging the evidence could take a very long time.

We don't have a long time. A search of the Millhouses' home and their hardware store had yielded no sign of Ford or Kimberly. This hadn't surprised Joseph. He hadn't expected the Millhouses to stash the kids where they could be easily found. They didn't have many leads. Yet. This crime scene was key.

CSU had uncovered Isaac Zacharias's body. Two pairs of Taser electrodes were embedded in the victim, one pair in the abdomen and the other in his thigh. Joseph stopped at the red socks, studying the body. Didn't appear to be any other wounds. If his throat was slashed postmortem, then how did the man die?

"Hear you had a close call," Dr. Brodie said, appearing from behind the Dumpster.

"I'm fine," he said. "Lots of folks aren't."

"You'll find who did it," she said simply.

"I know who did it. Stevie Mazzetti killed who did it."

"Was that person connected to this death?"

"I'd say that's a fair assumption. Exactly how, I'm not yet certain."

Brodie walked around the body, shining a UV light at the walls and pavement. "What's missing?" she asked and he felt like he was in her class at the academy again.

"No spatter," Joseph said. "He was dead or close to it when his throat was slit. The Taser wouldn't have killed him, so something else did."

"Why slit his throat if he was already dead or close to it? Seems like wasted effort."

Joseph had been mulling over that point as he'd driven from the ER. "I figure his killer wanted to be sure Zacharias didn't survive to talk."

"Or his killer was just a sick sonofabitch who liked slitting throats," she said.

"That, too." He pointed to the AFID tags, discharged with every fired Taser cartridge. "There are enough tags here for him to have fired at least two or three times."

"Four, actually." Brodie swept her UV light over the scene, revealing dozens of round disks. "I found four sets of serial numbers. Sets one and two are consecutive. Three and four are also consecutive, but nowhere near the one/two range."

"Two different cartridge lots. Two different Tasers?"

"Sounds right," she said. "There's a small pool of blood near the alley entrance, about ten feet from Kimberly's Toyota. A set of smeared handprints lead away from it."

"Ending on the handle of the girl's car," Joseph said. "I saw the blood on the car handle when I first arrived this morning."

"Agent Novak found the handprints," Brodie told him. "He's got a good eye."

Joseph looked around. "Where is Agent Novak?"

"He went into the office to run phone records. Said he'd be back when he could."

"Okay, what about Ford's SUV?"

"No blood on the outside. I had it towed to the lab to check the outside for prints and the inside for blood. Oh, and I found one of the sets of Taser electrodes against the far wall."

Joseph frowned. "He missed one of his shots."

"That's my take."

"So how did this go down?" Joseph muttered to himself. "Four serials, two lots. Could have been four separate Tasers were fired or two, if they were X2s."

"With the backup-shot feature."

"Two X2s makes sense, especially if there was only one attacker." He glanced over at her. "You find anything suggesting we had multiple attackers?"

"No, but also nothing suggesting it was only one. Run scenarios for one and two attackers. Start with one attacker and we'll list the assumptions that have to be made."

"Okay. Firing two Tasers would take skill and coordination, but one person firing four as quickly as they needed to would require too much juggling to make sense. So for one attacker we're talking two X2s."

"I'm with you."

"Ford and Kim leave the theater, walk this way. Ford didn't know about Zacharias, so I assume he was keeping some distance, staying in the shadows."

"If Ford didn't know about him, maybe the shooter didn't, either," she said.

"Possibly. Probably, even." Joseph visualized the scenario in his mind. "Four cartridges fired, two hit Zacharias. One misses. Kimberly makes it as far as her car. Blond hair and blood in the middle of the alley are probably Ford's, so he goes down."

"Still with you," Brodie said.

"So, I'm the shooter. I target Ford first, because he's a big guy and I want to eliminate his threat." He lifted his left hand, forefinger pointed like a gun. "Bang. Ford falls. Bang, same Taser because they're next to each other, but he misses. Kimberly runs. Then there's Zacharias, exploding from the shadows. Not expecting him." He turned ninety degrees, lifting his right hand, forefinger extended. "Bang, bang with the second Taser and Zacharias falls."

"Maybe. I reserve the right to change the order. But I agree that Kimberly runs."

"She leaves a bloody handprint on the car door handle, but she's injured ten feet away, still in the alley. How much blood did you find?"

"More than she would have bled by falling down. She was stabbed, struck, or shot."

"Shit. Why do you think it's a different order?"

"Response time. We're still talking one attacker. Unless he shot a gun, he had to catch up to her at the end of the alley to stab her."

"Maybe he had a gun."

"Then why not shoot all of them?"

"True. And later he uses a blade on the victim's throat."

Brodie shrugged. "It might not matter in what order they were tased."

"But it's bugging you and I learned a long time ago to respect that," Joseph said.

"What's bugging you, Joseph?" she asked.

"He had two X2s and cartridges. They're only legally sold to cops and the military. Whoever did this was a cop, stole from a cop, or bought them on the black market, but he didn't even make an attempt to gather up the AFID tags. It's like he didn't care."

"Maybe he was in a hurry," she said.

"But he took the time to slit the throat of a man he'd already killed. Why? And how did Zacharias die? Unless he had a heart condition, the Taser wouldn't have killed him."

"And even then, it'd have to be one hell of a heart condition," she said. "I didn't see any evidence of trauma other than the slit throat and the two pairs of electrodes."

That were still stuck in Zacharias's thigh and abdomen. Joseph crouched, studying the victim's knees. "His trousers are dirty. He crawled. He kept coming, even after getting tased."

"So the killer tased him again," Brodie said slowly. "Where are you going with this?"

He glanced up at her. "Once he was down, he didn't get up again because Ford and Kimberly are gone. He didn't stop it. What kept him down?"

"He died?" Brodie asked, a touch of sarcasm in her response.

"Lucky break for the killer," Joseph returned with equal sarcasm. "Even two Taser blasts shouldn't have kept Zacharias down that long. A few minutes at the outside and he would have at least been able to fight. There's no sign of a struggle. No abrasions or ligature marks to indicate that he was restrained. He went down and stayed down, giving the killer time to get Ford and Kim to his getaway vehicle."

"At some point between going down and staying down and getting his throat slit, Zacharias died," Brodie said.

"Exactly. Death by Taser is less than one in a thousand. Maybe one in a hundred thousand. If it happened just when Zacharias's killer needed it to . . ."

"Then I want him picking my lottery tickets," she said.

"Exactly," Joseph said again. "Then there's Ford, the target. He's a big guy and he would have been trying to protect Kim. I wouldn't have wanted to be the one to drag him off, fully conscious, even if I'd cuffed him—especially if I was going for stealth."

A healthy young man fighting for his life would put up a hell of a lot of resistance. If he was protecting his lover's life as well, he'd be as unstoppable as a fucking freight train. Unless he'd been drugged. Then he'd be rendered as helpless as a newborn baby.

This Joseph knew firsthand. The ropes had hurt. The blows he'd taken resisting hurt more. But the helplessness . . . That had been sheer agony. It still was.

He cleared his throat. "If I'd been kidnapping Ford Elkhart, I'd have wanted him heavily sedated. I'd have come prepared."

Brodie leveled a long look at him and Joseph wondered how much she knew about his past. She'd never mentioned it, in all the years she'd known him. To her credit, she didn't mention it now.

"So let's say Zacharias was drugged," she said. "Maybe his killer OD'd him. Maybe that's why he was dead before his throat was slit."

Joseph rose, even more troubled now. "OD'ing on a sedative is a lot more likely than a heart attack from the Taser."

Frowning, Brodie said what he was thinking. "Zacharias died. Is Ford dead, too?"

"That depends on why he was taken. I'm not going to borrow trouble till I have to."

"Agent Carter? Dr. Brodie?" The voice came from the alley entrance where ME tech Ruby Gomez was waving to get their attention. "You ready for me to take him?"

Brodie motioned her in. "Come on in, Ruby. We're done with him." She looked up at Joseph. "What will you tell Ford's mother?"

Joseph cringed at the thought of sharing any of this with Daphne. "As little as I can get away with. She doesn't need to know how Zacharias died or that his throat was slit."

Brodie sighed. "Agreed."

Six

Joseph stepped back to give the ME tech room to work. He'd been glad to see Ruby pushing the stretcher into the alley. Skilled at her job, she ensured that evidence was preserved while showing compassion for the victim. She'd increase their chances of finding Ford and his girlfriend while still taking good care of Maynard's dead friend.

"Pretty exciting morning you've had, Agent Carter," Ruby remarked as she prepared the body bag. "Glad to see my favorite FBI guy still in one very nice piece."

Ruby's flirtation was more about her personal style than any come-on. She flirted like most women breathed. "Gotta love Kevlar," he said pleasantly.

"Absolutely. I have to say, I held my breath while all those bullets flew. And when you leaped through the air to save Daphne . . ." Ruby fanned her face. "Majorly hot. Especially in slo-mo. And Daphne's my favorite prosecutor, too, so it was all good. I'd hate for anything to happen to her." She winked. "The woman's muffins are to die for."

Joseph frowned. How many TV stations were showing the courthouse crime scene anyway? Because every time they did, they were compromising his investigation. *I should have grabbed the cameras.* Except shooting video wasn't a crime. *Dammit.*

"Where did you see it?"

"Her muffins? She brings us a basket every time she attends an autopsy."

"Not the muffins," Joseph said, annoyed. "The leap. Which TV station showed it?"

"All of them. But that's not where I saw it." Ruby glanced up at him, her eyes twinkling. "I saw it on the Internet."

Joseph's frown became a snarl. "I'm on the Internet?"

"All of you cops are, but you, Agent Carter, are a bona fide sensation."

"But I don't want to be on the Internet," he said, sounding like a disgruntled child.

Ruby lifted a brow. "It could be a whole lot worse, *papi*. You might have missed."

"Good point," he muttered, chastised.

"I thought so." Turning her attention to the body, she looked at it from different angles as if studying pool balls on a billiards table, her mouth bent in sad concentration. "*Dios*. How do we move you?" Then abruptly she rose and looked toward the street, her posture shifting as she eyed the man hurrying toward them. "Oh, yeah. That'll work."

The man wore a distracted expression on a face that looked like it belonged in a photographer's studio, not at a crime scene. Both Ruby and Brodie stood straighter, staring with undisguised appreciation. Joseph's eyes narrowed in irritation. With a pretty face like that, the guy had to be a reporter. Which meant he was leaving.

Joseph stepped in front of him, blocking his view. "No media. You have to leave."

"But, Agent Carter—," Ruby started and Joseph cut her off with a harsh look.

"No media, Ms. Gomez."

"I'm not media. I'm Dr. Quartermaine, the new ME. Here's my ID."

Joseph studied the seemingly legit ID. "What happened to the old ME?"

Ruby blinked up at him, incredulous. "You mean Lucy Fitzpatrick, who's on maternity leave because she's big as a goddamn house? She'll be out for at least six months and our old department head just retired. Neil is the new boss."

Feeling a little foolish, Joseph returned the man's ID. "I'm sorry, Doctor. Reporters make me crazy. I'm Agent Carter and this is Dr. Brodie. We're with VCET."

Quartermaine's brow bunched slightly. "VCET?"

"Violent Crimes Enforcement Team," Ruby murmured to him.

"Oh, right. The acronym was in the join-up materials Lucy Fitzpatrick left for me to read. The FBI/BPD joint task force." He turned back to Joseph with a nod. "No worries. I hate reporters, too. So what's the situation here?"

Joseph stood back to let him pass. "Victim's a cop. Was a cop."

"Then we'll take good care of him." He tugged on the gloves Ruby handed him. "You said it would be exciting, Ms. Gomez. I had no idea it would start my first day."

"Your first day?" Brodie was sympathetic. "Hell of a way to start."

"Better than being my last day," Quartermaine said soberly. "Like this man's." He crouched beside the body, brows knit. "This victim was dead before his throat was slit."

"We know," Joseph said. "We're just not sure why." Joseph's phone began to ring. "Excuse me. I have to take this." It was Deacon Novak. He stepped away from the group and answered. "What do you have?"

"A lot," Deacon said. "But I'll give you the top four—Kimberly MacGregor's parents have been trying to reach her since yesterday evening. Seems Kimberly's fourteen-year-old sister, Pamela, is missing. Philly PD put out an AMBER at ten last night."

Joseph truly hadn't seen that coming. "So it *is* about the girl?"

"Maybe. Second item—Kimberly has a record. Felony theft. She was cleaning houses and helped herself to a diamond ring. Guess who the prosecutor was?"

Joseph's heart sank. "Not Daphne."

"Yep," Deacon said. "Didn't she recognize the girl?"

"She probably would have, but Kimberly didn't want Ford to introduce them. He told his mother about her, but asked for a little space."

"Hm. Shouldn't the bodyguard have checked her out?" Deacon asked.

"Somebody in Maynard's organization definitely should've, since Ford was their responsibility to protect. That Maynard didn't mention that Kim had a record, especially given the connection to Daphne, makes me think that he didn't know."

"I totally stand on my 'Not much of a bodyguard' statement from before."

Joseph sighed. "I'm actually inclined to agree with you. Whether Maynard's group didn't bother to check or somebody did check and somehow fucked it up, I don't know. But they should have had that information. Not knowing might have cost Isaac Zacharias his life." *What a waste.* "What's the third item?"

"We dumped Ford's and Kimberly's cell phones. Kim got a text at seven last night."

Joseph checked his notes. "She told Ford about the movie about fifteen minutes later, according to Ford's Facebook post."

"How'd you get access to his Facebook page? I couldn't guess his password."

"I didn't. One of the other interns at my father's company is Ford's Facebook friend. He showed the post to my father this morning when Ford failed to pick him up for work. Ford posted that he wished Kim had given him more notice about the movie, because he had to bail on plans to watch the hockey game on TV with the guys."

"The text to Kimberly's cell came with a large data attachment."

"A photo," Joseph murmured. "Of her abducted sister, maybe?"

"That'd be my guess."

"Hell, she set Ford up. What's number four?"

"Ford's cell phone record showed that a text was sent to his mother at ten this morning."

Joseph frowned. "*This* morning? Are you sure? What the hell?"

"I'm sure. There's been no other activity on either phone, Ford's or Kimberly's. Both phones are turned off, not responding to pings."

Joseph's neck tensed. "Did you get a location on that last text?"

"Yes. I'm there now. It's an alley a few blocks from the courthouse. Nobody here but me. I texted you the address."

"Why didn't you tell me that one first?" Joseph demanded, exasperated.

"The facts flowed more logically my way. Should I wait for you?"

"No!" Joseph barked, then took a breath, calmed his voice. "No. Start searching."

"Good, because that's what I did. I found a backpack and that's it. No ID."

"I'll be there as soon as I can." Joseph hung up and rejoined the others. "We have another missing person—Kimberly's younger sister. Dr. Brodie, I need a Taser fire scenario that assumes Kimberly knew the abduction would occur."

Brodie's face fell. "Don't tell me she set him up."

"For the missing sister," Ruby murmured.

"Possibly," Joseph said. "Probably. Dr. Quartermaine, if you could provide an analysis of any drugs in the victim's system as soon as possible, I'd appreciate it."

"You think Zacharias was using?" Ruby asked.

"No, I think that's how the attacker kept him down." Joseph needed to get to Novak, but the scene was cooking in his mind and he needed to get it straight. "He planned to hit Ford first, but the Taser would have kept him down for thirty seconds at the outside."

Tasers used by police didn't incapacitate as long as those used by civilians. Police needed the suspect quiet only long enough to cuff him. Civilians needed time to escape.

"Based on his firing skill," Brodie said, "I'd assume that the attacker knew this."

"Agreed. He needed something to knock Ford out that acted fast—before the Taser effects wore off— and lasted for as long as it took to transport them."

"Not many things act that fast and last a long time," Quartermaine said. "It would have to be a cocktail, with a second medication taking effect before the first wore off."

"That makes sense," Joseph said. "Let's assume Zacharias was a surprise. Our shooter tases Ford, then is startled. He shoots Zacharias twice because he keeps coming." He looked to where the missed electrodes had landed. "That leaves the girl."

"Who'd already started to run," Brodie said. "That's what was bothering me—where those electrodes landed. He aimed for her when she was several feet from where Ford already lay. She'd gotten a good head start."

"Because she knew it was coming," Ruby said.

"Exactly," Brodie murmured. "He probably stabs her.

She's bleeding, but crawls to her car and grabs the door handle. He had to have left her alone after stabbing her."

"Because Ford and Zacharias are only down temporarily," Joseph said. "He's got two hundred pounds of angry cop that he wasn't expecting. So he adapts. This guy thinks fast on his feet. He'd planned to knock out Ford and the girl for transport."

"He can't give the girl's cocktail to the cop," Quartermaine said. "She's too small. I listened to the BOLO details on my way over here—Asian female, five feet one inch tall, one hundred five pounds. She weighs about half what the cop did. Her dose wouldn't have kept the cop down. He had to give the cop Ford's cocktail."

"And Ford got the girl's dose," Joseph said slowly. "It slows him down, but not enough, so the attacker grabs his hair and smacks his head on the pavement."

"Thus the blood and blond hair," Brodie said.

"So why did the cop die?" Ruby asked. "Did the attacker intend for Ford to die? And why slit the cop's throat if he was already dead?"

"Good questions," Joseph said. "And how did he get Ford and Kimberly out of the alley? Where was his vehicle parked? Did he roll them out? Dolly, cart, wheelchair?" He saluted the doctor. "Welcome to Baltimore, Dr. Quartermaine. Call me as soon as you have anything. Dr. Brodie has my contact info. I have to meet Agent Novak."

Tuesday, December 3, 1:20 p.m.

"Watch your head, Daphne." Detective Hector Rivera hovered over her as a nurse transferred her from a wheelchair to the backseat of an unmarked FBI car. Black, of course. She'd protested the damn wheelchair, but it was "policy" and she'd finally given up, too weary to argue anymore.

A decorated Baltimore PD Vice detective, Hector was clean-shaven today, but dirtied up he made the most convincing drug addict she'd ever seen. She'd been relieved to see his familiar face on her security detail.

I have a security detail. Before, it had been Paige and Clay providing security "just in case" the Millhouses were serious. It hadn't seemed real. But they were serious. It was real. *They have my son.*

Obediently she slid into the backseat of Hector's sedan. Leaned back. Closed her eyes. Tried not to be sick. *Ford.*

"Daphne, wait!"

Recognizing Grayson's voice, Daphne leaned forward and out the door. Grayson was jogging across the hospital parking lot.

Hector immediately blocked her view, pushing her back into the car. "Don't *do* that."

"But it's only Grayson," she said quietly.

"'Only Grayson' could be the break a lurking gunman out there is waiting for."

She nodded dully. "I'm sorry. I didn't think."

Hector crouched in the open doorway, his face creased in sympathy. "I don't mean to bark at you, Daphne. It's my job to keep you alive for when your son comes home."

He stepped aside and Grayson took his place, holding out his hand palm up. "I brought you this."

"My phone." She took it, feeling the return of a small level of control. "Thank you."

"J.D. found it in the pocket of your coat. These are from me." He handed her a thick folder. "A copy of your Millhouse file. VCET has the original. If you need to keep busy, you might want to look for connections. Maybe something only you'll recognize."

"Thank you," she said quietly. "For everything."

"I should be thanking you. You risked your life, throwing that camera bag at Marina. If there's anything I can do to help you, just name it."

"Where are you going from here?" she asked.

"To draw the arrest warrants, then on to Interview. I want first crack at Bill."

Fury bubbled up from her gut. "Then make him tell you where he's taken my son."

"If it can be gotten, I'll get it," he promised. "Paige will be coming to stay with you. Please," he said when she started to protest. "I need to know you're okay. Clay can't protect you right now. He's too distracted. Paige can carry his load for a little while."

Poor Clay. Daphne hadn't had a chance to think about him. He'd lost a colleague and a friend. And he'd hold himself personally accountable for Ford's abduction.

Shouldn't he? Daphne was disturbed to realize that she

held Clay accountable as well. She needed to deal with that before she saw him again. "It will be good to have Paige there, for me and Mama, too. And if you see your brother, thank him for me."

"We need to go." Hector slid behind the wheel. He pointed to the woman in the passenger seat, a striking redhead who oozed sex appeal, despite the heavy SWAT-style bulletproof vest she wore over the jacket of her FBI-standard black suit. "Riding shotgun is Special Agent Kate Coppola. From Iowa."

Daphne winced. "'Riding shotgun' isn't the expression I would have chosen today."

"Except that I am, ma'am," Coppola said. She reached down at her feet and brought up an impressive-looking assault rifle.

"At least now we're evenly matched with the bad guys," Daphne murmured.

"If there's any incident," Hector said, "Agent Coppola leads the defense. I cover her. You hide in the floorboards. This car isn't bulletproof, but it is bullet-resistant. You're wearing a vest?"

"A new one," she said. "My old vest was taken by CSU." *Because it was riddled with holes from Marina's bullets.* Daphne shuddered as the thought of how close she'd come to death briefly snuck through her terror over Ford. Then the moment was over and fear for her son threatened to paralyze her once more.

She closed her eyes, knowing there was a call she needed to make. Dreading it. *Travis.* Ford's father needed to know.

Her hands trembled as she dialed Travis's number from memory. It wasn't in her contact list. She hadn't wanted to desecrate her phone with his name. It began to ring and her stomach turned inside out. Like a coward, she hoped no one would answer.

"Elkhart residence." *Damn.* The nasal tone belonged to Remington, the butler who was proud to be descended from a long line of butlers. In Remington's mind, being a butler trumped being a mountain girl like Daphne, no matter how polished she became.

"Remington, this is Daphne. Please connect me with Judge Elkhart."

"Daphne? I'm afraid I can't place the name."

Her temper snapped. "Dammit, I'm *not* in the mood for

your games." Since the divorce he'd thought it funny to not remember her. "I need to talk to Travis about Ford."

"He's not in at the moment," Remington said snidely.

"Then connect me with wherever he is. This is not a social call. This is . . ." She exhaled carefully, controlling her temper. "This is a matter of life and death."

"One moment, please." There was a minute of silence and then the phone picked up.

"This is Nadine. What is this matter of life and death, Elizabeth?"

Oh God, no. Not today. Please. Travis's mother hated her. And the feeling was mutual. *But this isn't about you, Daphne.* Or even Elizabeth, the middle name that Nadine insisted on calling her by since forcing her marriage to Travis. *This is about Ford.* And in Nadine's own praying-mantis-type way, she loved her only grandson.

"Ford has been kidnapped."

Nadine's gasp was audible. "What? What is this?"

"What I just said. Ford has been kidnapped. I need to talk to Travis."

"He's not here. He's in court this morning. Oh my God."

Daphne could hear Remington in the background. "Madam? Madam, are you unwell?" The old lady's heart had never been that strong.

Daphne hated her, but didn't want her to have a heart attack. "Are you all right?"

"No," she whispered. "I am not all right. Elizabeth, what have you done?"

"I don't have any details," she said, ignoring the accusation. "I'll keep you apprised."

"Don't you *dare* hang up on me, Elizabeth. Have you received a ransom demand?"

"Not to my knowledge."

"Have you informed the FBI?"

They informed me. "They are involved."

"When did this happen?" Nadine's voice was thinning. She'd be hysterical in a minute or two. This time Daphne couldn't blame her.

"Last night. He went to a movie and didn't return to his dorm."

"How could you let this happen, Elizabeth?" she demanded shrilly.

Daphne bit her tongue. There were so many ways to reply. Most of them unproductive. "If you could pass this message on to Travis, I'd appreciate it. As I said, I'll keep you apprised. If you hear anything, please call me. You have my number."

Daphne hung up, staring at the phone crunched into her fist. There, that was done. At least she hadn't had to talk to Travis. She didn't think she had the strength to deal with him at the moment.

She had scarcely drawn a breath when her cell began to ring. The caller ID read BLOCKED NUMBER.

Her heart stopped, then began to race. *It's the one who took Ford. He has my son.* "There's a blocked number calling in."

Coppola turned to meet Daphne's eyes. "I'm texting Bo Lamar. Keep the caller on as long as possible. We'll try to trace."

"I can record the call. Should I?"

"Answer it while I find out if recording it will impact triangulation."

"Okay." Daphne sucked in a breath and answered. "Hello?"

"What the fuck is going on, Daphne?"

She flinched for the second time in five minutes, meeting Coppola's gaze with a shake of her head. "It's just my ex," she said quietly.

Travis's mother called her Elizabeth, because her first name was "far too vulgar for an Elkhart." When they'd been married, Travis had bowed to his mother's wishes, also calling her Elizabeth. When he called her anything, that was. He'd pretty much ignored her from day one. Once the divorce papers were signed, he'd taken to calling her Daphne, in a way that made her name sound . . . like trash. Which was exactly how he'd treated her for the twelve years she'd borne his name. And raised his son.

"*Just* your ex?" Travis said icily.

"Yes, Travis. Just my ex. You'll be contacted by Agent Lamar to have your phones tapped. Until then I suggest you start answering your phone, in case they call you instead of me."

"'They,' meaning whoever kidnapped my son."

Daphne pressed her fingertips to her throbbing temple. "Yes, that would be the 'they.'"

"How could you let this happen?" he asked, fury in his tone.

Again she bit her tongue. "Ford is twenty. He is independent. I did not 'let' this happen." *Except that the Millhouses took him to punish me.*

She should tell this to Travis, but somehow couldn't bring herself to say the words.

"That's what comes from going to college in the ghetto. If he'd gone to Princeton . . ."

She let him rant. Arguing never did any good. Not when Travis knew he was right. Which was always. When he paused to breathe, she cut him off. "I have to go. Next time I call, please make yourself available." She hung up and leaned her head against the seat. "That was fun."

Hector was frowning. "With all due respect . . . Wow. I thought my ex was bad."

"Yeah. Well. You probably should set up a phone tapping at the estate. Just in case." *In case this isn't because of me. Except it is. My fault. All my fault.*

"The estate?" Hector asked carefully.

"River Oaks, in Northern Virginia, Loudoun County. About an hour west of here."

"Horse country," Hector said. "Is it a ranch?"

Daphne laughed bitterly. "No. That would be vulgar. It's an estate. Family money. They have stables and grooms. But the land is not an 'economic enterprise.'"

"Okay," Hector said slowly. "Upper crust?"

"The crustiest. They'll cooperate because my ex-husband is very politically minded. He won't want to anger law enforcement. His mother will observe all the proprieties."

Hector looked genuinely confused. "But this is his son, too."

"Yes, he is. But there's . . . friction. In the divorce, they made Ford choose."

"He chose you." Hector sighed. "Hell of a thing to do to a kid."

"Ms. Montgomery." Kate Coppola kept a vigilant watch on the cars that crawled alongside them in the midday traffic. "Why do you record your calls?"

"Because of the death threats from the Millhouses. I got a wiretap warrant first. I didn't want to give them any ammunition." She winced at her word choice. "Hell."

"Do you have any of those threats saved on your phone?" Coppola asked.

"Yes. The police have them, too." Daphne scrolled through the screens on her phone, then froze. "Wait. I got a text from Ford this morning."

"When?" Hector asked tersely.

"I was in court." Hands shaking, she managed to find the message. "Here it is. He texted me at 10:04. 'Good luck, Mom.'" She looked up, hope trembling through her. "He's okay. He texted me. This is all a mistake."

Not looking hopeful at all, Coppola dialed on her cell phone. "I'll call Agent Carter. He'll need this information."

Anger burned her chest. "He texted me, dammit. We can find out where he texted from. We can find him."

"Joseph, it's Kate . . . No, no, Ms. Montgomery is un-harmed. She remembered that her son texted her this morning at—" She listened, then glanced over her shoulder carefully. "Yeah, that's the time."

All the air left her lungs. *No.* Daphne didn't realize she'd whimpered it aloud until she heard the sound of her own voice. Her hand lifted to cover her mouth, to keep the other whimpers in, but they escaped, keening sounds of pain.

That's me, she thought. *That sound is coming from me.* The last time she'd heard that sound . . . *I was in a doctor's office.* The doctor had just delivered the bad news, using words like "diagnosis" and "chemotherapy" and "metasta-size," but all she'd been able to hear was the keening sound of pain ripping from her throat. *I'd rather be back there than here. I'd trade places in a heartbeat. I'd go through it again if it brought Ford back.*

But those kinds of bargains were fruitless. This she knew. Her lungs were working now, hard. Each breath hurt. *Hurt.*

Ford, where are you? Where are you?

Kate looked at Daphne from the corner of her eye. "Straight home." She hung up. "They knew about the text already. They dumped Ford's cell phone records."

There was more she wasn't saying. "Where did he text from?"

"The text was sent from an alley, a few blocks from the courthouse."

"Is Joseph there now?" she asked.

Kate hesitated. "Yes."

"Then take me there." She met Hector's eyes in the rearview mirror. "Now."

"Daphne," Hector started.

"Now!" Daphne shouted and both agents flinched. She quieted her voice. "Or I will get out of this car and hail a cab. Hitchhike if I have to. What's it going to be?"

Tuesday, December 3, 1:35 p.m.

Joseph got out of his car and jogged to the alley where Deacon's car was parked. Deacon was nowhere to be seen. "Novak," he called.

"In back of the Dumpster," Deacon called back. A few seconds later he emerged, a backpack dangling limply from a pen, hanging by the shoulder strap. "This is all I found."

"Then let's have a look," Joseph said.

Deacon unzipped the compartments and took a little whiff. Then coughed. "Somebody carried their lunch in this. Whoever that was ate a lot of garlic." He looked up, blinking rapidly. "That'll curl the hair on your chest."

Joseph waved the pungent odor away, then paused, studying Deacon's strange eyes as he cleared them of moisture. "You're not wearing contacts, are you?"

Deacon looked amused. "Nope. What I got is what I got."

"Your eyelashes are white, too. Why?"

Deacon shrugged again. "All my hair is white. Even the ones on my chest."

It bothered him, Joseph realized. "I'm sorry, Deacon," he said. "I figured you were pretty impervious. I was wrong."

"It gets old," Deacon confessed.

"The eyes work, though?" Joseph asked. "No vision issues, blind spots that I need to know about? No vulnerabilities in a firefight?"

"No. My vision is at the top of the chart, actually." Deacon's odd eyes took on a thoughtful gleam. "You're worrying about me?"

"'Worry' isn't the word I'd use," Joseph replied, hedging.

Deacon grinned. "You were worrying about me. You like me, you really like me."

Joseph snorted. "You're an ass, Novak."

"I know. Makes life more interesting. To answer your

question, I have no vision defects. It's all cosmetic. My good vision is unrelated to the color. Dad had great eyes, my mother's side provided the ice-breaking conversation topic."

"Well, it's a damn fine weapon if you ask me," Joseph muttered. "Catches people off their guard. As well you know."

"Hell, yeah." Deacon opened the backpack. "What do we have?"

Joseph shined his flashlight inside. Reaching in, he brought out a plastic . . . something. "What the hell?"

"Looks like a shoehorn," Deacon said.

"A bit." Joseph opened the backpack wider. "And a single dollar bill. That's all."

Out on the street a car came to a screeching halt. Doors slammed and arguing voices approached. Joseph stood, the backpack in his hands. Beside him Deacon also rose, his hand on his weapon.

"Where is he?" a woman demanded, and Joseph sighed.

"Have you met SA Montgomery?" he asked Deacon.

"No, but I have a feeling I'm about to."

"Yep." Joseph started walking, meeting her as she entered the alley from the street.

She walked faster when she saw him and for a tiny second he let himself stare. Then he saw her red eyes and knew she'd been crying and abruptly checked his lust. "Joseph, he texted me. From here. Ford did."

"Somebody holding his phone texted you," he said gently.

"But why?" she asked plaintively. "Why go to the trouble?"

"I don't know. All we've found so far is this backpack. Do you recognize it?"

"No. What's in it?"

Joseph took out the plastic piece and watched her flinch. "What? What is it?"

"It's the same color as the knife Reggie used to stab Deputy Welch," she said. "Kind of the same shape, too. But that's not a knife."

Deacon took it from Joseph and sniffed it. He made a face. "It smells sour. Like unwashed skin. But it's not a knife. It's not even sharp."

Daphne carefully turned, and began walking away.

"Daphne." Joseph grasped her shoulders and made her look at him. Her blue eyes were filled with tears. And devastation. "Aw, honey," he whispered. "You hoped."

She blinked, sending tears down her cheeks. "How stupid was I?"

"No, no. Not stupid. Never stupid. You're a mother who loves her son."

She dropped her chin to her chest and her shoulders shook as she tried to contain her sobs. "Where is my son, Joseph? Where is he? What are they doing to him?"

He gave the backpack to Deacon and put his arm around her shoulders. "Come on. Let's get you home."

She looked up at him, that terrible pain in her eyes. "What can I do?"

"For now, believe he's alive, because it's the only way you'll be able to breathe."

She blinked at him. Then her eyes changed and he knew she realized that he truly understood. "I believe," she said firmly.

"That's my girl. Come on. You have to go home. I have bad guys to catch."

She squared her shoulders and walked away, pausing at the edge of the alley to look back at him. "Thank you, Joseph."

His heart squeezed in his chest. "Just doing my job." He watched her go, then turned back to Deacon, who had avidly witnessed the entire exchange. "What?"

"Nothing," Deacon said. "Who's got the knife Reggie used in the courtroom?"

"BPD was inside the courtroom processing the stabbing scene when the shooting started outside. All evidence is being taken to their lab and we'll coordinate who did what when the crime scenes are secure. The head of BPD CSU is Drew Peterson. I'll have him coordinate with Dr. Brodie. I'd like her to examine that knife."

There were so many players here, Joseph thought. He needed all of them to hear the same info at the same time. He hated meetings, but he needed to call one.

Deacon inspected the plastic plate. "Bet we can get prints off of this."

"Get it to Latent, then watch for a text from me. I'm call-

ing a debriefing with BPD." And after that, he and Grayson
would have a chat with the Millhouses.

Tuesday, December 3, 2:10 p.m.

I believe. I believe. Her eyes closed, Daphne repeated the
two words in her mind again and again as Hector and
Agent Coppola drove her home. *I believe.*

She pictured herself opening the door and finding Ford
on the front porch. Whole. Alive. *Smiling at me.* And she
continued to breathe, just like Joseph had said.

Joseph. I wonder who was stolen from him? The thought
snuck in among the litany of affirmations. He'd said he understood better than she knew. Now she knew he'd been
telling the truth.

That the person he'd lost was a woman was only a guess.
But Daphne was pretty good at reading people. Unfortunately many of the people she met on the job had lost someone who'd completed them. Spouses and lovers wore a
different look from the parents and siblings. It was a stark . . .
aloneness. The knowledge that you'd never be the person you
were, ever again, because part of you had been hacked away.

For a moment Joseph had worn that look, there in the
alley. But for a while he'd believed. He must have. He still
breathed.

The car stopped moving. "We're here, Daphne," Hector
said.

The terror abruptly returned in a wave, smashing through
all that lovely, completely pretend positive energy. *Please
don't let them be hurting my son.*

Coppola reached over the seat, gently shaking her
shoulder. "You're home."

"I know," she whispered, lifting her eyes to her house,
the elegant Victorian she'd fallen in love with at first sight.
It looked impossibly the same. But it didn't feel like her
house. Arduously, she reconstructed the mental picture.
Opening the door, seeing Ford standing on the front porch.
Smiling at me. I believe. If it kills me, I believe.

"Wait." Hector engaged the door locks when she reached
for the door handle. "Until this is over, you don't go anywhere unprotected. If you're walking out in the open, we're

flanking you. We'll go in and out through the garage. You stay inside until the garage door is back down. Got it?"

She nodded. "Got it."

Hector's expression softened. "I know you're worried about your son, but you were a target this morning. My priority is to keep you safe. That allows Agent Carter to focus on finding your son." He dialed his cell. "We're here. You can open the garage."

The door slid up and he glided them in, then turned the car motor off as the door started back down. Daphne stayed put as she was told—until she heard a familiar voice.

"Daphne! Daphne! Wait!"

Before Daphne could blink, Coppola was out of the car, then out of the garage through a side door, her rifle on her shoulder.

Hector reached over the seat to push Daphne's head down, twisting to aim his gun out the back window, all in one motion. Reluctantly impressed, Daphne struggled against his hold.

"Hector. Hector, let me up. I know that guy. He's okay."

He loosened his hold. "Who is it?"

"His name is Hal Lynch. He's a friend."

"Your boyfriend?" Hector asked.

"Oh no. No. Just an old friend. He used to be my ex-husband's head of security. Hal was my bodyguard during most of my marriage. He's retired now." She winced when she heard a loud thump against the closed garage door.

"*Let me go.*" Hal's voice was muted, but his fury came through. "*Daphne!*"

"He needs to know I'm okay. Old bodyguards' habits die hard."

Hector exited through the same door to the outside that Coppola had used. A minute later, Hal appeared, his hands cuffed behind him. Hector and Coppola followed him inside and shut the door.

Of average height, Hal had a stocky build and a slightly crooked nose—like he'd boxed one too many rounds with the champ in his youth. At the moment, he looked ready to go a round with the FBI agents, his normally calm disposition anything but, and his usually charming smile replaced with a fearsome scowl.

Daphne got out of the car and saw the scowl fade. "Can we lose the cuffs?"

Coppola unlocked the handcuffs.

Hal rubbed his wrists. "Your protection detail, I assume?" he asked, eyeing the two agents appraisingly. He gave a single nod of approval. "They'll do."

"I'm sorry, Hal," she said, her voice unexpectedly cracking. "It's been a bad day."

He wrapped his arms around her in a hard hug, then let her go, tipping her chin up so that he could search her face. The scent of lemon oil was strong on his hands. *He must have come straight from his boat.* Or what might eventually become a boat. Someday. He'd been working on it for years, long before her divorce. Whenever she smelled lemon oil, she thought of Hal.

"I needed to know you were okay," he said gruffly. "I saw the attack on TV. Live. Scared the shit out of me."

"I'm okay," she assured him, grasping his hands and holding on tight. He was her oldest friend—the first smiling face she'd seen when she'd been absorbed into the Elkharts' strange and rarefied world. He'd been one of the first people to hold Ford when her son was just minutes old. He'd been a part of so many of the milestones of their lives, both hers and Ford's. She hated to break the news to him now.

She drew a breath. "Hal . . . Ford is missing. He's been kidnapped."

Hal swallowed hard. "I know. Your mother called. What can I do to help?"

"Right now, nothing. The FBI is on it."

"Do they have any leads?"

"Not really." She closed her eyes, battling new tears. *I believe.*

"Do you want me to call Travis for you?"

She opened her eyes, her face heating. "No. I called him already."

His face darkened. "He blamed you, didn't he? That sonofabitch."

"It wasn't anything I couldn't deal with."

He studied her carefully. "I can see the headache in your eyes. You should sleep. I'll see you later."

"I'll try." She frowned. "I can see the anger in your eyes. Promise me you'll stay away from Travis."

He smiled, but it was grim. "I promise I won't hit him."

"Hal. Please. Don't make this any worse. I can't take any

more drama from the Elkharts. And you know Nadine's got a bad heart."

"She's actually got a heart?" he asked dryly. "Don't worry. I won't cause trouble. I promise." He kissed her forehead. "Get some sleep. Call if you need anything."

"I will. Thank you." When the door closed, Daphne's shoulders sagged. "Just don't do anything stupid," she murmured.

"I take it that he doesn't care for your ex," Agent Coppola said.

"No. Hal ran a tight ship as Travis's head of security and he respected him as his boss, but he doesn't care for him as a person. They at least used to be friendly, but something happened between them a bunch of years ago. I don't know what, but it festered for at least five years. I just hope Hal doesn't hit him again."

"He hit his boss?" Hector asked, surprised.

"Later, when Travis and I were divorcing. I think Hal retired before he hit him. Or maybe during." She blinked hard and rubbed her head. "I think I will lie down. I do have a headache." She paused at the door into the house. "I have a big dog. I'll go first."

"Dog's under control," Hector said. "Your mother put her in your room. Let's go."

Her mother was sitting in semidarkness in the living room, Maggie by her side. Her mother rose, her face ashen. "Baby," she whispered.

Baby. Daphne froze, her heart racing, her lungs contracting, and instantly she was eight years old again. Her mother had been sitting in the dark that day, too, her face smooth and young, but ashen. That living room sofa hadn't been expensive leather, but cheap fabric. Maggie hadn't been there. They hadn't met her yet.

It had been her father sitting beside her mama. *Daddy.* Her father's handsome face had been red, his eyes swollen from crying. *I'm so sorry, Daddy.*

Aunt Vivien was sitting in the rocking chair, rocking with a mindless, sightless rhythm. They'd stood together, their expressions a mix of desperate hope and dread as they waited for the sheriff to speak. He'd been a big man, the sheriff. He stared at them, then twisted to look behind him, surprised.

Daphne had crunched herself into a ball, hiding behind the sheriff's legs. Like trees. They'd been tall as trees, his legs. "What're you doin', child? You're home," he'd boomed, then plucked her from the floor, frowning when she screamed, clinging to him.

It had been chaos. Her mother and father grabbing for her, tears of joy running down their faces. Aunt Vivien demanding hysterically, "Where is Kelly? Where is she? Where is *my* daughter?"

Still there. Back there. With the cats and the man.

I'm back. Did you miss me?

No. Don't. Don't think about it. Don't ever think about it. Don't remember.

"Daphne. Come back."

Daphne sucked in air, filling her lungs again. Her back stung. *Somebody hit me.* She blinked and Maggie came into focus, an encouraging smile on her face. But her eyes were fearful. Daphne looked over to her mother, who stood wringing her hands, then she caught herself searching the room for the oldest of her mother's sisters. But Aunt Viv was gone. She'd died five years ago.

And her father? *Daddy, I'm so sorry. Wherever you are, I hope you can forgive me. I'm so sorry.* Sadness overwhelmed her as Maggie walked her into the kitchen. Daphne was aware of Hector and Coppola sharing puzzled glances behind her. She noted two more agents in her formal dining room, where they'd set up their computers to trace incoming phone calls. She ignored them all for now.

In the kitchen doorway she stopped. A tall man with silver in his dark hair stood at the stove, where he'd just put a kettle on. "Scott," she whispered, swallowing back new tears. "You came, too."

With a look of fierce sorrow he held his arms open. She walked into his embrace, holding on as he rocked her gently. She inhaled, smelling the barn on his clothes, feeling her racing pulse quiet. Hal's hands always smelled like lemon oil. Scott's smelled like saddle soap. Both scents soothed her.

Both men had played important roles in her life. Both had been friends when she'd been lonely. Both had made personal sacrifices for her along the way.

It was fitting that both of them would show up to support her today.

"Of course I came," Scott murmured. "Did you really think I wouldn't?"

Hearing a thread of hurt in his voice, she leaned back to meet his eyes. "Only because I didn't know you were home. I thought you were at the horse show in Florida."

"Got home last night. Two of my kids brought home blue ribbons." Scott's "kids" were his equestrian students. One of the best show jumping trainers in the state, he'd coached Ford since he could sit in the saddle and loved him like he was one of his own sons. Together, Hal and Scott had been the fathers that Travis had never even tried to be.

Scott tried to smile, but it didn't come close to reaching his eyes. "And I brought you and Maggie a present. When you're feeling up to it, you have to come meet him."

She found her lips could still curve. "Another rescue?" she asked and he nodded.

"Found him tied to a tree. He's a bag of bones right now, but he's got heart. You need to hurry out before Maggie names him," he added teasingly.

"I'll come out as soon as I can." She swallowed hard. "After we find Ford."

Scott dropped his head so that his brow touched hers and dropped his voice so that none of the curious ears behind them could hear. "If you need me, I can be here in twenty minutes. And if you need to brush a horse, I'll bring Reese to you."

Daphne's heart squeezed. "I bet my neighborhood association would have something to say about that."

"Fuck 'em," he said soberly. "Say the word and I'll bring you the whole damn barn."

She tried to find her voice. "Thank you," she whispered hoarsely.

"Don't you worry about Ford," he said, ignoring her thanks. "He's a smart boy. And tough. We raised him well." He walked her to the table, pulled out her chair, took off his jacket, draped it over her shoulders. She turned her face into the warm suede.

He brought the barn to me.

"I'm making tea," Scott said. "Anyone else want any?"

"I'll have some," Daphne's mother said as she sank into the chair next to her. "You remember how I like it, don't you, Scott?"

"Of course, Simone. One part tea, four parts of whatever's the highest proof."

"You're the man," her mother said, but her eyes never left her daughter's face. Daphne knew she had to address what had happened in the living room.

"I'm sorry, Mama. About . . . in there. I wasn't thinking."

"Nothing to apologize for, baby. You were remembering. So was I."

"You called me 'baby' that night."

"Did I?" Her mother's mouth bent, her posture melancholy. "I didn't remember that."

"I didn't think about what you'd be going through today, reliving all that," Daphne said. *And I should have. God.* "It's been a . . . difficult day."

"I know, baby. I know." Her mother sighed. "I wouldn't have had you experience this for all the tea in China."

Hector sat down at the table, extended his hand to her mother. "Ma'am, I'm Detective Rivera. I'm working the abduction of your grandson with the task force."

"I'm Simone Montgomery and the woman standing behind Daphne is Maggie VanDorn, a family friend. And over at the stove is Scott Cooper."

"Scott owns the farm next to mine in Hunt Valley," Daphne said. "He helps Maggie take care of our horses and he's been Ford's trainer for more than fifteen years."

"Trainer?" Hector asked.

"Jumping," Daphne said. "On horses. Ford competes at the state and national level. He's always trained with Scott."

And he will continue to do so. Daphne lifted her chin slightly. *I believe this is true.*

Hector's head bobbed politely as he greeted them all, then turned his gaze on Daphne. "So what happened in the living room?"

Daphne's cheeks heated, embarrassed now. "I had a cousin disappear when I was eight years old, nearly thirty years ago." She hesitated, then felt Maggie's hand rubbing her back. She forced the words from her brain to her mouth, remembering too keenly how she hadn't been able to speak that day or any of the days that followed.

She'd come home that horrible day . . . mute. For months. She'd hadn't lost her voice. She'd lost her *words.* They'd fled. Whatever pathways connected the verbal area of her brain to her mouth . . . they'd snapped.

No matter how hard she'd tried or how much her father

begged, pleaded, cajoled, even threatened . . . she could do little more than stare up at him, desperate to do the right thing. *I'm sorry, Daddy. I never wanted that to happen to you. To Mama. To me.*

She was no longer eight years old, but the fear had never gone away. Now, at thirty-five she felt the words slow, start to recede. *No. Not again.* She concentrated, inhaled the scent of Scott's jacket. Shoved the words free.

"Me, too," she said on an exhale. "I . . . disappeared, too." She swallowed hard, aware of every eye watching her. "I was just remembering the night the sheriff brought me home. Everyone was sitting there waiting, just like tonight. It was a life-defining moment."

Hector was watching her closely. "What happened to her? Your cousin?"

"She was found, later."

Hector's brows lifted. "Alive?"

"No." Daphne swallowed, her mouth dry as sandpaper. Scott put a cup of tea in front of her and she sipped at it gratefully. Hector was waiting, his head tilted, and Daphne sighed. "My cousin's body was found in some woods in Ohio, about a week after I came home. She was seventeen."

"And the perpetrator?"

"Never caught. It was just . . . one of those times when the bad guy didn't pay."

"I'm sorry," Hector said sympathetically, but his eyes were sharp. Watchful.

"It was a long time ago," Daphne said.

"It was yesterday," her mother murmured. "Any word on where Ford could be?"

"No," Daphne said. "But good people are looking." She straightened her shoulders. "And we're going to believe he's all right."

"Of course we are," her mother said. "It's all we can do. That, and wait." She met Daphne's eyes, hers a steely, determined blue. "We've been through hard times and we survived. Ford is your son. He'll survive and he will come home to you."

"I believe," Daphne murmured. *And I'll continue to take one breath at a time.*

Seven

Joseph's debriefing and strategy meeting with VCET and BPD was set to begin in ten minutes. Walking from the parking garage to the conference room, he checked his e-mail on his phone. One message stood out, the subject header in all caps: READ ME ASAP.

It was from his father. *Damn.* His father had been waiting for him to call back. *He must be worried.* Hell, his whole family would be. Joseph didn't normally check in after a close call on the job, but then his close calls had never been on TV before. Ruby's words came back to him in a mocking rush. *I'm an Internet sensation. God.*

Waiting for the elevator, he read the e-mail. *Joseph, please call your mother. She and Judy were watching the news live when the bullets started flying. She needs to hear your voice. Plus, it seems we have houseguests that you didn't tell us were coming.*

Joseph winced. He'd asked Bo to send officers to watch over his family, but he'd forgotten to tell his parents about it.

He dialed home and his mother answered on the first ring. "Hi, Mom."

"Joseph." His name came out on a little rush of air. She'd been holding her breath.

"I'm fine," he said mildly. "I didn't want you to worry."

"I wasn't worried," she said archly.

"Yes, she was!" a woman chimed in. It was Judy, Grayson's mother, on another phone extension. Joseph and Grayson shared no blood, but Joseph had considered them brothers since the day Grayson and Judy had come to live with them, close to thirty years ago.

"Are you all right, son?" his father asked, having picked up yet another extension of the landline at the house. "We saw it live."

"I'm fine," he assured them. "I was lucky. It could have been much worse."

"I wouldn't call it luck, Joseph," Judy said. "That was skill. I was very impressed with you—after my heart started beating again, that is. It stopped when Grayson and that . . . killer were pointing guns at each other."

"You saved Grayson," his mother said proudly. "Then saved Daphne, too."

"Actually, Daphne saved Grayson," Joseph said. "She threw a cameraman's bag at the shooter and that distracted her."

"We never saw that," his mother said.

"Must've been a bad camera angle. Daphne distracted the shooter, then Stevie fired the kill shot."

"Really?" His father sounded both surprised and relieved. "It looked like you did."

"Another bad camera angle. If I'd fired, they'd have put me on admin leave."

"That makes sense," his mother allowed, making Joseph smile.

"We're just glad you're okay," his father said gratefully. "That bad camera angle gave us the scare of our lives. It looked like she'd shot you in the back."

"She did. I was wearing Kevlar, which thankfully worked as designed."

"Oh my dear Lord," his mother murmured weakly.

"But I'm okay, Mom," he assured her again. "Just a little bruised."

"Oh my dear Lord," his mother said again.

"Just breathe, dear," his father said. "How is Ford?"

"And Daphne," Judy added. His entire family had known Daphne since she started working with Grayson. She and Ford were like family. "How is she holding up?"

"The news said that Ford is missing," his mother said.

"Which your father apparently already knew," she added in a mutter, her panic attack apparently bypassed thanks to his father's deft subject change. Many of Joseph's deflection skills had been learned by watching his parents argue over the years.

"I asked Dad not to say anything until we had more information. We don't know a lot, and that's the truth."

"Can we help?" his father asked.

Joseph thought about what he needed. A timeline around Ford and Kimberly's relationship was critical. "Actually you can. I've got Ford's laptop in custody." It had been retrieved by the uniform standing guard at the dorm. "But we can't get into his system. Can you get that intern friend of Ford's to give us Ford's log-in info if he knows it or log back in to Facebook and create screenshots of Ford's posts?"

"I've still got the Facebook page open," his father said. "How far back do you want to go?"

"To the day he met Kimberly and then a few weeks beyond that."

There was silence on the other end. "Why?" his mother asked.

"I need a timeline." And then borrowing his father's trick, he said, "So you've got guards now? I hope they're not tracking snow on your carpet."

"Your father's subject changes are smoother," his mother said dryly. "But, yes, we've got guards now. It would have been nice to know they were coming, but we understand you've been a little busy. Don't worry about us, Joseph, and we'll try not to worry about you. You focus on finding Ford."

"Fair enough. I've got to go now. I've got a meeting in a few minutes and I called it, so I can't be late. I just wanted you to know I was okay."

"Be careful, Joseph," his mother said. "Love you."

"Love you, too." Stepping into the elevator, Joseph hit the button for his floor. The doors were nearly closed when a pair of hands shoved into the gap, pushing them back open. Joseph drew his weapon on reflex, then relaxed when Deacon entered the elevator with a scowl. "What the hell, Deacon?"

"Didn't you hear me yelling for you to hold the damn elevator?"

"No. Sorry," Joseph added, unconvincingly.

"No, you're not," Deacon said.

"You're right." Joseph eyed the deli bag in Deacon's hand. "Did you get any extra?"

"No. Sorry," Deacon added, mocking Joseph's tone.

Joseph chuckled, surprising himself. "No, you're not." As he followed Deacon to the conference room, Joseph's phone buzzed with a new text message. It was from Judy.

You never said how Daphne is. I'm worried about her.

So am I, he thought. He typed his reply as he walked. *She's holding. She might welcome a phone call.*

He hesitated, then typed a new message. *Believe.* He entered Daphne's cell phone number from memory, only a little ashamed that he'd known it by heart for nine months, having peeked at Grayson's contact list shortly after laying eyes on her for the first time. Joseph sent the message and squared his shoulders. *Time to get to work.*

Tuesday, December 3, 2:25 p.m.

Oh, girl. Daphne sat at her vanity, regarding her reflection in the mirror with a serious wince. *You look like you were rode hard and put away wet.*

She'd finally made it to her bedroom. Finally had a moment alone. She loved her family, truly she did. But sometimes they hovered. *I hope I'm not that way with Ford.*

Her words hit her hard. *I should have hovered. I'd have him with me right now.*

You can't think that way, she chided herself as she plugged her phone in to charge. Then she placed it on the vanity's surface, taking care to center it so she'd be able to see the screen the moment it rang.

Please ring. Please.

A wet nose nudged her arm and automatically she smoothed her hand over Tasha's wiry head.

Daphne had gone her whole life without a dog, never wanting one. But within a week of the Giant Schnauzer's arrival, Daphne didn't know how she'd lived without her. Tasha always seemed to know when she was upset or stressed. And when Ford moved into the dorm, her wagging tail had helped make coming home at the end of a long day something she no longer dreaded.

Until today. "He's coming home, girl. He has to." Tasha

rested her muzzle on Daphne's leg and blew out a little sigh. Commiserating. A soft knock on her bedroom door made the dog growl. "I'm all *right,* Mama," she said firmly.

The door opened a crack and in the mirror Daphne could see long black hair swinging gently. "I know you are," Paige said softly. "But I'm not."

The reflection suddenly grew blurry when Daphne's eyes filled with tears. She was nowhere close to all right. "Come on in, then," she said quietly.

"Peabody, too? He wants to play with Tasha."

Daphne huffed a watery chuckle. "As long as he stays off the bed."

"He knows not to jump on the bed." Paige closed the door behind her. The Rottweiler sauntered in, ready to play, but Tasha remained where she was, giving comfort the only way she knew how. "Besides, all this pink lace gives him a complex."

Daphne tried to laugh, but it came out a sob. Once the first tear broke through, she couldn't stop, the sobs ripping at her chest. *I should have hovered. Why didn't I hover?*

Paige stood behind her, massaging her shoulders, saying nothing. Letting her cry. Finally the tears were shed and Daphne closed her swollen eyes. "My head hurts."

"I'm not surprised. If you take off the wig, I'll give you a scalp massage and use pressure point therapy to make your headache go away."

Daphne jerked her chin up, meeting Paige's knowing eyes in the mirror. "How long . . . ?" She looked away, embarrassed. "Never mind."

"Do you remember the day I met you last April? You were wearing a lime green suit with a miniskirt and four-inch stilettos, dyed to match. And big hair. I mean *big.*"

Daphne's puffy eyes narrowed. "So?"

"You offered to go undercover as my rich sponsor and Grayson turned you down."

Daphne scowled. "He said I was 'too memorable.' " But Joseph hadn't found her so. He'd met her that very day but had never called her afterward. Not once. "So?"

"So . . . you left Grayson's house and an hour later you were back, unrecognizable. Shiny French twist. Wearing a dress I dreamed about trying on for months after."

"The McQueen," Daphne said. "I told you that you

could have it, that same day. You can have the whole damn closet."

Paige's eyes widened in the mirror. "Hold that thought, but first, fast-forward to last August. You and Maggie took your mother to Vegas for her birthday."

Paige started massaging between her shoulders and Daphne's eyes grew heavy. "If you do this for Grayson, how does he stay awake for all that sex you brag about?"

"I never said *where* I massage him. Stick with the program, girl."

"Vegas. Mama's birthday."

"While you were gone, I watched your house, got your mail. Watched your DVDs and soaked in your Jacuzzi. And I tried on your clothes."

Daphne sighed, knowing where this was headed. "You went in my closet?"

"I did. I have to admit I was a bit startled by all those Styrofoam heads staring at me." She met Daphne's eyes in the mirror, an affectionate smile on her face. "All those months I'd wondered, how the hell did Daphne change so fast that day I met her? The clothes weren't the problem. But the hair? It should have taken you three shampoos just to get all the hair spray out of that beehive. There was no way you could have made it back to Grayson's place in an hour. When I saw the wig heads it made sense."

"Didn't you want to know why?"

"Of course I did. I still do, because I'm nosy. I figure it has something to do with your having cancer. I also figure you'll tell me when you're ready." She lifted a shoulder. "Or if I ever 'accidentally' knock it off your head in self-defense class."

Daphne hiccupped a laugh, but whatever she'd been about to say fled her mind as her phone buzzed with an incoming text. It was from Joseph. One word. *Believe.*

She exhaled in a rush. "Oh." *Thank you, Joseph. I needed that.*

Paige leaned over to look. "Huh. Brother Joseph finally got off his damn stick."

"What do you mean?"

"Oh, come on." Her black eyes widened. "You're serious. You never noticed?"

"Obviously not," Daphne said stiffly. "Noticed what?"

"Joseph has been watching you for nine months, Daphne."

"He has not." Daphne stared at his message. "He's just doing his job."

"What*ever*. I'm just sayin' that Peabody's got nothing on Joseph Carter in the puppy dog eyes department." She stepped back, crossed her arms over her chest. "You do know why he transferred from Homeland Security to VCET, don't you?"

Daphne met Paige's eyes in the mirror. "For . . . ?"

"Little old you. Yeah." Paige tilted her head. "Do you wear that hair to bed?"

Daphne's cheeks heated. "No." She closed her eyes. "Oh God. Thanks for putting that worry in my head." But for a few moments she hadn't been out of her mind with worry for her son. Her friend was smart that way. "I mean that. Thank you."

"Part of the service. Come on. The others are downstairs waiting to see you."

Daphne's eyes flew open. "Others? Who's here?"

"Clay, Alyssa, and Alec." She met Daphne's eyes, hers resolute. "They stopped by on the way to the office. But Clay needed to see you first." She hesitated. "If you're angry with him, I'll tell him that you finally fell asleep. He's terrified to see you."

"Tell him I'll be down in a few minutes. I need to freshen up."

Paige left with the dogs and Daphne picked up her phone, staring at Joseph's text.

I wonder what he did when she was stolen, whoever she was. Daphne was pretty sure he hadn't sat around his house crying. *Neither will I. I have the entire Millhouse file.* And it was stuffed full of financials, friends, neighbors, associates, business partners . . .

She gave herself a stern stare in the mirror. "I'm going to do more than believe, Joseph Carter. I'm going to find my son."

Tuesday, December 3, 2:30 p.m.

When Joseph entered the conference room Bo gestured to the vacant chair at the head of the table. Joseph had Bo on his right and BPD Homicide Lieutenant Peter Hyatt on his left. Hyatt was crusty, tending to make enemies when he didn't need to, but Grayson liked him, which said a lot.

Rounding out the table were Brodie and her BPD counterpart, Drew Peterson; Deacon, who sat munching his deli sandwich unapologetically; and J. D. Fitzpatrick, who sported one hell of a shiner received during Bill Millhouse's resisted arrest.

J.D. gave him a grim nod. "I'm on temporary loan to your team."

"Good to have you. I'll keep this as brief as possible so we can get back to the investigation. We'll connect with Detective Hector Rivera, who's heading up the team guarding Ms. Montgomery, and SA Grayson Smith by speakerphone," Joseph said, dialing the phone as he spoke. "The ME said he'd call if and when he found anything."

On the speaker, Hector answered. "Rivera here. I'm at SA Montgomery's home."

"Grayson Smith here," Grayson said through the speaker. "I'm calling from my office, where I'm preparing the charges against a hell of a lot of Millhouses."

Eyes narrowed around the table, the tension palpably increasing.

"Then let's get moving," Joseph said, "so we can grant them their right to a speedy trial. Before we begin, I have a few medical updates. Deputy Welch is out of surgery and in good condition. The cameraman is also out of surgery, but in serious condition. I don't have anything new on Detective Mazzetti, so I assume she's still in surgery. My last voice mail from her parents said the doctors were saying there was extensive damage to her femoral artery and that it would take a while to repair."

If they could repair it, Stevie's mother had added in a teary voice. Joseph decided to keep that detail to himself. "And we need to take a moment to remember the officers we lost today—BPD's Officer Winn and MPD's Sergeant Zacharias."

The room went quiet as they observed a moment of silence. "All right," Joseph said soberly. "Let's begin. Dr. Brodie, you're first. Please report on the crime scene."

Brodie detailed the layout of the scene, including Joseph's analysis of the most likely scenario. "I've traced the serial numbers of the Taser AFID tags," she said. "Two Tasers and ten cartridges were reported stolen by a Pennsylvania state trooper a year ago. They'd been assigned by his department and he kept them in his gun safe, which was in his home. The thieves also got his service weapon, several antiques, and two semi-automatic pistols." Her eyes gleamed. "And guess where those pistols were found?"

J.D. leaned forward. "In Bill Millhouse's trunk with his ten assault rifles."

Brodie's smile was sharp. "Very good, Detective. We're running ballistics on the other weapons found in Bill's and Marina's possession. So far nothing's popped."

"But now we can connect Bill Millhouse to the murder of Officer Zacharias and the abduction of Ford Elkhart," Joseph said. "Even if we can't prove Bill was in the alley, we've got a connection through whoever supplied the pistols and Taser cartridges. What about the knife that Reggie used in the courtroom? Has anyone had time to look at it?"

"I did," Drew Peterson said. "I've never seen anything quite like it." He passed photos of the knife down the table. "It's curved, like a sickle. When it's taken apart, the halves align, one on top of the other. Hector and Grayson, I'll e-mail you the pictures."

"Thanks," Grayson said. "I want to know how they smuggled it into the courtroom."

Joseph studied the photo. Daphne had said that the plastic strip they'd found in the backpack was the same color as the knife. It was also the same shape as both halves, when stacked on each other. He saw that Deacon had also noted the connection. "Show them what you found," he said to Deacon.

Deacon put the plastic plate on the table, tagged in an evidence bag. "Ford's cell records led us to an alley where we found this in a backpack. It smells like a gym shoe."

"Let me see that," Peterson said. "There are prints on the surface."

"I was going to send it to Latent when we were done," Deacon said.

Peterson typed a text into his phone. "I'm requesting a tech to come up here and get it. We'll put a priority on running the prints."

"You say Ford's cell phone record led you to this alley?" Grayson asked.

"Yes. Daphne Montgomery received a text from Ford's

phone today at about ten a.m.," Joseph said. "She thought it was real, that Ford had texted her and he was safe. She was devastated to find that wasn't true."

There was a rumble around the table followed by a moment of intense silence.

Deacon spoke up. "Why take SA Montgomery's son now? I mean, I get the notion of payback, but they took him before the guilty verdict was in. There was still a chance the jury would acquit. If they'd failed or if Ford had been discovered missing before the trial reconvened this morning, it would have made things even worse for Reggie. If it'd been me, I'd have taken one of the jurors' kids. Just sayin'," he added when everyone stared at him. "Kidnapping Ford *when* they did it served no purpose."

"Neither did shooting innocent people," Hyatt said coolly. "I don't think we're dealing with great intellect in the Millhouses."

"I don't know," Joseph said. "Zacharias's killer came with a plan. He was surprised by Zacharias, but he adapted. I don't think he's stupid. Marina? Stupid or maybe suicidal. Bill Millhouse showed up with a trunk full of weapons this morning. He had a plan, too—to break Reggie out. And in the absence of that, kill as many as he could."

Hyatt's face flashed fury. "Millhouse family Plan B. Scorch the earth."

"Having said all that," Joseph said, "Deacon has a point. We can see purpose to Millhouse's actions at the courthouse today. But why they took Ford when they did? It's a damn good question. We have to keep an open mind."

"Fine," Hyatt muttered. "Just don't go looking for any grand design to all this."

Joseph nodded. "So noted. What else do we know?"

"Kimberly MacGregor may have set Ford up," Deacon said, registering surprise around the table. "She had a felony record for theft. SA Montgomery dealt her down. And her younger sister went missing last night. Out of Philly."

This sent up a flurry of exclamations. "That changes things," Hyatt said.

"And underscores Deacon's question on the timing of the abduction," Bo added.

Deacon looked satisfied, but wisely said nothing.

Joseph frowned as a fact clicked in his mind. "Dr. Brodie, did that Pennsylvania trooper's theft report have an address?"

Brodie checked her phone. "E-mail says . . ." She looked up. "Broomall, P.A."

Deacon's fingers were flying over his phone. "Google says it's just outside Philly."

"Not a coincidence," J.D. said. "How long have Kim and Ford been dating?"

Joseph checked his phone again and smiled. His father had come through. The e-mail was short. *Screen shots you asked for are attached. Ford met Kim at a frat party in early September. Let me know if you need anything else. Love, Dad.*

"They met in September at a frat party," Joseph said. "Daphne knew about her, but had never met her. I've got his Facebook posts here. We'll read through those, and ask around the dorm, see if any of the students can add any detail. Let's search Kim's dorm room top to bottom. We need to know everything about her. Let's talk possible places they could hide Ford, Kimberly, and her sister. I think the Millhouses have him, but not at their principal properties. Where else might they hide him?"

"If they haven't already killed them," Brodie said quietly. "They've shown themselves to be ruthless and capricious. They have a taste for revenge. And they've made no ransom demands. Why wouldn't they kill them?"

Why indeed? "Then we'd better hurry," Joseph said. "The search of the Millhouses' primary address and their business turned up nothing. J.D., can you search for any other properties owned by the Millhouses and their relatives?"

J.D. nodded. "Did we get their computers?"

"Yes, but they're encrypted, unfortunately. IT's working on breaking in to their network, so check with them. Deacon, give a call to the trooper who reported his weapons stolen. Find out if he knew Kimberly. And pull up her felony conviction. She stole some jewelry, right? Find out how she took it."

"Her arrest report said she was with a cleaning service," Deacon said. "But I'll get more info on her employment history. I may need to drive up to Philly."

"Plan on it. I'll go with you if I can. I want to talk to MacGregor's parents. Bo, can you coordinate with the

Philly field office? We'll need to interview witnesses ourselves. And we need to be plugged in to the investigation into the little sister's kidnapping."

"Consider it done."

"J.D., you've also got the dorm. Talk to Ford's roommate and Kim's, too. I want to know everything about them, especially Kimberly. I want to know who she hangs out with and where. If she set Ford up, she knows the abductor, so uncover *any* connection she has to Millhouse or his family. And if you find anything involving the little MacGregor girl, call me right away."

"Okay. I can go to Philly with Novak if I need to dig more."

"No, the rest of us can travel. You stay close to home. I hear your wife's about to deliver." Joseph lifted a brow. "Ruby Gomez said she's 'big as a goddamn house.'"

"Lucy'll love that," J.D. said dryly. "I appreciate not leaving town. Lucy will, too."

"No problem. Moving on to Isaac Zacharias. We have to wait on the new ME to figure cause of death, since it wasn't the slice across his throat. Quartermaine's thinking Zacharias was drugged. Probably a mixture, something that would have knocked him down fast, kept him down while Ford and Kimberly were carted off. Given that Zacharias was a surprise, he thinks the killer gave him Ford's dose."

"Which was strong enough to kill a two-hundred-pound cop." Bo frowned. "Was he trying to kill Ford, too?"

"That assumes the drug mixture was the cause of death," Joseph said. "But it's a good question. If he meant to kill Ford all along, then why didn't he?"

"Assuming that he hasn't," Brodie said gravely.

"Which I am, until I know otherwise," Joseph replied firmly. "There was no weapon found at the scene, but we know a knife was used—definitely on Zacharias and maybe on Kim. Lieutenant Hyatt, can we get a canvass of all the storm sewers in the area of the crime scene, in case he tossed it?"

Hyatt nodded his shiny bald head. "Consider it done."

Joseph turned to Brodie's BPD counterpart. "Drew, you have all the weapons found in Millhouse's trunk, right? Any knives?"

"About fifteen knives, along with the ten assault rifles

and two pistols. When the ME releases the autopsy photos we'll see if any of the knives fit your wound."

Brodie had picked up the photo of the knife Reggie had used in the courtroom. "Quartermaine will tell us for sure, but Zacharias appeared to be sliced with a nonserrated blade about this depth. This could be the knife," she said.

"I was thinking that, too," Joseph confessed. "It just seems very . . . tidy. See what you can find on the knife. From a print standpoint, we're pretty sure it was handled by George, Reggie, and Cindy."

"And Daphne," Grayson inserted. "Reggie had dropped it on the floor and Daphne grabbed it while the deputies were restraining him. She crawled right into the thick of it."

The mental picture had Joseph's stomach rolling over even as his chest filled with pride. "That woman is too damned intrepid for her own good," he muttered.

"We'll check every square millimeter of the knife," Peterson promised.

"Good." Joseph tapped the table again, thinking of all the unexplored angles. "Kim got a text, possibly about her sister's abduction, at seven last night. If Kim did set Ford up, she had him in position by eleven, because that's when the movie ended."

"That gives whoever snatched her sister four hours to stow the kid and get to the alley," Deacon said. "Philly is a two-hour drive, so the little sister can't be stowed any farther than two hours from town."

"Unless he kept her," J.D. said. "He may not have stowed the girl right away."

"Possible," Deacon said thoughtfully. "He'd need a pretty big vehicle. Kim and her sister would have been small, but Ford's a big guy. How did he get them out of the alley? In a van? A car with a really big trunk? Is Bill Millhouse's car big enough?"

"We've examined Millhouse's car," Brodie said. "Our first inspection didn't reveal any blood and both Kim and Ford were bleeding when they left the alley."

"His trunk's also too small," Peterson added. "Millhouse would have been hard-pressed to fit Ford in his trunk, even if he hadn't been carrying enough assault rifles to kill everyone in that crowd."

"It could have been so much worse," Bo said quietly, "if J.D. hadn't noticed Bill Millhouse skulking around."

"And if Stevie hadn't shot Marina," J.D. added gruffly.

Joseph considered the teenaged killer. "When Daphne saw that Marina was dead, her worry was for the unborn child. Marina had been very pregnant during the trial, but when I checked her body, she was wearing a maternity pad."

"She missed the last days of the trial," J.D. noted. "We thought she'd had the baby."

"Maybe she wasn't pregnant to start with," Deacon said.

"Quartermaine can tell us for sure, but she looked like she'd had a baby recently. Assuming it was a live birth, that baby's out there somewhere. With Marina dead and all the Millhouses in jail, who's taking care of him? Or her. And where?"

"Maybe the 'where' is the same place they've stashed Ford and Kim," Deacon said.

"I was thinking that, too," Joseph said. "We need to find out where the baby is. We know it's not at the Millhouse home."

"I'll put a team of my detectives on it," Hyatt said. "I'll have them check with the hospitals, find out where it was born."

"Thank you," Joseph said. "Does anyone have anything else?"

"I do," Hector said. "Something that is too big a coincidence in my book. Ford isn't the first person in this family to be abducted. Daphne and her cousin were kidnapped almost thirty years ago. Daphne was eight, her cousin seventeen. Her cousin's body was found a week later in another state."

Joseph frowned, a shiver skittering down his back. "That's way too much coincidence. Why didn't she mention that?"

"I got the impression that it's something she's buried pretty deep. When she walked into her house, she had this moment of major déjà vu. I honestly thought she would pass out. When I asked what happened, she said that the night the sheriff brought her home, everyone was gathered together, like today, and that it was one of those times when the 'bad guy didn't pay.' She and Simone talked about it without really talking about it, if you know what I mean. It was damn eerie."

Joseph's head was spinning as reaction slammed him from multiple directions.

First and foremost was helpless fury. *Daphne was abducted.* The very thought made him sick. That she'd reacted so violently to the reminder of her homecoming made him even sicker. *Someone hurt her. My God. She was only eight years old.*

The man in him wanted to *hit* something. Someone. *Goddammit.*

But the cop in him kept his cool. She'd been abducted and then her son was abducted, too? What were the odds of those events being independently random? Probably less than being struck by lightning. The two events were somehow connected. He could feel it. But how? And why?

Finally, the victim in him could only blink. She'd been abducted, too? *Really? Just . . . Wow.* He'd known from the moment he met her that she was the one. She'd drawn him like a lodestone. Was this why? Had he sensed this?

Roughly he cleared his throat. "We'll look into it, Hector. You and Kate keep talking to Daphne and her mother. See what else you can find. We need more data."

"Will do," Hector said. "Also, she's had two visitors, both old friends. One was her ex's security head and Daphne's former bodyguard—name's Hal Lynch. The other was Scott Cooper. He helps take care of her horses and trains her son, who competes in show jumping. Both of them have been father figures to Ford."

Joseph noted the names in case they needed a look at Ford's childhood from a male point of view. He distrusted both men on principle, but that was the male in him talking. "If the father figures visited, what about Ford's father? Has he been in contact?"

"Well . . ." Hector hesitated. "Ford's father is Travis Elkhart. He's a judge. The family is seriously wealthy. Like snooty-butler wealthy. Elkhart and his mother were quick to blame Daphne for Ford's abduction. So far they've made no attempt to contact her here."

Joseph had to fight the urge to grind his teeth. Blaming her. *As if she hasn't been through enough.* "We'll send a tech to their residence to monitor any incoming calls, just in case

this really is about money and they get a ransom demand.
If there's nothing else, we're adjourned. I've got a date with
the Millhouses."

Tuesday, December 3, 3:05 p.m.

Daphne inhaled deeply as she left her room. *Mama's bak-
ing cinnamon buns.* Her mama always cooked when she
was upset. From the sound of it, most everyone had gathered in the kitchen.

Everyone except the two agents in her dining room
waiting for a ransom call and the two cops patrolling her
property. And Clay.

He stood at her front window, staring out at the gray sky,
his handsome face completely expressionless. Daphne worried about him on the best of days.

Today she'd worry about him more than usual. Because
then she wouldn't be thinking about Ford out in this
weather. The forecasters were calling for a bitterly cold
night. *He'll freeze to death. And . . . I'm not thinking about
that. I'm worrying about Clay.*

"I'd have to say as days go, this one has sucked," she
said. "Epically."

"I'd have to say I agree," Clay replied evenly, not looking at her.

She tugged at the sleeve of the black T-shirt he wore.
"You join up after lunch?"

He looked down at the big BPD in block letters on his
chest, then shrugged. "J.D. had it in his car. I ripped mine."

"Making bandages and a tourniquet for Stevie. I saw. Is
she out of surgery yet?"

"No." A muscle ticked in his cheek. "And it's been way
too long."

She chanced touching his arm. He flinched, but didn't
pull away, so she kept her hand there, gentling him. "If it
was bad news, we'd know. You probably saved her life. She
would have bled out if you hadn't helped her."

Clay said nothing for a long moment. "Her name is Kimberly MacGregor."

"Ford's girlfriend? I know. He told me about her." She
rubbed her temple. Her headache was worse. *I should have
let Paige do that pressure poking thing.*

"I don't think he told you nearly enough."

"Clay, I don't have the energy for puzzles. Whatever you have to say, say it."

"She has a record, Daphne. Felony theft. You cut her a deal."

Daphne gaped at him. *"What?"*

"She stole a diamond ring from the woman whose house she cleaned. You cut her a deal for two years' probation and five hundred hours' community service. I assume Ford didn't know. He's not the kind to hang with criminals."

"No. He's not." Cold fury started to bubble in her stomach. "Exactly when did you find this out?"

"This afternoon. I ran a background on her."

"You mean you hadn't before?" Her voice had grown louder with each word. She consciously lowered it to a hiss. "Zacharias had been following Ford for *two weeks* and you hadn't checked out the girl he was seeing?"

"He said he had."

She tried to stay calm. She knew Clay wouldn't and couldn't check up on everything his employees told him. *And maybe it doesn't mean anything.* "So she had a record. I might not want to meet my boyfriend's prosecutor mother, either."

"Her little sister went missing last night. Pamela is fourteen."

Daphne opened her mouth but no words came out. *Breathe.* "And?"

Clay braced his shoulders. "Kimberly's French teacher hadn't assigned any movie."

Breathe. "She . . . she set up my son?"

"I think so, yes."

Oh God. Oh God. "This changes everything," she said quietly.

"I'm s—"

"Don't you *dare* tell me you're sorry," she said, rage making her voice tremble. "This could have been avoided if your *trusted employee* had done his *job*. Your friend is responsible."

He turned, his dark eyes flashing. "No, whoever killed my friend is responsible."

Daphne took a step back. "I can't talk to you right now."

"Guys?" Paige asked from behind them.

Daphne didn't even acknowledge her. "Does Joseph know?"

"I've sent him a text, an e-mail, and left him a voice message," Clay said tersely. "If he's picked up any of those things, he knows."

"All right. I want you to tell Detective Rivera about this. And then I want you to go."

"Daphne . . ." Paige put her hand on Daphne's shoulder.

"Not now, Paige." Daphne turned away from them both. "Not now."

Eight

Clay watched Daphne walk away, his heart in his throat. "That went well."

Paige stared at him, bewildered. "What just happened, Clay?" He told her and her eyes slid shut. "Oh my God," she whispered. "What the hell was Tuzak thinking?"

"I don't know. I know he was tired. I should have found somebody else for the job. His report on Kimberly said her background check came in clean. I believed him. He'd never lied to me before." *That I knew about.*

"Does Phyllis know?"

"No. She gave me everything she found in his pants pockets when she did the wash yesterday. There was a to-do list. *Take Phyllis's car in for service, pick up milk. Do background on KM.* Plus about ten other things. He'd crossed off everything but the background. I think he kept meaning to do it. And just didn't."

Her eyes had narrowed. "Tell me you're not about to make an excuse for him."

He shot her a cold look. "No. I'm not even trying to understand why he lied to me, because it doesn't matter why. That he didn't do the background check is bad enough. That he deliberately falsified his report . . . He made me believe that Kim was no threat to Ford. And now Tuzak's dead and Ford is taken."

Paige sighed heavily. "God, what a nightmare. Let's tell Rivera. He needs to know."

"I've already spoken to Carter, so I assume Rivera knows."

"You spoke to Carter? In person? Not just by text?"

"In person on the phone. Turns out Carter knew already."

"So he didn't tell Daphne, either."

"No, but Tuzak wasn't his responsibility. He was mine."

Paige ran her hand over his back, a gesture of comfort. "Let's go fess up to the Feds. Just in case Joseph hasn't had time to tell them yet."

"You don't have to go with me."

"You're my partner," she said simply.

"What if Ford dies?" he asked, barely able to say the words.

"I'm not going there. Neither should you." She walked with him a few steps, then looked up, brows knit. "You didn't tell Daphne that Joseph already knew. Why?"

"Because he's . . . got it bad for her. I didn't want to fuck it up for him."

"You're a sentimental fool, Clay Maynard," she said softly.

"You're half right," he muttered.

He had finished telling Rivera everything he knew when Simone came into the dining room carrying a wicker basket covered with a red-checkered napkin.

"Cinnamon buns," she said, her expression grave, and he knew that she'd heard how he'd failed her daughter and her grandson. "Daphne insisted you take them, so don't think of saying no."

His young assistants, Alec and Alyssa, filed in behind Simone, waiting for direction.

"It's time to work," Clay said, because he didn't know what else to do.

Tuesday, December 3, 3:30 p.m.

Daphne glanced up when Paige slid into the seat across from her at the kitchen table, then resumed reading the top page of the stack in front of her. "They're gone?"

"Yeah."

"I'm sorry I shouted at you in there," Daphne murmured. "It was wrong of me."

"It's okay. Just give me the white Chanel suit and we'll be even."

"It's yours." Daphne sighed. "Look, I know Clay didn't mean this to happen."

"But Ford's your son. How could you not have reacted the way you did? We have a big responsibility when we promise people to keep their loved ones safe. Tuzak lied to Clay. Clay can't change that, but he'll do what it takes to find Ford."

"I know he'll try." Daphne sighed again. "And I'm upset, but I don't blame him." She returned her gaze to the stack of papers in front of her and tapped them. "This is my file from the Millhouse case. Grayson made me a copy. The original's with the Feds."

Paige came around the table to sit next to her, her eyes going wide. "Wow. You've got everything here. I wish Clay had a copy. This would save him a lot of time."

"He has one," she murmured.

Paige's eyes widened. "How? When? Oh . . . The cinnamon buns. Why the subterfuge?"

"Coppola. They're marked *Confidential* and she's a by-the-book girl."

"Can you get into trouble for giving them to Clay?"

"Probably. If it helps us find Ford, it'll be worth it. If it doesn't . . . it won't matter." Squaring her shoulders, she gave a portion of the stack to Paige. "I wanted Clay to have a copy so he could help."

"You know he will." Paige began sorting her pile of papers. "Reggie, Bill, Cindy, George . . . Huh. You have financials on the whole family. How?"

"We got a tip that Reggie had robbed other motorists and hocked their valuables. I found two pawnbrokers who said they'd bought jewelry from him. Since he was only a senior in high school, I convinced a judge that he had to have had the help of an adult. I was able to subpoena the entire family's tax and banking records for the last three years."

"And?"

"Bill's and Cindy's accounts were okay, but Reggie's weren't. I matched his deposits with receipts from local pawnshops. He'd robbed other people, so his self-defense plea didn't hold water. The testimony of the pawnbrokers turned the trial."

"There's a reason we always follow the money," Paige said briskly, sorting papers as she spoke. "You want me to start reading? Or sort your piles?"

"You sort, I'll read. We're looking for anyone who appears in major cash transactions—salary, deposits, personal checks. We can then identify any businesses and property those people might own. They have to hide Ford somewhere and Bill would only trust someone in his circle."

"What businesses am I looking for?" Paige asked.

"Start with anything connected to the defense fund Bill started for Reggie. They raised a hell of a lot of cash. Bill made a point of saying he was keeping his hands off the funds, to keep everything on the up-and-up. Somebody's managing it. Following the money will lead us to Bill's most trusted associates."

"Wouldn't relatives be the most trusted? All the uncles and cousins and aunts?"

"Not necessarily. Bill Millhouse used Reggie's arrest as a platform to push his own agenda. In the months between the arrest and the trial he drew a very devoted following, preaching that the country's going to hell in a handbasket because we've become so politically correct that we're weak."

"I know. I watched him on the talk show circuit. He makes his argument seem almost . . . mainstream when he's on camera."

"He's very savvy. He's made himself appealing to a disturbingly broad group, challenging 'ordinary people to take back their country.' He preaches a return to core values and a simpler way of life."

Paige froze, blinking at one of the bank statements. "When you said a hell of a lot of cash, you weren't kidding. My God."

"Some of that cash was earmarked for Reggie's defense fund. The rest goes to support 'taking back their country.' I wasn't really surprised that he had all those guns in his trunk. Bill's been edging closer to militia-type statements since the trial started. I think that's his true agenda."

"Any thought on who his right hand is?"

"I got the sense that nobody was. He doles out info on a need-to-know basis."

"Not even his wife and sons?"

"Bill doesn't trust Cindy with money. She spends too much."

"What about the sons? Either of them the right hand?"

"Reggie would be, if he hadn't been in jail. Bill doesn't like George. He uses him, but doesn't trust him. Because Bill doesn't trust anybody."

"So on top of being a racist, he's a paranoid sonofabitch."

"Paranoid, definitely. Sonofabitch? Absolutely. But it's more than that. At the beginning, long before the trial started, he thought 'the cause' was a means to an end and if people were dumb enough to donate, they deserved to be taken to the cleaners. As the trial progressed, it seemed like Bill believed more and more of his own rhetoric. He stopped playing a role and starting becoming that voice in the wilderness, the one who would lead armies to victory."

"Culminating with his bringing weapons to the court-house today."

"Exactly. Bill has always been a paranoid sonofabitch and that caution has probably kept him out of jail."

"Till now."

"Exactly. Because now he's graduated to being one *crazy* sonofabitch."

Tuesday, December 3, 3:45 p.m.

"That Bill Millhouse is one crazy sonofabitch," Joseph said as he walked into the interview room where the aforemen-tioned crazy SOB waited. Bill sat a few feet from the table, wrists and ankles manacled, wrists behind his back. The manacles were chained to the chair, which was bolted to the floor. Behind him stood two armed officers. No one was taking any chances.

Bill Millhouse was a large, hulking man and he'd passed his size on to both of his sons. His face was bruised, his left eye swollen nearly shut, his upper lip split nearly in two. He kept his eyes forward, not acknowledging anyone's presence.

Joseph had read the Millhouse profiles in Daphne's file, read their testimony in the trial transcripts, and reviewed a few tapes of Bill on some talk shows. Joseph's interview plan was pretty simple. He'd get Bill to talk about the guns he'd brought to the courthouse and why he had so many. From there he'd try to lead him from the pistols in his car to the Tasers in the alley and from there to Ford.

He picked up a chair and placed it a calculated distance from Bill. "One crazy sonofabitch." He sat down, casual only on the outside. "That's what they're all saying, anyway. The media, that is. Not that I blame them. Seems crazy to try to break your son out of jail. I mean, who does that anymore? Well, obviously you do. Gave it the old college try, anyway."

Millhouse didn't flinch. Didn't say a freaking word.

Okay, so we can play it this way, too. "*You* gave it the old college try. Can't say the same for your team."

The tiniest twitch in Millhouse's cheek.

Now we're talking. He'd considered the guns in Bill's trunk carefully as he watched the talk show tapes, with all of Bill's "Take the country back" rhetoric. There was no way Bill could have used all those guns. Joseph guessed that Bill had planned a bigger party, but he'd been caught by J.D. before he could arm his followers.

"Not like you didn't give them every opportunity. Could've done some serious damage with ten assault rifles. Bunch of cowards if you ask me. They ran, just when you needed them most."

No response.

That's not the team he's angry with. Or maybe Bill didn't have followers lined up to fight. Bill had definitely had a plan inside the courtroom, though.

"I don't suppose those rifles would have made any difference, though, since your wife and sons failed to accomplish the mission inside the courtroom. Although Reggie did do some damage to a deputy with that blade you smuggled in."

Millhouse's eyes stayed forward, but his lips curved, a deliberate fuck-you.

Fuck you, too. But Joseph kept his expression congenial. "But Reggie failed, too. It's fascinating that the most serious damage was done by a girl with a modified Glock."

Again the smirk.

"Of course, *she's* dead. Your only casualty."

The smirk disappeared abruptly.

Oh, yes. "Marina took seven bullets altogether. Six in the extremities. Whoever came up with the idea of her wearing the pregnancy pad . . . Kudos. It worked. Mostly. The seventh bullet, though, hit her right between the eyes."

Millhouse's chest rose and fell with the deep breaths he was now taking.

"Maybe you're wondering who killed her. Who could have been a big enough sonofabitch to shoot a pregnant girl right between the eyes? To put a bullet right through her brain? To blow her head right off her shoulders?"

Millhouse's chest was pumping like a bellows. A little bit more would push him over the edge. But getting Millhouse angry at Stevie would be a waste. She wasn't here for Bill to attack. *But I am.* Joseph didn't think Stevie would mind if he borrowed her glory.

He spread his arms wide. "*I'm* the sonofabitch who killed your brave soldier."

Millhouse turned his head then, his eyes so full of hate that Joseph might have been nervous had the man not been shackled with two rifles pointed at his head.

Joseph smiled. "Yep, it was me. And I'm glad I did it. The look on her face right before I pulled the trigger . . . It was fear, Bill. She begged me not to shoot, but I did anyway. I'd do it again in a heartbeat. Right between the eyes."

The only warning was the subtle tensing of muscles before Millhouse sprang. Because Joseph had been expecting it, he didn't flinch, just remained in his chair, arms loosely crossed, while Millhouse came crashing to the floor. His head landed only inches from the tips of Joseph's shoes.

The uniforms had their rifles cocked and aimed at Millhouse's head before it hit the floor. Millhouse lay breathing hard, his cheek pressed into the concrete, his body fully extended, his feet at awkward angles to the legs of the chair, the bolts of which had held. *Thank God for that.*

"My engineering degree always comes in handy at the strangest times," Joseph said blandly. "Like when I calculate the exact trajectory a body will take when it's hurled through the air toward me. You disappoint me, Bill. You're predictable. Now your little girl, Marina. Not predictable. I wonder if she was supposed to open fire like she did. What possible purpose could that have achieved? I wondered this. I did."

He paused. "And I came to a conclusion. Do you want to know what I think?"

Millhouse spat at him, the gob of phlegm hitting the edge of Joseph's shoe.

᾿ *That's just nasty.* But Joseph didn't flinch. "I'll take that as a no," he said, pulling a handkerchief from his pocket. Taking care to stay out of Millhouse's reach, he cleaned his shoe and tossed the dirty hankie on the table.

"That's okay. I'd planned to tell you all along. See, I think you anticipated they might fail inside the courtroom. I think a smart guy like you always has a Plan B. When I first walked in here, I thought Plan B was to create chaos outside the justice center, just like your family was supposed to do inside, but on a much bigger scale. I thought you had a team, like helper bees. I thought they'd all buzzed away when they saw that you'd been taken down by Detective Fitzpatrick and that your plan had disintegrated into one little girl shooting people in the front row. But now I think Plan B was simply to kill Daphne Montgomery for the pain she'd caused your family. Payback for Reggie's unfortunate incarceration. Of course, Marina also failed to do that. How'm I doing?"

"Go to hell," Millhouse growled.

Joseph ignored him. "I think you circled around like you did because you were planning to swoop in and grab Marina once she'd shot Montgomery. I think Marina took things into her own hands when you didn't show up like you had planned."

Millhouse's expression changed. Softened.

Pride, Joseph thought. *Affection? Tenderness? Love?*

"There is one piece I don't get. What was the purpose behind the abduction of Daphne Montgomery's son?"

Millhouse lifted his head to stare at Joseph, his eyes narrowed. Then without a word Millhouse lay back down and Joseph got the feeling one of them had missed something.

Joseph sat quietly for a minute, waiting. Finally Millhouse raised his head again, stared briefly, and then resumed his position on the floor, brows bent.

Millhouse doesn't know about Ford. Joseph's mind raced, trying to build a theory inside this scenario. *If Millhouse didn't do it, who did? And why?*

He kept coming back to the ten rifles in Bill's trunk. There had to be helper bees. Had to be followers. What if the followers saw the crazy futility of Bill's plan?

What if they'd enacted their own plan? A preemptive counterattack, as it were.

And even if they hadn't, what if he could make Bill believe they had? His goal was to lead the conversation, little as it had been, to Ford. What if one of the followers took Ford? Why, Joseph had no idea. Maybe Bill would know.

"I've always thought," Joseph said slowly, "that the hardest thing for a leader is to receive a no-confidence vote. For a politician, it means a fade into obscurity. No more office, no power. No statue on Main Street. But for a military leader like yourself, it's anarchy. Not to have had your troops rallying around you at the courthouse has got to be hard to swallow. But to have them doubt your success so much—in advance—that they create their own Plan B? Second-guessing you even before you had the chance to prove yourself? Humiliating. And infuriating. I'd be totally pissed off if I were you."

"You're not me," Millhouse hissed through gritted teeth.

"True. I'm sitting in a chair wearing Armani. You're on the floor, wearing an ugly orange jumpsuit. You're facing a long stay at Hotel Don't-Bend-Over and I'll go home to a soft, warm bed. I'm glad I'm not you for those reasons alone. But the biggest difference between us is that my people believe in me and yours don't."

"Don't know what you're talking about," Millhouse muttered.

"You really don't, do you? And it's driving you crazy because you want to know. But you don't want to ask me." Joseph's phone buzzed three times in quick succession. He checked and found texts from Grayson, Daphne, and Hector Rivera, all sent within seconds of one another, all telling him to halt his interview, as there was new information. "I'll see you later, Bill. Should I give your regards to Cindy and George?"

He didn't have to look to know Bill's teeth were grinding. He could hear them. He told the cops to return Bill to his seat, then left to find out what had just happened.

Tuesday, December 3, 4:10 p.m.

Alyssa had been blessedly silent as she drove them back to the office, leaving Clay to lick his wounds in peace. From the passenger seat, he stared at the sky, worrying. More snow was on the way. *Ford's out there. Somewhere.*

Clay had never been a hard-assed boss, demanding paperwork for paperwork's sake. He'd always had good people who pulled their weight. Except for Nicki. And now Tuzak. *I need to either get out of this business or become a cross-your-t's paper pusher.*

Neither sounded like a good choice. God. *What if Ford dies, too? How will Daphne survive that? How will I?*

Behind him, Alec Vaughn made an impatient noise. "The smell of those cinnamon buns is making me crazy. If nobody else wants any, pass the basket to me."

Clay handed it to him over the backseat. It had been very Daphne-like to insist that they take food, even through her fury. Which she had every right to. Still . . . it hurt. In the past nine months they'd become friends. She knew things about him that he'd never told another living soul. *She'll never forgive me. If she does, she'll never trust me again.*

"Um, Clay?" Alec said, his mouth full.

Clay didn't turn around. "What?"

"These cinnamon buns are a Trojan horse."

Clay twisted in his seat to stare at his newest staff member. Deaf from toddlerhood, Alec wore a cochlear implant and, after years of therapy, could speak clearly. But there were times Clay still had trouble understanding what he'd said. Like now. "What did you say?"

"These cinnamon buns are a Trojan horse," Alec repeated more slowly.

"What do you mean they're a Trojan horse?"

Alec dug his hand under the checkered napkin and brought out an envelope. "Weighs a ton. Which means all this weight isn't cinnabun-ly goodness after all."

He handed the envelope to Clay, who slid the contents to his lap. On top was a smaller, sealed envelope, addressed to him in Daphne's perfect penmanship. He opened it, not sure what he'd read.

Dear Clay,
    As a dad yourself, I know you have some sense of what I'm going through. I pray you never have to feel what I'm feeling. This is the worst hell I've ever endured. I know you didn't mean for this to happen. It doesn't change that it has and we're both going to have to live with it, no matter how things turn out. Please know that I still need your help and value your exper-

tise. I've enclosed my file for the Millhouse case. I hope inside is something you can use to help me find my son. I count you ever my friend.

Yours,
Daphne

I count you ever my friend. It was far more than he deserved and, in her place, far more than he would have given. Clay folded the note and slipped it in his pocket.

"Alyssa, I need you to drop me off at the university. The two of you go back to the office and start going over these papers. I'll take a cab back to the crime scene when I'm done to pick up my car."

"What's in those papers?" Alec asked.

"Daphne's file on the Millhouses. She told me at one point they were checking all their financials. I want to know how they paid the guy last night. It probably won't be in this file because these financials were taken weeks ago, but you can get bank account numbers. Do whatever you need to do to see their bank transactions."

"So we look for a money trail," Alyssa said. "What do we do when we find it?"

"Send it to me. I'll get it to Carter in a way that doesn't implicate either one of you." Clay tilted his hips, fishing deep in the pocket of his jeans and drawing out a handful of the AFID tags from the crime scene. "Also, I need to find out where these came from."

Alyssa glanced over with a frown. "What are they?"

"AFID tags," Alec said, impressing Clay that he knew. "Came from a Taser. Give them to me. I'll trace them for you."

"Thanks, kid." Clay's phone buzzed. It was Paige. "Hey."

"Hey yourself. How did you find those cinnamon rolls? Tasty?"

"Yeah. Tell Daphne thank you."

"You bet. Not the reason I'm calling, though. Grayson just let us know that Stevie's out of surgery. They've got her in ICU until she's stabilized, but the doctor told her folks that the surgery went well."

"Oh God," Clay breathed. "Thank you."

"The surgeon also told them that whoever administered

first aid on the scene probably saved her life. Her parents want to meet you."

Clay's head was still spinning from the relief. "Not sure Stevie would want that."

"I don't think they were asking Stevie," Paige said softly. "I've met them, Clay. They're really nice people. They want to thank the man who saved their daughter's life."

"You'd go?"

"Considering how long you've mooned over Stevie un-requitedly? Hell, yes. You and Joseph, I swear to God. Peas in a damn pod. Now I gotta go. I'm conferencing with brother Joseph in . . . crap, two minutes ago. I'm late. Bye. And good luck."

She hung up, leaving Clay to stare at his phone. Until he was thrown into the door when Alyssa cut through three lanes of traffic to get to the exit. "What the hell?"

"Hospital exit," Alyssa said. "I assumed that's where you'd want to go first."

He frowned at her. "You could hear Paige's end of the call?"

"No. You said, 'Thank you' like a prayer and didn't im-mediately tell us Ford was found. The mention of Stevie was also a clue. Plus you're blushing. It's cute."

"I'm not blushing," Clay growled. Except his face felt like it was on fire so he probably was.

"You used to blush like that when I'd catch you kissing Lou," Alyssa said teasingly. "My sister," she added as an aside to Alec. "She and Clay were engaged for a while."

"Hey, wait," Alec said. "You mean Sheriff Lou Moore, out at Wight's Landing?"

"Yeah. You know my sister?"

"I met her once," Alec said. "I haven't seen her since . . . well, that summer."

The summer six years ago when Alec had been kid-napped. *Shit.* "I'd forgotten about that," Clay confessed. "Crazy, considering I'm the one who found you." Twelve years old, tied, gagged, drugged out of his mind, Alec had been shoved under a bed in a dirty hotel room by an evil, deranged woman. "I just don't think of you as that little kidnapped kid anymore."

"That's good to hear," Alec said. "I don't think of myself that way, either."

"Are you okay with all this? No PTSD or anything?"

"If you're asking if I'm going to fall apart, then no." Alec's eyes shifted and Clay could see the withdrawn kid he'd been back then. "Is this easy for me? No. When I saw Daphne I thought about how scared my mom must have been. But I was lucky. The bitch who took me had a 'grand plan,' so she didn't hurt me. Just drugged me so I wouldn't cause trouble. I hope the Millhouses have a grand plan for Ford. It'll give us time to find him. If not . . ." He shrugged. "It'll be hard. On everybody."

"Then let's hope for a grand plan," Clay said grimly.

Alyssa pulled into the hospital parking lot. "Be careful. Call if you need us."

"I will." Clay stood in front of the hospital doors for a full minute trying to bring himself to go inside. He'd tried to start a relationship with Stevie several times. But, still grieving for her husband and son, she'd never been ready. *Maybe nearly dying will show her how precious time really is.*

Or not. Either way, he would meet her parents and smile and pretend like he wasn't as lovesick as a damn dog over their daughter.

Nine

Joseph had left Bill Millhouse to cool his heels in Interview and joined Bo and Grayson for a conference call with Daphne, Paige, and Rivera.

It had been Daphne's meeting from the first moment. She'd opened with a quietly dignified statement: "Nobody here has more to lose than I do. But nobody knows the Millhouses better than I do. Let me help you find my son."

What had followed was her incredibly complete assessment of the Millhouses, their associates most likely to be trusted with both Ford and the baby, and the properties where they might be held.

God, she was smart. Even if she hadn't had legs to her shoulders, he would have found her brain sexy as hell.

"So if I can summarize," he said. "George is the weak link. Reggie would be the heir apparent were he not in prison. Bill is making tons of money, misrepresenting himself to hundreds of thousands of followers as a 'patriot' who just wants to protect the ordinary guy when in reality he's tried to raise a small militia."

"It's the money that interested us," Daphne said. "And what he was doing with it."

Joseph searched his memory. "In one of his talk show interviews he said it would go toward Reggie's defense fund."

"You know, it's a funny thing about lawyers," Daphne

said wryly. "We can't talk about anything regarding a case, but spouses don't take any such vow. The wife of a defense attorney who hasn't been paid can be quite talkative. Especially when she now has an ER bill to cover because the client broke her husband's arm."

"And his ankle," Paige added. "In three places. Ellis is going to have to have surgery to get his ankle pinned because Reggie tossed the table on him this morning."

"Ellis hasn't been paid by the Millhouses?" Grayson asked.

"No," Daphne answered. "Only about a third of what he's billed out."

"How do you know this?" Grayson asked, brows lowered.

"Because I asked," Paige said evenly, "when Ellis's wife, Shannon, called me to ask if I had any places open in my next self-defense class."

Grayson sat back, surprised. "*She* called *you*?"

"She called my school. I have it set up to forward to my cell phone."

"Shannon Ellis was in the courtroom today," Daphne said. "She saw Cindy attack me, saw me block her—right before one of the Millhouse cousins hit her hard enough so that she had to be taken to the hospital."

"I'm missing something," Bo said. "Why did Ellis's wife come to you, Paige? How did she know you, much less that you gave Daphne self-defense lessons?"

"We can thank that reporter Phin Radcliffe for that," Paige said. "Shannon said she saw one of his TV news reports on my school. He's given our center a lot of good press. Which was the least he could do after making me an Internet sensation," she added grumpily. Then her voice brightened. "Kind of like you are now, Joseph."

It's not the same thing at all, Joseph thought. Paige had been filmed while attempting to save the victim of a shooting, the video instantly uploaded to the Internet and shown on every news network in the country. *Okay, I guess it's completely the same thing.* Of course it marked the beginning of Paige and Grayson's relationship and now they were engaged. *So maybe being an Internet sensation bodes well.*

"Back to Shannon Ellis . . . ," Joseph said.

"Shannon was scared," Daphne said. "She's the wife of the guy who represented the monster who'd just stabbed a deputy while trying to escape. The monster whose girlfriend killed a cop, then injured a detective and a civilian. Shannon sat in the ER for two hours, and while her medical needs were met quickly, not one cop came to take her statement. They took everyone else's, but not hers."

"So she came to us," Paige said. "She's got three children and she is terrified the Millhouses will blame Ellis for losing the case and want revenge. I think she figured that any information she gave to me would be passed to Daphne, who would square things for her with the cops. Then the police would actually come if the Millhouses made trouble and she had to call 911 in the night."

"She shouldn't have to worry about that," Bo said with a frown.

"You're right," Paige said. "But cops will blame the Millhouses and anyone that helped them. Defense attorneys are up there on the cops' shit list."

"Shannon didn't want her husband to take Reggie's case," Daphne said. "She begged him not to. But they needed the money."

"We're back to the money," Joseph said. "If Bill never paid Reggie's attorney, what has he done with the money people donated for Reggie's defense?"

"That's what we wanted to know," Daphne said. "I knew Bill filed a certificate of incorporation for a new nonprofit organization four months ago. That's where all the donations are going. This is the good part. Richard Odum, who's on the nonprofit's board of directors, recently bought several bank-owned homes that had been foreclosed on. But in his own name, not in the name of the nonprofit."

"Odum has his own plumbing business," Paige added. "He's not poor, but he shouldn't be able to afford three investment properties. We sent you the addresses of the houses and the board of directors list."

Joseph looked at Grayson. "Can we get warrants for the houses Odum bought?"

"Eventually. But not just for being on Millhouse's board and buying property. I'd have to show that he didn't have the personal funds to buy the property and that would require a warrant into his bank records. I could get you one in five minutes if you can get one of the Millhouses to confirm he's taking nonprofit funds."

Which was what Joseph had expected him to say. He sat back, thinking. "This Richard Odum . . . has he been giving interviews today?"

"Yes," Daphne said. "Hector and I checked while Paige was talking to Shannon Ellis. There's a lot of money at stake here, and now, with all the Millhouses being in prison, a power vacuum. Conditions are ripe for a coup. Anybody who knows enough to take control may also know where Bill Millhouse is hiding Ford."

Again Joseph was impressed with her quick thinking. But she was missing a puzzle piece. "I'm not sure that Bill Millhouse was involved in Ford's abduction," he said, drawing protests from the other side of the phone. "Hear me out. When I mentioned Reggie's stabbing of the deputy, Bill smirked. When I mentioned Marina shooting people, his smirk grew. When I gave him the opportunity to smirk about murdering Zacharias and abducting Ford, he didn't react. He didn't know what I was talking about. I'm wondering if someone else in his organization kidnapped Ford."

"Like Richard Odum," Bo said thoughtfully.

"Possible," Grayson allowed. "Still need more than you have to get a warrant."

Again, Joseph was not surprised. "We need one of the Millhouses to link Richard Odum's spending to the defense fund. Who would you start with, Daphne?"

"Cindy," she said. "She's the most volatile. But you'll have to get her mad enough to betray Bill. I saw the way Bill treated Marina during the trial—like she was spun glass. Cindy wasn't so keen on the girl. If Cindy felt threatened, I don't know, because maybe she believed that the father of Marina's baby was Bill and not Reggie . . . That would ignite her temper. Especially since Cindy sacrificed her freedom for Bill's grand scheme."

Bo nodded. "If it doesn't work with Cindy, we can try it on Reggie. To think his dad's been poaching on his territory might make him even madder than Cindy."

"I'll prepare the warrants," Grayson said. "If you can't get any of the Millhouses to tie Richard Odum to the defense money, I'll try to get a judge to sign without it."

"It's a plan," Joseph said. "I'll contact you if—"

"Wait," Daphne interrupted. "I want to be there when you interview—"

"No," Joseph snapped. "You'll stay where you're safe."

Grayson winced and Bo looked up at the ceiling, his gray head wagging in pitying disbelief. The silence on the other end lasted so long that Grayson turned the speaker up. "Hello? You guys still there?"

"Yeah, we're here," Paige said. "I muted the phone. I didn't think you'd want to hear Daphne's true feelings about Joseph's little pronouncement. Daphne's coming down there, Joseph. Like it or not."

"She's not safe here," Joseph gritted out.

"You're not her keeper," Hector said mildly. "Kate and I will accompany her."

Grayson shot Joseph a sympathetic look. "Paige, you'll stay with her, too?"

"Of course. See you in about twenty minutes."

The phone disconnected as Paige hung up.

"Fuck," Joseph muttered.

"Nobody knows the Millhouses like she does," Grayson said softly. "Do you believe Kate and Hector are good at their jobs?"

"Yes. I just don't want her to get hurt," Joseph said.

"None of us do," Bo said. "But she's one of our best resources right now, so we will use her. I'm more interested in your theory that Bill wasn't involved in Ford's abduction. If Bill didn't know about Ford and Zacharias in the alley, why did he have pistols in his trunk that were stolen from the same Pennsylvania state trooper who owned the Taser?"

Joseph shrugged. "If one of Bill's followers wants to push him out, he might know where the Tasers and pistols came from. Hell, the follower could even have been the one to steal them from the trooper to begin with." His cell buzzed and he checked his e-mail. "It's from Brodie. She and Drew Peterson examined the knife Reggie used in the courtroom. The blood types match Welch and Zacharias."

Joseph's phone buzzed again. "Peterson said they got a fingerprint match on that plastic strip Deacon and I found in the alley. George. They looked at photos of George. Every day in court he wore a wrist brace. When he was arrested, he didn't have it on. CSU is looking for the brace in the courthouse." He looked up at the group. "The knife was smuggled in by George. Maybe George used it on Zacharias last night."

"George?" Bo shook his head. "The son who's not that bright? You said yourself that the person in the alley last night was a planner, a quick thinker. If George pulled off that abduction and murder, Bill had to have been involved."

"I don't think so," Joseph said. "Bill didn't know what I was talking about. But since George smuggled in the knife, I'll start with him. If I don't get what I need, I'll move on to Cindy. By that time Daphne should be here."

Tuesday, December 3, 5:00 p.m.

"Have a brownie. They're good for the soul."

Daphne looked at the brownie Paige held in the palm of her hand, then turned back to watch the traffic they were passing easily on I-83 due to Agent Kate Coppola's Formula 1 approach to driving. "No, thank you. I can't eat."

"Then just *sniff* the chocolate," Paige said. "It'll calm you down."

"Maybe I don't want to be calm."

"But *I* do. Daphne, you are making me crazy." Paige forcibly stilled the foot Daphne couldn't stop bobbing. "You're going kick yourself in the chin."

"She's right," Coppola said. "You're not doing yourself any favors, getting so upset."

"I'm not upset. I'm angry with Joseph and that's canceling out the upset."

Hector twisted in the front seat to look back at them. "That weirdly makes sense."

"Thanks. 'You'll stay,'" Daphne mimicked. "I'm not a dog, to be told to stay or heel."

"Maybe you'd prefer he teach you to play dead," Paige said, an edge to her voice.

Daphne looked at her hands, twisted together in her lap. "Ford is my son, Paige."

"I know that. And he'll be so happy to come home and find you dead."

"That's not funny."

Paige's jaw tightened. "Nor was it meant to be."

Paige is angrier than I am. At me. Which is unfair and just plain mean. "You think I should let Joseph Carter dictate my actions?"

Paige gave her an I'm-disappointed-in-you look. "I think 'dictate my actions' is a slightly dressed up way of saying 'you're not the boss of me.' I also think you need to remember that Joseph already saved your life once today. Which I know he'd do again in a heartbeat. It just doesn't seem fair to ask him to do so unnecessarily."

Daphne sighed. "Now you make me feel like I'm being childish."

"Because you are. Look, Daphne, I get that being angry with Joseph is taking your mind off the hell I know you're going through right now. Joseph would be happy to have you be angry with him—as long as you're safe. You ramping up all that energy, all that's going to do is muddle your mind. And the minds of everyone around you. If someone shoots at you now, your reflexes are slowed. So are mine."

"Mine aren't," Coppola said smugly and Paige snorted back a surprised laugh.

"So hers aren't, which is good, because she's seriously exceeding the speed limit." Paige sobered. "Be angry with Joseph. He's insensitive and drags his knuckles. But don't lose your head or you'll get yourself killed. That won't bring Ford home."

Hector had been watching the entire exchange. "That makes more sense."

"Thank you," Paige told him.

Now Daphne really felt childish. "You think I should have stayed home?"

Paige shook her head. "No. But we're headed back to the place where somebody tried to kill you today. Not ideal from a security standpoint. When we get there, you'd best be settled in your head. I mean it. No foot bobbing, prissy prancing, or hissy fits."

Daphne lifted her chin. "I do not prance, prissily or not."

"But you're not denying the hissy fits," Coppola said. "Just for the record."

"On that I'm taking the fifth. Okay, Paige. I hear you. I will be settled in my head before we arrive at BPD. And I'll take that brownie. Thank you."

Paige draped her arm over Daphne's shoulders. "You're welcome."

As Daphne nibbled, she thought of Joseph's heroics, leaping through the air to shield her from Marina's bullets. All of a sudden he'd been there, larger than life. And he'd taken care of her. *Even my hair.* He'd been terrified, but not for himself. *He was terrified for me.* "Not insensitive," she murmured.

"Hmm?" Paige studied her face. "What did you say?"

Daphne stared at the brownie, breaking off tiny pieces. "He's not insensitive."

Paige squeezed her shoulders. "His knuckles do drag the ground sometimes, though. It's just how he rolls. He has a deep need to take care of people. I think once there was a— Wait, that's my phone." She listened for a long time, her expression too smoothly serene. "Okay. Thanks." She hung up, studied the two agents sitting up front. "Clay just saw Stevie's parents," she said to Daphne, all the while typing a text message. "They said that the doctor sounded hopeful that she'd make a full recovery."

"That's wonderful," Daphne said. Then her phone buzzed and she found herself reading the text Paige had just sent her from the other side of the backseat.

Call was from Clay. Taser used at Z crime scene this morning. AFID tags trace to guns rept'd stolen from cop near Philly. 20 min from KMacG parents. C going to PA.

This is progress, Daphne thought, *so why the cloak and dagger?* She waited, because Paige was still typing.

"I'm searching for the ICU visiting hours," Paige lied. "Do any of you know how late Stevie can receive visitors?"

"They close for a few hours around breakfast and dinnertime," Hector said.

"Thanks," Paige said. "I don't suppose you can send flowers."

Hector shook his head. "Not till she's in a regular room."

Paige put her phone away. "Hopefully that'll be tomorrow. Grayson will want me to send flowers as soon as she's able to receive them."

Daphne read the second text. *Don't say where you got the Taser-Philly link. C'll get in trouble. Delete this message.*

Feeling like Jim Phelps, Daphne deleted the message before it could self-destruct.

"How are we planning to get Daphne to the interview rooms?" Paige asked Hector.

Hector turned in the seat, his brows lifted. "I left instructions for our entry to the interview unit on a microfiche
hidden in an envelope hidden under your seat. Better read
it in a hurry, before the film goes up in smoke."

Paige looked reluctantly impressed. "That text thing's
worked, like, so many times."

"I know," Hector said. "I use that technique often myself. What's the secret?"

"Busted," Paige muttered. "Oh, look, we're here!"

Hector gave both Paige and Daphne a sharp look. "I'm
serious."

"Truthfully," Paige said, "it's all stuff you already know
but haven't told us."

"Uh-huh," Hector grunted. "We called ahead and have
two uniformed officers waiting for us. At all times you stay
within our circle. You're still wearing your vest?"

"Absolutely," Daphne said, pulling her turtleneck sweater
down to her collarbone to prove it. "Let's go. I want to
watch Joseph make Cindy Millhouse squirm."

*And when he's done with that, I want to know what else
he's keeping from me.*

Tuesday, December 3, 5:15 p.m.

George Millhouse didn't look like a murderer. That was Joseph's first impression after walking into the interview
room where Bill's son was being held. Despite his size, he
looked like a lost boy who was waiting in the mall security
office for his mother to come claim him. *Could be why everyone thinks he's not so bright.*

Joseph took the seat at the far end of the table and
waited for George to look up. After about ninety seconds
of silence, he finally did. He had two black eyes and his
nose had bled profusely at some point. Blood soaked the
sleeve of his shirt. He'd probably used his shoulder to wipe
the blood from his face since his hands were cuffed behind
his back. His feet, however, were free.

While Reggie was enormously well muscled, George was,
well, not muscled at all. But he was a big guy, maybe two
seventy-five.

Joseph wasn't lulled into complacency by the young
man's physique. He'd played football in high school and

some of the most effective offensive tackles were the big guys who just walked through the defensive line, steamrolling the other players. Usually they moved at little more than a stroll, but sometimes they were fast.

"Are you fast, George?" Joseph asked when he met his eyes.

George blinked, confused and in pain. And scared. Tears had run tracks through the grime and dried blood on his face. "I don't think so. I don't know. Why?"

Joseph shrugged. "Your dad took a flying leap at me. I wanted to know if I could expect the same from you."

"Why? Why did he do that?"

"I guess I just got on his bad side. Do you know who I am?"

"A cop?"

"My name is Special Agent Carter. I'm with the FBI."

"I'm not going to tell you anything. You might as well give up and go."

"That's not going to happen," Joseph said, "but I think you know that. I don't think you're as stupid as everyone seems to think you are." This earned him a narrow-eyed glare. As narrow as George could manage with his eyes swollen.

"If you think you're going to insult me into telling you what you want to know . . ."

"Yeah, yeah, you're not going to tell me anything. And I have to wonder why. It could be loyalty. Maybe pride. Could be fear."

"Loyalty," George said in a low growl. "Not that you'd understand that."

"Frankly, you're right. I don't understand that. I mean, your family gives you all the dirty work while Reggie doesn't lift a finger all day."

George shook his head. "You're just bullshitting me. Reggie's in jail."

"So are you," Joseph pointed out cordially. "Because your family gave you the dirty work. An impossible mission that you accomplished. You smuggled a knife into the courtroom and didn't get caught."

Ah, there it is. The slight lifting of George's chin. The gleam of pride.

"No, I didn't," George said. "I don't know what you're talking about."

Joseph smiled. "You *do* remember the knife, right? The one that Reggie had in his hand? The one he used to stab a deputy?"

"Yes," George said with disdain. "I saw it. Doesn't mean I smuggled it in."

"Your fingerprints are all over it. Just sayin'."

George's mouth clamped shut.

"We know how you did it, by the way. Pretty ingenious. Pretending to need a wrist brace, switching the supports at the last minute. You waltzed through security. Hit the men's room, assembled the knife, walked into the courtroom—just in time for the verdict. You handed it to Cindy, who gave it to Reggie. Who blew it. All your work, all your risk . . . and your golden-boy brother blows it. So here you are. That's gotta chafe."

George looked away.

"Yours was the most dangerous part," Joseph went on. "You had to get the knife. If you made it, kudos. They might find a place for you in the workshop in prison." Joseph exaggerated a grimace. "Except they don't let death row prisoners have jobs."

George's gaze came back around in slow motion, stunned at first, then disbelieving. "I didn't kill anybody."

Joseph shrugged again. "Reggie did."

Fear flashed in his eyes. Fear and guilt. "The deputy . . . ?"

"He died," Joseph lied harshly.

George wasn't that stupid. And the boy seemed to have some thread of conscience. *I can use that.*

"You brought Reggie the knife. Therefore you are as guilty as if you stabbed the deputy yourself."

George's reaction was the polar opposite of Bill's. There was no glee. No smug joy. Just cold-blooded fear. "But I didn't kill anybody," he insisted desperately. "I didn't."

Joseph thought of Isaac Zacharias and wanted to cause George great pain. He said nothing, though. Just watched as George thought through the possibilities.

"I did *not* kill anyone. They can't give me the death penalty for bringing the knife."

Joseph wondered if George even realized he'd just confessed. "See, this is what I meant by the dirty work, George. Reggie gets himself jailed for murdering that couple on the side of the road. He's found guilty by the jury. He has nothing to lose. What's one more once you've killed already?" He paused a moment, letting the statement hover. "You, on the other hand, you didn't kill the couple on the side of the road. Yet now, here you sit. Because they gave you the dirty work. 'Bring me the knife, George. Create a disturbance in the courtroom, George. Help your brother escape, George.'"

George sat silently, his massive chest moving up and down.

"You might be right, George," Joseph said softly. "The jury might not give you the death penalty since you didn't actually touch the deputy. But I can guarantee they'll give you the death penalty for the murder of that DC cop."

George's swollen eyes widened and his mouth dropped open. "Wh-what? No. No. No fucking way. I did not kill anyone. I really didn't kill a cop."

Joseph took a photo of Zacharias's body from his pocket and slid it down the table.

George paled. "They cut off his head. Oh my God. I don't know him. I swear it."

"I can believe that," Joseph said. "You didn't know he was there. He surprised you in the alley. I can believe you'd never seen him before."

"What? That guy was not in the alley. I would have noticed *that.*"

"When were you in the alley, George?" Joseph asked silkily.

George realized he'd said too much.

"CSU found the dead cop's blood on the knife Reggie used in the courtroom. He was killed last night. With the knife you had possession of this morning."

"You're lying," George said, his body starting to rock. "You're lying."

"No, I'm not. I found the cop's body this morning. Long before the verdict was read. You smuggled the knife into the courtroom. You had it last night. You killed Officer Zacharias. You slit his throat."

"No, I didn't! I *didn't* have it last night! I just got it this morning. *I swear.* I never saw it before this morning and I wish I'd never seen it at all." Tears cut new streaks in the dirt on his cheeks. "Oh my God." George's rocking grew more pronounced. "Son of a motherfucking *bitch.*"

"You slit his throat, George. And then you did the dirty

work you were sent to do. See, I believe you when you say you never saw Officer Zacharias before last night. You didn't know he'd be there when you carried out the real reason you were sent to that alley. You killed the cop, then kidnapped those two college kids."

George scrambled to his feet. "No, I did not. I don't even know what you're talking about. Kidnapping? That's crazy. You're crazy."

"Sit down, George," Joseph barked.

George sat, almost missing the chair because his legs were trembling so badly. "You've got to believe me."

Joseph was very conscious of the time. He needed to get Grayson something linking Richard Odum to the money so they could get a warrant. "Why should I?"

"Because I didn't do it!" George cried.

"The real killer did it," Joseph deadpanned. "I've never heard that one before. But let's say I believe you. I don't, but let's just say I do. Where did you get the knife?"

"From Doug. He sold it to me. Promised that nobody would detect it."

"Okay. And who is this Doug?"

"I don't know his last name."

"Of course you don't. You're just wasting my time."

"I don't! He's a friend of my father's. He sold us the knife."

"And the Tasers?"

George frowned. "What Tasers? I bought a knife. No Tasers."

"What about the assault rifles?"

George opened his mouth. Closed it again. "I don't know."

"Doug didn't sell them to you?"

George sighed wearily. "I don't know."

Joseph stretched out his legs, made himself comfortable. "Marina's dead."

George flinched. "You're lying." When Joseph continued to study him in silence, horrified acceptance began to fill his eyes. "When? How?"

"She opened fire on the crowd outside the courtroom. A cop shot her, right in the head." He made a gun with his thumb and forefinger. "*Pow*. She dropped like a rock."

George closed his eyes. "Oh my God. Oh my God."

"You keep saying that," Joseph said blandly.

George shook his head. "Shut up," he whispered. "Oh God. Just . . . shut up."

Joseph gave him a minute. Then casually threw out the name he was most interested in at the moment. "Richard Odum."

George's eyes flew open, the flash of hatred unmistakable. And then he schooled his features to mimic mild resentment. "What about him?"

Not so stupid after all. "You tell me. Since you're so eager to have me believe you."

George's shrug was forced. "Friend of my father's. On the board. All I know."

"I got that from the Internet, so you haven't helped me at all. You should know that the state's attorney is on the other side of the mirror. The charges against you are already signed. It'll be first-degree murder and two counts of kidnapping. And all that's before we even start discussing the courtroom drama—and the aftermath."

"Marina," George said hoarsely. There was real grief in his eyes. Like he'd lost a lover. Joseph had planned to turn Cindy by telling her that Bill had an unholy affection for Marina. He wondered if it would work with George.

"Interesting. Seems like for such a young girl, Marina has attracted an awful lot of strong emotion from you Millhouse men."

George's eyes narrowed, his breaths very shallow. "What do you mean?"

"Well, Reggie was sleeping with her. You obviously carry a torch for her. And your dad . . . well, his *torch* got *extremely* intimate with her, if you know what I mean." Joseph was deliberately vulgar, just to see what George would say.

"No, I *don't* know what you mean," he hissed, furious now.

"Oh, but I think you do. Daddy was poaching on Reggie's territory. That baby Marina had a few days ago? Daddy's."

Again George leapt to his feet. "No!" he roared. "You're lying."

"You'd better be sitting in the next five seconds or I'll have you hauled off to a cell."

George viciously kicked his chair, sending it sliding

across the room to crash against the wall. "That baby is not his. That baby is *mine*."

Well. That one I wasn't expecting. Keeping his expression bland, Joseph calmly stood and slid the chair back to George. "Sit. Down. *Now.*"

Breathing like a bull, glaring up at Joseph with hate, George obeyed.

Joseph stood close to George now. "You've got a big problem, then, *Daddy*. Your baby-mama is gone. Pushing up the proverbial daisies. Your dear old dad is in jail, as are your mother and brother. Nobody's taking care of *your* child."

George looked away, shaking his head numbly. "She'll be okay."

Yes, yes, yes. Just a little more. "A baby that small could die if she's not cared for properly. Still not sure I believe the kid's yours, though. Your father . . . he reacted very badly to the news of Marina's death. Attacked me and everything. There was something in his expression. Made my skin crawl, George. Face it. Your daddy had an improper liaison with your baby-mama."

"Sonofabitch," George snarled. "Motherfucking sonofabitch."

Interesting. He'd said the same thing when he'd learned the knife had killed the cop.

"He's not gonna win Father of the Year, that's for damn sure. Then again, neither are you. An infant that age needs to be fed every few hours. By the time you get out on bail, *if* you ever get out on bail, that baby will be dead."

George looked completely poleaxed. "No. Someone will take care of her."

"Who, George? None of your family. They're all arrested with you."

"A . . . friend. A friend will find her."

"You keep on thinkin' that. With friends like yours . . ." Instinct had Joseph backing off. "Fine. We'll leave the baby all alone for now. Let's get back to dear old Dad who gave you all that dirty work. You know, kidnapping a state's attorney's son, killing a cop, smuggling the knife, supporting his mini revolution."

George's mouth fell open again. "State's attorney's *son*?"

"Did I fail to mention that? The college kids you kidnapped last night were SA Montgomery's son and his girl-friend." George slumped into the chair looking like he couldn't absorb one more word. "*Now* do you understand the severity of your situation? You're going down, George. Murders of cops, kidnapping. You can't change that. But you *can* be a father to that baby. Tell me where she is. I'll make sure she's cared for."

Joseph sat in what he hoped was nonchalant repose when inside he was holding his breath. *Please give me Odum. Give me a location for the baby. Give me something.*

"You'll give her away," George murmured. "To strang-ers."

"That's not mine to decide. I just don't want her to die. We've lost two people today. Three if we count Marina. I don't want to bury your baby, too."

George clenched his eyes tightly closed. "Can I see her?"

"I'll do my best."

"I didn't kill anyone." It was a desperate whisper.

"Then don't start with your own daughter."

George's sigh was tortured. "Richard Odum. He's got a house, a couple houses. There's one in Timonium. It's nicer than the others. I, um—" His voice broke. "I fixed her up a room there. Painted it yellow. Bought her a crib."

There you go, Grayson. Richard Odum, wrapped in silver paper. Now get me my damn warrant. "What's your daugh-ter's name, son?" Joseph asked quietly.

"Melinda Anne." George opened his eyes and Joseph saw a lot of pain and maybe a little truth. "I didn't kill any-one. I swear it. I only got the knife from Doug this morn-ing."

"Where did you go to buy the knife? And when?"

"I met him in an alley near the courthouse. I almost didn't get back in time."

"Where were you last night, George?"

"I was supposed to meet Doug to buy the knife last night at ten thirty. I waited until after midnight, then I texted him to ask him where the hell he was, but he never answered. He never showed up, so I left."

"When was that?"

"About one a.m. I was almost home when he texted me to meet him the next morning at nine. So I did and he was

late again. I almost left, but I knew my father would . . . not
be happy if I showed up in court without the knife. So I
waited until he showed."

"And nobody saw you? Either time?"

"Nobody," he said glumly.

It was on the tip of Joseph's tongue to ask about the text
to Daphne's phone from the alley, but he decided against it.
George would just deny sending the text, and revealing its
existence would give the defense a reason to confuse a future jury as to the timeline.

"Why?" Joseph asked. "Why would you go to all this
trouble to get Reggie out?"

"Because . . . that was the plan. Reggie's next in line."

"For what, George?"

"For everything." It was said in the way of a person long
trained in a dogma. "He'll run the family when my father
dies." But then his face hardened. "Which I hope is soon."

"On that we agree. Tell me about Doug. What does he
look like?"

"Ordinary. Brown hair, cut short. Brown eyes." He
shrugged. "Ordinary."

"Height? Weight? Tattoos?"

"Maybe five nine. One eighty? No tats that I ever saw."

"Ordinary," Joseph murmured. "He's your father's friend?"

"Yeah. His father served with my father in the first Gulf
War. Army buddies."

"Did he sell you anything other than the knife?"

George's eyes flickered, as though he were considering
the best answer. "No."

Which meant yes. But George seemed back in control
and looked like he was considering how to best cut his
losses. Joseph decided to come back to the Taser and guns
later, when he could catch George off guard again. "Okay.
Why did Reggie say Marina's baby was his?"

Again Joseph saw a little gleam of pride. "Because he
thought it was. But Marina was mine and the baby is, too.
She had to let Reggie think it was his, or he'd be angry when
he got out. Marina's small." He closed his eyes for a second.
"Was. She *was* small. If Reggie got mad, she'd get hurt."

"So why would you try to help Reggie escape?"

Weary confusion clouded his eyes. "Because that was

the plan." His chin dropped to his chest, as if he couldn't hold his head up anymore. "I need a lawyer, don't I?"

You need the best damn lawyer money can buy. "Yeah, George. I'd say you do."

Joseph let himself back into the observation room, feeling like he needed a long nap, but instantly he came to attention. "Daphne."

She stood at the window, watching George, who sat in the chair, quietly weeping. Joseph found himself feeling a little sorry for the young man, but then he thought of Zacharias's family and whatever pity he'd felt vanished.

"Nice interview," Daphne said, her voice distant. She didn't look at him, keeping her eyes on George. But something was off. Joseph could feel it.

Paige stood on her left. She'd angled her body so that she could see the whole room, ready to protect Daphne even here, in BPD's headquarters. Which, considering that Daphne had already been attacked twice while surrounded by cops, seemed prudent.

When Paige met his eyes, Joseph knew his instincts had been right. Something wasn't right. He and Paige had developed a friendship over the months, a respect that had always seemed mutual, but at this moment Paige's eyes held a wary distrust. That she was letting him see it was significant. For good or bad, he wasn't sure.

Hector Rivera and Kate Coppola stood shoulder to shoulder about ten feet away. They seemed to be waiting to see what would happen next.

Feeling at a distinct disadvantage, Joseph walked to Daphne's side. Rarely had he seen her in anything but suits and evening gowns. Now she wore soft, faded jeans tucked into a pair of equally worn hiking boots. Her sweater wasn't cashmere or angora, as he would have expected, but an oft-washed acrylic that she might have bought at Walmart.

She was dressed for the outdoors, he realized. Dressed for snow. Dressed to join in a search for her son, should it become necessary.

She'd changed her hair, too. Literally, he supposed, wondering how many occasions she had wigs for. Her hair was down, held away from her face by a barrette at the nape of her neck. This way, she looked more like a college student

herself instead of the mother of one. Heartbreakingly
young. Vulnerable. Fragile.

He wanted to touch her so badly he could taste it, so he
shoved his hands in his pockets to avoid temptation. "I'm
sorry we started without you. Grayson wanted a connection to Richard Odum."

"Yes, he told me. He's getting the warrant signed now
and Agent Lamar is organizing search teams."

If Bo was organizing the teams, it meant Joseph could
afford to stay a minute or two. To recharge. To be near her,
just a little. "That's good." Feeling as awkward as a boy asking a girl on a first date, he barely resisted the urge to stare
down at his shoe.

Paige gave him a pitying look, then rolled her eyes, making him feel even more like an idiot than he had before.
"That was good work, Joseph, getting George to tell you
about Odum."

"Thank you. We should start with the house in Timonium. If the baby is there, Ford might be, too."

Daphne swallowed hard. "Hopefully."

He gave in to the need to touch her, taking his hand
from his pocket long enough to give her upper arm a brief
squeeze. "Hold on," he said quietly. "Just a little longer."

And then he practiced what he preached, sliding his
hand down the length of her arm and threading his fingers
through hers. Holding on.

She never took her eyes from the window, but her hand
gripped his with a desperate strength that broke his heart
all over again. "A small part of me has always felt sorry for
George," she murmured. "I don't know what I think now.
Part of me still feels sorry for him. I guess that makes me
crazier than he is."

What it did was make Joseph want her even more. He
cleared his throat. "I think he made his choice, Daphne.
And I don't think he's as stupid as everyone thought."

"Maybe not stupid. Maybe just alone." She turned to
look up at him, her blue eyes searching his. "Do you think
they took Ford? Bill or George?" The way she asked let
him know that she wasn't sure anymore, either.

"I'm leaning toward no at the moment. I sure as hell
want to know who Doug is."

She was still looking at him, still searching. "Have you told me everything?"

Paige gave him a look, her black brows arched. Like, *Don't fuck this up, buddy.*

Which meant they'd learned something he hadn't told them. Consorting with PIs was making this situation more difficult than it otherwise might have been. He pitied Grayson, always having to worry about what his fiancée was capable of digging up.

No, I don't. His brother had found what most people spent their whole lives looking for. The woman made just for him. The thought that maybe, just maybe, the woman made for Joseph himself was staring up at him with blue eyes full of questions . . . Joseph wanted the questions gone, answered. He wanted to see trust. And other things.

"No, I haven't, but not because I don't trust you. There are some aspects of the Zacharias crime scene I thought you'd be better off not knowing."

"Like?"

Like Zacharias's head was nearly severed from his body, which means that the person who took your son is capable of doing the same to him. But there was no way he'd tell her that. Even if it meant she never trusted him.

"Like Zacharias was shot with a Taser stolen from a cop who lives about thirty miles from Kimberly's parents' house in Philly." None of this surprised her, he could see. "Kimberly's got a record for theft. You dealt her down. And her sister was reported missing last night. Tell me when I say something you don't already know."

Trust crept into her eyes. "Why didn't you tell me about the Taser and Kimberly?"

"Because if it was used on Zacharias, it was probably used on Ford and it's not a pleasant experience. The Kim connection?" He shrugged. "I wasn't thinking about it. Any more than I was thinking about the guns in Bill's trunk that were also stolen in that Philly burglary. That blood matching Zacharias's type was found on the knife that stabbed Deputy Welch was information I didn't have until after we'd hung up."

"Wait," Paige said briskly. "*Bill* Millhouse had guns linked to the Tasers at Tuzak's crime scene and *George*

Millhouse had the knife that was used to kill Tuzak and we're still considering that they didn't take Ford? What's wrong with this picture?"

"I said I was leaning toward no," Joseph said, irritated, "not that I'd decided. I'm checking every house that Richard Odum bought with Bill's donation money. We are looking for Ford and that baby, whoever it belongs to. We're digging into Kimberly, finding out if she connects to the Millhouses and how. I'm proceeding as if the Millhouses kidnapped Ford, okay?"

Paige blinked at his sudden show of temper. "Okay."

Daphne tugged on his hand, reminding him he still held hers. "But?"

"But the timing bothers me. The involvement of Kimberly bothers me. That text from the alley bothers me."

Daphne frowned. "I just figured they sent the text because they wanted to delay us looking for Ford. Buy themselves time. What bothers you about it?"

"I don't know," he said honestly. "Other than why they'd need to buy themselves time? They'd planned violence at the courthouse, either from within or without. Either way, they'd be kicking up a huge cloud of dust. So why try to hide that they'd taken Ford?" Joseph's cell phone buzzed in his pocket. It was Bo. "You ready to roll?"

"Just waiting for you."

"I'll be there in two." Joseph hung up and squeezed Daphne's hand. "No," he said when she opened her mouth. "You'll just have to be angry with me, but you can't go."

"I was going to say 'hurry,'" she said.

He made himself let go of her hand and took off through the halls at a run.

Ten

"And be careful," Daphne murmured. She clasped her hands together, warming the one he hadn't touched with the hand he'd held. *Hurry. Please hurry. Please find him.*

Paige put an arm around her shoulders, urging her to a chair. "Breathe, honey."

Daphne's knees gave out as she lowered herself into the chair. She pressed her folded hands to her lips, trying to quell the panic that rose in her throat, threatening to choke her. She inhaled deeply . . . and smelled Joseph's aftershave on her hand.

His scent calmed her. Greedily she covered her nose and mouth and breathed until the heartbeats in her head had quieted. The panic was gone. For now.

Dropping her hands to her lap, she looked up. Hector and Coppola stood in front of her. "How long does it take to get to that Timonium address from here?" Daphne asked.

"Not too long," Hector said. "Thirty minutes."

"Thirty minutes," Daphne repeated. "Then we'd best get busy."

"Doing what?" Coppola asked.

"Figuring out who the hell this Doug guy is."

"You don't think they'll find Ford there," Paige said softly.

"No. I don't. I think George was telling the truth." She leaned left to look around Coppola. George was still in the interview room, still sitting in the chair. He'd stopped crying, now sitting with the expression of a man who knew he'd lost everything that mattered. "I think they'll find Marina's baby in the Timonium house, unless one of Bill's devotees has whisked her away. But Ford's not there." She squared her shoulders. "Let's go upstairs to one of the conference rooms. I can't think in this room."

Because it was dark and she was underground. Normally she could lie to herself that Interview was just a windowless room on the first floor, but today her mental walls were weak and she could feel the panic closing in.

When they reached BPD's Homicide floor, they were met by Lieutenant Peter Hyatt. To Daphne's utter shock the lieutenant wrapped his beefy arms around her in a bear hug, nearly lifting her off her feet. He released her, his expression fierce.

"Anything you need, Miss Montgomery, and I mean *anything*, you need only to ask."

"Thank you." Daphne didn't dislike the man, but she didn't always trust him. He liked to grandstand and he could be a real prick. But there was honest pain in his eyes today and it helped ground her somehow. "We came up here to explore some new leads. Can we use the conference room?"

"Of course. I happen to know the commander isn't using his right now and it's a lot more comfortable. Come with me." He set off with long strides. "Nice to see you, Miss Holden," he tossed carelessly over his shoulder.

Paige's lips twitched. "Always a pleasure, Lieutenant."

Paige and Hyatt had really gotten off on the wrong foot while working the Muñoz case nine months before, Daphne recalled. But after helping Hyatt's detectives catch a killer, Paige had earned his trust and respect, and maybe even a little affection. Daphne had always suspected that Hyatt had a softer heart than he let on. That bear hug confirmed it.

He led them to the conference room and showed them in. "There's a washroom through that door and snacks in the cabinet. I'll make sure no one disturbs you."

When Hyatt had closed the door behind him, Hector let out a low whistle. "Can we make whoever stole the real Hyatt keep him?"

"He's not so bad," Paige said, raiding the snack cabinet. "Mostly bark, minimal bite."

Daphne sat down near the whiteboard. "Would one of you mind being the scribe? The smell of those markers makes me dizzy and my head is already killing me."

"I'll be scribe," Coppola said. "I love the aroma of markers. Especially the red ones."

"You have a headache because you haven't eaten," Paige said, dumping several boxes and cans on the table. "We've got most of the major food groups here. Nuts, raisins, crackers, and Cheez Whiz is dairy. Kind of. Eat, Daphne."

Daphne grimaced. "Cheez Whiz is not even close to dairy." But she took a few cashews to keep Paige from nagging her. "What do we know about Doug?"

Hector leaned back in a chair, getting comfortable. "We only have George's word that he exists," he said and Coppola noted it on the whiteboard.

"He's Caucasian, average everything," Coppola added. "Height, weight, coloring."

"George said he texted him," Daphne said. "We can get a phone number."

"Nice," Paige said. "I'm betting everyone has disposable cells, but George probably had his cell on him when he was arrested. We can check the call and text logs."

"Let's get CSU on the line," Daphne said. "They need to hear this, in case they have evidence we don't know to ask for." She dialed the CSU lab.

"Lab. This is Peterson."

"Hi, Drew. It's Daphne Montgomery."

"Daphne." His voice warmed. "How are you?"

"Keeping busy. I'm on the Homicide floor with Rivera, Coppola, and Paige Holden." She told him about the mysterious Doug. "Do you have George Millhouse's cell phone?"

"I have it inventoried. I just hope it's not encrypted. I'll put you on speaker so I can listen while I look for it. I'm going to mute you because the lab is busy tonight."

The line went quiet and Coppola pointed to the board. "What else?"

"He's a weapons dealer," Hector said. "Tasers, knives, semi-autos. Assault rifles."

Daphne nodded. "Assuming Doug sold the knife to

George this morning, Doug may have had it in his possession the night before. He could have killed Zacharias."

May be Z's killer, Coppola wrote. "If this is the case," she said, "he's smart. He's capable of planning and quickly adapting."

"Yeah, Tuzak showing up in the alley must have been quite a shock," Paige said. "If Doug killed Tuzak and took Ford, he's got some muscle, or he had help. Ford's a big boy. He had to be able to lift him into a vehicle." Paige cast Daphne a nervous glance as she said this.

"It's okay, Paige. I'm not going to fall apart. I'm . . . compartmentalizing." Which was keeping her barely sane. "Doug connects to the theft of those weapons from the cop in Philly because he used the Tasers. Semi-automatic pistols from the same theft showed up in Bill's trunk. Either he stole the weapons himself or he knows who did."

"He's ambidextrous," Hector said. "He shot two Tasers in rapid succession, probably one in each hand."

"He's probably right-handed, though," Coppola inserted. "He missed the shot that he aimed at Kimberly. She was a bit farther away by then and his aim was off. That would have been his left hand."

"He's good with drugs," Hector said. "Joseph believes that Zacharias was drugged with a cocktail meant for Ford, that the killer had customized doses for Ford and Kim. Customizing for size is more complicated than it appears. He may have a medical degree or have access to medical knowledge."

He drugged my child. Daphne had gotten stuck at that point, barely comprehending anything else Hector said. Fury whipped up within her, making her jaw clench. Paige patted the hand she'd balled into a fist.

"Down, girl. You'll get your chance with Doug, but we have to catch him first."

"You're right. Sorry." Daphne forced her fist to relax. "George said that Doug's father served in the Army, in Desert Storm with Bill Millhouse. I have Bill's military record in my file." She pulled the folder from her bag and searched. "Bill served in the Persian Gulf with the First Infantry Division, attaining the rank of sergeant. So we have to find out who was there with him who has a son named Doug."

Hector shook his head. "Possible, but unless Doug's father listed him as a beneficiary on his benefits paperwork, it'll take a while to find him. Anytime we deal with the Army, we've got red tape. Hyatt's request might carry some weight. He was Army."

"He offered to help," Daphne said. "I'll ask him when we're done here."

There was a slight lull as everyone read what they'd captured on the whiteboard so far. Daphne wouldn't let herself stare at the clock on the wall. Her millions of small glances had been enough. It had been only twenty-two minutes. Joseph should be there soon, assuming they drove north to Timonium with sirens blaring. They'd do a silent approach to the house itself, but the sirens would cut most of the travel time.

"Hey, Daphne." The speakerphone crackled as Drew Peterson un-muted his end. "Got George's cell phone. I got lucky. It wasn't encrypted. You want calls or texts?"

Yes. "Both, please. The abduction happened at eleven. Maybe then?"

"How about six p.m. yesterday?" Hector said. "Kim got a text at seven with a large file. We think that was the photo of her kidnapped sister. We want to start before that."

"Here we go," Drew said. "Between six and ten last night George sent ten texts. Nine were to the same number—Marina. All a variant of *How's my little girl?* Marina answers, *She's fine, She's pretty, She's sleeping.* With one she sends a photo of the baby sleeping in a room with yellow walls."

"What was the tenth text?" Daphne asked.

"It went to Bill. That's how he has him labeled in his contact list. 'Bill,' not 'Dad' or 'Father.' Bill sends the first text at nine fifty-five p.m. *Do you have it?* George answers, *D supposed to come at ten thirty.* Bill responds, *If you fuck up, don't come home.* George doesn't respond. From ten till midnight there are eight more texts to Marina, asking about the baby. She responds to four of them, responses pasted from earlier texts."

"Now *I* almost feel sorry for him," Paige commented.

"Not me," Drew said harshly. "At midnight there's a text to Doug. *Waiting for you. Where are you?* There's no reply. He gets a text from Bill at twelve thirty. *Do you have it?*

George responds right away, *D didn't show.* There are three texts at one thirty, one each to Bill, Cindy, and Marina. *Let me in. It's cold.* Nobody answers."

Hector winced. "They locked him out of the house? Bill meant what he said."

"I guess so. Then nothing until four a.m. This is a text from Doug. *Sorry, got tied up. Meet me at nine a.m. Same place.* George asks if they can meet earlier, but Doug doesn't reply. Between nine thirty and nine fifty-seven, George sends six texts. Four are to Doug, asking where he is. Various expletives are used. One is to Cindy saying he's waiting. One is to Bill, same thing. Then at ten oh-one he texts Cindy, *Finally. Got it. On my way.*"

Daphne checked her own cell phone. "I got the text from Ford's phone at ten oh-four."

"George sends a text at ten oh-three. *At Balt n Calv. Running.*"

"He couldn't have sent the text from Ford's phone," Daphne said. "He would have had to run backward. Or he lied to Cindy and he wasn't at Baltimore and Calvert."

"I can check the security cameras around the court-house," Drew said, "to see where he was at ten oh-four. Anything else?"

"Not right now. Thanks, Drew." Daphne hung up, looked at the clock, then closed her eyes, fighting off a new wave of panic. "Joseph should be arriving at Odum's house in Timonium any minute now."

Tuesday, December 3, 6:30 p.m.

"Go!" Bo barked into his radio. "Now!"

In a coordinated wave, three teams busted through the doors of the three houses belonging to Richard Odum. Joseph's team barreled into the Timonium house, along with a SWAT team carrying enough firepower to wipe out a neighborhood. They'd expected resistance, shots fired.

Instead they were met with an oppressive quiet. By previous agreement Joseph and Bo took the top floor and the SWAT guys took the main floor and the basement.

Joseph had just started up the stairs when he heard it — the squall of a newborn baby. He ran upstairs, where there were four closed doors. Joseph grabbed the doorknob to the first door. And froze as his training kicked in. *What if this was a trap?*

He backed away as Bo made it up the last stair, breathing hard. "What is it?"

Joseph pressed his ear to each door. The crying was coming from behind all the doors. "It's the same baby's cry, played on a loop. How long before the bomb dog gets here?" Joseph asked, sniffing at each door.

"A few more minutes. Are you vying for the dog's job?" Bo asked him.

"No. I'm hoping for fresh paint." Through the last door he smelled it. "This is the nursery. George said he just painted it." Joseph pressed his ear against the door and listened. "There's real crying in here, muffled, but I can hear it." He went to the banister and leaned over to where an officer waited at the door. "Evacuate the neighbors in the surrounding houses and tell the handlers to hurry up here when they arrive."

Then he went back to each door, called Ford's name loudly, and listened, trying to block out the recorded baby's cry. The only response was at door number four. The muted crying grew a little louder before quieting altogether.

"Dammit, Bo, that baby's suffocating."

"You don't know that," Bo soothed. "And you're not opening the door until it's safe."

One of the SWAT guys jogged up the stairs. "We've called for both Ford and Kim, but get no response. There's a basement. There could be rooms down there."

"When the bomb guys come," Bo said firmly.

Three excruciating minutes went by, then Joseph heard barking. "Finally."

"Everybody out!" A burly cop came up the stairs with a dog. "I'm Innis. This is Rascal and the guy behind me is Poehler."

Poehler lugged a large trunk. Both cops carried riot shields.

Joseph pointed at door number four. "There's an infant in there, a few days old."

"We'll be careful," Innis promised. "Now get out and let us work."

Joseph and Bo left the house to wait at the curb. Joseph could picture Daphne waiting by the phone and frustration clawed at him. "I can't just stand here," he muttered. "I'm going to interview the neighbors, see if anyone saw anything."

He didn't have to look far. The neighbors who'd gathered when they arrived had been moved two houses down, where they watched from a front lawn. There were six of them, four women and two men, ranging in age from thirty to eighty. A woman in her sixties who looked every inch the corporate executive approached him. Apparently she was this group's representative.

"Hello," Joseph said, showing them his badge. "I'm Special Agent Carter, FBI. I'd like to ask you some questions about this house. Can I have your names, please?"

"I'm Arwen Jacobsen," the executive said, then introduced the others—two teachers, a retired nurse, a bus driver, and a pastor. "We've been hoping somebody would do something about that place, but we were afraid to call."

"Why?"

"We thought a family would move in. Instead, it was a place of business. We're not zoned for business. This is a nice neighborhood."

"It was," the pastor said morosely.

"What kind of business?" Joseph asked.

"We think it was drugs," Arwen said. There were murmurs of assent. "A black van would come two or three times a week, pull into the garage, unload, then leave a few hours later."

"How do you know it was unloading?"

"The van was several inches higher off the ground when it left," Arwen said.

Joseph was impressed. "Not many people would notice that."

"We did because we were looking," the retired nurse said. "Mainly because the people who lived there were suspicious. About a month ago we realized who they really were. That terrible Millhouse family that's been in the news. You know, because the oldest son murdered those two people on the side of the road? At first it was just the mother and the other son. Then that girl, that pregnant girl, moved in."

"She was just a kid," one of the teachers said sadly.

"Old enough to shoot up a crowd at the courthouse today," the other teacher said. "I know it sounds cruel, but I'm happy that cop shot her."

Me, too. "Tell me more about the baby."

"She had it," the retired nurse said, "at home."

Arwen shuddered. "Without a single drug. You could hear her screams through the walls. It was horrible."

"It wasn't that bad," the nurse said, rolling her eyes. "I've heard a lot worse."

"She sounded like she was being skinned alive," Arwen insisted.

"Did anyone attend her?" Joseph asked.

"Mrs. Odum," the first schoolteacher said. "She's a mid-wife."

The nurse gave her a puzzled look. "How do you know that, Bea?"

"I asked. I live right next door," Bea explained to Joseph. "Our upstairs windows are only a few feet apart. The girl *did* sound like she was being skinned alive. I was looking out my window and saw Mrs. Odum come out to smoke on the front porch. I took her a loaf of bread I'd baked and asked her how it was going and if they needed help. She said she'd attended lots of births, that she knew when to call for help. The screams stopped three days ago, around midnight. I waited for Mrs. Odum to leave, but she didn't. I went to work the next day and never knew if it was a boy or a girl."

"Have you seen anyone else go in or out?"

"Mr. Odum," the other teacher said. Her name was Angie. "He came in the black van this afternoon around three. I was coming home from school and drove in behind him. He had someone with him. Another man."

Joseph went still inside. "Had you seen him before?"

"Yes, twice before today." She looked uncomfortable. "I have to tell you because you look interested in this guy, but . . . well, I'm not a pervert or a stalker."

Joseph blinked. "Why would I think that?"

"I teach life science and birds are my passion. I have binoculars for bird watching." She looked at her neighbors. "I've never used them to look in *your* houses."

Joseph felt a sizzle of energy prickle his skin. "But you used them on this house?"

"Yes. I wanted to know what was going on in there. My

nieces and nephews come to visit me here," she said defensively. "I didn't want drug dealers across the street. And what if they were making meth? They'd blow us all sky-high."

"Understandable concern. So what did you see?"

"Mr. Odum and two other men in the basement. They were walking around, pointing at the walls. The next day the window was covered with black paper. I only saw them together that once."

"Who were the two men with Odum?"

"One was the Millhouse father, Bill. The man I saw that one time was shorter. Top of his head came up to the father's shoulder. So maybe five nine? Brown hair, cut short. He was pretty ordinary-looking, to be honest. If I hadn't seen him in Odum's basement, I never would have given him a second look the second time I saw him."

"Second time? When was this?"

"Two weeks ago. I stock shelves at my cousin's drugstore at night on weekends." She shrugged. "Teacher pay cuts. Anyway, the ordinary guy came in. First I thought he'd come for me, because I'd been peeking in the window, but he ignored me. Went straight to the school supply aisle and picked up two packs of Super Glue."

Joseph frowned. "Super Glue? Are you sure?"

"Positive. I waited till he got to checkout and watched from the fem-hygiene aisle. Men never go in that aisle. My cousin was working the register and she asked to see his ID. They card for Super Glue because teens huff it."

Joseph stood straighter. "Would your cousin remember his name?"

"No, because he wouldn't give her his ID. At first he was incredulous. He said, 'I'm twenty-nine years old. Why are you carding me?' My cousin told him that she'd have to card him if he was seventy, that it was store policy. He opened his wallet like he was going for his ID, then said he didn't have it. Made a big deal of how stunned he was to see it missing. He tried to wheedle my cousin, told her the glue was for his kid brother's science project, that they were making model rockets. He had to have it the next day and couldn't he come back with his ID? Carol was firm because she can get in trouble, especially if he's undercover, looking for carding violations."

"What did he do?"

"Left all angry. I wish we'd gotten his name."

Joseph felt like kissing her. He'd been helped by busy-body neighbors before, but never by one who was so well organized about it. "You did very well. Thank you. Would you mind sitting with a police artist? You've seen his face."

"Of course, but I might be able to do one better. Carol has surveillance cameras in the store. Hopefully she still has the tape. Let me go get her information."

She'd turned to go when a blast rattled the windows in the Odum house.

"Get down! Everybody down!" Joseph made sure everyone was okay, then ran back to the house. Ford could be inside. The baby definitely was.

Philadelphia, Pennsylvania
Tuesday, December 3, 6:50 p.m.

"Did you decide where to go first?" Alec asked. "The Mac-Gregors' or Trooper Gargano's house to ask about the stolen Tasers? Because we're almost there."

When Alec called with the results of the traced AFID tags, he'd offered the use of his car to get to Philly—but only if he drove. "You're rattled," the kid had said and Clay knew he was right.

I'm not objective anymore. Having the kid around for perspective might be wise.

Clay scrubbed his palms over his cheeks as he contemplated his choices—Gargano, the trooper who'd been stolen from, or the MacGregors, whose daughter had set Ford up. "I need a shave before I go anywhere."

"A shower wouldn't hurt, either," Alec commented. "And a change of clothes. If you get stopped by a cop, you'll be answering questions about the blood on your pants."

His pants were black, so the patches of Stevie's dried blood didn't show that much. "I'm less worried about that than the fact that I'm still wearing J.D.'s T-shirt." With BPD in huge letters. "Never a good idea to talk to a cop when you're impersonating one."

"Turn the shirt inside out. If you keep your jacket on, nobody'll see the seams."

"That's not a bad idea," Clay muttered.

"Works like a charm for me. Especially the day before laundry day."

Clay shot the kid a disgusted look. "You're so lazy that you'd walk around with your shirt inside out rather than do a load of laundry?"

"Oh, like you were Martha Stewart when you were my age."

"When I was your age I was in boot camp," he said sourly. "My uniforms were spotless. The pleats in my shorts were sharper than a Ginsu knife."

"What's a Ginsu knife?"

Clay rolled his eyes. "Forget it."

Alec chuckled. "I know what a Ginsu is. I'm just yanking your chain. The inside-out trick works best when I've run out of clean clothes and the only ones that don't smell like ass have a ketchup stain. You know. In an emergency."

"And you wonder why you don't have a girlfriend."

Alec scowled at that. "I could throw plenty of rocks at your glass house, Mr. Casanova. Oh, wait, you're dateless, too."

"I'm beginning to wish I'd brought Alyssa with me."

"I'm that bad?" Alec asked, amusement back in his voice. "Okay, okay, I'm sorry for the dateless comment."

Clay shifted, looking out the window. "Nah, it was fair. It's true anyway."

Alec sobered. "How was she? Detective Mazzetti?"

Clay had asked her parents for a few minutes alone with her after they'd finished talking in the ICU waiting area. He knew her parents hadn't believed his claim that he and Stevie were just friends. They'd even seemed pleased by the notion that there was something between them. Clay had felt a twinge of hope . . . until he'd seen her.

"She's still unconscious." And so fragile. He'd never seen Stevie fragile before. He'd seen her angry and he'd seen her terrified. He'd even seen her cry, nine months ago. She'd just been confronted by the betrayal of one of her oldest friends and her heart was breaking. She'd wanted him to hold her, to walk into his arms. But Stevie didn't let herself have what she wanted.

I should have held her anyway. But he'd given her space, hoping she'd come to him on her own. But as the months passed, it became clear that wasn't going to happen.

Stevie was Cordelia's mom first. Then a cop. Being a

woman came dead last, which meant her interest in Clay came last, too. He knew it, understood it. Didn't like it worth shit. It sure didn't change how he saw her—strong, confident, smart. *One hell of a beautiful woman, one I've wanted from the moment I saw her.*

But today, she'd been fragile.

"She's going to be okay, right?" Alec asked.

"The doctors told her parents she has a good chance." But Clay didn't believe it. He'd seen more war wounds than he cared to remember. Men at death's door had more color in their faces than she had. She'd lost so much blood.

He'd almost been too afraid to touch her, lying in that hospital bed, so pale. But he'd been more afraid he wouldn't get another chance. So he'd touched her face, cupped her cheek. Kissed her forehead. Then her lips.

And then he'd pasted a smile on his face, gone back out to the waiting room, and lied to her parents. Told them he believed she'd pull through.

"I'm sorry," Alec whispered.

Maybe Alec hadn't heard him. "I said the doctors were optimistic."

"But you don't believe it. And you care for her." Alec glanced at him sadly. "I may be horrible at talking to girls, but I'm good at reading people. You should turn your shirt inside out now. We're almost at Trooper Gargano's house. You seemed preoccupied, so I picked for you. If you want to stop and buy a razor, this is the time to say so."

Not trusting himself to speak, Clay shrugged out of his leather jacket, pulled the shirt over his head, then put it back on, surreptitiously wiping his eyes as he did so. He figured if nobody noticed the shirt seams under his jacket, they weren't likely to notice the damp spots on his sleeve, either.

"I just want to get this over with," Clay said, then focused on talking to Trooper Gargano, the man whose stolen property was at the core of one very bad day.

Baltimore, Maryland
Tuesday, December 3, 6:50 p.m.

Joseph skidded to a stop at the front door of Richard Odum's house. Bo had gotten there first and had stuck his head through the doorway, looking up.

"Report!" Bo shouted.

"We're fine." Innis appeared at the top of the stairs. "You can come up now. I want you to see what would have happened to you if you'd opened the nursery door."

Joseph followed Bo up the stairs, then did a double take. *"Holy fuck."* The wall directly across from the nursery door now had a hole the size of a toaster oven.

"It was rigged with a shotgun," Innis said. "Basic setup. String ran from the doorknob up through a hook in the ceiling and down to the trigger. Shotgun was pointed straight at the door. You would have taken a gutful if you'd run in there."

"I can see that," Joseph said. "What about the baby?"

Innis's partner, Poehler, appeared, carrying a small bundle wrapped in a pink blanket. "She seems okay. They'd wrapped a blanket around the crib."

"To muffle the sound of her crying," Bo said.

"And maybe to protect her from plaster if the ceiling got shot out." Poehler handed the baby to Joseph. "Here you go." He grinned. "Her diaper needs to be changed."

"That's okay. I've done it before." Joseph looked down into the baby's face. She was so small. And very pretty. "You really do forget how small they are."

"You have kids, Agent Carter?" Innis asked, surprised.

"No." Which left him feeling . . . sad. "But we all pitched in to help with my youngest sister." He looked up at Innis. "What about the other doors and the basement?"

"Rascal here didn't detect any explosives on this level." Innis scratched the Belgian Malinois behind his ears. "We'll open these other doors using the riot shields to absorb any shots. Then we'll start Rascal on the basement. It's just going to take a while."

"I've instructed the other crews as to what you've found," Bo said. "When you're done here with Rascal, I've got the next addresses for you."

"Gonna be a long night," Poehler said dismally. "And I had a date."

I wish that's all I had to lose. Joseph thought of Daphne, waiting by the phone. *I don't have your son.* "I have to call Daphne and let her know where we are."

"Tell her we'll look under every rock," Bo said, but there was no hope on his face.

When Joseph went outside, he frowned. Dr. Brodie had

arrived in a CSU van, but so had the media and now TV vans lined the street. The officers who accompanied them had set a crime scene perimeter, but it wasn't nearly far enough away. Having spotted the bundle in his arms, reporters crowded the crime scene tape.

"How did they know?" Joseph asked coldly.

Bo scowled from the doorway. "How do they ever know? One of the neighbors might have called or they might have even followed us up here."

"Hell." Joseph turned his back to them to keep them from photographing the baby as Dr. Brodie trudged up the walk, her hands filled with her toolboxes.

"Who have we here?" she asked.

"Melinda," Joseph said, tilting the baby away from his body enough to show her.

Brodie set her cases on the ground and reached, then grinned when Joseph reflexively backed away, cradling the baby closer to the warmth of his body. "So what are you going to do with her?"

Joseph looked down at the baby with a sigh. "Call a social worker, I guess."

"It's awful cold out here," Bo said. "But she can't stay in the house. Just in case they find another booby trap."

"One of the neighbors is a retired nurse." Joseph called over an officer, carefully transferred the infant to his arms, and pointed out the nurse, who still stood on the lawn.

When she saw Joseph point her out, the nurse ran over, taking off her own coat as she approached. "A little girl, Agent Carter?" she asked.

"Her name is Melinda. Would you mind if this officer keeps the baby in your house until the social worker gets here?"

"Of course not." She wrapped the baby in her coat. "Come with me, Officer."

He turned back to Brodie and Bo. "We may have a lead." He told them about the science teacher, the Super Glue, and the drugstore surveillance video.

Bo's face lit up. "So Doug is real. Very nicely done."

"We could have his face in less than an hour," Brodie said. "I'll get started on it."

"Thanks." Joseph didn't smile. He had to call Daphne. He'd put it off long enough.

"Agent Carter, Agent Lamar . . ." Innis called from the doorway. His face was grim. "You need to see this. You, too, Dr. Brodie. You'll need your equipment."

Dread washed over Joseph. He followed Innis once again, this time down the stairs and into a basement room. "This is the room the next-door neighbor saw them in a few weeks ago," Joseph said. "The window is covered with black paper, just like she said."

He turned and saw the wall behind him, his arm dropping to his side, his stomach dropping to his knees. "Oh my God," he whispered. "Oh my God."

The seconds ticked as they stared at the wall, at the words that had been painted there with a wide brush. In blood.

Joseph read them aloud, his voice thick and hoarse. They were familiar. He'd heard them quoted recently, by Daphne. "'Now you know how it feels.'"

So much blood. It was pooled on the floor, already congealing. A wide streak ran to the door that led to the garage, like someone had been dragged through the blood.

A pile of clothing had been left in the pooled blood on the floor. Joseph crouched beside it, dreading what he'd find. Brodie snapped photos, handing him a metal rod, which he used to lift each item so that she could photograph them one by one.

On top was a striped rugby shirt that had absorbed the blood unevenly. The bottom was soaked, consistent with how it had folded on itself in the pile. The collar was saturated, still glossy and wet even though it hadn't touched the pool of blood. Still untouched by the blood was the name of Ford's university, stitched across the back.

"Oh God," he whispered, his stomach turning over. He thought of Isaac Zacharias, lying in that alley, his throat slit wide-open. Unlike the alley, the wall in front of them was covered in spatter. "His throat must have been slit. And he was alive at the time."

Brodie cleared her throat roughly. "It appears so. It also appears he put up a fight." She pointed to the collar, where dozens of short blond hairs lay at haphazard angles.

"His hair was yanked out during the struggle," she said, then removed a wallet from the back pocket of the jeans that were next in the pile. When she opened it, Ford's face stared out at them from his driver's license.

Any hope Joseph still clung to disappeared like mist.

Brodie dropped the wallet into an evidence bag and, using a pair of tongs, lifted the jeans. At the bottom of the pile, covered in blood, was a gold watch. Carefully she picked it up, held it to the light. "It's a Rolex. The back says 'Elkhart.'"

Joseph choked back the bile that had risen to burn his throat.

We're too late.

Eleven

Pennsylvania State Trooper Jim Gargano lived in a two-story house at the end of a dead-end road. Lights were on in the living room and two upstairs bedrooms.

"This is it," Clay said.

Alec stopped the car at the curb. "No trooper car in the driveway."

"Trooper Gargano was banned from using a take-home car again," Clay said. He reread the e-mail Alyssa had sent on the investigation. "He reported the theft of his weapons as soon as he discovered they were missing. The department found him in violation of policy. He insisted he'd locked his gun safe, but the department could find no reason that the safe would have malfunctioned."

"So he was screwed."

"Basically. The thief took the Tasers, his service weapon, and a bunch of antiques, then found the keys to the cruiser and drove off in it with everything he'd stolen plus Gargano's uniforms and the SWAT uniforms that were in the trunk of the car. He filed a claim with his insurance and got a settlement, which the department found suspicious. They never actually accused him of insurance fraud, but that's how they treated it. He was suspended for two weeks without pay, took a permanent pay cut, lost his rank."

"That sucks," Alec said, frowning. "I'd have quit."

"He probably wanted to, but he's only a year away from retirement and he wants his pension." He closed the e-mail and checked his texts.

"Anything new from Paige?" Alec asked.

"Nothing on the house raids yet." Paige had been texting him with the updates she'd learned from Joseph Carter. Now Clay knew that the knife used to slit Tuzak's throat was the same knife Reggie had used on the courtroom deputy. He knew to look for a guy named Doug who'd sold the knife to George. And finally, he knew to pray because by now Carter and a SWAT team should be converging on a house in Timonium where Ford's abductor might be hiding him. "You coming with me?"

Alec's eyes widened. "Me? I thought I was just the driver."

"I changed my mind," Clay said. The kid noticed things that other people didn't. "Get your gear and follow me. And close your mouth before the birds fly in."

Clay's knock was answered by Gargano. Who immediately slammed the door.

"That went well," Alec murmured.

Clay knocked again. And a third time. The door opened again, but this time Trooper Gargano was armed. In one hand he held a Glock nine millimeter, his finger on the trigger. In the other hand he held a cordless phone, his finger poised over the keypad. "Go the fuck away."

"I'm not a cop," Clay said. "And I'm not selling anything."

Gargano's eyes were cold. "Then you're a reporter and I hate them even more."

"I'm not a reporter," Clay shouted as the door was slammed again. "Dammit."

Alec pulled out his cell phone, did a quick search, punched in a few buttons. Then he connected the phone to his cochlear implant with a special cord and waited.

"Got the answering machine," he said to Clay. A few seconds later he said, "Hello, sir. I'm standing on your doorstep. We have a dead friend with two of your X2 cartridges in him. If this is one of those seriously old-fashioned answering machines and you can hear me, please pick up. If it's voice mail, I hope you listen in the next few minutes—"

The door opened. Gargano was still armed, but most of his anger was gone. "Who the hell are you people?"

"My name is Clay Maynard. I'm a PI. This is my associate, Alec Vaughn. We're from Baltimore."

"I figured as much. You're really late. The other guy left two hours ago."

"Would you mind telling me who was here two hours ago?"

"Yes, I mind. You said your dead friend has my cartridges in him. How?"

"That's what we're trying to find out. I run a security firm. The victim was one of my contract employees, an off-duty cop doing after-hours bodyguard work." Clay gauged the man's reaction and decided he needed to lay it on a little thicker. "He was trying to make a little extra for his fourth kid that's due any day."

Gargano looked suspicious. "Quite a story."

"It's true. You've heard about the shooting spree at the Baltimore courthouse?"

There was a flicker in Gargano's eyes. "You were there?"

"Yes. I got there just as the shooting started."

"Why were you there?"

"I've given you some information. I want a little from you."

"Why should I?"

"Because two of your cartridges ended up in my dead friend."

He and Gargano locked stares. Finally Gargano blinked. "It was a Fed."

Clay sighed. "White hair, creepy eyes?"

Gargano grimaced. "Hell, yeah. What's with him, anyway?"

"Personally, I have no idea. Professionally, we have the same objective. Two kidnapped college kids. We want them back. Before they're dead, too."

Gargano looked upward and Clay guessed one of the upstairs lights belonged to his own kid. "What do you want to know?"

Beside him Alec's teeth were chattering. "It's freezing cold. Can we come in?"

"Are you carrying?"

"Yes. He's not, though." Clay looked at Alec doubtfully. "Tell me you're not."

"Okay, I'm not," Alec said. "Really, I'm not."

"Let me see your ID," Gargano said, then nodded when

Clay showed it to him. "Keep your hands where I can see them. I don't trust anybody anymore."

"I can understand that." Clay sat down on a well-worn sofa and put his hands on his thighs. Alec sat beside him, looking around the room, openly curious.

I'm going to have to teach the kid a little subtlety.

"All right," Clay said once Gargano had sat down. "I think the question of the day is how your Taser cartridges ended up in an alley in Baltimore. The cop's name was Isaac Zacharias. He was providing security for a young man named Ford Elkhart. Ford was last seen in Baltimore, walking his girlfriend to her car after a movie. They cut through an alley and the abductor was waiting. He didn't know about Zacharias, though."

"Zacharias was tased?"

"And then drugged. His killer slit his throat with a non-metal blade."

"The blade's not mine, I can tell you that for certain. I don't keep blades."

"Then do you know anybody named Doug?"

"No." There wasn't even a flicker of recognition in Gargano's eyes.

"Kimberly?"

"No." But he frowned. "The Fed asked me about Kimberly, but not Doug."

"He might not have known about Doug yet. He'll be back. What did you tell him?"

"Nothing more than he could have read in the police report. Because there isn't anything else," Gargano said, frustration making his tone harsh.

"There has to be," Clay said. "We just haven't found it yet. Did Novak tell you why he'd asked about Kimberly?"

"Just that she'd been kidnapped with the Elkhart boy."

"She has a record for theft. She stole a diamond ring from a home she was cleaning."

"Novak did ask me if we had a cleaning service. I laughed at him. We're barely surviving now, putting one daughter through college and saving for the younger one."

"And then they cut your pay," Clay said and watched Gargano's eyes flash fury.

"Yeah, well, they're all sonsofbitches," he said bitterly. "I was a damn good cop. Nineteen years without a single blemish on my record. And they turned on me."

"Daddy?" The alarmed little voice came from upstairs. "Are you all right?"

Gargano hid his gun between the chair cushions before looking over his shoulder with a smile. "Go back to your room, MeiMei," he said gently, lovingly. "Daddy's fine."

Clay's ears perked up. MeiMei? It was a Chinese endearment meaning "little sister."

"Who are those men?" she pressed, coming down a few more steps. She was about nine years old and had black hair. She was Chinese.

Quickly Clay scanned the room for a family photo, but saw none. Was Mrs. Gargano Asian or was the little girl adopted? Gargano had just said he was putting a daughter through college. Was she adopted, too? Like Kimberly MacGregor?

Beside him, Alec sat up straighter. He'd made the connection, too. *Smart kid.*

"They're just visiting, honey. Go back upstairs and finish your homework. Mom will be home from work soon and she'll want to see it done." The little girl did as she was told and Gargano's gun hand reappeared. He still had his finger on the trigger.

Clay barely noticed. His mind was spinning. "You called your daughter MeiMei."

"Yes. So?"

"She's Chinese. Adopted, yes?"

"Yes. We adopted her when she was six months old." His eyes narrowed. "Why?"

"Your older daughter," Clay pressed. "The one in college. Is she also Chinese?"

Gargano's face darkened. "What the hell is this?" He stood up. "You need to leave."

"I'm sorry. Wait." Clay lifted his hands, palm out. "Kimberly MacGregor is also Chinese, adopted by her family. Aren't there groups for families who adopt from specific parts of the world? Is it possible your daughter met Kimberly at a local function?"

This made Gargano even angrier. "Are you saying my daughter stole from me?"

"No, not at all. But what if she knew Kimberly, trusted her, invited her in, unwittingly gave her access? We know Kimberly stole once. Maybe she stole from you, too."

Gargano's expression changed from fury to stunned disbelief. "I don't know."

"Can we talk to her, your older daughter? Please, this is important."

"Yes, of course. She's lives in the dorm."

"In Baltimore?" Clay asked.

"No, why?"

"That's where Kimberly goes to school."

"My daughter didn't go away to school. She's here, in the city, but living on campus. She's a freshman at Drexel in Philly. She doesn't have a car, so we'll have to go to her. If we can make this connection stick, I can appeal my demotion."

"*After* I find my missing college kids."

"Of course. I'm sorry." Gargano holstered the gun and ran to the staircase. "Jessica, we need to leave the house, baby. Get your coat and bring some homework."

"Clay," Alec said urgently, "look."

Pushing himself to his feet, Clay looked over his shoulder and blinked. Alec had grabbed a chair from the dining room table and was standing on it, peering between the vent blades of the heating duct on the ceiling. "What the *hell*, Alec?"

"Good God!" Gargano shouted. "Were you raised in a barn? Get down! Now!"

"In a minute," Alec said, pulling a penknife from his pocket. "This'll be worth it."

"You said he wasn't armed," Gargano said accusingly.

"It's just a screwdriver set." Alec held it out for Gargano to see. "Was your gun safe against that wall?" he asked, pointing to a large built-in bookcase. A large rectangular area was empty, shelves having been built around it.

"It was. I got rid of it after the theft. Why?"

Alec unscrewed the vent cover and grinned. "Right there in the duct. A camera."

"In my heating duct? Why the hell would a thief leave a camera in my duct?"

"To watch you dialing your safe's combo," Alec said. "I've heard of this before, but usually when the safe contains high-value goods, like trade secrets or diamonds. Whoever did this went to some trouble. They knew you'd have something they wanted."

"But why me?" Gargano asked, bewildered.

"We'll ask Kimberly—if we find her," Clay said. "For now, this explains a lot."

"It does," Gargano said, new hope in his eyes. Footsteps clattered down the stairs and Gargano met his daughter with a huge smile, swinging her in a circle that had her squealing with delight. "Let's go for a ride, MeiMei. We need to talk to your sister."

Baltimore, Maryland
Tuesday, December 3, 7:30 p.m.

The conference room was silent except for the sound of Daphne's boots as she paced. Paige was out in the hallway, doing a kata, one of the ways she relaxed.

Daphne stopped pacing long enough to watch her. It was a little like ballet, Daphne thought, lithe and fluid. Powerful.

And then Daphne saw Grayson at the other end of the hall. He was watching Paige, his expression intense. Paige saw him watching and came out of a spinning kick, landing gracefully in front of him and walking straight into his arms.

Daphne turned away, her throat suddenly too tight to breathe. *I want that. I want someone to look at me like I'm everything. That can't be too much to ask. Can it?*

She closed the door to the conference room and walked to the window. Resting her forehead against the cold glass, she tried not to fall apart. But the walls she'd built in her mind had broken down and all she could think about was Ford.

Where are you? Are you still alive? Are they hurting you? Please don't be hurting. She opened her eyes to stare at the snow that had started to fall. *Please don't be cold.*

The door opened and Grayson and Paige came in together. In the glass Daphne could see that neither of them smiled. Her blood suddenly colder than the glass, Daphne turned to look at them. She opened her mouth, but no words emerged.

The floor began to shake. Someone was running. The shaking slowed and Grayson moved away from the door. Joseph was walking toward her. His eyes were bleak.

Hector and Coppola were leaving, Grayson motioning

them out. Daphne took a step back and hit the window, the cold a jolt to her body. "No."

This isn't happening. Wake up, dammit. Wake up, because this isn't real.

"Daphne." Joseph's voice was rough. *Real.*

Unable to run, she stared up into his face as he walked to her and took her into his arms. "No," she whispered.

"We found a crime scene at Odum's house. We found Ford's watch. Some of his other personal effects." He drew a breath. "He could still be alive. But we found blood. A lot of it. We have to face the fact that he could be . . . in trouble."

She wanted to look away. Run away. Cover her ears and not hear. But her body wouldn't move. Trapped, she stared up at Joseph. "Where is he? Where is my son?"

"I don't know. We didn't find . . ." He hesitated, swallowed hard. "A body."

Daphne jerked out of his arms and ran for the washroom.

Philadelphia, Pennsylvania
Tuesday, December 3, 7:55 p.m.

"Daddy?" Laurel Gargano jumped up from the coffee shop table where she'd been sitting when Trooper Gargano rushed in, Jessica's hand tight in his. Clay was right behind him. Alec was looking for a spot to park his car, Gargano having slid his aging Toyota into the last parking place on the street.

Laurel's face was tight with fear. "What's wrong? Is it Mom?"

"No," Gargano said. "Your mother's fine. I just needed to talk to you."

Laurel pressed her hand to her heart. "You scared me. Your text said that it was urgent." She shot her father an indignant look. "Who is this man?"

Gargano took her arm. "He's a PI from Baltimore. He has a few questions for you. It's important, honey. Really important. He might be able to help us."

"Okay, Daddy," she said, still wary. She let her father lead her back to the table, glancing sideways at Clay. "What's this about?" she asked when they were seated.

"Do you know a girl named Kimberly MacGregor?" her father asked.

"Yes. I know her from Chinese school. You know her, too, Dad. Her father's the veterinarian. You met him at one of the picnics for the adoptive families." When her father still didn't remember, she crunched her eyebrows, thinking. "Oh, I know. Her dad is the one you lost the bet to, the one I wasn't supposed to tell Mom about."

"Which bet was this?" Clay asked.

"I have no idea," Gargano said.

"You bet him that the Lightning would never take home the Cup."

Gargano frowned. "What?"

She sighed patiently. "You were mad that they scheduled the annual social during game seven of the Stanley Cup, but when we got to the MacGregors' house all the dads were in the TV room watching the game, and you let me come in and watch with you. You bet Kimberly's father a hundred bucks that Tampa wouldn't take it."

"Honey, that was in *2004.* You could have come up with something more recent."

She shrugged. "We stopped going to the socials after you made SWAT in 2004."

He looked away. "I'm sorry about that, baby."

"That's okay." She patted his hand. "I didn't like them anyway. I went for Mom."

He kissed her forehead, then looked at Clay. "That family is wealthy. Nice house, nice part of town. He had one heck of a man cave—three different beers on tap."

"Which was why you bet him the hundred to start with," Laurel said affectionately. "And why I wasn't allowed to tell Mom." Her brows crunched again, this time in concern. "Is this about Kim's sister, Pamela? The one who went missing last night?"

"Possibly," Clay said. "There's been an AMBER Alert since last night."

"I didn't know. I wasn't on duty today." Gargano turned his attention back to Laurel. "Was Kimberly ever in our house?"

"Yes," Laurel said, her wariness returning. "Why?"

"When, Laurel?" Clay asked quietly.

"Last winter, before Christmas. It was a sleepover for my birthday. My mom invited all the girls from the Chinese school. I was a little surprised Kim came. She and I were never really close and she's two years older than I am. She was home from college for the break. I figured she'd have better things to do than have a party with kids. Why?"

"Where was the sleepover?" Clay asked.

"In the basement. We have a rec room downstairs," Laurel explained.

"Did you notice if Kimberly left the party at any time that night?"

"I don't remember, but she could have. There were ten girls and only one bathroom downstairs." Laurel looked at her father. "Daddy? What's going on here?"

"It's possible that Kimberly could have been involved in the burglary," Gargano said. "Mr. Maynard's associate found a camera in the ceiling vent. Whoever put it there may have been watching me dial the safe's combination."

Laurel was shaking her head. "Kimberly wouldn't do that."

"She's been caught for stealing before," Clay said gently. "In Maryland."

"Why would she steal?" Gargano asked. "Her father is loaded."

Laurel shook her head. "Not anymore. Her father's practice got hurt in the recession. She used to drive a BMW, but I heard her parents sold it. When she came to the party she got dropped off by her boyfriend."

Clay had to remind himself to breathe. "Did you see him?"

"No. I don't even remember what he drove. I'm sorry."

"Don't be," Clay assured her. "You're doing great. I'm asking all these questions because the Tasers taken from your dad were used to kidnap a young man about your age. Kimberly's new boyfriend. We're trying to bring him home."

A tap on his arm had him looking down. Gargano's younger daughter looked up at him with intelligent eyes. "Do you have a picture of her?" Jessica asked.

"I do." Clay checked his cell phone and found the photo of Kimberly that had come up with her background check. As he was about to show Jessica the picture, his phone rang, the caller ID sending the photo to the background. It was Paige. He'd call her back in a second. He hit DECLINE, then showed the photo to the little girl. "Do you remember her?"

Jessica took his phone and stared. Then nodded. "I'd

gone downstairs to get some cake before the girls ate it all. She was standing in front of the bookshelves, talking on her cell phone and smiling like she was getting her picture taken. Looking up, you know? Like when you take a picture of yourself." She frowned. "But she was talking on the phone. So how could she be taking her own picture at the same time?"

"What happened next, honey?" Gargano asked.

"Nothing. When she saw me, she hung up fast and went back to the party." Her lower lip trembled, her eyes filling with tears as she returned Clay's phone. "I'm sorry, Daddy. If I'd remembered before, the police wouldn't have been so terrible to you."

Gargano lifted the child to his lap. "It's all right, MeiMei. None of this is your fault." He kissed the top of her head. "You remembered now and that's the important thing."

"Absolutely," Clay said. "Laurel, what day was your party?"

She checked the calendar on her phone, scrolling back a year. "December 20."

"Great. And Jessica, what—" His phone buzzed. It was Paige again. *There must be news.* Carter should have been at the Timonium house already. *Please. Please let it be good news.* "I need to take this," he said to Gargano, then answered. "Paige?"

"Don't you dare decline my calls again," she stormed. She was crying. *Oh no.*

Dread settled on his shoulders. "What's wrong?"

"Joseph's here. Oh, God, Clay." She was sobbing so hard her words slurred.

"Slow down. I can't understand you." But he did understand. He just couldn't accept. *I was too late.*

He heard Grayson's voice, faintly. "Give me the phone, baby." A long pause. "It's Grayson. Joseph found a crime scene. No body, but lots of blood and signs that a body had been dragged to the garage. There was a message to Daphne on the wall, written in blood." His voice broke and he cleared his throat. "'Now you know how it feels.'"

The air left Clay's lungs. "We were too late," he said numbly.

"Joseph's in with Daphne now. Where are you?"

"Philadelphia. With Trooper Gargano." Clay exhaled,

trying to think. "I found the link between Kim and the weapons taken from Gargano. Check her cell records for the night of December 20." He looked at Jessica. "What time did you see her, honey?"

"After midnight. Maybe one or two?"

"Look at her calls made between midnight and three. There's a camera in Trooper Gargano's ductwork. Maybe it can be traced to this Doug guy you're looking for."

"Okay. I'll check those records now. Thanks."

His throat was so tight he couldn't breathe. "Is Daphne . . . ? Forget it. Of course she's not all right. Tell her . . . I don't know what to tell her."

"This isn't your fault, Clay," Grayson said soberly. "Novak's up there somewhere. Where can I have him meet you, so he can check out the camera?"

"I'm at a coffee shop." Clay gave him the address. "I'll wait here for him. Then I'll get home as fast as I can." He hung up and closed his eyes, fighting the tears that burned his throat. Another little tap on his arm had him looking at Jessica again.

"I'm sorry," she whispered, her little face pinched with sorrow.

"Thanks, honey. I appreciate it."

Gargano sighed wearily. "Should I go home and wait for the creepy Fed?"

"That's probably best."

Baltimore, Maryland
Tuesday, December 3, 7:55 p.m.

She hadn't cried. Not a single tear. Joseph sat on the floor of the washroom, Daphne curled up on his lap. She clutched his shirt in a white-knuckled grip, the strength of her hands the only indication she wasn't asleep.

He stroked her back, saying nothing. What could he say? They'd been too late. All he could do was watch helplessly as she knelt in front of the toilet, rubbing her back as her body convulsed. Then he'd washed her face and pulled her into his arms.

He rested his cheek on the top of her head and exhaled, bone-weary. A noise had him looking up. Paige and Grayson stood in the doorway. Paige's eyes were swollen and red. She'd cried, a lot. She knelt and put her arms around Daphne.

"He could still be alive," Paige whispered fiercely.

But even though Joseph had said that himself, he didn't believe it was true. If Ford had been alive when he was dragged from that basement, he hadn't lasted long. Not with all the blood they'd found in that basement room.

So much blood. He'd been on autopilot, helping Brodie with the scene. Not even realizing that he himself had grown pale as they'd examined each piece of clothing.

When he'd stood, he'd actually stumbled, nearly falling into the pool of the boy's blood. He'd quickly recovered, blaming his light-headedness on not having eaten all day, but Brodie wasn't fooled. She'd sent him out of the house to get some air.

Joseph clenched his jaw, thinking about the moment he'd exited the Timonium house. The reporters had nearly come over the crime scene tape again, their instinct—and his own pallor—telling them something had happened. They started shouting questions. Then one of them took a gamble and shouted the right one.

Does SA Montgomery know her son is dead?

It had taken Joseph a few seconds to realize the reporter was baiting him, but a few seconds was all the vipers had needed. They rushed to get in front of their cameras so they could be the first to break the "development."

And short of killing each one of them, there wasn't a damn thing Joseph could do to stop them. But he could make sure Daphne didn't hear it on the news.

Commandeering a squad car, he'd driven back to the city like a bat out of hell, his siren screaming, his only thought that he couldn't let her find out that way. She deserved better than that.

He'd called Grayson on his way, warning him to keep Daphne off the computer, away from the TV, the phone, and anyone outside their team who might tell her before he got to her. But now she knew and Joseph didn't have a clue as to what to do next.

"My mother," Daphne said quietly. "Does my mother know?"

"Grayson and I were going to tell her for you," Paige said.

"Thank you, but no." Daphne released Joseph's shirt and pushed away from his chest, turning to face her friend. "Mama needs to hear it from me. But if you could go with me, I'd appreciate it. I'll meet you outside. Give Joseph and me a minute."

When they were alone, Daphne rose, then extended her hand, urging him to his feet. "We have things to do. I have to tell my mother. You still have to find that baby."

"I found her," he said. "She was a little dehydrated, but otherwise fine. She's with social services now."

"Good. I'm glad." She walked out of the washroom and pointed to a whiteboard, filled with notes. "We made a list of everything we knew about Doug."

He read Coppola's notes. "This is good stuff. It'll help."

"Good." She dropped her chin to her chest. "Thank you, Joseph. For everything you've done for me today. I don't know what I would have done without you."

"I wish everything had turned out differently," he said. "If it helps at all, I do know how you feel. A little, anyway. When it's your child . . . I know it's different."

"Who was she? The person you lost?"

"My wife."

Daphne lifted her head slowly, stunned. "You were married?"

"For a few days. A long time ago."

Her eyes flickered. "You were on your honeymoon?"

"Yes."

"Did you catch who did it?"

"Yes."

"Are they still alive?"

He shook his head slowly. "No," he said coldly.

Her lips trembled and she sternly firmed them. "Good. Now I have to . . . I have to go." But she didn't move. She just stood where she was, lost. "Joseph."

He put his arms around her again. "I'm here."

She slid her arms around his waist, the second hand on the wall clock ticking away as she held on tight, her cheek pressed against his chest. They were standing that way when there was a light rap on the door and it opened a crack.

"Agent Carter, it's Fiona Brodie. I need to talk to you both."

"Now?" Joseph asked.

"Yes. *Now.*" Brodie opened the door. "This will make a difference."

Joseph felt Daphne swallow. "Okay." She released him, then grabbed her bag from underneath one of the chairs. "I need a minute." She disappeared into the bathroom and closed the door. Seconds later, water was running.

Brodie took the chair next to the one Daphne had been sitting in. And said nothing.

"What the hell's this about?" he asked.

The look she gave him was one of reproach. "When you called me from the squad car, I told you I wasn't ready for her to be told. You said you'd wait to tell her until I called you, but you didn't. Now I'm here to talk to Daphne."

"When I got here, there were fifteen reporters camped around the front door."

"That didn't give you the right to—"

"Fiona." He rarely used her first name and she quieted. "I had to throw two reporters out of the elevator. They'd signed in with the desk downstairs, claiming they were going to a different floor, intending to come here all the time. One told the other that their producer wanted her face when she learned the news. That they'd top the ratings. I couldn't wait for your go-ahead."

She sighed. "I get it. You didn't want her to find out the wrong way. But—"

The water shut off and Daphne emerged, holding her hiking boots by the laces. She'd changed her heavy sweater for one of lighter weight and now wore sensible loafers. *No need to be dressed for an outdoor search now.* She'd applied lipstick. Her version of body armor, he suspected.

She sank into her chair, smelling faintly of toothpaste and peaches, the latter from her hand lotion. He knew this because he'd smelled peaches on his own hand after holding hers in the observation room earlier that afternoon.

She squared her shoulders. "All right, Dr. Brodie. I'm listening."

Hunt Valley, Maryland
Tuesday, December 3, 8:00 p.m.

Mitch took a step back, frowning at his handiwork in the glow of his flashlight. He'd done better work in Odum's basement, but it was harder to line up the letters out here in the dark. He wondered how the message would appear in the light of day, if the human blood would dry a different color than animal blood.

It wasn't the message he'd really wanted to paint. That would come after Ford got himself fucking found.

Did you miss me?

So far, Ford was still missing. What was wrong with that boy? He should have arrived in the nearest town by now. But there had been no reports on any of the police radio channels within a fifty-mile radius of Wilson Beckett's cabin.

He'd known there was a chance he'd have to go back and help the kid, but he'd really thought that Ford could handle a measly twenty-mile trek. He turned off his flashlight and stored his materials in the van.

He hoped the roads were clear through the mountains. He needed to be home by midmorning. *Thank you so much, Cole.* Mitch had woken from his nap to a message from Cole's guidance counselor, who wanted to discuss his brother's behavior issues with his "guardian," Betty Douglas.

Mitch hoped the counselor continued to buy his story that Betty was housebound, that the cold weather was a risk to her health. Otherwise he'd have to hire another old woman to play Betty. He'd had to do so in Florida because he'd been on parole and hadn't wanted the cops knowing he'd left Maryland without their permission.

He'd had to do it again when they'd first returned to Baltimore, because Betty had died. Mitch had wanted to stay under the radar then, so he'd buried her quietly in the back garden, notifying no one. He'd read Betty's will. It was enough to know the house belonged to him. He didn't need—or want—his name listed as the new owner of the house. And, of course, he didn't mind the Social Security checks that continued to be deposited in her bank account month after month. It wasn't a lot of money, but it kept the cupboards full. Because Cole ate like a horse. Mitch scowled. When the boy wasn't getting into trouble at school.

If possible, Mitch wanted to be back here at Daphne's farm by dawn. Just to see the reaction of whoever found his barn art. He wished it could be Daphne herself, but the Feds had her locked down. They wouldn't let her come all the way out here.

But that was okay. All this—the barn, the basement—it was all warm-up. Just the windup before the pitch. The tease before the huge roller-coaster dip. Is Ford alive? Is he dead? Is he alive? Soon enough she'd find out her son wasn't dead after all, but then Ford would say the magic words and Daphne's world would turn upside down.

Did you miss me?

Those four little words were the key to unlocking Daphne Montgomery's personal nightmare. *And to think . . . Had I not gone to prison, I would have never known about them.*

Mitch had his stepfather to thank for the whole prison experience, but he supposed he also owed some thanks to his old cellmate, Crazy Earl. Earl was convinced that the warden had hidden cameras in the ductwork so that he could spy on the inmates.

Mitch had tried for weeks to convince Earl that the warden didn't *need* to hide cameras in the vents—there were cameras in plain view on nearly every freaking corner of the cellblock. But Crazy Earl was not to be dissuaded because he was crazy.

Later, when the good people of the state prison board had enrolled Mitch in HVAC training, he remembered Crazy Earl and wondered if it could be done. At first his thoughts were purely prurient. After months of forced celibacy he wanted to catch a little T&A action. But then he realized that he was thinking way too narrowly. Having the ability to spy in people's homes could be commercially lucrative.

And it had been.

Mitch tried it for the first time in the little house he'd rented in Miami. During the months he lived there, he experimented with camera brands—some worked better than others—and placement in the ceiling ducts. Too close and the camera would be visible. Too far away and the vent cover got in the way of the picture. He practiced installation over and over until he could place a camera in under five seconds flat.

When he came back to Maryland he decided he was ready to try it for real.

His first target? His stepfather, of course. It was incredibly poetic, since the bastard had sent him to prison in the first place. Also, who was his stepfather gonna go to if he found the camera—the cops?

Placing the camera was ridiculously simple. On the night he'd gotten Mutt drunk and obtained the code for his brother's password file, he had also stolen his house keys and made copies. Discovering the security alarm code wasn't much more difficult. Mutt kept the alarm access code, along with his ATM sequence and all of his other passwords, in the same iPhone app.

All Mitch had to do after that was wait until Mutt and his daddy went away for the weekend to some stupid trade show, giving him time to install the camera. Waiting for his stepfather to open his damn safe was the hard part. He'd expected the old guy to open the safe every day. Instead, he'd had to wait three weeks.

But it had been so worth it. Mitch had expected to find deeds and maybe a few bonds and some cash. And he did. But far better was the manila envelope labeled DE.

The initials jumped out at him—he'd just found his mother's diary a few weeks before. Just learned the identity of the woman who'd broken his mother's heart. DE.

Daphne Elkhart. Mitch had been tempted to look inside right there as he stood by the safe. But he'd controlled himself, waiting until he got home. What he'd found was a gold mine, a treasure trove of every detail of Daphne's life.

It was damn creepy. His stepfather's obsession was evident in the detail. *Detail after detail.* Mitch now knew everything there was to know about Daphne Montgomery—her birthday, Social Security number, underwear size . . . The record stopped about the time of her divorce, but that was okay. The most important piece—the childhood trauma that left her terrified of underground places and four little words—was all there.

With some old-fashioned ingenuity, a bit of con artistry, and the power of Google, Mitch used what he'd read in the envelope to locate Wilson Beckett and his cabin in the West Virginia woods. And all that lay beneath.

And because Mitch had done his research, gaining Beckett's trust was a snap. *Hi, I'm Robert Jones. I think you knew my grandfather—you served in the same regiment in 'Nam.* That Beckett had served in the military wasn't a big leap—most men his age had, in some capacity. All Mitch had to do was locate a list of men who'd served with him and pick one with a very common last name who'd already died.

Then he laid it on thick. *My granddad used to talk about how you two dreamed about going home and doing nothing but fishing. He always said he wanted to find you and catch those fish. I lost him last year. Would you mind if I went fishing with you, for old times' sake?* One day of fishing had led to more. A few months of fishing and a case of Jack Daniel's later and Beckett was primed for the hook.

You need money? I know this kid whose daddy is a rich judge. I'll nab him and you hide him. That's all you have to do.

Mitch had always known Beckett was bad. He'd read it in his stepfather's obsession file. So he wasn't surprised by how easily Beckett had fallen, hook, line, and sinker. Mitch just reeled him in. In Beckett's mind, Ford's escape was a terrible thing—ransom lost and the danger of capture.

Mitch had made sure Ford never saw his face, but Ford had seen Beckett's. Now Ford would hopefully get himself found soon. His mama would be so happy! Then Ford would tell her what he'd heard.

Did you miss me?

Daphne would know her secret was out. Ford would lead them back to where he'd been kept. Then the show would begin. Mitch had prepared the venue very carefully.

That he'd miss her reaction to the basement and barn art wasn't such a big deal because when he got Daphne exactly where he wanted her, he'd have a front-row seat.

Baltimore, Maryland
Tuesday, December 3, 8:05 p.m.

Joseph stood behind Daphne's chair, his hands on her shoulders.

Brodie focused her attention on Daphne. "I wanted to know if you'd seen this before." She put the watch they'd found in Odum's basement on the table in front of Daphne. Sealed in an evidence bag, the watch was stained with blood.

When Daphne flinched, Joseph had to control the urge to shake his old mentor.

"Sit down, Joseph," Brodie said mildly, but with an undercurrent of sharp command. He took the chair next to Daphne and he could have sworn Brodie rolled her eyes before turning to Daphne, her expression gentling. "Have you seen it before?"

"Yes," Daphne said faintly. "It's Ford's. His grandmother Elkhart gave it to him for his eighteenth birthday. It's a tradition. Elkhart men wear Rolexes." Her mouth tightened. "He hates that thing."

"Why does he hate it?" Brodie asked.

"He doesn't have the best relationship with his father's family."

"Tell me, does Ford wear this watch often?"

Daphne was speaking of Ford in the present tense, Joseph noted. Common in these situations. But Brodie was, too, and that wasn't common. Guilt slid through his gut as he waited for Daphne's reply.

He'd compounded his momentary lapse in front of the Timonium house by rushing off to do the right thing, to make it right. His intentions had been pure but his logic completely clouded. He drew a breath and let it out slowly. *I fucked up. Big-time.*

Daphne was still frowning at the watch. "No, he rarely wears a watch at all and if he did it wouldn't be that one. So why did he have it last night?" She looked up at Joseph. "And why did whoever did this leave it behind? It's worth fifteen thousand dollars. Why didn't they take it?"

Damn good questions. *I should have asked them myself.* He met Brodie's eyes, telegraphing his apology, saw it was accepted. "Tell her, Fiona," he murmured.

"Tell me what?" Daphne demanded.

"Daphne, I found two types of blood in Odum's basement. Neither matched the blood found in the alley where the abduction took place."

Daphne gasped. "What? You mean that wasn't Ford's blood?"

"Do you know his blood type?" Brodie asked.

"Yes, of course. O negative, like mine."

"Type O neg was what I found in the first alley, but I found Type B on the wall and Type A on the floor in Odum's basement. There wasn't enough B blood to have caused death. But there was plenty of Type A."

Daphne closed her eyes. "Oh God. It's not Ford." She

pressed the heel of her hand between her breasts. "My head is spinning."

Joseph picked up the evidence bag containing the Rolex. On the back of the watch ELKHART was engraved in a spidery script. "What about this? Is it real?"

"It's real," Brodie said. "I imagine whoever did this planned to come back for it, Daphne. Especially given what else we found in that room."

Daphne looked up at Joseph. "What?"

"Guns," Joseph said. "The neighbors thought the Millhouses were moving drugs through that house, but it's weapons. Crates of assault rifles, just like the ones we found in Bill Millhouse's trunk this morning."

"They're dealing?"

"Either that or arming one hell of a militia," he said. "If they had a fifteen-thousand-dollar Rolex, they'd sell it and buy more guns."

Daphne took the watch from his hand. "Why? Why go to all the trouble of making us think they'd killed Ford in Odum's basement? Why the charade? They had to have known the first thing you'd do is test the blood. We'd know it wasn't Ford's."

Dammit. Joseph wanted to kick his own ass, because she was right. *I played right into their hands.* He walked over to the whiteboard and studied the text history from George's phone. "George didn't call you from the alley using Ford's phone."

"We figured he couldn't have. It must have been Doug," Daphne said.

"When you read the text from Ford's phone you felt hope, like this was a mistake."

"Yes. And when I realized it wasn't Ford texting, I was devastated."

"And just now?"

"Just now, I was devastated, and now I have hope." She sat back in her chair. "You're saying that they're playing with me?"

"Yes," he said tightly. *And I helped.* "Doug has been seen at the Timonium house." *And the black delivery van was there today.* He turned to look at her. "He was there today. Setting all this up. Manipulating us." And then a puzzle piece dropped into place in his mind. "He wanted us to find that house, that 'crime scene,' just like he wanted us to find that alley with the backpack."

Daphne's eyes narrowed. "He lured us to the alley with the text from Ford's phone."

"Why else would he text you at that moment, from that place? He had to know we'd trace the location the text was sent from. He wanted us to find the plastic support plate with George's fingerprints all over it."

"A tidy link," Brodie said, "from George to the knife to the murder of Zacharias and the abduction of Ford."

Daphne's brows knit. "But didn't Doug think that George would mention him?"

"I think he believed he'd taken care of that," Brodie said. "Joseph, what if that neighbor hadn't seen this Doug person through the window with her binoculars? What would you be thinking right now?"

"That George was lying," Joseph said. "And I'd be madder than hell that he sent me to that house to check for his baby, considering the booby trap he'd left behind."

Daphne looked from him to Brodie. "What booby trap?"

"The nursery door was rigged," Joseph said. "If I'd barged in like I'd wanted to . . ."

"You'd be dead." Brodie turned to Daphne. "The shotgun blast took out a wall."

Most of the color that had returned to her face drained away again. "Joseph, I'm . . . Oh, dear Lord. This is because of me. He's taunting me. You could have been killed."

"Don't even think it," he said harshly. "I was cautious and I'm not dead. But I would be thinking that George had lured me into a trap."

"We'd disregard everything George told us," Daphne said. "Including the existence of Doug. We'd have charged the Millhouses with the murder of Zacharias and the abduction of Ford." She'd grown more shaken as she spoke. "We never would have pursued Doug. We'd have kept following Millhouse leads to look for Ford, diverting us from where he really is. Oh my God."

"But we do know Doug really exists," Joseph soothed. "We won't be diverted."

"You're right," Daphne murmured, visibly regaining control of herself. "Doug has made this personal. I wonder if I've prosecuted him before."

She's one hell of an amazing woman, Joseph thought, admiring her ability to think under circumstances like these. "It's a distinct possibility. A witness says he claimed to be twenty-nine. Maybe you can go through your files for anyone that you either convicted or dealt that would match his age and 'ordinary' appearance. Hopefully I'll have a photo for you in a few hours."

"I'll start looking through my files right away. But first, since it wasn't Ford's blood, whose blood *did* you find, Dr. Brodie?"

"I don't know. I've submitted samples for PCR analysis so we'll have DNA profiles by tomorrow. I also submitted a sample of the baby's DNA, just so we'll know paternity."

"How old was the crime scene in the basement?"

"A few hours, maybe. The blood pooled on the floor had started to congeal around the edges. The blood on the wall had already dried, but it had been applied thinly."

Daphne contemplated the watch. "My ex-husband has Type B negative blood. And he wears his Rolex every single day. I called him an hour ago to give him an update on Ford, but he didn't answer. I didn't think anything about it because he rarely answers me right away. B negative is a fairly rare type. Was it B negative?"

"Yes, it was, actually."

"We'll get someone out to his house to check," Joseph said.

"Maybe this is about Travis," she said. "He's pissed off people in his career. If the Millhouses are a diversion, maybe whoever took Ford is trying to get back at Travis."

Brodie tilted her head. "What does your ex-husband do?"

"He's a judge, district court in Loudoun County. You're frowning, Joseph. Why?"

"Because there was a message, written on the wall. *Now you know how it feels.*"

Daphne let out a breath. "What Cindy said to me. But she's in jail. If this was done a few hours ago . . . We're back to Doug. What about Kimberly? What blood type is she?"

"I'm still waiting on her medical records," Brodie said, "but the blood I found in the alley near her car was O positive. It wasn't her blood in the basement, either."

"Do we know where Richard Odum is?" Daphne asked. "Was he at the courthouse today? Maybe one of Bill Millhouse's followers who got cold feet?"

"I put a BOLO out on Odum when I was on my way up to Timonium, but we've got no hits yet," Joseph said.

"Actually, we did," Brodie said. "While I was typing the blood in the Timonium basement, Bo heard from the other SWAT teams. Odum was found dead in one of the other houses he bought with Reggie's defense fund. His throat was slit. The blood in the Timonium basement could be his, but I can't be certain until I've run the tests."

"And his wife?" Joseph asked.

"Her body was found with his," Brodie replied.

Doug's getting rid of loose ends, Joseph thought, but kept it to himself. At some point Ford would become a loose end, too. They had to find him before that happened. And Joseph wanted to shift the topic before Daphne realized that fact.

"My team's going to be gathering downstairs for a debrief soon."

Her gaze became challenging. "And I should stay here?"

"You're welcome to join us. I may not be the most enlightened man on the planet, but I can be taught."

The challenge softened to gratitude. "Yes, I'd like to join you. Thank you."

Brodie put the watch in her briefcase. "I'll go break the not-such-bad news to SA Smith and his fiancée. I'll meet you in the team room, Agent Carter."

When they were alone neither of them said anything for a moment.

Joseph sighed. "I'm sorry, Daphne. I didn't wait for all of the evidence. I just raced down here to tell you and I put you through hell."

"Why did you? Race down here to tell me, I mean."

"The media. One of the reporters saw me leave the house and guessed Ford was dead. Three of the stations had already broadcast the story of 'rumors' that Ford was dead before I was even halfway down here. I didn't want you to hear it that way."

She was watching him, her expression suddenly inscrutable. "That addresses the urgency, I suppose," she said softly. "But you could have called me."

"Oh no, I couldn't," he blurted out, his face heating as her eyes widened. He backpedaled, trying to salvage his pride. "Daphne . . . you're an amazingly strong woman. But even a strong woman shouldn't hear news like that on the phone. It needed to be in person."

"Grayson was here."

"Dammit," he snapped. "I didn't want it to be Grayson. I wanted it to be *me*."

Her expression abruptly changed, swinging from inscrutable to wide-open. In her eyes he saw a deep yearning that gave him the courage to say to hell with salvaging his pride and to give her the honesty she deserved.

"I wanted it to be me because I'm a selfish bastard," he said quietly. "If you'd needed anyone after you were told, I wanted it to be me. I wanted you to need me."

"I did," she whispered. "And I will again before this is over."

And then? "Whatever you need," he managed.

And then she stunned him by walking into his arms, once again sliding hers around his waist. "I need not to have to be strong. For just a little while. Please."

His arms tightened around her. *Finally.* He was holding her, not because she was light-headed or ill. *Because I'm me. She came to me.* He ran his hands up and down her back, learning the feel of her. "For as long as you want."

"Joseph?"

He loved the way she said his name. "Yes?"

"If you had gotten yourself killed today, I would have been very angry with you."

He smiled against her hair. "I certainly don't want to make you angry."

"I'm serious." She pulled back far enough to see his face. She *was* serious, her blue eyes dark with worry. "I want my son back. But I don't want you killing yourself to make it happen. Please. Promise me."

He swept his thumb over her lips. Just once. "I promise."

"Thank you." She continued looking up at him, searching his face for something he couldn't guess. He only knew that she was the most beautiful thing he'd ever seen. Soft and vulnerable. But underneath she was tempered steel.

And he knew that he needed her. Wanted her. He cupped her cheek in his palm, closing the distance between them. Watched her eyes slide closed as he covered her mouth with his. He spread his hand across her back to bring her a little closer. And let himself sink a little deeper.

It was a chaste kiss that rocked him to his core. And when he raised his head he knew that once would never be enough.

She opened her eyes and he saw no regret. Just quiet acceptance of what had just transpired between them. And trust. It was the trust that had his heart knocking out of his chest. *She trusts me. Needs me.*

"Now what do we do?" she whispered.

"We find Doug and we follow him to Ford." And then . . . more. *I need more of her.*

Twelve

"I have to say I'm impressed," Alec said as they walked into Philly PD's headquarters. "And, truthfully, relieved. You're better connected than I thought."

"We shouldn't get trouble from the locals," Clay murmured. "Novak's another story."

The Fed had been excessively annoyed to find Clay had "interfered" with Gargano. Novak had curtly summoned him to Philly PD's headquarters to "debrief."

"They say we're six degrees of separation from everybody on the planet. I never really believed that until just now," Alec said, glancing nervously at the uniformed officers giving them hard stares as they walked up to the main desk.

Probably because I look like a drug dealer. Clay was dirty, unshaven, his pants still stained with Stevie's blood. "You stay in this business long enough and everybody's connected, kid. You just got a head start."

Clay had reached out to an old friend to smooth his way with the Philly PD, but he was on his own with Novak and the local Feds. Carter wouldn't be able to bail him out of any trouble Novak made for him. Carter was too busy containing the mess in Baltimore.

Which had become the most royal of clusterfucks. Ford was dead. Daphne was shattered. *I was too late.*

"'Scuse me." The man had just come out of the elevator

and was walking toward them. He was no more than thirty, his sandy blond hair cut military short. "You the PI?"

Clay nodded to the man. "I'm Maynard," he said.

"Detective Wiznewski. Come with me, please."

"This is Alec Vaughn, my associate. He stays with me, if you don't mind."

Wiznewski shrugged and hit the elevator button. "Whatever. I'm supposed to take you straight to the LT. How is it that you know Chick? Are you related? Because he's got, like, a million brothers and sisters and cousins."

"He's a friend of a friend. Ciccotelli's sister is married to a Chicago homicide cop."

"Him, I've met. Nice guy. Reagan, right?"

"Right," Clay said. "Aidan Reagan. Aidan's brother is also a homicide cop. My old partner and I worked with the brother on an abduction case in Chicago about six years ago." Which is how Clay had met Alec. *We aren't always too late.* "My old partner decided to stay in Chicago and is tight with the locals there."

The elevator doors opened and Wiznewski shepherded them in. "Why'd he stay?"

"Ethan got married," Clay said. "He left my firm."

"The new wife made him quit?" Wiznewski was clearly a man who liked his gossip.

"Dana wouldn't have done that," Alec inserted loyally, but the sideways glance he gave Clay was questioning, as if he'd wondered.

"She didn't make him quit," Clay said firmly. "Ethan wanted to settle down, have a family. Plus, his godson had moved to Chicago. He wanted to be close to the kid."

Alec's lips curved. He was the godson. "Because the kid was awesome."

"And very humble," Clay said dryly.

Thinking about those old days was a double-edged sword. He was happy for his old friend, because Ethan had definitely gotten his wish. Dana had just given birth to their third child. Between their kids and all the fosters they had running around, their house was pretty damn exciting. And pretty damn happy.

But Clay envied his old friend, too, because thinking about Ethan's happy home made him wish for one of his own, which made him think of Stevie, as it always did.

The elevator doors opened. "Chick's office is over here," Wiznewski said.

A man was leaning against the doorframe of a perimeter office, scrutinizing them as they approached. Tall and lean, he had black hair threaded with silver at the temples.

That would be Vito Ciccotelli, Clay thought. Alec stayed at his side, but his stance changed as they stopped in front of Ciccotelli. The kid stood tall, shoulders back just enough to be firm without appearing defiant.

He's protecting me, Clay realized, incredibly touched.

"Lieutenant Ciccotelli?" Clay asked and the guy nodded.

"You're Maynard." He stuck out his hand and Clay shook it. "I've heard stories. I wish we weren't meeting under these circumstances."

"Thank you." Clay pointed to Alec. "Alec Vaughn, from Chicago."

Ciccotelli's dark brows shot up. "Really? I've heard stories about you, too, but you're always twelve years old in them."

"Twelve was a pretty action-packed year," Alec said lightly. "I've led a relatively uneventful life since then."

Ciccotelli shook Alec's hand. "I think you've broken your streak of uneventful, son." He gestured them into his office. "Come have a seat."

Ciccotelli's office was tidy, his desk cleared of paper, every book neatly arranged on the shelves. It might have been stark, except for a toddler's artwork taped to his office door. In the bottom right corner of each drawing an adult had written "Anna."

And, of course, there was the photo on his desk—a blonde with a radiant smile. She sat astride a motorcycle, her helmet tucked under her arm.

"Your wife?" Clay asked.

"Better be," Ciccotelli said. "If Sophie found me with the picture of another woman on my desk, she'd . . . well, let's just say she's very skilled with sharp objects. Add to that she's eight months pregnant and *very* cranky, and I toe the line." He checked the time. "The others should be back soon."

"Who are the others?" Clay asked.

"The detectives I've assigned to this case, plus Agent Novak."

"*You've* assigned to the case? You're Homicide."

"So it says on my badge."

Oh no. Dread pooled in Clay's gut. "But Pamela Mac-Gregor is a missing-person case. Have you found her?" *Please let it not be too late*.

"No, we haven't found her. But this afternoon we were able to link her disappearance to a homicide that occurred yesterday afternoon."

Clay closed his eyes. "Who?"

"Elmarie Stodart, a young au pair from South Africa. She'd taken her two charges, a toddler and a five-year-old, to the mall to see Santa. From what we've been able to piece together from the older child's testimony, Elmarie saw that the toddler had dropped a toy on the floor of the parking garage, locked the kids in the van, and went to get it. We think she discovered Pamela being forced into a vehicle, tried to help, but was stabbed in the process. By the time she was found, she'd bled out."

"And the children?" Clay asked, afraid to hear the answer.

"The baby had fallen asleep, but the five-year-old saw everything. She's in shock."

"Security tapes?" Alec asked.

"The cameras don't see between vehicles. Elmarie's killer stabbed her between two vans, then pushed her body under a car. None of that action was captured. We know her killer left in a black van. We ran the plates—they were stolen off another vehicle. We put it on the wire as soon as we knew, but I imagine they've already been changed."

Clay dragged his hands over his face. "Was the child able to describe the killer?"

"No. She was too hysterical. My sketch artist is going to try tonight. At the moment, we have nothing. That's why my detectives want to talk to you. Linking Kimberly Mac-Gregor to this Doug person is the first real lead we've had."

"You need to be in contact with Agent Carter in Baltimore. I have his number."

"Already talked to him. And he already knew about the black van. We'll conference with them at eight fifteen. Before then, I'd appreciate any information your PIs have dug up."

"I want to sit in on the meeting," Clay said baldly.

Ciccotelli went still. "And if I refuse?"

"I'll still tell you everything I know. I want this Doug stopped."

For several seconds Ciccotelli said nothing. Then he lifted his brows. "How do you feel about being an unpaid consultant?"

It was an invitation, and far more than Clay had expected. "Favorable. Thanks."

There was a knock on the door and Wiznewski stuck his head in. "Maynard, you have a call. Your partner has been trying to reach you on your cell for a half hour."

Heart hammering, Clay took the receiver Ciccotelli offered, checking his cell phone at the same time. "No bars in here," he said to Paige. "I wasn't avoiding you."

"Clay, it wasn't Ford in that basement! We don't know who it was, but it wasn't Ford's blood type. *We aren't too late.*" She sobered suddenly. "At least, not yet."

Relief had him light-headed. *Thank you.* "Have you heard from Stevie's folks?"

Her voice softened sadly. "No change."

Clay cleared his throat. "What about Tuzak? Have you heard from the ME?"

"He's supposed to be at Joseph's eight fifteen meeting. Says he should have preliminary tox results."

"Tell Carter that Kim's father is a veterinarian. Ask the ME if any of the drugs he finds in Tuzak's tox screen could be found in a vet's supply closet. MacGregor treats horses. Those meds should be stronger and Kim may have had access."

"Nice, Clay," Paige said. "I'll let him know. Listen, you didn't ask, but Daphne tried to make this call. She couldn't because she had to go to her office to pull trial records to see if she ever prosecuted Doug. She told me to keep at it until I found you."

A little warmth curled around his belly. "Thanks. I wanted to ask, but was afraid to. Tell her . . . tell her I won't rest until we know where he is. I'll talk to you later." Clay handed the receiver back to Ciccotelli. "We got a brief reprieve. That wasn't Ford Elkhart's blood in the basement."

"Thank God," Alec breathed. "Whose is it?"

"Damn good question, kid."

"Damn good observation about MacGregor being a

vet," Ciccotelli said. "Who's Tuzak?" Clay started to answer, but Ciccotelli held up his hand. "Wait. Sign this." He pulled the page he'd been typing from the printer and slid it across the table.

Clay had to laugh. "My contract saying I'm an 'unpaid consultant.' So formal."

"I learned the hard way to get everything in writing, Mr. Maynard. My first consultant was Sophie there." Ciccotelli pointed to her photo, laughter in his eyes. "I didn't have a signed agreement with her and I ended up marrying her."

Clay smiled as he signed the contract, then drew a breath, sobering. "Tuzak is Isaac Zacharias. This is what's happened so far."

Baltimore, Maryland
Tuesday, December 3, 8:15 p.m.

Joseph went straight from his debriefing with Bo Lamar and the brass to the conference room where his team waited for their call with Philly PD.

"Everyone ready?" he asked as he took the seat at the head of the table. He did a quick head count. Grayson and J.D. were here, as were Kate and Hector. Brodie was representing CSU and Quartermaine had texted that he'd be late.

Daphne sat at the end of the table looking composed. Until she met his eyes and he saw the strain. He wished he could make all of this go away. Wished that they were just two people who had nothing but time to explore an attraction that, thank God, was mutual. But they weren't two normal people.

Her son was still missing. *And I won't rest until he's found.*

The side conversations ceased as Joseph dialed Philly PD on the speakerphone. When the phone began to ring, everyone got quiet.

"This is Ciccotelli." The man had a smooth voice. "Agent Carter?"

"Yes," Joseph said. "I'll tell you who I have here, then you can introduce your crew." He introduced his team, providing rank and role. "Our ME will be here soon. You have one of ours up there. Is Special Agent Novak with you?"

"He is," Ciccotelli said. "I've also got private investigator Clay Maynard here, acting as a special consultant."

"We're glad for any help we can get," Joseph said, surprised at Clay's inclusion until he remembered that the PI was connected to the Ciccotellis through friends and family.

Joseph knew all about consulting with family. Grayson pulled him in on cases from time to time and both of them consulted with their younger sister, Zoe, a police shrink. Her perspective had helped Joseph understand—and catch—several suspects over the years. He made a mental note to call her later about Doug. *Because we need all the help we can get.*

"We're happy to help however we can," Ciccotelli said. "In addition to your two, I've got Yelton from IT, and McFain, CSU."

The door opened and Quartermaine slipped in, taking the seat beside Daphne.

"And we've just been joined by Dr. Neil Quartermaine," Joseph said, "our new ME. I've briefed my team on the murder of the au pair, Elmarie Stodart. Any luck with the sketch artist talking to the five-year-old witness?"

"Not yet," Ciccotelli said. "But if anyone can coax it out of her mind, it's our guy."

"He knows how to do that correctly, right?" Daphne asked. "You push too hard, you can make it worse. You can break the child." This she knew from personal experience.

"He understands that. He's good with kids. I'd trust him with my own daughter."

"I hope he's successful," Joseph said, looking annoyed. "We thought we had Doug's face on video at a local drugstore, but their system tapes over itself every two weeks. We missed it by a day. We've got a sketch artist meeting with the one witness who saw him. We'll compare sketches, but a photo would have been really nice."

"What about the house you mentioned?" Ciccotelli asked. "Any prints there?"

"Tons of prints," Joseph said. "None that match any of our databases yet. Latent is still processing the scene. What about mall security tapes? Any possible face shots?"

"No. Pamela was walking through the parking garage with a man, five nine, one eighty-five, but a hoodie hid his face. They walked between two cars right about the time the au pair got out of her van. Neither Elmarie nor Pamela reappears on the tape. A black van pulls away, driven by what appears to be a woman."

"But was really hoodie-guy wearing a wig," Novak told them. "I've studied the tapes. This guy's build is slight enough that he passed for a woman."

"How did Pamela get to the mall?" J.D. asked. "Was she with anyone?"

"Pamela told her parents she was going to a friend's house," Wiznewski said. "We pulled her cell LUDs and she got a text from 443-555-2320. Prepaid."

"Mr. Maynard told us about the call Kimberly made from Laurel Gargano's birthday party," Ciccotelli said. "We've requested Kimberly's back phone records."

"We have them," J.D. said, thumbing through the printout. "We requested them when we discovered Kimberly's arrest record. And . . . yeah. The 2320 number is the same one Kimberly called the night of Laurel Gargano's birthday party."

"So we're one step closer to Doug," Joseph said. "Those prepaids are traceable, but we'd have to lure him into making a few phone calls so we can triangulate."

"How about Richard Odum?" Hector asked. "He's Bill Millhouse's second-in-command. Odum might be able to persuade Doug to call a few times."

Joseph shook his head. "He's dead. One of the SWAT teams found his body in one of the houses he bought with Reggie Millhouse's defense fund. His throat was slit. As was his wife's."

"The CSU team I sent to that house typed the blood," Brodie said. "Odum's type matches what we found in the basement with Ford's watch. Unfortunately, we'll have to find someone else Doug trusts enough to call from his cell phone."

"We might be able to trace him another way," Ciccotelli said. "Yelton from IT is working on tracing the Webcam he put in the ceiling of Trooper Gargano's house to his own server, which must have downloaded the images."

"How long will that take?" Joseph asked.

"Depends on how clever he is," Yelton said. "An hour or a day or never. The Webcam was no longer connected to its host server. It had run out of battery. We'll know if it's still transmitting within a minute after hooking it back up. We'll let you know."

"Good," Joseph said. "Anything else from your end, Lieutenant?"

"We thought Dr. MacGregor was going to let us search his medical cabinet without a warrant, since, you know, both his daughters are missing. But his attorney was there when we arrived and advised the father not to allow it." Ciccotelli sounded extremely annoyed. "He told the father that if Kim had stolen any of the drugs she could be found complicit in the death of Officer Zacharias. So we started a warrant app for Dr. MacGregor's supply cabinet."

"Dr. Quartermaine?" Joseph asked. "Did you get my message about one of the abductees' fathers being a vet?"

"I did," Quartermaine said. "I was late because I was waiting for the results of Officer Zacharias's tox screen. Short answer is that you shouldn't have any trouble getting a judge to sign the warrant. The victim had high levels of fentanyl and ketamine in his system, both of which would be found in a vet's drug supply—especially a large-animal vet. I'm happy to fax a copy of the autopsy report with the tox screen results to your office, Lieutenant Ciccotelli."

"Excellent," Ciccotelli said with satisfaction. "Thank you."

"What was Zacharias's cause of death?" Joseph asked.

"Official cause of death was asphyxiation," Quartermaine said.

"What?" Clay sounded stunned. "He was strangled?"

"Yes, but chemically, not manually. As I said, he was given a cocktail of fentanyl and ketamine, after being tased. The Taser jolt incapacitates for thirty seconds at the most. Fentanyl is a fast-acting narcotic—within thirty seconds, but it doesn't last that long. Ketamine kicks in before the fentanyl wears off and lasts thirty to ninety minutes, depending on the dose. He was tased twice, then injected with the fentanyl into a vein. The ketamine was given intramuscularly." He said the last sentence with a frown.

"So how did he asphyxiate?" Clay asked through the speaker.

"Laryngospasm. It's a side effect of the ketamine. The vocal cords spasm and slam shut, blocking the airway. It's seen in operating rooms where ketamine is used as an anesthetic, but not often. Because the patient is monitored in the OR, his head would be repositioned, opening the airway. But this victim wasn't repositioned because he wasn't monitored. In more than two-thirds of the cases the ketamine is given intramuscularly, which was the case with this victim. It was a perfect storm—everything went exactly wrong. The victim would have been dead within seven to ten minutes." Quartermaine paused to stare at Daphne. "Miss? Are you all right?"

Daphne was white as chalk and for the second time that night Joseph wanted to kick his own ass. *You just let her sit there, listening to what happened to Zacharias, knowing the same drugs were given to her son.* And what was Quartermaine thinking?

He wasn't, Joseph realized. Quartermaine had come in at the end of the introductions. He didn't know he'd been talking to the abductee's mother.

He opened his mouth to explain when Daphne managed a strained smile.

"I'm okay. You came in after introductions and this is a very special situation. I'm Daphne Montgomery, state's attorney's office. Ford Elkhart is my son."

Quartermaine's mouth dropped open. "Oh my God. I'm sorry."

"It's all right," Daphne said, her persona having changed before their eyes. Her voice had dropped a few notes and smoothed. Her posture changed, her body becoming more . . . Zen. "How could you have known?"

She'd become the woman he'd met at Grayson's house nine months ago, cool, composed, collected. His Daphne was bold and inviting. This woman . . . wasn't. He glanced at Grayson, saw that his brother was staring at her, too. With the exception of Quartermaine, everyone around the table had noticed.

Hector Rivera scribbled a note and passed it down to Joseph. *She spoke with this same voice when she told her ex that Ford was missing and again when she talked about her cousin's abduction. Does she even know she does it?*

Damn good question, Joseph thought. Then, it was like a switch flipped in his brain. *Would she change like that during sex?* He shifted in his chair, suddenly erect. *Oh, for God's sake,* he thought, disgusted with himself. *Not now.* With an effort, he pushed the mental image to the side and focused.

"Still, I'm sorry," Quartermaine was saying to her. "Now you're wondering if the same thing happened to Ford. And the answer is no."

Her brows lifted, elegantly. "No, definitely? Or no, in your opinion?"

He hesitated, a little rattled. "Both. Look, Mrs. Montgomery—"

"Miss," she interrupted. "It's Miss."

Quartermaine drew a deep breath. "Okay. Miss Montgomery. First, Ford fought him. We found his blood in the alley, but only enough to indicate he'd have a nasty bump. He couldn't have fought if he'd had the same reaction as Officer Zacharias."

She nodded. "Thank you, Dr. Quartermaine."

"Neil," he said, still flustered. "Please."

"If you call me Daphne," she said. She made no mention of the way she'd just changed, but her cheeks flushed and Joseph knew she was very aware.

The speakerphone crackled. "Excuse me. This is Clay Maynard. Officer Zacharias was working in an off-duty capacity for me."

"Hell," Quartermaine muttered, looking like he'd rather be anywhere but where he was. "I'm sorry, Mr. Maynard. I didn't know you were acquainted with the victim."

"It's okay," Clay said in a flat voice. "I can deal. I just wanted to know, was he wearing any body armor at all?"

"No. He had his badge on a chain, under his sweatshirt, but no vest. His holster was also empty and no weapons were found on or around the body. I am sorry."

"It's okay," Clay repeated. "Thank you for taking care of him. We appreciate it."

Joseph turned his attention to Brodie. "Have you figured out how he got Ford and Kimberly out of the alley?"

"We did," Brodie said. "I went back to the alley after the techs had moved a lot of the trash. The garbage on the street had been mixed around, erasing his tracks, but the techs found oil mixed with hydraulic fluid on the pavement at the end of the alley and on some of the debris in the area where Ford would have fallen."

"He used a cart with a hydraulic lift," Joseph said. "And it needs maintenance."

"We found the same oil/fluid mix in the garages of all of

Odum's houses," Brodie added. "I bet that's how he unloaded the guns. He definitely visited all three houses."

Joseph frowned. "He's not hiding Ford at any of those houses, though. J.D., did any other Millhouse properties come up in your search?"

"None. The house and business that we searched today were rentals. I had Hyatt's clerk run a property search for 'Doug' in Maryland and Pennsylvania, both as a first and last name. I also searched variants on 'Doug,' such as 'Douglas' and 'McDougal.' We got thousands of hits. I'll start narrowing them down tonight."

"Good. Let me know if you need support to do any physical searches." He reviewed his notes. "Daphne, you're checking all of your old cases to see if you prosecuted Doug. What's the status?"

"I keep all my cases in a database, which I checked before the meeting. In my first year and a half with the state's attorney's office, I was Grayson's assistant. When I wasn't sitting second chair in court, I mainly handled cases like Kimberly MacGregor's, where the defendant was taking a plea. I dealt over five hundred misdemeanors and class D felonies. Since I've been lead prosecutor I've closed less than a hundred cases. Reggie Millhouse's case has sucked up most of my time."

"Did anybody jump out?" Joseph asked.

"Not yet. I know that I never prosecuted anyone with 'Doug' in the first or last name or any of the variations J.D. just mentioned, but that doesn't mean he wasn't a family member. There's an army of clerks researching the cases I did when I was assisting. They're also checking photos of all my defendants, pulling every male between twenty-five and thirty-five who has brown hair and who's between five six and five ten. They should be done by midmorning tomorrow. I offered to help, but my presence would require too much security." She frowned. "I'm banned from my office until Doug is caught."

Joseph was secretly thrilled that she wouldn't be going back to her desk or into the courtroom until the threat to her life was gone. But he knew she'd just lost a major occupier of her time—a way to keep herself busy so she didn't think about her son.

He shot her a look of silent sympathy. "If they come up

with any photos, we'll get them in front of our eyewitness, that teacher in Timonium, as soon as possible." He turned to J.D. "What did you find out about Kimberly?"

"From Ford's Facebook posts that you sent to us, we know Kim and Ford met at a party in September and he told his friends that she had more in common with him than any other girl he'd ever met." J.D. put an evidence envelope on the desk. "I found this in her dorm room. It's a list of all the things Ford liked and her to-do list to find out about them. It's handwritten. She did a lot of research."

Joseph bit back a wince. Just looking at the list was painful. "Kimberly is a . . . calculating young woman. Did anyone else see her that way?"

"Nobody I talked to," J.D. said. "She was funny, smart, laughed at their jokes. Baked them cookies . . . Didn't complain when Ford went out with his friends. She was the perfect girlfriend."

"Joseph, it's Deacon. I talked with the MacGregors for a while tonight. They live in a very nice house and the parents drive luxury cars. I wondered why Kimberly stole to begin with. The parents said that they'd hit some hard times two years ago and had to cut back Kim's allowance. They put her BMW in storage so they wouldn't have to pay for the insurance and on-campus parking. She didn't take that well. A month into the school year she wanted a new laptop and her parents told her she'd have to get a job. The next thing they knew, she'd been arrested for stealing the diamond ring."

"That's consistent with what I'd noted in my file," Daphne said. "She was caught trying to trade the ring to a pawnbroker for the laptop. I might have dealt her down to a misdemeanor, but she was disrespectful to me and to her parents. They'd hired an expensive attorney and paid her bail and she treated them like crap."

"Well, they sold her BMW to pay for the bail and the fancy attorney," Deacon said. "And Mrs. MacGregor said Kim cussed you out to anyone who'd listen. The MacGregors hoped the experience would teach Kim a lesson. They were devastated to hear she'd had a hand in Ford's abduction. They kept telling me to tell you how sorry they are."

Daphne seemed to be struggling for the right words.

"Um, tell them thank you and that we're working to find both their girls."

Joseph understood her hesitation. "I think it will be much easier to accept their apology once Ford is home safely."

She smiled gratefully at him. "Exactly."

Joseph lingered on her face another second, then dropped his gaze to his notes. "Lieutenant Ciccotelli, can you send us a photo of the man in the parking garage?"

"Sure. We'll make some stills of him in the wig and in the hoodie," Ciccotelli said.

"Thanks. The objective is to find Doug, whoever the hell he is. Recapping—J.D.'s got property searches, Agent Coppola and Detective Rivera continue to be primary security for Daphne's family. Ciccotelli's sketch artist will continue working with the five-year-old witness who saw Doug's face and his IT will try to route the Webcam Doug used in Gargano's house. Deacon, I'd like you back here unless you think you're needed there."

"I think they've got it covered up here," Deacon said. "I'll head home tonight."

"Good. Anything else?"

"Yes," J.D. said. "Where's Agent Lamar?"

"He's working with the ATF on finding the origin of the rifles that were found in Odum's houses. He'll keep us updated as he's able. Everyone good with the plan?"

Heads were nodding—and then the cell phones began to buzz, up and down the table. A group text had been sent, resulting in considerable whooping and clapping. Grayson's eyes grew moist and he wasn't the only one. Joseph found himself blinking at tears as well and J.D. didn't even try to hide his.

Joseph leaned into the speaker. "Hey, Maynard. You get that text?"

"Yeah." Clay cleared his throat. "Stevie woke up. I'll be home as fast as I can."

Joseph looked down the table at Daphne, who sat with her eyes closed, her lips soundlessly moving. *Praying,* he thought. *Giving thanks or begging for equal mercy.*

Or both.

"On that note, we're adjourned."

Marston, West Virginia
Tuesday, December 3, 8:30 p.m.

Ford choked down a few bites of the old man's beef jerky
and ate a few mouthfuls of the snow, tossing the remainder
to the ground before his lips touched the filthy glove he'd
taken from the cabin. At least he wouldn't get dehydrated.

He'd freeze to death first. There were no stars, just a
blanket of white, falling snow. There were no lights anywhere. This was the blackest night he'd ever experienced.

Ford hunched his shoulders against the wind. *One foot*
in front of the other. He had to keep walking or he'd end up
dead. For the first time he entertained the notion that he
might.

I don't want to die. So move. Move your feet. One foot in
front of the other.

Thirteen

"Home or hospital to see Stevie?" Joseph asked when she was buckled in the front seat of his Escalade.

"Home," Daphne said. "I think Stevie needs to rest."

"And so do you," Joseph said, waving to the car behind them. Rivera and Coppola took their place behind the Escalade, escorting her home. "Parents of missing kids don't remember to take care of themselves. It's like they believe if they slow down they're betraying the child."

Daphne turned in her seat to study him. Here in the quiet she could finally think. And she did not want to think. So she talked. "Did you slow down when your wife was missing?"

He glanced at her, surprise in his eyes. Then he shrugged and looked at the road, slick with the new snow that was still falling. "No."

"Will you tell me about her?"

He blew out a breath that puffed into a cloud. "Daphne, I don't think—"

"I'm sorry. It's just that it's cold and it's snowing and my son is out there. And if I can think of anything else then maybe I won't lose my mind. But I won't ask about her again. I don't mean to hurt you. How about hobbies? Sports? I'm not very good at sports, I'm afraid." *And now I'm babbling.*

"You don't hurt me by asking. It's just I didn't think women liked to know about the tragic love of a guy's life." He said it dramatically, making fun of himself.

Daphne didn't smile. "You loved her. She was part of your life, if only for a little while. I don't need to know the details of her abduction. I guess I want to know what about her made you . . . fall."

Another sideways glance her way. "You didn't fall for Ford's dad."

"No. I was a fifteen-year-old girl who'd lied on her job app about being eighteen so that I could wait tables to make money for community college. Travis was much older and polished. A lawyer from the big city, which was what I desperately wanted to be."

"Which? A lawyer or to live in the city?"

"Both. I started talking to him. I just wanted to ask questions about being a lawyer. He thought I was offering myself. You know."

His jaw had grown tight. "I can guess."

"Next thing I knew, my shift was over and it was wine and roses in his hotel room at the Greenbrier."

His brows shot up. "The five-star golf resort? You worked there?"

"No, I wasn't lucky enough to work there, but I still made better tips at a restaurant nearby than I could have made in any other town around. I thought I knew how rich people lived from watching my customers. I had no idea."

"You must have been swept away," he said quietly.

"It was more than this country girl had ever thought to dream. I was goggle-eyed. Then I was drunk. By the time I realized what was happening, it had happened."

His jaw had clenched. "And then?"

"I woke up. Travis was long gone. His head of security, Hal, was waiting to take me home. I was so hungover. I'd never had champagne before. I'd never had a *lot* of things before. A month later, I was still praying to the porcelain God, every morning."

"It was your first time."

"Joseph, if you clench your jaw any tighter you're gonna break your teeth," she said dryly. "It was a long time ago."

He made a visible effort to relax. "So you had Ford."

"I did. I thought the Greenbrier was the fanciest place

on earth, but I was shocked yet again when I went looking for Travis to give him the glad tidings. I was struck speechless. I'd turned to go without ringing the bell when the front doors opened and Hal came out. I tried to hide, but he saw me and remembered me. I think he took one look at me, pale and scared, and it didn't take a rocket scientist, as they say."

"What did he do?"

"Sat me down in the kitchen and gave me milk and cookies. And then he took me to Nadine—that's Travis's mother. Talk about scared . . . She was like Cinderella's stepmother and the Queen of England all rolled into one." Daphne frowned, remembering. "She took one look at me and turned almost as pale as I was. Hal had told her who I was and how I'd been with Travis at the Greenbrier while I was down in the kitchen. She took my chin and tilted my face to the light. Then said, 'What is your name, child?' I told her it was Daphne Elizabeth. 'Elizabeth is a suitable name.' I think that made me mad, because I pulled away and said, 'Suitable for what?' She said, 'For the mother of my grandchild.'"

"She wanted the baby, then?"

"Oh, yes. Turned out that Travis's current wife was infertile."

"His current wife?"

"I was wife number three. And too young and stupid to know any better. Not that I would have made a different choice at the time. I mean, I was pregnant and fifteen and poorer than a church mouse. The Elkharts could give my baby a life that I never could have. And I didn't know that he was married at the beginning."

"Did Travis just divorce the current wife? Just like that?"

"Pretty much. I don't think Travis cared who he was married to. It took a few months to get his divorce from wife number two. Nadine made good use of the time. She whisked me to the family house in DC. She didn't want me seen by society until I was more polished."

"And less pregnant?"

"Absolutely. I stayed in that house until Ford was born and a little after that."

"What did your mother have to say about that?"

"She was kind of flattened by Nadine. That first day, the

day I showed up pregnant on her doorstep, Nadine called for her limo, said she was taking me to my mother. I had to tell my mother that I was pregnant, with Nadine watching. Poor Mama. She was devastated. Nadine told Mama that I'd be moving in with the Elkharts and told me to pack my things. Like she owned us."

"What did your mother do?"

"She said no. Then Nadine listed all the things the Elkharts could provide for my baby and for me—mostly education and financial stability. My mother relented, but only on the condition that Nadine's promises be in writing and reviewed by Mama's attorney. I was shocked—I didn't even know Mama had an attorney. I found out later that she didn't, that she was totally bluffing. But requiring a contract earned her Nadine's respect. Mama's foresight was what allowed me to go to college and get my degree when Ford was a little boy. She also made sure that Travis couldn't just divorce me after the baby was born—the marriage could only be dissolved if I agreed to it or if there was proof that I'd been unfaithful."

"What did Travis say when he was confronted with you being only fifteen?"

"Travis swore he thought I was eighteen, and that was fair. I'd lied to get a job in a restaurant that served booze. Higher tips."

"We wouldn't want to be unfair," he said dryly. "Was it even legal for you to marry?"

"It was legal in Maryland if you were pregnant and you had parental approval."

"It must have been quite a change for you."

"In the beginning it was very hard. I missed my mother, I had morning sickness for weeks, and Nadine was a taskmaster. There was the academic tutor and all the how-to-be-an-Elkhart lessons. How to stand, eat, sit, dress. I was a regular Eliza Doolittle. But in her own way, Nadine tried to do right by Ford and, in the beginning, by me."

"I have to say that I'm surprised Travis's mother agreed to any of this. I know a lot of rich women through my parents. Most of them would die before they allowed an uneducated, penniless waitress to marry their son, much less force the issue."

"I always wondered about that. I asked Nadine, several

times. She always said that I 'fit her requirements.' I kept poking and one day one of the housemaids showed me a picture of Nadine's daughter, who'd died in a boat accident when she was about fifteen. The resemblance was very strong. I figured Nadine wanted me because I looked like her daughter."

Joseph cringed. "Travis must have known that, too. That he slept with you to begin with . . . Sorry, that's just . . . Well, I have three sisters and I can't imagine that."

"I worried about that for a while, too, until I realized that Travis's requirements were far less specific than his mother's. I mentioned once to Hal that I was disturbed that Travis had even considered me and he told me that the night Travis met me he'd already had two women in his room. Apparently this was during Travis's 'Neopolitan' phase. You know, blonde, brunette, redhead. That actually made me feel better."

"So what finally happened to Travis?"

"I got old. I was twenty-seven. I should have seen it coming."

"But you didn't?"

"Nope. Well, not until I walked into his office unannounced one day. Then I saw him coming. And his secretary, too." She exaggerated a shudder. "Bleach for my eyes, stat!"

He laughed, long and deep, and Daphne went completely still. Serious, stern, and focused, Joseph was compelling and sexy. Dangerous, even. But laughing . . . he was beautiful. As she'd always known he would be.

He turned his head, abruptly sobering, and she wanted to sigh at the loss. "What?" he asked. "What's wrong?"

"I like it when you laugh," she said simply. "It feels nice."

He stretched his arm over the center console, palm up, silently waiting. She slid her fingers through his, almost wincing when he closed his hand, hard and tight. When she lifted their joined hands to her cheek, brushing his skin against hers, his exhale was audible. She pressed her lips to his knuckles before lowering their hands back to the console. "Thank you," she whispered.

"For what?" he asked, his voice rough, raspy.

"For helping me get through this awful day." Her eyes stung and she blinked to clear them. He said nothing in response, just brought her hand to his lips as she'd done his. Kissed her knuckles. As she'd done his.

But when he lifted her hand to his face, he turned his head so that he nuzzled her palm like it was a soft blanket while keeping his eyes on the road.

"You smell so good," he murmured and she remembered breathing his scent from her own hands and how it had calmed her.

"So do you."

He kissed her palm again, then rested their joined hands on the console, not letting her go. Minutes went by, the two of them in a quiet, warm cocoon.

But it's cold outside. Ford is out there. The thought snuck through her relaxed defenses and she was about to start talking again to banish it.

Except he started talking first.

"Her name was Jo Carter," he said.

"Jo Carter?" That made her smile. "Really?"

His mouth curved. "That's how we met. Her name was Joella Priscilla Carter. I got a package addressed to 'Jo Carter, USS *Theodore Roosevelt*.' A lot of people called me Joe when I was younger, so I figured it was a typo. Until I opened it. It was a care package from her best friend with . . . feminine things. The Girl Scout cookies were cool, but the rest . . ." The face he made was comical. "Makeup and panty hose and . . . hygiene things. And, um, other things. Rather unexpectedly naughty things."

Daphne laughed softly. "Oh dear. I imagine that was a bit of a . . . jolt."

He coughed. "Oh yeah. Especially when my buddies saw me frowning into the box. They had a lot of fun ribbing me about that . . ."

"Pocket rocket?" Daphne supplied helpfully.

Another rich laugh burst from him. "I prefer the term 'personal massager.'"

"Tomato, to-mah-to. So what did you do?"

"Well, I ate the Girl Scout cookies, and then—"

She laughed again. "Joseph! You ate her cookies?"

"They were Thin Mints," he said, as if that explained everything. "Plus, she owed me for all the shit I got for that . . . pocket device. I looked her up and hand-delivered the box, just to see her blush. But she didn't blush at all. She said,

'Hot damn, my bunk's gonna rock tonight.'" He grinned at the memory. "She made me laugh that night and every time I saw her after that. And . . . and I knew she was the one." His grin faded. "She was . . . everything."

Daphne's eyes started to sting again. "She sounds wonderful."

"She was. She was a helicopter pilot, damn smart."

"What were you?"

"Pilot. Flew a Prowler."

"You were a fighter pilot? Really? I'm surprised you went into the Navy and not the family business. You're an engineer, right?"

"Yes. My dad wanted me in the business. Never entered his mind I wouldn't want the same thing. He had my future all planned out, from the day I was born. When I was a kid, I hated that. It chafed, you know? Feeling like you had no control of your destiny."

"I do know," she said. "Although mine came from the opposite end of the socioeconomic scale. My mama cleaned rooms at one of the hotels in town. She wanted more for me. That's why she was so upset when I got pregnant."

"Understandable," he said. "My struggle with my dad must seem petulant to you."

"Different," she said, and he gave her a disbelieving glance. "Okay, petulant works."

"It's just that I wanted to be someone other than Jack Carter's boy. My dad is a great guy, a great dad. But . . . he throws a really long shadow and I'd lived in it my whole life."

"You wanted to throw your own shadow," she said and he squeezed her hand.

"I wanted it so much that I applied to the Naval Academy without Dad's knowledge. Or any of his connections. I got in on my own. It was one of the best days of my life."

"And your dad?"

"He was so hurt." Joseph shook his head. "And then I explained. And because he's a great dad, he listened and remembered pulling himself up by his own bootstraps. After that, he bragged to anyone who would listen."

"He's so proud of you." Daphne watched his chest expand. "As he should be."

"Thank you. That means a lot."

They finished the ride to her house in silence, Daphne not able to stop herself from wondering what it would feel like to mean everything to someone. To him.

And then the respite was over, reality intruding in the form of the new snowflakes falling from the sky to the windshield. *Please don't let him be cold. Or in pain. Or afraid.*

Tuesday, December 3, 9:45 p.m.

Joseph stopped the car at Daphne's curb, waiting for Hector and Kate to clear her garage. Her fingers were still twined with his, the strength of her grip the only indication she hadn't fallen asleep in the passenger seat.

"Hey," he said softly. "We're here."

"I know. I'm trying to screw my courage to the sticking place."

"And we'll not fail," he said, finishing the quote.

Her eyes opened, regarding him curiously. "You quote *Macbeth*?"

"Like I said before, I can be taught. Plus it made me the chick magnet of the twelfth grade." When the sight of her lips curving minutely made him feel like a king, he knew he was completely lost. "I need to tell you something." He dropped his gaze to their joined hands. "I applied for the transfer to VCET nine months ago. Monday, April eleventh," he added.

"The Monday after we wrapped the Muñoz case," she murmured to herself.

"I can't tell if you're pleased or surprised or thinking that I'm a stalker."

Her lips curved. "Very pleased. Not really surprised, but only because I heard it from a little bird earlier today."

"Paige?"

"Who else? Up until that moment, I thought you didn't notice me."

He laughed at that, then saw she was serious and, abruptly, so was he. "Daphne, I noticed you the first moment I saw you walking up to Grayson's front door wearing that lime green miniskirt. Dreamed of you that night. And almost every night since."

"Then why didn't you say something before? You've

been with VCET for months now. I can tell you exactly how many times you've seen me and haven't said a word." She rolled her eyes, embarrassed. "Because I counted."

He let go of her hand long enough to brush his thumb over her lips. "You were with Maynard. Every one of those times. Because I counted, too."

"Clay and I, we're not—" She grew flustered. "We're friends. That's all."

"I know. He told me today. And I know this is the most horrible time to tell you anything like this, but I find that I'm selfish yet again. I didn't want you to go to sleep without knowing." He laid his finger over her lips when she started to speak. "Not now. When this is done, I want to . . ." He exhaled. "Just know that I'm waiting. And if Rivera weren't ten feet away, I'd be kissing you senseless right now."

Her cheeks grew beautifully rosy as he let her hand go and turned to roll his window down. "We clear?" he asked Rivera.

"Yep. Coppola and I will stay the night. Kate's got the upstairs and I've got the main floor. The phone guys will sleep in shifts, too." He leaned down so that he could see in the window. "Daphne, you've got a visitor. He's with your mom in the living room or parlor or whatever she calls that room with the forty-five-foot ceilings."

"I think they're only twenty-five feet. Who is it with her?"

"Hal Lynch."

The man who'd been here before. The man who'd been her ex-husband's head of security. And her bodyguard. Joseph's neck went tight as he watched her face for a reaction. It wasn't nearly what he'd hoped for, which would have been utter disgust.

"Poor Hal," she murmured. "It's got to be rough having to watch when you used to be in charge. I'll be there in a minute."

"Sounds good," Hector said. "What about you, Carter? You staying?"

Hell, yeah, he wanted to say. But he knew he couldn't. He'd just told her he'd give her time and Hector was good at his job. "No. I need to tend to a few things at home. I'll be back in the morning to drive Miss Montgomery into the city." Joseph looked over at Daphne. "I assume you're not going to want to stay at home tomorrow?"

"You assume correctly. Let's go inside now, Hector. The sooner I get Hal taken care of, the sooner I can take off my wi-w-wardrobe."

Joseph was careful to keep his lips from twitching until his window was closed all the way. "Wi-w-wardrobe?"

"I'm tired," she said. "I almost spilled the beans and said 'wig.'"

"Look, I don't want to pry."

She gave him an incredulous look. "Yes, you do."

"Okay, I do. I need to know that you're okay. I'm guessing it was breast cancer."

Her eyes widened. "How did you know?"

"You've made helping women with breast cancer your focus. I paid attention at all those fund-raisers, even though that damn bow tie was cutting off my air supply. One of the services you're going to provide is wig fittings, right? And there's the new dorm for single mothers and their families. I'm wondering why the hell you don't tell people that you're a survivor, but I don't need to know now. Just tell me that you're okay."

She caught her bottom lip between her teeth, making him want to do the same. "I'm past the five-year mark," she finally said. "I'm okay."

Relief sent a shiver across his skin. "Good. Let's go in." He drove the Escalade into the garage, parking it by a cherry red Jaguar. "Nice. Yours?"

"I drive a Chevy Silverado. Lets me haul stuff. The Jag is Mama's," she said with a shake of her head. "As is the Harley."

"Really? She ever take you for a ride?"

"A few times, but she's wicked fast. Scares the hell outta me. She's a terrible influence on Ford." She drew a sharp breath, realizing what she said.

"He's out there, Daphne. We will find him."

"I know. I'm just . . . I know."

He went around to her side and helped her down. Then put his arms around her, gratified when she snuggled deep. "Come on. Let's get you inside where it's safe."

"You're coming in? I thought you said you weren't going to stay."

"I'm not, but I'll go in and say hi to your mother." *And to make sure Hal leaves quickly.* He walked her into her house, his hand resting lightly on her lower back. As soon as he entered the room, the smell of pine smacked him in the face, dominating Daphne's own delicate peach.

"Mama?" Daphne called out as she went into the great room and stopped short. "What the hell is that? And where did it come from?"

"That" was a Douglas fir that had to be fifteen feet tall. Daphne's mother knelt on the floor at the tree's base, sorting through a box of holiday ornaments. A lady with a sweet face was muttering over a string of lights. And a man dressed in jeans and a suede jacket sat on the sofa.

Glaring at me. Or more precisely, glaring at Joseph's hand, which still rested lightly on Daphne's back. Joseph returned the man's stare coolly, arching his brows. It was a petty middle-school-boy challenge that he wasn't proud of, but he didn't look away.

Simone looked at the tree, her expression determined. "It's a Christmas tree. I bought it and it's staying. Any other questions? Hello, Joseph."

"Hello, Mrs. Montgomery. Nice to see you again."

"But . . ." Daphne trailed off, looking up at the height of the giant tree.

"Simone," Simone said absently. "Call me Simone."

"But . . ." Daphne looked back down to her mother. "Mama, we said we'd do a tree in the parlor, a normal-sized tree. This is enormous."

"I know," Simone said. "That's what I was going for. Fucking enormous."

"Language, Simone," the lady with the lights said mildly. "She bought a tree for the parlor, too, Daphne."

"And one for the upstairs hall," the man on the sofa added affectionately.

Daphne's mouth opened, but no words came out. "Why?" she finally asked.

"Because," Simone said with a firm nod, "we are going to decorate every one of these damn trees so that when Ford gets home, he'll see them from the parkway."

Daphne's expression softened. "Oh. Kind of our version of 'Every Light in the House Is On.' " She looked at Joseph over her shoulder. "It's a country song."

"I've heard it," Joseph said. "It's a beautiful tree, Simone. And a wonderful idea."

"Thank you," Simone said, but her lips trembled. She turned her face away and Joseph watched the lady with the lights press a tissue into her hand. Seconds later Simone was back to her task, her expression as determined as before. Maybe more.

It wasn't hard to see where Daphne had gotten her strength.

Daphne turned to the man on the sofa. "Hal, I'm sorry. I was about to tell you hi, but then I saw the tree."

"It's okay," he said with an easy smile. "I did the same thing when I came in." He rose and walked up to them, then leaned forward to murmur, "Let her have the tree, Daphne. It's keeping her sane right now."

"You're right," she whispered, then cleared her throat. "Hal, this is Joseph Carter. He's with the FBI. Joseph, this is Hal Lynch, a very old family friend."

Hal shook his hand, his eyes wary. "Do you have any leads?"

"A few," Joseph said, trying not to sound terse and aware that he failed utterly.

"But you can't discuss them," Hal said. "I understand. I do hope you can answer a few of my questions, though. Both Nadine Elkhart and I got visits from the FBI tonight, looking for Travis."

"That's because we're looking for Travis," Daphne said.

"Why? Has something happened to Ford that no one's telling us about?"

"Oh, no," Daphne said. "I'm sorry you thought that. The FBI wants to find Travis so that we can get a list of criminals he's sentenced or represented in the past. It's routine."

Joseph kept his expression bland, even though he frowned inside. Brodie had told them that the blood in the basement matched Odum's, but Daphne had still been worried that it was the same type as Travis's. She hadn't mentioned that and Joseph wondered if she had a reason.

Hal was frowning. "I thought those Millhouses were responsible."

"They may be," Daphne said seriously. "But they're not narrowing the focus just yet. The girl who was with Ford when he was kidnapped was one of my first cases. I cut a deal with her. It's possible she had nothing to do with Ford's disappearance, but it brought into the light that both Travis and I have jobs that make enemies. We'd be foolish not to track those possibilities. Did you see Travis?"

"No. I talked to him on the phone this afternoon. He was very upset when you told him about Ford. But I don't know where he is right now."

"At what time did you talk to him this afternoon?" Joseph asked. "And was he calling from his cell or home phone?"

"It was at about three. Maybe four. And neither. I called him and he was at the office. Which I already told the other FBI agents. Don't you guys talk to each other?"

"They do, Hal," Daphne soothed, "but it's been a very long day. If you don't mind, I'm exhausted. I'm going to sleep now. If you talk to Travis again, please tell him that the police need his cooperation. For Ford's sake."

"I will. For Ford's sake. And yours."

Daphne slipped her arm through Hal's, leading him to the front door. "I'll call you as soon as I hear anything. I promise." She paused with her hand on the doorknob, looking around as if she'd suddenly realized something. "Where is Tasha?"

"In the solarium," the lady with the Christmas lights said. "When Hal arrived she became a bit . . ."

"Vicious," Hal said, disgruntled.

"Agitated," the lady corrected.

"Tasha's not a vicious dog, Hal," Daphne said. "She's just protective. You said yourself that you worried about me by myself, so I got a protection dog. Plus she's got to be on edge. So many people coming in and out." She handed Hal his hat and overcoat from the entry table. "Be careful. The roads are slick."

Hal nodded, searching Daphne's face. "Are you really all right?"

"No," she said, very seriously. "I'm falling apart, inside. I have been terrified every minute of this horrible day. But I want my son back and if that means staying lucid and not being hysterical, then that's what I'll do."

"Then get some sleep." Hal pulled her to him and for a moment Daphne clung, looking like she was fighting tears. "You'll call me if you need me?" he whispered.

"I will."

Hal finally left and Joseph let out the breath he'd been holding. Daphne bowed her head, resting her brow against the closed door, her face intensely still.

"Daphne?" he said softly.

"Just . . . a panic attack. I'm okay."

She was not okay. Joseph went to her, put his arms around her. She was trembling from the strain of holding herself together. "What can I do for you?"

"Just stay here for a minute." She turned her face into his chest and breathed deep, even breaths that slowly grew shallower. Finally she stepped back. "Thank you."

"Anytime." They turned to find her mother and the light lady staring at them.

Daphne braved a smile. "Show's over, girls."

The woman who'd been working on the lights approached him, extending her hand. "I'm Maggie VanDorn. I'm *also* an old family friend."

Daphne's eyes closed. "I'm sorry, Maggie. It was the damn tree. I swear."

Maggie patted her cheek, then turned to Joseph. "I was Daphne's nanny."

He met Maggie's eyes, found them filled with worry. "Good to meet you, ma'am."

"Stay as long as you like," she said to Joseph. "Come along, Simone. I'll fix us a hot toddy. It'll help us sleep."

The ladies went to the kitchen, leaving Daphne and Joseph alone. Joseph ran his hand down her back. "Before I leave, is there a place we can talk privately? I have some questions about your friend. Hal."

"Sure," she said. "This way." She led him to the solarium, where a hundred-pound Giant Schnauzer waited. "Follow my lead. She might look cute, but she's fierce."

Great, he thought sourly. *Another protection dog to dislike me.* Paige's dog still barely tolerated him. Nevertheless, he followed her in.

The dog immediately began to bark frantically.

"Tasha," Daphne said sharply. "Down." The dog dropped to her belly, eyeing Joseph as if he were a giant pork chop. "Now come. He's okay."

Unbelievably the dog came—warily, but she came.

"Crouch down with me," Daphne said, and together, they did. Daphne laid her head on Joseph's shoulder and patted his knee. "It's okay, Tasha. He's okay." When the dog came closer, Daphne took Joseph's hand and held it out to the dog. Within a few seconds, she'd licked him and gone back to her corner and curled up to sleep.

Daphne straightened, pulling Joseph up with her. "There. Now if you need to come in the house when I'm not here, she'll most likely leave you alone."

She hadn't let go of his hand. That was very good. He needed to ask his question and leave her alone to sleep. He wanted to kiss her senseless.

He wanted too many other things that he couldn't have right now. "I need to go."

She held tight to his hand. "Not yet. What was your question?"

With difficulty, he brought his body into check. "Why didn't you tell your friend about the blood in the basement?"

"Hal? I didn't want to upset my mother and Maggie. They hate Travis, but hearing about all that would terrify them more than they already are."

"That's it? I thought maybe you didn't trust him."

"I do trust him. He would never hurt me. But Joseph, he's a friend, no more." She met his eyes. "You have nothing to fear from him."

The need to have her hit him like a brick, and before he knew what he was doing he'd started to reach for her. He backed away. "I have to go."

"Wait."

He stopped, hanging on to his control, but barely.

"I did tell Hal something that wasn't true. I told him that I'd been scared every minute of this horrible day. But there were a few seconds when I wasn't scared. When I believed everything could be all right."

"When?" he whispered.

"When you kissed me. That moment with you in the conference room was the only time all day that I didn't feel afraid." She swallowed hard. "I know you have to go, but . . ." She looked up then. "Please?"

The air left his lungs in a slow, steady exhale and he let her see how very, very hungry he was. Her breath hitched when he lifted his hands, cupping her face the way he'd wanted to all day. The way he'd wanted to for nine fucking months.

"My hands are shaking," he whispered.

"Why?"

"I've wanted this for so long . . . I'm afraid I can't go slow."

"Then don't. Don't go slow. I don't want to be able to think."

God. With a groan he snapped, taking her mouth with no finesse, no control. Just . . . need. Raw need. He devoured her in a big, greedy surge. He couldn't get enough. *Never enough.* And then she was kissing him back. Her arms were around his neck and she was lifting herself higher. *Closer.*

More. His hands slid down her body, down that beautiful body that he'd watched so many times. *Mine.* His hands closed over the roundness of her butt and he kneaded hard and fast. She was on her toes, her arms straining, her hips lifting. Seeking.

He spun them, pressing her against the door, pressing himself against her. Rocking up into her. Good. She felt so good.

And it still wasn't enough. Need boiled over and he ripped his mouth away, forced his hips to freeze. But his cock failed to get the memo, throbbing against the softest part of her. He rested his forehead against hers, watching her face, waiting for the moment she opened her eyes. He needed to see her eyes. Needed to know she needed this, too. Needed to know he hadn't gone too far.

"Daphne?" Her name came out gravelly. She opened her eyes and he managed to swallow his groan. The blue was dark with desire. Alive with need. "I want you. You understand that?"

She nodded, the pulse at the hollow of her throat beating so fast. He kissed her there, felt her go languid in his hands. She was still staring up at him. Wonder and want swirling in the blue. "Joseph."

"Soon," he whispered. "Soon I'm going to do all the things to you that I've dreamed about." She swallowed hard, bit her lip harder. He kissed her there, taking her lip between his teeth and tugging. "I've dreamed a lot, Daphne."

She licked her lip. "So have I."

"I need to stop. Or I won't be able to." He lowered her feet to the floor, unwilling to let her go. "I need to stop. God, I want you naked."

She closed her eyes, opened her mouth to breathe. "You do things to me."

"You have no idea what I'll do to you."

"Soon." It was uttered on an exhale. "Please. Oh God."

He forced himself to step back, forced his hands to let her go. "Soon." He removed her hands from his neck and pressed them together, kissing her fingers. "I'll be back for you tomorrow morning. Try to sleep."

She nodded. "I'll try. Thank y—"

He silenced her with a last hard kiss. "Don't you thank me. Not yet. Not until I give you something to be thankful for."

Exercising every ounce of discipline he possessed, he left her there. When he looked back she stood in the doorway, her fingertips lightly covering her mouth, the big black dog at her side.

Tuesday, December 3, 11:20 p.m.

Clay tapped his foot impatiently. The elevator was so damn slow.

"Clay," Alec said softly. "You can't go to Stevie's family like this. They're scared enough without you barging in looking like a drug dealer on meth. Your eyes are wild, man."

Clay closed his wild eyes, slumping against the elevator wall. The kid was right. "Okay. I'm calm." He opened his eyes. "How's this?"

"Sixteen cups of coffee and a handful of uppers. But down from meth. Keep going."

Clay had to smile. "You know, you're actually proving useful, kid."

"Gee, thanks. I'm touched." But Alec's tone was amused and his eyes were kind. "Sometimes I'd be at Ethan and Dana's when they'd get a new foster. Those kids can be wild, too, like wounded animals in cages, ready to bite even a friendly hand. Ethan's just a rock, you know? He can get them calm when nobody else can."

"So you're channeling him?"

"Something like that. He's pretty much been my dad for the last six years. There are worse people to wanna be when you grow up."

Yeah, like me. Helluva dad I turned out to be. His daughter wouldn't even see him, no matter how many times he tried. "Not many better." The elevator opened, but instead of running out like he wanted to, he looked at the kid seriously. "Now?"

Alec studied his eyes. "Okay, now you're down to a case of Red Bull. If you promise to play nice, you can go in."

"Thanks, Alec. I mean it."

The kid's cheeks heated. "That's what you pay me for."

No, it wasn't, actually. They walked down the hallway to the ICU security door, but Clay didn't push the call button. "I'm not trying to get rid of you."

"But?"

"But while I appreciate the many wild-animal-calming skills you've picked up from Ethan, what I *pay* you for are the technical skills he taught you."

Alec's brows lifted. "What do you have in mind?"

"I'm not sure yet. But I got loose ends flapping around in my head. One of them that I keep thinking about is the Webcam stuck in Gargano's vent. That was a crime of opportunity that Doug made work for him. I mean, Kimberly was invited to the party through an outside association. She didn't crash it. But it worked."

"And because it did, maybe Doug and Kimberly tried it again?"

Clay nodded. "Exactly. But in a planned way instead of relying on chance party invitations to homes of cops. Kimberly was arrested for stealing from a cleaning client."

"Working for a maid service would get her into people's houses. But if she had a record, nobody would hire her." Alec considered it. "Maybe she worked for herself. If so, we'd need to find her clients."

"Gargano filed an insurance claim," Clay said. "I'm wondering if any of Kim and Doug's other victims did the same thing."

"Gargano was suspected of insurance fraud but they couldn't prove it. Maybe there have been other insurance claims that were denied or dicey—places where Kimberly might have worked." Alec's eyes had begun to sparkle. "Let me see what I can do."

"I'm not asking you to hack into anything," Clay warned.

"I would never do anything like that," Alec said sincerely. "Unless absolutely necessary," he added under his breath. "Hey, you're down to a pot of hi-test Starbucks. I think you're safe."

Clay watched the kid jog to the elevator and disappear through its doors. Then he set his shoulders and told the hummingbirds crashing around in his gut to settle down as he hit the call button and requested admittance to ICU.

When he got to the waiting room he was met by Stevie's parents, their faces beaming. A man Clay hadn't met earlier rose deliberately from the chair in which he'd been sitting, watching silently as Stevie's parents welcomed him back.

Zina Nicolescu reached up from her tiny four feet eleven inches and grabbed Clay's face, dragging him down to kiss both cheeks soundly. "I hoped you'd come back," she whispered.

Like anything on this earth could have kept me away. "I was a few hours away. I had to drive," he whispered back, "or I would have been here already. How is she?"

Zina shrugged happily. "Trying to give orders, even though she can't say a word."

She let him go and Clay straightened, having to look up at Stevie's father. Clay didn't have to look up to most men, but Emil was extremely tall. "I would like to see your daughter for just a minute, if I could."

Emil nodded and Clay got the uncomfortable feeling that the man saw a great deal more than Clay would have liked. "Of course. But first you need to meet Stefania's brother, Sorin. He just arrived from California."

Sorin crossed the small waiting room, his eyes scrutinizing. "She never mentioned you," he said abruptly, earning him a swat from his mother.

"Sorin. Your manners. This is the man who saved your sister's life."

"I see," was all the man said. He shook Clay's hand, but only because his mother appeared ready to swat him again. "What do you do for a living, Mr. Maynard?"

"I'm a private investigator. Please call me Clay."

Sorin nodded, clearly not convinced. "I see," he said again, giving him a once-over that made Clay look down at his clothing.

And then the source of Sorin's blatant disapproval was clear. "Oh. I don't normally look like a drug dealer. This has been a long day."

"I've traveled across three time zones," Sorin said. "And still I found the time to shave."

"Sorin!" his mother snapped.

Clay drew a breath. "My friend was murdered last night and we have two missing college kids and one missing teenager. That was before your sister was shot."

Sorin had the good grace to look ashamed. "I suppose shaving wasn't foremost on your mind."

"No. It was nice to meet you, Sorin. I'll go see your sister now, if that's okay."

"It's more than okay," Emil said. "Before I forget, Stefania's daughter made this for you." He handed Clay a folded-up piece of paper. "She wanted to give it to you herself, but we sent her home with our youngest daughter, Izabela, to get some rest."

When Clay opened it, he sucked in a breath. Cordelia Mazzetti had made him a thank-you card. With crayon she'd drawn her mother in the hospital bed, a frown on her face. A man stood next to her, crudely drawn blood dripping from his clothing. With a yellow ring over his head. *An angel.* Clay didn't have to ask who the angel was—Cordelia had drawn a bold arrow pointing to the ring with his name written over the line.

Clay almost laughed, but his throat was too damn tight. "I think this is the first time anyone's ever called me an angel," he murmured.

"Sometimes Cordelia gets scared when Stefania is at work," Emil said. "Especially since last year." When a killer had held a gun to Cordelia's head, then Stevie's. "We tell her that both she and her mother have guardian angels watching over them. Today that angel was you."

Clay stared at the paper, remembering the art on the back of Ciccotelli's door and wishing that he had a crayon drawing of his own. Now he did. He rubbed the back of his hand across his mouth, hard. Then swallowed harder.

Very carefully he folded the paper and slid it into the inner pocket of his jacket. "Tell . . ." He had to clear his throat. "Tell Cordelia that I will keep this forever."

"I will." Emil patted his back. "Now go see my daughter so that you can go home and sleep. You look exhausted."

Clay nodded, waved to them lamely, and hit the call button to be let into the unit itself. He sanitized his hands as he waited, aware that the three Nicolescus watched his every step. Finally the door opened and he was waved in.

"You only have a few minutes," the nurse warned. "Did you wash your hands?"

"I used the hand sanitizer."

"Well, wash your hands here." She pointed to a sink, then scrutinized his face. "Your face, too. Especially if you plan on kissing her again," she added in a mutter.

Clay's face heated. He hadn't even considered that anyone had been watching him before. "Yes, ma'am."

"But first, lose the dirty pants. I'll get you some scrubs."

"Yes, ma'am," he said again. He changed into the scrubs, then washed his hands, scrubbing until it was a wonder he had any skin.

Then he steadied himself and walked into her room. She was asleep again, her face still so pale. But maybe she had a little more color. Or maybe that was just what he wanted to see.

He sat on the edge of the chair by her bed, elbows on his knees, hunching over until his forehead rested on the cold metal of the bed rail. *I'm so tired.* But not just of this day. "I'm so damn tired of my life," he whispered.

He wasn't sure how long he sat there with his head down, certain that any minute the nurse would make him leave. Then the bed rail trembled and his hair was brushed off his forehead. *Stevie.* Slowly he lifted his head, afraid he'd scare her. Or that he'd been dreaming again.

Her eyes were open and staring at him. Her hand had fallen back to the bed, as if that was all the energy she'd had to spare.

"Hi," he said quietly. "I won't stay long. I just wanted to see you."

She shook her head, just a little, and his heart sank.

"All right. I'll go now." He stood and her eyes flashed annoyance. She lifted the hand that wasn't connected to any tubes and crooked her finger before letting the hand fall again. She wanted him to stay. "Okay." He started to sit again when she rolled her eyes. "What?" he asked, frustrated.

The look she gave him left no doubt that she was more frustrated. She crooked her finger again and he bent close. "What?" he whispered.

She searched his face, then once again lifted her hand. To touch his lips. She touched the corner of her own mouth before sinking into the bed, her body drained. Her eyes were narrowed in question.

"Did I kiss you?"

A single nod.

"If I say yes, am I going to get yelled at?"

Another nod. And the slight curving of her mouth around the tube.

His heart began to race. "If I do it again, what will you do?"

Her eyes changed, grew very serious. Sad. Her shoulder lifted.

His racing heart slowed, stuttering. "This didn't change anything, did it?"

She looked away.

"I never took you for a coward, Stevie," he said quietly and her gaze swung back, angrily. "Did I make you mad? Good. I'm glad. Because you make me mad. If today didn't change anything for you, then you're either a liar or a fool. And I never took you for either of those." He leaned closer, until he could see every dark eyelash. "I'm not a coward or a liar, but I might be a fool because I'm not giving up on you. Nor am I giving you up. So consider yourself on notice, Detective Mazzetti. Things will be different when you get out of here. I'm not going to wait forever, because we don't *have* forever. If things had been any different this morning, we might not even have this moment. So if you're not 'ready,' then you'd best spend your time in here figuring out how to *get* 'ready.'"

He let the words hang between them while she stared up at him, her nostrils flaring slightly. "And you need to know that if that tube weren't sticking down your throat I'd be kissing you the way I've wanted to for a long, long time." He flicked a glance at the heart monitor, his lips quirking at the jump in her pulse. "That's really cool. I can see exactly how much that affects you."

Her eyes narrowed dangerously and he knew he'd pushed too far. "I'm going now," he said, softening his voice. "But I'll be back. I promise." He brushed his lips over hers, watched her eyes drift closed and all his bravado fled. "God, Stevie." His voice broke. "I thought I was going to lose you before I ever had you."

Because you've never had her. You just have a lot of wishes.

He straightened with a weary sigh. "You know, just forget what I said. I can't make you want me. I can't make you be ready. I won't stalk you or force you in any way. That's not who I am. If you decide you want to see what we could have together . . . well, you know where to find me."

His step heavy, Clay walked back to the waiting area. Sorin was waiting by the door, blocking his path. "What?" Clay asked dully.

"She's my twin, you know. I'm five minutes older."

Clay shook his head. "No, I didn't know. I hope she recovers."

Sorin huffed a rueful chuckle. "I know Stefania better than anyone. She will recover because she's too damn stubborn to do otherwise. She's also doomed to be alone for the rest of her life for the same reason. Which makes her a coward and a fool." He lifted a shoulder. "I listened at the door of her room just now."

Clay's jaw clenched. *Keep it together. Don't knock his head off his shoulders in ICU or that nurse will yell at you again.* "I suppose that's your right."

"No, it wasn't, but I did it anyway. You were right, you know. Up until the end when you folded."

Clay's chin lifted. "I didn't fold. I reconsidered."

"Whatever. Just please don't give up on her." Sorin stared at him hard, then offered his hand. "Be well, Mr. Maynard."

Clay shook his hand. "You, too. Your folks have my cell phone and e-mail. Can you let me know if she needs anything?"

"Other than a swift kick in the pants? Sure." With that he stepped back and let Clay pass. Mercifully, Stevie's parents weren't in the waiting area. Hopefully they'd gone home to sleep.

Which is where I'll go. Home. But not to sleep. Because Ford was still missing. And because his heart physically hurt like it never had before.

He'd never gotten a chance to talk to the MacGregors. Maybe he'd drive back up to Philly and do that tomorrow. Because there was always a tomorrow. *Just ask Stevie,* he thought bitterly. *She thinks she has a million of them.*

Fourteen

Joseph parked in his parents' driveway behind the police cruiser he'd had stationed there after the shooting. He hadn't checked on his family all day, so he showed his badge to the officer and let himself into the house, only to be met with a low growl.

"Oh, for God's sake," he muttered. "It's me, Patty." He turned on the foyer light and the growling immediately ceased, an adult Rottweiler jumping up on him to say hello. "No." He pushed the dog down, glaring. "You could learn a lot of manners from Tasha."

He hung his coat over the banister and cut through the living room to the kitchen—

Where he stopped short, not sure what he was seeing. Not because the room was dark, but because . . . His mind registered the men's Nikes on the floor next to a lacy white bra before he saw his youngest sister poking her head up over the back of the sofa, a pair of boxers in her hand.

Oh. My. God. He spun around, clenching his eyes shut. "Holly?"

"Joseph?" Holly said tentatively. "Didn't know you were coming home."

"I guess not." He shook his head, hoping to dislodge what he'd seen, and thought of Daphne waving her hands, saying *Bleach for my eyes, stat!* "Who is he?"

"His name's Dillon. We met at our social center. Say hi, Dillon."

"Hi?" Dillon squeaked, then cleared his throat. "Hi," he said in a deeper voice that still trembled a little. "Is he going to kill me?" he added in a whisper.

Joseph rubbed his pounding temples. "It depends. Is this . . . consensual?" He choked out the word.

"Of course. I'm twenty-eight, Joseph! I'm not a little girl anymore, so back off."

He knew Holly thought he was overprotective because she had Down syndrome, but that wasn't true. He'd felt this way about his other sisters, too. But Holly was more vulnerable, even if she didn't want to accept the notion.

He thought about the bra and the boxers. This seemed a situation better handled by his mother. Because he just might kill the guy and that might be wrong.

"Just put on your clothes. Please." He hurried to his father's study, where there was a light on under the door. He knocked, then went in, not waiting for a reply. "Dad, have you seen Mom? She needs to—Oh, *hell*, no." He spun around for the second time in as many minutes. "Goddamn hell."

Yes, his father had seen his mother. *And now, so have I.*

"God put doors on rooms for a reason, Joseph," his mother said impatiently.

"Next time wait for me to say 'come in,'" his father added in a sour voice.

Joseph could hear zippers zipping and wanted to stick his fingers in his ears. "What is *wrong* with you people? Is this house under some kind of sex spell?"

"What are you talking about?" his father asked.

"I just caught Holly and some guy named Dillon . . . You need to do something."

"She is twenty-eight, Joseph," his mother said. "You can turn around now."

"No. I'm never turning around again. You're okay with her doing it on the sofa?"

"Well, no," his mother said. "I'll have a talk with Holly about appropriate spaces. But, Joseph, you need to know . . . Dillon's asked to marry her."

Joseph turned around at that, staring at his mother. "Is that okay with you?"

"Maybe you didn't hear the first time?" his mother said. "She's twenty-eight. So is he. They are adults with Down syndrome who work full-time and are quite capable of living independently, with a little help from us. We like him. And he loves her."

Joseph blew out a breath, humbled. "I guess I can't ask for more than that."

"This is what we've prepared her for, Joseph. A life of her own, just like any of our other children. I'm sure Holly wanted you to find out a little differently, though."

"I could live my whole life without seeing any of this again."

His mother climbed out of his father's lap, lightly slapping Jack's hands away when he tried to drag her back. "I'd better take Dillon home."

"He doesn't drive?"

"Most of the time, yes, but he's wise enough to ask for a lift when the weather is bad, like tonight. I hope you didn't threaten to kill him. He's a sensitive young man."

"I would never threaten to kill him."

"You threatened to make her last three boyfriends into eunuchs," his mother said, exasperated. "And then *I* had to explain to Holly what a eunuch was. I love you, Joseph, but you're uptight. Other people have sex lives, including your father and me. We did make four children."

"Please," he begged. "No more. I'm sorry. I just . . . Bleach my eyes."

His mother's eyes twinkled. "Well, *sugar*, that just answered my next question. You've been spending time with Daphne." She sobered. "How is she?"

Joseph's body hardened, just remembering how she was, then he felt guilty as hell. "She's holding up, for now. Stevie woke up, so we've had *some* good news."

"We heard. Paige called." She studied Joseph's face, suddenly sad. "You don't think you're going to find Ford, do you?"

"There are so many possibilities. I don't even know why he was taken."

She patted his cheek tenderly. "I'm sorry, son. You never said why you came tonight. What can we do for you?"

"I wanted to be sure you all were okay, that the police had been providing good security. I should have come earlier, but I've had kind of a busy day."

"We know," his mother said dryly. "The police have been kind. We don't need them, though. You've always had us locked up tighter than Fort Knox."

"I didn't want to take any chances."

"And we appreciate that. We're really fine, so stop worrying. I'll go see to Holly now. You visit with your dad."

Joseph had a hard time looking at his father. His father, on the other hand, seemed to find Joseph's discomfort wildly amusing. "If you could have seen the look on your face," his father said, chuckling.

"Look, Dad, I'm really happy you and Mom have a healthy . . . God . . . love life, but no kid wants to think of their parents that way."

"I know." His father walked over to his desk, where he kept the good Scotch. "Are you here for the night? Can I pour you a drink?"

"Yes and yes. Make it a double, please." He sat down next to the fire. "Zoe's supposed to stop by after her date tonight. I need her advice."

His father handed him his Scotch, then settled in the other chair. "About women or killers?"

"Killers. I'm okay on the women."

"Bleach my eyes," his father said, mimicking Daphne's drawl. "I am so glad you finally made your move, Joseph. I was ready to draw you a damn diagram. What took you so long, anyway?"

"I thought she was taken."

"By whom?"

"Maynard."

"Hell, Joseph. Clay Maynard's all sloppy-eyed over Stevie Mazzetti."

Joseph stared at his father. "How do you know all this?"

"Because I listen when the ladies come over for 'major mojitos.'"

"What the hell is that?"

"Girl time. Paige apparently started it with Daphne, and before I knew it Zoe and your mother and Holly and Lisa and Judy were card-carrying members of the major mojito club. Daphne's mother and Maggie come, too, and sometimes Stevie. Not often. Her sister Izzy comes occasionally. But whoever comes, they talk and talk and watch sappy movies and do their nails." He shook his head. "Your mother absolutely loves it. They gossip and I listen and learn all kinds of stuff."

"They just let you hang around and listen?"

"Who do you think makes the mojitos? I've become a damned good bartender. I can even make chocolate martinis." His father grinned and then it faded to a wistful smile. "Your mother and I don't pry in our kids' lives. Not a lot anyway. But we know how unhappy you've been, Joseph. We want you to have a life as good as the one we have. I want you to have someone to grow old with and embarrass your children with when they catch you in compromising positions."

Joseph's throat closed. "I would love to have what you have, Dad."

His father's swallow was audible. "You know, I've been worried all day about Ford. He's such a good kid and I can't stand the thought that he could be hurt or worse. Your mother came in here tonight and found me staring at the fire. She sat in my lap to comfort me. It just kind of . . . got better from there." He was quiet for a long moment. "After all these years she still knows what I need before I do. If you can find one-tenth of what your mother and I have, you'll be a lucky man. And I will be the world's happiest father."

The flames got blurry as Joseph's eyes filled. When he could finally clear his throat, he whispered, "What if I can't find him for her, Dad?"

"You'll cross that bridge when you get there, Joseph. I never said it would be easy."

His father hadn't spouted empty promises and Joseph appreciated that. "Worthwhile things never are," he said quietly.

"That's bullshit," his father declared. "Whoever said that was full of it."

Joseph's mouth curved. "*You* said that to me when I was in high school."

"I did? Huh. Well. It's not true. Sometimes the most worthwhile things are right in front of our eyes. We just make them hard because we think that gives them more value. You make things too difficult, Joseph. It doesn't have to be hard." His father stood up, clapped his hands together. "Are you hungry?"

"Yes. Yes, I am. I haven't eaten all day."

"Then come with me. I'll make you some food."

West Virginia
Tuesday, December 3, 11:50 p.m.

One foot. In front of the other. Head down against the wind, Ford forced his frozen feet to trudge upward. Just a few more steps to reach the top of the hill.

How many hills had he climbed? Fifty? Sixty? A hundred? *So tired.*

No longer did he think of saving Kim with every beat of his heart. He'd been reduced to a single word, pounding in his head—

Frostbite. Frostbite. Frostbite. Every time his foot thundered into the snow, pain sliced up his legs. *I'm going to lose my feet. God, please. Let somebody find me. Please. Before it's too late.*

The ground under his feet leveled. He'd reached the top of the hill. He was afraid to look. He'd been disappointed too many times.

Please. A house. Anything. Just let me see light. Gritting his teeth, he forced his chin to lift until he could see the world before him.

"No," he moaned. All he could see was shades of dark. No lights. No houses. Just trees. More road. And the next hill.

Fuck it! Fury rushed up, momentarily energizing him, and the next thing he knew, his backpack was flying through the air, landing twenty feet away.

His shoulders sagged as the fit of temper rushed out as fast as it had rushed in. His eyes stung. *No.* He willed himself not to cry. A tear would leave his face wet.

That was really stupid, you fuck. The pack had landed on the side of the road, in the snow. Now he'd have to wade through a snowdrift to get his shit. The pack still had a strip of jerky. And that girl's purse.

Heather. Perspective returned and with it, determination. The girl might be alive. Kim might be alive. *But you won't be alive if you don't move your ass.*

Keep going. One foot in front of the other. Grimacing, he threw his right foot forward and prepared for the pain. And then he heard it. Ford went still, afraid to hope. But there it was, behind him.

An engine. A car was coming. *Thank you, God. Thank you.*

Shuffling, he turned around. Headlights. *Thank you.* The lights came closer, growing larger, then blurred as his eyes filled with tears. This time he let them fall. His face burned and he didn't care.

Finally. Hurry. Please hurry.

He lifted his arm to wave as the car grew closer.

Not a car. A van. It slowed, then rolled to a stop.

The headlights blinded him and he shielded his eyes with his forearm, wincing. The door opened. Someone got out. Ford couldn't see the face. The headlights . . . *So bright.*

"Hel—." Only a croak emerged. He cleared his throat. "Hello."

A sharp crack split the air. Sharp points puncturing his leg.

"No!" The roar burst from his chest and then all he knew was the pain. *Not again.* He fell to his knees, convulsing. *Not again.* Then he fell facefirst into the snow. He saw the shoes, inches from his face, felt the pressure in his back. A knee.

Fight. Dammit, fight. But his body was disconnected from his brain.

A hand yanked back the collar of his shirt a split second before the needle plunged into his neck. Ford could smell the aftershave. Same as before. *Him. It was him again.* Warm breath bathed his ear and he knew what would come next.

No. Not again. Please.

"I'm back," the man purred. "Did you miss me?"

It was happening again. And there wasn't a thing he could do about it.

Baltimore, Maryland
Tuesday, December 3, 11:50 p.m.

Joseph was following his father to the kitchen when he heard a small voice calling his name. He looked up the stairs and smiled.

"Holly-bear," he said softly.

She was dressed in a soft, thankfully modest robe, pink

bunny slippers on her feet. She padded down the stairs, her expression tentative. "You're staying here tonight?" She got to the bottom step and looked up at him. Holly was only four ten, so she tended to look up a lot.

"Yep."

"Good. I'll make you breakfast."

"I'd like that. Dad's making me dinner now."

"But it's almost midnight. It's not good for you to eat dinner so late."

"Been too busy to eat today. I have this case."

"I know. Ford. I wanted to call Daphne, but I know she's busy."

"What do you want me to tell her for you?"

"Just give her a hug and tell her it's from me," she said with a small smile that quickly faded. "Joseph, are you mad at me?"

"You mean about the sofa? No. Of course not."

"Because it's normal for couples to kiss." Her eyes went sly. "Even you kiss girls sometimes."

The memory of kissing Daphne against the door came back with a rush and he felt his face heat. "Sometimes," he allowed.

Holly smiled, delighted. "You're blushing, Joseph."

"Maybe I am. Maybe I caught some of your blush from earlier. As I recall, that's all you were wearing."

She rolled her eyes. "Joseph."

"Mom says he's getting ready to pop the question."

Her chin lifted slightly. "You think I shouldn't."

"I never said that. I'd like to meet him. And I'll try not to kill him," he added wryly. "He's just got to be good enough for my little sister."

"Paige likes him. She says he's good for me. So does Daphne."

Daphne knew about those two? "You and Dillon take karate together from Paige?"

"Not in the same class. I'm with the girls. I met Kimberly there."

"You mean Ford's girlfriend?"

She nodded, frowning. "Yeah."

"Talk to me, Holly. What did you see?"

"Nothing." She leaned close to speak in his ear. "I *heard*, but I didn't know if I should say anything."

"Tell me and I'll help you decide."

"She's got another boyfriend. That's wrong, Joseph. But it would hurt Ford to know."

"I think it would hurt more to think someone loved you and find out they didn't. Did you see him?"

"No," she said and his hopes faded. "But I heard her on the phone, talking to him. She told him that she found a job for them to do." Her face scrunched as she tried to remember. "She said he needed a GC something. Then she made kissy noises."

"Are you sure she wasn't talking to Ford?"

"Positive. Ford came driving up to get her and she said, 'Gotta go, he's here.' That's when I knew she had another boyfriend. That's wrong, Joseph."

"You're very right. When was this?"

"About a month ago. It was before Thanksgiving."

"Excellent. Did she see you?"

"Yeah, but she ignored me. Most people do," she added ruefully and his heart broke a little.

"Then they're fools," he said and kissed her forehead. "I want you to go to sleep now. Sweet dreams."

She grinned mischievously. "Of Dillon."

He winced. "Just no dreaming of him on the sofa down here, okay?"

"Okay. Joseph?"

"Yeah, baby?"

"I love you."

He wrapped her in a hug and spun her in a circle. "I love you, too, Holly-bear. Do I have to stop calling you Holly-bear when you get married?"

Her smile was huge. "You said 'when.'"

"I guess I did. You go to sleep now." He watched her pad back up the stairs.

GC. What is a GC?

He caught a whiff of something cooking in the kitchen. He'd worry about it after he ate. And maybe slept. He wondered if Daphne was sleeping.

He wondered what it would be like to watch her sleep, to watch her wake. For the rest of his life. *Find her son. Then you can find out.*

West Virginia
Wednesday, December 4, 12:15 a.m.

The kid had almost made it. Another few miles and he would have reached help, although not the help Mitch had originally intended. If Ford had taken the straight route through the wildlife management area, he should have stumbled right into the next town. Instead he'd ended up on a lonely stretch of road with an occasional farmhouse set way back out of view.

The snow was heavy and part of the time Mitch hadn't been able to see five feet in front of him. Ford must have gotten lost, unable to use the sky for navigation.

Switching off all the van's lights, Mitch moved the van forward until the back bumper was three feet ahead of Ford's unconscious body. He lowered the lift to the ground and rolled Ford in, huffing a little at the effort. Kid was a goddamn bruiser.

Sometimes genetics just weren't fair.

He raised the lift and shoved Ford into the back of the van. It was a tight fit. The hydraulic cart took up more than half the width of the van.

Closing the back doors, he returned the lift to its upright position and considered the next step. He'd have to ditch the kid and drive away quickly. Ford was wedged in so tight that he'd have trouble getting him out at all, much less in a rush.

He opened the side slider, grabbed hold of Ford's jacket, braced his feet against the running board, and pulled for all he was worth. After a few heaves his back was killing him, but he had Ford exactly where he wanted him—close to the door, folded into the fetal position.

That'll do. He closed the side door and climbed behind the wheel, sweating. *Give myself pneumonia, sweating in weather like this.* He rested his head against the seat for a moment, breathing deeply, focusing on the muscle in his back that was starting to spasm. When the burning began to subside, he popped a few pain relievers and put the van in drive.

He used to be able to bench-press a respectable weight for a guy his size. Moving boxes? No problem. Until he turned his back on Jimmy Cooley in the prison shower. The man had tried to make Mitch his bitch. Jimmy Cooley had ended up dead. *My shiv in his back.* But Mitch had hurt his back in the fight. He'd never been the same.

For that reason alone, his stepfather deserved to die.

Whoa. Driving without lights, he'd nearly passed by the first house he came to. It was a small place, fairly close to the road compared to its neighbors. Close enough for Ford to crawl to the front door once the ket wore off and he came to.

Mitch slowed to a stop, opened the sliding door, pulled Ford into the snow, and drove away. He planned to circle around and head back to Beckett's truck, still parked on the side of the road where Ford had run out of gas. *Right about where I figured he would.* He had time to tow Beckett's truck back to his cabin and set the man free before driving home.

He was looking forward to seeing how Beckett would react to having lost his ticket to "half of five million" . . . especially since Ford had seen his face.

He was especially looking forward to how Daphne would react to seeing Beckett's face after all these years. It had been twenty-seven years since Daphne had seen Beckett's ugly mug. Twenty-seven years since her mother moved her far, far away from their hometown. In a matter of hours, she'd be running back here as fast as she could.

Daphne, you're home. We missed you.

Fifteen

The screaming woke Daphne up. She lay in her own bed, staring up at the dark ceiling, trembling. Listening. To nothing. The house was quiet. She knew the screaming had only been in her own mind. It always was.

The last time she'd looked at the clock it had been midnight, so she'd slept less than an hour. She hadn't expected to sleep at all, so waking up was a surprise in itself. She hadn't slept at all the night before, the jury verdict heavy on her mind.

I should be too exhausted to dream. But it didn't work like that. The more exhausted she was, the more intense the nightmare. Lying beside her, Tasha lifted her head, and Daphne could have sworn the dog was listening, too. To nothing.

She got out of bed and peeked around her bedroom door. Agent Coppola had dragged a chair out of the spare bedroom and was sitting comfortably, keeping watch in the upstairs hall. When she saw Daphne, she came over.

"Everything okay?" she whispered.

Daphne nodded. "Did you hear anything?"

"Just now? No. Did you? Are you okay?"

Yes, she'd heard something fierce and terrifying—but in her own mind. It was the nightmare. It happened occasionally, usually when she was stressed. *I think today counts as one of those stressful days.*

"No, I heard nothing," she lied. "And yes, I'm all right."

"Usually when people say that, they're not. Your eyes say 'nightmare.' Bad one?"

Busted. "Yes, but I'm all right."

Coppola smiled. "Second verse, same as the first. Will you sleep now?"

Daphne wagged her head. "Doubtful."

Coppola pulled a deck of cards from her pocket. "We could play a game . . ."

Daphne opened the door wider. "Please."

Coppola came in and sat on the edge of the bed and dealt two piles of cards. "Your mother had a nightmare, too. She called out for 'Michael.' "

"My father." He broke Mama's heart. *And mine.*

"What's the story on him?"

"He left one night and we never saw him again. I should go to her."

"No need. Maggie's in there with her. Your mother played her music box and it seemed to help quiet her down."

" 'Edelweiss.' My father used to play it for us on his guitar."

"I'm sorry about your dad."

"Long time ago." He'd left them twenty-seven years ago. *Because of me. Because he couldn't stomach the sight of me. Because everyone knew what I did.*

His voice lingered in her memory, another by-product of the nightmare. *Where is she, baby? Where is Kelly? You have to know. You have to tell.* His hands, on her shoulders, shaking her. *Snap out of it, Daphne. You have to snap out of it.*

And then her mother. *Stop it, Michael. You're making it worse.* And then . . . the sound of their fighting with each other. *Over me.*

I should have told. I could have told. Why didn't I tell? Familiar panic rose in her throat and she tried to shake it off. *Can't do this. Can't let myself get so wound up. Got enough problems in the here and now, I don't need to be adding problems from the past to my plate.* Especially since the time for helping her cousin Kelly was long, long gone.

She sat on the bed, closed her fingers around the cards. "What are we playing?"

"Rummy 500." Coppola eyed Daphne's white-knuckled

grip on the cards, on her foot that bobbed almost convulsively. "What can I do to help you, Daphne?" she asked so gently that Daphne felt churlish for wanting to reply *none of your business*.

"Nothing. It has to work through my system on its own." It was like withdrawal from a drug. She got the shakes, violent trembles. Yesterday she'd warded off a panic attack by breathing in the scent of Joseph's aftershave on her hands. But now when she lifted her hands to her face all she could smell was her hand cream.

Abruptly she slid off the bed and walked into her bathroom, feeling like a marionette on a string. From the side of her tub she plucked the sweater she'd last worn to the barn and buried her face in the soft wool. Inhaling deeply, she pretended she was in the barn, with the horses. Slowly, slowly, the panic began to subside.

She looked up and saw Coppola standing just outside the bathroom door, watching her with a puzzled frown. Annoyance mixed with embarrassment. "I'm all right."

Coppola said nothing and even though Daphne knew it was a ploy to get her to fill the silence, she couldn't seem to help herself. "It's the barn," she said. "I'm calmer when I go to the barn. Like . . . stress therapy."

"I personally am into scented candles, but hey, whatever floats your boat."

"Scented candles make me sneeze. Look, can we keep this to ourselves? People will think I have some weird fetish, going around sniffing barn clothes."

"Of course, although it's nothing to be ashamed of. It's a little different, I give you that, but a helluva lot healthier than a lot of ways people let off steam. A lot of cops could take a page from your notebook."

"Who?" Daphne asked, because the woman looked lost.

Coppola shrugged. "Your dad left. My dad stayed. Impact much the same."

"He was a cop?"

"Oh, yeah. Still is. When he had his own nightmare, he drank. Still does."

"I'm sorry, Kate," Daphne said softly.

"Thanks." Brusquely, she held up the cards. "You ready to play?"

"Sure."

Wednesday, December 4, 1:10 a.m.

"Joseph?" The muffled greeting was accompanied by a soft knock.

Joseph swung his gaze from his laptop to the back door in his parents' kitchen where his middle sister, Zoe, had her face pressed against the glass.

He opened the door and she ran in, stomping her feet. "Cold, cold."

He stared at her legs. "You're wearing shorts. In the snow."

"I was rock climbing."

"After midnight? In the snow?"

"Not in the snow. In the gym." She shrugged. "Gym's open twenty-four/seven and my date works nights. I was on my way out of a workday and he was on his way in. We met in the middle." She sat at the table and pointed to the bottle of wine. "Please?"

He poured her a glass while she blew on her fingers. "Where are your gloves, Zo?"

She shrugged again, sheepishly. "Gave them away."

And that was Zoe in a nutshell. He loved all three of his sisters, but Zoe was the one he felt most comfortable with. Lisa was older, bossier. She'd kept them in line growing up. Holly was the baby and he'd always taken care of her.

But he and Zoe had always been tight. Two years between them, they'd grown up in step. He'd gone to the Naval Academy and she'd followed in his footsteps. He'd joined the Bureau, she'd become a psychologist with DC police. And when he'd come home from his final deployment, and the nightmares had kept him awake for days, she was the one he'd called and she'd always known what he needed.

Sometimes advice. Sometimes companionable silence. Sometimes a punishing hike or a run. She'd been there for him as he worked through his grief over Jo.

Joseph prayed that he never had to return the favor. The thought of any of his sisters being hurt, having their hearts ripped apart . . . He would move heaven and earth to spare them that.

She took off her coat and Joseph shook his head. In addition to the bike shorts, she wore a tank top and rock-climbing boots, her auburn hair pulled into a plain-Jane ponytail that was as much Zoe's trademark as Daphne's big hair was hers.

"Where is everyone?" she asked.

Joseph tugged on Zoe's ponytail as he took the seat beside her, moving his laptop out of her way. "It's after one. Everyone's in bed."

She grimaced. "Sorry I'm late. That snow is coming down. Took me twice as long to get up here from Bethesda. Visibility sucked."

"No problem. I was working." He'd been trying to search for anything on Daphne's abduction, twenty-seven years before. But he'd come up completely empty. He didn't have enough information to request specific newspaper clippings and the local paper wasn't archived online that far back. "Did you have a nice date?" he asked her.

"It was fun."

"Mm. Who's the guy?"

"A cop. His name is Jim. Very nice guy, but just a time passer." Zoe pushed one of the wineglasses across the table. "You know how that is."

"I do. I hate it." He so hoped he was done settling for time passers.

"I know. Me, too." She raised her glass and her brows. "To the end of time passers." She winked. "To Daphne."

He couldn't fight the smile that took over his face and didn't even try. "Hear, hear."

Zoe looked surprised. "No denials?"

"No." He drew a breath, remembering that last kiss. "It's too important."

She smiled at him. "Good. It's long past your turn, Joseph." She settled back in her chair, sighed contentedly. "It's so quiet. But it smells like burgers."

After the day he'd had, the burger had hit the spot and the quiet was a balm.

"Dad made me a late dinner, then Mom came back from driving Holly's boyfriend home. I, um, sent them up to bed." He winced. "At least I won't walk in on them up there." His father had obvious plans to take up where he and Joseph's mother had left off when they'd been so "rudely interrupted."

Zoe snorted. "You walked in on them? Where?"

"In Dad's office. Oh my God."

She grinned. "I hear you also met Dillon."

"How'd you know that?"

"Holly texted me. She was afraid you'd be mad."

Joseph frowned. "She said the same thing to me. Why did she think I'd be mad?"

The look she shot him was wry. "Because you threatened to make her last three boyfriends eunuchs. And because you often seem mad," she added quietly.

Joseph blinked, taken aback. "But I'm not mad."

"I know that, Joseph." She sipped her wine, watching him.

"But Holly doesn't? Is that why everyone knows about Dillon but me?"

"I think Holly knows you're not really angry with her." Zoe's words came carefully. "She worries about you."

"What, about those bullets today?"

Zoe's brows went up. "No, but we'll come back to that. She worries about your heart. She remembers what it was like when you came home, brokenhearted. She's worried that seeing her happy will break your heart even more."

"Oh." He frowned, hating that his little sister had seen him that way. Hated that he'd been that way at all. "But that's not true, not at all."

"I know that, Joseph. Maybe you should tell her."

"I will. I don't want her to worry about me."

"That's going to happen, whatever you do. Like those bullets today. I saw it live. I didn't breathe until you stood up." She paused, studying him. "Are you all right?"

He didn't pretend to misunderstand. "I had a bad moment or two." He fixed his gaze on his glass so he didn't have to see the concern in her eyes. "Daphne had blood all over her blouse. Took me back to Jo. Those last few minutes."

"Oh, Joseph. I'm sorry. But you got through it."

"Didn't have a choice."

"We rarely do." Leaning over, she pulled a spiral notebook from her backpack. "I have to be in court tomorrow, so let's talk about your killer so I can go to sleep."

"His name is Doug. Last name unknown. He's twenty-nine, Caucasian, and completely ordinary. He wants to hurt Daphne and I don't know why."

"Start at the beginning."

He did and she took pages of notes as she listened, her expression growing more troubled with every detail.

"Daphne was abducted as a child? That is too damn weird, Joseph."

"I know. I tried to look it up, but I don't have enough information. I know the year was 1985, that it happened somewhere in West Virginia. I know that Daphne was eight, and that her cousin's name was Kelly and that Kelly was seventeen. The newspaper archives I searched didn't go back far enough."

She blew out a breath. "I can write you up a profile, but that abduction is what you have to focus on."

"I will tomorrow." He could have tonight, but he hadn't. A piece of him was afraid to ask, afraid of what he might hear. *Afraid of what you'll have to relive?* No. He was sure it wasn't any reason so shallow.

She was watching him. "If you need me to help, I will. I feel like I know Daphne well enough by now to offer."

One side of his mouth lifted. "All those major mojito nights? Dad told me he played bartender for you girls."

Her smile didn't reach her eyes. "You got it." She looked down at her notes, circled a few things, underlined a few others. "Okay. I'll give you the bare-bones profile I see right now. Tomorrow I'll type it up and make it pretty enough for you to share.

"Doug is a white male, approximately thirty years old. He's intelligent and cunning. Proud of his cleverness. He enjoys predicting the behaviors of others and planning for contingencies. He probably graduated high school. Likely no college. His interest in weapons *could* indicate military service. It might be that he just *wishes* he were a soldier. If he was in the military, his service record is not blemished but probably not distinguished." She hesitated. "He's been abused. He may have done time."

"What makes you say that?" Joseph asked.

"He has a pathological need to control the lives of others. Somehow he knows about Daphne's abduction. He's abducted Ford, very elaborately. He wants to make Daphne hurt. He went out of his way to kidnap Pamela MacGregor to force her sister's hand. This man has had all the control taken from him at some point in his life. Probably from a young age. He's taking power back."

"But why?"

"Million-dollar question. He blames Daphne for some-thing deep."

"She checked to see if she'd prosecuted him. If any part of his name is 'Doug,' then she hasn't."

"This is more than a hard-nose prosecutor offering a lousy deal. Doug lost something, or someone. This kind of intensity . . . it's hard to maintain. Exhausting. I think some-body died and he blames Daphne."

Joseph drew a breath. Nodded. "Okay. At least we'll know how to narrow it down."

"One more thing. The very absence of Google hits means something."

"This is no casual Web surfer," Joseph said grimly. "Doug has information that I don't have." *Because I haven't asked. That will change, first thing in the morning.*

"When Daphne tells you the story, you need to find out who else would be privy to that information. Joseph, be careful. This man doesn't give a rat's ass about collateral damage."

Joseph thought of the dead au pair. Of Isaac Zacharias. And all the others who'd been killed or injured by this man and his cohorts. "I will." He leaned forward, kissed his sister on the cheek. "I'll keep you apprised. Thanks, Zoe."

Marston, West Virginia
Wednesday, December 4, 1:30 a.m.

Ford Elkhart was nicer than I would have been. The kid had closed the door to Wilson Beckett's cabin and hadn't turned off the heat after stripping Beckett naked earlier. *I would have let him freeze to death.*

Mitch rolled his shoulders, preparing to deliver a grade-A rant. He threw the door open. "What the *fucking hell* happened? Where's the kid?"

"Close the goddamn door," Beckett gritted out. "And untie me."

He slammed the door and stalked over, wincing at the sight of Beckett's bony ass. "What happened?" he repeated, opening and closing drawers. "Where are your knives?"

"Asshole kid took 'em all."

Mitch took his keys from his pocket and sawed at the

twine. Ford had done well here, tying the twine so tight that it had dug into Beckett's skin. The twine snapped and Beckett's shoulders sagged forward.

"The knives aren't all he took. He stole your truck, too. I found it on the side of the road, out of gas. I towed it back for you."

He cut the twine at Beckett's ankles, then moved out of the way quickly. A wise decision as Beckett rolled over, swinging his fist where Mitch's face had been seconds before. Hitting air, Beckett flopped onto his back like a fish.

Now that's nasty. The front view was far worse than the back. He grabbed a blanket from the bed and tossed it over Beckett's crotch. "How long ago did he escape?"

Beckett didn't answer, slowly pushing himself to his feet to search through the drawer that had held ammo for his rifle. "Where's my ammo?"

"I don't know." Which was totally untrue. He hadn't wanted Ford shot while trying to escape, so he'd emptied all the ammo boxes the night before. "Maybe the kid took it."

Beckett's eyes narrowed. "My gun was unloaded."

"You tried to shoot the kid?"

"No, he tried to shoot me."

"While he was escaping?"

Beckett's face reddened. "Yes."

Mitch was impressed with Ford, although he didn't let it show. He scowled at Beckett. "Wonderful. I suppose he took your gun and the ammo with him."

"He said the boxes were empty."

"He *wanted* to *escape*. He would have said anything. You've got one helluva knot on your head. Did he knock you out?" Which Mitch knew had happened. He'd seen it on the Webcam.

"Not for long."

"But you *were* unconscious. No telling what he did while you were out."

Beckett went to his dresser, searching for clothing. All of the drawers were empty, as Mitch had known they would be after seeing all of Beckett's clothes in the cab of the truck. Ford was pretty damn clever.

"Sonofabitch," Beckett growled, yanking open the door to the basement. "Stay here. I'll be back." Stiffly the old man descended the stairs.

Beckett's basement was a thing of beauty. Not nearly as historically cool as Aunt Betty's bomb shelter, but a lot more functional. The front half, accessible from the cabin stairs, was home to a washer/dryer and Beckett's man cave with its sixty-inch television illegally connected to every cable station on the planet through the satellite on the back exterior wall.

It was also how Beckett got his Internet, which the man used almost exclusively to download porn and play online poker. Mitch had tapped into it to get a signal to the Webcams he'd planted.

The back half of the basement was Beckett's very dirty secret, one that Beckett had no idea Mitch knew about. One that Mitch never would have dreamed to look for had it not been for his stepfather's obsession file. One that still left him shaking his head in disbelief. He'd been to prison. He'd thought he'd seen depravity. He'd been wrong.

Beckett . . . well, the man was one sick bastard.

Mitch remembered the day he'd first crept down there, having waited for one of the rare day-trips Beckett took, going across two states for his supplies. Mitch hadn't expected much—it had been almost thirty years since the incident detailed in the obsession file. At the most he thought he might find some forgotten shard of evidence that two girls had been kept here. He'd never expected what he did find.

The shock almost had him backing away from his entire plan. Until he remembered cleaning his mother's blood and brains from the bomb shelter. Until he remembered the years of nightmares that tormented Cole because he'd found her. Until he'd reread his mother's diary and re-stoked his own hate.

With the exception of its location, none of what he'd seen had been documented in the obsession file. Mitch knew what he knew only because Beckett had created his own record, one the old pervert thought was for his eyes alone.

Accessible only by a trapdoor in the garage floor, the back half of the basement housed Beckett's . . . hobby. The hobby changed over time. Sometimes it was a blonde, sometimes a brunette. Occasionally the hobby would be a redhead.

The back half of the basement was a single room that contained a bed and a nightstand, a sink and a toilet. Nothing else.

Beckett's current "hobby" was a brunette named Heather. He'd had her for six months and would probably keep her another six. Or until she died. Hobbies tended to die by their own hand, driven mad by Beckett's perversion. When Beckett grew weary of them, he'd cut off their food and water and leave a bottle of pills on the nightstand by the bed. Inevitably they took that way out. If not, Beckett shot them.

Or so Beckett had told Heather when he'd first installed her in his little chamber of horrors. It had been one of the few times Mitch had regretted the placement of a Webcam. The image of Beckett taunting the girl with what would happen to her had been hard to watch.

But Heather wasn't his responsibility. None of Beckett's hobbies were.

However they died, Beckett would capture the moment with a photograph. One which he framed and mounted on the wall of the back half of the basement so that the new hobby would know exactly what her future held.

Because Wilson Beckett was a real sonofabitch. But a smart one. After a bumpy beginning, he'd had smooth sailing for nearly three decades. It nearly wasn't so, though. Because his earliest hobby got away.

That the escapee hadn't revealed Beckett's location or his scheme was a testament to his ability to scare little girls completely out of their minds.

The day Mitch had first descended into Beckett's little hell, the girl on the bed had been the hobby before Heather and she'd been in very bad shape. If Mitch hadn't needed Beckett, he would have anonymously called the cops that day and walked away. But he had needed Beckett, so he'd forced the pills he'd found on the nightstand down the girl's throat.

It seemed more merciful that way. Besides, he couldn't have the girl telling Beckett he'd been down there. But first he'd asked her what Beckett said when he opened the trapdoor and prepared to climb down. Her voice was faint and hoarse, but he'd understood every word.

Did you miss me? The same four words he'd read in the obsession file.

Apparently much like Mitch's great-grandfather, Beck-ett was a sonofabitch who believed in not fixing what wasn't broke.

But Beckett's fun was about to end. Ford would lead the authorities back here and they'd catch the perverted old goat. If they failed, Mitch would anonymously turn him in. *I'm a bastard, but I'm not a monster. Beckett . . . he's a monster.*

The clomping of Beckett's boots on the step startled Mitch back into action. He put his fists on his hips and glared when the old man appeared with a filled laundry basket under one arm. He was fully clothed, thank God.

"Beckett, I want to know how long ago he escaped."

His question was met with a shrug. "A couple hours. Maybe."

More like thirteen. "This is a disaster. Did the kid phone for help?"

"He said the phone was dead."

He rolled his eyes. "He *said*. He *said*. Good God, man, I thought you had a brain." He went to the phone and lifted the ancient receiver. "It's dead. Did you cut it?"

"Hell, no!"

Mitch had done that himself, also the night before. "Then the kid did. Of course he called for help first. He's not stupid."

"He couldn't have called for help. The law woulda been here already."

"We can kiss the ransom good-bye. At least he didn't see *my* face."

Beckett paled. "We need to find that kid."

"Yeah, *you'd* better. Because I'm not going to jail with you, old man. I don't care if you and my grandpa were joined at the hip in 'Nam. You're on your own." He walked to the door, turning back to point at Beckett. "You find him and shut him up."

"Which way did he go? Where did you find my truck?"

"When you get to the end of the driveway, turn right. Do you have gas?"

"Got a can in the garage."

Actually, no you don't. Mitch had taken it last night. He'd carefully planned where he'd wanted Ford to run out of gas and had left only that much in Beckett's pile of rust.

"Good, 'cause your tank's dry as a bone. Are we clear? You're going to find him?"

Beckett sneered. "He probably headed home to his daddy."

"Yeah, the daddy who's a very wealthy judge who was willing to do anything to get his boy back." Half true. *He's wealthy anyway.* He couldn't see Travis Elkhart going to any trouble to get his kid back. Because Travis Elkhart was a pretty lousy father. "You just cost me a fucking fortune."

With that he slammed out of the cabin, got back in his van, and started the engine. *Your move, Beckett. Make it a good one.*

Mitch's next move would be the long drive home. He dreaded it. His back was killing him and he'd just be turning around to come back tomorrow. When Ford's mother got word of where he was, she'd race up here to collect him. Beckett would be chasing the kid, trying to eliminate him, since Ford had seen his face. *If my luck is good, their worlds will collide. If my luck is stupendous, I'll get to see it go down.*

Normally he'd just stay at the studio apartment he rented for the times when it didn't make sense to drive all the way home. He'd had a few of those over the months— especially the times he'd been courting Beckett, convincing the man that he and Mitch's grandfather had been best buds in 'Nam.

But he wouldn't be staying there tonight. He had an early-morning appointment with Cole's guidance counselor. *The kid better not be suspended again. I swear to God I'll kick his ass,* he thought as he turned the van toward home.

Baltimore, Maryland
Wednesday, December 4, 6:30 a.m.

"That is one large tree," Maggie said. "Da-yum."

Daphne looked at the tree over her coffee mug. "Mama needs it right now."

"I know, but still. How're we gonna get a star on top?"

"Ford can do it when he comes home." Daphne lifted her chin. "Because he's coming home." *I have to believe.* Day two. *This will be the day he comes home.*

She wondered how many parents of missing children thought the same thing. Day after day. *How do they stand it?* She was suffocating and it had been only one day. One long, horrible day. *Except for the moments Joseph held me. Those moments . . . they got me through.*

"Did you sleep at all, Daphne?" Maggie asked quietly.

"About an hour." She patted the sofa. "Come and sit. You were up a good part of the night, too."

"Off and on. Your mother had nightmares last night."

"I know. I went in a few times to calm her down."

"Who's gonna calm you down, Daphne?"

"Joseph does a pretty good job of it."

Maggie's brows went up. "So he was 'calming' you in the solarium?"

Daphne's cheeks heated. "Maggie! Were you peeping?"

"No. But you don't need to be a detective with a fancy badge to know that pink cheeks and heaving bosoms and swollen lips mean . . . well, not calming."

"My bosoms were not heaving. Much. Fine. They were heaving. I know this isn't the time for such . . . interludes." She sighed. "But for a minute there, I didn't think about being scared." She just hadn't thought. Period.

Maggie put her arm around Daphne's shoulders. "Then it was the best time for such an interlude. You should have more interludes. You've been interlude-free for too long."

"I've been interlude-free forever," she said glumly.

"Then you have a lot of catching up to do. As specimens go, he's a damn fine one to catch up with. He'd make my bosoms heave except for that whole gravity thing."

Daphne smiled. "You're bad, Maggie."

"And you need to give yourself permission to be. Every now and again."

Daphne rested her head on Maggie's shoulder. "I don't remember how."

"I imagine Joseph can jog your memory."

Daphne chest felt suddenly tight. "I imagine he could."

"That's supposed to be a good thing, child."

"I know. And it is."

"Except?" She reached back to give a tiny tug on Daphne's wig.

"That. And the heaving bosoms that are gravity-proof."

"Does he know?"

"Bits and pieces. Maggie, I'm scared." The admission opened the door for all her fears, a wave that came crashing down. "I thought I knew fear. Being taken, knowing Kelly was being hurt like she was, terrified he'd come for me next. That was . . . indescribable. I thought the moment the doctor said 'cancer' was the worst moment I'd ever face. But this . . . is worse. Every minute it's worse. I think I'd go back to the day I was diagnosed if it meant Ford would never be taken. Right now I'm scared to breathe."

"I know. And I won't insult you by telling you not to be afraid for your child. We all are. But breathing is important. We had this conversation eight years ago when you were too scared to breathe. We had this conversation every time you had a nightmare when you were small. So, keeping this conversation specific to the topic of Joseph and interludes, what would make you not be scared?"

Wise, Daphne thought. But Maggie always had been. "To have it over with. Part of me wants to yank off the wig and strut stark nekkid in front of him. Just to have it done. He can leave and I can get back to my life in the real world."

"You think he won't like what he sees?"

"I think he'll want to. And I think he'll be kind."

"Which means you won't know if he means it when he says he wants you."

"Or if someone will come along that he'll want more."

"Travis was an asshole, Daphne."

"I know that. And I never loved Travis anyway. But Joseph isn't an asshole. I think if he made a commitment to me, he'd feel obligated to stay. Then he'd hate me."

"You've played this whole hand out in your head, haven't you?"

"Yes. Because he makes me wish for things I might never have."

"Horsehockey," Maggie declared. Standing up, she held out her hand for Daphne. "You got too much time to think, child. Idle hands and all that." When Daphne didn't move, Maggie yanked her to her feet. "Go change into barn clothes. We're going to do morning feedings." She whistled. "Tasha!"

The dog bounded around a corner, sliding to sit in front of Maggie, who gave Daphne an impatient look. "Get goin'!"

"I can't go to the barn," Daphne said. "I've got body-guards. And work." Loud clomping on the stairs had them both turning to look. Daphne blinked. "Kate?"

Coppola hopped down the last two steps, doing a spin and flourish. "Do I look equestrian or what?"

"You do actually." And it chafed a little. *She looks better in my clothes than I do.* Daphne walked closer. "Are those my jeans?"

"I took them to her," Maggie said, which translated to, *Down girl. She didn't go in your closet.* "As well as the boots."

"Boots are a little tight, but the jeans are really roomy in the butt." Coppola lifted innocent brows in Daphne's direction. "And I can squeeze acres of denim." She grabbed hold of the thighs of the jeans, pinching excess material.

Daphne laughed. "Bitch," she said, without heat.

Coppola grinned. "Gives me lots of room for my arsenal."

Daphne smiled in spite of herself. "It's really okay to go to the farm?"

"Yes. Hector and I will stay with you. Now go change."

"Who will stay with Mama?"

"Paige is coming," Maggie said. "She's five minutes out, so that's all the time you have."

"I'll be ready."

Sixteen

It was more a ranch than a farm, Joseph thought as he drove along the single-lane road leading from the main thoroughfare. He'd arrived at Daphne's house only to find her already gone, headed out here.

He remembered Clay telling him that this place was a security nightmare. He'd been completely right. Joseph counted eight outbuildings of various sizes. All looked to be in a decent state of repair. Any could be concealing a psycho whack-job with an assault rifle. He wondered what Hector and Kate had been thinking.

By the time Joseph parked his SUV in front of the largest of the barns he was primed to give the two guarding Daphne a piece of his mind.

"What the—" He broke it off when he saw Hector's face. "What's happened?"

"She's okay," Hector said. "But." He pointed at the side of the barn.

"Holy God," Joseph said quietly, staring. It was a message in brown letters a foot high, painted on the side of the barn.

NOW YOU KNOW HOW IT FEELS.

"Blood?"

"Yeah. Whether it's human or not I don't know."

Kate came around the other side of the barn, looking grim. "I think it's cow."

"How can you tell?" Joseph asked.

"Because there's a dead cow in the back," she said. "Slaughtered. It was wearing a collar and a bell. I think it might have been their pet."

Joseph's heart lodged in his throat. "Did Daphne see the message?"

"Yes," Hector said. "She and Maggie are in the barn now, along with the caretaker. They're making sure the horses are all right."

"Who's the caretaker?"

"Scott Cooper. He was at her house yesterday when we got there. She trusts him. Apparently Cooper and Daphne go way back, since before her divorce. He has the next ranch over, but he works this one for Maggie." He pointed at a tidy, white wood-framed house. "That's Maggie's — Simone's friend."

"I met her last night. She was Daphne's nanny," Joseph remembered.

"Now she lives here, generally oversees the horses. Cooper does the heavy work."

"How often is Daphne out here?"

"Every day when she's not in a big trial," Hector said. "She hadn't been out in over two weeks, though. Before you ask, cameras were installed, but the power was out. Still is. Line was cut."

"Generator?"

"Natural gas, and that line was turned off. I think someone knew they'd all be gathered down at Daphne's, that Maggie wasn't here. Cooper said he did the six p.m. feeding yesterday and the power was just fine."

"Have you called CSU?"

"I did," Coppola said. "Brodie's on her way."

"All right. Let's get Daphne and Maggie out of here." Joseph went into the barn, where Maggie was standing watch, her mouth pinched tight. "Good morning, Maggie," he said softly, not wanting to scare her. She was holding a shotgun.

"Agent Carter. This has to stop."

"I agree. I need to get you two out of here."

"I'm ready. She's not." Maggie pointed to the stall at the end of the barn. "Give her a few more minutes if you can."

"I can't. It's not safe here."

"It's not safe for her anywhere," Maggie said harshly.

"It's especially not safe here, for either of you. We can't secure all the buildings."

"You sound like Clay."

"He's right. I'm sorry. I know this is your home."

She tried to smile. "No, it's all Daphne's. I still have my place back in Riverdale."

"West Virginia, right?"

She nodded. "I came out here eight years ago, thinking I'd stay for a few weeks. Six months, tops. Life doesn't always behave the way you expect."

"That's true. What brought you out here eight years ago?"

"Daphne and Simone needed me."

"Because Daphne got cancer." The word made his stomach clench.

"She said you knew. Yes. When I came down eight years ago she was nearly broken. And that wasn't enough for those damn Elkharts. They wouldn't have rested until she was in the ground."

"They wanted her to die?" he asked, incredulous.

"They didn't care if she did as long as they got their way. Rich people play dirty." She looked around her. "But Daphne got the last laugh."

"Must have been one hell of a divorce settlement."

"It was."

Joseph gave a hard nod. "Good for Daphne."

"The settlement made a difference in the broad sense, but it also allowed Daphne to cut all ties with the Elkharts. She didn't have to put up with their bullshit or sacrifice Ford to pay for his education or her doctors or . . ." She clamped her mouth closed.

"Are you saying that Elkhart divorced her and wouldn't pay for her health care?"

"You should ask Daphne these questions."

Joseph studied her a moment. She met his gaze so squarely that he wondered if her "running on" had been calculated, that these were things she wanted him to know. Questions she wanted him to ask Daphne.

"And I will," Joseph said. He gestured to the small office. "But first I'd like to talk to you some more, privately." She followed him into the office and Joseph closed the door, shutting them in. "Daphne's under attack," he said baldly. "We don't know who's responsible, but we're not sure it's only the Millhouses. This threat on the barn wall is personal. It's written in blood, for God's sake. And this is the second time we've seen it."

Maggie drew a sharp breath, her hand flying up to cover her mouth.

"The more personal information I have on Daphne's past, the better I'm prepared to protect her. Tell me about the divorce. Please."

"What a nightmare. Okay then, the divorce. The court probably wouldn't have allowed Travis to do what he threatened, which was to leave her destitute, but Daphne didn't know that for sure at the beginning. Travis made a horrible situation even worse for her. He told her she'd be left with nothing, that he'd get custody of Ford. She'd been an Elkhart long enough to know what influence their money bought."

"But *he* cheated on her with his secretary."

"Yes. And with hundreds of other women during the twelve years they were married. Except this time she caught him in the act. So he set her up to look like she was having an affair as well."

"With who?"

Maggie grimaced. "Let me explain before you get bent outta shape. It was Scott."

"The Scott who's standing with her right now?"

"Yes. Daphne met him when she first married Travis. He stabled the Elkharts' horses. She missed my horses and spent whatever free time Nadine gave her down at Scott's. Scott was one of her true friends during the years she lived with the Elkharts. Later, when Ford was old enough, Scott started training the boy to jump. He was one of the best trainers around, but poor. He grew up with money but his dad left him and his mother destitute. He used his contacts with his old school friends, like Travis Elkhart, to build his business, but he never made much money."

"So what happened?"

"What did she tell you about her split with Travis?"

"That she caught him having sex with his secretary during lunch."

"Hm. What she didn't tell you is that she never visited

Travis in his office, but that day she did because she was rattled to the core and Travis's law office was only two blocks away from her ob-gyn. She'd started walking and ended up there."

Joseph stared at her. "No way."

Maggie lifted a shoulder. "It was not a good day, by all reports. She walked in, saw them, walked out. She did what she always does when she's upset. Went to the barn."

"Why? Why horses?"

Maggie looked away. "That *is* something you'll have to ask her."

"All right, then. I will. So she went to the barn. And?"

"Scott found her there, crying. He did what anyone would do. He held her, not realizing that snake Travis'd had one of the PIs that worked for his law firm following Daphne for months. Travis couldn't divorce Daphne unless he could prove she'd been cheating."

"Her mother's contract with Nadine."

Maggie looked surprised. "She told you a lot. Travis figured she had to be cheating, because she wasn't getting any from him."

Joseph wasn't proud of the childish spurt of pleasure he felt at the last few words, but the relief he could live with. Travis was a womanizer and men like that, more often than not, brought STDs home to their wives. That she hadn't been with Travis meant she'd been protected. It also meant she hadn't been with Travis and that his jealousy could sit the hell down now.

"He got pictures of this embrace, and used them against her when she had *cancer*?"

"Basically, yes. In any other *normal*, non-Elkhart world, what that PI had pieced together would have been laughed out of court. But the Elkharts run in more rarefied circles. Travis let a few 'hints' drop and the rumor spread like wildfire. Standing up for Daphne cost Scott his business and what property he had left. The bankruptcy cracked his marriage.

"When Daphne bought this place, she immediately reached out to him. He was alone at that point, so he moved up here. He started coaching Ford again, Ford started winning, and things turned around for Scott. Clients started bringing their kids to train with him again and he was able to buy the next farm over a few years ago. Scott's very loyal to Daphne and he's been *the* male role model in Ford's life."

"So what happened with Travis and the cancer doctors?"

"Oh." Maggie smiled and Joseph relaxed a little. "Travis was holding a settlement over her head—but she had to cede custody of Ford to get it. It was one of those time-sensitive choices. She could fight him and probably win, but it could take a long time to get to court. She needed care then."

Part of Joseph wished the watch they'd found in a pool of B negative blood really did belong to Travis Elkhart. *No, all of me wishes it.* "What did she do?"

"Cried a lot. That's when I came down. Simone was at her wits' end, trying to get Daphne the care she needed. Daphne was having X-rays and biopsies and having to make some hard choices about her health. Travis made it so that she also had to choose between her son and her life."

"Sonofabitch."

"You'll get no argument from me there."

"But she got the care she needed."

Maggie's smile widened. "Yeah. I'd only been in her house for about four hours when Ford approached me. He was twelve. So that day, he comes downstairs in a suit and tie and asks me if I'll drive him to his grandmother's estate in Virginia. I was very curious why, but he didn't seem inclined to share. I took him there, and waited in the 'parlor' while he met with his grandmother behind a closed door. When he came out he was slipping a piece of paper into his pocket, looking damn satisfied. Nadine, though, she was pale. Ford turned and said, as adult as you please, 'We have an agreement. All bills will be paid on time.' Nadine said they would and that she'd inform Daphne's doctors of the new billing address the next morning. Then the kid gave her this look and patted the pocket where he put the paper."

Joseph's brows shot up. "He blackmailed his grandmother?"

"I guess so. He never told me what he'd said and I never brought it up. After that, things were different. Daphne got treatment and pretty much anything else she wanted. It was a good settlement. I'll admit, I've always wondered what

Ford had in his pocket. But I never told Simone or Daphne. That was between me and Ford. I'd appreciate it if you wouldn't tell unless you have to."

"I'll do my best. That Ford has been blackmailing his grandmother might also explain why the judge and his mother haven't taken a great interest in Ford's being missing." She shrugged and Joseph shifted the subject. "You said you were Daphne's nanny. When was this, and where?"

"Daphne was eight and in Riverdale."

"Why did Daphne need a nanny? At eight, a lot of kids are latchkey kids if their parents work. Especially poor kids."

"Oh. Not a babysitter nanny. A granny nanny. Simone was by herself and needed a little moral support. I wanted people to take care of."

"Where was Simone's husband?"

Maggie's face turned to stone, and she changed the subject. "I haven't introduced you to Scott yet. Come."

Wednesday, December 4, 7:45 a.m.

Joseph followed Maggie to the last stall in the barn, his step slowing as he approached. Daphne was brushing a chocolate brown horse that appeared to be falling asleep on his feet. Something about her had changed. A serenity that hadn't been there before. The worry was still there, but muted.

Joseph got a little closer to see her better and noticed a set of human knees behind the horse. A man crouched, inspecting the animal's back leg.

Maggie leaned into the stall. "How's our girl?" she crooned.

The man rose. "She needs to be re-shoed. I'll do it while she's up at my place. "

Daphne turned and her smile bloomed. "Joseph." The smile faded. "You saw the wall outside. Is it human?"

"Don't know yet. Brodie's on her way." He looked at the man, who was studying him carefully. "I'm Special Agent Carter, FBI."

"Scott Cooper."

"Scott says he can take the horses for a few days," Daphne said. "He's got some empty stalls right now. We're not taking any chances." She gave Maggie a careful glance. "With the horses or you. I want you to stay with us until all this is over, Maggie."

Maggie looked apprehensive. "That's a lot of work for Scott."

"My son will help me. He's always looking for extra income. I wouldn't sleep a wink knowing you were alone out here, Maggie. Not with that psycho on the loose."

"It would be safer," Joseph said.

Maggie sighed. "We'll try it for a few days. Scott, that new rescue might have a touch of colic. Can you come look?" She shot Joseph a look of make-this-count over her shoulder as she walked with Scott to the other side of the barn.

Bless her heart, Joseph thought. "Can I come in?" he asked Daphne.

"Please do." Uncertainly he picked his way over the hay and she smiled at him. "Not your cuppa, huh?"

"Just not used to it. Are all of these horses yours? Or just this one?"

"They're all technically mine. The four over here belong to me and Mama and Maggie and Ford. All of our horses were rescues except for Ford's. Ford's horse is a hunter—way different price bracket. We usually keep at least two rescues, sometimes more. Scott just brought one of them home a few days ago. He finds abused and abandoned animals while he's on the road. If he has room in the trailer, he'll persuade the horse's owner to sell it or give it up. We rehab them and find them homes."

"Where do they go during the day?"

"Pasture. They're in here at night and in bad weather. I tell you, I saw that paint on the side of the barn and I was terrified of what I'd find inside. But it doesn't look like he came in. Everything's the way it should be."

Except for the dead cow. He figured he'd tell her once he got her safely away from the farm. There wasn't anything she could do and no reason she should see such a senseless slaughter. Joseph edged his way to her side, realizing that cowboy boots were in his immediate future. "Why horses?"

She shrugged. "There's something about caring for an animal. It's healing."

A curious choice of words, he thought. And then he couldn't think because she'd moved close enough to touch. "How did you sleep?" he asked, dropping his voice.

She looked away. "Not well."

"I can't tell." He skimmed a fingertip under her eye.

"The miracle of a good concealer. I'm ready to go, Joseph. I know we should have left already. I'm putting everyone in danger every minute we stay."

"I was going to wait for Brodie. But if you want to go, we can."

She gave the animal's neck a final stroke. "Maybe we can see Stevie?"

"We'll have to get our names on the waiting list." He followed her out of the stall and Tasha fell in line behind them. "There was a thirty-minute wait this morning."

Daphne shook her head. "Stevie's as popular as Olive Garden. We can call from the car. It'll take us at least forty-five minutes to get into town."

"Let me talk to Cooper first. He does the maintenance around here, right?"

"His son does." She frowned. "Why are you talking to him? Scott's a good guy."

"I didn't say he wasn't. I have some questions about your power lines and generator. You can stay here a few more minutes while I talk to him."

Cooper was standing next to his truck, filling a syringe topped with a seriously large needle. "Agent Carter, what can I do for you?"

Joseph's radar went off at the sight of the syringe. "What's that you're filling that syringe with?"

Cooper gave him a calm sideways glance. "Banamine. Non-narcotic pain reliever. Use it for colic. One of the rescues is on it. You can call the vet and ask."

"Okay. Do you keep any narcotics on your property?"

"Not on this property because it's not that secure. I've got narcotics up at my place. Keep 'em locked up. You're free to check."

"You're very cooperative."

Cooper's mouth curved, not quite enough to be a smile. "Daphne likes you. I want her to be happy. She'll be happy if I cooperate with you. And I got nothin' to hide."

"Do you keep ketamine?"

"Nope."

"What about fentanyl?"

"Yes. Don't use it very often. May be expired. You're free to check."

"I will."

"Now I've got a few questions. You've got quite an entourage around Daphne, protecting her. How long can you keep that up before you eat through your budget?"

"Not long."

Cooper stared at him with sharp eyes. "So what the fucking hell are you doing about this pissant psycho drama queen?"

The fear Joseph saw in the man's gaze kept him from snarling back. "Not enough," he said quietly. "Do you have any thoughts?"

"Yeah. He wants to be seen. Like any punk that does graffiti. His fascination with blood scares the hell out of me. And he knows how to butcher a cow," he added bitterly.

"I'm sorry. Detective Rivera thought it was a pet."

"Maggie's. She rescued that damn cow. Bottle-fed it because it was weaned too soon and left to die. And then some punk kills it to do *graffiti*?" Cooper's voice shook with suppressed rage. "He'd want to see her reaction. Daphne's." He lifted his eyes, swept his gaze across the trees. "He's out there now. Or was. Guaranteed."

Joseph agreed. "Does Maggie know about the cow?"

"Yes. She'll fall apart later, in private. That's her way. She's far more worried about Daphne right now. As am I. Who the hell would kill a defenseless cow for graffiti?"

"Same person that kidnapped Ford."

Cooper flinched. "My mind can't accept that he's being held against his will. I've known that boy since before he was born. I taught him to ride. To shoot. I gave him his first razor." He looked up at the sky, his throat working as he fought back tears. "First box of condoms, too. Don't tell Daphne."

"Our secret," Joseph said. "I think you're right. I think there's a good chance he's going to want to watch. Where would he get the best view?"

"A few places. I know this land. If it would help, I can take you or your investigators to those places. A man stands in one place long enough, he'll leave something behind."

"I've got a CSU team on the way. Thank you. Now about your generator."

"I sent my son back to the house for the maintenance books. He should be back in thirty minutes if you can wait."

Joseph thought about Doug, out there watching. "I need

to get Daphne out of here. You can give the manual to Detective Rivera. Excuse me." The cell phone in Joseph's hand had begun to buzz, the number on the caller ID unfamiliar. The hair on the back of his neck lifted. "This is Agent Carter."

"Carter, this is Agent Kerr in the Pittsburgh field office. We got a hit on your BOLO."

Joseph didn't breathe. "Which one?"

Wednesday, December 4, 8:00 a.m.

"Something's wrong," Daphne murmured. She'd come out of the stall just as Joseph took a phone call, his body going still as a statue, his face blank.

Maggie tugged on her shoulders. "Come on. Scott brought a thermos of coffee."

"No." She pulled free, not wanting to watch but unable to turn away. Joseph had stopped breathing. He was listening to his phone, his chest frozen. Daphne's heart began to pound, hard and fast. He turned then, as if feeling her watching him. His mouth curved into a smile, but his eyes were still blank.

"I'll be just a minute," he called. "Don't worry."

Daphne closed her eyes. "All right." *Exhale, inhale. Rinse and repeat.* "I'm going to sit in the office, Maggie. Can you ask Joseph to come talk to me when he's ready?"

"Of course." Maggie cupped her neck loosely, bringing her head close until their foreheads touched. "Whatever happens, we will do this. Together. You and me and your mama. Just like we've done everything else."

"I know. But for now I'd like to be alone." She left Maggie with a hug and made it to the office and sank into a chair, trembling so hard her legs were jelly. She twined her fingers together in her lap. Fixed her gaze to the clock. And waited. Four and a half times the second hand swept around. And finally the door behind her opened.

"It's me," Joseph said. He came around the chair to crouch at her feet. His warm hands covered hers. But all she could see was the clock. She couldn't look at him. Because then it would be real.

"Daphne, honey. Look at me." He gently pinched her chin and tugged her face down until she had no choice but to look into his eyes.

Kind. Not blank anymore. *Still can't breathe.*

"He's alive. Did you hear me? Ford is alive."

Her chest imploded. "What? I thought . . ."

He smiled at her, so gently. "I needed to be sure before I gave you news again."

"Where? Where is he?"

"In a hospital in West Virginia, just past the Pennsylvania state line."

Hospital. "West Virginia? How did he get all the way out there?"

"They don't know yet. He's not conscious."

The room tilted. "Joseph."

"The cop I spoke to said the doctors were saying mild hypothermia, exhaustion, and dehydration. Maybe some frostbite, but not severe. No major injuries, Daphne."

Her face was wet. And she still couldn't breathe. Boneless, she slid from the chair to her knees, collapsing against him. He was there, warm. So warm.

His arms came around her, bringing her close, cradling her head against his chest, kneeling with her while the sobs wracked her body. "It's okay, cry it out," he murmured.

She had no choice. The floodgates had opened and she couldn't seem to make it stop. She just held on to Joseph, sobbing and gripping his shirt like a life preserver.

The door opened behind her. "Daphne?" It was Maggie. "Honey?"

Daphne sucked in a lungful of air and gritted her teeth. The tears didn't stop, but the noise did. Her fingers tightened their grip on Joseph's shirt.

"She's okay," Joseph said, rubbing her back. He dipped his head to murmur in her ear. "I told them the news. Because they had pitchforks and wouldn't let me pass."

Daphne hiccupped a watery laugh and nodded against his chest.

"I brought her some things," Maggie said.

Keeping Daphne's head cradled against him, he reached forward and one at a time dropped a box of tissues, a bottle of water, and her bottle of headache pills on the floor beside them. "You're a good nanny, Maggie. Does Daphne have any extra clothes or toiletries up at your house? We're going to get Ford."

"I'll pack her a bag." There was a pause, then Maggie's

hand was stroking her hair. "I called your mama. She's crying, too."

Then she was gone and Daphne plucked a handful of tissues from the box. "So stupid . . . so stupid to cry. He's alive. Why can't I stop crying?"

"This is normal, Daphne. So much emotion, all bottled up. Let it out."

"Tell me again," she whispered. "Please. Say it again. I need to hear it."

"Your son is alive," he said. "Ford is alive and he is safe. And I'm going to take you to him as fast as I can drive."

"You're sure?"

"Triple verified," he said wryly. "I had Bo call the Pittsburgh field office, then I called the local cops and the hospital. He's there, honey. He was brought in five hours ago, but he didn't have ID on him. One of the nurses had seen the TV reports on the shootings yesterday. When Hyatt and Bo gave their press conference after the shooting, they included photos of Ford and Kimberly. The nurse notified the locals, who called the Bureau's field office. They got patched through to me."

Finally the tears had slowed enough for her to think. "Who brought him in?"

"Local PD. They responded to a 911 call from an elderly lady who discovered him on her property after her dog wouldn't stop barking. Ford was unconscious by then."

"Why was he there to start with?"

"That's what we have to figure out. Hopefully he'll be awake by the time we get there and he can tell us."

She let go of his shirt and inanely tried to smooth the fabric. "I keep messing up your shirts."

"I don't mind." He lifted her chin, brushed his thumb over her lip. "Better now?"

"Yes. Thank you."

His dark eyes changed, heating. "I haven't done anything yet."

Last night. The solarium door. *Not until I give you something to be thankful for.* Her emotions swung again and the relief that had so overwhelmed her disappeared like mist in sunshine. Rising to take its place was lust, simple yet potent.

She framed his face with her hands. "You're here," she

said fiercely. "Right now, that's a lot. More than I've ever had. And right now, what I need."

"And later?"

The way he looked at her gave her the courage to speak when she might otherwise have faltered. "You make me greedy, Joseph," she whispered. "You make me want more than I need."

His eyes flashed, hungry, but his movements were slow. Precise. He bent his head, kissing the pulse point of her left wrist, then her right, never taking his gaze from hers. It was simple. And very potent. He took her breath away.

"I think we need to work on your definition of 'want' and 'need.' And 'greed.'" His voice dipped, each word a featherlight caress that made her skin feel way too tight. "And we will. Later." He rose in a single powerful movement, capturing her hands in his and tugging her to her feet. "Now, we drive."

Wednesday, December 4, 8:20 a.m.

Finally. The Fed was driving Miss Daphne away in his Escalade, another Fed covering his back, while the others waved good-bye. Mitch took one last look at his handiwork on the barn wall before lowering his binoculars.

He'd expected the message to be discovered by whoever did the morning feeding. He never expected it would be discovered by Daphne herself. Amazing luck, fantastic show, and well worth the loss of one cow.

The Fed's black Escalade should be passing this way soon. Once it had, the coast would be clear for him to head back home. Anytime now he'd be getting a frantic call from his brother Mutt about the guns that were found in the houses Millhouse and Odum had purchased with Reggie's defense fund. Mutt and his daddy would soon be very unhappy because they'd do a check on the books and see that somebody had been skimming guns from the deliveries.

Mutt's father would be blamed and Mitch doubted his stepfather's Russian boss would leave the old man alive.

Mitch would pay good money to see the old man's face once he realized he'd been set up. *He'll blame me, like he does for everything. Only this time he'll be right.*

Of course, what Mitch most wanted to see would be

Daphne's face when Ford gave her his message. *I'm back. Did you miss me?*

He heard the low roar of the Fed's Escalade as it passed by, followed by the quieter unmarked sedan. *I'm good to go.*

He walked through the woods to where he'd left his black van. He'd have to retire it now. He'd planned to store it only for a while, once the Feds found the Millhouses' gun stash. But after that woman he'd had to kill in the parking garage . . .

Shit. He did hate waste. It was a perfectly good vehicle.

Hagerstown, Maryland
Wednesday, December 4, 9:55 a.m.

It was at times like this that Joseph was very happy to have an SUV with four-wheel drive. Western Maryland had received four inches of snow the night before and the roads were slick. It would be even worse once they got to the higher elevations.

Flying Daphne to West Virginia would have been faster and safer from a security standpoint, but after she hit her head the day before, her doctor friend at the ER had nixed air travel for another twenty-four hours.

At least he had them covered. Hector drove behind them, watching for any speeding vehicles that came too close. Kate Coppola was leading the investigation at Daphne's farm, checking out Cooper's medicine cabinet. When she was done, she would follow them up to West Virginia with Daphne's mother and Maggie and the dog. Joseph felt better when Daphne had Tasha around.

He himself was well armed and he'd had the SUV outfitted with bullet-resistant glass when he'd bought the thing. Still, he'd felt nervous until they'd reached the more open road west of Baltimore. Now he wasn't so much nervous as watchful.

He'd spent the last hour touching base with each member of his team. He'd started by informing Ciccotelli that Ford had been found and where. Ciccotelli had reported that the MacGregors had still received no word, no calls, no communication regarding their missing daughters. A search of MacGregor's veterinary hospital had shown that several boxes of fentanyl and injectable ketamine, as well as other controlled substances, were missing.

Joseph had called Deacon to West Virginia to coordinate with the Pittsburgh office in the investigation. He wanted to know where the hell Ford had been for a day and how he had magically shown up on some lady's snow-covered lawn.

He had called Bo Lamar next. The FBI/ATF task force formed to track the source of the assault rifles recovered from yesterday's raid was moving rapidly. The assault rifles had a connection to organized crime. Specifically a Russian "businessman" named Fyodor Antonov.

The Bureau had been watching Antonov for a year now, but had never been able to put their hands on the goods to connect with him. Bo would spend most of his morning arranging a warrant and planning a raid on Antonov's warehouse.

J. D. Fitzpatrick had spent the entire night checking out the properties he'd found belonging to Dougs, Douglases, or MacDougals within a two-hour radius of Baltimore. Two hours was how long Doug would have had between coming home from Philly with Pamela and arriving at the alley to attack Isaac Zacharias and Ford Elkhart. It was tedious and time-consuming work, but that's what detective work was usually like.

Joseph had told J.D. about his conversation with Holly the night before, that Kim had told Doug about a possible job, but that he'd need a "GC" to do it. J.D. was adding that to his rapidly overflowing plate.

Daphne had called everyone in her world to give them the good news. She'd smiled and laughed and sometimes cried with her family and friends.

When she'd finished her last call, she'd become abruptly quiet, as if she'd expended all her energy being happy. For the last half hour she'd stared out of her window, deep in thought. He let her have her space, well aware that for the last twenty-four hours she'd had precious little time to herself.

When she finally did speak, she took him by surprise.

"It was stage one. I was twenty-seven years old."

He looked right so hard and fast that he nearly hit a tractor-trailer. The trucker blew his horn but Joseph barely heard it. He got back in his lane and drew a breath.

She hadn't looked at him, still staring at the passing countryside that he didn't think she saw at all.

Stage one. *That's . . . the least bad, right?* But he couldn't ask that question.

Twenty-seven? He hadn't done the math for some reason. "That's not . . . usual, is it?" He'd caught himself before "normal" left his mouth. "To be diagnosed so young."

"It's rare and I certainly wasn't expecting it. I figured it was something innocent, like a cyst. When he said 'cancer' I went into a state of shock."

So much so that she'd wandered to her ex-husband's office. "How did you find it?"

"Monthly self-exam . . . that I didn't do every month because I was twenty-seven. 'Old women' in their forties and fifties got breast cancer. But women in their twenties do get it, and when they do it's usually a lot more aggressive."

His heart stuttered at the word. *Aggressive.* "Was yours?"

She lifted a shoulder. "Could have been a lot worse. I'm still here. I come with an awful lot of baggage, Joseph. I think you need to know that."

"We all have baggage."

"Mine still hovers over my head. Anyone who wants to be with me needs to understand that. I'm seven years clear and with every year my chances of dying from something else get better and better. I sometimes get paranoid over the smallest sniffle or bruise, worrying that it's come back, because if it does . . . that would be very bad."

He took a minute to think, to use the logic that normally served him well. But at the moment the fear clawing at his gut was kicking logic out the door. She waited for him to speak, still not looking at him.

"I've got a million different thoughts running through my head right now and I'm terrified I'm going to say the wrong one," he confessed.

"I don't think there is a wrong one, Joseph."

"Yeah, there probably are several wrong ones. The wrong ones would be ones that hurt you. A right one would be one that makes us both feel better."

"What makes you feel better?"

"That numbers don't lie. Statistically speaking, I'm more likely to get hurt because I have a dangerous job."

She grimaced. "That doesn't make me feel better at all."

"I just mean that anyone who wants to be with me needs to understand that my job comes with certain risks." He

cast her a sideways glance and caught her peeking at him
from the corner of her eye. "Although lately, your job is a
helluva lot more dangerous than mine."

"That's fair."

"My dangerous job could end me with less warning than
cancer would end you."

"That's true. But while it's the end that scares people, it's
the getting there that puts the strain on a relationship."

He reached across the console and tugged her left hand
free of the choke hold the right had it in. He threaded their
fingers together and kissed her hand as he had the day before. "I'm thirty-seven years old and not getting any younger,
so I'm going to be blunt, okay?"

She shifted in her seat so that she could look at him.
"Okay."

"I like you. I think you're beautiful and smart and . . .
colorful."

She'd looked happy until the last word. "Colorful?"

"Yeah. Full of color and . . . life. And that's a good thing
for me."

"Okay," she said warily. "I'll let you have that one."

"No, I want you to understand. For a long time I've felt
like my life is Dorothy in Kansas. All gray. You are . . . color."

Her smile had bloomed. "Thank you, Joseph."

"You're welcome. I'm still in blunt mode, okay?"

"I'll try to keep up," she said dryly.

He smiled. "There are things I want and there are things
I need. I want a challenging job, but I need someone to
come home to when I'm done with that job. I need that
somebody to need the same thing. That might be you. It
might not. But I'm tired of wasting time and I get the impression you are, too."

She nodded, her eyes wide.

"So," he continued, "if it does turn out to be you and you
come with baggage, it becomes my baggage, too. Same goes
the opposite way, but we're talking about your baggage
now. If you got sick again, I wouldn't run away. I'm not
made that way."

"I know you're not," she said softly.

"I'm about to get blunter," he warned. "I want you. Any
which way I can have you. And some ways I haven't even
thought of yet. I've wanted you for nine months and I've . . .

thought about how it would be between us. Often." He glanced over, saw her cheeks had pinked. "And since I'm not getting any younger, I'd really like to find out sooner versus later. Much sooner."

"In the spirit of bluntness, that scares me more than anything else. I'm . . . different now. Almost certainly different from any other woman you've been with. You can say that it doesn't matter, but if it does when the time comes . . . that will be hard."

"But in the grand scheme, if none of the baggage existed . . ."

She drew a deep breath. "Sugar, I'd be on you like white on rice," she drawled.

He laughed. "That's something at least. Not sure I'll ever look at rice the same way again." He sobered. "Daphne, nothing I can say now will alleviate your concern. That's kind of an in-the-moment thing. I'll probably be more nervous than you."

"I know." She looked down. "And I'd do nearly anything to spare you that."

"It's not your job to spare me." He said the words more curtly than he'd intended.

She looked up, surprised. "Excuse me?"

"I'm not your mother or your nanny who you buy houses for and take care of. I'm not a rescue animal that you take in. You take care of people and that's what's wonderful about you. But that's not what I want from you."

"Then what *do* you want from me?" she asked quietly. "Besides sex."

"Sex is a damn good start. Don't dismiss the multilayered benefits of sex," he said lightly and saw her smile. "Daphne, I don't want a mother. I have a mother and she's pretty wonderful."

"You want a mate." She went back to looking out the window. "So do I."

"Then I'd say we're off to a good start."

Her lips twitched. She didn't agree, but she didn't disagree, either.

"I'll be less nervous if I'm prepared," he said seriously. "Mastectomy?"

She stiffened at the question, but answered nevertheless. "Bilateral, radical."

"Reconstruction?"

"Yes. So at least when I'm eighty, the girls'll still be perky."

"Sugar, ain't nothin' wrong with perky," he said, mimicking her accent.

She turned to smile at him. "I never expected you to be charming. There's always this intensity that swirls around you, but it's tempered by charm. I like that."

"Don't disclose my secret weapon," he teased. "You know what I first noticed about you? Your legs. I said, 'Grayson, there's a woman coming up your walk wearing a lime green suit and four-inch heels with legs up to her shoulders.' When my eyes finally got up to your breasts, I was distracted by the basket of muffins in your hand."

Her laugh was full and throaty. "So if I bake for you, you'll be blind to all my flaws."

And there it was. What she wanted. Someone to love her, "flaws" and all. He could relate to that. "If you bake for me, I'll be your slave. As for your 'flaws,' we'll add that word to our vocabulary list for later."

"When we discuss wants and needs. And greed," she murmured.

"The lady learns fast." He pointed to a restaurant sign up ahead. "I had breakfast a million years ago. Let's get some food."

"I might actually be able to eat, but let's use the drive-through, okay? I want to get to Ford as fast as we can."

Joseph hadn't intended to stop long enough to allow her to become a target. Because even though Ford had been found, Doug was still out there.

Seventeen

Mitch pulled into his garage, tired but pleased. Ford was "found" and Daphne was on her way to her boy. Wilson Beckett was on a mission to find the rich kid who'd seen his face, a mission that would send him running straight into Daphne.

Daphne would remember things he'd done. She'd remember the room in the back half of Beckett's basement, with its bed and nightstand, its sink and toilet. Leading the police back to that place would be agony for her. And when the truth came out, she'd be ruined, personally and professionally.

Everyone she loved would be ashamed.

She'd be cut off from everyone and she'd limp home and try to pick up the pieces. *But then it'll be my turn. And she'll finally know who's ruined her life. And who's ended it.*

He hadn't yet heard from his brother, but it was only a matter of time before Mutt and his dad discovered that the rifles found by the cops the day before were Antonov's. Mutt's father had made a lot of money discreetly distributing the Russian's goods—some drugs but mostly guns.

He got out of the van and moved the bookshelf covering the entrance to the old bomb shelter. He needed to be sure Kimberly was still alive. Because he still needed her for when it came time to lure Ford back.

Because Ford would lure Daphne. *And then it'll be Daphne's turn for payback.*

I'm fine if somebody else kills Mutt's daddy. But Daphne is mine.

Claysville, Pennsylvania
Wednesday, December 4, 2:40 p.m.

Daphne had not only been able to eat, she'd slept a little, too.

Ford. He's alive. Those were her first thoughts as she opened her eyes. *Thank you, God, so very much.* To say that she was relieved . . . The word was far too mild.

His ordeal was a long way from over. This she knew. There would be emotional hurdles to scale. His sense of personal safety and control had been irrevocably altered. He'd been betrayed by the girl he'd trusted. And whoever had taken him was still out there.

But he was alive and in that reality she let herself steep, finally able to breathe again as joy bubbled up like champagne, filling her lungs from the inside out. She felt energized. Invigorated. As close to giddy as she'd come in a very long time.

Most of that was because her son was alive. But she'd be a fool and a liar not to acknowledge the role played by the man behind the wheel.

Because she could breathe again, she did, filling her head with his scent. She rolled her head sideways to look at him, saying nothing yet. She just wanted to look a little bit. He drove with one hand, his forefinger tapping the wheel, as seemed to be his preferred position.

Which made her wonder if he did have a preferred position. Heat that had nothing to do with the SUV's climate control rushed to her cheeks as she contemplated the thought for a moment. Somehow she couldn't see Joseph being content with anything as vanilla as missionary, which was the sum total of her limited experience.

He was a massive man, but he moved with a grace that sent her imagination in all kinds of lovely directions. And he wanted her. It made her draw a deep breath as her pulse thrummed low and for a moment she wasn't thinking about her inexperience or her scars. She was thinking about how he'd feel next to her, on top of her. Inside her.

Daphne's eyes slid down his body, happy to observe him when he wasn't looking at her. He wasn't a bodybuilder like his brother, Grayson, and Daphne rather liked that. Instead he was broad of shoulder, lean of hip, and . . .

Holy God. She sucked in a small gasp as her gaze froze on his lap, which left no doubt as to what he was thinking about right now. *Wow. Just . . . wow.*

The sound she'd made had him turning to look at her, the expression on his face making her hot. And wet. Her mouth opened and not a blessed word emerged.

His grin was wicked. "Well?" It was a purr and she shivered.

"Mercy," she whispered.

He looked back at the road. "I don't think so."

Her brows crunched, her mind too addled to follow. "Don't think so, what?" A notion intruded, altogether unpleasant. "You changed your mind?"

"Do I look like I changed my mind, Daphne?" he asked, his voice pitched low. It was like he'd petted her and he hadn't laid a finger on her. Yet.

"No. I'd have to say the evidence is pretty definitive that you haven't."

His chuckle was rich and deep and she thought if he'd been holding her at the moment, she would feel the vibration of his body. The thought of climbing over the console and straddling him suddenly didn't seem all that crazy.

"I've just been thinking," he said.

She smiled at him. "That I can see."

"You want to know about what?" he teased.

"I think I can guess."

"Maybe. Maybe not." He reached for her hand, pressing her palm to his thigh. His leg was solid. Thick. And her eyes were once again drawn lower, to where his body visibly strained against the zipper of his trousers, trying to get free. And her fingertips tingled, wanting to touch.

No mercy. "Oh." She got it now. "What were you thinking about?"

"That I'll have to be inventive, think outside the box." He looked over, brows lifted. "Your breasts. I assume they're not as sensitive as they were before."

Her mouth fell open again, this time in shock. "What?"

"True?"

She shook her head, no words emerging again.

"True or false?"

"True," she said, her voice rising a few notes.

"I told you I was done with wasting time. I'm going to be blunt because I need to know. Now, can I also assume you have full . . . feeling everywhere else?"

The rush of heat returned. "Yes." She shifted her hips, unable to resist the urge to squeeze her thighs together. A movement he noticed.

"Good." He drew a breath, his nostrils flaring. "That's what I've been thinking about. All the ways I can make you feel good, without ever leaving . . . Well, you get the idea."

The image of his dark head between her thighs slammed into her mind, front and center, and she bit back what would have been a moan. "Um, yeah. I do. Get the idea."

"Good." He released her hand to turn the heater down and tug at the knot in his tie. Then he surprised her by pressing his palm against the hard ridge in his trousers, adjusting himself with a grimace.

She wanted to do that for him. She wanted to see what he looked like, what he felt like in her hand. Inside her body. Sooner versus later. Which meant she'd need to be prepared. Protection. The doctors weren't sure if she'd ever conceive again, but she had no intention of finding out the hard way.

Hard way. Damn. Her fingers itched again, this time to give herself some relief. Instead she squeezed her thighs tighter. *There'll be plenty of drugstores in Morgantown.* It was a college town, so they'd have no shortage of condoms.

"If you keep looking at me that way, we might never get to Wheeling."

She lifted her eyes to his face. Saw no hint of a smile. Just raw need. He'd laid himself bare to her, letting her see what he felt. What he wanted.

Me. He wants me. This big, beautiful man wants me.

Then the word "Wheeling" sank in and she frowned. "Morgantown," she said. "We're going to Morgantown."

His brows knit. "No, we're going to the hospital in Wheeling. That's where Ford is."

Her breath was hitching up in her lungs, the warmth she'd felt cooling to ice. "You said we were going to Morgantown. You said . . ." She looked away, aware that he was looking at her in consternation. *What had he said?* "You said . . . that Ford was in a hospital in West Virginia, just across from Pennsylvania."

"That's Wheeling. Daphne, what's wrong? What's in Wheeling?"

Dark rooms. Screaming. Always screaming. Did you miss me?

No. Don't think it. It's not real anymore. She was dimly aware that she was rocking and forced herself to still.

"Daphne?"

She bowed her head, stared at her hands. "I lived there for a while. My whole family did. And something happened to us. We were never the same."

"Your cousin was abducted," he said, his voice oddly tight. "As were you."

She frowned, then remembered. Hector Rivera had asked the question when she'd zoned out upon entering her house the day before. Of course he'd told Joseph about it.

"Yes, my cousin was abducted. Kelly." *And so was I.* But those words didn't want to come. They never did.

"They found Kelly's body."

"Yes. She'd been missing for three weeks altogether." She chanced a glance at his face. He looked like he'd swallowed something too large to get down.

"You were taken, too," he said.

She exhaled. *You can do this. You're an adult now. He can't hurt you. Nobody is going to hurt you. Say it. Yes. I was. Say. It.*

"I was, but not the way Kelly was. I can't talk about this right now. I'm . . ." *Having a panic attack.* "I can't quite breathe."

"All right," he said quietly. "We'll be at the hospital in ten minutes."

Baltimore, Maryland
Wednesday, December 4, 3:00 p.m.

The banging on his bedroom door woke him up. It was Mutt and he was frantic. "Dammit, wake up, Mitch. Wake up!"

Mitch squinted at the clock. Five hours' sleep. That's all he really needed. He got out of bed and checked his gun. It was loaded and ready to go in case his brother got confrontational. Mitch opened the door to find Mutt deathly pale.

"We've got trouble. Antonov is about to be raided by the Feds. He's clearing everything out of his warehouse."

"Why would the Feds raid him?"

"They found a stash of rifles yesterday. What do you know about this?"

Mitch made his eyes go wide. "Me? What would I know about anything? I just drive where you tell me and drop off what you tell me. I've got signatures from the buyer on every delivery."

"I know. I know. It's just that Dad is scared. Antonov isn't a man to screw with."

Neither am I. "Antonov has other distributors, so don't panic. We didn't do anything wrong, so they can't be angry with us. Go home, have a glass of that wine you like so much. It'll be fine."

When Mitch heard Mutt leave the house, he grinned. It wouldn't be long now before his stepfather got exactly what was coming to him. *I'm glad the bastard is scared. So was I my first day in prison and every day after that for three years.*

He'd always wondered if his mother had been, too, right before she pulled the trigger. Or if she'd just been so devastated that she'd shot herself that way . . . He wasn't sure which was worse—hopelessness or fear.

Either way, she'd have her justice. The people who'd driven her to kill herself would be punished.

Good old stepdad was well on his way and Daphne would be soon enough.

Mitch went online and checked the police scanner feed for the Wheeling, West Virginia, area. No mention of a BOLO on anyone matching Beckett's description. *That means either Ford is still unconscious or they found the old bastard while I was asleep.*

Checking the Web sites for the Wheeling local newsrooms he found that Ford's rescue was the big story. But so far no one had the Beckett connection, so Ford must still be out of it, unable to tell his mother the four magic words.

Did you miss me?

The kid had to be waking up soon. *I didn't give him enough ketamine last night to keep him unconscious this long. I hope he's okay. I need him to say those magic words.* Otherwise, everything would fall apart. *Come on, Ford. Wake your ass up.*

Either way, things would start to pop because Beckett was tracking the kid and was certain to have seen the same stories Mitch had just read. It would be only a matter of time before Beckett arrived at the hospital to silence Ford—and then the real action would start. That's what he needed to be there for.

He'd see to his hostages' comfort, then unload everything he needed from the van into the Jeep he'd bought back in Florida, in the days before he was delivering guns for Mutt. On his way to the garage he realized how quiet the house was now that Mutt was gone. *Cole isn't home yet.* He should have been.

Mitch scowled. He had a few things to say to the boy, his ears still burning from the talking-to he'd received from Cole's guidance counselor. Cole was out of control and Mitch was going to have to institute heavier punishments whether he liked it or not.

Because I'll be damned before I let you end up like me, kid.

Wheeling, West Virginia
Wednesday, December 4, 3:00 p.m.

She was pale as a ghost and shaking like a leaf. Joseph had to get the story out of her, but knew he'd have to be careful. She was incredibly fragile.

But this was important. Critical. He could feel it with every nerve in his body.

He parked the SUV and came around to help her down. When her feet hit the ground she turned to him, holding on like she'd never let go. He wrapped his arms around her, trying to absorb her trembles.

"Sweetheart," he whispered, fear rising to burn his throat. "You're okay. You're safe. Nobody's going to hurt you."

Her arms tightened and he knew he was right. Someone had hurt her. Rage simmered, but he kept it controlled. He needed every piece of information he could get.

"Come on, baby," he said softly. "You're going to get sick out here in the cold." He pulled her coat from the backseat and put her arms in the sleeves, like she was a child.

Then she drew a deep breath. "I'm okay. Ford is here. Nothing else matters."

Joseph wasn't so sure of that as he walked her into the hospital. Hector had parked while Joseph had been holding her and now he shadowed them as they headed to Ford's room. He would continue to be Daphne's shadow until Doug was no longer a threat.

Ford's room had a uniformed officer standing guard outside. Joseph showed his ID. "This is the boy's mother."

The officer's face softened in sympathy. "We're glad we found him, ma'am."

Daphne looked up and Joseph was struck by the transformation. She was serene, her smile contained. "Thank you, Officer." She was Stepford Daphne.

She'd transformed several times the day before, always when she was scared shitless or stressed beyond her breaking point. "I'm here," he murmured.

She nodded almost regally and walked into the room where her son lay, her trembling hands the only sign that she wasn't really composed. She stood by Ford's bed and stroked his forehead like the boy was made of glass.

Joseph didn't realize he was holding his breath until it came out in a relieved hiss. "He looks good, Daphne," he said. Ford's face was a little red in places, but there was no sign of the frostbite Joseph had secretly worried about.

"Excuse me." A doctor came into the room. "Are you Ford's parents?"

"She is," Joseph said, when Daphne didn't turn or respond. She stood by Ford's bedside, still stroking his forehead. "This is Daphne Montgomery and I'm Special Agent Carter with the FBI."

"Ma'am?" The doctor touched Daphne's shoulder and she turned then, her face composed. "I'm Dr. Rampor. I wanted to let you know that your son is stable and that we don't see any long-term damage from the exposure. He does have some injuries, but none are life-threatening." The doctor smiled kindly. "He's a lucky young man."

Daphne nodded. "Thank you. What injuries?"

Joseph tucked her under his arm. The trembles had become pronounced and he wondered how she was even standing up.

The doctor met Joseph's eyes, deeply concerned. "Is she all right?"

"It's been a long day and a half, Doctor," Joseph said. "She's holding."

"Well, if we need to treat Ms. Montgomery, we certainly can."

"I'm fine," Daphne said coolly. "And I'm right here. Please, just focus on Ford."

"Of course. Your son has a laceration on the back of his head, some abrasions on his face. Nothing needed stitches. Do you have any questions for me?"

"When will he wake up?"

"I would think soon. There don't appear to be any injuries that are causing him to sleep. It's more likely that he's simply exhausted. We've administered an IV with some antibiotics in case there's any infection associated with the head injury. Everything else is just fine."

"Thank you," Daphne said. She turned around, leaned over the bed rail, touched her forehead to her son's. "Ford. I'm here. It's Mom."

Joseph drew the doctor out into the hall. "Did you find any needle marks?"

"We did, but I was hesitant to mention them in front of the mother," Rampor said softly. "Several needle marks around the neck. And Taser punctures. Two sets."

"Two sets? Are you sure?"

"I see a lot of Taser punctures in the ER," Rampor said, "so yes, I'm sure. One set in the middle of his back are starting to heal over. The set on his thigh are fresher."

"How much fresher?"

"Hard to say exactly. Maybe as long ago as last night."

That didn't make sense. "After he was out in the snow or before?"

"I'd have to examine the affected area under a scope to know that and even then I might not be able to tell. Is it very important?"

"I don't know. It's something Ford can answer when he wakes up. Did you do any tox scans?"

"Yes. We found very high levels of ketamine."

"What about fentanyl?"

"We didn't test for that."

"Why did you test for the ketamine, Doctor?"

"Because of the way he woke up the first time—terrified

and out of control. He's a big kid. It took three of us to hold him down."

"Emergence phenomena from the ket," Joseph murmured. Hallucinations were a common side effect, especially when used at sedative levels.

"I'd say so. He was screaming 'Kim' and 'Heather.'"

"Heather? Maybe MacGregor? That's Kim's last name."

"Could have been, I suppose. We were too busy holding him down to dissect what he was screaming."

"When did he wake up?"

"About a half hour after the EMTs brought him in. I hesitated to tell his mother, but we had to sedate him. But the sedative should have worn off some time ago."

"What if the ketamine was mixed with fentanyl?"

"Then his sleeping so much longer would make sense."

"He was probably dosed with a fentanyl-ketamine cocktail at the same time as the second Taser attack. The question is why."

"That and how did you know about the ketamine in the first place?" Rampor added.

"One person was murdered at the scene where Ford was abducted. Our ME found traces of fentanyl and ketamine in the victim. It made sense that Ford was drugged up at the same time so that he could be transported. But why he was dosed again, so close to being found . . . that makes no sense. Not yet, anyway."

"If you think I should tell Ms. Montgomery about the extra sedation, I will."

"No—not as long as he wakes up soon. I don't want her to have to worry about why he was dosed a second time. Let her be happy that she has him back."

"He really is lucky. If he hadn't been discovered when he was and by whom, we could be talking about the loss of several toes, at the very least. But he was found by a retired nurse who knew what to do. By the time the EMTs arrived, she was warming the boy's extremities according to best practices."

"I'll make sure Ms. Montgomery knows. I know she'll want to thank that person when she's feeling more like herself."

"Call me if she needs anything."

Joseph thanked the doctor and went back into Ford's

room, pulling up a chair to the side of the bed and gently pushing Daphne into it. "Don't worry, honey. He'll wake up soon and you'll take him home."

Again the nod. "I'm fine, Joseph. Really. You go do what you need to do."

He kissed the top of her head. "All right."

He stepped back into the hall and was joined by two men in suits. They introduced themselves as Agent Kerr from the Pittsburgh field office and Detective McManus from Wheeling PD. They'd shaken hands when the elevator door opened and out walked Deacon Novak, sunglasses shielding his eyes.

More than one of the nurses gave Deacon the up-down once-over, fanning themselves as he walked by, but he behaved as if oblivious. Joseph had witnessed the women in VCET flirting shamelessly with Deacon, but Novak let it roll off his back.

Joseph didn't see it, but more power to the guy if he had it.

"How is Ford?" Deacon asked, peering into the boy's hospital room.

"He hasn't regained consciousness yet," Joseph said, "but he's stable. Gentlemen, this is Special Agent Novak. I'd like him to work with you in your investigation. We need to know where Ford was being held. Two others are still missing."

"Happy to have the help, Novak," Agent Kerr said. "Ford Elkhart appears to have been pushed out of a vehicle into the yard where he was discovered. The woman who lived there was on her toes. She saw him lying there, saw the tire treads on the road were filling up with snow, so she grabbed the shower curtain out of her bathtub to lay over the tire prints."

McManus smiled a little. "That's Miz Cornell. She really loves her TV cop shows. She covered the tracks before she covered the boy. Tire tread suggests we're looking at a van, an F-150 cargo model. I've got photos you can take to your lab."

Joseph frowned. "The black van."

"You know of this van?" Kerr asked, and Joseph nodded.

"Black van with a hydraulic lift that's leaking oil and

hydraulic fluid. It's been used in several crimes back in Baltimore."

"That's what we found on his clothing, hydraulic fluid along with a few carpet fibers," Kerr said. "What doesn't make sense, then, is who dumped him and why."

"He'd been walking a long time," Detective McManus said. "We figured he'd been picked up from the side of the road somewhere and dropped in Miz Cornell's yard. But why would someone do that? We assumed it was a good Samaritan who didn't want to get tied up in the investigation because they had something in the van they didn't want the cops to see. Pot, pills, whatever."

"But if it was the van you all know about," Kerr added, "why drop him off at all?"

"And why drug him up and tase him before dropping him off?" Joseph said. "The doctor just told me that he was brought in with ket in his system. He woke up violent."

"None of this makes sense," Deacon agreed. "But we might be able to match the tire prints, just to find out if it's the same van, or the same type at least. Carter, did we get any prints from the floor of the Timonium house?"

"Brodie got dirt from the treads. She may have gotten a print, too."

"I'll call her," Deacon said. "Were you able to tell where the van came from before it dropped Ford off?"

"Not really. We followed the tire tracks from Miz Cornell's to the main road, then lost them," Detective McManus said. "We think Ford walked along the road for a long time, so we know the general direction he was coming from before he got picked up. But before that, he walked through the woods."

"Why?" Deacon asked. "Why do you think he walked through the woods?"

"For one thing, the road he was on originates in the wildlife management area. He had to have come through there. The burs on his jeans confirm it," McManus said. "He could have walked through that wildlife management area for miles without seeing a soul. He had to have been on a road when he was picked up because that van wouldn't have functioned off-road. If we can find where he was picked up, we can try using dogs to track him to where he started."

Joseph looked over his shoulder at Daphne. She was bowed over, one of Ford's hands sandwiched between hers. "I need to do a search of your archives." He turned back to McManus. "It'd be a thirty-year-old case."

"Her cousin's abduction," Deacon murmured. "Daphne went missing, too."

"When she realized we were coming into Wheeling, she was not happy. Apparently she lived around here when it happened. Where can I check old property records and police reports, Detective?"

McManus handed Joseph a business card. "If you call the main number and ask for Junie Bramble, she'll get you what you need. She knows those archives like the back of her hand and can save you hours."

"Thank you. It's too much coincidence, Ford turning up in the same area where Ms. Montgomery and her cousin were abducted."

"Agreed," McManus said. "If you can't find what you're looking for, I know a few of the retired cops who didn't move to Florida. They'd be happy to bend your ear about any thirty-year-old case you want."

Joseph gave him one of his cards. "Can you put them in touch with me? I'd like to talk to them regardless of what Miss Bramble finds in the archives. Keep me in the loop as you search and I'll do the same."

Deacon looked in on Ford again. "He gonna keep his fingers and toes?" he asked quietly.

"Doc said yes. I'm going to stay with her in case Ford wakes up." Joseph hesitated. "Be careful out there, Deacon. I don't like that we were drawn out this way."

"I hear you. You, too. She's the target. He's just the lure."

"I know." And the knowledge made Joseph's blood run cold. "I wish I knew why."

Baltimore, Maryland
Wednesday, December 4, 3:00 p.m.

Clay tossed his hat on his desk and sank into his chair, gratefully accepting a cup of coffee from Alyssa. "It is cold out there," he said, wrapping his hands around the mug.

"It can get to fifty below if it wants," Alyssa said with a big smile. "Ford's found."

It had been a call he would never forget. Daphne had called him first. Even before she'd called Paige. Well, Paige technically knew already because Carter had told Maggie, who'd called Simone and Paige was standing right there. But the thought was sufficient. Her son was safe and Clay's and Daphne's friendship was mending.

He'd been on his way to Philly to speak with the Mac-Gregors when he got the call. He'd cried like a baby and was mostly not ashamed to admit it. "Hopefully Daphne will bring him home soon. Hopefully we'll have found Kim before then."

Because the girl has a helluva lot to answer for.

"Did you find out anything from Kim's parents in Philly today?" Alyssa asked.

"Not much, but at least it wasn't a wasted trip. I got the name of Kim's first roommate at the university. The roommate remembered her getting arrested and the conviction. She went to court with Kim for moral support. She said that a week later Kim met this guy named Doug who made her nervous—the roommate, not Kim."

"Why did Doug make the roommate nervous?"

"I couldn't get her to say exactly. I think it had something to do with sex and she wasn't comfortable talking to me about it."

"You want me to follow up?"

He frowned. "Yes. I'm not sure why I didn't just ask you to talk to her to begin with."

She patted his knee. "You're still a little rattled from yesterday, big guy. Kim was red hot and ready for revenge after her plea bargain with Daphne and Doug reeled her in like a fish. Eighteen-year-old girls can be *so* stupid."

Clay bit back a smile. "So says the twenty-year-old girl."

"I can't help being twenty. But at least I'm not stupid."

"No, you're not. Talk to the roommate, see what you can find."

She started for her desk, then came back to give him a peck on the cheek.

"What was that for?" he asked gruffly.

"You looked like you could use it," she murmured. "For what it's worth, I think Stevie will come around."

He tried not to be annoyed with Alyssa for prying. "Alec has a big mouth."

"He never said a word. Didn't have to. That you would run to her when she woke up was a given. That it didn't end well is written all over your face."

He looked away. "Wonderful." Then, because he was a fool, he asked, "Why do you think she'll come around?"

"Because she's not stupid. And I've seen how she looks at you."

"She doesn't look at me."

"Oh, yeah, she does. I saw her at the Halloween benefit Daphne did for the center."

Stevie had come as Mata Hari and Clay had had a hard-on for days afterward. He got one now, just remembering. Discreetly he lowered his coffee mug to his lap, but not discreetly enough. Alyssa's eyes sparkled.

"She watched you, Clay, like she wanted to gobble you up. So give her some time."

She walked out, but Alec showed up as soon as she was gone. "Got something."

Clay scooted his chair so that his legs and his lap were under the desk. "On what?"

Alec sat on the edge of his desk as Alyssa had done. "Thefts from gun safes. There haven't been too many and they're spread out—one each in Maryland, DC, Northern Virginia, eastern Pennsylvania, and West Virginia. After Ford turned up there, I added West Virginia to my search radius. I looked for insurance claims that were either rejected or that resulted in a police inquiry."

"Not going to ask how you got into the insurance database."

"That would be wise on your part. I called each person who filed a claim, saying I was an internal auditor for the insurance company and was reopening their case. Two of the four talked to me, both of them wives of cops. Both had weapons stolen. Neither of them used a cleaning service, but both had AC work done which included having their ducts cleaned out."

Clay sat back, impressed as hell. "What's the name of the company?"

"Two different companies, both legit. But the cops both got a flyer in their mailboxes offering a 'special.' The number didn't belong to the real companies and neither had offered a special. Both said the team that came was a man

and a woman. Woman was Kimberly MacGregor. The man
fit Doug's, five-nine, totally average description."

Excitement buzzed down Clay's spine. "Get me the information. I'll give Carter a call. He can get a sketch artist
out to those two homes. If they saw Doug, they can provide
a description. Hopefully we can get a likeness of this guy
that's more helpful than we've had so far. Good work, Alec."

"Thanks. How will you hide that I got information
through . . . inventive means?"

"I'll think of something. Don't worry."

Wheeling, West Virginia
Wednesday, December 4, 3:30 p.m.

After Deacon had left with the locals, Joseph returned to
Ford's room. Daphne sat still as a statue in the plastic chair,
her hand over Ford's. He knew she wouldn't leave her son
to sleep in a proper bed, so he mentally urged the boy to
wake up fast.

Standing behind her, he rubbed her shoulders, satisfied
when she dropped her head, elongating her neck. In minutes her tight muscles began to loosen.

"You need to sleep, Daphne."

"I need him to see me when he wakes up. Then I'll
sleep."

"I was in the hospital for three days once, unconscious,"
he said. "My mother talked to me. I remember just wanting
to hear more, to get closer, and I woke up. So maybe you
should talk to him."

She looked back at him, eyes wide. "What happened to
make you unconscious for three days?"

"Skateboard accident when I was a kid. Once I finally
woke up and Mom knew I wasn't going to die, she ripped
me a new one. I wasn't wearing a helmet."

"I would have ripped you one, too."

He grinned. "Yeah, but I didn't fall until after I'd popped
an ollie and ridden the rail all the way down the middle
school steps. Totally worth it." His grin faded. "Except for
how much I scared my mom. I always hated that I'd done
that."

"I suspect she's forgiven you," she said with a smile, then
turned back to her son. "With Ford it was always the horses,

which I suppose was my fault. I took him to the stable with me from the time he was an infant. When he was five he saw a jumping competition and he was hooked. My heart would routinely stop, watching him compete." She stroked the boy's hand. "He loves to fly."

"Talk to him about the horses or Simone's gigantic Christmas tree. Just talk to him."

She did, but the topic she chose was the women's center that she and Paige were building, the one for which she hosted all those fund-raisers. At first he listened with half an ear, thinking instead about all the colors she'd worn to those charity events, how bold she'd looked among the sea of little black dresses. *How alive.*

And then he remembered all those hours he'd watched her from across the room, imagining peeling those bright dresses off her body. Imagining all the things he'd do to her if she were only going home with him. To his bed. If she were his.

She could be his. *Mine.* He liked the sound of that.

And then he realized she wasn't talking to Ford. *She's talking to me.* She was telling him how scared the women were, how hard the treatments were on their bodies. And spirits. How devastating it was for the women she served to lose their hair, their curves. Their femininity. How terrified they were to think they might leave their children motherless. And how hard it was to take care of their children when they could barely take care of themselves.

And Joseph knew she was really telling him how it had been for her, helping him to understand all the things he'd need to know. *If she decides to belong to me.*

"I was lucky," she murmured. "I had Mama and Maggie. I always knew that if anything ever happened to me that they'd take care of you. So many aren't so lucky, and I always said, 'Someday I'll do something about that.' Then Paige started talking about starting her school, offering self-defense classes to the women in Holly's social center. It brought her back from a dark place where she was afraid all the time. I'd been there, too, in that dark place. For a long time I just held my breath, waiting for the doctor to give me bad news. But he didn't and then he didn't again, and then years had gone by. I knew the time had come to give back." She exhaled on a sigh. "When I get to the end of my life, I want to be able to look back and know that my being here made things better."

And in that moment he knew. *I have to have her. Nobody'd better stand in my way. Or threaten to take her away from me. She is the one made only for me.*

"I think you already have made things better," he said quietly.

"Not as much as I will," she said. "We've got a good start. In six months we'll have facilities for twenty single mothers and their kids. Not all those women will make it, but I'll be damn sure they leave their kids with some good memories."

"Is that why you bought the farm?" he asked.

She looked up at him, eyes filled with disbelief. "Did you really just ask me that?"

He frowned, then winced when he realized what he'd said. "Not what I meant. I meant, buy the . . . property that the farm is . . . on," he finished lamely.

Her lips twitched and he realized she was laughing at him. "You're easy, Joseph."

With someone else he might have been annoyed. With her, he couldn't help but chuckle. "Not really. I like to at least be taken to dinner first."

She stared for a moment. Then she swallowed hard, obviously trying not to laugh. He blinked innocently. "What?"

She clapped her hand over her mouth, but it was too late. She started to laugh, more a release of stress than anything else. Still, *king of the world* raced through his mind. Her laughter subsided and her eyes changed, darkening. His body immediately responded and he leaned down, needing to taste her mouth.

"Mom?"

They broke apart like guilty teenagers. Ford's eyes were struggling to open, his broad shoulders lurching as he threw his body forward, disoriented and afraid. Joseph leaned over Daphne, holding the boy down so he didn't yank the IV out of his arm.

"Ford." Daphne cupped his face in her hands. "It's me. Mom. Open your eyes."

His lids fluttered open, green eyes filled with confusion. "Mom?"

"I'm here, baby. Right here."

"Where?" It was a pathetic croak.

Joseph hit the call button and hurried to the bathroom to wet a cloth, handing it to Daphne. She dabbed Ford's cracked lips and squeezed a few drops into his mouth.

"In the hospital," she said. "In West Virginia."

He searched her face. "Feet?"

"Your feet are fine. Hands, too."

"Kim?"

"She wasn't with you?" When he shook his head, her expression grew pained. "We're still looking for her."

A sob caught in Ford's throat. Daphne leaned in until her forehead rested on Ford's. "It's okay, son. Cry all you want to."

A nurse ran into the room, stopping when she saw that Ford wasn't violent this time. She approached, watching carefully, standing by as tears silently ran down the boy's face. When the wave had passed, his shoulders sagged back to the bed.

"So tired," he whispered.

"Then sleep, son."

"How long?" he whispered, his eyelids drooping. "Gone how long?"

"A day and a half," Daphne said softly. "Longest day of my life."

"I'll sleep . . . if you sleep." He struggled, his eyes popping open. "Mean it."

"I'll sleep. I promise."

Ford's eyes closed. "You get sick. When you don't sleep."

Joseph leaned over. "Ford, I'm Joseph Carter with the FBI." The boy's brow creased in confusion, so Joseph added, "I'm Jack Carter's son," and Ford nodded. "Do you know where you were?"

"Cabin. Woods. Walked miles. So tired."

"Did they say why they abducted you?"

"Money. Ransom." Ford was fading back into sleep. "Miss me."

Daphne kissed his forehead, his cheeks. "Rest, baby. I'll be back. Love you, son." She straightened and Joseph pulled her close. "I don't want to leave him."

"The hotel is next door. You can be back in two minutes when he wakes. This is your chance to sleep. Besides, you promised."

Eighteen

Having checked on both of his "houseguests," Mitch was jogging up the stairs from the basement when he heard the garage door go up. Cole was home from school. The kid ran up the stairs and slammed his bedroom door so hard the house shook. *What now?* He left his room and knocked on Cole's door.

"Go away."

"What happened, Cole?"

"Nothing."

Which meant it was probably pretty bad. "I'm going to find out."

The door abruptly opened and he found himself looking up into Cole's angry green eyes. "I said, *go away*, and I meant it."

Damn. The kid hadn't just grown tall. He was filling out, too. Give him a few years and he might be as big as Ford Elkhart. Who, Mitch's still-aching back could attest, was as big as a damn ox. "Are you suspended?"

"No." But he looked away. "Leave me alone."

"Don't take that tone with me, boy. I had to take time out of my schedule today to meet with your guidance counselor. She says if you get suspended one more time, you're out. I'll have to find you another school. I don't have time for that just now. So whatever the hell you just did, it better not be a suspendable offense. You got me?"

Cole glared down at him. "Loud and clear. Sir."

Mitch flinched when the door slammed in his face. He knocked again. "I've got an HVAC job tonight. Office building, so it's an after-hours job. I should be home by the time you have to go to school tomorrow, but if I'm not, you'd better get your ass out of bed and go to school."

"Fine. Whatever."

Meaning no, Mitch thought. He'd figure out what to do about Cole when he got home. Tonight he would be in West Virginia. Beckett had to have figured out by now that Ford was in the hospital in Wheeling. *If I were Beckett and that kid had seen my face, that's the first place I'd go.*

Mitch took out his keys and jangled them in his hand. "The van's having engine problems, so I'm taking the Jeep. I saw a pile of your schoolbooks in the backseat. Do you need any of them tonight, to maybe do . . . I don't know. *Homework?*"

Silence met his ears and Mitch felt a dull ache behind his eyes. *I wish to God you were still here, Mom. Because that kid's making me crazy.*

His mother still would have been here had it not been for Daphne. Just one more reason she needed to pay.

"When I get back from this job we need to talk, Cole," Mitch said quietly. "I want a better path for you than the one you're on. Please go to school tomorrow." More silence met his ears and Mitch let out a frustrated sigh. "Just don't get into any new trouble till I get back. Okay?"

His head pounding, he got into the Jeep and left for West Virginia. At least everything was moving in the right direction there. And it was only a matter of time before Mutt's daddy would be getting a visit from his very unhappy Russian boss.

Things could be a lot worse, all in all.

Wheeling, West Virginia
Wednesday, December 4, 4:30 p.m.

There's something illicit about adjoining hotel rooms, Daphne thought as she watched Joseph slide her key card through the lock. He went in first, put her bag on the dresser, and proceeded to check every window, nook, and cranny for . . . for what?

"I don't think a killer could fit in there," she said when he opened the tiny microwave in the kitchenette.

He slanted her a look. "Camera might."

Her eyes widened. "Camera?"

"He used one to rob Trooper Gargano." He checked the cupboards. "I'm nervous that we're here, that Ford was found here, that you used to live here. Feels like a trap."

She wished he was teasing her. But he wasn't. He was on high alert and had directed Hector to be as well. The Vice detective was currently patrolling the perimeter of the hotel, checking exits, watching for anyone who looked like Doug.

Joseph checked all the vents, then turned off the lights and pulled the draperies shut, pitching the room into total darkness. "I'm looking for pinpricks of light," he said, even though she hadn't asked. "Holes that could be drilled."

"Wouldn't they have to know we were staying in this room?"

"Or they could have bribed the clerk at the front desk," he said, as if not believing she could be so naive. He had a point. She was purposely being obtuse. Defense mechanism, right up there with her Stepford face. He unlocked the door between their rooms, then left through the hall door. "I'll be right back," he promised, then shut the door, again plunging her into darkness.

She could sit down, put her feet up. It was a mini-suite, with a sofa and a kitchenette and a bedroom with a separate door. She could move, but she didn't. She could turn on a light, but she didn't do that, either.

Because something was going to happen. She could feel it. Blindly she put her purse on the kitchen counter, listening.

Joseph was in his room. She could hear him doing all the checks he'd already done in her room. The dead bolt on the other side of the adjoining door was thrown and . . .

Her heart was pounding and had been since they'd come up in the elevator. His jaw had been clenched, his fists shoved in the pockets of his coat. His expression dark.

She might have thought him angry, but her gaze had dropped to the zipper of his trousers. Not angry. He was aroused. Intensely so.

She might have been surprised, except she'd done her

part to get him that way. He'd been about to kiss her when Ford woke up. She'd switched to mother mode, but even as she'd comforted her son, even as she'd wept with him, sharing his relief, even then she'd not forgotten that Joseph was there. And that he'd been about to kiss her.

So when he helped her out of the SUV in front of the hotel, she'd kissed him first. Hard and fast, her hands in his hair. She'd let him go with a single word. "Sooner."

Now, something was about to happen.

Thank God. She'd nearly jumped him on the interstate when he'd seeded her imagination with all the things he'd do to her. Below the waist.

The door flew open and it was suddenly "sooner."

He didn't pause to chat. Time for sweet nothings was done. In a fluid movement his hand gripped her jaw, lifting her face, taking her mouth with a ferocity that left her lips tender and her lungs empty.

She was hot, her skin tight and tingling in all the right places. She drew her head back to gasp in a breath and he took advantage, thrusting his tongue in her mouth. And what had always seemed . . . puzzling as to its appeal now made perfect, perfect sense. It was a prelude. A promise. What he was doing with his mouth was what he'd do with that rock-hard flesh that pressed against her, down low.

He broke away, his voice a growl that made her shiver. "Say yes."

"Yes."

He backed her against the door, hands on either side of her head, hips surging against her center. "Anything I want. Say it."

"Any . . ." She faltered. "What do—"

"Anything I want," he repeated harshly. Then softly, "Everything I want will make you feel good. You have my word. So tell me, Daphne. Anything I want."

She nodded. Found her voice. "Anything."

He kissed her again, gentle plucking kisses that made her want to sigh. He nuzzled her throat, licking a line to where her pulse throbbed. "Nervous?"

"A little. Yes."

"Don't be." He rolled his hips and she sucked in a breath. "Are you wet?"

A shiver sensitized her skin. *Oh God.* "Yes."

"A little?"

She let out a breath. "No."

His exhale was ragged. "Good." He kept his hands flat against the door on either side of her head and took her mouth in another blistering, hard kiss. She grabbed his coat and held on.

"Unbutton your coat," he said. Hands shaking, she did so, dropping it to the floor without a second thought. "Now the sweater." She pulled it over her head, hesitating when the turtleneck caught her wig, fearing what he'd ask next. Carefully she tugged it free, smoothing her hair as she dropped the sweater on top of her coat.

His mouth descended to hers again, this kiss lush and unhurried, and when he lifted his head she hummed a protest. "This time you get to choose what you take off," he murmured. "Jeans or the bra."

"I still have boots on."

"I'll take care of that," he said smoothly and she shivered again, all kinds of images flitting through her mind. "Take off your jeans for me, Daphne."

How she managed the snap and zipper she didn't know, but a shove and a shimmy of her hips sent her jeans to pool around her ankles. His breath shuddered out, warming her shoulder. Which he kissed. He moved to her collarbone, letting his breath warm her skin there, too. He traced the center of her throat with the tip of his tongue and she sucked in a breath.

"Joseph." She felt him smile against her skin.

"You're not shy, are you, Daphne?" He didn't wait for an answer, walking his hands down the door in a prowling motion, his shoulders rolling like a big cat. He kissed his way down her stomach until he was on his knees, kneeling before her, his nose a fraction of an inch from where she was very wet indeed.

He inhaled, the exhale a rough sound that weakened her knees.

"You make me impatient, Joseph."

He chuckled darkly. "Good. Because you're driving me crazy. Do you know how good you smell? How much I want to dive in and taste you?"

She had to lock her knees, which made him chuckle again. "Why don't you?"

His swallow was audible. "Because I want your legs free. The first time I saw you, I imagined your legs over my shoulders, my tongue buried so deep inside you." Again the dark chuckle. "I bet you had no idea that while I was eating your muffins I was thinking about eating you alive."

"No," she whispered. "No idea whatsoever." Her hips had a mind of their own and they tilted toward him. He backed up a few inches, a warning growl in his throat.

"When I start, I won't be able to stop. So don't tempt me."

"Then for God's sake, hurry."

Abruptly he grabbed her foot and yanked at the boot, sending it flying over his shoulder. The other boot followed. "Step out of the jeans."

She did and he rose, grabbing her butt in both hands and lifting her off the floor. Her knees lifted to grip his hips, hands grasping his shoulders as he spun her around.

"Hurry, Joseph. Please."

Seconds later she was on her back on the bed, her legs over his shoulders, his mouth . . . "Oh God." He was sucking her through the lace of her panties and she arched, increasing the friction, rolling her hips, finding the rhythm that drove her higher.

Abruptly he pulled away, drawing a protest from her lips. "Wait," he ground out. "Just wait." She could see the outline of his body in the darkness. He knelt between her legs, his head bowed, his fists at his sides. His chest rose and fell as he panted.

"What? What's wrong?"

He gave an incredulous laugh. "Wrong? Daphne, I'm about to come and I haven't even gotten started yet. I need to slow it down." He ran his hands down her legs, then back up again. "These have to go." He pulled her panties off, one leg, then the other, then brought them to his nose and inhaled.

"Oh," she whispered.

He tucked the panties in his pants pocket, then slowly brought her legs up over his shoulders, dragging her to his mouth. His tongue lapped, teasing, and she thought he was watching her, that even though she couldn't see in the dark, he could.

"Joseph. Please." She thrust her hips toward him. "Please." With a groan he dropped back down to the bed, his tongue stabbing deep. She thrust her fingers into his hair and pulled him closer, dug her heels into his back to push herself higher, all while he sucked and licked and sent her flying.

The orgasm took her by complete surprise and she arched off the bed, gasping his name. After . . . she lay on the bed, her fingers still clenched in his hair, breathing like she'd run a mile.

"Oh my God," she whispered. He'd lifted his head and hung over her, panting.

"Better than I dreamed," he said quietly. "And I dreamed a helluva lot."

She forced her fingers to let go of his hair and flopped back on the mattress. "I can't believe I didn't know about this."

He pressed a kiss to the inside of her thigh. "You say the nicest things," he teased.

"We aren't finished, are we?"

"Oh no," he said. "But I'd rather not go off like a teenager."

She bit her lip. "I forgot protection."

"I didn't."

She drew a breath. "Hurry," she whispered.

"No." He pushed himself off the bed slowly and she got the impression he was stripping for her benefit, to give her time to get used to him. Suddenly she needed to see him. She hit a light switch and froze. His lips glistened. *Me. That's from me.* It was erotic as hell.

He was shrugging out of his shirt, his muscles flexing with each twist of his body. He dropped the shirt on the floor and he stared her fill. His chest was . . . beautiful. *My chest . . . not so much.* She closed her eyes.

"No," he said harshly. "Don't you dare go there. Look at me."

She opened her eyes in time to see him drop his pants. He stood there, his shirt unbuttoned, his erection straining to escape his boxer shorts.

"Joseph," she murmured.

"Does this look like I have any issues with what I see?" he demanded, pointing at himself. "Does it?"

"No." She looked up at his face, then back down to his shorts. "It doesn't."

"Damn right, it doesn't," he growled. He shoved the boxers down and bent to find his wallet and pull out a condom. He rolled it down his length and her mouth went dry.

Never taking his eyes from her face, he crawled across the bed until he hung over her. "Say yes," he demanded.

"Yes." She reared up, kissing his mouth, tasting herself on his lips. Surprising the hell out of him. With a low roar he pushed her down to the bed, pushing into her body with one thrust. She arched her throat. Felt him filling her. "Yes."

"You're tight. Feels so damn good."

"You're perfect," she whispered. "Show me."

He set the pace, slow at first. She knew when he'd reached the limit of his control because his eyes grew darker than black, the muscles in his jaw bulging slightly, his biceps quivering under the strain.

"Wrap your legs around me."

She did, humming when he went even deeper. Sweat beaded on his brow and his eyes grew unfocused. Then he was pounding faster, harder, teeth clenched until he arched his back, his body jerking convulsively as he found his release.

He sagged, his body heavy on top of hers. She wrapped her arms around him and sighed. He didn't move, his voice muffled when he said, "Good sigh or bad sigh?"

"Very good sigh." He tried to move, but she tightened her hold. "No. Stay."

"I'm too heavy for you."

She pressed a kiss to his shoulder. "So many years of being alone . . . Feels good to have you be too heavy."

He kissed her chin, rested his forehead against hers. "Anything I want?"

She had to smile. "Now you're asking?"

His lips winged up, then he sobered. "When I was . . . tasting you . . ."

Daphne's cheeks heated. "Yes?"

"You had your fingers in my hair and I liked that. I want to touch you. Everywhere." He kissed her temple, brushing her hair with his lips. "I'm going to think you're beautiful, no matter what. Next time . . . will you at least think about taking it off?"

"Yes."

He smiled ruefully. "You'll do it or think about it?"

"Both. Joseph? Thank you."

Satisfaction gleamed in his eyes. "You're welcome."

Wheeling, West Virginia
Wednesday, December 4, 5:25 p.m.

Joseph closed the door to her bedroom, leaving her sleeping deeply. He felt . . . damn good. Muscles loose, stress low. He felt like he could run a marathon.

That had been amazing. So many times he'd fantasized about those long legs of hers, wrapped around his waist. It had been better than his fantasies. He already wanted her again.

But first he needed to make the threat to her go away.

He had a team meeting in five minutes, but that should give him enough time to start the ball rolling on a search for the report on the abduction of Daphne's cousin Kelly. He found the card Detective McManus had given him and called the number.

"Wheeling Police Department, Junie Bramble speaking. How may I help you?"

"Hello, Ms. Bramble. My name is Special Agent Carter. I'm with the—"

"FBI," she said. "Detective McManus said you'd be calling. He said you were interested in an old case. The abduction of the Montgomery girl and her cousin."

"Yes, ma'am."

"I've already started digging. I should have something for you soon."

"Thank you."

"That was a big case here, Agent Carter. Everyone I knew volunteered to search for those girls. I understand the cousin is with you."

"State's Attorney Montgomery, yes."

There was a beat of silence. "Ex . . . excuse me? Kelly Montgomery died."

"Right. I'm talking about Daphne Montgomery, Kelly's cousin."

"Oh. Daphne wasn't a Montgomery then. She was a Sinclair. Daphne Sinclair. Her mother was a Montgomery until she got married . . . Oh, right. Simone must have gotten divorced and gone back to her maiden name."

Joseph remembered the way Maggie's face had gone hard as stone at the mention of Daphne's father. "Do you know why they got divorced?"

Junie hesitated. "He left them, as I recall. So, Daphne's a prosecutor now? How lovely is that. How's her mother doing?"

"Do you know Simone?"

"I went to high school with Simone's sister, Vivien, who passed on a number of years ago. She was Kelly's mother."

"Oh."

"Yes. It was tragic. Vivien nearly lost her mind when Kelly went missing. And then when the girl was found dead . . . Vivien snapped, poor thing. It was a dark time for our town. I file police reports all day, every day, Agent Carter. I see all the bad, all the ugly. It's not just victims, but their families and communities. Everyone suffers, and here at the police station we hardly ever see a happy-ever-after. I'm glad little Daphne found a good life. Please tell her I said so. I won't go home until I have your reports to you."

"You're working overtime," Joseph said. "I wish I didn't have to ask you to do that."

"If you can bring closure to that family, it'll be well worth it. This will be my little part."

Joseph thanked her, then hung up, curious. No one had ever mentioned Aunt Vivien. And what was up with her father? He'd get the whole story from Daphne when she woke up. Now he had to get presentable, as his team meeting was via videoconference through the computer.

He hated videoconferences. He liked the visual anonymity of regular telephone meetings. But the group had some photos that he needed to be able to see, so he put some clothes on and set up his laptop. When the call connected, he got a close-up of J. D. Fitzpatrick's left eye.

"Sorry," J.D. said. "I'm adjusting the camera." He stepped back, his brows shooting up. "You might want to . . ." He tapped his cheek. "Before everyone gets here."

Joseph jumped up and looked in the mirror. "Shit," he muttered and heard J.D.'s low chuckle. He had lipstick smeared all over his cheek. He wet a cloth and scrubbed his face. And scowled. The stuff had a half-life.

Still, it had been worth it. He removed most of the evidence and went back to his laptop. Most of the team had filed in. "Can we get started? Who's there?"

"Everyone except you and Daphne, Deacon, and Hector," J.D. said.

"I'm calling from the road," Kate said through the speakerphone. "Simone and Maggie and I left for West Virginia two hours ago. Simone had to finish putting the lights on that big Christmas tree. When she flips the switch, it'll drain the power grid for the East Coast."

"Keeps her off the street," Joseph said with a smile. "Deacon's out with the local PD and the Pittsburgh field office. They're trying to track Ford's steps to find where he'd been held. Hector's on break."

Hector had secured the hotel and handed off the patrol to local agents from the Pittsburgh field office. He'd been on duty since the morning before and Joseph needed him rested. Just in case.

Joseph had booked the adjoining rooms for himself and Daphne, then a room across the hall for her mother and Maggie. Kate and Hector would each have a room on either side of Simone. Deacon and Hector would share. Everyone had a place to lay their heads.

"Daphne finally went to sleep." And Joseph had to work hard to hide his cat-in-cream smile at what had made her tired enough. "Ford's stable. He woke up for a minute or two, then went back to sleep." He told the team about the second dose of ketamine and the second tasing.

"That makes absolutely no sense," J.D. said. "Why would Doug pick him up only to drop him off again? It's like Doug wanted Ford to be found."

"That's my take," Joseph said. "He lured us here, just like he lured us to the house in Timonium."

"I have some information for you on the crime scene in the basement there," Brodie said. "I ran the DNA on the blood on the wall and it belongs to Daphne's ex-husband, Judge Elkhart. However, it's frozen blood, like from a blood bank."

"And the judge is very much alive," Grayson said. "I got a visit from him this morning. He was upset that we'd sent the FBI out to his estate like he was a 'common thug.' I asked him if he was going out to see Ford in the hospital and he said that Ford's mother was there and he wasn't needed."

"Did you ask him if he froze his blood?" Joseph asked.

"No, because we didn't have that info then."

"I called the judge's mother," Brodie said. "She confirmed that they did put blood away for emergency surgeries because the judge had one of the rarer blood types. It was supposed to have been stored on estate grounds, but it's not there."

"Doug is a sick puppy," Joseph said. "Did we find any sign that he was there watching Daphne at the barn?"

"We did," Kate said. "Scott Cooper showed us the places a man could stand and get the best view of the barn. There was evidence that someone was there today. Fresh footprints in the snow. We were probably being observed the whole time."

"Shit. How close are we to having a picture of this asshole?"

"Not close at all." J.D. sounded disgusted. "We've had uniforms canvassing every place up and down the college strip, restaurants, bars . . . Nobody's got him on video. This guy is careful not to get his picture taken. The police artists we've used have given us nada and it's not their fault. The teacher who saw him in Timonium gave a description that could be anyone."

"What about the girl in Philly?" Joseph asked. "The one who saw her au pair killed?"

"She's still under sedation," J.D. said. "We did get the photos the Philly mall's garage camera picked up. This is Doug getting out of the black van on Monday night." The team flashed away, replaced by the still photo.

Joseph leaned forward, frowning at the sight. "Fuck him. Daphne used to wear her hair that way." Doug wore a wig that had been teased into Daphne's old beehive hairdo. "One more check in the this-is-personal column. How are we doing on her caseload files? Did you find anyone who hates her this much?"

"None that fit Doug's description," Grayson said. "Lots of hate, though."

"See if anyone she prosecuted died or had a family member die," Joseph suggested. "The fact that Doug is this

personal and focused indicates that he blames Daphne for
more than a few parking tickets."

"We will," Grayson said. "Have you heard from Bo?"

"Not since this morning," Joseph answered. "They're
planning the raid on the Antonov warehouse, which should
be going down tonight. If Doug is Antonov's employee, we
might get info on him as part of what's recovered in the
raid. How's the search for Doug's house coming?"

"Got it narrowed to thirty properties owned by anyone
with 'Doug,' 'Douglas,' and even 'McDougal' in the name.
Until I know a little more about Doug, I'm stuck. I started
checking out the properties, though. Maybe something will
pop. So far, nothing."

"Keep looking. Kate, since you're with Simone, ask
her about her older sister, Vivien. Vivien's daughter was
Kelly, the cousin who was killed. They lived here, near
Wheeling. I'd like to get the story from Simone so I can
compare details to the newspaper reports I requested
from the local PD's archives. I'll be asking Daphne when
she wakes up. We've obviously been lured here. I want to
know why."

"I will," Kate said. "I'll contact you when I have that information."

"Thank you. Hopefully we can get Ford up and moving
so we can bring him home. I'm very uncomfortable being
here at Doug's invitation."

*And you want to have Daphne in your own bed. Well,
yeah. Duh.*

"Keep in touch and keep your phones with you. I'll text
you any outcome from the search to backtrack Ford's trail
to where he was held. Kimberly and her sister are still missing, so the priority is finding Doug's house and wherever
Ford was held. Let's connect at seven tomorrow morning
unless we have a breaking lead."

Joseph disconnected and went straight to the bedroom.
Daphne was so deeply asleep, she hadn't moved. He'd
thought she'd be more comfortable in the dark for their
first time together. He'd been utterly stunned when she
turned on the light. More stunned when she kissed him full
on the mouth when his lips were covered in her juices. She
surprised him at every turn.

He dropped his pants, shrugged out of his shirt, selfishly

hoping her son slept a little longer, because he wanted to be surprised again.

Baltimore, Maryland
Wednesday, December 4, 7:40 p.m.

Cole checked his gym bag, making sure he had everything he needed. Cell phone, charger, Game Boy, box of ammo, T-shirts, clean briefs, spare set of keys to the van. And a Ziploc bag full of cash, money he'd grabbed by the fistful from Mitch's stash.

Two thousand dollars in small bills. He hoped they were unmarked. He had no idea where to look for a mark. He hoped nobody he planned to buy stuff from knew where to look, either. There was something wrong with money you could grab by the fistful like candy at Halloween.

I need to get out of here before the cops come. He'd wasted a lot of time planning, but it was cold outside and he needed to know exactly where to go. First to the bus station and then thirty miserable hours with a Greyhound full of people who hadn't showered in a week. Rico, Cole's pal from his old school in Miami, would pick him up at the bus station there. Rico lived in a condo complex that was three-quarters empty. There were plenty of abandoned units that Cole could hide out in while he figured out what to do.

I never should have taken the stupid gun to school today, he thought miserably. *What was I thinking? I'm just a stupid kid, like Mitch says.* Cole looked in the mirror, unimpressed. He'd grown six inches since the summer. Six inches. *I should be king of the hill.* Instead the guys still wouldn't leave him alone.

He hadn't planned to take the gun to start with. Hadn't planned to take it to school, for sure. But that fat-ass Tulio wouldn't let it go. He kept pushing and pushing . . . *Calling me names. Threatening to . . .* Cole swallowed, his hands going clammy just thinking about the stairwell and how they'd pushed up against him.

So he'd taken the gun to school just to show them. Just to scare them off. *Because they wouldn't leave me alone.* But that fat-ass Tulio had called his bluff and grabbed the gun right out of Cole's hand and wouldn't give it back.

Enough of the guys had seen Tulio walking around with

it. Of course the principal had seen them. That old guy had eyes in the back of his damn head. They'd scattered, but the principal had seen the gun. *There is no way any of the guys will lie for me.* The principal would tell the cops and the guys would give Cole up in less than a heartbeat.

So I'm outta here. But he didn't want to go empty-handed. He'd gotten used to the feel of cold metal at his back. He wouldn't take a gun to school again, but he sure as hell wanted one when he walked into a bad neighborhood. He'd lost the first one he'd taken, but he knew where to find more.

Cole didn't want to know why Mitch kept a bunch of guns and thousands of dollars in that little room in the basement—the hidden room that Mitch didn't want him to know about. Mitch had his hands in some serious shit and Cole did not want to follow in his brother's footsteps. "Ex-con" didn't look good on your permanent record.

But this once, he needed the help. There had been fifteen normal guns plus some that looked like antiques. He'd left the antiques alone the first time. He wouldn't touch them this time, either. Just a normal pistol. *That's all I need.*

He crept down the stairs, grateful that Mitch was gone, leaving Cole all alone in the house, which had more nooks and crannies than an English muffin. Mitch thought he was too stupid to know about all the hidden corners and rooms.

Cole knew about them and more. He pushed the boxes away from the wall and frowned. Then his heart started pounding even harder. The door had a new padlock.

Oh no. Hell, no. Now what?

A clatter upstairs had him jumping away from the supposed-to-be-secret door.

"Mitch! Where are you? Goddammit, you mother*fuck*ing sonofabitch, where the *fuck*ing hell are you?"

That couldn't be Matthew. Matthew didn't swear. But it was. Stowing his shock, Cole replaced the boxes and listened. Matthew charged up to the second floor, so Cole jogged up the basement stairs. If he hurried, he could slip out through the garage before Matthew came back down, because he didn't want to listen to another one of Matthew's rants about what a problem Mitch was becoming.

Cole had gotten through the kitchen when a hand clamped onto his shoulder. He turned and looked down into Matthew's glaring face. Matthew was bigger than Mitch. *But I'm bigger than them both. Why do I have to be such a fucking loser?* "What?" he snarled.

"Where's Mitch?" Matt demanded.

"Not here. Said he had a job. He took the Jeep, left the van."

Matthew looked away. "Damn him. Damn him to hell."

Don't ask what's wrong. Don't ask. "What's wrong?" *Dammit.*

Matthew was pale. "Mitch set Dad up with some dangerous men. Stole from them, made it look like Dad did it. Fucking nightmare."

See, now this is where I'm smarter than Mitch. Mitch would be all sarcastic, but I will pretend to care, just so I can get the hell out of here before the cops haul me off to juvie. "Why would he do that?"

Good tone, good concern. Go, me. But Cole was really grinning inside. *Go, Mitch.* Asshole stepfather made Mitch take the blame years ago. That's why Mitch went to jail. *Paybacks are a bitch.*

"I don't know. Still holding a grudge, I guess."

Well, it was three years of his life in prison getting it up the ass every day. Which is why I'm having problems now. Thanks, Dad.

Cole grimaced. "It wasn't like that was Dad's fault or anything." *Man, even I can't pull that one off with a straight face.* "But it *was* three years of his life, Matt."

"This is going to get Dad killed," Matthew said bitterly. "What's wrong with you two?"

"Look, I don't want anything to happen to Dad. If Mitch did this, he was wrong."

"If? *If?* I don't know why I *bother* with you people."

Cole raised his hands. "Whoa. What did Mitch steal? Maybe we can give it back."

Matthew gave him a look that said he was trying to decide if Cole was old enough to be trusted.

Cole shrugged. "I can't help if I'm runnin' blind."

Matthew sighed. "Guns. Lots of guns."

"Guns? They're downstairs in the basement."

Matthew's jaw dropped. "You knew?"

Cole shrugged uneasily. "Fifteen guns didn't seem like that big a deal. Not anything to get Dad killed over."

Matthew's shoulders sagged. "I don't know what you're talking about, kid. These are lots of guns. Crates of semi-automatic assault rifles. AK-47s."

Cole went still. "Like the ones they found in that guy's trunk at the courthouse yesterday?"

"Yes. Those were the guns Mitch stole. The number recovered in the raids yesterday was exactly what's missing from our inventory. We didn't know till we did the count today. This is a nightmare."

"Oh my God." *This is way worse than what I did. Hey. Wait a minute.* "How did Dad have them for Mitch to steal in the first place?"

Matthew rubbed his forehead. "Welcome to the real world, Cole. Dad has a shipping and distribution business."

"Yeah, antique furniture." Which had been Matt's father's story for years. "It's how your father met our mother. She told me the story when I was little, right before . . . You know. Before. Mom said she owned this antique furniture store before she married him. She let him run it while she took care of us. That's how he made his money."

Which Cole knew was a lie. He wondered if his mother had known her husband distributed drugs through her furniture store. If she'd suspected. Or just didn't care.

Something flickered in Matt's eyes at the mention of their mother. Guilt or sorrow? Matt had chosen his side in the divorce. He stayed with Dad. Turned his back on Mom.

"No," Matt said. "Not furniture. He distributes guns from Russia and . . . other things."

Cole's brows shot up. "Drugs?"

"Sometimes."

At least Matt was truthful about that. Cole frowned. "People?"

"Not to my knowledge."

Fucking hell. That was not anything close to a no. "What do you do?"

"My MBA's in accounting. I keep the books. And other things. I was the one who hired Mitch to make deliveries. I was trying to give the guy a break."

I didn't think he was doing HVAC work. "That actually explains a lot."

"Now Dad is terrified. You don't screw with the Russians."

Cole kept his voice sincere. "What are we going to do?" *I will be running like hell.*

"I have to find Mitch. He has to make this right."

It was, Cole supposed, a gorgeous piece of revenge. "Will they come after us?"

"Probably not. I don't think Antonov even knows about you, Cole."

And don't that make me feel special? "Look, I'd love to stay and help, but I've got a few problems of my own."

Matthew grabbed his arm. "What's more important than this?"

Two cars pulled up in front of the house and panic jacked him. *Sheriff's department. Shit.* "Them." He looked around wildly. "Dammit. Now it's too late."

"What have you done, Cole?"

"Nothing." *Have to hide. Hide.* Basement or garage? The garage was closer.

Matthew grabbed his arm again. "Goddammit, *stop*. What happened?"

"I found the guns, okay? Not your dad's guns, but some of Mitch's. And I . . . took one to school."

"Holy shit, Cole. Why'd you do that?"

"Guys giving me a hard time. About Mitch being in prison."

"So?"

"About him getting . . . you know . . . there. And how it's just the two of us pussies in this big house and does he do me here, too? They tried to do it to me. They grabbed me and yanked my pants." The words came bursting out and Cole felt his face flush with shame. "So I took a gun to school. But some punk stole it right out of my hand."

"Holy hell." Matthew looked around the garage, thinking. "Where can you hide?"

There was only one place and the thought of it made Cole's skin go clammy. "In the bomb shelter." He swung the fake shelf back as he hadn't done since the day he'd discovered his mother's body. He hadn't been down there since. *I hate this house.*

Thank God. Mitch hadn't padlocked this door, like the one in the basement. *I just hope the combination hasn't changed.*

Matthew's mouth fell open. "What the hell? I never knew about this."

"Because you didn't have to live here with Aunt Betty. You got to live with your father." Cole glared at Matthew. "You weren't here when Mom . . ." He couldn't make himself say the words. "When she ended it. I was. I found her. Down there, in the shelter. So, that you didn't know about it is a fucking huge shame."

Matt was staring at him, all confused. "What? No. That's not what happened."

Cole balled up his fist, so tempted to knock Matt's head off his shoulders. "It is so. I found her. Mitch said you were in Europe."

"I was. It was my senior year in high school. I was an exchange student that year. When I came home, she was gone. Dad said she killed herself in the garden."

"That would have been a lot less trouble for Mitch to clean up," Cole said bitterly. He could hear the muted echo of the doorbell. *The cops are on my doorstep.* "I don't have time for this. Believe what you want to believe. Just tell the cops I'm not here."

"Cole, wait. I'm sorry. I never thought . . . I went away to college. I didn't know . . ."

"You didn't know because you didn't want to know. If you'd visited here just once. Just once. Then you would have seen. You would have known."

"Dad wouldn't let me come out here. I should have made him bring you home."

"Yeah, you really should have. You can start making it up to me by telling those sheriffs that I'm not home."

"Is there water down there?"

"I have no idea. I haven't been down there since I was five."

"Hell. Stay there until I come for you. I will come back for you. I promise."

"Thanks," Cole grunted. "Bang on the door when it's safe for me to come out. "

"How will you know it's me?"

"Do it to . . . 'The Star-Spangled Banner.' Hell, I don't know. Just don't be long. Please." He pulled the shelf back into place and twisted the vault-style lock to secure the door from the inside. He then crept down the stairs into the darkness, his heart thundering to beat all hell.

He felt sick. *Oh God, please don't let me throw up.*

"I hate this goddamned house," he whispered. Then he drew a breath, sat on the hard cement floor, and went absolutely quiet. He couldn't hear anything happening up in the house and could only pray that Matt had gotten rid of the sheriff.

He hated this house and he hated the dark. There had been lights down here before, when his mother came down here to drink herself unconscious.

Cole pulled out his cell phone and turned it on, shining the light at the walls until he saw the light switch. He flipped it on, his eyes widening as he turned to view the room. It was different. Smaller. Way neater than Aunt Betty had kept it.

Mitch must have come down here. His brother hated clutter.

The two doors along the far wall were new. One was open. Behind it was a tiny room, big enough for a cot. The other door was closed. Locked. Cole yanked on the doorknob, jiggled it, but the door did not open.

And then he heard it. A girl's voice. "Hello? Is someone there? Help me. Please."

There aren't any ghosts. No such thing as ghosts. Cole swallowed hard. "Mom?"

"What? Hell, no, I'm not your mom or anyone else's. Who are you?"

"Cole. Who are you?"

"Kim. My name is Kim. Please help me."

Nineteen

"You needed more sleep," Joseph said, studying Daphne's face in the harsh light of the hospital elevator. She looked fragile, her skin too translucent.

She lifted her brows at him. "I feel remarkably rested. I'm thinking that would be one of those 'multilayered benefits of sex' I was recently told not to dismiss."

His body surged to life, instantly remembering, instantly wanting her again. "That it would." He cupped her cheek in his palm, brushed his thumb over her mouth. "Still, when this meeting is over, we're going back to the room for sleep. For both of us."

Her eyes laughed at him. "You're going to keep your hands to yourself? Really?"

He shoved his hands in his pockets. "I'm capable."

"Hmm." She took a step closer, lifted on her toes so that her mouth was a breath away from his. "So when we get back to the room, you don't intend to pick up where we left off when the phone rang? Because that would be a real shame."

He was unable to control a shudder. She'd fallen asleep in his arms, but he hadn't been able to keep his hands off her. "That was . . . stealth reconnaissance."

That's how he'd started anyway. He'd wanted to know which areas of her breasts were sensitive and which were not. He'd read that women who'd had mastectomies were more likely to have feeling on the edges of their breasts, with the sensitivity decreasing the closer one came to the center. The next time they made love he wanted to include her breasts, but he didn't want to touch her anywhere there was no feeling. It would make her self-conscious, take her out of the moment. Rob her of pleasure.

And he wasn't going to let that happen. She deserved pleasure.

Areas of her breasts were very sensitive, he'd found. A single touch had her legs opening to him and the next thing he knew he was between them, tasting her again.

"Since it woke me up, it wasn't so stealthy, was it?" she murmured.

"Did you mind?"

"Did I look like I minded?"

That would be a no. He'd known the moment she'd awoken by the slight tensing of her thighs followed by a throaty hum of satisfaction and the tilting of her hips as she tried to get closer. He'd glanced up—and nearly come right then and there. She'd pushed herself to her elbows and was watching him tonguing her, her eyes hooded and hot. She'd said nothing and neither had he, the two of them suspended in a darkly erotic moment that seemed to stretch on and on until she came on a low, quiet moan, throat arched, her head lolling back like a flower too heavy for its stem.

He swallowed hard, aware that the elevator would open any moment. "You watching me was the sexiest thing I've ever seen."

She kissed his chin, then licked it. "Does this mean we take up where we left off? Or are you really going to make me sleep?"

"I think you win."

She grinned at him. "Thank you."

The doors opened and her grin disappeared as she managed one of those quicksilver changes he'd come to appreciate. She was professional, cool. Collected. This was Prosecutor Daphne, ready to work.

"Where did Agent Novak say we should go?"

Deacon had called Joseph's cell phone as he'd been slowly building Daphne to a second orgasm. Leaving the warmth of her body had nearly killed him, turning his brain back on nearly impossible.

He hoped she still wanted him to take up where they'd left off after his next statement. "Room 602 is where *I'm* going. I need you to go to Ford's room." Which was 636, at the other end of the hall.

Her chin lifted. "Why?"

He held up a hand to stave off her argument. "It's not about you not having a right to be there or about you not being able to handle it. Because you do and you can."

"Then what is it about?"

"Unfettered communication. The locals aren't going to feel comfortable being candid if you're in the room because you're his mother. Think about poor Quartermaine last night. He felt terrible about making you upset. Do you think he'll be straightforward again? We need answers and we need them fast. I don't have time for the investigators to tiptoe around the facts."

She frowned for a moment, then nodded reluctantly. "Okay. You're right. We've still got Kimberly and Pamela out there. You'll tell me everything later?"

"Everything. You have my word."

"Then I'll be down the hall with Ford. Hopefully I can get him to wake up so we can get out of this town." She glanced down, then back up at him, her brows lifted. "You might want to make a stop in the men's room before you join the other boys."

Because he had a tent in his pants again. He folded his coat over his arm and held it in front of him. "You're enjoying this."

"I am indeed. I hope to enjoy it more later."

He laughed. "Go. Call if you need me."

Baltimore, Maryland
Wednesday, December 4, 8:00 p.m.

Clay shook his head at the list of stolen merchandise. "Doug and Kim were busy."

"Guns, cash, and jewelry," Alec agreed. "But at least now we can give the info to the cops and not get put in jail ourselves."

Getting the list of items stolen by Doug and Kim as they posed as HVAC techs had taken Alec less than an hour by hacking into the insurance companies' databases. It took him and Clay hours more to find the same information legally, now that they knew where to look. But it was solid and Alec was in no danger of repercussions.

"Not going to jail is always good." Clay checked his cell phone. No new messages or texts. "I called Carter an hour ago, but I haven't heard back. If he doesn't call me by ten, I'll send the list to J.D. and Grayson and let them run with it. Now I've got to go. They're having Tuzak's wake at his house tonight."

"They don't have the body, like, *there*, do they? In the house?" Alec asked.

"No. This is for Tuzak's friends and family. We'll just tell stories and remember him the way that he was." He stood up and tightened the knot of his tie. "I wanted to talk to Alyssa before I left, but she's not back from talking to Kimberly MacGregor's roommate at the dorm and I can't wait any longer. Tell her to call me when she gets here, okay?"

He was in his car when Alyssa pulled up beside him in hers, her driver's-side window next to his. "I'm sorry, Clay. I hit traffic."

"It's okay. Did you find anything?"

Alyssa lifted her brows. "Doug likes it rough. Really, really rough."

Clay grimaced. "Could you not say those words again?"

"Hey, you asked me to find out why Kim's roommate didn't like Doug. The first few times they went out, Kim came back to the dorm bruised and barely able to walk."

"That is rough."

Alyssa nodded. "The roommate said Kim told her that Doug really liked to be in charge. And he liked to hurt her. Roomie told Kim to run away, fast. Kim just laughed and said they were both getting something out of it."

"Sexually or revenge?" Clay asked.

"Good question. Roomie said that Kim liked to 'punish herself.' Usually denial of food or an activity. But sometimes she hooked up with angry boys. That's why her roommate was surprised when she took up with Ford. He was too nice for her. Too respectful. She said that in the last few weeks Kim had blossomed, that after one of their dates last week Kim said she'd never had any guy be as good to her as Ford was. And that seemed to make her sad."

"Because she was planning on betraying him," Clay said acidly.

Alyssa grimaced. "I hate to say this, but I hope Ford practiced safe sex. That Kim is a skank. He's going to be devastated when he finds out, but I'd rather have him be alive and devastated than dead with his pride intact."

"Well said. I have to go. Call me from your home phone when you get in."

"Home phone, yeah, yeah, yeah," Alyssa grumbled. "I will. See you tomorrow."

Wheeling, West Virginia
Wednesday, December 4, 8:10 p.m.

Room 602 was an empty patient room that the charge nurse was allowing Joseph, Deacon, and the locals to use as a meeting room. Joseph wasn't sure why the others had come back here rather than going straight to the precinct with whatever they'd found. He guessed he was about to find out.

Deacon was sitting on the bed, computer on his lap, legs stretched out, his feet bare. His wet socks were draped over the bed rail to dry. He was typing at fever speed, frowning at the screen.

Wheeling PD Detective McManus stood at the window, reviewing a stack of papers, and Agent Kerr from the Pittsburgh field office was gone.

Joseph knocked on the doorframe. "You rang?"

Deacon looked up, his eyes more intense than usual. "We found something. Come in and shut the door."

"Where is Agent Kerr?"

"Setting up a search," Deacon said, "after he took what we found to the lab."

McManus handed Joseph an envelope that had been sealed, but no longer was. "I stopped by the precinct on my way back here. Junie Bramble found the report you asked about in the archives."

"We read it already," Deacon said. "Where do we start?"

"What did you find, Deacon?" Joseph asked calmly and Deacon drew a breath.

"The kid's backpack, or at least the one he was carrying. McManus had figured all the roads that would lead to that WMA."

Joseph wished he'd stopped for a cup of coffee. "WMA?"

"Wildlife management area," Deacon said. "We got two teams of dogs to search, using the coat Ford was wearing when he was found."

"Which wasn't his coat," McManus said. "It was a size too small and smelled like skunk. The scent led us to the backpack. It was off the road in a snowdrift."

"It held some beef jerky, three knives, a dead flashlight, and this." Deacon swung his legs over the edge of the bed and angled his laptop so that Joseph could see.

It was a photo of a purse, the kind with a wrist strap. The hairs on Joseph's neck lifted. "And inside the purse?"

"ID." Deacon clicked to the next photo.

It was a girl, seventeen years old, dark brown hair. Her address was Wheeling, West Virginia. "Heather Lipton. Ford said 'Heather' when he first woke up."

"When did he wake up?" McManus asked.

Joseph told them about the second dose of ketamine and the violence with which Ford had woken thirty minutes after being brought into the ER. "The doctor said he screamed Kim's name and Heather's. I assumed they'd heard him wrong and that he was saying 'MacGregor.'"

"Heather Lipton disappeared last summer," McManus said. "She'd been on her way to a concert with her friends. Their car broke down and Heather decided the concert was too big to miss. She set off hitchhiking, even though the other girls begged her not to. She never showed up at the concert. We had search crews out every day for a month. Cops, Feds, community volunteers. It was like she vanished into thin air. This is the first lead we've had."

Dread building in his gut, Joseph slid the contents of the envelope onto the bed. There were copies of newspaper articles and a series of police reports, typed on an old-fashioned typewriter. Grace Kelly Montgomery had been abducted in November of her senior year of high school. She was seventeen. Also missing was Daphne Sinclair, age eight. The report included photos, taken on school picture day. Daphne had blond pigtails and an engaging grin. Kelly's photo was her senior portrait.

"Seventeen," he murmured. *Like Heather Lipton.* What the hell was this about?

He leafed through the pages that documented the search for and subsequent discovery of little Daphne hiding in a bathroom stall at a rest stop off the interstate near Dayton, Ohio. She'd been dirty and half frozen. And unable to tell them where she'd been or how she'd escaped. Or even if her cousin still lived. "'A week later Kelly's body was found,'" he read quietly, "'in a state park north of Dayton, Ohio.'"

"I remember this now that I've read the report," McManus said. "I was only five and my mother and all the neighbors were scared to let us walk to and from school alone."

"What the hell is all this about? Where's the connection to Doug?" Joseph whispered, staring at the grainy copies of the old photos.

"We need to talk to Ms. Montgomery," McManus said. "And we need that kid to wake up and tell us where the hell he found that purse."

"You said Agent Kerr was setting up a search," Joseph said. "Over what area, and what kind of support?"

"Canine units and foot teams for now. We've got a helicopter coming from Charleston. We're starting from where we found the backpack."

Joseph rubbed his mouth with the back of his hand, thinking. And as he breathed, he could smell Daphne's scent on his hands. "Let's go talk to Miss—"

A shrill scream cut him off, quickly followed by another scream.

"Joseph!"

Daphne.

Baltimore, Maryland
Wednesday, December 4, 8:10 p.m.

It took Cole a few minutes to find something to pry the door open. Luckily it was a regular door, not a super-secure steel model like his great-grandfather had used when he built the place. Or so Aunt Betty had told him.

All the good tools were up in the garage, but he'd found a fire axe in the storage closet. It looked very old. Cole hoped he didn't break it. He slipped the axe blade in between the door and the frame and yanked.

The door flew open like it was butter, revealing the girl who'd begged him for help. She was small and still, lying on a cot like the one he'd seen in the other room. Cole leaned over her, studying her. She was college age, Asian. He touched her forehead. She was also burning up. *I hope she doesn't have a contagious disease.*

He sat on the floor next to her, his back to the wall. "Great," he muttered. "I'm stuck in a bomb shelter with Typhoid Mary."

"Kim."

Startled, he flashed the cell phone light in her face again. "Excuse me?"

"My name is Kim," she said in a voice that sounded like sandpaper. "And I don't have typhoid. Your brother stabbed me and my leg is on fire."

"Which brother? I have two."

"Doug."

"I don't have a brother named Doug."

"You're Cole, right? The one who gets suspended all the time?"

He scowled. "Yes."

"Then you have a brother named Doug."

Wheeling, West Virginia
Wednesday, December 4, 8:28 p.m.

Daphne's scream still ringing in his ears, Joseph threw open the door and ran the length of the hall to Ford's room, where there was chaos.

The uniformed officer who'd been on guard duty was on the floor, bleeding profusely, a knife embedded in his gut. A nurse knelt beside him, already administering first aid.

Daphne stood beside Ford's bed, shielding him with her body. Her eyes were wide and filled with abject fear as she pointed to the door. "Scrubs. He's wearing scrubs. Old man, gray hair. Six feet, maybe. Hector followed him."

Joseph took off again, looking over his shoulder. Deacon was behind him, laptop under his arm, shoving his feet into his shoes as he ran. "Deacon, pull up hospital security video. Get a description, put out a BOLO." He drew his weapon and pointed to McManus. "Let's go."

He entered the nearest stairwell, taking the steps three at a time. He heard a door slam below and ran faster, blowing through the exterior door in time to see a white truck peeling out of the parking lot. Hector had started to chase the truck on foot but had given up and was running back.

By the time Joseph got to his car, the truck would have been on the interstate already. McManus ran past him, carried by the momentum of running down the stairs.

"I got his license plate." Hector called and, breathing hard, recited it to McManus.

"Call it in," Joseph said. "White truck, taillights looked like a Suburban."

McManus nodded. "Dispatch, this is Detective McManus."

Joseph turned in a slow circle, searching the parking lot as McManus put out the BOLO, eyes narrowing at the sight of a car with its trunk partially open. He ran over to find the car's tire flat and blood spattered on the hubcap. A cell phone lay on the ground about ten feet away. Another slow turn had his racing heart sinking.

Against the building was a Dumpster. From behind it extended a bare arm. Again he ran. The arm was attached to a man, stripped down to his briefs. Blood had pooled beneath his head and torso, the latter the result of a stab wound that had split his abdomen wide-open.

Joseph knelt, pressing his fingers to the man's throat. "He's still alive, barely. Hector, run upstairs and get a doctor. They'll need something to stop the bleeding."

McManus ran up, phone in hand. "I called Dispatch and they're calling the ER. They should have someone here in a minute." Then McManus sighed. "That's Billy Pratchett, a guy I went to school with. He's a nurse here." He nodded to Joseph. "I'll wait with him. You go check on Ms. Montgomery."

"Thanks." Joseph made his way back up the stairs, more slowly than he'd come down. *What the hell is going on here?* He walked back to Ford's room, where things seemed more under control. The uniformed officer must have been taken to another room, because he wasn't there anymore.

Ford was awake and sitting up, peering at his mother through bloodshot eyes.

Daphne sat in a chair, her back to him. Her wig gone. *Curls.* Her head was covered in tight blond curls. But she wasn't looking at him now. She was staring at her hands. Joseph imagined that this wasn't the way she'd envisioned laying herself bare. So to speak.

Why would she want to cover up curls like that? His hands itched to touch her, but he stayed where he was, in the doorway. Later he could touch all he wanted.

"Are you all right?" she asked quietly. "Did you find him?"

"No, but we did find a nurse named Pratchett. It looks like he was attacked for his clothing and ID badge. Detective McManus is with him now. We got a BOLO out on the man and his vehicle. Now, please tell me what happened here. Where is the uniformed officer who was here before?"

"He was taken to surgery," Daphne said. "I wondered how the intruder got in. I guess now I know."

She still hadn't looked at him. "Daphne, what happened?" He touched her shoulder. "Talk to me."

"Hector got here right after I did and we went to get a cup of coffee," she said. "I thought Ford would be all right with an armed guard. When we came back, the officer was standing guard and the door was closed. He said a nurse had come in to give Ford a new IV. But a nurse had just finished doing that. I pushed at the door, but the old man had put a chair across it. I could see him through the window." Her voice shook and big tears plopped onto the hands she'd twisted in her lap. "He had a pillow over Ford's face."

"I'm okay now, Mom," Ford said thickly. "Please don't cry anymore."

"How'd you get in the room?" Joseph asked her.

"The officer broke the window with a fire extinguisher and reached through to move the chair. We pushed the door open and rushed in. The man grabbed me and held a knife to my throat. Tried to drag me out with him. I fought him and he grabbed my hair." She smoothed a hand over her curls self-consciously. "When it came off in his hand . . ." Her chuckle was watery. "It surprised him. He yelled and threw it. That's how I got away. If my hair hadn't . . . you know, come off, then he would have gotten me across the throat. Bye-bye me."

Joseph's blood chilled. When he'd entered the room, he'd been so focused on the chaos that he hadn't noticed that the wig was gone. He hadn't realized how close he'd come to losing her yet again. "Then what happened?" he asked hoarsely.

"He was fast for an old guy. He threw me down, stabbed the officer and threw him into Hector. He ran like hell and Hector chased him. I screamed for you."

"Did you know him, Daphne?"

Her eyes flickered uncertainly. "I didn't see his face. He was either bent over putting the pillow on Ford's face or he had my back pulled against his chest. But it wasn't Doug. He was too tall and too old."

"That's okay," Joseph soothed. "Hector got a good look at him and Novak's looking at security videos. Between them we can get an ID."

"I'm back," Deacon said from behind him. "We got his face. I made a still and faxed it to the local PD and to the Pittsburgh field office. They're putting up roadblocks. They said McManus called in a white pickup."

Crouching next to Daphne, Joseph looked over at Ford. The boy was still out of it, but some clarity had returned. "It was a white Chevy pickup, son."

Ford's mouth fell open. "He . . ." He closed his eyes, then opened them, his effort to focus admirable. "Can I see his photo, please?"

Deacon crossed the room. "I'm Special Agent Novak, FBI. It's good to meet you, Ford." He showed the photo to Ford and the boy flinched.

"Yeah, that's one of them."

"There was more than one?" Joseph asked, sharing a glance with Deacon.

"Yes. There were two. One was this old man. He had the cabin and the truck was his. Heather. Last name, last name." He closed his eyes, murmuring to himself. "Ice tea." His eyes opened. "Lipton. Heather Lipton. I found her purse under the seat of his truck. I didn't see her in his cabin, but I got free and pretty much got out of there. I took all of his knives and all his clothes and put them in the truck. Stripped him naked and took his shoes. Tied him and left him in the cabin. Figured that even if he got loose from the twine I used, he wouldn't get far buck naked in the snow."

"Smart," Joseph murmured.

Daphne sat like a statue, her eyes on the paper in Ford's hands. She could see the face, upside down. *She knows him,* Joseph thought, his heart beginning to race.

"I drove about thirty miles, I think," Ford said, "then the piece of shit ran out of gas."

"So you walked?" Deacon asked.

"For miles. Oh, wait." Again he closed his eyes. Then

rattled off a license plate number, the same one Hector had noted earlier. *Kid's got an amazing memory.* "That's the white truck. I think I remember it right."

"You remembered it perfectly," Joseph said. "We spotted it driving away."

"Good. I rolled his fingerprints across the blade of one of his knives before I left the cabin. I didn't want to drag him with me, but I thought you could run his prints."

"Very smart and incredibly practical," Joseph said, impressed. *No wonder my dad thinks this kid's a genius.* "I don't know that I would have thought of that."

Ford leaned forward, touched his mother's knee. "Mom? I'm okay."

She nodded. "I know, honey. It's just . . . I'm emotional."

"Do you remember which way you walked?" Joseph asked.

"For a long time I stayed on a road, but then the road ended and there was nothing but woods. At one point there was a fishing area with picnic tables. I sat there for a while. Looked like it was only accessible by boat. It was really snowing hard by then. I couldn't see a thing. I followed the waterline inch by inch and finally I found a road and stayed on it until . . ." He frowned. "There was a van. It stopped and I thought I was okay. But . . ." He lifted the hospital johnny to look at his thigh. "Sonofabitch tased me. Again. And shot me up. Again. That's all I remember until I woke up here."

"What about the other guy?" Joseph asked.

Ford's expression changed, becoming grave. "That was him, the one who tased me last night. The old guy said it was the other one's idea, that they were asking for a ransom. Five million dollars."

"No one ever called in a ransom demand, Ford," Joseph said.

"There was something else going on. Strange stuff. There was a shed. When I first woke up, I was in this shed that had been a garage. Detached. Which was weird because when I finally got to the cabin, I think it was smaller than the garage. I woke up the first time and the guy who tased me was there, whispering in my ear, then shooting me up. What was it? It wasn't heroin or meth, was it? Please say it wasn't."

"Ketamine, which is used as a sedative," Joseph said.

"Addictive but not at the levels you've received. Also fentanyl, which is a narcotic. Again, not addictive at the levels you received. Don't worry. What else do you remember?"

"When I woke up the next morning there was this smell. Something dead. I got the blindfold off and it was . . . cats. One was decomposing and the others were just bones." He paused, remembering. "Another weird thing, the decomposing cat had been dug up. It was wearing an old collar, but a brand-new tag. The tag had a cat's name."

Daphne had begun to tremble. "Fluffy?" she whispered.

Ford's frown was immediate and sharp. "Yes. How did you know that, Mom?"

Abruptly Daphne reached for the photo in Ford's hand. "Let me look."

Joseph held his breath because she was holding hers. She gripped the paper and spread it across her thigh to keep it from shaking. Then jerked her chin down to look.

"Oh God," she whispered. She'd started to hyperventilate. "Can't be can't be can't be." The words ran together, like a prayer. "What did he say, Ford? Exactly?"

Ford cleared his throat. "I'm back. Did you—"

The little color left in her face drained away. "Miss me?" she finished.

"Yes," Ford said, alarmed. "Mom? What's happening here?"

Joseph gently turned her so that she looked at him. "The old man, the man in this picture. It was him, wasn't it? The one that took you and your cousin."

She nodded, tears welling in her eyes. "Why is he doing this?"

"I don't know, but we will find out. I promise you. But you know what I need from you. The whole story. Because somewhere in there is a connection to a guy named Doug who wants your life to be a living hell."

"There are still two girls out there," she whispered.

"Maybe three," Joseph said. He pointed to the picture of the old man. "Ford found evidence that this man's taken another seventeen-year-old girl."

"Another?" It wasn't even a whisper. More an exhale. She fixed her gaze on Joseph's and the temperature around him seemed to plummet. There was knowledge in her eyes, terrible knowledge. And terrible guilt. "I'll tell you everything. But you should update the BOLO."

"With what?" Joseph asked, almost afraid of the answer.

"Now you can add his name. He's Wilson Beckett."

Joseph couldn't control his reaction. Utter shock. And then anger as the implication set in. "You knew his name?"

She flinched slightly but didn't break eye contact. "Yes. I've always known."

Twenty

"Thank you." Daphne took the cup of coffee Hector offered, her hands shaking with a combination of cold and shock.

Ford had insisted that he be allowed to listen. He'd earned the truth, he'd said.

Daphne didn't think he could handle the truth. *I'm not handling the truth.*

Joseph agreed with Ford and now arranged a few additional chairs in her son's hospital room. A minute later Daphne was facing what felt like a tribunal. Joseph, Hector, Agent Novak, and Detective McManus. Pittsburgh's Agent Kerr had returned from setting up the search for the missing girl, Heather Lipton, and squeezed into Ford's room with them. And then it was time.

Joseph hadn't looked at her after that first stunned, furious reaction. The others wore expressions of horrified disgust. All but Ford. He looked heartbroken. Betrayed, even. And he didn't even know about Kimberly yet.

You knew and you never told? No one had voiced the question aloud, but she heard it just the same. It was written all over their faces.

Daphne pressed her fingertips to her temples. Her head hurt. Her heart hurt because Joseph still wouldn't meet her eyes.

And Beckett had another girl. *Another girl.* The words were like knives.

It's been twenty-seven years since he took Kelly and me. How many had he taken in between? There was so much blood on her hands. *Dear God.* There could be no coming back from this. No forgiveness. *What have I done?*

She drew a breath that hurt, her chest was so tight. *Get it over with. And then you'll have to accept the consequences.*

"I thought he was dead," she said flatly. "I searched for him and received a death certificate from the county court-house. I just want you to know that before I begin." She looked at each of the men in turn. "So you don't think that I'm a total monster."

Joseph looked at her then, the rage in his eyes now mixed with surprise. And regret. *But regret for what? Being angry? Being with me?* She wished she could ask him, but there were too many people here. And this wasn't about her anyway.

It was about Beckett's victims, however many there had been.

"I never thought that," Joseph murmured and she so wanted to believe him. "Not once."

"Neither did I," Hector said.

With an effort, Ford sat up enough to take her hand. "I've known you a long time, Mom. You're not a monster."

The others remained silent, watching. Withholding judgment. *It'll have to do.*

"Thank you, Ford." Her voice wobbled and she had to clear her throat. "Okay." She let out a harsh breath. "I have to tell you about my family. So you'll understand. My father was a musician but he worked in the coal mine to put food on the table, just like everyone did around here. We got by and we were pretty happy. Mama was one of five, and her family lived all around us. All except Vivien, Mama's oldest sister, who had a sales job that kept her on the road all the time. Vivien was Kelly's mother. I don't know if anyone knew who Kelly's father was.

"I remember Vivien having a lot of boyfriends. My parents would whisper about it, how it wasn't healthy for Kelly, having all those men around. When Vivien was on the road, Kelly stayed with us. It got to where Vivien was only home on weekends so Kelly had practically moved in. Then

Vivien surprised everyone by getting married to a guy she'd
met on the road. A preacher, of all things. The family was so
happy that she'd finally settled down and got her heart
right.

"She had a church wedding, but I got a cold and couldn't
go. I heard all about it later, because it did not turn out the
way Vivien planned. Kelly showed up in a short skirt, got
tipsy, and flirted outrageously with all the men there. At
seventeen years old that would have been bad enough, but
then she actually disappeared for a while with the groom's
brother and they were caught having sex in the baptismal
pool. Vivien was so angry that Kelly had spoiled the wedding. Kelly was out of control, her behavior 'not appropriate for a minister's daughter.'"

"Sounds like she just wanted her mother's attention,"
Joseph said.

"I'm sure she did, but it didn't work. After the wedding,
Kelly lived with us even on weekends. Vivien wanted no
part of her 'drinkin', whorin' ways.' I mean, hello, pot meet
kettle, but Vivien didn't see it that way. And neither did I.
But I was only eight years old.

"It was Kelly's job to walk me home from school and
that day I couldn't wait to get home. My cat had just had
kittens and I wanted to play with them. But Kelly dawdled
and I kept telling her to hurry. A car passed us, turned
around, and came back. The man asked if we wanted a ride.
I said no, I didn't ride with strangers. But Kelly told me it
was okay, that she knew him, that she'd met him at her
mother's wedding. The two of them laughed, like it was a
joke. It was Beckett, of course, but I didn't know him."

"She'd arranged to meet him that afternoon?" Hector
asked, very softly, as if Daphne was breakable. Daphne figured she probably looked that way.

"She might have arranged it. I never knew for sure. I
knew about the groomsman she'd disappeared with at the
wedding. I thought this was him. I didn't know that much
about sex, but I knew enough to know that it wasn't right for
Kelly to have done what she did at the wedding when she
was only seventeen, and in the baptismal pool at that. I also
knew never to get in anyone's car that I didn't know. I pulled
Kelly's hand, told her I wanted to go home, to my cat."

"Fluffy?" Ford asked in a strained voice.

"Yes." She patted her son's hand. "This isn't going to be pleasant. Nobody will blame you if you leave. I'll be honest and tell you that I don't want you to hear this."

Her son met her eyes. "I haven't left you before. I'm not starting now."

Her throat closed. "Okay. So . . . Kelly got annoyed. She wanted a ride home and I was making her walk. Her job was to walk with me and maybe she'd figured I'd tell on her to my parents. So she told me that if I didn't want a ride that I could just walk alone and she got into the car with him. I didn't know what to do, so I just started walking home. A few minutes later, the car stopped again and the man got out. He wasn't so friendly looking anymore." She swallowed hard. "I was eight years old. I tried to run, but he caught me. Pressed a hankie over my face . . ."

She closed her eyes. "I woke up in a garage and it was cold. I was tied up and gagged. There was a trapdoor that went underground. The trapdoor was open and I could hear Kelly crying, screaming from down below me. She screamed for help, mostly. Then it was just screams. I don't know how much time passed. Beckett would go down the stairs to the room with food. Every time I'd hear him say, 'I'm back. Did you miss me?' And then she'd scream some more. But nobody came to help. Nobody came but Beckett.

"He took my gag off so I could eat, but stood there, watching me with a knife in his hand. Told me if I made a sound he'd kill me. I believed him. When I'd eaten, he'd gag me again and go back into the basement room and Kelly would scream some more. I wondered why he kept me gagged and not her, then I realized he liked the screaming. But other than to take off the gag, he never touched me." She looked at Ford, but his eyes were closed. "Do you understand me, Ford? He left me alone."

Ford nodded unsteadily. Said nothing.

"For maybe a week, Beckett would go down the stairs saying, 'I'm back. Did you miss me?'" She closed her eyes. "Always with the trapdoor open. Eventually she stopped screaming. She must have gone into shock. But I could still hear her screaming inside my head. I still can."

"God." It was a horrified whisper from Agent Novak.

"I think it was at the beginning of the second week that he took me to the cabin. I thought he was going to do to me what he did to Kelly, but he didn't." She shook her head, laughing incredulously. "He made me clean his cabin. Told me if I tried to run, I couldn't get far. The next town was forty miles away and there were no neighbors. If I tried, he'd kill my mother. He laughed and said he knew where she lived.

"He felt confident enough that I wouldn't escape to go out to the garage and leave me in the house. He locked me in and locked up his knives. One day he was in the garage and the phone rang. I wanted to answer it, but was scared it was a trap, that it was him and he'd kill my mother. He had an answering machine, and the volume was turned up. It was the gas company telling him they were coming to fill his tank that afternoon. He had one of those old steel tanks outside the house."

"He still does," Ford said dully.

"I wish you didn't know that," she said, looking at her hands. But then she took a deep breath and went on. "It was the first time anyone had come to where we were, the first contact with anyone outside since he'd taken us. I knew that would be my only chance to get away. I didn't have a weapon, but Beckett kept hornet spray under the sink with the cleaning supplies. I waited until he'd opened the door." She cocked her jaw, still feeling the grim satisfaction of the moment all these years later. "He said, 'I'm back. Did you miss me?' and I sprayed the hornet spray in his eyes and ran as fast as I could. He was coming, thundering after me." Her heart still raced at the memory. "I knew there was nowhere to run, so I climbed a tree to hide. I was a tomboy in those days, thankfully. He was still crashing around, screaming, tears streaming down his cheeks. He couldn't see me because his eyes were burning."

"Good for you," Hector said fiercely and made her smile a little.

"I got to the top of the tree and looked around and he was telling the truth." Her tiny smile faded. "There was nothing for miles. Just trees and mountain."

"Still is," Ford muttered and she patted his knee.

"I stayed in that tree for hours. He went back to the house and came out with a gun—and Kelly. He was dragging her, the gun up against her head, yelling for me, calling my name, saying that he'd kill her if I didn't come out. I almost did. But I was too scared to move. And I figured he'd kill us anyway. He passed right under me as he dragged her through the woods, looking for me. I was sure he could hear my heartbeat. And then Kelly yelled, 'Run!' He hit her in the head with the gun but she yelled again, this time that she was sorry. That he'd told her I was dead. He hit her again and she went really still. He dragged her back to the garage." She sighed. "And that was the last time I saw her."

"That's why he kept you gagged," Joseph said quietly. "He didn't want her to know you were there."

"I figured that out, much later. After a while he got in his car and drove away. I guess he figured I'd made it down to the road. While he was gone, the gas truck came and I got down from the tree. It was a guy with a pickup truck and he hauled the tank with a hitch. I'd almost run up to him for help when Beckett came back and asked if he'd seen a girl running around. Said his sister had left her brat with him and that I'd run off again. The gas man said if he saw me, he'd bring me back. So I said nothing, just waited until Beckett went back into the garage and the gas man took the hose around the back to fill the tank. Then I climbed into the bed of the man's truck and hid under a tarp. I didn't breathe until the truck started and we'd been driving for a while."

"The police report said you were found in Dayton, Ohio," Novak said. "How did you get there?"

"The gas man stopped at a convenience store. I got out and hid in the next truck over. It had a camper top, so I opened the hatch and crawled in. I figured I'd wait till the gas man drove away and then I'd find help. But the driver of the camper came out at the same time. I was too scared to come out and then the camper was moving. Didn't stop for a long time. I fell asleep. Next I knew, we were at a rest stop and it was night and I was so cold. I climbed out when the driver went to the men's room and I went into the la- dies' room where it was warm."

"Why didn't you ask the driver for help?" Hector asked kindly.

"I don't know. I think I was so scared at that point . . . I didn't want to go with a man and I didn't know how far I'd gone. I was afraid they'd take me back to Beckett. A few weeks in isolation can mess with your mind."

"Not to mention the trauma," Agent Kerr murmured. "Who found you?"

"A nice lady. I don't even know her name. She called the police, who told me I was in Dayton. They asked me what had happened, but by then all I could hear was Beckett's voice in my head, telling me he was going to kill my mom. I was too scared to talk. They didn't have AMBER Alerts then, so it took a while for them to figure out who I was. Once they did, the police took me home."

She pressed her hand to her stomach. This was one of the worst parts to recall. "My parents were waiting for me in the living room with Aunt Vivien when the sheriff brought me home. And in the kitchen doorway was Beckett."

Baltimore, Maryland
Wednesday, December 4, 9:30 p.m.

"I don't believe you," Cole whispered, but Kim didn't answer. After telling him all kinds of lies, she'd gone unconscious, or maybe was pretending to be.

He didn't believe a word she'd said. Couldn't.

But deep down he knew some of what she'd told him had to be true. He prayed all of it wasn't. Although he knew it probably was. She said Mitch had killed people. Enjoyed killing people. And was apparently pretty damn good at it.

She'd told him she'd met "Doug" in September, fifteen months ago. That's when he and Mitch had just moved back here from Florida. Mitch had been one mean SOB to live with. He was on the run again, although he pretended it was just another job change.

But a week after they'd moved back into this house, something happened to Mitch. Cole had come home from school to find his brother sitting at the kitchen table, pale. He'd been reading an old book which he'd whisked out of sight when Cole came in the room for an after-school snack.

The book and Mitch disappeared to the garage. *Probably he came down here,* Cole thought. Mitch came down to the bomb shelter to remember their mother.

Cole didn't need to come down here. The memory of this place was branded into his brain. *I hate this house.*

The day after Cole had found him reading the old book, Mitch was a changed man. Calm. Happy. He'd even whistled. He'd gotten his HVAC license, bought some equipment, and started a business. Gone straight. Or so Cole had wanted to believe.

But he'd peeked at Mitch's "license." It was not in his own name or any combination of his names. His brother couldn't get a license with his felony record, so he'd bought a fake ID. If Mitch got caught, he could go to jail for that, too.

I'm so tired of being afraid. Of cops, of school, of the kids. Of my own family.

"I wish I was adopted," he muttered.

"Not always an improvement," Kim croaked. "Do we have water down here?"

"Yeah." He brought her a bottle and held it to her dry, cracked lips as she chugged it down. "Easy." He pulled the bottle away and capped it. "You'll make yourself sick."

"Thanks. I was so thirsty. Can you untie me?"

He hesitated. Then shook his head. "No." *Not until I can figure out what's true.*

She sagged back to the cot. "Have you at least been thinking about what I said?"

Yes, and I still don't want to believe you. Don't want to believe my brother could do those things. That he could kill in cold blood.

"Why did you say adoption wasn't always an improvement?" he asked instead. "Are you adopted?"

"Yeah. Me and my little sister."

"The one my brother kidnapped."

"Yeah. Her name is Pamela. We're not really sisters but we were both born in China. I'm telling you, kid, your brother is not who you think he is."

His brother who went by Doug. Aunt Betty's last name was Douglas. Cole knew that everything she'd said was probably true. *Damn you, Mitch.*

Cole sighed. "He's exactly who I think he is. I'm just not sure who you are."

"We're wasting time. We need to get out of here before your brother comes back."

"Sorry, no can do. We're down here until Matt tells me to come back up. Mitch won't be back till tomorrow. He had a job in an office building. They do a lot of the HVAC at night."

"You still think he works an HVAC job?" She coughed

and Cole held the water bottle to her lips again. "Thanks. He worked with me, kid. We steal stuff."

"Like what?"

"Guns mostly." She went on to describe every one of the guns in detail. They were the same ones Mitch had hidden in the basement storeroom. "We steal from cops."

Which actually made sense. Mitch hated cops. *I guess most ex-cons do.*

"The HVAC job is a cover," she said when he didn't say anything. "He's got some plot to take down a state's attorney. Montgomery." She spat the name.

"That doesn't make sense. He doesn't even know any state's attorneys."

Kim laughed, which made her start coughing again. "He knows *her*. He hates her. I hate her, too. That's how he reeled me in."

"Why does he hate her?"

"You'll need to ask him that question. He never told me."

Cole wasn't sure he believed her. "Then why do *you* hate her?"

"Montgomery stabbed me in the back. Best deal she'd give came with a conviction. Now I've got a record and I can't get a job. Bitch."

O-kayyy. "You said my brother killed people. How many?"

"That I know of? One. Directly."

Cole swallowed. "Who?"

"A cop who was guarding the guy I was with two nights ago."

"I thought you and Mitch . . ."

"*Doug* and I . . . Well, we *were* a couple. But never again. I was with the other guy—his name is Ford—only because Doug wanted him. At first. I was supposed to bring Ford to meet Doug, so they could talk. They were just supposed to talk. But . . . I didn't want to do it."

"Why not?"

"Because . . . Ford's a nice guy. I started to feel sorry for him, not to want Doug to talk to him at all. That's when your brother kidnapped my sister. She's just a kid, about your age. I don't know where she is."

"Did you set the nice guy up?"

"Yeah. Because your brother had Pam. I brought Ford to that alley where Doug was just supposed to talk. Instead

Doug goes all Rambo with a Taser in each hand and kills Ford's bodyguard. Why does he call himself Doug if his name is Mitch?"

"Our aunt's last name was Douglas. This was her house."

Oh God. Cole felt like he'd been kicked in the gut. "Mitch killed a bodyguard? In an alley? A big black guy?"

"Yeah."

"Oh my God. That was on the news. That guy was a cop."

"That's what Doug said. Look, Cole, you seem like a decent kid. I need to get out of here. He's got my sister. She could be dead."

Cole thought of the new padlock on the door in the basement. It hadn't been there three days ago. "When did he take her?"

"Monday night. You know where she is, don't you? *Don't you?*"

"Maybe." He looked up to the door that led to the garage. Matthew would tell him when it was safe to leave. He didn't want her sister to die, but he didn't want to go to jail for taking a gun to school, either. "We'll wait a little longer."

"Why?" She struggled to sit up. *"Why?"*

"Because I said so. Shut up," he snapped when she started to yell. "If you want, I can tape your mouth. But we don't leave until the coast is clear."

"I'm going to kill you," she muttered. "If my sister dies, you're dead."

"Good to know," he said grimly.

Wheeling, West Virginia
Wednesday, December 4, 9:45 p.m.

There was a collective gasp and looks of shock from everyone but the local detective, McManus, who looked grim. He'd known the story, Daphne realized, but had let her tell it her own way. Whether out of pity or suspicion, she wasn't sure.

"Beckett was in your *house*?" Novak demanded.

"In my house. I couldn't believe that he was there. *In my house.* I didn't understand at all how he could be. I remember cowering behind the sheriff's legs and him lifting me up, to give me to my father. Then Beckett drew his finger across his throat. I started to scream and my parents didn't know what to do. Vivien was screaming, too. 'Where is *my* daughter?' Then Beckett went to her, put his arms around her, soothed her, called her 'sweetheart' and 'dear.' And that's when I figured it out."

"He was Vivien's new husband," Ford said softly. "Oh my God, Mom."

"Yeah. Then my mother told me that he was my Uncle Wilson. Beckett just smiled at me. My parents brought me here to this hospital to do an exam. That just made everything worse. They were relieved to find out I hadn't been assaulted but I couldn't say a word. I didn't speak a word for almost eight months, I was so traumatized."

"Did you ever tell them?" Agent Kerr asked.

"No. My folks brought me home from the hospital and Aunt Vivien was there, waiting for me. She screamed at me again, but I couldn't speak. My dad told me that I had to talk. We had to get Kelly back. Aunt Vivien shook me so hard my teeth rattled. The whole time Beckett stood where no one could see him and then he drew a line across his throat. My father dragged Vivien away and he and my mother had a huge fight with her. And while they were screaming, Beckett made it look like he was helping me, but he whispered in my ear, 'Did you miss me?' "

"Bastard," Ford whispered.

"The next morning there was a commotion downstairs. I crept down, peeking through the rail. My cat had been hit by a car and my parents and Vivien were arguing over whether to tell me. Beckett saw me watching, drew the line across his throat. Then he winked and I knew he'd done it. Three days later they found Kelly's body about twenty miles from the rest stop in Dayton where I'd been found. Her throat had been slit."

"And the investigation moved north," McManus said. "They assumed you'd both been held in the Ohio area. Nobody looked around here anymore."

"What happened then, Daphne?" Hector asked.

Joseph had been quiet for a while, she realized. His fists were clenched, the muscle in his taut cheek twitching. He was angry, *for* her. That helped. A lot.

"We had Kelly's funeral. Beckett delivered the sermon. I . . . threw up."

"Your parents made you go to the funeral?" Novak asked disbelievingly.

"My dad thought it might shake me out of my 'hysteria,' but it just made it worse. Then my mother compounded it by a million when she invited Vivien to stay with us."

"What?" Ford exploded. "Why?"

"Vivien was a wreck. Mama said she needed her family close. And it may have been guilt that Mama got her daughter back and Vivien didn't. But that meant Beckett moved in, too. I didn't sleep, didn't eat. I wouldn't leave my mother's side. I avoided my father because he kept trying to make me talk. He became almost desperate."

"Why?" Agent Kerr asked. "Kelly was his niece by marriage. I would have thought the family pressure would be on your mother."

"There was tremendous pressure on my mother from her family. But my father wasn't from around here. And Kelly had lived with us. Looking back, I think he was worried from the beginning that people would accuse him. I was oblivious to that then."

"Everyone kept trying to get me to talk, but I just withdrew. We went on like that for a few weeks, through the holidays. Everywhere I turned, Beckett was there. He'd whisper, 'Did you miss me?' Sometimes he'd whisper that I had to sleep sometime."

Joseph's eyes were closed, his throat working as he tried to swallow.

Beside her, Ford trembled with anger but kept his mouth closed.

"They took me to a therapist who kept trying to get me to speak. She finally told me to draw the 'bad man.' So I did."

"You drew a picture of Beckett?" Joseph asked.

"I tried to draw a picture of Vivien, Beckett, and Kelly—but I was eight years old and a very bad artist." She sighed, remembering the agony that had followed. "They thought I was drawing my own family. They thought I was accusing my father."

"Oh no."

She wasn't sure who'd said it, because she'd closed her eyes, battling back tears. "I'll never forget the look on my father's face when the police came that night. The therapist had told them about my picture and they came to question him. He stared at me, so betrayed. And I couldn't speak. I tried to scream, to tell them 'No!', that it wasn't my father. They took him in for questioning and when he came home . . . he just looked at me. He was so damn hurt.

"The news picked up on it. My mother's family ganged up on him because they'd never really trusted him. He was a musician Mama had met in California. Beckett was a minister and he went on TV calling my father all sorts of names. It was a nightmare."

"What did your father do?" Agent Kerr asked.

"He and Mama had been fighting about me all along. My father had been saying they needed to make me talk. Mama protected me, saying I'd talk when I was ready. I remember hearing them fight that night—it would be the last time I heard my father's voice. He accused Mama of believing the lie. She was crying so hard. So torn."

She opened her eyes, met Joseph's sorrowful gaze. "I've seen this happen in my job," she said. "A child is abused and the father is blamed, maybe by the child or maybe by a social worker. There's that one moment that the wife has to choose—do I protect my child or do I believe the man I love could never do such a hideous, heinous thing? Mama found herself in that moment and she stood by him. But my father had seen that flicker of doubt in her eyes and he confronted her with it when he came home from being questioned. She tried to tell him she was sorry, but he was so hurt . . .

"He came into my room that night and stared at me. Just stared, saying nothing at all. He looked so sad and I wanted to yell at the top of my lungs that it was not true! That he didn't do anything. But I couldn't make my mouth speak. I don't know if he was waiting for me to say something, to do something—I just don't know. He looked . . . sorrowful, but so angry, all at once. The next day he went to work, and after work went straight to play with his band. After that, no one saw him again. He never came home." She swallowed hard. "The next morning I woke up and my mother was screaming. Someone had killed one of Fluffy's kittens."

"Beckett," Ford said coldly and she patted his hand.

"I knew that, of course. Mama thought it was somebody angry at my father. The community rose up against him, but my father was nowhere to be found. They assumed he was guilty, that he'd run before he could be arrested. It got bad, like pitchforks and burning torches bad. I withdrew even further." She sighed. "Seeing Beckett gloat over my father being the perpetrator was so hard. Vivien ripped into my mother, so furious that my father had butchered her child. The family sided with Vivien and Mama broke relations. She and I moved to Riverdale and Mama got a job cleaning hotel rooms. She got a divorce a few years later. In absentia, of course, because he never came back."

"Did you ever tell your mother about Beckett?" Joseph asked.

"Yes and no. When I finally started talking again, I went to her and said, 'It wasn't Daddy.' I needed her to know that much. But I was afraid to tell her who it was. The morning after I told her that, I woke up to find my new cat dead. Mama had been on the phone with Vivien the night before, telling her what I'd said. It hadn't made a difference to Vivien, but I knew she must have told Beckett. After I found my cat, I knew I could never tell my mother Beckett's name. I knew he'd kill her, just like he promised."

"Did you ever see Beckett again after you moved?" McManus asked.

"He'd pop up from time to time."

"What do you mean?" Novak asked.

"He'd . . . pop up. I'd turn around in the grocery store or the library and he was there, whispering in my ear or slicing his finger over his throat. That didn't stop until I moved in with the Elkharts. Their security kept me safe from him, but Mama was still living in Riverdale and still vulnerable."

"When did you check him out and hear he was dead?" Agent Kerr asked.

Joseph still hadn't said a word. He looked tortured. Furious. Deadly. She wanted to beg him not to do anything crazy for her, but she kept those words to herself.

"When I was fifteen. I was pregnant." She looked at Ford, remembering the exact moment she'd decided to act. "I'd just felt you move and you were suddenly so very real." She smiled at him sadly. "I remember thinking that now I had another life to consider. I couldn't risk him trying to hurt you, too. I knew I needed to tell, but I had a lot of questions—like could he even be prosecuted? What if the statute of limitations on his crime had run out and I accused him and the cops couldn't even arrest him? I'd be

putting my mother in even bigger trouble. So I wrote a letter to the FBI asking about statutes of limitations and
whether a parent could be placed in witness protection."

Detective McManus's brows rose. "You wrote to the
FBI? What happened?"

"I got a visit from an Agent Baker. Claudia Baker was
her name. We met a couple more times and then she told
me Beckett was dead. She even got me a copy of his death
certificate."

"Did you tell your mother then?" Hector asked.

"No. Beckett was no longer a threat. She believed me
about my father, but there was no way I could prove any of
it to anyone else. There didn't seem to be any point. I just
wanted to put the whole thing behind me." She sighed. "I
never dreamed he was still kidnapping girls. When I saw
him tonight it was fast and I wasn't paying attention to his
face, just to his hands and the pillow he had over Ford's
face. I had this . . . déjà vu, you know? But I thought it was
just being here."

"But none of this tells us why he's doing this now," Novak said. "Why draw you here? And how does Doug and
his black van connect with Beckett and his white truck?"

"It was a van that stopped for me last night," Ford said.
"Could have been black. He shined headlights in my eyes
so I couldn't see." He frowned. "Beckett said that he and
Doug's granddad were Army buddies in 'Nam. That that's
how he knew him."

Daphne sighed again. Joseph and Novak both swore.

"What?" Ford asked, concerned.

"That's how he got into Bill Millhouse's trusted circle,"
Daphne said. "Told him that their fathers had served together in the Gulf War. We've had the Army searching for
troops who went on to have sons named Doug. If it's just a
ploy, we wasted our time."

"Now we're back to Kim as our key connection to
Doug," Novak said.

Ford went still. "Excuse me? What are you talking
about? Kim isn't connected to this guy. *She's a victim.*"

Daphne's heart sank. "Ford, there are some things you
need to know."

Twenty-one

Joseph leaned against the doorframe connecting their rooms, holding on to both ends of the towel he'd hung around his neck, the jeans he'd pulled on clinging to his wet skin. He hadn't taken time to dry off, worried about leaving Daphne alone. His concern at the moment was far more for her emotional state than her physical safety.

Her mother and Maggie had arrived, bringing Daphne's dog. Tasha lay directly across Daphne's door into the hall. Nobody was getting in Daphne's room without getting past the dog first.

No, he'd sped through his shower because she'd cried through hers. He didn't think she knew he could hear her. She'd waited till the water was full blast before letting go. But he'd heard. Her sobs tore at his heart.

Now she stood at the window, looking down at the street, which was steadily being covered by the falling snow. She wore no wig. Someone from CSU had found it, but Beckett had touched it. She hadn't wanted it anymore. Joseph had to admit he was glad of that small plus. In front of him stood the real Daphne.

Or as real as she could allow herself to be. She held herself gingerly, as if she'd break if anyone pushed too hard. But Joseph wasn't fooled. There was nothing weak about this woman.

But she was . . . softer. The curls that had been so tight right out of the shower were drying into chaotic peaks, like a wind-tossed sea. Her face was bare, her silk pajamas a soft pink. She looked impossibly young. And so very sad.

She'd had to tell her son the truth about Kimberly Mac-Gregor and at first he didn't believe her, certain that she was mistaken. But one look at Joseph's and Deacon's faces told the boy it was true. He'd withdrawn, not letting his mother touch him.

She hadn't wanted to leave him but Ford commanded her to go. No, not just to go. To "leave him the hell alone." Deacon promised that he'd stand watch and would let no new harm come to her son. It had been the only thing that allowed her to leave.

Then she'd come back to the hotel to find her mother and Maggie pacing the floor of their room across the hall under Kate Coppola's watchful eye.

Kate had texted Joseph of their arrival in Wheeling about a minute before he and Daphne had walked into Rampor's office. Joseph had told Kate to keep the women in the hotel until further notice. Daphne had been poised to tell her story and he didn't want anything to disrupt her. Plus, he figured anything that Daphne knew, Simone knew, too.

He'd been very wrong about that, which he hadn't found out until she'd told her story in Ford's hospital room. And so after telling her story once, Daphne had to tell it again. Simone hadn't moved a muscle—until Daphne got to the part about the picture she'd drawn, the one that had caused her father to be accused.

Simone began to cry, silent tears that had all but ripped Daphne's heart out.

Mine, too. He hadn't been much help, though. He'd been strung so tight while she told her story, it had been all he could do not to break something. Or someone.

Joseph had dealt with child molesters, kidnappers, murderers. In every case he'd wanted the perpetrators to be punished. He'd wanted to ease the victims' pain.

But tonight . . . It had been a long time since he'd battled such a pagan urge to kill. Not since he'd held his dying wife in his arms. It had been Simone's agony that had brought his rage to a grinding halt. Daphne's mother had lost so much—her marriage, her daughter's childhood, her family. But she'd also been denied the opportunity to heal her child because Daphne had been terrorized into silence.

Simone's reaction had broken his heart. But Maggie's . . . Maggie's reaction had left him puzzled. He'd expected her to be there for Simone, to put her arm around her friend, to cry with her. But she hadn't. Instead she'd separated herself from the group, almost an observer, her affect flat. Maggie's "reaction" was to have no reaction at all.

It might be the way she deals with loss. But Joseph's instincts told him it was something different. He just didn't know what. But he'd deal with that later.

Right now, Daphne stood at the window looking lost. He didn't know which piece to address first—her son, her mother, her trauma, or his reaction to hearing it. He decided to tackle the easiest one first. Ford.

"It doesn't have anything to do with you, you know," Joseph said softly.

She didn't turn to look at him. "Which thing? There are so many to choose from."

He crossed to her, sliding his arms around her waist from behind. She leaned into him and her quiet sigh was one of despair.

"Ford's a man now, Daphne," Joseph said. "There are some things he's got to get through on his own. When my wife died I pulled into myself. I didn't want to be touched. I didn't want anyone to speak to me, even my parents. I had to lick my wounds and move on. This is worse than a death for Ford, in some ways. He's just found out Kim isn't the girl he thought she was. He has to lick his wounds. Find his dignity."

"I know. I guess it's not *my job* to spare him from it." He wasn't sure if the subtle edge to her words was meant for him or for herself.

"No, it's not. But it's your job to *want* to spare him from it. You're his mother. That's what good mothers do. Better mothers step back and give their sons room to grow."

"I guess I got used to being the one he depended on," she said in a small voice.

"He hasn't rejected you. He'll always need you. But pain is part of life and he has to learn to face the pain without your help." He kissed her ear. "Knowing you're there if he does need you is sustaining him right now. He's working with a safety net. You."

"Thank you," she said, her voice breaking. "That helps. It really does." She swiped her fingertips under her eyes, then cleared her throat. "What would help me more is to stab Kimberly in the eye with a really big knife, but . . ."

He chuckled. "But you can't have everything. You're a fearsome woman. I like that."

"Not a monster?" It was asked uncertainly and he sobered. Sighed.

"Daphne, I'm sorry. I was shocked when you knew Beckett's name. But I never thought you were a monster. I was angry that you'd had to go through that. That any of this ugliness touched you. That there wasn't a damn thing I could do to make the past go away. But never once did I think you were a monster."

Her expression reflected in the window glass was one of abject misery. "I wonder how many he took," she whispered.

"However many it is, they're not your responsibility."

"Try telling that to their mothers and fathers. Try telling that to myself. He went free for seven years before I reported him."

"Seven years that he terrorized you with mind games."

"I always thought that he'd picked Kelly because she was Vivien's daughter, that he knew we were coming or that Kelly might even have arranged it. I never once thought he'd do the same to anyone else. Why didn't I think of that?"

"Because you were a child. A little girl who was forced to grow up way too soon."

"I know. But I can't stop thinking of all those parents standing at the window waiting for their daughters to come home. Not knowing where Ford was for a day nearly broke my mind. How have these parents borne the pain for all these years?"

"You're assuming there were others between Kelly and Heather."

"Aren't you?"

"Yes."

"I don't want their blood to be on my hands, Joseph. But it is."

"No, it's not. It's on the hands of whoever declared Beckett dead twenty years ago. That could have been Beckett, faking his own death. It could simply have been a clerical error—but you didn't make it. You told what you knew, honey. It's not your fault that Beckett somehow managed to cheat the system. We'll find out how. And if it was Beckett who's responsible for the deception, we'll make him pay. If it was an honest clerical error . . . I wouldn't want to be in that clerk's shoes because they'll feel as culpable as you do now."

"Can we contact Agent Baker? Ask her who she talked to when she investigated?"

"I've sent a request to the DC field office for the report she filed when she closed the case and for her to contact me, day or night. It'll probably be morning before I hear anything, though."

"I hope by morning it isn't too late for Kim and her sister. And for Heather. She could still be alive. How can finding one cabin be so hard?"

They'd received word that the teams had aborted their search for the evening. The dogs had lost Ford's scent as they backtracked his path.

"They'll try again tomorrow at first light. They won't give up."

"They may not have a choice. Look at that snow. It's erasing everything. And what if Beckett's gone back to the cabin already? He'll kill her."

"If he goes back to the cabin he'll be seen. The Bureau has all the roads into that wildlife management area under surveillance. If someone drives in, they'll know."

"And if he never goes back and we never find the cabin? If by some miracle she's still alive, she'll die anyway."

She was coming unraveled so he tightened his hold. "*Stop this.* You'll make yourself crazy. You didn't cause this, Daphne. And their blood is not on your hands."

"I hear you. And I appreciate it. It's just . . . never mind."

He squeezed her again, more lightly this time. "Talk to me."

She met his eyes in the glass. "When I was thirteen years old I decided to be a prosecutor because they were . . . righteous. And they made a difference, even if it was after the fact. They got *justice.* And I wanted justice. *Needed* it."

"I understand."

"I know you do. The day I met Travis, all I wanted was information on being a lawyer. He was the first one I'd ever met."

"He was a prosecutor, too?"

"Oh no. He was defense. And if I'd known *that*, I wouldn't have approached him to begin with." Her mouth winged up briefly, then drooped again. "If I'd known Beckett was still alive, I would have reported him."

"I know that, honey."

"And I appreciate that you do. What you think matters."

"But?"

She sighed again, this time so wearily it made his heart ache. "I worked hard to get my law degree. I've worked hard to become a prosecutor. To be fearless. Fearsome. Dedicated to getting victims justice. But now . . . God, this is going to sound so selfish."

"So? It's just us, Daphne. Talk to me."

"It's just that nobody's going to care that I've worked for the victims. Or how many bad guys I've put away. When this comes out—and it will—everyone will say, 'She waited *seven years* to report him?' I'll have to explain why . . . which will rip me open, for everyone to see. This could ruin my career, everything I've worked so hard to do."

Which would be, Joseph thought darkly, an excellent motivation for someone with a grudge against Daphne to orchestrate this revelation. Still, why now? And how did any of this connect to Doug and the Millhouses?

She blinked and two tears rolled down her cheeks, followed by more that fell as steadily as the snow outside. There was no explosion of emotion, no sobs to wrack her body. No drama. Just simple despair that filled her up and had nowhere else to go.

"It's so selfish of me to care about myself or my career," she whispered brokenly, "because Beckett's got more victims. Their families will want to know why I said nothing when I knew his name. I'm going to have to tell them. They'll despise me, Joseph, because I was *weak*. And I can't disagree with them."

She was breaking his heart. She hadn't been weak. She'd been a traumatized child. There was no weakness in this woman and he'd defend her from anyone who said there was. Even if it was herself.

"They won't despise you. Come on." Pulling the drapes shut, he turned her in his arms and nudged her toward the stuffed chair in the corner. "Sit with me."

Wednesday, December 4, 11:30 p.m.

Well. Mitch lowered the binoculars, no longer able to see them through the window once Carter pulled the drapes. Agent Carter and Daphne. That he hadn't expected.

Shame on you, Agent Carter. Fraternizing with a witness. And a perpetrator. Although he shouldn't have been so surprised. The expression on Carter's face as he'd leapt to save her from Marina's bullets had been chilling. A man saving his woman.

But just now, he'd looked helpless. A man comforting his woman as she cried like a baby. It would all be jelling for her now.

Wilson Beckett had been a busy man this evening. *Took him long enough to get here, though.* Filling his tank with gasoline had taken him longer than Mitch had expected.

But once Beckett had arrived, he'd made good use of his time. The first BOLO that Mitch caught on his police scanner described Beckett wearing nurse's scrubs, armed and dangerous. He'd stabbed a cop after attempting to murder a patient. *Go, Beckett.*

A few minutes later the BOLO was upgraded to include a white pickup truck at the same time that emergency personnel were called to the southwest corner of the hospital. Sounded like Beckett had hurt somebody for those scrubs.

Idiot. He hadn't needed to hurt anyone for the scrubs. There would have been plenty in the hospital's laundry room. Plenty more if he'd just followed the guy home and stolen the scrubs from his clothes hamper. Now there was a new victim and an even higher price on Beckett's head. Which was Beckett's problem.

Beckett's problems were mounting.

Because shortly after the cops went back in the hospital, the BOLO was updated with the suspect's name. Wilson Beckett. Daphne had come clean.

Mitch was surprised. He hadn't been sure that she'd ever tell, that she wouldn't take her secret to her very early grave. He'd predicted that she might reveal Beckett's name, but only when she was shamed into it by being shown proof that she'd been in that little bunker twenty-seven years ago. That she'd known all along.

But she'd shared straight up. And now the shit would rain down on her head. Her career would be over. Her family would know the truth.

The families of over two dozen dead girls would be asking why she didn't reveal Beckett long before he tortured and killed their daughters. The families of over two dozen dead girls would want their pound of flesh.

Sorry, guys. You'll have to stand in line. Daphne Montgomery is mine.

Wednesday, December 4, 11:30 p.m.

Daphne let Joseph lead her to the stuffed armchair, where he tugged her onto his lap. She melted into him, pressing her cheek to his warm chest, listening to the steady beat of his heart as her tears continued to fall. She was too tired to make them stop.

She let herself go, let herself lean on him. Inhaled the scent of him—soap from his shower, his aftershave. He held her close, one hand closing over her hip, anchoring her to him, the other rubbing her back. Slowly, firmly, rhythmically.

Calming her. The tears slowed. Stopped. Until all that was left was the bare, unavoidable truth. *All these years.* She'd thought Beckett dead. *But he's not. He's been out there. Doing it again and again.* How could she face his victims? Their families?

Her own family. Her friends. Herself. *It's not my fault. I didn't know.*

How many times had she heard that excuse in court?

"What have I done, Joseph?" she whispered.

"Nothing wrong," he murmured. "You were a child."

He sounded so sure, and in her mind she knew he was right. She desperately wanted to believe him in her heart.

The hand that rubbed her back lifted to stroke her hair, gently at first, gradually increasing the pressure until he massaged her head, taking care to avoid yesterday's bump. She let her head fall forward and for precious minutes she didn't think about anything except how good it felt. He seemed to know just how hard to press.

He seemed to know exactly where it hurt. Even if she'd had another wig with her, there was no way she'd put it on now. His touch against her scalp felt too good.

The quiet moan escaped her before she knew it was coming. His chest expanded in a giant exhale as his hips shifted beneath her. He was aroused, but not demanding.

"Feel good?" he asked, his voice a deep rumble in his chest.

"Mm-hm. Thank you. I've had a headache since yesterday morning. I thought the worst was over when Ford was found. And for me as a mother, it is."

"But for you as a person?"

"My worst nightmare."

"Coppola said you had one last night. A nightmare. Did you dream of Beckett?"

"Yes. And that little room and Kelly's screaming. And . . ." She hesitated, not wanting to tell but knowing she must.

She could feel his dread as he held her, his arms tensing. "And?" he said, his voice gone darkly menacing.

She sighed. "I wasn't entirely truthful earlier."

"You said he didn't touch you." He went still. "No, you said he didn't touch you the way he touched her. Why didn't you say it before?"

"He didn't touch me. He would have, though. That's why I ran. I didn't say it before because Ford was there and I didn't want him to know. But somebody needs to know the truth because now . . . there are others."

"What did he do?" he growled.

"It wasn't what he did. It's what he said. Can you settle down? The growling is making me edgy." She sighed, trying to calm herself. "I was an early bloomer. Always looked older than I was. I was the only eight-year-old in my class with a training bra." She shrugged. "Beckett noticed."

Joseph quietly seethed. "And then?"

"He'd pet my hair and tell me that I needed 'to cook' for a while longer. I think he'd planned to keep me until I'd developed more. It wasn't like he was going to let me go."

"He needs to die."

His expression was deadly, but Daphne felt safer than she ever had in her entire life. "I completely agree. But I don't want you to do it."

Dark, determined eyes met hers. "Why not?"

"One, it's against the law. Which I know I'm supposed to say, but which doesn't make it less true. Two . . . I'm very much an eye-for-an-eye kind of girl. But there are consequences to every decision we make. I don't want you to have to live with any negative consequences on my account. At least any that aren't absolutely necessary."

"Killing him feels necessary," he said darkly.

"Stopping him is necessary. Justice is necessary." She ran her finger over his frowning lip. "Giving the victims the closure of a guilty verdict is necessary."

He closed his eyes. "You're right. I still want to kill him, though."

"So do I, but I only told you about the needing-to-cook comment because it might help you catch him. Kelly was seventeen and so was . . . is Heather. He might have only shown interest in me because I was convenient. But his attraction may not be based on chronological age. So don't narrow your field of possible victims."

"I understand," he said grimly. "Is there any more you remember?"

"His smile. When he'd come back up the stairs from . . . from raping Kelly, he'd smile at me like everything was normal. Like he was . . . Ward Cleaver or something. Later, when I'd come home and he wanted to keep me in check—"

"You mean terrorize you?" Joseph interrupted harshly. "Because that's what it was. An innocent child being terrorized by an adult with all the power."

Another voice punched through the memory of Beckett, echoing Joseph's words. "That's exactly what Maggie said."

She could feel his momentary surprise. "Maggie knows?"

"She and the FBI agent I gave my statement to are the only ones who did."

"His name, too?"

"No. Maggie couldn't get me to say his name. My statement to Agent Baker was the only time I gave his name to anyone. Until tonight."

He processed this. "So he'd smile when he terrorized you?"

"Yes. It would make me throw up. The last time was the day before I met Travis. I was walking to the bus stop after work and there Beckett was, standing under a streetlamp. He smiled at me and drew a line across his throat. I ran back to the restaurant, got sick. Called Maggie to come get me. She begged me to tell her the name of the man, but I was too terrified."

"Maggie told me she was your adopted grandma. How did you meet her?"

"After my father left us and Mama moved us to Riverdale, she rented a little apartment in this nice woman's basement."

"Maggie was the nice woman?"

"Yes, she was. She had a big farmhouse with a lot of land. And horses."

"Ah, I wondered how the horses factored in."

"They were Maggie's. Her husband had been a breeder, pretty famous in their neck of the woods. Anyway, Mama and I arrived in our station wagon, which was packed full of everything we owned. She took me into the house, introduced me to Maggie, and started down the basement stairs. I freaked out."

"I can understand why."

"I still have trouble being underground. Mama was trying to calm me and Maggie was staring. Not like she was appalled, but like she was assessing. I was having a major meltdown without saying a word or even making a sound."

"You said you didn't speak for eight months. You mean nothing? No words?"

"Not one. Mama was getting frantic, telling me that I was going to get us thrown out. And Maggie stopped her. Told her that nobody was throwing us out and that I didn't have to go down the stairs. She gave me a room, decorated for a girl who loved horses. Maggie was a social worker and she and her husband had been foster parents. Her house had always been filled with kids. Now it was empty because her husband had died and she hadn't had the heart to take in anyone new."

"Until you and your mother."

"Yes. She'd decided that her time for grieving was past. She was so patient with me, taking care of me so that Mama could work. When the husband walks out, it's sometimes financially worse than if he'd died. We were destitute."

"If he'd died, you would have at least had his pension."

"Exactly. After a few months, I ventured into the barn. And met Lulu. That horse—and Maggie—were my salvation. At first I was like a little ghost, always watching. Then one day Maggie put a brush in my hand. I'd brush that horse and feel connected again. Like I was part of the world. When I'd have a nightmare or a panic attack, Maggie would carry me out to the barn and put the brush in my hand. It's a wonder Lulu wasn't bald after all that brushing. But I'd brush Lulu and bathe her. Later, I'd ride her and whisper my secrets in her ear. The wind in my face, the freedom of being able to go anywhere I wanted, the act of caring for an animal . . . It healed me, a little at a time."

She sighed. "And then one day it was just me and Maggie in the barn with the horses and it all came out, all in a rush. That's the only time I've ever seen Maggie cry. I was terrified after I'd told her. I never wanted Mama to know. Mama stood up for me with her family, lost them because of me. My dad was gone, because of me."

"Please tell me that you know now that it wasn't because of you."

"I know that in my head, but I still don't believe it. The other reason I didn't want her to know was that Mama would have never let me rest until I told her Beckett's name. And then he'd kill her. Of that I had absolutely no doubt."

"I guess I can understand that."

"I was homeschooled for a long time, because even when I started talking again, it was years before I was ready to go to a normal school. Years before I'd let anyone touch me other than Mama and Maggie. If I heard anyone say, 'Did you miss me,' I'd be a mess for days and poor Lulu would get the brushing of her life. If Beckett popped up and said it, I was back almost to square one."

"It's a wonder you didn't have a nervous breakdown."

"I did have one. The first time he popped up was when I'd finally started at the local school. I was eleven. My first day, I was headed for my bus and somebody bumped me from behind. I dropped my books. I'd bent down to gather them and a man stopped to help. I looked up to say thanks and there he was."

"My God."

"Yeah. He said, 'Did you miss me?' then said, 'You look pert near cooked' and tried to grab me. The next thing I knew, I was in the hospital, waking up. I'd run away, screaming in my mind. Ran into the street and nearly got plowed by a bus. I tripped trying to get away, hit my head. Ended up in the hospital."

Joseph's face had grown very dark. "He needs to die, Daphne."

"I know. But that's not why I'm telling you this. These are the things that will come out if I have to tell grieving, angry parents why I didn't turn him in sooner. Why I waited seven years to turn him in to the FBI."

"Who told you Beckett was dead."

"Because the county records department told them so. You think that Beckett faked his own death?"

"It's the most straightforward explanation. If he was dead, he'd be off the grid. He wouldn't have to worry about anyone looking for him."

"He could kill with impunity. I'd like to read the autopsy report. I wonder if he found a body or procured one by murdering the person. Somebody has to be dead to get the ME to sign off on the document itself."

"McManus was going to the county records office first thing in the morning, but we may be able to see a copy of the certificate online."

"Can we do it right now?"

"Sure. Let's put at least one of these questions to rest right now."

Wheeling, West Virginia
Wednesday, December 4, 11:45 p.m.

"Hey, kid. Ford. Are you okay?"

No. I'm not okay. Ford looked up at the ceiling. Numb. When he'd first opened his eyes and seen his mother's face . . . *I thought everything would be all right.* His biggest worry had been for her. When she let herself get worn down, she got a cold.

And every time she sneezed he still worried that the cancer had come back.

When he'd opened his eyes the next time? It had been to see . . . nothing. *Because there was a goddamn pillow in my face.*

He'd heard his mother. Her war cry. If he'd been Beckett, he would have been terrified. *Now I know his name.*

Because my mother told it to me. Because she'd always known.

She'd yanked the old asshole off him like the guy was a fifty-pound third grader.

Don't mess with my mama, he thought with a tiny spear of pride. *She was like a mother lion, defending me. No. I don't want to be proud of her. I want to be mad at her. Saying those things about Kim. They can't be true. They just can't.*

She didn't set me up. She didn't fake wanting to be with me, just to give me over to Doug. Whoever the hell he is. She didn't. She couldn't.

Could she?

"Hey, kid." It was that Fed. Novak. Ford continued to ignore him. *Maybe he'll go away.* "You okay, Ford? You might as well say something to let me know you're all right, at least physically, otherwise I'm capable of annoying you until you do. It's one of my special skills. So one more time. Are. You. Okay?"

Ford blew out a breath. "Do I fucking *look* okay?"

"No, you fucking look like shit. But you've been through a lot in the past two days. I figure you're entitled. You got any questions?"

"Like what?"

"Like, did your mother tell the truth?"

Ford turned his head to stare at the Fed. Novak leaned against the doorframe, appearing calm, but there was an intensity to the man that hummed under the surface.

"Come closer, please," Ford said politely and Novak complied, coming to the side of Ford's hospital bed, holding his gaze steady so that Ford could study his eyes. Each iris was two different colors, brilliant blue and chocolate brown, split right down the center. He looked like a comic book superhero, too brawny and rugged to be real. "Do they hurt?"

"My eyes? No. Because you've had a bad day, I'll allow you one more personal, then you gotta get back to business. Got me?"

"Yeah. What causes this . . . uniqueness?"

Novak's lips twitched. "You are your mother's son, aren't you? Flatter and dig in one motion. It's a genetic anomaly that runs in my family. Not contagious, not fatal, just cosmetic."

"Okay." Ford had many more questions, but he'd been allowed only one, so he respected the limit and got back to the subject he knew the Fed wanted to discuss. "*Is* she telling the truth?"

"Yes. In fact, she left some things out, either because she simply forgot or because she didn't want to hurt you more."

"Tell me, then. Please."

"All the stuff about Kimberly having a record for theft is true. We don't know yet how she met this Doug character. We know they've worked together on several heists—important to your story is the theft from a state trooper's gun safe. That's where Doug got the Taser gun he used on you. Kimberly was an acquaintance of the trooper's daughter. That's how she got her entrée to the trooper's house."

"How did she know the safe's combo?"

"Planted a Webcam in the heat vent above the safe. Turns out she and Doug have used this method several times since. We have a list of guns they've . . . purloined."

"Are they . . ." Ford swallowed hard. "She and he . . . ?"

"Lovers? Probably. Recently? That I don't know."

"Hell."

Novak looked sympathetic. "Pretty much sums it up."

"So Kim did set me up, just like my mom told me."

"Yeah. I'm sorry, Ford. Your mother's PI dug up a lot of this information. See, he has huge motivation to catch Doug."

"Finding me. Right?"

"Partially. This is the other thing she didn't tell you. I feel like you should know. She wanted to hire a bodyguard for you."

"I said no."

"So she hired one anyway."

Ford's eyes widened. "She did *what*?"

Novak lifted a shoulder. "You'd find out sooner or later. The BG worked for Maynard. Name was Isaac Zacharias. Maynard's a pal of yours, right?"

"Yeah, we're tight. Mainly because he's just my mother's friend. I don't have to call him 'daddy.' Unlike some other people who were touching her way too much tonight."

Novak arched his ultra-white brows. "Not bad, trying to dig dirt on Joseph Carter. I got nothin' there, other than he seems to care for your mother a great deal. So, back to

Maynard. That night you were taken? His pal gets killed. Doug nearly severs his head right off his neck."

Ford gripped the bed rail when the room began to spin. "Holy shit."

"Exactly. That's why Maynard's a man with a mission. Zacharias was his old partner when he was a cop. Not sure your mother knew the severed head bit. I think Carter was trying to protect her from hearing it."

"Oh my God. Poor Clay. That poor man . . . Zacharias. He died protecting me."

"That was his job. He also fucked up, though, just so you know it all. Zacharias never ran a background check on Kimberly, even though he said he had. He told Maynard that Kim was clean. If he'd done his job . . . well, things would have turned out differently. But Maynard seems like the loyal type."

"He is. I don't think that's a failing."

"Never said it was. I just meant he knows his friend fucked up, but he's still keen on finding Doug. He and his assistant found the Webcam in the trooper's house. They also found the other cop houses that Doug and Kim broke into."

"She seemed so perfect," Ford said angrily. "Played me for a sap."

"Fitzpatrick searched her room. Found her crib notes. She'd been researching what you like, don't like, music, food, hobbies. That's why she seemed so perfect."

How humiliating. "Hell."

"Was she your first?"

He scowled. "Because you've been nice you get one personal and that was it. Yes."

"Then this is gonna take a while to heal, man. Most guys get garden-variety betrayal. You know, she cheats with a football player. You, it's like you chose the *Titanic* for your first cruise. Upside is, if you ever go on a boat again, it'll never be that bad."

The Fed looked like he had more to say. "What else?" Ford asked.

"Your mom doesn't know this part and I only know because I asked Maynard directly. According to Kim's girlfriend, Kim and Doug may not have practiced safe sex."

Ford's stomach turned over. "What?" he whispered.

"Look, I'm not your dad. I'm not anybody's dad. I'd

probably be a lousy dad. But I am a big brother and, um, one of my sisters trusted her boyfriend when he said he was clean. He wasn't and now my little sister's not, either."

Ford swallowed hard. "Is your sister's condition curable?"

"Not at this time. Nobody's saying Kim has any STDs. If you used a condom, you're likely okay. You still need to get tested. Got me?"

"Yeah." Overwhelmed, Ford covered his face with his hands. A sob was building in his chest and he didn't know what to do. He heard a chair scrape on the floor, the plastic squeaking as Novak sat down.

"It's okay," Novak said softly. "If you need to let it out, let it out. I'll close that door and nobody will come in. Or I can stay. Your choice. My feelings are fine either way."

"I don't want to let it out," Ford said hoarsely. "Last time it wasn't pretty."

"When was the last time?"

"When my mom was sick and my dad was being a real prick. And my grandmother sold my horse to get back at my mother."

"How old?"

"Me or the horse?"

"You," Novak said, amusement in his voice.

"Twelve."

"Hell of an age. What'd your mom have?"

"Breast cancer. She was twenty-seven. If she'd been her age now, she'd have had a nine in ten chance of being fine. Then, they gave her six in ten of making it five years."

"She made it."

"My mom's a fighter. But me . . . I've never been so fucking scared in my life. Until last night. I thought I was gonna die all alone out there and no one would ever find me. And I thought Kim was out there and I couldn't save her."

"Well," Novak drawled, "somebody would have eventually found you. When the snow melted." He sobered. "As for Kim, she didn't want to set you up in that alley. It sounds like she was having major second thoughts because she was getting attached to you. Doug stole her sister, only fourteen. We think that's how he got her to do his evil bidding."

"I guess that's something."

"That's what your mom was trying to tell you when you told her to leave."

Ford rolled his eyes to the ceiling, miserable again. "God, I'm an asshole."

"Hey, I know assholes. I *am* an asshole. You ain't one, kid."

Ford looked over at him. "Thanks, Agent Novak. I appreciate it. All of it."

Novak shrugged. "We've used the word 'condom' in a conversation. I think you should call me Deacon." He stood abruptly and pushed the chair against the wall. "Try to get some sleep. I'll make sure nobody bothers you."

Ford waited until Novak was at the door. "Deacon, I hope your sister stays well."

"Me, too, kid. Me, too."

Twenty-two

Joseph got his laptop from his room so that he could search the online archives for Wilson Beckett's death certificate. When he rejoined Daphne, she was pacing back and forth in front of the window, arms crossed tight over her breasts. Pausing for a moment, he let himself watch her move. The silk she wore flowed around her legs like water and he was keenly aware that she wore nothing under those pajamas.

He'd been keenly aware of that the entire time she'd been on his lap.

The entire time she'd explained what she should never have had to explain to anyone. *Especially to me.*

Beckett deserved to die for what he'd done to Daphne alone. Add to that her cousin Kelly, Heather Lipton, and the others . . .

But why now? Why was all this coming together now? *Doug.* They'd been so fixated on Beckett that they'd lost focus on Doug.

"Doug did this," Joseph said. "Set this plan in motion. He kidnapped Ford, somehow convinced Beckett to be his accomplice. He found Beckett, for God's sake. How did he find Beckett to start with? How did he even *know* about him?"

"Damn good questions," she said. "I've been wondering that myself. The only time I said Beckett's name was to that FBI agent, Claudia Baker. I imagine she filed a report. Could Doug work for the Bureau?"

"God, I hope not. What's Doug's game? He makes sure Ford is found *here*, drawing you back to the one place you probably never would have come back to in a million years. You think it's coincidence that Beckett came here to kill your son tonight?"

"No. I think Beckett was manipulated by Doug just like we were. Doug wanted us to find the connection between George Millhouse and the knife used on Isaac Zacharias. He wanted us to find those weapons in the basement of Odum's house. He wanted us to find the connection between the pistols in Bill Millhouse's trunk and the Tasers used in the alley. Doug has manipulated us into finding exactly the evidence he wanted us to find. That he'd manipulate Beckett isn't such a stretch for me."

"He brought Beckett back into your life."

She stopped pacing, her back to him. "I know. But why?"

"To discredit you. To ruin you. To make you hurt."

"I got that much. But *why*? What did I do to him?"

"Once we figure out who the hell he is, then hopefully we'll know. But it must have been major, at least in his eyes. This is . . . a lot of effort." He sat on the bed and patted the mattress next to him. "Sit."

"Actually, I need to pace."

"Actually, I need you to sit. I can't concentrate when you move like that."

She turned to frown at him. "Like what?"

"Like any way you move," he said dryly. "So please . . . sit." He opened his laptop and signed in to his Bureau account. The mattress depressed next to him, the whisper of silk taunting him, the scent of peaches filling his head. He adjusted the computer on his lap. *Maybe I should have just let her pace.* "I want to see that death certificate."

"I have a copy. It's in my safety-deposit box."

"I should be able to get to it online now." Joseph focused on the screen, not chancing a glance in her direction. "It was a West Virginia death certificate, right?"

"Yes, Ohio County."

"And you got it from Agent Baker?"

"Yes. At first she just told me he was dead, but I wanted proof. It was my mother's life we were talking about. I'd called the records office to corroborate it myself, but they wouldn't give me any information over the phone. I had to

mail in a request, which I did, and I was told it could be a
month before I got the actual piece of paper, but when I
told Agent Baker that I'd requested it, she said she'd get it
for me faster. She did and then a few weeks later I got another copy in the mail from the state. If I hadn't used the
mail or Baker's connection, I'd have had to go in person all
the way to West Virginia. There wasn't an Internet back
then."

"Yeah, there was. Just not for civilians."

"Which both of us were at the time. Therefore my statement holds, Mr. Phelps."

His lips curved at her grumpy retort. "Phelps? I'm flat-
tered. He's one of my childhood heroes."

"Then your ears should have been burning all those
times Paige described you as tall, dark, and dangerous, with
a 'this-tape-will-self-destruct-Jim thing' going on."

His smile faded. "All that 'raw danger,'" he said, hating
the term he'd heard so many times over the years. Paige
had not been the first to use it, not by a long shot. Probably
just the first to use it with honest affection.

"I imagine that drives the women crazy," Daphne said
quietly.

He looked at her then. She sat with one knee drawn to
her chest, resting her chin atop it. Once again he was struck
by how very young she looked.

"Maybe it did. But I never cared. Not until I met you." A
shadow of doubt passed through her eyes that irritated
him. "You want to know what drove the women crazy?" he
asked with an edge that he couldn't contain, yet knew she
didn't deserve. "It wasn't me. Most of the time it was money.
My father's money. And for the few that were attracted to
the badge, it was the perception of danger that wasn't really
danger at all."

Her gaze met his head-on, unwavering. "Then what
was it?"

"Just the stink of the animals I deal with every day. It
rubs off on you, a . . ."

"Malevolence," she supplied, understanding.

"Yes. Perfect word. If any of those women had had to
face real danger, they would have turned tail and run like
scared rabbits. If they'd had to face one percent of what you
see on a daily basis as a prosecutor, they'd have dissolved.

If, as adults, they'd had to face a millionth of what you dealt with as a defenseless child, they would never have survived." He blew out a breath, listening to himself. He sounded bitter and he didn't mean to. "Some of them were very nice women. Others were gold diggers that didn't get a second date. But none of them . . . mattered. They fed a basic hunger."

Her eyes skittered to the pillows they'd left jumbled before Novak had called them back to the hospital. "Sex," she said, her voice going husky, her cheeks going pink.

The erection that had been uncomfortable became painful. "Yes. I won't deny it. I haven't been celibate, but I've never been indiscriminate. And I've always been safe."

"Good to know," she murmured.

"But it was more than sex, Daphne. It was . . ." He hated admitting it, but her opinion of him was too important to let it go unspoken. "After Jo, I was dead inside for a long time. As time passed, I healed, but I was so incredibly alone. The women I've known kept the loneliness at bay. For a little while."

Her eyes flew back to his, darkly turbulent. "I find myself terribly conflicted," she said. "I know lonely, and I never would've wanted that for you. But I'm still wishing every woman who's ever had you to a fiery perdition. And I have no right."

He might have smiled at her phrasing, but she was dead serious and so was he.

"I think you believe there are more to wish to perdition than really existed. There haven't been that many. And none since the day I met you."

She swallowed hard. "What about the bank executive, the flight attendant, the surgeon, the actress?"

All of the women he'd brought as dates to her fundraisers. "Nice women, all of them. None of them looking for a relationship any more than I was. They wanted a night out, where they could wear their bling. Not even one nightcap in the bunch." He shook his head with a small smile, remembering. "They're all old friends. A few of them actually wished *you* to a fiery perdition."

Her brows shot up. "Me? Why?"

He lifted a shoulder awkwardly. "You were breaking my heart."

Her lips parted in surprise. "Because of Clay?"

"Yep." He trailed a fingertip across her smooth, rosy cheek. "You say you don't have a right to resent anyone who came before. You have every right, just no need. They didn't matter to me. All of them were a pale imitation of what I'd lost. Of what I want. Which is what I see right now." She went statue still, not breathing even though her pulse fluttered wildly at the hollow of her throat. "I knew it the moment you walked through Grayson's front door. You matter, Daphne. You matter to me."

Her eyes closed, new tears seeping from beneath her eyelids. "I've waited so long to hear somebody say that to me," she whispered, breaking his heart all over again.

Joseph put his laptop on the floor, the search he'd been running forgotten. Threading his fingers through her hair, he pressed his lips to her forehead, her wet cheeks, the corner of her trembling mouth. "You matter to me," he repeated hoarsely.

Then her hands were gripping the back of his neck and she was on her knees beside him, leaning over him, kissing him with a hunger that wiped every thought from his mind except getting inside her, as fast as possible. He palmed her butt and swung her over so that she straddled him. She hummed against his lips, breaking contact only long enough for them both to gulp a lungful of air before returning to his mouth with a different kind of kiss, this one luscious and full of movement. He ran his hands up and down the backs of her legs, brushing her inner thigh with his thumbs, a little higher, a little closer to where he really wanted to be on each upsweep.

God. He could smell her arousal, all musky and sweet. Unable to wait, he yanked the pretty pink silk pajama bottoms down and plunged two fingers up into her warmth. She was tight and wet and she writhed against him, working herself against his hand.

Abruptly she pulled away from his mouth to stare down into his eyes. "Any which way I can have you," she whispered. "And some ways I haven't thought of yet."

It took him a few seconds to realize she was quoting him. He'd said those words. While they were driving up that morning. When he was being blunt. "Yeah? So?"

"Have you thought of them yet?"

"A few. More than a few. Why?"

She leaned down and nipped his lip, making his pulse roar in his head. "Where are your condoms?"

"One's in my back pocket."

"So get it."

He pumped his fingers into her more slowly, teasingly. He could press his thumb to her clit and finish her off, but he liked seeing her this way. She glowed. *She's mine.* "Then I have to take my fingers out of you and I don't want to."

She leaned to whisper in his ear. "But then you can put something better in me."

She laughed breathlessly when he yanked his fingers free and rolled to one hip to reach his back pocket. He fell back on the mattress, ready to unzip his jeans when she stayed his hands. *Shit. Don't make me stop. Please don't make me stop.*

He forced his voice out of his throat. "Do I need to stop?"

"No." She moved his hand, grasped the zipper herself. "This is mine. Mine to do."

This was about power. About her taking back what had been stolen from her. By Beckett and Elkhart. By cancer. This was important. He linked his hands behind his head. "Just be careful. I, uh, didn't take the time for shorts."

She was careful and she was slow. He was ready to beg when she finally got the zipper all the way down, freeing his erection, grasping it in her hand. She squeezed and his hips lifted off the bed. "God. Daphne."

With her other hand she touched his chest, sweeping him with her palm. Learning him. "You're beautiful," she murmured. "Really."

He wanted to be. He wanted to please her. Wanted to be better than that prick of an ex-husband and any other men who'd touched her since her divorce. Men he hoped he never met because he might do violence. "If you could hurry, I'd really like that."

Her mouth curved. "You made me impatient. It's my turn." With agonizing slowness she ripped open the condom wrapper and rolled it down him, her touch feather-light. His eyes rolled back in his head.

"Mother of God. If you don't hurry, I'm going to take over."

"No, you won't." She slid off him and he pushed himself up on his elbows to protest. Except she'd shucked her pajama bottoms and was grabbing his jeans. "Lift." He did and she yanked until he was naked, then got on the bed still wearing her pajama top and crawled toward him. She leaned in, kissing him thoroughly. "You won't take over because you know this is important. For me."

Her eyes had lost the glaze of passion and were now determined. He wound a lock of her hair around his finger. "Yes, I get that. But I want it to be good for both of us and you're . . . out of the moment. Can I help ease you back in?"

She tilted her head warily. "What did you have in mind?"

"Straddle my chest like before." She did and he had to work hard to keep his hips flat on the mattress. She was open to him, glistening and wet. "Scoot closer. Closer." He could see the moment she'd figured it out. Her eyes widened and she blushed.

"Mercy," she murmured.

"No. None." He held his breath as she hesitated the last few inches. Then she grabbed the headboard and pulled herself forward until her knees slid off his shoulders and she was pitched forward, her lower legs pressed against his chest for traction. He could have lifted his head, but he waited. Waited . . . Waited until a growl rolled out of him. "Daphne."

Finally she relaxed her body, lowering until she made contact with his mouth and he was back in heaven. Greedily he licked, tasting, feeling each quiver, the rumble of each moan as she rocked against him, finding her own rhythm, and it didn't take long for the passion to return. Better still, from this angle he could see up her top, getting his first view of her bare breasts. No bra, no lace, nothing between her skin and the silk.

He let out a silent sigh of relief, his worst fears not being the case at all. If they had been, he'd have dealt, but he was relieved as hell he wouldn't have to. They were fine, beautiful. They were scarred, but part of her. He was looking at all of her.

And they were perky. When she was eighty, the girls would still be perky.

Even as her words made him smile, he felt curiously like weeping. He didn't think he would have cared if they hadn't been perky or the shape hadn't been so nice. But she did. *She would have wanted to spare me the loss of . . . perfection.*

Because that's who she was. *Thank God she doesn't have to
spare me anything.*

It might be a while before she trusted him enough to
take off her top. He'd have to show her that the scars didn't
matter. And he had time for that. For now, he was all about
making her feel so good that the only anxiety she'd feel
would be about when they got to do this again.

He reached up, running his finger along one of the places
he'd explored while she slept before, lightly caressing her
left breast. Now she froze, her back arched.

Her breath shuddered out. "Do that again. Please."

He complied, gently taking a breast in each hand, tracing his finger across them lightly. Then he pulled her clit
into his mouth and sucked as hard as he could and she
came apart. Crying out, she jerked against him and he
could hear the headboard creak behind him.

She hung there for a minute, breathing hard, trembling.
Then she eased back until she straddled his pecs and looked
down at his face. She didn't say anything, just sat there, staring.

"Daphne?" he whispered.

Her eyes closed. "I thought I'd lost it all. All the feeling."

"You didn't try to see for yourself?"

"I was too afraid to. All these years and I was afraid to
know."

"Now you do."

She opened her eyes and he saw contentment and relief.
"Thank you, Joseph."

He grinned despite the throbbing in his groin. "You're
welcome."

She looked back over her shoulder. "Wow. All for me?"

"Yeah, all for you. But you don't have to feel—"

She cut him off with a look. "You aren't about to say 'obligated,' are you? 'Cause that would make me damn mad."

He had been, but he shook his head. "I was going to say
'intimidated.'"

She shook her head, a smile on her face. "Can we say
'full of himself'?"

He opened his mouth to return the volley, but she was
sliding down his body. Then it was his turn to glaze over
when she took him in.

All in one stroke, so smooth. Deep. He groaned and
lifted his hips, unable to control their movement. Her

breathing shattered and she began to move, fluidly, like she'd done this a million times. She fell forward to grip his shoulders and . . . rode him.

Somewhere in the back of his mind he told himself to thank Maggie, the next time he saw her, for teaching Daphne to ride. And then he didn't think at all, giving himself over to the friction, the tightness of her body gripping him, the pleasure of it all.

"Feels so good," he groaned. "Don't stop."

"I won't. I can't."

I can't. He liked that. He tried to make it last, but even though he'd had her once that night, he was starved. He gripped her hips and pulled her down on him, harder and faster until he bowed, his heels digging into the mattress, his head flung back. She came this time on a quiet moan that was all he needed to hear.

He closed his eyes and followed, letting himself fall.

She melted onto his chest, one hand cupping the back of his neck, the other right over his heart. He wrapped his arms around her, unwilling to let her go.

"Thank you," he murmured into her hair.

She patted his heart. "You're very, very welcome."

Seconds stretched into minutes. He knew she wasn't asleep because her forefinger traced lazy circles around his nipple and lightly fussed with the hair on his chest. He had enough energy to press a kiss to the top of her head.

"Daphne, why the wigs? There's nothing wrong with your hair."

"I hate it," she murmured sleepily. "Too wild. Won't behave. Stupid chemo."

Like waves on a wind-tossed sea. He ran his fingers through the misbehaving locks, enjoying the haphazard way they winged this way and that, as well as the knowledge that he was seeing a Daphne that no one else got to see. *Mine alone.* "What was it like before?"

She was quiet for a moment. "Smooth and pretty," she said, awake now. "But I lost it all. I hated the surgeries, the reconstruction. I hated losing my breasts, but to look in the mirror and be bald . . . I think I hated that more."

"So you started wearing the wigs then."

"Yes. And I found they did more than hide my bald head. They let me be someone else. For twelve years I'd had

Nadine saying an Elkhart does not do this or that. Elkharts don't swear, they are not loud, they wear respectable clothing. I wanted to do the opposite, so I looked for the biggest, Dolly Parton–est wig I could find and wore it to every single divorce settlement meeting. Nadine was appalled. Ap-*palled,* I tell you. It was worth every penny."

He smiled at the smug satisfaction in her voice. "I bet it was. But why did you keep wearing them? Once your hair grew back, I mean."

"At first, because I hated the new color."

"It changed?"

"Did it ever. Before the chemo my hair was like corn silk, white blond and smooth. When it came back in, it was reddish brown, this really ugly, muddy color, and really curly. Much curlier than this. And coarse. I'd read about the possibility of color changes, so I expected it to be different, but not like that. I cried all the time. Finally Mama and Maggie told me to just keep wearing the wigs. So I did. Eventually it lightened a little, enough to color it blond. Over time, it got better, softer. Like it is now."

"Then why keep wearing the wigs?"

"Some of it's convenience. It takes a lot of work to get this hair the way I want it to look for court, and sometimes it doesn't behave at all. The wigs are a lot faster and that gives me more time for riding in the morning."

His brows lifted. "I like riding in the morning."

She frowned, then snickered when she caught his innuendo. "I bet you do."

"If convenience is some of it, what's the rest?"

She lifted one shoulder in a self-conscious shrug. "By the time it started to come back in, I was in law school and people were used to seeing me in the wigs. If I took them off, they would know I'd been wearing one all along. I didn't want the questions. I didn't want to call any attention to myself."

He blinked in disbelief. "Daphne, you wore a neon green miniskirt and Dolly Parton hair the day I met you. You *love* calling attention to yourself. But maybe you just like to control the kind of attention you draw."

Her eyes widened, startled. "I hadn't thought about it that way. I guess that's true. But it still looks like I stuck my finger into a light socket."

"It does not. In fact, the curls are gone now that it's dry, which is too bad because I liked them. I guess I'll just have to think of ways to keep you all wet."

She smiled. "I have every confidence in your creativity."

"Your hair is beautiful because it's yours. It wouldn't matter to me how it looked. You might wish it looked different, more like it did before, and I understand that. But to me, every misbehaving wave is proof that you're still here. Same goes for the scars. You fought cancer and you won. They're like . . . badges of courage."

She pushed up on her elbow to study his face, her eyes soft. "You're a sentimental fool, aren't you?"

"Just telling the truth."

"We'll see how you feel come summer," she said with a yawn. "The humidity makes these 'badges of courage' so damn frizzy, I turn into Bozo the Clown."

She was already thinking about summer. His heart squeezed hard. The last time he'd planned more than a few weeks out with any woman had been Jo.

I'm happy. How long had it been since he'd thought those two words? Same answer. Not since Jo. *I'm holding on to this one. Nobody will take her away from me.* Not Beckett, not Doug, not Millhouse. Nobody.

He stroked her back until her breathing evened out and she fell asleep. Then he slid out from underneath her, covering her up. He pulled on his jeans and plucked his laptop from the floor.

On his screen were the results of the search he'd started for Wilson Beckett's death certificate before he and Daphne had gotten so pleasantly distracted.

But what the results said was that there was no death certificate for Wilson Beckett in the county or state records. He ran the search again, with the same result.

On one hand, this was no surprise, since Beckett wasn't dead. Any certificate in the system would have been a fake. But the lack of its existence in the official system raised a different set of questions—where had FBI Agent Claudia Baker obtained the proof of Beckett's death? And who'd created it to begin with? And if the death certificate didn't exist, did Agent Claudia Baker?

With a sigh, Joseph typed a quick e-mail to Bo asking him to request the service record of Special Agent Clau-

dia Baker, calling in favors if he had to. Joseph had requested it himself, but he didn't expect an answer till
morning. Bo should have connections that could access
personnel records twenty-four/seven. Crossing his fingers,
he hit SEND.

   I sure as hell hope Baker's real. Because if she wasn't . . .
it was going to get very hairy. Because they'd be right back
to the question of motive. Beckett faking his own death had
a clear payoff. But who would have motive to fake a federal
agent? And what the hell could that motive be?

Wheeling, West Virginia
Thursday, December 5, 12:30 a.m.

Joseph took his laptop into his own hotel room and quietly
closed the adjoining door before dialing Grayson on his
cell phone. It was answered on the first ring.

   "Joseph," Grayson said. "What's happened? How are
Daphne and Ford?"

   "Daphne's okay. Finally went to sleep. Ford's okay, physically. Deacon's with him. Daphne told Ford about Kim and
he was about like you'd expect. He shut down. Shut her out."

   "Poor kid. What's happening with the search for the girl
and the cabin?"

   "Called off for the night. It's snowing here."

   "Here, too. I could give you a full weather report, but I
don't think that's why you called," Grayson said dryly.

   "No. Where are you?"

   "Just leaving the hospital. I went to see Stevie."

   Something in his brother's voice gave him pause. "I
thought she was improving."

   "She is. They took out the breathing tube. But she's not
talking. She's not *not* talking, but she's not complaining or giving orders or anything. She seems depressed, which I guess
can be normal after an injury like this, but it's not like her."

   "Maynard wasn't there?"

   "No, he's with Paige at the wake for Zacharias. I'm on
my way over there now to pick her up. Why?" Suspicion
had sharpened Grayson's voice. "Why did you ask . . . No
way. Maynard and Stevie? No. Way. Really?"

   "He's got it bad, but it doesn't sound like she does. I'm
sure Paige can fill you in."

"Paige is a bit too discreet, I think. Luckily for me, J.D.'s a gossip."

Grayson's words were pointed and Joseph thought of the lipstick on his face before the video call. "If you wanted to know, you could have just asked."

"Fine. What's going on between you and Daphne?"

Joseph was suddenly glad this was not a video call because the stupidest grin had just overtaken his face. "It's good. Really good."

"Then I'm glad. I'm really glad. I've worried about you for too long."

"You can stop, because I've got more pressing things for you to help me think through." He filled Grayson in on Daphne's story and how Beckett had terrorized her by "popping up from time to time."

Grayson had grown very quiet, and when he spoke it was with deadly calm. "I hope that when you catch him, he tries to resist."

So that I can kill him. "I hear you. The bigger problem at the moment, though, is that there is at least one more victim and probably more in the almost thirty years between. I don't think their suffering has completely filtered through her mind yet." And when it did, it would devastate her beyond what Joseph was able to imagine. "For twenty years she's believed Beckett was dead, on the say-so of the FBI."

"Obviously somebody erred. But Daphne can't be held responsible for anything he's done. She tried to turn him in, and believed he was dead."

"She's more concerned about having to explain why she didn't say anything before she thought Beckett was dead."

Grayson's sigh was weary. "I wish I could say she's worried about nothing. I don't think anyone rational would blame her for what happened, but just having her name in the headlines could hamper her effectiveness in the courtroom. Instead of being the voice of the victims she represents, she'll become the story. It'll die down after a while, but it won't be easy while she's going through it."

"It gets worse," Joseph said, looking at his computer screen. "I can't find any death certificate on file for Wilson Beckett in West Virginia, yet Daphne says she's got a copy in her safety-deposit box."

"That's not good."

"I know. That's why I called you. I need help in thinking this through before I tell Daphne. She's been through enough. I'm certain she didn't lie about having the copy of the death cert. We have two options."

"Clerical error or somebody's fucking with her," Grayson said harshly.

"That sums it up pretty well. If it's a clerical error, it could just not have been entered into the online system. Still, there would have had to have been a body or a complicit coroner to provide the certificate. I talked with the woman who works in the police archives tonight and she seems to know her stuff. I'm hoping she'll know if one might have existed twenty years ago when Daphne requested it."

"Do you think it's a clerical error?"

"No. I think somebody wanted her to believe Beckett was dead."

"Who would want that? Beckett himself?"

"Maybe. She was getting older. By then she was living with the Elkharts. He didn't have proximity to 'pop up' and scare her anymore. He might have thought she'd get brave and report him. But if he falsified the death certificate, it means he knew she'd requested it."

"That holds true for whoever did it. Who else?"

"He's the only one whose motive makes any sense. And there's the question of how she got the document to begin with. She'd contacted the FBI to report Beckett and they told her he was dead. She wanted to be sure, so she mailed in a request to the state records department and ended up with two copies. One the FBI agent got for her and one that she received from the state through the mail about a month later. Now all this assumes that Agent Baker exists."

"You should request her personnel record."

"I did. After I heard Daphne's story, I requested her report on the investigation and for Baker to call me. Just now I sent a note to Bo, asking for her personnel record. Hopefully we'll know something by morning."

"How did she contact the FBI? Did she go to the office or call them on the phone?"

"Neither. She wrote them a letter."

"Why didn't she call?"

"I don't know. I'll ask her when she wakes up. I get the

impression that she was watched pretty closely by her mother-in-law, Nadine. Maybe she was worried her calls would be screened. If so, maybe her outgoing mail was, too. Anyone who knew she'd contacted the FBI is suspect. The only people she had contact with in those days were the Elkharts—Travis and his mother. The staff. Her own mother to a smaller extent. And Maggie, also to a smaller extent. I don't think Daphne got to see them often."

"I can't imagine the Elkharts would have appreciated Daphne's coming forward at that point. Huge scandal. I'm actually surprised the Elkharts allowed the marriage to happen at all. They had to have known what happened to her as a child. They would have done an extensive background check. I would have thought Travis would want a wife with no skeletons in her closet."

"The skeletons wouldn't have been easy to find. Daphne was only eight at the time and they'd moved to a different town. Her mother changed her name, too. She'd been Sinclair, but she went back to her maiden name when her husband left."

"Elkhart had the money to buy a damn good PI, Joseph. They would have left no stone unturned."

"The only people who knew the whole story before tonight were Maggie and the FBI agent, Claudia Baker. Even Maggie didn't know Beckett's name." He blew out a breath. "But Daphne did call the state death records office to ask about Beckett's death. If someone was monitoring her calls . . . Shit."

"They didn't even have to be monitoring her calls. They could have been inspecting her mail and seen the request for the death certificate. All they'd have to do is whip up a fake, make it look official. Daphne was only— How old was she?"

"Fifteen."

"Oh, Joseph, she was just a child herself. She wouldn't have known what to look for on a fake document."

Joseph didn't think Daphne had ever been just a child. "You could be right. But that would mean Agent Baker was involved. Again, assuming Agent Baker exists." Joseph checked his e-mail. He'd asked Bo's help in speeding things up only a short time ago, but miracles did happen, even in the world of the FBI.

"Who else knew about Beckett, Joseph? You said Maggie knew. How?"

"Maggie knew about Beckett, but not his name. Maggie did therapy with Daphne, letting her take care of the horses." Then Joseph went still as he heard Daphne's voice in his head.

I'd whisper my secrets in her ear. Daphne had told Lulu the horse all about her agony. And then Maggie's voice. *She did what she always does when she's upset. She went to the barn.* Had a fifteen-year-old Daphne whispered her troubles to one of the Elkharts' horses? And who had overheard?

"Shit," he muttered. "Daphne still takes care of the horses when she's upset. She said she whispered her troubles in their ears. The Elkharts have a stable on the grounds." He knew this because Maggie had told him that Scott Cooper had been the Elkharts' groom before he'd started his own business coaching kids to jump.

"If Travis had a PI following her, he could have overheard Maggie tell her story, maybe even say Beckett's name."

"Or Scott Cooper could have overheard. He lost his business because Travis accused Daphne of having an affair with him." He told Grayson the story Maggie had told him that morning. "His wife left him and he had nothing. Had to depend on Daphne until he got his business back up and running."

"Could make a guy resentful," Grayson said. "You want me to check him out?"

"If you would. Also check Elkhart's former head of security, Hal Lynch. He was there from the beginning, from the night she met the prick. If someone hired a PI for a background check, it probably went through him."

"You met him, too?"

"Yes," Joseph said. "But neither of those guys is Doug. Doug's twenty-nine. Cooper's a good fifty and Hal's pushing sixty."

"And Doug would have only been a kid himself when Daphne requested that death certificate. Nine years old."

Joseph thought hard, abruptly ceasing his pacing. "Cooper has a son. He said the son could help him move Daphne's horses to a barn on his property."

"Cooper's got property up by Daphne's farm? That is

pricey real estate. Starts in the six figures and goes up fast. I thought you said he had nothing."

"That's what Maggie said." A dark suspicion crossed Joseph's mind and he shook it away. "I don't want to believe Maggie would be involved in anything to hurt Daphne, but almost everything I know came from her."

"I can check her out, too, if you want. But we know she's not Doug."

"True. And she could have harmed Daphne long ago if she'd really wanted to. Damn. I'm so twisted up in my mind that I'm suspecting sweet old ladies. It's making me crazy, knowing Doug's out there, gunning for Daphne, and I don't even have his face. And not even his whole name."

"He's careful. He hasn't left a print anywhere so far."

"He leaves prints," Joseph grumbled. "Just not where we know to look for them."

Grayson yawned. "Go get some sleep, Joseph. You'll be able to think better when you're rested. I'm at Zacharias's house and it looks like this wake is breaking up. I'm going in to get Paige and go home and practice what I preach."

"I can't sleep yet. I've got to let the locals know what I found on Beckett. Thanks, Gray. I appreciate it."

"You know you can call me at any time. I'm always there for you. And Daphne. She's a good woman, Joseph. Makes damn good muffins."

Joseph thought about her muffins. "Yeah, I know."

"And, ah, we're probably not talking the same kind of muffins."

Joseph laughed. "We'd better not be. I wouldn't need to kick your ass. Paige would have it all pre-kicked for me."

He hung up and slipped into Daphne's room to get his briefcase. Once there, he couldn't resist the urge to stand at her bedside and watch her, just for a moment. Or two. She slept deeply, her brow uncreased. She wasn't dreaming, for now.

He made sure she was covered up and crept back into his own room, closing the adjoining door behind him, even though he really wanted to climb under the blanket with her. To hold her and . . . be happy.

He would. Once he made sure she was safe. He rummaged through his papers and found contact information for McManus and Kerr.

He got McManus's voice mail, but Kerr answered. Turned out the Pittsburgh Fed had come to the same conclusions that Joseph had. Kerr had also put in a request for information on Agent Claudia Baker. Whoever got the info first would call the others.

With no more that could be done till morning, Joseph was ready to crawl back into bed with Daphne when he saw the big black dog still stretched across her door.

He grabbed her leash. "Tasha, let's go outside." He hoped the dog remembered him—specifically he hoped the dog remembered that she liked him. When she didn't take a bite out of his hand, Joseph figured he was safe.

Out in the hall he tapped on Hector's door. And blinked when Kate Coppola answered. "Don't even think it," she warned. "We're sharing out of necessity."

Joseph looked over her shoulder to see Hector sprawled on the sofa, a can of cola in one hand and a slice of pizza in the other.

"What necessity?" Joseph asked.

"Simone and Maggie had a fight. Simone wanted to get her own room, but the only vacancies were on other floors. I told Simone to take my room. Therefore, necessity."

"Why did they fight?"

"I only caught the tail end of it, after Simone broke a music box."

"Why did she have one of those?"

"I'm not sure, but I know I heard the melody last night when Simone had nightmares and Maggie tried to get her to go back to sleep. I'm guessing it's a sleep aid."

"How did she break it? Tell me she didn't throw it."

"No. She threw a pillow that knocked it off the dresser. I came in to find Simone snarling at Maggie, who was trying to help her pick up the pieces. She said she'd had enough of Maggie's help for a lifetime. I gathered that up to that point the fight was about Daphne. Simone said 'betrayal.' A lot. That's all I know."

"I can guess. Maggie's known about Beckett, almost since the beginning."

Kate winced. "And she didn't tell Simone?"

"Maggie was acting in a therapist role. Daphne made her promise not to tell. Daphne was afraid that if her mother knew, she'd go after Beckett."

"And then Beckett would kill her." Kate's mouth bent sympathetically. "Finding out after all this time that Maggie knew would cause a rift. I'm staying out of that one."

"Wise. I actually knocked to see if Hector would keep an eye on Daphne while I walk the dog, but now that I'm standing here that pizza smells really good."

"You might as well come on in and join us," Hector called from the sofa. "We're expensing it to your budget."

Let's see . . . eating a relaxed meal or crawling back under the covers with Daphne?

"I'm beat. I think I'll take a slice to eat while I walk the dog, then call it a night."

Hector came to the door, a slice in his hand and a look of knowing amusement on his face. "I kind of thought you'd say that. Eat up, boss. You never know when you'll need that sudden burst of energy."

Kate bit back a smile and Joseph knew his jig was up.

"Thanks," Joseph said, taking the slice with as much dignity as he could muster. "Status meeting in my room tomorrow morning at seven. Don't be late. Good night."

But when he got to the elevator, Joseph let himself grin.

Twenty-three

The screaming woke her up. On a sharp indrawn breath Daphne's eyes flew open, her body going rigid in the bed. And she listened. To nothing.

Slowly she exhaled. Just the nightmare. She'd expected it. After everything that had happened yesterday, how could she not?

A strong arm curved around her waist, pulling her against a warm, hard body. *Joseph.* His hand slipped up under her nightshirt, cupping her breast gently but possessively.

"I'm here," he murmured. "You're safe."

"I know." *Now.* "It was just a dream."

"Same one you had last night?"

"Yeah."

He pressed his lips to the side of her neck, not kissing, just firm contact. "Tell me."

"It's just screaming."

"Kelly?"

"Sometimes. Sometimes it's me. I run and I run and I can't breathe. And there's a hole . . . in the floor. I always stop in time. But the hole is dark. I know something evil is there. And I back away from the hole. But he comes and pushes me in."

His arm tightened around her. "And then?"

"I wake up. I guess it's not exactly subtle on the symbolism. I never scream out loud, at least not that I know of. I kept thinking I'd grow out of it, that I'd move past it, but I never have. I mean, it wasn't like I even saw anything. I just heard it. But I can't forget the screams. And the nightmare never goes away."

He was quiet for a long time. Only the fine tension in his body told her he wasn't asleep. "I know."

His voice had gone hollow. Haunted.

Daphne turned in his arms, looked up into his face. His jaw was taut, his eyes open but unblinking. Staring straight ahead. At nothing at all.

"Tell me," she murmured, laying her hand against his jaw. "What do you know?"

He blinked then, looking down at her, pain in his dark eyes. "I know what it's like to hear the screams and not be able to make them stop."

"You heard Jo scream?" she asked, very quietly.

He nodded. "They wanted a ransom. Thought my family needed incentive."

Oh no, she thought, fearing what had made his wife scream. "What happened?"

He said nothing, rolling to his back and tucking her up against him. His fingers were in her hair, his palm cradling her head. She spread her hand over his heart and let him hold her, cocooned against him. And she waited.

"She wanted a big wedding," he finally said. "I just wanted my ring on her finger. We were both still deployed, but her unit had been assigned to another ship. I guess I felt making it official would make it more real. So we compromised. We'd have a civil ceremony with a military chaplain, take leave for a short honeymoon, then do the big church wedding when we both got home."

"Where did you go?"

"Paris. In the end it wouldn't have mattered where we went. She'd been a target for a long time."

"Because she was a pilot?"

His chest moved in a single bitter huff. "Because she was mine. And I was rich. And so damn naive I thought nobody knew it."

She thought about what he'd said the night before, about wanting to be his own man. About getting into the Academy on his own. "You didn't tell anyone about your family."

"No. I wanted people to respect me . . . to like me for myself. Not because I was my father's son. But it turned out quite a few people on the ship knew I was my father's son, that I had millions at my disposal. One of them, an ensign, wanted a few of those millions. He knew I was going on leave because he worked in the admin office, processing the requests. He knew Jo was, too."

"What did he do?"

"Hired some pals from the States to be there when we got to Paris. We had three days together and it was . . . beautiful. I'd hired a car to take us back to the airport and that's where everything unraveled. The ensign had a driver waiting in the lobby. He'd canceled the reservation I'd made weeks earlier. So the car that picked us up at the hotel pulled off an exit halfway to the airport, overpowered us, drugged us, and the next thing I knew I was waking up in the dark. Jo was in another room, screaming. Begging for help. For me. But I was tied up and couldn't get to her. I have never felt so helpless."

"I know." She had to force the words from her throat.

"I know you do. One of the kidnappers shoved a phone to my ear, told me to talk to my father, tell him to get the money to them fast and not to contact the police. Dad got on a plane with the cash. He also contacted the Parisian police. One of the kidnappers went to get the money, the other stayed to guard us. I'd been working the rope they used to tie me ever since I'd woken up and had made a little progress, when the one who'd stayed behind got a call. When he hung up he told Jo that they'd gotten their money, but that he'd have 'one last go' for the road. He started again and I . . . lost it. Just raw rage."

She didn't know what to say. What to do for him. She'd been a terrified child. He been an adult, Jo the woman he'd loved. "What did you do?" she whispered, horrified.

"I clawed at the rope until finally I could rip my hands free. It took the top layers of skin off my hands, but I didn't even feel it. Not then anyway. I got the ropes off my ankles and charged. But I was too late. He'd . . . finished and was dressed. I don't know if he'd ever gotten completely undressed. He hadn't completely undressed Jo. She was still wearing her blouse, but that was all. I remember that. It was white, or it had started out that way. When I got to him, he had his gun pointed at her. He saw me and went pale. I threw myself at her, over her, but he'd hurried up and pulled the trigger, trying to kill her first. I guess he didn't want to fight us both at the same time. He shot her in the chest."

She remembered his panic on the courthouse steps. He thought she'd been shot, had been on the verge of ripping her shirt off to get to her wounds before Grayson had made him understand that she was wearing Kevlar, that the blood on her white blouse wasn't her own.

He'd been reliving that moment with Jo. *Oh, Joseph.* "I'm so sorry."

He held her tight, so tight she could barely breathe. "She was bleeding, a lot. And then he shot me. I barely felt it. I was . . . beyond pain. I surged up, grabbed him and took the gun."

The air seemed to seep out of his lungs and he lay there, very still. And something changed. His arms still wrapped around her, but all the previous need was gone. She felt him pulling away from her, even though he never physically moved an inch.

She remembered the commander's conference room when she'd thought Ford was dead. She'd asked him if the men who'd taken his wife were alive and he'd said no. So coldly. She lifted her head, resting her forearms on his chest. His expression was shuttered. Wherever he'd gone, he didn't want her there with him.

Which was too damn bad.

"What did you do to him?" she asked, her voice low.

He closed his eyes. "I'm tired. Let's go to sleep."

"Pffft." The sound she made was one of derision. "I don't think so, sugar."

His jaw tightened. "Please." His voice was even. Reasonable. "Go to sleep."

"Joseph, I'm not getting any younger, so I'll be blunt. You said you wanted a relationship. And so do I. But I don't do threesomes."

His eyes flew open. "Excuse me?"

"Right now there are three people in this bed. You, me, and whoever the sonofabitch was that you killed that day. If you shut me out now . . ." She trailed off, knowing a threat would damage what they hadn't even started to build.

Which was exactly what Joseph would be doing with his silence.

She kissed his mouth, felt him stiffen in surprise, and realized he'd hoped to make her so angry that she'd roll over and go to sleep. He didn't know her very well. Yet.

"Joseph, I've told you my worst secrets. If you shut me out now, you'll hold power over me, and I'll have none over you. I lived that life for twelve years as Mrs. Travis Elkhart. I am *so* not going down that road with you."

He met her eyes then, and she saw misery. "How do you know I killed him?"

"Because you told me the men who took your wife were no longer alive."

"I have a big mouth," he said grimly.

She kissed that mouth, traced his lower lip with her fingertip. "What did you do?"

His shoulders tensed. All of him tensed, the facade of calm he'd projected suddenly gone. "We fought. He was strong. But I was . . . wild. I broke his neck. Snapped it. Like a twig. I can still hear that sound to this day." He swallowed hard. "It still brings me satisfaction."

His eyes grew piercing and he seemed to hover over the statement, waiting.

She cupped his tight jaw, felt the muscle twitch under her palm. "If he'd overpowered you, what would he have done?"

"The same damn thing."

"Then there you go. Eat or be eaten. I, for one, am very glad you won. You survived."

He stilled once again. "I didn't even care about survival at that moment, Daphne. I just wanted him dead."

He'd used her name for the first time since starting his story. He was back with her. Re-engaged. Relief shivered down her back. She considered her answer carefully, knowing it was an important one. And that he held his breath, waiting for it.

"Joseph, if you're waiting for me to condemn you for wanting him dead, you'll be waiting a long time. If you're waiting for me to be horrified that hearing that snap still brings you satisfaction, you'll be waiting even longer. He hurt your wife in unspeakable ways. He killed her. For money. That he paid for his evil with his life . . . that's justice."

His eyes flickered, his throat worked as he swallowed, but he said nothing.

"The satisfaction . . ." She shrugged. "I'd label it 'comfort.' I envy you, in a way. You got the closure most victims can only dream about. And whether you accept it or not, you were fighting to survive. It's a basic instinct. It's only after the fact that we question our motives. You killed him before he killed you. End of story. If I were in your shoes, I'd consider the satisfaction at the neck-snapping memory as a gift."

He closed his eyes. "I never thought about it that way."

"Well, you should. What happened after that?"

"I found a phone. Called for help, hoped the police could trace our location, because I didn't know where we were. I went back to Jo, tried to stop her bleeding but I couldn't, so I just held her. She stopped breathing, but I couldn't let her go. I just held her as her blood drained away and there wasn't anything I could do."

"Oh, Joseph." Her lips trembled.

"I don't know how long I sat there, but I heard a noise. The second guy had come back for the first, taken one look at the scene and charged me, his gun drawn. He fired, twice. Hit me once. I tackled him before he could fire again and we fought for his gun. I grabbed his hand, got control of the gun." He paused. And sighed. "I could have thrown the gun away but I didn't. I forced his hand so that he jammed the barrel into his own gut. And I made him squeeze the trigger. Just as the cops burst in."

"What did they see?"

"Me, fighting for my life."

"Which you were, Joseph."

"Not really."

"I'll ask again. If he'd won the fight, what would he have done? Left you alive to identify him?"

"No."

"Then you did what you had to."

"I could have held him off till the cops came."

"Did you know they were coming at that moment?"

His eyes flickered. The notion surprised him. "No," he murmured. "I didn't."

"You were wounded, too. Bleeding, right?"

Again the flicker. "Yes."

"How long were you in the hospital afterward?"

"Two weeks."

"Because your injuries were that bad. So could you really have held him off for long? And if he wrested control of the gun away from you, what would he have done to you?" She gave him a moment to consider it before answering the question herself. "He would have finished the job. You'd seen him. He had the money with him. He wasn't going to let you live from the beginning, Joseph."

"You make it sound so simple."

"Because it is. You're making this harder than it needs to be."

His brow furrowed slightly. "Someone else said that to me recently. Someone smarter than me." He reached up, smoothed the hair away from her face. "I wasn't fighting for my life that day, Daphne, no matter what you think. I was fighting for their deaths, because at that moment my life was gone. Holding Jo as she died . . . It was like my life drained away with hers. I didn't care about living for a long, long time after that. Everything was dark. All the color was gone. If I hadn't had my family and my job . . ."

"Finding other people's missing loved ones?"

"It gave me a reason to want to wake up in the morning. And little by little the darkness faded." One side of his mouth lifted. "To sepia, maybe. But there was never color. Until one day . . ."

His eyes were on hers and she knew this was one of those moments she'd carry with her always. She held her breath, waiting for it. "One day?" she whispered.

"One day I looked up and saw this . . . goddess walking up to my brother's front door in a lime green suit and legs up to her shoulders. And it was like I'd just been dropped from Kansas into Oz. Brilliant, bold color where there had been none. Warmth when I'd been so cold. My heart . . . started beating again."

Her heart stuttered, her eyes filling. "Joseph."

He tugged her head down until she covered his mouth with hers. The kiss was lush and utterly lovely. "How many people are in this bed now, Daphne?"

"Just you and me."

"Good. Then let's go to sleep. Just you and me. No more nightmares tonight."

Baltimore, Maryland
Thursday, December 5, 6:00 a.m.

Cole woke slowly, his neck so stiff that he winced. The floor was hard and cold and he hadn't slept more than an hour at a time all night because Kimberly wouldn't shut the hell up. Finally, out of self-preservation, he'd duct-taped her mouth shut.

He sat up, rubbing his neck. Checked his cell phone for the time. School started in an hour and a half. The cops would probably be waiting at the school for him to show up so they could arrest him. When he didn't show up, they'd come back here.

He couldn't wait on Matt's all clear any longer. He forced himself to stand up, then looked around for a toilet. Damn but if the shelter didn't have one. He found it in the back corner behind a curtain—a camping toilet that looked brand-new. *Mitch* would *have thought of this.* His oldest brother had a plan for everything.

When he came out, Kimberly was giving him the evil eye. He removed the tape from her mouth, careful to keep his fingers away from her teeth.

"Water." She was croaky again and he felt a little bad that he'd made her go without water all night. He gave her a few sips, then pulled the blanket off her.

"Come on," he said. "Let's go."

"I need to go, too. Really bad."

Cole hesitated. "I'm not untying your hands."

She gave him a weary look. "I weigh a hundred five pounds, probably less since your asshole brother's been starving me to death. You're what, like two hundred? Like I can be a threat to you."

One sixty-five actually, but hearing he looked bigger was nice for his ego. "I don't know . . ."

She huffed angrily. "Come on, kid. Use your brain. I can't take you. Let me pee and then tie me back up if you want. I just want to get to my sister."

Cole didn't want her sister to die. And she couldn't take him. She was too tiny. "Okay, fine. But when you're done, I tie you back up."

"Whatever."

He untied her, taking care to stay away from her feet.

"Hurry up." He watched her limp to the toilet, dragging her hurt leg behind her. His brother had done that to her. He still didn't believe it.

Mitch, what the hell are you doing? And where are you? For that matter, where was Matt? It wasn't like Matt to just not show up.

This was really bad. He'd taken a stolen gun to school. Stolen from a cop, if Kimberly was telling the truth. *If it gets traced back to me . . .* The cops would never believe he wasn't part of whatever Mitch had going. Whatever the hell that was.

I am so tired of this family. I wish I was adopted.

Kimberly came out of the toilet, her limp more pronounced. "I need to rebandage my leg. It started bleeding again while I was in there."

"Fine, just hurry."

She hobbled back to the bed and grabbed the roll of gauze that sat on the floor beside it. She started to unbutton her jeans, then stopped, glaring. "Do you mind?"

Rolling his eyes, he turned his back. He needed to get out of here and to the bus station. He'd call Rico in Miami and tell him he was going to be a little late, and—

Cole groaned, the pain in his head worse than anything he'd ever felt. He sat up, the room doing a slow spin that left him nauseated. *The bitch.* She'd hit him with something. He blinked hard until the room came back into focus. A fire extinguisher lay on the floor on its side. Cole vaguely remembered seeing it on the wall by the toilet.

I'm a stupid idiot. He staggered to his feet, wondering how long he'd been out. He patted his pockets for his cell to check the time—and found his pockets empty. She'd cleaned him out. And stolen his backpack.

He ran for the stairs and sighed with relief when he got to the garage. The van was still here. She had to be on foot and she couldn't go far with her leg messed up. He thought of the little room in the basement. Her sister was probably in there.

He looked around the garage for a weapon, because a hundred five pounds or not, the girl was fucking dangerous. *I shouldn't have listened to a word she said.*

Weapon, weapon, what can I use? He scanned the shelves, everything neat as a pin, the way Mitch demanded.

Shovel. *I'll use a shovel.* He ran to the wall where all the garden tools were arranged on a pegboard.

The big empty space where the shovel had been registered in his mind a second before he heard the grunt behind him, then felt the blow crash into his head. He turned, his legs weak and the room spinning. He felt himself falling, his knees cracking as they hit the concrete floor.

The sight of the shovel coming at his face was the last thing he saw before everything went dark.

Wheeling, West Virginia
Thursday, December 5, 6:00 a.m.

Joseph inhaled deeply as he came awake in stages.

Peaches. Warm body curled against him. *Mmm.* Curvy warm body. Pretty hand resting over his heart. Long leg buttressing his hip. Curls tickling his jaw.

He'd always felt envious of men who woke with soft women in their arms who were meant for only them. Now he didn't have to. *Because I've got one.*

He hadn't wanted to tell her about Jo. About what he'd done. But he was glad, so damn glad, that he had. Many people knew the play-by-play of his story. Anyone who was fluent in French could read the police report, he supposed. His family knew, even Holly. And he knew they'd been afraid for his sanity those first few years. He knew they worried about his temper sometimes.

He'd never told anyone that he still heard the snap of that man's neck. That it still brought him . . . comfort. He liked that word a lot better. He kissed the top of her head and slid from the bed, reluctantly. He wished he could stay. Wake her with slow kisses and make love to her for hours.

But he had a job to do and so did she. He needed to find three still-missing girls—Kimberly, her sister, and Heather Lipton—assuming any of them were still alive. He needed to bring Doug and Beckett to justice. But he had to find them first.

She needed to confront a past over which she'd had no control. When they found Beckett's cabin—and Joseph had no doubt that they would because Doug was driving them in that direction—she'd insist on being there, no matter how much it hurt her. And even though every bit of him screamed in protest at the very idea of letting her go there, he knew he couldn't keep her from doing so. Nor should he.

She was a grown woman, smart and logical, and the decisions she made would be wise ones. Necessary ones. He just needed to keep her safe through the process.

He wasn't sure which of them had the harder job.

Joseph snapped a leash on Tasha, then left Daphne's room, quietly pulling the door closed behind him. And then he froze as Simone came out her own door, across the hall. Their eyes collided and Joseph felt his cheeks heat. *Busted,* was his first thought.

"Good morning," he said quietly.

She studied him for a long moment. "Good morning, Joseph. Is she all right?"

"Yes." *She's more than all right. She's amazing.* "Yesterday was a hard day."

"For all of us," Simone said and he could see she was still angry. On one hand, he didn't blame her. But as Daphne's . . .

What am I? he wondered. "Boyfriend" sounded way too juvenile. Lover? Yes, but that didn't begin to describe what he felt. Suddenly he heard Daphne's voice in his mind from the day before, as they'd driven through the mountains. *You want a mate. So do I.* Warmth curled around his heart. He liked that. Very much.

As Daphne's *mate*, her welfare was at the top of his agenda. Daphne's welfare would be improved if her mother could forgive what had never been intended as a slight.

"May I offer my opinion as an outsider, Simone?"

She lifted a shoulder. "Doesn't seem like you're an outsider anymore."

"Then I'll take that as a yes. You're angry and you have a right to be. But seems to me that the person you need to be angry with is Beckett. Not Daphne and not Maggie."

She closed her eyes briefly. "I understand why Daphne didn't tell me, but Maggie wasn't a scared little girl. She should have told me."

"I don't know about that. I think that Daphne's having someone she could trust with her pain, someone she didn't think she was hurting in the process . . . it made a difference. And kids know when you betray their trust. If Maggie had told you, Daphne might never have opened up again. And particularly not to you. Not because she didn't trust you or love you. But in telling you, she would have hurt you. That would have pushed her deeper into herself. You might never have gotten her back."

"I'm her mother," Simone said stubbornly. "I should have known. I could have helped her." Then her eyes filled. "You think I was unaware of her pain? I knew. Every god-damn day I knew she was in pain, but I never knew how to help. Maggie knew. She kept that from me. She kept me from taking care of my own child. Do you have any idea how that feels?"

"No, because I'm not a parent. I would never discount your pain. But at the same time, don't discount how difficult this was for Maggie."

Simone made a rough, scoffing sound in her throat and Joseph frowned.

"Simone, don't you think she always knew this day would come? That she dreaded it? She loves you both. Last night you heard Daphne's pain and it nearly tore you apart. But last night it was only an echo of what it was twenty-seven years ago. What do you think it was like for Maggie, to hear it fresh and not have anyone she could share it with? She's carried a heavy burden all these years. And I think, even knowing how angry this has made you, she'd do it again the same way. For your daughter."

"She could have shared it with *me*. She didn't have to bear it alone. She had no *right* to." Her voice rang with con-viction. He wasn't getting through.

He mentally backed up, came at it from another angle. "My dad taught me to drive."

She blinked. "What?"

"Yeah. I was a hothead when I was a teenager and not about to let anyone push me around. I remember sitting at a four-way stop. Another driver took my right-of-way and I wasn't going to have it. I put my foot on the gas and went through the intersection. Next thing I knew, I was in the ER getting stitches and my dad's car was totaled."

"And the point of this is?"

He smiled at her, gently. "I'm getting there. My father wasn't happy, especially when I tried to defend myself. I was in the right, the other guy in the wrong. Dad got real quiet and told me I could be right, but I could be dead right.

You had the right to know, Simone. But you could have been dead right. And where would that have left your daughter?"

She faltered. "I don't understand."

"Beckett has killed to keep his secret. He killed your niece. Just last night he nearly killed a nurse at the hospital, just to steal his ID so he could sneak inside. We found that young man just in time. Beckett was smothering your grandson with a pillow when Daphne walked in on him, and he stabbed the officer standing guard outside Ford's door. God only knows how many he's killed in the past twenty-seven years. He threatened to kill *you* if she told. He threatened her with that over and over again. Your daughter may have saved your life by keeping this secret. So be mad if you want, but be mad at the right person."

"Daphne didn't tell me about the nurse," she said, as if that one fact was enough to tilt the scales toward belief from disbelief. Sometimes it worked like that, that one detail tipped the balance one way or the other.

"I think she was pretty overwhelmed at the time. I don't think a lot of this has sunk in. It may not for weeks."

"But when it does, you'll be there for her?"

"I promise." *Because I'm her mate.* He knew it as clearly as his own name.

"Thank you," she said hoarsely.

"Don't thank me for that. It's the smallest thing I can do for her. Simone, you've had a terrible shock and it probably hasn't sunk in with you, either. But Daphne's in a different position."

"She's still in danger."

"Yes, but we'll find Beckett and we'll find Doug." He knew that as clearly as his own name, too. He wouldn't let Daphne go through life looking over her shoulder in fear. "I'm talking about her career. Everything she's worked so hard for. This will all come out and even though she was a victim in all of it, people will ask why she didn't turn Beckett in earlier."

"It's nobody's business," Simone said fiercely.

"No, but she's a prosecutor. She expects victims to come forward, to testify. That she didn't . . . nobody will blame her per se, but as Grayson told me last night, she'll become the story in the courtroom. It'll die down eventually, but she's going to need all of us around her, supporting her until it does. She's going to need you *and* Maggie. She loves you both."

Her shoulders sagged. "You're saying I have to let my anger go for her own good."

He shrugged. "You *are* her mother. Isn't that what mothers do?"

She regarded him for a long, long moment. "You, Joseph Carter, are damn good."

He smiled. "I know. Now, I'm going downstairs to walk Tasha and get coffee. Can I bring you anything?"

"Coffee would be nice. But I'll walk with you. I could use the exer . . ."

She trailed off as the door next to her opened and Maggie came out, a music box in one hand and a small suitcase in the other. She stopped short when she saw them, her expression carefully blank. "Joseph, Simone."

"Where are you going?" Simone asked, pointing at the suitcase.

"Home."

Joseph frowned. "Maggie, the farm's a crime scene. You can't stay there."

"Not Daphne's farm. My farm. I'm going home."

"To Riverdale?" Simone's face fell. "No. You can't."

"I can and I should and I'm long overdue. I meant to stay with you two for eight weeks and it turned into eight years. I miss my own place." She drew her shoulders back. "It's time I went home. I've already talked to Scott. He'll take care of the horses until you find another hired hand."

Simone's mouth fell open. "You're . . . you're not a hired hand. Maggie . . ."

Maggie looked down, then back up again. "That's not what you said last night."

Joseph couldn't control a wince. *Ouch.*

Simone let out a ragged breath. "Maggie, I'm sorry. I said a lot of things I shouldn't have. I was wrong. Please don't go."

"No, you were right. I kept important information from you. You had every right to be angry. Maybe not to express it like you did, but that is what it is. I left my farm eight years ago because Daphne needed me. She doesn't need me anymore. She's got you and Ford. Grayson and Paige and Clay. And now Joseph." She extended the hand that held the music box. "The desk downstairs had some Super Glue. It's not exactly like it was before, but it was the best I could do."

"Maggie . . . I know I said some terrible things and I can't take them back. But we've got twenty-seven years of friendship." She swallowed hard. "We've seen each other through a lot, good times and bad. And we . . . we raised an amazing woman together, Maggie. You and I. And she does still need you. She's going to need both of us because this nightmare is far from over for her. Please stay, for just a little longer."

Maggie hesitated. "I don't know."

Simone took a few tentative steps toward her. "You gave my daughter back her voice and for that I owe you a debt of gratitude. But you gave *me* friendship when I was all alone." Sadly she took the music box from Maggie's hand. "Daphne gave this to me for Mother's Day, the first one after Michael left us. You'd taken her to one of those pottery places where she got to paint it, and they glazed and fired it."

"I remember."

"It plays 'Edelweiss.'"

"From the movie. *The Sound of Music*." Maggie glanced at Joseph. "Her favorite."

Simone shook her head. "She doesn't love the song because of the movie. She loves the movie because of the song. Her father used to sing it to us, on the front porch at night when it was time for her to go to sleep. It was her lullaby."

"I never knew that," Maggie said quietly.

"I know. It hurt too much to say out loud. The day she gave it to me, it was hard to not break down in tears, right in front of her. She looked so hopeful that I'd like it, then so disappointed when I didn't. But I couldn't play it, not for weeks after. One day I came into my bedroom to find her sitting on my bed, holding the music box to her ear. She shut it off quickly, like she knew it hurt me." Simone sighed. "And she spoke her first words in eight months. 'It wasn't Daddy.' Then she ran to the barn. I had no idea that she blamed herself for Michael's leaving because I was too busy blaming myself."

Maggie's eyes filled. "Oh, Simone."

"After that I made it a point to play it every night. Because I wanted her to know I didn't blame her. That I was all right. Now I can't go to sleep without it."

"It still plays," Maggie said hoarsely. "The box is cracked, but it plays."

"Last night I thought it was a goner." Simone wound it up, smiling sadly as the tune tinkled out. "Amazing what a little Super Glue can do." She met Maggie's eyes. "I know I said some terrible things to you and although I would do anything to take them back, you can't unring a bell. I just hope I haven't broken us beyond repair."

Maggie shook her head. "No. You haven't."

Joseph found his eyes stinging as Maggie dropped her suitcase and the two women embraced. And then his eyes focused on the music box. The broken pieces had been lined up precisely, the cracks barely visible.

Amazing what a little Super Glue can do. He frowned, then went still. *Super Glue.*

"Oh my God," he breathed. He laughed aloud. "Oh fucking hell."

The women turned to stare at him, faces puzzled and mildly disapproving, but he barely noticed. He had his phone out, dialing Dr. Brodie. "Come on, wake up."

"Joseph?" Brodie sounded sleepy. "Meeting's not till seven, right?"

"Right, but this can't wait." His heart was racing. "We need to get your techs back to that drugstore. The one that tried to card Doug."

"We tried to get the surveillance video, Joseph. I told you they'd taped over it."

"Did you get the Super Glue?"

"What?" There was a long pause. "No. We didn't. We should have, but we didn't."

"He wasn't selling weapons to the Millhouses. He was just being a normal guy, buying school supplies for his brother. Maybe his guard was down. He could have left a print on the package."

"I'll get right on it. It's a twenty-four-hour store. I'll get a uniform out there to watch the shelf until my techs can get there. It's a long shot, but worth a try. I'll let you know as soon as I have something."

Hanging up, Joseph smacked a kiss on Simone's cheek,
then Maggie's. "Wish me luck." He left them staring, and
was still grinning when he got outside with Tasha, despite
the fact that it was snowing again and he'd left his coat in
the hotel room. His cell rang and he answered it with near
euphoria. "This is Agent Carter."

"Joseph, it's Bo."

"Did Brodie call you already?"

"About what?"

Joseph told him about the Super Glue, fighting the urge
to dance.

"That's great," Bo said, but he didn't sound enthused.

"What's wrong? How did the raid on Antonov's warehouse go?"

"Not well. It was empty when we got there. They'd just
moved hundreds of crates. Bomb dogs found traces of ammunition, but no actual evidence."

"Damn. I'm sorry, Bo."

"Me, too. Antonov has been on ATF radar for months.
Stopping him would have kept Russian organized crime
from getting a toehold in the area, but now we're back to
square one. But that's not why I called."

"Then why?" Joseph's mind clicked. "Oh. Yeah. Sorry. I
haven't had coffee yet. I sent you an e-mail last night, asking for Agent Claudia Baker's info. You got anything?"

"Yeah. She doesn't exist. She never did. The Bureau has
no record of a Special Agent Claudia Baker, in the DC field
office or anywhere else."

"Shit," Joseph snarled. "I was afraid of that."

"Are you sure Daphne wasn't mistaken?"

"As sure as I can be considering I wasn't actually at their
meeting twenty years ago. Did you check married and
maiden names?"

"I checked everything. I've been working it for hours.
We need to talk to Daphne, because assuming she really
did talk to someone, it wasn't an FBI agent."

Assuming? "She's not lying, Bo. Somebody lied to her."

"And you weren't there twenty years ago, Joseph. Playing
devil's advocate, it wouldn't look good for her to have kept
that information secret all these years. She's a prosecutor
now. She might have found herself grasping for an out."

Joseph's temper rattled its chains. "I'll talk to her. Find

out exactly how and where she met this alleged agent. I'll have her sit with a sketch artist if necessary. Because whoever was pretending to be Claudia Baker stopped her from reporting a murder."

"Why would anyone want to do that?"

"I don't know. I do know she was living with the Elkharts at the time. If they found out her plans, they might have feared she was going to cause a scandal. Most rich families don't like scandal, especially if they have political aspirations. Travis Elkhart is a judge—that wouldn't have looked good for him."

"He wasn't a judge then."

"Maybe he already wanted to be. I don't know. I can stand here speculating all day long but it won't get us any closer to the truth, plus I'm standing outside freezing my ass off. We're having a status meeting at seven. Should I patch you in?"

"Yes. I'd like to hear Daphne's story for myself. Be careful, Joseph. You might think you know this woman, but remember you weren't there. You can't know."

"I'll talk to you at seven," Joseph said, grimly reentering the hotel. He took the stairs, needing the mild burn of a seven-flight run to cool his temper and figuring it'd be a good workout for the dog as well.

When he came out of the stairwell into the hall the first thing he heard was a bloodcurdling scream coming from down the hall. *Daphne.*

Joseph started to run, passing a few hotel guests who'd opened their doors to investigate. Another, louder scream met his ears as he reached Daphne's room. It was coming from inside. *Oh, God. I shouldn't have left her alone.*

Twenty-four

The screaming woke her. Daphne's eyes flew open and she sat up in bed, breathing hard. Her throat was raw.

That was new. Her throat had never been raw before. She lifted her hand to her throat, trying to control her breathing. The bed was empty. Joseph was gone.

And then the door flew open and there he was, weapon drawn, shouting her name, and she clapped her hand over her mouth to muffle her shriek.

Joseph ran through both rooms, checking every closet, the shower. Under her bed. Through it all she sat motionless in the bed, the blankets tangled around her legs.

"Joseph? Everything okay in there?" Deacon Novak's voice spurred her to action and she jerked the covers up to her chin.

Joseph sprang up from checking under the bed, poised on the balls of his feet. Slowly he turned and stared at her. "What happened?" he panted.

"I don't know." She coughed, her throat dry as dust. "Should I assume that I screamed out loud this time?"

"Did you ever." Deacon stood in the doorway looking rattled, his white hair askew, like he'd been sleeping. "If everything's okay, I'll get out of here until seven."

"We're all right," Joseph said. "Thanks."

"Wait," Daphne said. "If you're here, Agent Novak, who's with Ford?"

"Hector. We switched places so I could sleep. Which I'll get back to."

Joseph sank to the bed when Deacon had gone. "Oh my God," he said, still panting. "You scared the fuck out of me."

"I'm sorry." She closed her eyes, mortification setting in. "I didn't mean to. I don't think I've ever done that before."

Joseph lightly grasped her chin. "Bad dream? Open your eyes, honey."

She obeyed, finding his expression both fierce and gentle at once. "I think so. It wasn't the same one. I was at Beckett's, but as I am now. Older. I was always a little girl before, but this time I was me. A shrink would have a field day with this."

"Don't worry. Talk to me. You were at Beckett's. What happened?"

"The gas man came in his truck and I climbed inside, but I was too big and he and Beckett caught me. And then they were . . . monsters. Like you can't see them, but you know they're bad?"

"I've had those dreams, too. What did they do?"

"Chased me through the woods. I was just running through the woods." She eased from the bed, testing the stability of her legs. When she didn't fall down, she started for the bathroom. "What did Deacon mean about coming back at seven?"

"I have a status meeting scheduled on my side. I was going to let you sleep."

She paused at the bathroom door, not yet ready to face him. The terror was too fresh and she needed to be by herself for a little while. To regroup. Settle down. Get control. "What time is it now?"

"Twenty-five till."

"Let me wash up. I'd like to sit in, if it's okay."

"Sure."

She chanced a look over her shoulder, found him still sitting on the bed, frowning to himself. "What's wrong?"

"Nothing. Just . . . unsettled. Go, get ready." His mouth curved. "I love the view, but I don't think that's what you want to show to the others."

Her cheeks heated. She wore only her pajama top. "No. Can you order me some room service for breakfast? I don't think I've eaten since lunch yesterday. Thanks."

She closed the door, sagged against it. Her legs were like jelly and she had to lean against the shower wall to wash her hair. *Run. Run. Through the cabin, out the door.*

Sighing through clenched teeth, she shoved the damn dream aside as she toweled off and went through her morning routine mechanically. Brush the teeth, comb the hair.

Run. Run. Climb in the truck. Hide under the tarp. Get away.

She paused as she blended her makeup, frowning at her reflection. Jerking her mind back to the here and now. "Stop it," she muttered. "You'll make yourself crazy."

Bronzer. Blush. *If I find her I'll bring her back to you.*

Mascara. *He sees me. The gas man sees me. Hide. Make yourself invisible.*

She froze, her eyes wide as she stared at herself, mascara wand halfway through its stroke. "Oh my God," she whispered. "He was there."

She burst through the bathroom door, much as Joseph had burst in earlier. She found him sitting in the same position on the bed, a grim expression on his face.

"Joseph, he knew. The gas man knew."

Joseph's gaze shot over to meet hers. "What?"

"The gas man knew where Beckett's cabin was. What if we could find him? Track him down? We could find the cabin. Find Beckett. Save Heather?" She ended the last on a note of question because he'd come to his feet, his gaze burningly intense.

She looked down at herself and felt her heart sink. Naked. She was stark naked. Everywhere. Reflex had her folding her arms over her breasts, but he was crossing the room, purpose in every step. Carefully he closed his hands over her wrists, tugging until she let go of the iron hold she had on herself.

He held her arms out, his eyes fixed on her body, a flush rising up his unshaven cheeks. His chest rose and fell with rapid breaths as he looked his fill.

Finally he glanced up. Met her eyes and she saw . . . greed. Reverence. Want.

"Promise me," he rasped. Cleared his throat and started

again. "Promise me that you won't hide from me anymore. Because I like what I see. Very, very much." His voice had dipped low, like a caress, and she shivered. "Promise me."

She swallowed, unable to look away from his face. Unembarrassed now, despite the fact that he was fully clothed while she wore not a stitch. "All right."

He stepped closer, pressing his lips to the side of her neck while guiding one of her hands to his trousers. He was fully erect and very ready. "Do you have any doubt that I'm telling you the truth?" He undulated against her hand, and she shivered again.

"No. I think you've proved your case very well."

He kissed his way from her neck to her shoulder. "If I didn't have a meeting in five minutes, I'd have you up against the wall, your legs wrapped around my waist and I'd be inside you, making you moan."

She moaned anyway, making him smile as he pulled away, leaving her trembling. "You're beautiful, Daphne."

"So are you."

There was a knock on the door of his room and he cursed softly. "Damn early birds." He kissed the tip of her nose and took a giant step back. "Come next door when you're ready."

The knock was repeated, harder this time, and Joseph shook his head hard.

"Damn. How am I going to concentrate?" He leaned toward the open adjoining door. "I'm coming. Keep your pants on." He winked at her. "That goes double for you, until later." Adjusting himself, he walked stiffly, muttering under his breath.

Daphne blinked, disoriented. Then she remembered why she'd burst out of the bathroom stark naked. "Joseph, wait."

He looked over his shoulder, brows furrowed. "Don't tease me, please."

"I'm not. Joseph, listen. The gas man knew where Beckett's cabin was. He went there every quarter to fill the tank. What if we could find him?"

He blinked. "Could we, after all this time?"

"I don't know, but it's better than what we've got so far."

He nodded once. "Get dressed and meet me on my side. We'll figure it out."

When the door closed behind him, Daphne exhaled

slowly. *Whoa.* Her body felt tight, needy. Greedy. But she had priorities. *Find the cabin. Find Heather. Find and punish Beckett and Doug, whoever the hell he is.*

And then . . . A delicious shiver ran down her back, making her skin tingle. She went back into the bathroom and studied her reflection. Her eyes were bright, her cheeks rosy. All shadows from the nightmare were gone.

"I think you just found a cure for panic attacks, sugar," she murmured to herself, smiling at the notion.

Now she was late, though, and needed to hurry with her makeup and clothes. Rather than pick through the makeup bag Maggie had included when she'd packed her overnight suitcase, Daphne dumped its contents on the bathroom countertop, creating a small mountain of lipsticks, eyeliners, and compacts of blush.

Then she froze, staring. An antique silver compact sat on top of the pile. The compact had been at the bottom of her makeup drawer in her bathroom at the farm. In Maggie's haste to get her packed and on the road to Ford, she'd scooped the contents of the entire drawer into the bag.

Daphne had almost forgotten she'd left the compact there. She always almost forgot—until she needed it again. Or more accurately, until she needed what was inside.

Had she had the Beckett nightmare while sleeping at the farm, this compact would have been the first thing she would have reached for. She opened the compact now, revealing the folded paper tucked within.

Carefully she unfolded it. The letterhead read WEST VIRGINIA STATE DEPARTMENT OF HEALTH. Her voice was but a whisper as she read the first line aloud. "Name of the deceased: Wilson William Beckett."

The original document she'd received from Claudia Baker was in her safety-deposit box, but she'd hidden a copy wherever she slept—in a wig box in the closet of her bedroom at home, in a box of tampons in the drawer of her nightstand at the condo where Ford would never look, and in this compact in the bathroom drawer at the farm. And when the nightmares were bad, she'd pull out the copy as tangible proof that Beckett really was dead. That he could no longer hurt her.

But it was a lie. He *wasn't* dead and he *could* hurt her. He'd tried to kill Ford.

She refolded the paper, put it back in the compact, and dropped the compact in her purse. *Get dressed and get the certificate to Joseph.*

Thursday, December 5, 6:58 a.m.

Joseph firmly closed the adjoining door and adjusted himself again. Looking down, he cursed. The bulge against his zipper was obvious.

The early bird knocked a third time. "Joseph? You okay?" Deacon called.

"I am fine," he ground out, grabbing a sweatshirt from the gym bag he'd left on the table. Holding it in front of him as nonchalantly as possible, he opened the door to Deacon, who had a box of doughnuts in one hand, his laptop in the other. "You're early."

"Good morning to you, too." Deacon tossed the doughnuts on the table. "Last time I bring you breakfast. How's Daphne?"

Delectable. Joseph had to fight a shudder. The image of himself dropping to his knees and burying his tongue inside her taunted him and he drew a hard breath.

"She had a bad dream about Beckett." Joseph busied himself making a pot of coffee, giving himself a moment to regain his composure. "But she'll be okay. Did you see Kate this morning?"

"She left with Simone and Maggie just before the screaming started. Something about a quest for chocolate chip pancakes. Heavy on the chocolate. I'll brief her later."

"We should have McManus and Kerr here soon." Joseph looked over, saw Deacon reading the newspaper. "Any of our news make the front page?"

"Nope. Not yet. I expect that'll change, though."

"Especially when the reporters get wind of Beckett." Joseph groaned quietly. "Shit. I forgot to tell her."

"Tell who what?"

"Tell Daphne that Beckett doesn't have a death certificate in the system and that the FBI agent she talked to doesn't exist."

"Shit. That mucks things up."

"Exactly. I'd like not to blindside her with that in front

of the others." Joseph checked his watch. McManus and Kerr were a little late. "Can you call Grayson, Bo, and Brodie? I need to talk to her before the locals get here."

"Sure."

"And start wrapping your mind around this one—when she calmed down after that scream, she remembered that the gas man who unwittingly helped her escape knew where the cabin was. It was on his route."

Deacon's eyes widened. "Holy hell. It's been thirty years. Hopefully the same gas companies are still around."

"Got a better idea?"

"Nope."

"All right then." Joseph went back into the hall and knocked on Daphne's door. Now that the locals were due, he didn't want to compromise anything by having them see him moving freely between their rooms.

She opened the door, fully clothed in jeans and a sweater, munching on a slice of toast. "I was leaving to come to your room when my breakfast arrived. You ordered me enough food for an army. You want some of it?"

"No thanks." He followed her into her room, giving her a cautious look. "I need to tell you something."

Her hackles rose as she closed the door. "What happened?"

He let out a breath. "There's no death certificate for Beckett in the system."

"That's impossible." She looked up at him, confusion in her eyes. "I have a copy. With a seal and everything."

"Well, since he's not really dead, that the certificate was a fake isn't that much of a stretch. That isn't the big thing. There never has been a Claudia Baker with the FBI."

She froze, then swallowed the toast with a gulp. "I don't understand."

"Somebody lied to you. Set you up to think you were giving a statement. There's no record of a Claudia Baker in the Bureau, in the DC office or anywhere else."

She sank onto the sofa, stunned. "That means . . . what does that mean, Joseph?"

"I don't know yet. But Bo wants answers. He might be less . . . friendly than before."

Her eyes widened. "He thinks I'm lying?"

"He doesn't know for sure," Joseph hedged. "He wants to talk to you himself."

She looked up sharply, studying his face. "Does he think you're covering for me?"

Joseph hesitated. Shrugged. "He doesn't know for sure," he said again. "Do you need a minute to regroup?"

"No." Her expression had grown hard. "Let's do this."

She grabbed her handbag and followed him back to his room, her breakfast forgotten. Kerr and McManus had arrived and were eating the doughnuts. On the phone were Bo, J.D., and Brodie. Kate wasn't able to get to a secure place to call, and Hector still stood watch over Ford.

"Good morning," Joseph said. "We've got a lot of new developments, so let's jump in. First up, a possible ID for Doug. One of the neighbors of Odum's house in Timonium reported seeing Doug trying to buy Super Glue at the local drugstore. We weren't able to get any photos from the store's surveillance video, but we forgot about the Super Glue itself. Dr. Brodie?"

"Local uniforms are at the store now," Brodie said. "J.D. and I are about five minutes away. We're hoping the package Doug touched is still in the store. If it's not, the store has a record of anyone who bought Super Glue in the past two weeks, since everybody who buys it is carded. If someone's bought that specific package, we'll try to track them down. Hopefully they'll still have the packaging in their possession. We'll keep you up-to-date."

"Thanks. We'll keep our fingers crossed. Second." Joseph glanced at Daphne, saw her jaw set grimly. It grew tighter as he explained the situation concerning Beckett's death certificate and the nonexistent Agent Claudia Baker.

Bo cleared his throat. "Can you tell us *exactly* how you were contacted by the woman claiming to be Baker?"

"I wrote to the FBI to ask whether they ever provided security for the families of informants whose information about a killer could endanger other members of the family. I said it was for a school project, a paper I was writing. I put the letter with all the outgoing mail at the Elkharts' DC house. A few days later I got a visit from Agent Baker."

"Why did you write a letter?" Bo asked. "Why didn't you call or go in person?"

"I didn't call because I didn't know who was listening to my calls. I'd just moved into my ex-mother-in-law's house in Georgetown. She was very strict and didn't let me have any contact with the outside. I had a tutor and a doctor, but that was all.

"When Agent Baker showed up, I was terrified that Nadine—my ex-mother-in-law— would find out. But she was taking her daily nap and my tutor was out sick, so nobody saw me talking to the agent at the front door. I didn't want Nadine to be angry. I was pregnant and fifteen and she had promised my baby a good life. I wasn't about to get thrown out for breaking the rules. The agent said she knew who I was, that she'd searched the files and had finally found my story."

"How did she say they found out?" McManus asked.

"She said that my letter sounded like more than a school project, so she checked unsolved cases, found Daphne Sinclair and Kelly Montgomery. She said it didn't take a rocket scientist to do the math. Plus, she could see my resemblance to the newspaper photos she'd found of me at eight years old."

"Plausible," Bo admitted.

"Thank you," Daphne said sweetly, but Joseph wasn't fooled. She was pissed at having to defend herself.

As well she should be. "What happened next?" Joseph asked her.

"She told me she'd wait for me in the park the next day if I could get away. My tutor was still sick the next day, so I slipped out during Nadine's nap and met Baker in the park. I told her the story. I even gave her Beckett's name. She said she'd see what she could find out and for me to meet her again the next day. I did, and that's when she told me that Beckett was dead, that there was no reason to proceed.

"I wanted to believe her, but I was afraid for my mother and then for my baby. I wanted to be sure that Beckett really couldn't hurt them, so I contacted the state records department in West Virginia. They sent me a form to fill out and return by mail to get the certificate. I had one more follow-up with Baker and told her I'd requested the death certificate, but that the records office said it would be a month. She got it for me faster. Later the copy from the records office arrived."

"Do you still have the death certificate?" Bo asked.

"I have the original one I was given by Baker in my safety-deposit box." She opened her handbag and took out a silver makeup compact. From it she withdrew a folded piece of paper, so worn it was falling apart. She gave Joseph a quick glance. "I have a copy with me. I'm giving it to Agent Carter right now."

Joseph stared at her for a moment before taking the piece of paper. "It's a photocopy of a death certificate, Bo. It's for Wilson Beckett, gives his date of death as the year before Daphne made the request. There appears to be a seal, looks like it's raised on the original. It's signed by the county coroner. Says cause of death is myocardial infarction. Beckett had a heart attack. It looks official."

Joseph passed it to McManus, keeping his eyes on Daphne's face. She wasn't looking at him and that bothered him.

"We'll check out the county coroner who signed this," McManus said, "but I think I recognize the name from other documents from that period. Why do you keep a copy with you, Miss Montgomery?"

Yeah, Joseph thought. *I want to know that, too. And why you didn't mention it when we were talking about this last night.*

Her cheeks had grown flushed with embarrassment and she kept her eyes on her hands. "I don't carry a copy with me all the time. I have nightmares. Most of the time they're about Beckett. When I wake up I have panic attacks and sometimes I get them in the daytime, too. I have various methods of controlling these attacks. When they get really bad, I look at that death certificate to prove to myself he's really dead. That he was, anyway. I've got several properties and often decide to sleep at one versus another on short notice. I needed to keep that certificate handy, wherever I was. I hid the copy I kept at the farm in this compact. It was in the makeup bag that Maggie packed for me yesterday. I didn't know I had it with me until I was putting on my makeup this morning. That's all."

"Okay," Bo said. "We'll need a description of Baker, if you remember."

"I'm happy to. It has been twenty years, but I'll do my best." She finally met Joseph's eyes and he saw apology. She hadn't wanted to surprise him with the copy of the certificate. He wondered why she had. "Can we talk about the gas man now?"

"In just a minute," he promised. "First we need to figure out who knew you were planning to reveal Beckett to the FBI, because somebody didn't want you to do it. Beckett himself would have a reason to keep you from talking, but he had no way to know your plans. We have to assume your mail was intercepted by someone. Who would have had access?"

"Nadine, Travis. My tutor. Any of the servants."

"Hal Lynch, too?" Joseph asked and she frowned.

"Yes. He was my bodyguard at the time. But he didn't."

"How do you know?"

"He wouldn't, any more than Scott would."

"Was Scott there?"

She frowned harder. "Yes. Part-time, but yes. Part of the agreement my mother and Nadine signed was that I'd have access to horses. It was . . . therapy."

"For the nightmares?" Agent Kerr asked kindly.

"Yes. Scott would trailer them up from the estate a few times a week for me to ride. If I had to guess, I'd say it was Nadine. She was hypersensitive to scandal."

Joseph remembered Maggie's story of Ford blackmailing his grandmother. He wondered what the boy had known. He sure as hell planned to ask.

"None of those people are Doug, though," Joseph said. "At some point Doug intersects with Beckett, but Doug isn't even thirty. He was a baby when you and Kelly were abducted. Somehow he had to find out about your history with Beckett, and if the woman posing as Baker was the only one you told, that has to be the intersection point."

"What about sons?" Deacon asked. "Does anyone have a son Doug's age?"

"Hal doesn't," Daphne said firmly. "Scott has three, but none of them would do anything like this."

Joseph leveled her a steady look. "Grayson, are you still there?"

The speakerphone hummed as Grayson un-muted his line. "I am. I'll check out the sons, too. How about the tutor, while I'm at it?"

Daphne's brows shot up. Her annoyed expression said, *Too?* "My tutor's name was Joy Howard. I have no idea where you'd find her after all these years."

"I'll see what I can dig up," Grayson said.

"*Now* can we talk about the gas man?" Daphne asked. "Heather could still be alive."

"Yes." Joseph briefed the team on Daphne's idea and McManus sat up straighter.

"Do you remember the name of the company?" he asked.

"No. But there was a cat on the driver's door. Like a bobcat."

"What about the driver, Daphne?" Joseph asked.

"He was about my father's age, black hair. That's all I remember."

Deacon took out a notepad and sketched an outline of a man, giving detail to his shirt. He added a round oval where a name tag might be, then sketched a bobcat above the oval. He slid the sketch to Daphne. "Take a look," he said quietly, "then close your eyes and see if you can fill in the oval."

She gave him a puzzled look, but did what he asked. She closed her eyes, her brows scrunching as she tried to remember.

"What color was his shirt?" Deacon asked softly.

"Blue."

"Good. Now I want you to picture his shirt. Can you see the oval?"

"Yes." She opened her eyes, dismayed. "But I can't remember his name."

"That's okay. Just close your eyes. Picture the oval and I'm going to read you some names. Think about how big the letters were, how curvy, how straight. How many. Are they wide or skinny. Ready?"

She frowned. "Okay."

Deacon looked at his laptop screen. "Dave," he said and after a moment she shook her head. "Jim. John. Bob. Mark. Bill. Tim. Chuck."

Her chin lifted and her eyes flew open. They shone with satisfaction. "Mark. It was Mark, with a 'k.' I remember the cursive 'k' at the end. But the letters were bigger—there were fewer of them. So Mark. My best guess."

McManus looked suspicious. "Where did you get the names?"

"Social Security Web site," Deacon said. "You can search the Social Security Administration's Web site for names in order of popularity by state and birth year. Daphne said he was about her father's age. I input that plus 'West Virginia' and that list was generated. Getting the name of the company might be trickier, although your Better Business Bureau may have a list of companies doing business back then. You can ask your state income tax department, but they'll put a yard of red tape around it."

"Or you could check the old phone books," Daphne offered. "I've searched old phone books for individuals before. The local library might have an archive."

"So we have to find the company and a guy named Mark," Joseph said. "Not a needle in a haystack, exactly, but not a simple Google. What else do we have?"

"General contractors," J.D. said. "I'll be checking with local contractors and hardware stores today to see if anyone matching Doug's description has bought any HVAC supplies."

Joseph frowned. "HVAC? You lost me."

"Heating, ventilation, air conditioners?" J.D. said tentatively.

"I know what HVAC stands for. Why are you looking at them?"

"Because Doug does HVAC work. It's how he got into all those cops' houses to plant cameras to watch them open their safes. He put flyers in cops' mailboxes offering a free duct cleaning. The cops who took him up on the offer said he did good work, so he's had training of some kind. If he'd been in the business, he'd need supplies. Also, you said your sister Holly heard Kimberly say that he needed to bring his 'GC.'"

"General contractor," Joseph murmured. "I remember now."

"GCs and HVAC operators are advertised together in the phone book," J.D. said. "Wait . . ." There was a long pause with a muffled conversation, then a very clear "shit."

"What?" Joseph asked, afraid he knew.

"Brodie and I are at the drugstore. She just checked with the clerk and all of the Super Glue inventory has been turned over. But we have a list of people who bought it, so that's where we're going. We'll be in touch."

Joseph bit back a curse of his own. "Anything else?"

"Yeah," J.D. said. "Brodie wanted me to tell you the paternity test came in for Marina's baby. George is the daddy."

"You're kidding." Joseph shook his head, still trying to

shake off the Super Glue disappointment. "I'm really stunned. Speaking of daddies, how much longer do you think we'll have you in the office? How is Lucy doing?"

"Don't ask. We've been at 'any day now' for a week. I'm losing my mind. Brodie and I are headed off to check the names on this list. We'll call when we know anything."

"Do you have any more questions, Bo?" Joseph asked, when J.D. had hung up.

"No, not right now. Daphne, I'm sorry if you were upset with me, but I couldn't assume you were telling the truth off the bat."

"Actually you could have," Daphne said quietly. "The questions would have been much the same, but the way you asked them would have been different. Tell me when to expect the sketch artist. I'll be happy to try re-creating the woman's face."

Good for her, Joseph thought. He'd wanted to charge to her aid with Bo, but she'd handled herself with dignity, without his help. "If there's nothing else, we're adjourned. We'll regroup by phone at noon." He turned to McManus and Kerr. "Tell us what you need and we'll support you. You have the necessary resources to find Mark the gas man."

"Assuming he's still alive," McManus cautioned. "And if he is, that he knows what the hell we're talking about."

Agent Kerr took a map from his briefcase. "This is the area we covered last night with the canine teams, tracking Ford's path. Maybe it'll jog his memory."

"Or maybe he has invoices or an old file of clients," Daphne said. "The company might still have route records. Let's find him first and see what happens."

When Kerr and McManus moved off to the side to plan, Joseph turned to Deacon. "I'm impressed with how you brought that memory out of Daphne's mind."

Deacon shrugged. "We'll see how impressive it is when we find him. If it's okay with you, I'm going to catch a little more sleep. I take over for Hector at noon, standing watch over Ford."

"Thank you, Agent Novak," Daphne said quietly. "For watching over my son."

He smiled at her. "He's a good kid. Who feels terrible about the way he treated you last night, by the way. He told me to tell you that. I think he could use a visit."

"I'll go as soon as Joseph can free up someone to go over with me. And don't volunteer," she said when Deacon started to do just that. "I want you to be alert and rested in case Beckett comes after Ford again. Go to sleep, Agent Novak."

When he was gone, Joseph leaned in closer to her. "Why didn't you tell me you had the certificate in your purse?"

"I forgot until I had the nightmare. Then you burst in and I didn't need it. I really didn't find it until after you'd left my room. I had a nightmare night before last, too, but Kate was there and I didn't want to show her the certificate I have hidden at home. I didn't know any of this was connected to Beckett then or I would have told her."

"But when I came to get you and told you Bo was suspicious, why not then?"

"You needed to be surprised in front of the others, I thought. Genuinely surprised. Otherwise they'd start doubting your objectivity. Bo did, didn't he?"

Joseph had no intention of answering that question. "I need to brief Hector. If you're ready to go, I'll take you with me and you can visit Ford."

She regarded him for a moment, head slightly tilted. "Five out of ten."

"Excuse me?"

"Your score. For diverting me from my question. If you want to improve, watch your father with your mother. He's a smooth diverter. I'm sorry Bo gave you a hard time."

"He's just annoyed because the raid on the Russians was a bust."

She smiled. "That was an eight out of ten."

"I'd give you the same score—for putting off the confrontation with your son," he said and watched her eyes flicker. "Come on, Daphne. Your son loves you. Let's go see him."

Baltimore, Maryland
Thursday, December 5, 10:30 a.m.

Cole woke to find everything dark. But not pitch-dark. More a hazy dark, like peeking through a blanket.

Reality returned in an icy wave. *That's because I'm under a blanket.* And not just one. Based on the weight that covered him, he was under at least two, maybe three of the fuckers. And he was tied. Hands behind his back, ankles crossed. He tried to open his mouth and couldn't.

Kimberly. The shovel. And . . . duct tape. The bitch had bound and gagged him with the same duct tape he'd used on her during the night.

Mitch, if I ever see you again, I'm going to fucking kill you. And Cole meant that. Mostly. He struggled against the tape, but the more he struggled, the harder it was to breathe. His heart pounding like the whole damn marching band, he gave up.

I will fucking kill you, Mitch. Now I mean that more than mostly.

Somebody had to come at some point. Mitch. Matt. Even the damn sheriff was starting to sound good.

No, I'm not going that far. The sheriff would arrest him first and ask questions, maybe never. Not with all the shit Mitch had in the basement. *Guns. Cash. A girl.*

God. He drew a breath and held it. *Relax. You'll never get free if you don't relax.*

But panic took hold and wouldn't let him go. *Relax or you'll suffocate.* The air was so totally not fresh. *By the time help comes you'll be dead.* Tears pricked his eyes.

God. What am I gonna do now?

Wheeling, West Virginia
Thursday, December 5, 10:30 a.m.

"How do you want to handle this?" Joseph asked Agent Kerr as the two of them plus Daphne and McManus gathered at the entrance to the bus station.

In the end, they'd used a combination of their ideas to locate Mark O'Hurley, who worked for Appa-Natural Gas, which had served a large portion of the Appalachian area thirty years before. They'd found an ad with the bobcat logo in an old-fashioned phone book in the library, used Better Business Bureau records to locate the name of the business owners, now retired, their company defunct. But the owner of Appa-Natural Gas had a good memory and a willingness to gossip. Unfortunately he had a wife who hadn't seen the need to keep thirty-year-old records. All of his client lists, invoices, and route maps had been thrown away in an office purge fifteen years before.

Then they'd done a new-fashioned Google search to find O'Hurley himself. He hadn't been home, but they found neighbors more than willing to talk about Mark.

The old gas company owner remembered needing to fire O'Hurley twenty-five years before, after several years of warnings and two DUIs. O'Hurley had developed a serious drinking problem, and had joined AA after he'd lost everything.

Now Mark O'Hurley worked for the bus station.

And here they were.

Daphne cleared her throat. "*Excuse* me? *I'm* talking to O'Hurley."

Joseph looked concerned. "He might feel too intimidated to talk to you."

"Joseph, don't you think it's interesting that the man starts drinking around the time my incident occurred?"

"Yes, I do. That's exactly what I meant by intimidating. You're his personal demon."

"He's gone through AA," Daphne said stubbornly. "He'll want to make amends."

"Lady's got a point," Kerr said. "Let her try, Carter. If he looks like he's shutting down, we can take over."

"All right," Joseph agreed. "Let's hurry."

Daphne searched the faces at the bus station until she found the night watchman. She knew it was the right face when her lungs suddenly deflated and her knees went weak. He was twenty years older, but the shape of his face, the placement of his eyes, hadn't changed. "There he is," she murmured, grateful that Joseph was there to put his arm around her waist, keeping her upright.

She drew a steadying breath before approaching him. "Excuse me. Mr. O'Hurley? Mark O'Hurley?"

He looked up from zipping his coat. "Yes? Who are you?"

"My name is Daphne Montgomery. I'm with the state's attorney's office in Maryland. These are my colleagues Special Agents Carter and Kerr, FBI, and Detective McManus, Wheeling PD. We'd like to talk to you about the days when you worked for the propane gas delivery company."

O'Hurley's eyes flickered. "All right. What do you want to know?"

"November, 1985," she said. "I know it was a long time

ago, but do you remember making a delivery to a cabin in what's now the wildlife management area?"

"That was nearly thirty years ago," he said, but he'd paled slightly. "I made a lot of deliveries out there in those days."

His hands were trembling, Daphne noted. *He knows.*

"This is very important," she murmured. "I'm interested in a day about a week after Halloween. You'd stopped at a cabin to make a delivery and it was late afternoon. Just starting to get dark. As you got out of your truck, the cabin's owner pulled up next to you in a car. He asked if you'd seen a little girl running around, told you that his sister had dropped off her brat and she'd run off. You told him that if you saw her, you'd bring her back." He'd closed his eyes. "You do remember, don't you?"

For a long time he didn't speak. When he did, his voice was hoarse. "I remember."

"What do you remember?" Daphne asked, forcing her voice to remain gentle.

He looked up at her. "What did you say your name was?"

"Daphne Montgomery. In 1985 I was Daphne Sinclair."

"It was you." His throat worked as he tried to swallow. "You were in my truck, weren't you? That's how you got away. You hid under my tarp."

Surprise had her eyes narrowing. "You knew I was there?"

"Not that day."

"When, then? When did you know I'd been there?"

"Not until a few days after the newspaper headline said you'd been found. I found a little girl's hair bow in the bed of my truck, under the tarp. Then I remembered a guy asking me if I'd seen a little girl. I wondered if it might be you."

"But you didn't tell anyone?" The question stuck in her throat. *I'm a damn hypocrite.*

"I didn't know for sure. I told myself that one of my own daughters had probably dropped it in the bed, although it had been a year since I'd seen my girls. Because their mother took them away from me." He swallowed hard. "Because I was a drunk. I was drunk the day you climbed into the back of my truck."

"Did you hear about my cousin?"

"Yeah, I did. I worried about it, worried that I should tell the cops what I'd seen. I even went back to the cabin when the man wasn't home. I snuck in to see if he was holding anyone. He wasn't, so I figured I'd got it wrong."

"I see."

"And then I saw the family interviewed on the news and there was the man from the cabin, cozy with you. I figured maybe the whole thing was a mistake. That you hadn't really been kidnapped. That you really had run away from that man at the cabin and that your family had . . . handled it in their own way."

"Hm." Handled it in their own way? Really? "I see."

"And then a few weeks later the papers said you'd identified your own daddy as the kidnapper. I figured the guy at the cabin was telling the truth after all."

It was Daphne's turn to go pale. *Oh God. This nightmare keeps going on.*

She felt Joseph's hands on her shoulders a moment before he spoke. "I can see how you might have thought that," he said, no recrimination in his voice. "There was a lot of confusion in the case back then. But today we got new information that the man you talked to at the cabin was the kidnapper. It's important that we find that cabin. Do you remember where it was?"

"I'm not sure. It's been almost thirty years. Even if the place still exists, the roads are going to look different. I just don't know."

"Will you try to help us find it?" Joseph asked.

"Now?" O'Hurley asked, dismayed.

"It's important," Joseph said again. "Please."

O'Hurley shrugged. "I'll try. I can't promise anything, but I'll try."

Wheeling, West Virginia
Thursday, December 5, 12:15 p.m.

The police scanner woke Mitch up. A glance at the alarm clock had his eyes bugging out. He'd overslept, seriously so. But all those nights with no sleep and all that driving had finally caught up with him. He'd slept like the dead.

Mitch turned the scanner up. The locals were rousing the troops. EMTs, uniforms, even a helicopter. *Good to know.* Dispatch was putting all personnel on alert. The location was the wildlife management area. Exact coordinates would follow.

Sounded like they'd finally found the cabin. Took them long enough. He wondered if they'd followed Beckett back to it or if the dogs had finally picked up Ford's scent and tracked him backward. *I have to see this for myself.*

He checked the phone he used with Cole and cursed. He'd missed a call from the school attendance office. The voice mail confirmed his fear that Cole was absent. *Again.* Mitch called the house, but no one answered. *Big shock.*

I am going to kill that kid. Then he forced himself to chill. Annoyed people made mistakes and this was too damn important a day. He'd deal with Cole tomorrow.

The phone he used with Mutt was loaded with messages. All from Mutt's daddy's phone. Mitch smiled. Fifteen messages. *Running scared, old man? Good.* Remembering his desperate phone calls from prison that went unanswered by the old man, Mitch hit DELETE. DELETE. DELETE. Fifteen calls, all deleted.

Now you know how it feels. His good mood restored, Mitch went to his closet and pulled out the uniform he'd stolen especially for this occasion. Minutes later he was standing in front of the bathroom mirror, straightening his tie.

The previous owner of the uniform was a West Virginia state trooper. Mitch had gotten some good stuff out of that heist. The trooper had excellent taste in baseball cards, guns, vintage *Playboy* editions . . . but, most important, the guy was exactly his size, so the uniform fit like a glove.

He placed the hat on his head. "This will make all of this worthwhile."

A banging on his door had him wheeling around, startled. Checking his Glock, he went to the door, his heart pounding in his chest. Who knew he'd be here? *Chill.* Nobody knew he had this place. *Must be a salesman or a Girl Scout selling cookies.*

He looked through the peephole in the door and his heart crashed to a halt. On his doorstep, his shirt bloody, his face haggard, swollen, and stained with tears, was his stepfather.

Wheeling, West Virginia
Thursday, December 5, 12:15 p.m.

"What the hell are you doing, kid?"

Ford looked up from tying his shoes. Deacon was standing in the doorway of his hospital room, fists on his hips, glaring. Ford glared right back.

"I heard you on the phone, talking to Carter. I'm going to that cabin, even if I have to hitchhike to get there."

"You're staying right here, so sit your ass back down."

Ford ignored him, pulling on the sweatshirt Gran and Maggie had brought him when they'd visited. He walked carefully across the tiled floor, every step painful, like there were millions of needles in his feet.

Deacon blocked his way. Face-to-face, Ford was startled to find he had to look up to meet the Fed's eyes. Because Ford had been sitting or lying down every time they'd talked, he hadn't realized Deacon was so tall. The guy had to be six three. The stark contrast of his white goatee and bronze skin combined with those weird bicolored eyes and the whole leather getup made him look like one bad motherfucker.

But Ford wasn't scared, because he was feeling like one, too. "Get out of my way, Deacon. I mean it."

"I could take you down with one pinkie, kid. You're weavin' on your feet."

Ford stowed his rage for a moment. "I know. I also know that getting help for that girl was what kept me walking, even when it hurt like hell." He thought of his mother's face as she'd told her story. "My mom's with Carter, isn't she? She'll go to that little room where Beckett held her cousin, even if Heather's not there to save. She needs the closure. When she comes up, she's going to be so . . . upset. I need to be there for her. So if you won't drive me there, please, just don't stand in my way."

There was a long pause. "Okay," Deacon finally said, his voice gruff. "On the condition that you remain in my vehicle until I tell you it's safe to come out. Agreed?"

"Yes."

Deacon pinned him with a hard gaze. "If you break your word, I will use a helluva lot more than my pinkie to take you down. Got me?"

"Yes," Ford said. "Thank you."

Deacon rolled his eyes. "Carter's gonna have my ass for this."

"No, he won't. I'll tell him I snuck after you and hid in your car. He already knows I'm willing to play dirty to get what I want."

"I somehow doubt that," Deacon said dryly, but Ford knew better.

Carter had taken him aside earlier that morning when his mother was getting an update from the doctor. The FBI agent had asked him what he'd held over his grandmother's head to get his own way. When he'd told him, Carter looked torn between laughter, respect, and dismay—the last because Ford had seen what he'd seen and been forced into trading secrets for his mother's welfare at an early age.

"Agent Carter knows what I'm willing to do to keep my mother safe. He won't blame you. Trust me. Let's go. We're wasting time."

Wheeling, West Virginia
Thursday, December 5, 12:20 p.m.

"I know you're in there, Mitch!" More banging. "Let me in!"

Mitch made himself breathe. His stepfather was making such a scene, people would come out to see. *I need to get him out of here. Fast.*

From his backpack Mitch grabbed one of the syringes of ketamine he'd prepared before leaving Baltimore. A small dose would make the old man look drunk. A guy in a trooper's uniform could explain away a lot of bad behavior from a drunk.

He opened the door and pulled his stepfather in, but he didn't need to work too hard. The old man staggered. He must be drunk already.

"What the fucking hell is wrong with you?" Mitch hissed, then flew backward when his stepfather's fist connected with his jaw.

The old man straightened to his full height. "You worthless piece of shit."

Okay. Not drunk after all.

Mitch came to his feet, his back protesting the movement. He said nothing, watching warily, waiting for the old man to speak again.

Mutt's daddy didn't say another word, though, instead reaching into his pocket, putting Mitch on full alert. But he didn't bring out a gun. He brought out a bundle the size of a child's fist, wrapped in a hankie. Soaked red with blood.

Deliberately his stepfather took one corner of the hankie and flung its contents in Mitch's face. He was pelted with small, hard objects, wet with blood. With horror Mitch stared at the floor where they fell, the syringe he held behind his back nearly forgotten. Fingers. And toes.

Fingers and toes. Bile rose in Mitch's throat as his gaze zeroed in on one of the fingers. It bore Mutt's ring. The one he'd gotten for being the true son. Mitch swallowed hard and looked up at his stepfather. His old man still stared at the floor. At Mutt's fingers and toes.

"I found them this morning when I went out for the paper," his stepfather whispered hoarsely. "I followed the trail, picking them up. Until I found him. In the garbage."

Antonov. Cutting off his victims' digits was one of his signatures. *Matthew. I didn't care if you got caught in your father's crossfire, but I didn't want anything like this.*

"It was supposed to be you," Mitch heard himself say. "Not Mutt. *You.*"

His stepfather lifted his chin, fury in his eyes. "You filthy son of a whore."

"Then so is Mutt. We share a mother. Or have you forgotten?"

His stepfather roared. "His name is Matthew!" He charged and Mitch stepped to the side, smoothly plunging the needle into his shoulder.

Like a fucking dance. Thirty seconds later his stepfather really *was* drunk.

"How did you find me?" Mitch asked.

"Tracker," the old man slurred. "I knew it was you yesterday. Matthew thought you were too stupid. I told him to put a tracker under your vehicles. Never expected to find you here. What's here, anyway?"

"Daphne."

The old man's eyes bulged out and he tried to fight but the ket was acting fast. His punch went wild and he ended up on the floor. "Daphne. Don't touch her."

"I'll do more than touch her. I'm going to kill her."

"Why?" It was an agonized cry and music to Mitch's ears.

"For my mother. My mother killed herself because Daphne stole the man she loved. I hate that she gave up her life for a worthless piece of shit like you."

"Noooo!" the old man wailed as he wound down.

Mitch slung his stepfather's arm over his shoulder and hurried him down the elevator to his Jeep. His stepfather was a deadweight by the time he got him in the backseat. This was unexpected, having both his stepfather and Daphne under his control at the same time. He'd take them both to Aunt Betty's bomb shelter, where he'd have more time to play. His stepfather had just lost his only true son. Now he was about to lose his obsession. Mitch covered him with an old blanket.

Then he took off for Beckett's little cabin in the woods.

Twenty-five

Marston, West Virginia
Thursday, December 5, 1:00 p.m.

She'd said little since the argument they'd had in hissed whispers outside the bus station. Joseph had planned to take her back to the hotel, but she'd refused to go, refused to get into the SUV until he promised to take her to wherever O'Hurley would lead them. She'd be in danger, he told her. Doug would be there, waiting for her.

Which was why she needed to be there, she'd fired back. He'd constructed this scheme for a reason. If she didn't go where he wanted her to go, he'd just postpone the inevitable until she did. Plus, she'd argued, she knew where the underground bunker was. If Heather was still alive, she could save them valuable time in rescuing her. Then she'd begged Joseph to let her help rescue the girl, begged him not to deny her what he did every day—save missing people to make up for not being able to save Jo.

It was the final point that silenced his opposition. If Beckett had taken more girls between Kelly and Heather, Daphne would internalize their loss, even though her mind logically knew it wasn't her fault. He knew firsthand that the heart sometimes didn't care what the mind knew. Bringing home other people's missing loved ones hadn't brought Jo back, but it did help him deal with the lingering guilt.

So he'd agreed, reluctantly. "What are you thinking about?" he asked quietly.

She didn't move her gaze away from O'Hurley's car in front of them. "That I could have stopped Beckett. That all I had to do was tell his name. And I keep thinking, would that really have been so hard to do?"

"I'd have to say yes," Joseph said. "Or you would have done it."

Her swallow was audible. "Thank you," she whispered.

"Daphne," he said gently. "How many times have you worked with a victim who had opportunities to tell but didn't? Women assaulted by a stranger or by someone they thought they knew. Children abused by someone they trusted—a priest, a coach, a relative. Their lives become insular. They're alone, even when surrounded by people."

"Sometimes even when they're surrounded by the people who love them."

"Exactly. If they let on that they're afraid or hurt, what little control they have over the situation is also gone. It's victim psychology that you've seen hundreds of times in your work." He took her hand, squeezed it lightly. "Is it so hard to accept that you're not so different from the people you fight so hard to protect?"

There was shocked silence on her side of the SUV. Long seconds later she shuddered out a breath. "I never saw myself that way. But I was. I am. Exactly like they are. Why was that so hard for me to see before?"

Joseph was quiet for a moment. "You feel their pain, see the world through their eyes, but you never see your own face. Now you hold a mirror in your hands. And now you can see yourself, too."

Again she was silent for long seconds. But this time she was considering, not shocked. "How did you come to understand this?" she finally asked.

"Because I finally saw myself. Every time I worked an abduction case it ripped open old wounds. I felt the family's terror, their despair. I felt their panic, the ticking of the clock. The hope every time there was a lead."

"And the devastation when the lead didn't pan out?"

"That, too. The last abduction case, before I moved to Homeland, I got too involved. And I finally snapped. I spied the kidnapper collecting the ransom but he sniffed me out, wouldn't lead me back to the child. I lost it. Used my fists on him to get him to tell me. I could have killed him.

Not that he didn't deserve it, but . . ." He shrugged. "We got the little girl back untouched, physically at least, and I earned the devotion of her family forever." One corner of his mouth lifted. "And all the pasta carbonara I can eat for the rest of my life."

"Giuseppe? The guy who owns the Italian place you and Grayson like so much?"

"He's the girl's uncle. He was very grateful. But I couldn't do that kind of work anymore. It got to the point where every victim was Jo. It was tearing me apart. It was just a matter of time before I exploded. Almost killing that kidnapper . . . that was my mirror. I saw myself and was terrified. So I got out for a while."

"This case . . . Joseph," she said, dismayed. "It's everything you wanted to escape. You said you transferred into VCET for me. I don't want you to— "

"Shh. It's been okay. I'm worried more for you. This case hasn't been about me finding the abductee because I didn't save Jo. This case has been about finding your son. For you. And finding the lost girls. For . . . themselves."

"That's good," she said softly. "I'd hate for you to be reliving Paris every day."

"I hate that you have to relive your past every time you stand for a victim by prosecuting all the murderers and rapists and general scum of the earth. But knowing what it costs you to do your job . . . It humbles me even as it comforts me. I know there will be times when this job gets to me again. But at least now I have someone to talk to at night. Someone who can keep me centered and won't let me bring anyone else into the bed with us. I want to be that someone for you."

"I want that, too. But right now, truthfully . . . I just want this to be over."

"It will be soon." *I hope.* "He's turning into the wildlife management area now." Joseph followed O'Hurley's car as it left the main road. "I don't know what we'll find at this cabin but I do know that Doug wants you here. When I try to analyze all the reasons why he could have orchestrated all this, something Scott said yesterday keeps nagging at me."

"Scott Cooper?" she said, surprised.

"Yes. We were talking about the message on your barn. Scott said it was just graffiti and that he bet that Doug was out there somewhere, watching your reaction. Turns out he was right. They found evidence that someone was watching you "

"Oh my God, Joseph."

"I'm betting that Doug will be somewhere near this cabin, too, watching. I'm worried that I'm taking you into an ambush. Doug wants you to suffer and we don't know why."

"But Doug isn't leading me here now. He couldn't have known about the gas man."

"True. But I think he thought Ford would lead us."

"Which is why he dumped him on that lady's front lawn. So he'd be found."

"I need to understand why Doug hates you so much. I know you don't want to believe anyone you care about could be involved, but will you at least entertain the notion? Because the only way Doug knew about Beckett is if Beckett told him or if that fake FBI agent told him. Because you and Beckett are the only ones who know."

"Unless another girl Beckett terrorized escaped, too."

"But Doug's not fixated on another girl. He's fixated on you. I'm beginning to believe that Beckett is no more than a tool. Doug's vendetta is personal. He might want you dead, but he wants you to suffer first. I talked to my sister Zoe this morning while you were visiting Ford." He'd brought her up to speed on everything they'd learned about Doug the day before. Once again his sister had helped. A lot.

"The psychologist. What did she think?"

"That this kind of intensity, this focus on Doug's part, says that he blames you for something that hurt him on the deepest level. Usually family—mothers, fathers, brothers, and sisters—are all wrapped up in that. That he used Ford makes her think that it has something to do with a parent-child bond, or the breaking of it."

"I guess that makes sense," she said, her tone guarded.

"That he knows about Beckett means he intersects with whoever manipulated you into talking to a fake FBI agent. Whoever did that knows everything about you that he needed to know. We need that intersection. I don't even have a photo of Doug yet, so I have to start with Claudia Baker and work my way forward. Who hired her?"

"Are you asking me?"

"You should be doing the asking. Somebody betrayed you, made you think Beckett was dead. Set you up for danger and allowed a murderer to go free. The only people who had access to you then were Nadine, Travis, Scott, and Hal. Doug intersects with one of them. And he blames you for something you did to him, real or imagined."

"Who are you liking for this intersection?" she asked coolly.

Joseph didn't let himself be deterred. "Jury's still out. Scott lost his business and his marriage because of his relationship with you. One of his three sons is the right age to be Doug and he might see you as the cause of their family's troubles."

"The background check Grayson mentioned during the morning meeting."

"Yes. I don't apologize for doing it, but I do wish for your sake that I hadn't needed to. Scott's wife divorced him after your husband accused the two of you of having an affair. She got the kids. Could have poisoned them against you."

"It's possible. But I trust Scott."

"Did you know his wife is dead?"

"Of course. She died soon after she divorced him and took what little he had left. She'd started drinking heavily during the time of their declaring bankruptcy. She had a car accident."

"One of his sons could blame you for all of that, even though none of it was your fault. Your alleged affair caused the string of events that left their mother dead." He paused a moment to let her think on that. "And speaking of the bankruptcy, how did Scott manage to buy the farm next to Maggie's if he'd lost all of his assets? That farm appraises at close to five million dollars."

"Scott came from old money, but his father walked out when he was a kid and left him and his mother destitute. He cleaned stalls to help his mother make ends meet and worked his way up, learning to train the horses. By the time I met him he'd built his business and had a lot of rich clients."

"But he lost it all."

She scowled. "Because of Travis. Anyway, his father died a few years ago. I don't know if it was guilt for having abandoned Scott and his mother or if he just never changed his will, but Scott got a sizable inheritance. He was able to buy the property and some really good-quality jumpers. Once he trains them and the horses start winning competitions, he can sell them for a lot more. One of his kids is a money whiz and invests well. Scott's pretty comfortable now."

The background checks on Scott Cooper's sons were still ongoing. Grayson had hoped to have a full report for him by the end of the day.

"Okay. Then let's talk about Hal Lynch. Did you know Hal owns four homes?"

She frowned. "I knew he had two. A house in Virginia near the Elkhart estate and a row house in Baltimore. He lives in the Virginia house."

"Not anymore. He lives on your street, Daphne. At the top of the hill."

She recoiled. "What?"

"He also owns a condo in your building at Inner Harbor. On your floor."

"That's . . . really disturbing." Her eyes were shocked. "But not a crime. And he doesn't have any sons Doug's age. His son is . . . maybe thirteen by now."

Joseph frowned. "No, his son is twenty-five."

Daphne shook her head. "I remember seeing his son, the night I saw his wife. He was small. Barely school age."

"Tell me about the night you saw his wife," Joseph said.

Daphne sighed. "You have to be careful being friends with men. Sometimes the wives don't like it. Hal's wife got the wrong idea about our relationship and confronted me one night. I knew he had a wife, but I'd only met her once, at one of Nadine's garden parties. I don't think we said more than hello to each other. Hal and I didn't have a friendship like that. We didn't hang out together, individually or with our families. He was my bodyguard."

"You told me a great deal just then, but not what I asked. Tell me about the night you met his wife."

She hesitated. "Joseph, I don't have any feelings for Hal other than platonic friendship and gratitude. He helped me a lot over the years."

"I believe you. And given that you still haven't answered my question, I have to assume that Hal's wife didn't believe you."

"No, she didn't. You need to know that I was alone for most of the twelve years I was married to Travis. After the night I conceived Ford, Travis touched me again a few dozen times, but never once after Ford was in elementary

school. Hal and I spent a lot of time together, especially
when I was going to college, after Ford was in school.
Once—just once—he kissed me."

Joseph kept his cool. "What did you do?"

"For a moment, just that tiny split second, I was tempted.
I was lonely and, honestly, kind of needy. But I told him no.
If I was caught cheating, I'd lose everything, according to
the agreement Mama's lawyer had negotiated with Nadine's lawyers before the wedding. I didn't care about the
money or the things, but Nadine would have fought for custody of Ford. And besides, it would have been wrong. I was
miserable in the marriage, but I'm no cheat even if Travis
was. So I told Hal absolutely no."

"Did he accept that?"

"Yes. His face got all red. He was embarrassed, too. Flustered. It was one of those heat-of-the-moment things that
never happened again."

"So . . . tell me about the night you met his wife."

She sighed. "By the time I left Travis, Hal had all but
quit. He and Travis had had a falling-out over something a
few years before and after that Hal cut back his hours and
did other things. Started another business. He'd always
loved the antiques at the Elkhart estate, so he opened a
small store in Baltimore. I've been there. He carries lovely
things. The only hours he worked for Travis at that point
were when he functioned as my personal security, which
wasn't so often then, as I'd finished school."

"What was their 'falling-out' about?"

"I don't know. I asked Hal once, but he evaded the question."

"Why did you need a bodyguard?"

"Nadine said it was because Elkhart wealth and Travis's
rising political career made me a target. He was a judge by
then and considering a run for Congress. But I think Nadine just wanted me observed. My college classes, shopping,
PTA meetings, even the Junior League—I was chaperoned
everywhere. The only time I ever really got alone time was
when I was riding or when I went to the doctor. I was the
only woman I knew who looked forward to her annual
physical. Until the day I got sick, anyway."

"Which was the day you discovered Travis with his secretary." He shrugged. "Maggie told me."

"Well, I guess I never told her not to. I was so distraught that day . . . I went to Scott's barn to brush the horse he boarded for me and Scott was there. He just held me while I cried. Kissed my forehead, like a brother. That's the 'evidence' Travis used to say I'd been unfaithful, plus he added a lot of innuendo that I'd been having an affair with Scott the entire time I'd known him. Nadine told me I had to be gone by morning. In the middle of the night I snuck out, grabbed Ford, stole the keys to the Bentley, and went to a hotel."

She smiled ruefully. "Nadine had canceled my credit cards, which I found out when I tried to check into the first hotel."

"What a peach." Joseph hoped he never had to meet Nadine. "What did you do?"

"Panicked. I'd been free to spend with the credit cards before, but my cash advances were minuscule. What I had in my wallet was enough to cover one night at a Motel 6." She shook her head. "It must have been the first time they'd ever had a Bentley parked out front. I needed cash, but couldn't call Scott. He'd been through enough because he was my friend. I couldn't let Travis go after him anymore.

"I didn't want to call my mother. I hadn't yet figured out how to tell her I had cancer. To tell her I'd been dumped by Travis, too? Oh, and by the way, I need money? But I didn't know what else to do, so I called her, but she and Maggie weren't home. The whole cancer, divorce thing isn't really something you leave on an answering machine."

"No, it's not. So you called Hal?"

"Yes, and he met me at the Motel 6. Gave me a hug, said everything would be fine, to not bother checking in, that he had a property in Baltimore that was unoccupied. He said I could live there until I got my settlement from Travis. I needed a safe place for Ford to live. There was a science and math charter school nearby that fit him to a T. And I knew I'd be going through cancer treatments soon, so I said yes."

"So . . . what happened the night you met his wife?" Joseph asked ponderously.

"I'm getting there," she snapped, then sighed. "I need you to understand that I'm not a cheat. I had no idea what would happen."

"I know you're not a cheat. You'd had the rug pulled out from under you. So . . . ?"

She sighed again. "The second night I was at Hal's house,

I got a visit from his wife. I was stunned. She was angry, saying I was a bitch, that I wasn't satisfied with the heir to the Elkhart fortune, that I had to steal her husband, too."

"What did you say?"

"You know, it was one of those moments you look back at and cringe." She shrugged. "I laughed. Not at her, of course, but that's how she took it. I had just been diagnosed with cancer, given a fifty-fifty shot at survival. I'd seen my husband doing his secretary, for God's sake, yet *I'd* been accused of cheating with married men—*twice* in the same week. It struck me as funny. Until she told me I was living in *her* house. She and Hal had lived there when they were first married. Now it was rented, but not to me."

"What did you say to that?"

"Nothing. She wouldn't give me a chance. She got in my face, told me to get out or she was calling the cops to throw me out. She had her cell phone out, ready to dial. So I took Ford back to the Motel 6. I hadn't told him about the cancer, either. He just thought his father had finally thrown us out. I went outside the room to call Mama so Ford wouldn't hear and I spilled out everything. I asked her if I could borrow whatever money she could scrape together. She said she was coming out that night."

She exhaled slowly. "Then I turned around and saw that Ford had opened the door a crack and was listening. He'd heard every word. And in that moment I wanted to kill Travis Elkhart. Wasn't terribly happy with God, either. Ford was in shock. Reminded me of how I looked when I came home after Beckett. Anyway, Mama came and the next day we put a security deposit on an apartment there in Baltimore, close to the hospital and Ford's new school. Hal called my cell phone, said he was at the town house and why wasn't I there. I told him about meeting his wife."

"What did he say?"

"Nothing for a very long moment. Then he said it was a misunderstanding and that he'd take care of it. I backed away from Hal for a while. I didn't want to jeopardize his marriage any more than I unwittingly had. And once chemo started . . . After I started law school he called me. His wife had died. Killed herself, actually. He told me that she'd been emotionally unstable for years. Based on what I saw that night, I believed him. We started meeting for lunch, just . . .

friends. He took me to the opera and ballet. Contributed to my women's center. We're platonic. End of story."

"Except he lives a hundred yards from you and you didn't know."

She looked troubled. "He was my bodyguard. Maybe it's an old-habits thing. I know you think I'm burying my head in the sand, but I'm not in a frame of mind to make a snap decision on him. Besides, his son is only thirteen. When I was walking out of his wife's house that night, I saw the little boy, asleep in the backseat. He was about five and this was eight years ago. He might even hate me if he thought his mother's account of things was right, but he's not Doug."

"Daphne, the check I had done showed that Hal Lynch has one son. His name is Matthew. He's twenty-five. His mother was Jane. Who committed suicide. That would make a son very bitter toward the woman he believed broke up his parents' marriage and drove his mother to kill herself."

Daphne frowned in confusion. "But that twenty-five-year-old son is still not old enough to be Doug."

"Unless he lied about his age to the lady who was carding him at the drugstore." He lifted a brow. "People do lie about their age, you know."

She rolled her eyes. "I know."

"Will you at least consider for a moment that he intercepted your letter to the FBI?"

She went still. "I guess I have to. I mean, Nadine never does anything herself. She gives orders and others do her bidding. If she'd told Hal to fake the certificate, I'm sure he would have. We weren't friends at that point. He owed more to Nadine than to me."

Joseph wasn't so sure Hal would have done the deed for his employer. "You still assume Nadine called the shots."

"Of course. She's the only one to have anything to gain."

"Avoidance of scandal," he said and she nodded. He said nothing more, waiting for her sharp mind to make the connection that her loyalty to her friends didn't want her to see.

"What possible motive could Hal have had?" she asked, doubt in her voice.

"Keeping you close by. If Nadine had found out then, before the marriage, what would she have done?"

She faltered. "I don't know. She probably would have sent me packing and found a way to get custody of Ford."

She looked out the window, her jaw tight. "And Hal lives up the street from me. Do you remember the date of his wife's suicide?"

She was finally starting to get it. Joseph gave her his phone. "Grayson forwarded it to me. Paige got all the info for us. You can look if you want."

"I don't want to, but I will." She inhaled sharply as she read. "Oh God. I was diagnosed on June 20, a Tuesday. I was thrown out by Nadine on Wednesday afternoon. Hal's wife threw me out on Thursday night. She died Friday night. She killed herself the day after I saw her. Because she thought I'd stolen her husband."

"Not your fault, Daphne."

"Funny how so many things aren't my fault," she said bitterly. "Hal did this. He faked that death certificate. For the past twenty years he's known. All along, he's known." Her expression changed, moving from bitterly aware to horrified. "He knew, Joseph. He knew that Beckett murdered Kelly. He let a killer go free just to keep me close to him? I thought I knew him. I trusted him. I trusted him with Ford. He stood there in my house, pretending to be sorry . . . What if he knew where Ford was all along?"

"I'll have him brought in for questioning." Joseph called J.D., asked him to pick Hal up, then called Grayson and asked for a warrant to search Hal's properties. Even if Hal wasn't involved in Ford's disappearance, Kimberly and her sister were still missing. Hal's son might have hidden the two girls somewhere on his father's property.

"Thank you," she murmured when he hung up his cell phone. "But, Joseph, why now? Why is Hal's son getting his revenge now?"

"I don't know. But we'll find out." He took her hand and held it as they followed Mark O'Hurley closer to where Doug had wanted her all along.

Baltimore, Maryland
Thursday, December 5, 1:30 p.m.

Cole had finally figured out where he was. Kind of. He could hear the echo of cars as they drove by and the occasional slam of doors as they parked. It was that ghostly sound that was peculiar to a parking garage.

He could smell the chemicals that Mitch used on his HVAC job. *I'm in the black van, covered with blankets.* He guessed that Kimberly knew how to use the hydraulic lift in the back. She was too tiny to have moved him on her own.

What he didn't know was where exactly he was or how long he'd been out. She could have driven them anywhere. He wasn't freezing at least, so maybe they were in an enclosed garage. He did know that his head was killing him. And he could smell blood. *Probably from getting hit by a damn shovel.* At least she hadn't broken his nose. He'd have suffocated on his own blood by now if she had.

When he caught the bitch, she'd be so sorry.

Marston, West Virginia
Thursday, December 5, 1:45 p.m.

Daphne sat in the Escalade while Joseph coordinated with Kerr and McManus, who'd followed them from the bus station. In front of her was O'Hurley's car. In front of O'Hurley was the cabin and garage from her nightmares. It had taken O'Hurley five wrong turns before finding the right one.

Now here she sat. Impatient and full of dread all at once.

Joseph opened the back hatch and she turned to see him buckling into a flak jacket. He looked up and met her eyes. "You sure about this?"

"Yes, Joseph. I'm sure. Do I get one of those?"

He was checking the magazine of a semi-automatic rifle. "A rifle? No."

"I meant a jacket."

"Yes, you definitely get one of those." He shook his head, like he couldn't believe he'd agreed to letting her go in with him. "I'm fucking insane," he muttered. Without waiting for her to respond, he grabbed a small case by its handle and gave it to Kerr, who also wore a jacket. "Explosive detector," he told Kerr. "Run the wand around the garage door before you open it."

"Sweet," Kerr said. "Where'd you get this?"

"My dad's company makes them for military and private use. He heard that I almost got blown up on Tuesday and insisted I carry one with me. Daphne, it's time. This vest is yours."

On shaking legs she got out of the car to put on the flak jacket, only to be stopped by O'Hurley.

"What's going on here?" he asked, panic starting in his eyes.

"We think that my cousin and I weren't his only victims, that he abducted a girl as recently as six months ago. She might still be alive."

"You can wait in your car," Joseph added, buckling her jacket. "Hopefully we'll know something soon. As soon as backup arrives, you'll be escorted to the police station and they'll take your statement. Until then, Detective McManus will see that you're protected."

His face horrified, O'Hurley backed away until he reached his car.

"Let's go," Daphne said. Then to bolster her own courage she added, "I'm doing this."

"You stay with me," Joseph said, his voice low and urgent. "Doug is here. Somewhere. He brought you here. He's watching. I know it. You're here to (a) point us toward his underground room and (b) draw him into the open. Maybe we can lure him out." He pointed to McManus. "Kerr goes in first. You cover our back. Make sure O'Hurley stays put and in one piece."

His body a shield, Joseph hovered over her as they crossed the open, unprotected area around the house. As she approached she was struck by the stench of decomposing flesh. The cat Ford had seen. With the "Fluffy" name tag. Realistically she knew it wasn't her Fluffy's body, but it was a damn fine way to mess with her head.

She'd told the impostor FBI agent the cat's name, too. *That's how Doug knew.*

Oh, Hal. Why? How could you? Her mind was still having trouble believing it was true. But she knew. *Good Lord. Hal.* Drawing a breath, she stepped into the garage . . . and back twenty-seven years.

"It looks the same," she said softly. "The shelf, the pile of wood, the chains. How can it look the same?"

"Where's the entrance, Daphne?" Joseph asked, his voice tense. He was watching, waiting. Worrying.

"Under the dead cat," she murmured. "Of course. Where else would it be?"

Joseph grabbed a snow shovel from a rack on the wall and pushed the carcass aside, tested the perimeter of the trapdoor for explosives, set the detector down. "When I call for you, bring down that bundle." He pointed to a brown blanket. "Wrapped inside is water, bandages, medicine. One last time—are you sure?"

No. "Yes."

"Okay." He pulled the door open.

Silence. Harsh silence. Daphne's heart sank. *She's dead.* She opened her mouth to say as much, but Joseph shook his head, laying a finger across his lips.

Weapon in hand, he started down the narrow steps and she knew true fear. It was the dark hole in her dreams, the one she always fell into. Doug could be down there. Or Beckett. Or a bomb or . . . *Stop it.* This is what cops' spouses went through every day. She needed to learn to be okay with the danger. Or at least try to handle it.

Daphne gritted her teeth and prayed.

She heard a click, then saw the beam of his flashlight moving across the small patch of floor she could see. Then a murmur, muted voices. Then his voice at full volume. "Daphne, come down. She's alive."

Daphne grabbed the blanket bundle and hurried down the stairs, ignoring the new fear clawing at her gut. As long as she'd been afraid for the girl or for Joseph, she hadn't been afraid for herself. Now she was.

Knees knocking, she reached the bed, saw the girl. Naked, chained. Emaciated.

Joseph turned his back to give the girl her dignity and was shrugging out of his wool overcoat. He wore the flak jacket under it. "Wrap her in the blanket, then in my coat."

Daphne hurried to the girl's side. "Heather?"

Heather's face was all bone, her eyes shrunken, lips cracked. "Water?"

Quickly Daphne covered her, tucking the blanket around her as best she could considering she was still chained. "My name is Daphne. That's Agent Carter. He's with the FBI. We're here to take you home."

Tears filled the girl's eyes, seeping down the sides of her face. Daphne poured a few drops of water into her mouth. "Easy. You'll get sick if you drink too fast."

She heard another click and the room was illuminated. Heather looked even more emaciated in the bright light and Daphne felt the unholy urge to kill Beckett. She wrapped Joseph's coat around Heather, felt the girl's hard shudder.

"How did you know I was here?" Heather asked, her voice hoarse.

"My son was kidnapped a few days ago. He was kept in the garage above you. He escaped and found your purse in Beckett's truck."

"That's the noises I heard? I thought I'd finally lost my mind. Who is Beckett?"

"The man who held you here," Daphne said softly. "But you're safe with us now."

Joseph had checked every corner. From his pants pocket he drew a felt pouch and from that a slim metal pick. In seconds he'd picked the locks that chained the girl and he and Daphne massaged Heather's shoulders, helping her to bring her arms down and under the blanket. He repeated the motion with the chains at Heather's feet.

"That's his name? Beckett? I didn't know." Heather closed her eyes. "All he ever said was 'Did you miss me?'"

Daphne stroked the girl's hair, trying to give her hands something to do so they wouldn't tremble. "I know, honey." She made herself look around the small room. There was a bed and a nightstand. A sink and toilet.

A fine layer of dust covered the nightstand. Cutting into it were two circles, one much larger than the other. A glass for water and . . .

"Medicine bottle," Heather whispered. "He always kept a medicine bottle there." She started to cough and Daphne lifted her enough to slide behind her to sit against the headboard, cradling Heather against her body.

"Why?"

"Sleeping pills. For when we don't want to stick around anymore. He told me so, the day he brought me here."

More rage exploded within her and Daphne had to clench her teeth to stay in control. And then she looked up. And froze. Her heart . . . stopped.

"Joseph," she rasped, the voice not her own.

He was halfway up the stairs, talking to Kerr who stood above them.

"Joseph," she cried, more loudly and shrilly. He came thundering down the stairs and, following her gaze, looked up.

"Oh my God," he breathed. It was pictures. Polaroid pictures. All in neat rows. The bottom row held ten, the middle row ten. And the top row held . . . six.

"Twenty-six." Sounds were coming from her throat, whimpering, mewling sounds. She could hear them, but she couldn't make them stop. *Make them stop.*

"The one at the very top . . ." she heard Heather say in a broken voice, "is me."

Get hold of yourself. Stop this.

Daphne closed her eyes, clenched them tight. Pursed her lips and breathed through her nose. *Twenty-six, twenty-six, twenty-six.*

"Sonofabitch," Joseph hissed, shining his light on each photo. When his beam passed over the bottom row she saw Kelly on the far left. Kelly had been the first.

And next to it . . . *Oh God. Can't breathe.* Next to it was a child. With blond pigtails, huddled into a corner of the garage, her knees pulled tight into her chest.

Beckett had taken it the day he told her she had to cook some more.

Joseph switched off the flashlight, his whole body shaking with fury.

Heather was crying pitifully. "I'm the last one. The last one," she kept saying.

Daphne's arms tightened around the girl and she began to rock herself, but held Heather so tightly that they rocked as one.

"He took my picture and I couldn't stop him," Heather sobbed. "He put it up there. He told me that when I died, he'd put a new picture up there, like he did with all the others. I begged him not to hurt me. I begged. But he did it. He did . . . oh God. He did things."

"I know." Daphne soothed out of habit, staring at the photos, no longer able to see any details but unable to look away. Feeling utterly dead inside. "I know what he did."

"No, you don't. You can't know. You can't know."

"Shh. I can know. I do know. The first girl was my cousin. Kelly. He kept her down here. I heard it all. The second girl . . . That's me, Heather. That little girl is me."

Twenty-six

This is priceless. Mitch had arrived at Beckett's place in the nick of time. *Hurry. Hurry. You can't miss this now.*

He pulled his Jeep off to the side of the road at the end of the long drive and started to walk through the trees. If anyone saw him, he would say he saw someone that looked like the BOLO description of Beckett and had pulled over to investigate.

He made his way to the place he'd scoped out weeks before—the place where the trees were cleared in a way that provided an unobstructed view of the garage door. He adjusted his binoculars so that when she came stumbling out, he'd have the perfect view. And now . . . on his smartphone he brought up his Webcam app and selected the router connected to Beckett's stolen satellite dish.

And . . . voilà. There was Daphne, sitting next to Heather, applying lip balm, giving her water. Sliding to sit behind her, propping her as she coughed and . . .

Yes. Daphne was looking up at the Polaroids. All twenty-six of them. This . . . this was the moment he'd been waiting for. When she realized there had been twenty-four more after her and her cousin Kelly. Twenty-four more lives ruined. Ended. Because she'd been a coward. Selfish.

Make that twenty-five more lives ended. Because Travis Elkhart and his millions hadn't been enough for her. Because she'd wanted what belonged to someone else. The selfish child had grown into a selfish woman who'd taken his mother's husband.

The selfish woman had pushed his mother into despair, so it was only fitting that despair was what was on Daphne's face right now.

Mitch wished this moment would go on for all time, but all too soon it ended.

Several squad cars and an ambulance raced past his Jeep and down the drive, parking near the garage. *Dammit.* The sudden influx of cops made him nervous. *I should go. Now.* But he'd waited so long for this moment. *Just a few minutes more.* EMTs jumped out of the ambulance, unloaded a stretcher and disappeared into the garage.

Three, two, one . . . And there they were on the camera. Daphne moved away to make room for them and the EMTs carefully lifted Heather to the stretcher. And then it was just Daphne sobbing into her hands. *Hope you choke on those tears, sugar.*

The EMTs were leaving with Heather Lipton. Soon Daphne would come out and he'd see her in all of her sobbing devastation.

The EMTs emerged from the garage and lifted Heather into the ambulance. *Heather Lipton.* Mitch was surprised she'd survived. The girl had grit. Beckett had tried his best to break her. Watching it on the Webcam, Mitch had nearly faltered once. Had come close to reporting her whereabouts to the cops. But it would have ruined everything. He was glad he'd stayed the course. Heather would be fine.

He looked around, half expecting to see Beckett lurking somewhere. The guy was still out there. A fugitive. That was disturbing. He'd hoped the cops would have taken Beckett out already.

Mitch lifted the binoculars to his eyes in time to see Daphne stumble out of the garage, weeping. In Carter's arms. Crying like her heart would break. *Good.*

Oh, and look at that. The door of one of the waiting cars opened and out came trusty old Ford Elkhart. Ford crossed the distance to his mother tentatively, then quickly. Carter transferred her to the boy's arms and Ford rocked his mother while she cried.

Mitch hoped the camera he'd hidden outside Beckett's garage was set at a decent angle. That cam was the old-fashioned kind. Tripped by a motion detector, it had been recording since Carter and Daphne had first arrived. It didn't stream to the Web, it just recorded. But it would give him a clear picture that he could keep forever, one that he could view again and again.

Like the juiciest parts of the novels his mother used to dog-ear. She'd read them over and over again.

Ford was walking his mother back to Carter's SUV. The first act was over.

That's my cue. Mitch started walking toward the cabin.

Baltimore, Maryland
Thursday, December 5, 2:30 p.m.

I am an idiot. Clay pinched the bridge of his nose as the elevator carried him up to the ICU where Stevie still lay. He knew it was hopeless but he couldn't stay away.

She didn't ask me to, he thought. Which made him pathetic. She'd had a tube down her throat. She couldn't have said a word if she'd wanted to.

But today the tube was out. She could speak her mind. He'd know for sure. And if she didn't want to see him, he at least had a final request. One that would give her some purpose as she started into the recovery and rehab phase.

Her family and a crowd of cops in the waiting room. It was SRO in the ICU, and pretty much had been since she'd woken up. Because it was Stevie and everyone loved her.

Her parents were working the room, shaking hands with the cops, kissing each person they greeted on both sides of the face. Her parents' faces lit up when they saw him and her mother threw her arms around him.

Clay had to smile despite his heavy heart. "How is she today?" he asked. Both Nicolescus shrugged.

"Not our Stefania," her mother said. "Not yet."

"She's too polite," her father complained. "We miss the fire."

"She'll bounce back," Clay predicted as brightly as he could muster. He felt a tug on his trouser leg and looked down. Little Cordelia sat on the floor, coloring with Stevie's

sister, Izzy. Cordelia shot him a shy smile and Clay immediately dropped down to crouch beside her.

"I got my picture," he said quietly. She'd given him an
angel's halo. It made his throat hurt every time he thought
of it. "Thank you. I really love it."

"Good," she said, beaming. "I'll make you another."

"I'd like that. I was going to say hi to your mom, but it
looks like there's a line."

"You get moved to the head of the list," Izzy said. "Mama's orders."

Less than five minutes later, Clay was scrubbed and approaching Stevie's room with sweaty palms. She lay in the
bed, her head slightly elevated now. Her dark hair was
mussed, the way he liked it. And there really was more
color in her face today.

When he walked in, she dropped her gaze to her hands.

"Hi," she said, her voice raw and raspy.

Clay didn't have any words now that he was there. He
just stood, looking his fill.

"Can I . . . help you?" she asked. So politely.

"You know you can." The words flew out of his mouth,
surprising them both.

She looked stricken, then looked away and the seconds
ticked by in the loudest silence he'd ever heard.

"Do you want me to go?" he finally asked.

"Yes. No." She looked up at him then, so conflicted. "I
don't know."

It was better than he'd hoped for. Because he was pathetic. And an idiot.

"Look, I don't want to crowd you." He came a little
closer, arms crossed over his chest because he so desperately needed to touch her. "Actually, that's a dirty lie. I
would love to crowd you. In every possible way. But . . .
that's not why I came. My friend, my old partner Isaac
Zacharias, was killed Monday night."

"By Doug," Stevie rasped and reached for the glass of
water on her tray. He stepped forward, putting the straw
between her lips. She sipped, then fell back against her pillows. "Thank you. I'm sorry about your friend."

"Yeah. My friend's wife is pregnant with their fourth.
She's due soon. She's . . . a zombie. Just stares into space. We
can barely get her to eat."

"I'm sorry to hear that, of course. But why tell me?" she asked, the question a warning to back off. But uttered so politely.

Her father had been right. Her fire was gone and it broke Clay's heart to see it. But he was here for Phyllis Zacharias as much as Stevie Mazzetti. *And for myself.*

"Because you've been there," he said flatly and saw her flinch.

She'd lost her husband and son when she'd been pregnant with Cordelia, but she'd made it through, coming out on the other side stronger by all accounts he'd heard.

"I thought you could talk to her. Maybe get through to her. She's got family to help with the kids, but that baby's gonna need her. And she's gonna need him. If I leave her name and number with your family, can you give her a call when you feel up to it?"

Her eyes lifted to his. Dark, lovely eyes. Now filled with a pain that made him wish he'd kept his mouth shut. "Of course," she said. "Any way I can help."

"Good." He took a moment, just to study her face. Until she dropped her chin, her gaze fixed back on her hands and he stepped away. "Be well . . . Stefania."

He'd wanted to use her given name for a very long time. It was what he called her in his mind when he dreamed of holding her in the quiet of the night, sated and content.

But she didn't look up, so he turned away. He was almost out the door when she called his name.

"Clay." Her chin still down, she looked up at him through her lashes, but not flirtatiously. She was hiding. "They told me that you saved my life. Thank you."

"I'd do it again in a heartbeat," he said quietly, "because I can't imagine a world without you in it."

She released a ragged breath. "I think . . . I think maybe you should try."

"Try what?" he asked, unable to mask his dread.

Then she looked up and his heart crumbled. "You want something I may never be able to give you," she whispered. "I don't want to hurt you. But I won't lead you on. You should find someone else to be in your world, Clay. I don't know if it can ever be me."

He stared as her words sank in. He'd come for a definitive answer. Now he had it.

He nodded, dimly aware that it hurt to breathe. "All right. Be happy . . . Stevie."

When he got out to the waiting room, he just kept going, not caring who saw him or what they thought. He didn't slow down until he was outside, the cold air smacking his face. He stopped then, closing his eyes, gritting his teeth through the wave of pain, grateful for the numbness left in its wake.

He started walking. One foot in front of the other. It was time to work. Because that's all he had left. Work. Always and only work.

He'd left Alec and Paige waiting in his car and they looked optimistic as he approached, then sad when they saw his face.

"Let's play hooky," Alec said when Clay was in his car and buckled in. "Go play video games in the arcade. Or paintball or something."

"Or go out for ice cream sundaes," Paige added. "Something."

"Nah. Got paperwork to do. Although I appreciate the offer." Clay's cell buzzed as he pulled into traffic. It was the security desk at Daphne's condo. *Time to work.* "This is Maynard."

"This is Tim Lasker, head of security at Inner Harbor. Someone entered Miss Montgomery's unit earlier today and you asked to be informed. Unfortunately the clerk who's on duty this shift just came back from vacation and didn't know to call this in. I just realized the error."

"Who signed in to the condo?" Clay asked.

"A Miss MacGregor. Kimberly MacGregor. The time is eleven thirty this morning."

"Is there a vehicle parked in Miss Montgomery's parking place?"

"Yes. It's a black van. What would you like me to do?"

"Just make sure Miss MacGregor doesn't go anywhere. I'll be there in ten." He hung up and hung a U-turn at the next light. "We're going to the Inner Harbor."

"Miss MacGregor?" Paige said excitedly. "Kimberly?"

"Apparently so."

"Are we calling BPD?" Alec asked.

Time to work. "Not yet. I don't want to spook her. If she's there, we'll call J.D. But I'd like to have a few words with her first."

Marston, West Virginia
Thursday, December 5, 2:30 p.m.

Joseph handed Daphne over to Ford, stunned to see the boy there. "Take her to my Escalade, okay?" he murmured to her son.

Ford shook his head, anguished. "What happened down there?" he demanded as his mother clung to him, sobbing as if her heart would break.

Deacon had joined them. "I might have known you'd bring him here," Joseph said.

"He said he needed to be here for her," Deacon said. "He was obviously right."

"I asked you what happened, Agent Carter," Ford snapped. He was pale and shaking. How much of that was the cold, emotion, or the simple fact that he should still be in a damn hospital, Joseph didn't know.

"Heather was alive and coherent. That was her in the ambulance that just left. She asked me to thank you for carrying her purse and setting her free."

Ford nodded, tight-lipped. "What else?"

Daphne had drawn a deep breath and was holding it, trying valiantly to regain control of herself. Her sobs were now silent, but her shoulders still shook from their force. Needing to comfort her, Joseph reached for her, but Ford held her tightly, unwilling to let her go.

Respecting the boy's feelings, Joseph cupped her head in his palm, applying gentle pressure to let her know he was there. Slowly, she calmed.

Joseph met Ford's turbulent gaze. "Beckett had amassed a collection of Polaroids of his victims. They're mounted on the wall in chronological order. Your mother's cousin was the first picture." Joseph watched her shoulders stiffen, massaged her head lightly to tell her that she had nothing to fear. He'd say nothing about the Polaroid of the frightened little girl she'd been. "Heather was the twenty-sixth. That was very hard to look at."

Ford gasped. "Twenty . . . *Twenty-six?* Oh my God."

"Why don't you take her to my SUV, Ford? She's shaking." *And so are you, son.*

He handed Ford his keys so that the boy could do as he'd asked. When mother and son were in the backseat of the

Escalade, Joseph turned to Deacon. "What the hell were you thinking, bringing him down here?"

"That he needed to be here for her and she needed him." Deacon's expression was like stone. "Haven't you ever looked back and wished you could do something differently? Be there for someone you loved who needed you?"

Joseph immediately thought of Jo. "Yes."

"So have I. And that's why I brought him down here." Deacon looked away, his jaw tight. "What didn't you tell him that I need to know?"

"That Daphne was the second picture."

Deacon blanched. "God, no."

"Yeah. It was something she couldn't tell us all together because Ford was there. Beckett told her that she needed more time 'to cook.' Yet he still put her picture on his wall like all of his other trophies. She's wearing clothes, unlike the others. But she's huddled in a little ball, terrified."

Deacon's eyes narrowed. "Beckett needs to die, Joseph."

I know. "After CSU is done, we'll have them take the photos down so we can compare them against the missing-children database. We should be able to ID at least some of the victims that way. As long as those photos are visible, the boy doesn't set foot near the place. Got it?"

"Got it. You see any sign of Kimberly or her sister?"

"No. There could be more hidey-holes, though. We should get the tracking dogs out here. And the cadaver dogs. Kelly's body was found in Ohio and Daphne and Heather escaped. That leaves twenty-three victims. Assuming no one else escaped, he had to put them someplace. We might as well start with the land behind his cabin."

"Before we start digging, let's map out the area with ground-penetrating radar. Then we'll know what we've got and we can preserve the evidence."

"Makes sense," Joseph said. "Good thinking, Deacon."

"Can't claim credit. Ciccotelli was telling me about it. He used GPR on a case up in Philly—a serial killer's burial site. It's how he met his wife. She was the archaeologist who did the map. He had nine graves. We could have him beat by a long measure."

"Would Mrs. Ciccotelli help us?"

"She's eight months pregnant, so I doubt it. But I'll call

him and see if she can recommend someone. Otherwise I'll
start calling universities."

"Good plan." Joseph looked back at the cabin. "I'm
handing off this part of the investigation to you. Whoever
the victims are, retrieve the remains and any belongings
you can find hidden in the house or garage. Let's get these
girls back to their families."

"What about the notifications?"

"I'll coordinate them. We'll do them together, all of us
on the team."

Deacon's eyes shot back to meet his and in them Joseph
saw panic. "You're better with the families than I am, Joseph. Any of the others are better than I am."

"None of us do it well." *Twenty-three more victims.
Twenty-three families waiting for girls who will never come
home.* Joseph had an overwhelming urge to run away as
fast as he could. But he knew that wasn't a possibility. "We
have to prepare ourselves for a wave of grief that can sweep
even a strong man away."

"Go take care of Daphne," Deacon said kindly. "I'll take
over from here."

"Thanks."

Thursday, December 5, 2:30 p.m.

Holding his breath, Mitch clutched a fresh syringe of fentanyl, hidden in his coat pocket. Agent Carter was coming
toward the SUV in which Ford and his mother sat in the
back, silent and numb. If Carter came any closer, it could
spoil everything.

And everything had been going so well. He'd watched
Ford help his mother into the back of Carter's Escalade,
then had stepped up to the vehicle before any of the real
cops could do so. He was dressed as a state trooper and
everyone assumed he'd been assigned to guard Daphne
and her son.

To protect them from big, bad . . . me.

But now Carter was approaching and Mitch clenched
his teeth, wondering how to distract him. But at the last
moment Mitch was aided by the white-haired Fed, who ran
over and grabbed Carter's arm. "Joseph!"

Mitch let the breath out. The white-haired Fed had gotten a phone call and pointed Carter back toward the cabin where the signal was clearest. *Thank goodness for the limitations of technology,* Mitch thought. It would take him about ten seconds to incapacitate her son, then about a minute more to walk her to his Jeep.

Carter's back was still turned. It was time to move.

Thursday, December 5, 2:35 p.m.

"Who is it?" Joseph asked.

"Ciccotelli," Deacon said. "I was about to call him to ask about finding a ground-penetrating radar specialist, but he called me. I'll put him on speaker." He hit a button. "You still there, Lieutenant?"

"I am. I understand you found Beckett's center of operations."

"We did," Joseph said. "And photos of twenty-six victims. Only two survivors that we know of. "

"Ah, hell. I'm so sorry, Joseph. I can't change what you found, but I might be able to help you with Doug. Our sketch artist just finished with the little girl who witnessed her au pair's murder. He sent me the scanned file about a minute ago. I forwarded it immediately, but it's a big file."

Deacon gave his phone to Joseph. "I'll go get my laptop from my car," he said. "It'll download faster than the phone. Be right back." He took off at a jog, his black trench coat trailing behind him like a cape.

"Can you recommend someone to do the GPR scan of this property?" Joseph asked Ciccotelli. "We've got about two feet of snow on the ground."

"Snow won't matter so much, except for the mess," Ciccotelli said. "We found our gravesite in February and we had a lot of snow, too. I just texted my wife with your question. She says she wants to come down and do the scan herself."

"I hear she's more than a little pregnant," Joseph said doubtfully.

"She's a lot pregnant, but she's not foolish. If she thinks she can handle it, she can. She'll arrive tonight and get her team out there to start mapping at first light tomorrow."

"I want to start as soon as possible," Joseph said, "but I want to be safe. I think Doug's around here somewhere. I think he came to see Daphne's reaction to Beckett's little room. I don't want your wife in harm's way. How about we assess at the end of the day and I let you know?"

"I appreciate that Joseph. So will Sophie."

Joseph turned in a full circle, doing a scan of the trees around Beckett's property. "Doug could be hiding behind any one of about a thousand trees. So could Beckett. We've got a BOLO on this area, but these are Beckett's woods. I'm sure he can slip through unseen. It's making me very nervous."

"Got it," Deacon called, jogging back to where Joseph stood. "We've got about a twenty-by-twenty area of cell phone coverage, so we have to stay put." He held out his computer for Joseph to see. "Meet Doug."

"Wow," Joseph said, studying a sketch so vivid that he half expected Doug to speak. He noted the signature in the corner. "T. Ciccotelli. Any relation?"

"My brother, Tino. He did his first police sketches on the victims of the burial site we found. Now he's in demand all up and down the East Coast. When he showed the little girl who witnessed the murder this sketch, she balled up in a fetal position again. So, sadly, we're reasonably sure it's close to how he looked—that night anyway."

"How's your brother?" Deacon asked. "Sending a little girl back into shock can't be easy on a guy."

"He's okay," Ciccotelli said, but he didn't sound so sure about it. "It's hard on him. Especially when they're kids. Call me when it's safe for Sophie to come down. She'll have her team waiting."

Joseph ended the call and Deacon raised his brows in question. "His wife's coming down to map it out for us, but I won't allow it until we clear these woods of threats. Take your laptop around and show everyone the picture. I want every Fed, cop, EMT, and state trooper on the premises to know who we're looking for. Thanks, Deacon."

Joseph looked around him again, feeling edgy. *He's here. I know he's—*

His cell phone rang. *Brodie.* Joseph's pulse kicked up as he answered. "Carter."

"It's Brodie. I'm here with J.D."

Something's happened, Joseph thought. He could hear it in her voice despite the crappy connection. *I'm ready for some good news.* "What do you have?"

"A name," she said with satisfaction. "Mitchell Douglas Roberts. I've e-mailed you a photo. He's five nine and utterly average."

Joseph couldn't stop the grin from spreading across his face. Sketches were great, but photos trumped any day. "*Yes.* E-mail it to Deacon, he's got better reception out here. How did you find him?"

Brodie sounded like she was grinning, too. "The third person on the drugstore's list of people they'd carded for Super Glue hadn't opened it yet and we got lucky. It was the one Doug tried to buy and we lifted prints off the cardboard package. Mitchell Douglas Roberts, aka Doug, was arrested for possession of heroin with intent to distribute six years ago and did three years at North Branch. Last known address was in Miami."

"We checked him against the database," J.D. said. "Father is deceased, mother is Jane Lynch, also deceased. Jane was later remarried—to Hal Lynch. You were right about Hal, Joseph."

It didn't make him happy, though. "Daphne and I figured Hal was the connection. Jane accused her of having an affair with Hal. Daphne tried to tell her it wasn't true, but she wouldn't listen. She died the next day. Suicide, according to the check Paige ran. So Hal is Doug's stepfather."

"Which explains a lot. A son would hate the 'other woman' who caused his mother's suicide," Brodie said. "Hal was Daphne's bodyguard. A wife could build all kinds of scenarios about a relationship like that."

"Seems like Hal has two other sons," Joseph said. "Paige found one son listed—Matthew, age twenty-five. But Daphne remembers Jane having a five-year-old with her the night she accused her. The boy would be thirteen now."

"I've got the report from Jane's suicide," J.D. told him. "She was found by her five-year-old son, Cole Lynch. God. Poor kid."

"Hell," Joseph said, rubbing his forehead. "That ratchets up the emotion even more. The Super Glue Mitch was buying was for his kid brother's science project. With the mother dead, Mitch must be the boy's caregiver. Knowing his brother had found the mother's body?" He sighed. "J.D., were you able to match Mitchell Roberts to any of the properties you've been investigating? Now that we know who he is, we need to find where he lives. He could have Kimberly and her sister there."

"Not yet," J.D. said. "We'll keep looking."

"If the boy had a science project for school, he has to be registered somewhere. Check with the schools. Get his records. They should have an address."

"I will. What's happening there?"

Joseph told them and could feel their energy level drop.

"Twenty-six?" J.D. whispered. "Oh God, Joseph."

"I know. I really, *really* want this bastard."

"How's Daphne taking it?" Brodie asked.

"Right now she's numb. I've got to go. She's—"

Joseph was cut off by the sudden shriek of a car alarm. He spun around, his heart dropping out of his chest. *Oh my God. No.*

It was him. The face from the sketch signed T. CICCOTELLI. In the flesh, as if he'd walked off the screen. Doug. And in his grasp, a gun to her temple—*Daphne.*

Thursday, December 5, 2:35 p.m.

Daphne had been numb. Blessedly numb, sitting in the back of Joseph's SUV, her son at her side. Ford's arm had been around her protectively, his other hand closed tight around Joseph's car keys. Her son had been shaking. She'd realized it on some subconscious level.

He's cold. He should be in the hospital. Those had been her thoughts when a state trooper had tapped on her window. She tried to roll the window down, but nothing happened when she pushed the button. With a grimace she realized that they hadn't thought to start the engine. *No wonder Ford's cold.* She opened the door a crack. "Yes, Officer?"

"We have to move this vehicle to make room for the flatbed truck. We're going to start moving Beckett's belongings to the crime scene lab." He opened the door wider, holding out his arm for support.

She forced her legs to move. "Of course," she murmured. The trooper helped her stand and then he turned to help Ford. Too late, she saw the flash of a steel needle as it punctured her son's neck. "Ford—" His name froze in her throat as the trooper pressed a gun to her back.

Not a trooper, she thought. *Doug. Shit.* Eyes wide, she

watched Ford fight the effects of whatever he'd been given. He was losing. She looked around frantically. Where was Joseph? *Over there. He's on the phone, his back turned. Look over here.*

But her mental telepathy went nowhere and Joseph didn't shift his stance. Ford was asleep, his arm stretched flat on the backseat as he'd reached for her. His tight fist was starting to open as his muscles went slack. She could see the tip of the black plastic key fob in his hand.

The man behind her leaned close, his breath tickling her neck. "I'm back," he said in her ear, his tone mocking. "Did you miss me?"

Clenching her jaw she pushed the panic aside. "Hello, Doug," she said calmly.

She felt his start of surprise. "You know me?"

"Yeah. You're Hal's kid," she said, throwing out her best guess.

He chuckled. "You had me there for a minute. Hal never calls me Doug. Now that Ford is in beddie-bye-land we're going to take a walk."

If he got her in a car, he'd kill her. *He might kill me anyway. Get him and the gun away from Ford.* She didn't want him able to take a direct shot at her son.

"Don't hurt my son," she said grimly. "And I'll do what you want."

The barrel of his gun poked her kidney. "You'll do what I want anyway. Now walk."

She turned, stretching her fingers as she passed Ford's hand. She looped her pinkie through the wire ring of the key fob, happy that Joseph didn't keep multiple keys on the ring with his SUV fob. That could have been noisy. And heavy. Moving with him, she curled her pinkie, palming the key fob herself.

"How did you know about Beckett?" she demanded. "I need to know."

"My daddy told me," Doug said. "Keep moving."

Hal. How could you? "Why are you doing this?" She grunted when he shoved the gun even harder. He was walking her toward the main road. Away from Joseph and everyone else.

"Just smile," Doug whispered. "Don't look scared or I will gut you where you stand."

"I guess you're handy with a knife," she said. "Like cutting Officer Zacharias or stabbing the au pair. You killed a cop, Doug. They'll give you the death penalty for that."

"They have to catch me first," he said, amused.

They were twenty feet from the rear of Joseph's Escalade and Ford was out of the line of fire. Keeping her hand as still as possible, she blindly depressed the fob buttons until she hit the panic button.

The alarm screeched, the Escalade's lights flashed and every cop at the scene came running. *Yes.*

She was yanked up against him, the gun leaving her back and reappearing at her temple. "Stop!" Doug yelled. "Or I'll blow her fucking brains out."

Everyone froze. Daphne searched the faces before her for the only one that mattered. Joseph stood stock-still, having covered most of the ground between them in the few seconds before Doug got over his initial shock.

His eyes were dark. Hard. Focused. Not meeting hers. That was okay. She needed him to stay calm, because now that her heroics were over, her heart was pounding and it was becoming harder to breathe.

No panic attacks. No panic attacks. Stay calm and stay alive.

"I want all guns on the ground," Doug barked. "All of them."

Everyone looked to Joseph, who nodded. The cops laid their guns on the snow.

"Good. Anyone who tries to stop me will have her blood on his hands."

Doug started marching her toward a white Jeep when Daphne caught a motion from the corner of her eye. It was the rear hatch of another black SUV, the Dodge emblem on its grille. It was parked midway between the cabin and the white Jeep. The rear hatch was opening by itself. Someone else had a key fob in their pocket.

Again Daphne scanned the faces and knew the second she locked gazes with Deacon Novak that he'd been the one to open the hatch. He lifted one snow white brow as Doug marched her past him.

Then she saw why. A blur of black leaped from the back of the Dodge, one hundred pounds of snarling Giant Schnauzer. *Tasha.* Deacon had brought Ford *and* Tasha.

The dog advanced, slowing to a deliberate prowl, blocking Doug's path to the cars parked down the drive.

"Call off the dog," Doug yelled. "Or I will kill it. And anyone who shoots me kills another little girl, because if I'm dead I can't tell you where to find Pamela MacGregor."

"If you're keeping Pamela at your house, *Mitch*," Joseph said, walking up behind Tasha, "then we'll find her."

Daphne didn't know who Mitch was, but Doug did. He jerked like he'd been shocked with a live wire. "Keep back," Doug shouted. "I will kill this bitch."

He began to back up, forcing Daphne to back up with him. Away from the vehicles lining the drive. This was not good. The minute she drove away with him, she'd be dead. As he backed up, Tasha followed, step for step, her teeth bared in a feral growl.

Doug took a step toward Joseph's Escalade and she realized she held the means of his escape in her hand. She threw the keys before he could stop her and they landed in the snow.

Joseph scooped them up, dropped them in his pocket. Still didn't look at her. He kept his eyes on Doug, who was vibrating with fury.

He jammed the barrel of the gun into her temple, so hard she cried out. "You'll be sorry you did that, bitch."

"I don't care. My son is in that SUV and you're not touching him again."

He pressed his forearm into her throat, making it almost impossible to breathe. From the corner of her eye she saw a wide-eyed Mark O'Hurley crouched behind his car as they passed. She'd forgotten he was there.

"I want a car," Doug hissed and Daphne could hear the desperation in his voice. "Give me those keys. Now."

"I can't do that, Mitch," Joseph said calmly. "You know I can't. Let her go and we'll talk."

"We have nothing to talk about. I will kill her."

"And then we'll kill you," Joseph said quietly. "Or worse maybe, in your mind, we'll send you back to prison. You think the three years you did was hard? You try the rest of your natural days." He tilted his head to one side, watching. "Either way it goes down, who will take care of Cole?"

Doug jerked again, his chest expanding against her back

as he sucked in a startled breath. "Don't you touch my brother."

"We won't. But he'll go into the foster system. And you'll never see him again. Unless you cooperate. Now." Joseph took a step forward.

Doug stepped back two, dragging Daphne with him. "Shut up!" He hit the garage's outer wall and froze. His forearm tightened against her throat. "She's yours, isn't she, Agent Carter? This bitch is yours. Don't even try to deny it." He started moving sideways, toward the door that was still open. "I saw you on TV. I saw how you leaped in front of bullets to save her. I saw you two last night, in her hotel room. You, holding her while she cried. Both of you half dressed. If you ever want to hold her like that again, you'll *back* the *fuck* away. Now."

Joseph didn't back away. But he didn't take any more steps forward. By the time Mitch dragged her into the garage she was seeing black spots floating in front of her eyes from lack of oxygen.

"You want her back, Carter? You get me that car. You drive it up to this door, leave the keys in it, and every last cop clears the premises. I'll give her back then."

The last thing she saw before he slammed the door closed was Joseph's face.

Doug backed them up until they were against the wall with the window. No sniper could get a shot this way. *Dammit.*

He let go of her throat and she dragged in a lungful of air, gagging on the smell of death. "Why the cat?" she asked him.

"To mess with you," he answered, shocking her with his candor.

She was surprisingly calm. Ford was safe. *Me, not so much.* She was . . . terrified. But her mind was clear. *My son is safe.*

Doug's mother is dead. "I remember your mother," she said quietly, then cried out when he jabbed the gun into her temple so hard she saw stars.

"Don't you *dare* mention my mother."

"Okay, then why are you doing this? Surely you want me to know. You went to a lot of trouble to get me here."

"You already know."

"I think I know why you *think* you're mad at me."

"Why?" he asked silkily.

"Can't tell you without using the 'm' word. So this stand-off will end with either me dead and you caught, or just you caught. Either way you won't be able to gloat. If you want me to know why you've done all this, now would be the time."

"We'll have time to talk in the car," he said, his tone cold.

She couldn't tell if he was being sarcastic or if he really thought Joseph would let him drive away. It didn't matter. Joseph wasn't going to let Doug drive away.

Joseph would come up with a plan. *My job is to stay calm until he does.*

They'll have cops ready to take Doug out. I have to be watching, ready to get away from him for even a fraction of a second. That's all they'll need.

Thursday, December 5, 3:00 p.m.

Joseph paced in front of that damn garage, trying to stay in control. They'd been in there for fifteen minutes without a sound. She could be dead. He'd let Doug take her, just waltz away with her. *What the hell is wrong with me?*

At least Doug hadn't gotten Daphne in his car, thanks to Tasha. The dog crouched in front of the door into the garage, every muscle tensed.

I know how you feel, girl.

Joseph stopped pacing when Deacon came to his feet, his laptop open.

"It's set," Deacon said. "You can watch everything from here."

Deacon had threaded a fiber-optic camera under the door and now they could see Daphne sitting on the floor of the garage. Mitch sat beside her, his gun pressed against her head. She was pale, occasionally stealing looks toward the still-open trapdoor to the bunker, and Joseph thought of her recurring nightmare—a mawing dark hole and Beckett pushing her in.

"As long as he sits there we can't get a bead," Joseph muttered.

"McManus says Doug needs to be about four feet from the window before they can get the right angle. We can't go through the walls. They're concrete."

The Wheeling detective had his sniper creds and had already positioned himself in a tree with a clear shot through the window if they could move Doug over a little bit. Joseph had called Kate from the hotel. She was their best marksman.

"We'll have to try a distraction to get his attention," Joseph said. His cell phone buzzed in his pocket, making him hiss a startled curse. He was wound tight. But watching his woman . . . his mate . . . watching her with a gun to her head . . .

It brought back a lot of majorly bad memories and messed with his mind. And with his heart, which was beating way too fast.

He answered his phone brusquely. "Carter."

"It's Clay. I heard about Daphne from J.D. What's happening?"

Joseph stared at Deacon's screen. "He's dragged her into the garage and is just sitting there with a gun to her head."

"Fuck. Just . . . fuck."

"What do you have, Clay?" he asked impatiently.

"Cole Lynch. J.D. says he could be a VIP to your gunman."

Joseph abruptly straightened. "Where are you?"

"In the parking garage of Daphne's condo unit. Security called to say that Kimberly MacGregor had signed in late this morning. We found her asleep in Daphne's bed."

"Hell, Clay, how'd she get there? Who's with her now?"

"Paige is with her until the EMTs we called arrive. Kimberly's not giving her any trouble at all. She got here in the black van. It's here, in Daphne's parking place. In the back under some blankets we found Cole Lynch, tied and gagged. He says Doug had been holding Kimberly hostage in their house. Apparently it's got a damn bomb shelter. He discovered Kimberly, but she hit him with a shovel and stole the van. He calls Doug 'Mitch.'"

"Doug's given name is Mitchell Douglas Roberts," Joseph told him.

"Cole says the property belonged to their great-aunt, Betty Douglas, so that makes sense."

"How'd she get in Daphne's condo?"

"She had Ford's key. Kimberly told Paige she was sleeping so that she could go back and look for her sister."

"Did she eat her porridge and break her chair, too?" Joseph asked bitterly.

"No, but she had Daphne's safe open and emptied. Alec found one of Doug's cameras in the AC vent and Paige found cash and jewelry in Kimberly's purse."

"I wonder if that's how Doug got his hands on Ford's Rolex."

"Wouldn't be surprised. We called the EMTs to pick her up. She's got a high fever and the stab wound on her leg is really infected. I called J.D. to let him know she was here, thinking he'd want to do the arrest, but he was on his way somewhere else, so he's sending one of the other Homicide guys."

"Somewhere else, like where? Like the hospital for his wife's delivery?"

"He wishes. No, he's on his way to Doug's house as we speak."

"How?" Joseph exploded. "Why didn't he tell me he found it?"

"Because you'd already found Doug. He didn't want to distract you from the Daphne situation. As for how, you remember the list of stolen property Doug got from the cops? One of the guns was used in a robbery last night. Punk carrying it said he got it from a kid at his school—Cole Lynch. Cole found Doug's stash. The sheriff got Cole's address from the school and J.D.'s meeting them there now. But this is important—Cole says he thinks he knows where Pamela is being hidden inside Doug's house. He says there's a hidden room in the basement that was padlocked in the last few days. He's going to show us, so as soon as the EMTs come for Kimberly, we'll head out there, too."

"That's good news. But that you found Cole . . . that I might be able to leverage."

"Kim did," Clay said. "Once she had Cole tied up, she sent a text to Doug with a photo attachment—just like Doug had sent to her about Pamela. She had Cole's phone in her purse. Doug hasn't seen the message yet, or at least he hasn't responded, for whatever reason."

"Okay." Joseph's head was spinning with the possible ways he could use that information. "Do me a favor and have the kid ready to talk to his brother. It might make a difference. And, Clay, good job. Thank you."

Twenty-seven

Thursday, December 5, 3:15 p.m.

"So, Doug," Daphne said, unable to take another second of the silence. "We really need to talk about your mother."

"*Shut up.* You don't get to talk about my *mother.*" He twisted his fingers in her hair and threw her to the floor.

She groaned when her head hit the concrete, pain bouncing around inside her skull. "Your mother misconstrued a few things."

"Shut. Up."

"I never had an affair with Hal."

"You laughed at her," Doug said fiercely. "Rubbed her face in your affair with her husband. You drove her to kill herself."

"If I had, you'd have a right to hate me."

Doug's eyes narrowed. "You're screwing with my brain."

"No, I'm trying to tell you the truth."

"Why would I believe your 'truth'? You'd say anything to escape me."

"That's true." She sat up, pressing her fingers to her temples. "But I think either you misunderstood your mother, or your mother misunderstood the situation. I suspect it's a bit of both."

He reached into the inner pocket of his jacket and pulled out a bound leather book. "This is the only truth I need," he said. He handed her the book, opened to the second to last entry. "Read that page and if you so much as make a smudge, I'll gut you."

She read the pages he'd told her to read, her heart heavy for Jane Lynch, but more for the boy who'd read these words and believed them true.

She closed the diary with a sigh. "I need you to know that I never laughed at your mother the way she thought I did. The night she came to see me, she accused me of having an affair with her husband. I laughed, it's true. But it wasn't at her pain. It was at the idea that I was having sex with anyone at all. I'd just been diagnosed with breast cancer and my husband was divorcing me on some trumped-up adultery charges with someone else I hadn't had sex with, either. Ever."

Doug's gaze dropped to her breasts. "I don't believe you."

"Too damn bad. Doesn't make it any less true. I'm sorry your mother thought I was laughing at her, but I was laughing at my own misery. I'm sorry that she thought I was having an affair with Hal, I truly am. The night she came to see me, I was shocked to find out I was living in her house. I felt terrible that she thought I was the kind of woman to cheat with her husband. I left that very day. Got my own place."

"She killed herself the next day," Doug said bitterly.

"I'm sorry that she did. But I didn't know. I tried to tell her she was wrong about me and her husband."

"You're not here to be sorry. You're here to pay." He twisted and suddenly the gun that had been pressed to her temple was shoved under her chin. "My mother shot herself in the head. Once I get out of here, you'll know exactly how she felt."

Thursday, December 5, 3:25 p.m.

Joseph stared at Deacon's laptop screen. *Mitch, Doug, whatever the hell he called himself, was a dead man.* Joseph had wanted to run in and strangle him with his bare hands when he'd slammed Daphne's head onto the floor.

"Deacon," he said, his voice strained. "What's McManus waiting for?"

"A clear shot," Deacon said grimly. "He'd almost need

to hang from the roof and shoot down to get Doug in his sight."

"Then tell him to do that," Joseph snapped.

"I will," Deacon said calmly. He drew a breath and Joseph angled his head so that he stared the younger man in the eye.

"Don't," Joseph warned.

"What? Tell you to calm down? Wouldn't think of it. I was going to suggest we call Clay. Tell him to get the kid to talk to his brother."

"I was waiting until McManus had a clear shot," Joseph said, his patience strained. "I'm saving the kid to throw him off balance."

"I'll tell McManus to figure something out."

"I'll tell Clay to prepare the kid." Joseph took his cell phone from his pocket, ready to dial, but it vibrated in his hand, startling him. Caller ID said it was Kate Coppola. Expert marksman. Maybe she could get the shot that McManus could not. "Where the hell are you?"

"Coming up the drive to the cabin. Thought you should know that I stopped to pick something up. You'll never guess who I just found climbing out of a white Jeep and trying to walk down the road on his own."

"Who?"

"Hal Lynch."

"What? What the hell is he doing here?"

"He's not talking. But his shirt's covered in blood that doesn't appear to be his."

Thursday, December 5, 3:25 p.m.

Daphne was scared out of her mind. *Keep it together, just a little longer.* Because as long as Doug was in the garage, he wasn't near her son.

"Did you know that my brother found her body? He was *five.*"

"That was a selfish thing for your mother to do." She winced when Doug shoved the gun harder up under her chin. "You're angry and you have a right to be. But if your mother was so keen on ending her life, she should have done it away from her five-year-old. She was selfish."

A muscle ticked in his jaw. "You drove her to it."

Goad him, push him, but stay in control. "I most certainly did not. Even if everything she said about me was true, I did *not* put a gun in her hand. *She* pulled the trigger, knowing her *son* would find her. What kind of mother does that? Tell me that."

"One in pain."

"*No.* Not true. My husband cheated on me every day for twelve years. Did you see me trying to kill myself? *No!* I got cancer, Doug. I was sick and scared and alone and *in pain*, but did you see me putting a gun to my head, knowing my son would find me? *No!* I fought to live. I fought to raise my son, to see him grow up. If your mother didn't do the same, then I'm sorry for you, but I will *not* accept the blame for her suicide." Her eyes blazed at him. *"I will not."*

Think, Daphne. Pretend like you're in court and he's just another witness on the stand. See the crime scene through his eyes. What did he experience?

"Your little brother found her. Where were you?"

"Iraq," Doug said tightly.

"Oh. I see. It must have taken you a while to get home."

"A week," Doug said.

"Who cleaned up the mess?" she asked and watched his face flatten in surprise.

"I did."

"I've seen photos of suicide scenes. Never had to clean one up. That must have been rough on you. Especially since it was your mother. You obviously loved her."

He swallowed hard. Under her chin he bobbled the gun a fraction before jabbing it hard against her once again. "I did. But she was sad. All the time. She drank." He snarled. "Because of you."

"Did you see her drink?"

"No. She told me she never wanted Cole to see her drink."

"It must be hard to reconcile that woman with the one who could let her son see her brains and blood sprayed all over." He flinched and Daphne knew she'd hit a nerve.

But then he stilled, the roiling emotion in his eyes settling to a cold, static calm.

"It is," he said levelly. "She must have been out of her mind with grief to do such a thing. That's the point you drove her to. Thank you for reminding me so clearly of why I hated you long before I knew your name."

He was no longer furious with her. He no longer trembled with rage. He was in deliberate control. *Way to go, girl. You brought a cold-blooded killer back in touch with his inner Zen.* Her mind raced as they locked gazes, his gun now steady under her chin.

How do I engage him? I pushed him too far. He'll kill me now.

The room was quiet, the only sound that of their breathing. His was slow and unhurried. Hers was rapidly speeding up as panic gained a toehold.

"Mitch!" The shout came from outside the door. Joseph. "You got that car, Carter?"

"No. But I do have something you want."

"I want the car. You want the woman. I thought we had an understanding."

"I think we will. Listen up."

"Mitch?" It was a young boy's voice, amplified as though he spoke through a speakerphone. "It's me. Cole."

Doug's head jerked up and the gun under her chin momentarily dropped away. If they had a sniper poised outside the window, this might be her only chance to give them a shot that didn't threaten her as well. She threw herself to one side, putting more distance between her and his gun. Then she looked up, and it was déjà vu all over again.

Doug straddled her hips, his gun in her face even closer than Marina's had been when this whole nightmare started. But his breaths weren't so steady anymore. "Are you okay? Where are you?" He spoke over his shoulder, toward the door.

"I'm okay." The boy didn't sound okay. He sounded scared. "Kimberly knocked me out. Stole your van. What the hell are you doing, Mitch? They say you have a hostage. For God's sake, let her go! Stop this craziness."

"I can't." The gun in Daphne's face began to shake as Doug's hands trembled. "I won't go back to prison. I won't."

"Mitch, dammit." The boy was crying, Daphne realized. And from the devastation in his eyes, Doug realized it, too. "They'll kill you before they let you take her, Mitch. You know I'm right. I'd rather visit you in prison than in a cemetery. Let her go."

"Thank you, Cole," Joseph said, his voice closer. He was

right outside the door. "I'm going to ask my associate to take back his phone now. Clay?"

Daphne blinked in surprise. But she said nothing, watching for the next opportunity to get away from the gun still pointed at her face.

"The boy isn't listening anymore," Clay said. "Do what you need to do."

"What you need to do is back the fuck off," Doug snarled, shoving his gun up against her forehead. "I'm not going back to prison. You'll have to kill me first."

"I'm okay with that," Joseph said quietly, still at the door. "Really okay."

Doug's smile was sharp and cruel. "I figured you would be. I also figure I have one good second to pop her head off before you kill me."

He's a man with nothing to lose, Daphne thought. *I'm going to die.*

Suddenly she had nothing to lose, either. He'd kill her if she didn't do something. *Divert him. Get him upset. Talk about his mother.* The mother who ate her gun with a five-year-old in the house. The little boy found his mother. Hell of a mother.

A thought occurred to her and her eyes narrowed. "Tell me about the gun your mother used to kill herself, Doug. Had she purchased it herself? Was it a family gun?"

Doug's brows drew tight. "No to all. Why?"

"Did she keep firearms?"

"No," he bit out. He shoved his own gun harder against her forehead.

"Hal was very angry with your mother the day I moved out of that row house and into my own apartment. She killed herself the day after she saw me. That would have been hours after I saw Hal." She had Doug's attention now. "Maybe she didn't kill herself after all, Doug. Maybe Hal killed her. If you kill me and Agent Carter kills you, you'll never know for sure."

"You're messing with my mind," Doug gritted out.

Whatever it takes. "How would she have gotten a gun to kill herself? She couldn't have. It's obvious if you think about it that Hal killed her! I'm just trying to help you see the truth. I may be the only one who ever has."

He stared down at her and she stared up, not daring to breathe.

A familiar voice broke the deadlocked silence. "Let me go!"

And once more with the déjà vu, Daphne thought. It sounded like Hal. But it couldn't be. Could it? Of course it could. She'd believe nearly anything at this point.

"Get your hands off her!" the familiar voice cried. "You worthless piece of shit. You're not fit to touch her. *Get off her now!*"

Doug twisted to look over his shoulder, a frown of disbelief on his face. In a split second the pressure of the gun pressing into her forehead lifted and Daphne rolled to the right, knocking him off balance.

The door flew open, a series of shots cracking the air, shattering the window over her head.

Doug fell on top of her. He didn't get up.

Daphne's heart was clawing out of her chest. Joseph was on one knee, arm outstretched, gun in his hand. Kate Coppola stood behind him, framed by the open door, slowly lowering a rifle from her shoulder.

Both stared at their target, which had been Doug's head. Which was now a good bit smaller than it had been. Daphne shoved at Doug's shoulder, but he didn't move. Didn't even budge. "Get him off me. *Please.*"

Joseph quickly pulled Daphne out from under Doug's lifeless body. His hands were shaking, his face pale as he knelt beside her, frantically searching her for injuries.

"I'm okay," she said. "I'm okay." Wordlessly he yanked her into his arms and rocked her back and forth. His whole body trembled. She laid her head on his shoulder. "I'm okay, Joseph. You saved me."

He shuddered. "Oh God. I thought he'd kill you. I thought . . ."

He thought he'd have to watch me die. Just like Jo.

He kissed her hair, then leaned back far enough to see her face, then he was kissing her mouth, long and hard and deep. When he was done, he hugged her hard and said, "You were brilliant, baiting him. Don't ever do it again." She patted his back until she felt his terror ebb. He pulled back, relief now mixed with embarrassment. "You're soothing me. I should be soothing you. What do you need?"

"To go home," she whispered. Daphne held on to Joseph as he gently lifted her to her feet. "I just want to take my son and go home."

Thursday, December 5, 3:50 p.m.

Ford was in a haze, just coming out of whatever Doug had given him. His head felt like it was filled with cotton, hungover and hurting. He pushed himself to his knees, realizing he was in the backseat of Joseph Carter's SUV. There was a cop standing near the SUV. Two cops. Standing guard. *What the hell?*

And then it came rushing back—his mother getting out of the SUV . . . The needle in his arm . . . The state trooper who—

My God. It was the trooper. He drugged me. The knowledge came at almost the same time as he realized he was alone in Carter's SUV.

"Mom?" His heart stopped. *She was gone.*

He scrambled to sit upright, fighting the nausea that had plagued him every time he clawed his way back to consciousness. The first thing he saw was Beckett's garage, the one that hurt his mother so much to return to.

Deacon stood near the door into the garage, his hand gripping Tasha's collar. Tasha had been in the back of Deacon's SUV. *Deacon must have let her out. Why?*

Joseph Carter was standing in front of the door into the garage, a woman standing behind him. The woman had a rifle on her shoulder. Joseph had his gun drawn, too, but the agent had his cell phone in his other hand and was holding it near the door.

What the hell?

Then . . . all hell broke loose and Ford had no idea what was going on. Joseph kicked in the door, then dropped to one knee, his arm coming up at the last moment, pointing the gun into the garage. And then he fired. And so did the woman.

Mom. His mother was in that garage. *With Doug.*

Ford yanked at the SUV's door, welcoming the bracing bite of the cold wind as the door opened. He threw himself forward, landing in the snow. He was fully awake now.

"Mom!" he screamed. *"Mom!"* He pushed himself up

and lurched forward, running on feet that felt like they were being stabbed by a million knives. He didn't care. Panic propelled him and he charged the door into the garage, only to be stopped by Deacon.

Deacon grabbed his arm and pulled him back. "Your mom's okay. Doug's dead, but your mom's okay."

Ford pushed in front of the woman with the rifle. She stepped back, allowing him to look inside. Horrified, he did.

Doug had been hit by the gunfire, but his mother was okay. *She's okay. She's not hurt.* Joseph had pushed Doug's body off her and was now kissing her like he owned her, and Ford felt the hackles rise on his neck. He wanted to yank the federal agent away from his mother, but she was kissing him back so Ford stayed where he was.

Deacon clasped his shoulder. "She's all right."

"Oh my God. Deacon." Ford's knees went wobbly and he started to fall. Deacon grabbed one of his arms, the woman who'd fired the rifle the other. They helped him to a folding chair that had been positioned in the snow.

"This is Agent Coppola, Ford. She fired one of the shots that freed your mom."

"Thank you," Ford said hoarsely.

"You're welcome." Coppola crouched beside him, studying his eyes. "You okay?"

"Just woke up when I heard the guns," Ford muttered.

"Doug drugged him again," Deacon explained.

"Oh," she said. "You have a right to look hungover, then. Hell of a way to wake up." She rose, then pointed behind a laptop that had been set up on a makeshift table made from a stack of plastic storage boxes.

The boxes had been in the back of Deacon's SUV when they'd stopped to get Tasha after springing Ford from the hospital. Ford had thought his mother might need the comfort of petting the dog once she came out of the bunker, since there would be no horses for her to brush.

"I'll put Lynch in the backseat of one of these cruisers," Coppola told Deacon. "We'll have to figure out how to get him back to Baltimore."

From behind the stack of boxes, she dragged a man to his feet. He was cuffed, hands behind his back. His butt was covered with snow, his shirt with dried blood.

Ford's eyes widened. "Hal? What the . . . Hal?" It was

Hal Lynch. He'd been a friend of his mother's for years. He'd been a friend to Ford as well, taking him to ball games, playing catch with him when he'd been small. *Hal?*

"Seems like Hal is Doug's stepfather," Deacon said.

Ford's eyes widened further. "How? I didn't even know he had a stepson."

"He's got two stepsons," Deacon told him as Coppola escorted Hal to a police car, "and one biological son. It's quite a story, but I'll give you a day to rest up before I give you all the details. Just sit for now."

Ford obeyed, staying that way until his mother appeared through the door of Beckett's garage, walking on her own, Joseph Carter's arm tight around her.

Ford came to his feet, watching every step she took. When his mother saw him, she threw her arms around his neck. "They got Doug. We're okay."

"They shot at you."

"At Doug. I don't have a scratch on me. I'm fine, I'm really fine."

And then everyone started to talk at once. Deacon had told him that Clay had found Kimberly and Cole Lynch, Doug's little brother. Cole had led them to Doug's house, where he'd shown them a number of hiding places. In one of them was Pamela MacGregor, who was now on her way to a Baltimore hospital, suffering from exposure and extreme dehydration.

Kimberly had been arrested, but she was at a hospital now, too. Doug had stabbed her the night he'd kidnapped them. They'd found her sleeping in Ford's condo, in his mother's bed, feverish and exhausted. And damned if Ford didn't feel sorry for her.

But nobody needs to know that but me. Because that's just damned pathetic.

Everyone had been found. Except for Beckett. He was still out there and none of them could rest as long as he was free.

Ford squinted again, staring at Hal, who was sitting in the back of the police cruiser. The man was staring at the trees, just past the line of cars parked along the drive.

Someone was there, in the woods. Another man. He was hiding in the trees, moving parallel to his mother and the others, who were walking toward the line of emergency vehicles. The man paused long enough for Ford to see long gray hair.

Wilson Beckett. Within him something snapped. Ford started to run, around the side of the garage, close to the cabin, toward the trees where Beckett lurked. From the corner of his eye, Ford saw an axe propped against the front wall of the cabin—the axe that Beckett had tried to use to kill Ford that first day.

Ford grabbed the axe and charged the treeline. He stopped thinking of anything but Beckett and crashed into the old man, knocking him to the ground. *Wilson Beckett.*

Beckett fought, grabbing for the axe, lurching forward, fighting like a wildcat. He bucked, trying to throw Ford off him. Ford pressed the axe handle into Beckett's throat, as he'd done days before.

And just as suddenly as he'd charged, Ford felt the energy drain from him. Beckett got in a good punch and Ford saw stars. Wavy stars. He blinked hard and Beckett grabbed the axe, rolling out from under him, shoving Ford away.

And then Ford was on his back, looking up at Beckett who held the axe high over one shoulder. *He's going to kill me.*

He could hear shouts, but they seemed far away. All he could see was that axe coming down. But the axe swung off to the side as Beckett howled with pain.

Tasha. She was growling, her teeth sunk into Beckett's thigh. Beckett swung the axe at Tasha, but fury gave Ford his second wind. He came to his feet, grabbed the axe, and hit Beckett with the handle as hard as he could.

Beckett dropped like a rock and Ford went down with him. He rammed the axe handle against Beckett's throat again, leaning into him with every ounce of his weight.

"You," Ford hissed, barely feeling a sting when his knuckles connected with Beckett's jaw. "You did this. You took her. You hurt her. You hurt them all."

"Ford. *Ford!*" His mother's voice broke through the haze. "Ford, stop!"

I don't want to. I want him to die. Ford stared down into malevolent eyes. An open, gasping mouth. Dirty hands that closed around the axe handle, pulling with desperation. *Beckett will die today.*

"Ford. Stop. Please, son." Ford looked up into his mother's face, inches away. She knelt behind Beckett's head, her hands gripping Ford's shoulders. "Don't do this. Don't ruin your life over him."

"He hurt you. He deserves to die."

"You're right. But he's not ours to kill. Think about all those families whose daughters aren't ever coming home. They deserve to have their voices heard. They deserve justice. If you kill him now, they won't get that. And you'll go to prison. Let him go, Ford. *Let him go.*"

Her words sank in, past the red haze of fury. She was right. Ford knew she was right. "Back up, Mom."

His mother stood, backing up a few feet, and Ford set the axe to one side. He caught the old man's wrists, pinning them over his dirty gray head. Beckett gasped for air, hate in his eyes. He continued to struggle and Ford had balled up his fist to hit him again when Joseph Carter appeared in his field of vision.

Joseph squeezed Ford's shoulder. "It's over, son. You can let him go. I'll take it from here. Daphne, honey, call off Tasha."

His mother did and Tasha backed away, still growling. Ford heard a click and, looking over his shoulder, saw that Deacon had snapped a leash on Tasha's collar.

Ford pushed to his feet, noticing with satisfaction that Joseph was none too gentle as he cuffed Beckett. The Fed hauled the old man up and shoved him facefirst into a tree, leaning forward to whisper in his ear, "Fight *me*. Resist. Just a little. Please."

"Go to hell," Beckett snarled.

Ford glanced at his mother. She'd crossed her arms over her chest, shivering. Her worried eyes didn't leave Joseph. She was afraid he'd kill the man.

Ford understood where Joseph was coming from. Beckett turned his head, letting his gaze rake lecherously down his mother's body, and Ford had to clench his fists to keep from hitting him again.

"You grew up real nice, little Daphne," Beckett drawled. "I'd say you're done cooking now. I wonder how you'd taste."

A warning look from Joseph had Ford shoving his clenched fists into his pockets.

His mother paled, but didn't back down. "I'm no longer

a defenseless child you can torment, Mr. Beckett. I think
you'd best be afraid of me."

Beckett didn't look afraid. He looked amused. "What did
you think of your picture, little Daphne? I saw you stumble
out, crying your eyes out. Didn't you like my gallery?"

She frowned at him, more confused than angry. "Why?
Why did you take us?"

"Kelly wanted me. You would have soon enough. I just
gave her what she wanted."

Ford had to close his eyes. He wanted to kill the man. He
didn't know how Joseph could stand there so calmly. Until
he looked at Joseph's face. It was a wonder the man didn't
break his teeth, his jaw was clenched so tightly.

But his mother had seemed to forget they were there.
All her focus was on Beckett. He was her nightmare, Ford
understood. This was her chance to face her worst fear.

"What about the others? Did they 'want it,' too?"

Beckett smiled at her. "Which others?"

His mother's eyes widened. "The twenty-four others on
your wall?"

"Which ones specifically?" Beckett mocked. "The six before you were fifteen or the eighteen after? Because the six
before were just time passers while I waited for you to cook."
His mother blanched and Beckett grinned. "The eighteen after were substitutes. I couldn't have you, so I had to make do."

His mother swallowed hard, blinking. She looked like
she wanted to flee. Ford started to go to her, but was once
again stopped by a warning look from Joseph.

Then something changed. His mother's expression went
from one of fear to one of understanding. "I bested you,"
she murmured. "I got away. An eight-year-old girl out-
smarted you. You're not my biggest nightmare. I'm yours."

Beckett's smug grin faltered, just for a moment, and
then it was back, but weaker. "You flatter yourself."

"Maybe. But it works for me and that's all I need to
know. Let's go home, Ford."

Joseph gripped Beckett's coat and shoved him forward.
When they'd started walking toward the car, Ford met Joseph's eyes. "Thank you," he murmured.

Joseph gave him a hard nod. "Same goes, both on catching him and not killing him. That took discipline. Your mom
is lucky to have you."

Ford thought his mother was lucky to have found Joseph, too. He hoped so. She'd been alone for so long. She deserved to be happy.

Thursday, December 5, 4:30 p.m.

Feeling hollowed out, Daphne watched as Joseph shoved Beckett into the back of one of the Wheeling PD squad cars. McManus would take him into custody.

"My boss has already contacted the Liptons," McManus said. "He was the one who coordinated the search when she went missing and had to give them all the bad news when we had no leads. This was one phone call he was happy to make. I'll keep you all apprised."

He got in his car and drove away with a wave. There were two other cops in his car—one in front and one in back. Both had weapons trained on Beckett. Two additional squad cars escorted them. Nobody was taking any chances of Beckett's escaping.

Daphne looked around. "Where's Tasha?"

Deacon pointed to the Escalade. "I put her in the back of Joseph's SUV, Daphne. That is one righteous dog. I might get one."

"Just to round out the whole badass look," Daphne said lightly. She pointed to his black leather trench coat. "Her coat would accessorize yours nicely."

Deacon grinned. "Never underestimate the look."

Joseph wrapped his arm around her shoulders. "Let's get you guys back to Wheeling. I don't know about you, but I want to drink a cold beer and sleep for a week."

"In a minute," Daphne said. She scanned the area again, finding the face she'd sought. She walked briskly to the black sedan that belonged to Agent Kerr, Joseph not leaving her side. Standing at the sedan's back door, hands cuffed behind him, was Hal.

"What are you doing here, Hal?" she asked.

Hal said nothing, just kept his gaze fixed forward.

"He was in the back of Doug's white Jeep," Coppola said. "He'd been drugged and was all groggy, trying to get away on his own. The blood all over his shirt doesn't appear to be his own."

"He's Doug's stepfather," Joseph said.

Daphne nodded. "I heard you tell Ford that earlier. But how did he get here?"

Hal's jaw tightened. "I want a lawyer," he said softly.

She found her palm slicing through the air and yanked it back a split second before she hit his face. "You want a lawyer?" she asked softly. "Too damn bad. Because I want some answers and I want them now. Whose blood is that on your shirt?"

Hal looked away, fixing his gaze anywhere but on her face.

"Probably his son's," Deacon said. "His son Matthew's body was found in the house on your street, Daphne. Whoever killed him left his body outside with the garbage. The body had been dragged into the kitchen. He was missing his fingers and toes. They weren't found at the scene."

"Why in the house on our street?" Ford asked, confused. "Why fingers and toes?"

"Because Hal lives there," Daphne said flatly. "Because he's a damn stalker."

"Cutting off fingers and toes is a signature of one of the heads of the Russian crime family that's trying to carve out territory on the East Coast," Joseph said.

Daphne looked up at Joseph, fury mixing with disbelief. "The Russian who owned all the rifles Doug sold to the Millhouses?" She looked back at Hal. "You deal in illegal weapons? Hal?"

Hal shook his head. "I. Want. A. Lawyer."

"You're not under arrest yet," Joseph said. "Sounds like Doug had revenge planned for both of you, Daphne. I'm looking forward to finding out what you did to your stepson, Lynch. I have a feeling there's a whole other story there."

"Hal." Daphne stared at Hal's face, trying to resolve the person she'd known for twenty years with the man who stood sullenly before her. "Did you intercept my questions to the FBI twenty years ago? Did you falsify Beckett's death certificate? Please. If I ever meant anything to you, tell me. I need to know the truth."

Hal looked at her then and Daphne fought the urge to take a step back. The look in his eyes was . . . damn creepy. "Yes. I faked the certificate. If you'd kept pushing, you would have stirred up an investigation and the FBI would have made you testify against Beckett. Nadine would never have allowed that. She would have made you leave. And I wanted you to stay."

"But . . . Hal, Beckett went on to kill more girls. Didn't that bother you?"

"Of course it did. I'm not a monster. I told him to stop, that he had to disappear. He promised he'd stop."

Daphne's eyes were wide. "You knew him? You talked to him? How?"

"I'd seen him, hanging around the house in Georgetown. The first time was after your mother visited from Riverdale. I assumed he'd followed her there. I was your bodyguard, Daphne. I knew who was a threat to you. He was. After you met with Claudia Baker and told her the whole story, she repeated it to me and I knew just how big a threat Beckett was. The next time he showed up, I followed him, to here. I told him that he was dead. He begged for his life. I'm not a killer. I told him he needed to disappear and never bother you again."

"Who was Claudia Baker?" Joseph asked.

He shrugged. "Just an actress I hired."

"Will we find her alive?" Daphne asked harshly.

Hal didn't answer, which was an answer in itself.

"How did Doug find out about Beckett?" Joseph asked.

Hal looked angry. "I don't know. I truly don't."

"Did you write everything down?" Joseph pushed. "In a file maybe? That you kept in a safe?"

Again Hal didn't answer.

Daphne met Joseph's eyes. "Doug stole it from Hal's safe," she said, and it was Hal's turn to look amazed.

"Told Matt not to trust that shit," he muttered. "I'm just glad that Mitch is dead, too."

"Hal, what did Travis know?" Daphne asked.

Hate flashed in Hal's eyes. "Travis is a drunk. A womanizing drunk. He never deserved you. You should have left him years ago. Now we're done."

"I have one more pressing question," Joseph said. "Since Doug is dead and your middle son is dead, who should we contact about your youngest son, Cole?"

"Cole is not my son," Hal said bitterly. "And I am done."

"Where does he go, Joseph?" Kate asked.

"Arrange for his transport back to Baltimore," Joseph

said. "Grayson's going to have a field day trying to figure out all the things to charge him with. Kerr, can you get your ME out here for the headless bastard in there?"

"Already called. We'll take care of processing the crime scenes. We've already started on the cabin. Beckett has a man cave in the basement with a sixty-inch TV, a pool table, and a keg." Kerr sighed. "And an entire wall of little cubbies, like you'd see at a post office. Lots of purses, jewelry, personal effects. We'll be out here for a very long time and that doesn't even start to cover the possible graves."

As a group they looked past the cabin to the field behind it.

Twenty-three victims unaccounted for, Daphne thought bleakly.

Joseph cleared his throat and she knew he was thinking the same thing. "Deacon, would you mind telling Ciccotelli that the coast is clear for his wife to start mapping the property? We need to find Beckett's victims and send them home."

"Sure. I'd like to stay while she's mapping, if that's okay with you, Kerr."

"We'd welcome the help," Kerr said. "I'll be here at first light. Let me know if Ciccotelli's wife needs anything and we'll have it available."

"Agent Kerr," Daphne said, "Doug had a diary that had belonged to his mother. It's in the garage. Can I get a copy once you've entered it into evidence? I'd like to read it."

"I think you've earned at least that," Kerr said kindly. "I'll get it for you."

Deacon clasped Ford's shoulder. "Come on, kid. I'll take you back to the hospital."

"No," Ford said. "I just want to go home. Mom?"

"If you promise to get checked out when we get home," she said. "I don't want any complications from frostbite or the drugs that Doug gave you."

Ford nodded wearily. "I will. I promise."

"Then let's go home."

Twenty-eight

Baltimore, Maryland
Friday, December 6, 8:30 a.m.

His team looked, Joseph thought, like victims of a ship-wreck, emotionally bedraggled and physically exhausted. They'd filed into the conference room to debrief, their usual chatter subdued.

He and Daphne had driven in together, which was nice. They'd rolled back into Baltimore late the night before. Ford had gone straight to bed, saying very little.

Now that all the danger was past, Ford still had to deal with Kimberly's betrayal. But for today he planned to sleep in and be spoiled by Simone and Maggie.

Joseph had already been spoiled a little by Daphne. Waking up with her body nestled against his had been like heaven, the morning sex quietly profound. Afterward he'd just held her and couldn't imagine letting her go.

When she'd come out of her closet, she'd been dressed in the lime green suit she'd worn the day he'd met her. He hadn't been sure if she'd done that on purpose or if she'd picked the first suit in her closet—until she'd passed him a basket of muffins at breakfast with a demure little wink. And then he remembered telling her that the first day they'd met he'd been eating her muffins while secretly thinking about eating her alive. Now he couldn't look at that suit without his mouth watering.

Tonight. As soon as we're done here . . . he'd take her

home and show her exactly what he'd been thinking about that day, nine months before.

But for now, there was debriefing to do. Joseph was more than ready to put this case behind him. He rapped the table and what little chatter there was ceased.

"Good morning," he said. "Let's start with the hospital report. J.D.?"

"Pamela MacGregor is stable," J.D. said. "Doug kept her sedated, so the days she spent in Doug's basement storeroom will mostly be a blur, which is merciful. If she'd been found much later it could have been very serious. Stevie is being moved from ICU to a regular room today, which is very good news. We're not sure how long she'll be on disability. Deputy Welch is doing very well. He should be going home soon."

"What about Mike, the cameraman?" Daphne asked.

"Stable. He'll be in the hospital a lot longer, but he's out of the woods."

"I have a list of fatalities," Joseph said. "Marina killed Officer Winn and was in turn killed by Stevie Mazzetti. Doug murdered Isaac Zacharias, Elmarie Stodart, Richard Odum and his wife, and was in turn killed by Detective McManus, Agent Coppola, and myself. Beckett . . ." He sighed. "The two men he attacked at the Wheeling hospital—the officer in Ford's room and the nurse whose credentials he stole—both died yesterday."

"Oh no," Daphne said softly.

"I'm afraid so. We don't know how many victims he has in total, but we're going to assume the number is twenty-six until we prove differently."

"I've been communicating with the Pittsburgh field office's CSU," Brodie said. "They began going through the personal effects of the victims yesterday afternoon. So far they've collected over a dozen driver's licenses from girls living in five different states. Once the body retrieval begins, they'll do DNA analysis for identification."

"Deacon called earlier," Joseph said. "Ciccotelli's wife and her team started GPR mapping of the area behind Beckett's cabin at dawn. She estimates it'll take her several days at least, so no retrievals or DNA analyses can start until then. Kerr and McManus both e-mailed me that their switchboards are going crazy with families of missing teenage girls. Hundreds of parents hoping they can get some resolution one way or the other."

"It'll be more," Daphne predicted sadly. "When the story breaks that his first victim was killed twenty-seven years ago, Pittsburgh will be inundated with cold cases."

Joseph shook his head, the thought of it overwhelming. "I can't even imagine. All right, what about—"

"Wait," Grayson said. "I have some names to add to the fatality list. I checked out your old tutor, Joy Howard. She died in a car accident shortly after she stopped working with you."

"Which was right before Ford was born," Daphne said with a frown. "I got a new tutor when I started back to school a few months later."

Grayson passed a photograph down the table to her. "Do you know this woman?"

Daphne's eyes widened. "This is Claudia Baker."

"I was afraid of that," Grayson said. "She's actually Claudia Howard. She's Joy's sister. Died in the same car accident."

"Hal," Daphne whispered. "Dammit. I guess my tutor getting the flu the week I talked to the FBI impostor wasn't coincidence, either."

"No," Grayson said. "I guess Hal couldn't depend on them to stay quiet."

"I'd also like to check into the circumstances of Jane Lynch's death," Joseph said. "I know you were just trying to get Doug agitated yesterday, Daphne." The memory of which still turned his gut to water. "But I think Hal's killing his wife is a possibility."

"Besides," Bo added, "any more crimes we can dig up on Hal, the more leverage the ATF team has to get him to flip on the Russian. The warrants we got to search Hal's properties turned up a sizable cache of illegal weapons yesterday. They were hidden among legitimate antiques he'd imported. Now our warehouse smells like lemon oil."

Daphne frowned. "Lemon oil?"

"Some smugglers think that strong odors like coffee or lemon oil will throw off the dogs' ability to scent," Bo explained. "It doesn't, of course. Why?"

Daphne closed her eyes briefly. "Hal has smelled like lemon oil for as long as I can remember. I never suspected a thing."

"He had two sets of books," Bo said. "He's been distributing drugs for decades. Looks like he started on the weapons more recently. I'm sorry, Daphne. He did it so well, and so far from where he lived, nobody suspected."

She nodded once, wearily. "Thank you."

"I talked with Cole Lynch yesterday," J.D. said. "I'd arrived at Doug's house with the sheriff's department and we were looking for Pamela and found the bomb shelter Doug used for his hideout."

"A bomb shelter?" Bo asked.

"Regulation Cold War model," J.D. said. "Once Cole got there and showed us where Doug had hidden Pamela, he told us that his mother had died there in the shelter. We think Doug meant to bring you back there, Daphne. I found a CD player in a small cell-like room. The CD inside would periodically say 'Did you miss me?' He wanted to make you crazy. Cole wasn't sure about your connection, but he told us that Doug hated Hal not only because he cheated on his mother but because he sent Doug to deal drugs for him and then let him go to prison when he got caught. Matthew, the middle brother with an MBA who cooked the books, told him that Doug had set Hal up to look like he'd stolen rifles from the mob."

"Payback's a bitch," Bo said. "Those stolen rifles were what Doug sold to the Millhouses."

"Which was why we were led to Odum's houses," Daphne said. "Doug wanted the Russians to believe Hal was skimming and making money on the side. So, was he trying to get Hal killed but they killed his brother instead?"

"The mob would have wanted Hal to suffer," Bo said. "Taking his son's life did that."

"We found all of Doug's papers, too," J.D. said. "Including a file on you, Daphne. It's a photocopy, so I think we'll find the original in Hal's safe. It had Hal's initial background check on you, a transcript of your meeting with 'Claudia Baker,' a copy of the death certificate Hal faked, and a map to Beckett's cabin. Doug found a gold mine. He could get his revenge on you and Hal all at once."

"Well, I think I found out what made Hal hate Travis so much." Daphne held up the photocopy of Jane Lynch's diary. "Jane suspected Hal of cheating with me for years, apparently. Jane wrote that at one of Nadine's garden parties she 'tried on my suit for size.' "

"She tried on your clothes?" Brodie asked.

"No, I didn't wear suits then, only dresses."

Brodie frowned. "Then why . . ." Her eyes widened. "Oh."

"Yeah, oh. There's a passage in here that describes Travis's bedroom to a T."

Grayson's brows rose. "So Jane accused you after doing the same thing herself?"

"Ironic, ain't it?" Daphne shook her head. "The date of that party is important, though, because nine months later Cole was born."

Mouths around the table dropped open.

Joseph wasn't surprised at this news, because Daphne had discovered the connection the night before after reading the diary on the drive home from West Virginia.

"Wait." J.D. frowned. "Cole, the kid I met yesterday, he's Ford's half brother?"

"Ironic, ain't it?" Daphne said again. "Cole's in emergency foster care. I'm going to go meet him today. If he is Travis's son, it raises a lot of questions about custody."

J.D. was still shaking his head when he pulled his cell phone from his pocket. Abruptly he came to his feet, a grin breaking through his frown. "Gotta go."

"It's time?" Joseph said, smiling.

"God, I hope so." J.D. left in a flurry of waves and good wishes.

"On that positive note, I think we're done. Good job, everyone. Next week we get back to ongoing caseload for a blissfully normal week."

"Normal?" Daphne asked, her mouth curving. "What's a normal week?"

"When I finally have one, I'll let you know."

Friday, December 6, 11:35 p.m.

Daphne was curled up on her living room sofa staring at the enormous, still starless Christmas tree when Joseph finally returned from the office. He let himself in the front door with the key she'd given him, locked the door and reset the alarm. He was headed straight up the stairs when he noticed her.

"I thought you'd be asleep," he whispered, crossing the room to where she sat. He leaned in to kiss her, keeping his hands in his pockets. "My hands are freezing cold or I'd be touching you right now," he murmured against her lips.

"Sit. I'll get you some coffee to warm your hands."

When she came back with two steaming mugs, he was sitting on the edge of the sofa, elbows on his knees, bowed at the waist. "You look exhausted," she said softly.

He looked up, a smile on his lips, but his eyes were stark. "Long day."

"I didn't get home till a few hours ago myself. Now that I'm not a target anymore, I was allowed to go back to work. Took me hours just to get through my mail and review my new cases." She curled up next to him, handing him one of the mugs. "Did you see J.D.'s text?"

He smiled. "I did."

Lucy had delivered her healthy baby boy a little past six. "He's beautiful."

"I know. He sent me pictures, too. We can go by and see them tomorrow."

"I'd like that. They're naming him Jeremiah, after the man who was Lucy's surrogate father. I think they're going to call him Jerry."

"J.D.'ll be a good dad," Joseph said, and she studied his profile. Something was off tonight, but she didn't know what.

"Did you ever think about kids?" she asked.

He looked at her sideways. "Of course. But if I never have one of my own, I wouldn't feel too terribly sad. Lots of nieces and nephews."

She stared up at the Christmas tree until the lights blurred and she had to blink. "Whenever anyone in the office has a baby, I think about having one, too. I don't know if it would be possible. After the chemo, I mean."

He squeezed her hand. "We have time to figure that out. I always thought I'd be happy adopting a kid, too. We have time, Daphne." He glanced sideways again. "Don't we?"

"Sure. It's just . . ." She sighed. "I met Cole today." She'd gone to visit the foster home into which he'd been placed while Joseph was still in his debriefing meeting.

"How did he seem?"

"Overwhelmed. Shy. Embarrassed about his family. Grieving for his brothers."

"Will he and I have any trouble going forward?"

"Because you shot Doug? I don't think so. He seemed to know Doug was doomed. He confessed that he'd wished he was adopted. And he cried. About his mom, about Doug, about getting expelled from school. I held him like I would have done Ford. He's just a boy, Joseph. He wants a family. A mom. I told him we'd take it a day at a time."

"You're going to bring him here."

It wasn't really a question. "If we get along, yes. I just wanted you to know."

"I kind of thought you would," Joseph said. "Both Clay and J.D. seemed to like the kid. I just want you to be safe and . . . he did bring a gun to school."

"Some boys were threatening to assault him, Joseph," she said quietly. "Sexually. He cried about that, too. The boys at school knew about his brother's jail time. Kids can be cruel."

"So he was defending himself?"

"Yes. I believed him."

"You planning to do a paternity test?"

"For Cole's sake, yes. I think he needs to know defini- tively. But I can see Travis in him. Cole's got his eyes."

"Will Travis want him?"

Daphne laughed bitterly. "No. Neither will Nadine. The boy represents too much scandal. But even if she does want him, I don't want that boy living with Nadine. He's got enough problems already." Then she frowned, perplexed. "I said something about it to Ford and he said to leave Nadine to him. That's all I could get out of him. Do you know any- thing about this?"

"Yeah. Ford's been blackmailing his grandmother for years."

"*What?* Why do you say that?"

"Maggie told me. Ford confirmed it. That's how you got the divorce settlement and all your medical expenses paid for."

Daphne stared at him. "Ford was blackmailing Nadine? With what?"

"I asked Ford yesterday. I needed to make sure it wasn't

connected to the forging of that death certificate. It wasn't. Seems that Ford had stumbled on Travis in a . . . compromised position one night. He had his phone, got some grainy photos. Nothing illegal about it. No one involved was underage."

"Joseph, what did my son see?"

"Ah . . . well . . . Travis had a dominatrix. He was licking her boot, stuff like that. The photos were pretty tame, actually, compared to the stuff kids see online these days. But if they had become public, Travis's career as a judge would have been over. Ford thought it was why Travis never ended up running for Congress. Nadine has stayed out of your hair over the years because of Ford."

"So that's why he thinks she'll back away from Cole. Good Lord."

"Kid had guts. And he loves you. He knew you'd stayed in that house for twelve years for him. He wanted you to have a life and be free of the Elkharts."

Her eyes stung. "I'm very lucky to have him. I hope we can give Cole a better life. He seems starved for . . . normality."

"That's kind of a relative term," he said.

"More normal than he had with Doug or would have had with Hal if Hal had wanted him, which he didn't. And I know how that feels, Joseph, to have your dad not want you."

Joseph flinched, then lifted his eyes to the tree, his brow furrowed in a frown. "There's something you need to know, Daphne. I don't even know how to tell you."

Dread had her heart fluttering unevenly. "Then just tell me."

He blew out a breath, took her hand. "Lieutenant Ciccotelli's wife has been at Beckett's all day mapping the graves we thought we'd find on the property. This is her area of expertise. She's one of the best in the country."

"Joseph, just tell me."

"So far they've found ten graves. Nine are filled with females. One an adult male."

"What?"

"They, um, decided to uncover him first, because it was so unexpected. Caucasian male, late twenties. His skull was cracked open. He had his wallet, so they had ID. It was your father, Daphne."

She shrank back to the corner of the sofa, staring at Joseph's face. "My father?"

"Yes. I don't know what happened to him. What I believe is that he suspected Beckett after you drew that picture of a mother and father with a girl, when the therapist asked you to draw your attacker. I think he knew what you were trying to say."

"But at that point no one would have believed him," she whispered. "They were all so sure he did it. I tried to tell them that he didn't. Oh my God, Joseph. How do I tell Mama? All these years she believed he left her. All these years . . ." Her throat closed. "All these years I thought I drove him away. I thought he hated me."

"He was trying to avenge his little girl. And clear his name, I'd guess. I'm sorry, Daphne. Beckett's taken so much from you and your family."

"I'm . . . well, stunned right now. I imagine it'll hit me later. But I kind of feel better knowing. It means my father was a hero, not a man who abandoned his family."

"That's the way I hoped you'd see it."

"Wow. Any other major bombshells?"

"Nope. I think that's it." He let out a long breath. "I feel so much better now. I was dreading telling you that. I hate to bring you bad news."

"Hopefully we're done with bad news for a while. But if it comes, we'll deal." She pulled his head down for a kiss that started out sweet but quickly became demanding, and when she pulled away they were both breathing hard. "We've had a long day," she whispered. "Let's go upstairs and end it right."

He smiled and her heart fluttered in her chest. "I like the way you think."

She rose and tugged him to his feet. "But I've been thinking all day. I'm ready to stop thinking."

"I think I might know a few ways to make that happen."

She slid her arm around his waist and walked with him to the stairs. "I kind of thought you might."

Read on for a sneak peek at
another thriller by Karen Rose

Watch Your Back

Available from Signet in February 2014.

Baltimore, Maryland
Thursday, April 3, 5:45 p.m.

I can't. I can't do this.

The words thundered in his mind, drowning out the beep of the cash register at the front of the convenience store. Customers milled around him as they went about their daily business, oblivious to the fact that the guy standing in front of the motor oil display was a cold-blooded killer.

But I'm not a killer.

Not yet.

But you will be. In less than five minutes, you will be. Desperation grabbed his throat, churned in his gut. Made his heart beat too hard and too fast. *I can't. God help me, I* cannot *do this.*

You have to.

The small print on the back of the bottle of motor oil he pretended to study blurred as his eyes filled with hot tears. He knew what he had to do.

John Hudson put the bottle back on the shelf, his hand trembling. He closed his eyes, felt the burn as the tears streaked down his wind-chapped cheeks. He swiped a knuckle under his eyes, the wool of his gloves scraping his skin. Blindly he chose another bottle, conscious of the seconds ticking by. Conscious of the risk, of the cost if he followed through. And if he did not.

The text had come through that morning. There had

been no words. None had been needed. The photo attached had been more than sufficient.

Sam. My boy.

His son was no longer a boy. John knew that. Knew he'd lost the best years of his son's life, because John couldn't recall much from those years. He'd spent them snorting and smoking and shooting up, filling his body with what he'd believed he couldn't live without. His addiction had nearly killed him.

Now it was killing Sam. *This is my fault. All my fault.*

His son had pulled himself out of the neighborhood, kept himself clean. Straight. Sam had a future. Or he would, if John did what he was supposed to do.

God. How can I? The photo flashed into his mind's eye, his son bound, unconscious, a thin line of blood trickling from his mouth. Tied to a straight-backed chair, his head lolling to the side. A gloved hand holding a gun to his head.

How can I? he asked himself miserably. *How can I not?*

The assignment had originally come via text yesterday morning from a number John had hoped he'd never see. He'd made a desperate deal with the devil and payment had come due. His target had been identified, the time and place specified.

The man came to this store every evening on his way home from work. John just had to show up. Do the job. Make it look like an accident. Wrong place, wrong time.

But he hadn't been able to do it yesterday. Hadn't been able to force himself to walk inside the store. Hadn't been able to force himself to pull the trigger.

So the ante had been upped. And Sam was the pawn. *Son. I'm sorry. I'm so sorry.*

He heard the quiet beep of the door as it opened. *Please don't let it be him.* Not the target. *Please don't let him stop here today. Please.*

But if it's not him, you can't kill him. And then Sam will die.

"Hey, Paul." The greeting had come from behind the counter. The cashier was a fiftysomething African-American woman who had greeted several of her customers by name. "What's shakin' in the hallowed halls?"

John's heart sank. *It's him. Make your move.*

"Same old, same old," Paul replied, a weariness to his

voice that somehow made John's task feel even worse. "Cops put them in jail and we do our best to throw away the key. Most of the time it feels like we just throw the key back in the bad guys' hands. They're on the street so fast, the door doesn't even hit them in the ass."

"Damn defense attorneys," the cashier muttered. "Same old, same old on the numbers, too?"

"My mother is a creature of habit," Paul said, his chuckle now rueful.

"You're a good boy to pick up her lotto tickets every day, Paul."

"It makes her happy," he said simply. "She doesn't ask for much."

Just do it, John barked to himself. *Before he makes you like him even more.* He edged to the end of the aisle, closer to the cash register. Pretending to scratch his head, he reached up under his Orioles' baseball cap to yank the ski mask he'd pushed to the top of his head down to cover his face. It could be worse. The three of them were the only ones in the store. If he had to dispose of a lot of witnesses ... That would be much worse.

"That'll be ten bucks," the cashier said as the register door opened with a *ping.* "So, how's that wife of yours, Paul? Pregnancy going okay?"

His wife is pregnant. Don't do this. For the love of God, do not do this. Ignoring the screaming in his head, John wheeled around, drawing his gun.

"Everybody freeze," John growled. "Hands where I can see them."

The cashier froze and John's target paled, his hands lifted, palms out. "Give him what he wants, Lilah," Paul said quietly. "Nothing in this store is worth your life."

"What do you want?" the cashier whispered.

Not this. I don't want this.

Do it. Or Sam will die. Of this John had no doubt. The gloved hand holding the gun to his son's head had killed before. He would kill Sam. *Do. It.*

Hand shaking, John pointed the gun at Paul's chest and pulled the trigger. Lilah screamed as the man went down. John caught a movement from the corner of his eye. Lilah had retrieved a gun from below the counter. Clenching his jaw, John pulled the trigger a second time and Lilah crumpled to the counter, blood pooling around the hole he had just put in her head.

It's done. Nausea churned in his gut. *Get out of here before you throw up.*

He took a step toward the door when he froze, stunned. Paul was struggling to his knees. There was no blood on the man's white shirt. Holes, but no blood. Understanding dawned. *Kevlar.* The man wore a vest. *What the fucking hell?*

He lifted his gun, aiming at the man's forehead.

The shrill beep of the door opening had him glancing to the left.

"Daddy!" *Oh hell. A little boy.* The devil had never said anything about a kid. *Fucking hell. Now what? What do I do now?*

Penguin Group (USA) Inc. is proud to continue the fight against breast cancer by encouraging our readers to "Read Pink®."

In support of **Breast Cancer Awareness** month, we are proud to offer eight of our bestselling mass-market paperback titles by some of our most beloved female authors.
Participating authors are Jodi Thomas, Carly Phillips, JoAnn Ross, Karen Rose, Catherine Anderson, Kate Jacobs, LuAnn McLane, and Nora Roberts.
These special editions feature **Read Pink** seals on their covers conveying our support of this cause and urging our readers to become actively involved in supporting The Breast Cancer Research Foundation.

Penguin Group (USA) Inc. is proud to present a $25,000 donation (regardless of book sales) to the following nonprofit organization in support of its extraordinary progress in breast cancer research:

The Breast Cancer Research Foundation®

Join us in the fight against this deadly disease by making your own donation to this organization today.

∞

How to support breast cancer research:
To make a tax-deductible donation online to The Breast Cancer Research Foundation you can visit: www.bcrfcure.org

You can also call their toll-free number, **1-866-FIND-A-CURE (346-3228)**, anytime between 9 A.M. and 5 P.M. EST, Monday through Friday. To donate by check or a U.S. money order, make payable and mail to:

The Breast Cancer Research Foundation, 60 East 56th Street, 8th floor, New York, NY 10022

About The Breast Cancer Research Foundation®
www.bcrfcure.org

The Breast Cancer Research Foundation® (BCRF) was founded by Evelyn H. Lauder in 1993, to advance the most promising breast cancer research that will help lead to prevention and a cure in our lifetime. The Foundation supports scientists at top universities and academic medical centers worldwide. If not for BCRF, many facts about the genetic basis of breast cancer would not be known, the link between exercise, nutrition and breast cancer risk would not be established, and the rate of mortalities would not continue its downward curve. BCRF-funded scientists are responsible for these and many other critical achievements.

**If you would like to learn more about risk factors, visit www.penguin.com/readpink.
Read Pink® today and help save lives!**

M742JV0513